A BROMFIELD GALAXY

THE GREEN BAY TREE
EARLY AUTUMN
A GOOD WOMAN

By

LOUIS BROMFIELD

H B

HARPER & BROTHERS PUBLISHERS
NEW YORK

A BROMFIELD GALAXY

FOREWORD

By general consent *The Green Bay Tree, Early Autumn* and *A Good Woman* are among the finest novels by the late Louis Bromfield. Published in the 1920's these three panels of American life immediately aroused the enthusiasm of the critics and achieved very wide readership both here and abroad. *Early Autumn* was awarded the Pulitzer Prize.

An author's work expresses the man, an observation which applies particularly to Bromfield. So it seems fitting that, as his publisher and friend for over twenty-five years, I should comment on some of his characteristics.

His vitality was that of ten men. It expressed itself in ceaseless activity and an avid interest in many things. He was both a manager and a person who loved to do things himself with his hands. The large farms he operated in Ohio and Brazil were world famous owing to his restless, imaginative, innovating spirit. At the same time he enjoyed the gift of the green thumb and could make flowers grow as no one else. He was a brilliant cook, and after he had produced a magnificent meal, his conversation would roam over every conceivable subject.

The man had a genius for people. Every type, from political and social moguls to the farmhands, would gather around his table and feel at home. And while he talked, as he did both entertainingly and incessantly, Bromfield would instinctively absorb the salient characteristics of those around him.

What distinguished him above all else was his huge appetite for life, which is reflected in his writing. He used broad strokes in his delineation of characters; they emerge sharp and clear, sometimes larger than life. In these three novels are found the qualities of an unforgettable personality who never lost his deep American roots in the course of his travels and long sojourns in foreign lands. They are also examples of storytelling at its finest, an art that has seldom been practiced so successfully in our time.

March, 1957

CASS CANFIELD

THE GREEN BAY TREE

Chapter 1

IF YOU CAN picture a little park, bright for the moment with the flush of early summer flowers and peopled with men and women in the costumes of the late nineties—If you can picture such a park set down in the midst of an inferno of fire, steel and smoke, there is no need to describe Cypress Hill on the afternoon of the garden party for the Governor. It was a large garden, indeed quite worthy of the name "park," withdrawn and shut in by high walls of arbor vitae clipped at intervals into small niches which sheltered bits of white statuary, some genuine, some of them copies. The Venus of Cydnos was there (in copy to be sure), and of course the Apollo Belvedere, a favorite ornament of formal gardens, as well as the Samothrace Victory dashing forward, it seemed, to soar high above the cloud of smoke from the neighboring blast furnaces.

Here and there the hedge displayed signs of death. There were patches where the green had become withered, and other patches where there was no green at all but simply a tangled wall of hard, dead twigs. Where death had touched the barrier it was possible to see beyond the borders of the garden into regions filled with roaring furnaces, steel sheds, and a tangle of glittering railway tracks cluttered by a confusion of semaphores and signal lights which the magic of night transformed into festoons of glowing jewels—emeralds, rubies, cabuchons, opals, glowing in the thick darkness. But it was not yet dark and no one at the garden party peered through the dying gaps in the hedge because by daylight there lay beyond the borders of the garden only ugliness of the most appalling nature.

The little park sloped away on all sides from a great brick house, conceived in the most bizarre union of Georgian and Gothic styles. It was large and square and faced with white stone, but beyond this the Georgian style played no part. The roof carried a half-dozen high pitched gables; the windows were tall and pointed in the manner of a church rectory, and the chimneys, built of white stone, were carved in the most ornate Gothic fashion. Over all clambered a mass of vines,—woodbine, virginia creeper and wistaria—which somehow bound the grotesque combination of styles into one harmonious whole, characterized by a surprising look of age, considering the fact that the house stood in the midst of a community which less than a century before had been a complete and trackless wilderness.

The vines, like the hedge, had been more green and exotic at some earlier day. In places there were now no leaves at all, and elsewhere, though the season was early summer, the leaves appeared sickly and wretched, surrounded by dead bare tendrils pressing desperately against the faded bricks.

On the whole, however, the garden was at its best. Along the gravel walks leading to the arbor, irises raised crowns of mauve, royal purple and yellow.

Peonies in the process of bursting from tight green buds into great pom-poms of pink and white tumbled across the flagged walk. At the feet of the flying Eros (made of cast iron and painted white), who carried a ring in one hand and thus served for a hitching post, ground pinks and white violets, brought from England by Julia Shane's grandmother, peeped from among the blades of new grass. But the greatest splendor had its being in the wistaria. High up among the branches of the dead oak that towered gauntly above the horse block, its cascades of mauve and white and purple poured like water escaping from a broken dam. From the black iron portico tumbled more torrents of blossoms. They appeared even high up among the tips of the pointed cypresses which gave the house its name. To be sure these were not true cypresses at all, for true cypresses could not have survived the harsh northern winter. In reality they were cedars; but their tall, green-black spires, swaying in melancholy fashion at the least breath of air, resembled cypresses as one brother resembles another. John Shane, perhaps because the name roused memories of some secret world of his own, always called them cypresses and such, to all purposes, they had become. None knew why he called the house Cypress Hill or why he loved cypresses so much that he called cedars by that name when nature cheated him out of his heart's desire. The Town set it down simply as another of his eccentricities. One more craziness no longer disturbed the Town. And John Shane had been dead now for more than ten years, so perhaps the matter was one of no importance whatever.

Under the wistarias on the wrought iron piazza his widow, Julia Shane, leaning on her stick of ebony filigreed in silver, surveyed the bright garden and the guests who moved about among the old trees, the men clad in sober black, the ladies in sprigged muslins or bright colored linens. She was a tall thin woman with a nose slightly hooked, which gave her the fleeting look of an eagle, courageous, bold, even a little pitiless and unrelenting. An air of dignity and distinction compensated the deficiencies of beauty; she was certainly not a beautiful woman and her fine skin was already crisscrossed by a million tiny lines no more substantial than cobweb. Like the women of the generation preceding hers, she made no attempt at preserving the illusion of youth. Although she could not have been long past middle age, she dressed as an old woman. She wore a gown of black and mauve of the most expensive materials,—a sign of mourning which she kept up for a husband dead ten years, a husband whose passing could have given her no cause for regret, whose memory could not possibly bring to her ivory cheeks the faintest flush of pleasure. But the black and mauve gave her great dignity and a certain melancholy beauty. On her thin fingers she wore rings set with amethysts and diamonds and about her neck hung a chain of amethysts caught in a setting of old Spanish silver. The chain reached twice about her thin throat and hung to the knees.

She had been standing on the piazza, a little withdrawn from her guests, all the afternoon because she knew that the mauve of her gown and the dull lavender sparkle of the amethysts blended superbly with the tumbling blossoms of the wistaria. She had not been, after all, the wife of John Shane for nothing. People said that he had taught his wife to make the best of herself because he could bear to have about him only those things which were in excellent taste. People also said that his wife was lame, not because she had fallen by accident down the long polished stairway, but because she had been thrown from the top to the bottom by her husband in an insane fit of rage.

From her point of vantage, her bright blue eyes swept the garden, identifying the guests—those whom she desired to have there, those to whose presence she was completely indifferent, and those whom political necessity had forced upon her. About most of them centered scornful, bitter, little thoughts that chased themselves round and round her tired brain.

Over against the hedge on the far side of the little pavilion stood a group which, it appeared, interested her more than any other, for she watched it with a faint smile that carried the merest trace of mockery. She discerned the black of the bombazine worn by Hattie Tolliver, her blood niece, and the sprigged muslin of Hattie's daughter, Ellen, who stood by resentfully with an air of the most profound scorn while her mother talked to Judge Weissman. The mother talked voluably, exerting all her power to charm the Judge, a fat perspiring Oriental and the son of an immigrant Viennese Jew. And the efforts of Hattie Tolliver, so solid, so respectable, so downright, were completely transparent, for the woman possessed no trace of subtlety, not the faintest power of dissimulation. She sought to win favor with the Jew because he was the one power in the county politics. He ruled his party with an undisputed sway, and Hattie Tolliver's husband was a candidate for office. Perhaps from the pinnacle of her worldliness Julia Shane detected a quality naive and almost comic in the vulgar intrigue progressing so blatantly on the opposite side of the pavilion.

There was also a quality indescribably comic in the fierce attitude of the daughter, in her aloofness from the politician and the intensity of her glowering expression. She was an obnoxious child of sixteen, wilful, spoiled, savage, but beyond the possibility of denial, she played the piano superbly, in a truly extraordinary fashion.

Presently Julia Shane, behind the shelter of the wistaria, sniffed suddenly as though the wind had carried to her among the delicate odors of the flowers the offensive smell of the fat perspiring Jew. He was there by political necessity, because the Governor desired his presence. Clearly she looked upon him as an intruder who defiled the little park.

Farther off at the side of the empty kennels, all buried beneath a tangle of vines, another group had gathered about a table where pink ices and pink and white cakes were being served. About the great silver punch bowl hung a dozen men, drinking, drinking, drinking, as though the little park were a corner saloon and the little table the accustomed free lunch. For a moment Julia Shane's gaze fastened upon the men and her thin nostrils quivered. Her lips formed themselves to utter a word which she spoke quite loudly so that three women, perfect strangers to her who stood just beneath the piazza, overheard it and spread the story that Julia Shane had taken to talking to herself. "Pigs!" she said.

Chapter 2

IN OTHER PARTS of the garden the bright parasols of the gossiping women raised themselves in little clumps like mushrooms appearing unexpectedly through the green of a wide lawn. The Governor was nowhere to be seen, nor Lily nor Irene, Julia Shane's two daughters.

The guests began to depart. A victoria with a driver on the box came round the corner of the old house. A fat dowager, dressed in purple and wearing a gold chain, bowed, and the diminutive young man beside her, in a very tight coat and a derby hat, smiled politely—very politely—Mrs. Julis Harrison and her son Willie, of the great family which owned the Mills.

Julia Shane bowed slightly and leaned more heavily upon her ebony stick. A second vehicle appeared, this time a high buggy which bore the county auditor and his wife . . . common people who never before had entered the wrought iron gates of Cypress Hill. The fat and blowsy wife bowed in an exaggerated fashion, never stopping the while to fan her red face vigorously until she discovered that her elaborate bows were expended upon the back of Julia Shane, who had become suddenly absorbed in the rings that glittered on her bony fingers. The smile froze on the fat lady's face and her heavy lips pursed themselves to utter with a savage intensity of feeling the word "Snob!" Indeed, her indignation so mounted under the protests of her tipsy husband, that a moment later she altered the epithet to another more vulgar and more powerful phrase. "Old Slut!" she said aloud. The two carriages made their way down the long avenue between the rows of dying Norway spruce to the gate where Hennery, the black servant, stood on guard.

Outside, with faces pressed against the bars, stood a score of aliens from the hovels of the mill workers in the neighboring Flats. The little group included a dozen women wearing shawls and a multitude of petticoats, three or four children and as many half-grown boys still a year or two too young to be of any use to the Harrison Mills. They pushed and pressed against the handsome gates, striving for a glimpse at the spectacle of the bright garden animated by the figures of the men and women who ruled the Town, the Flats, the very lives and destinies of the little throng of aliens. A baby squalled in the heat and one of the boys, a tall powerful fellow with a shock of yellow hair, spat through the bars.

At the approach of the carriage the black Hennery sprang up and with the gesture of one opening the gates of Buckingham Palace, shouted to the crowd outside, "Look out, you all! There's carriages a-coming!"

Then with a great clanging and shooting of bolts he swung open the gates and Mrs. Julis Harrison and her son William swept through. The hoofs of the dancing horses beat a tattoo on the cobblestones. The mother saw nothing, but the narrow eyes of her son appraised the group of boys and even the babies as potential workers in the Mills. These Dago children grew rapidly, but not fast enough to keep pace with the needs of the growing furnaces; and so many of them died before they reached manhood.

As the carriage swung into narrow Halsted street, Mrs. Harrison, leaning forward so that the gold chain swayed like a pendulum from her mountainous bosom, surveyed the wretched houses, the yards bereft of all green, and the shabby railway station that stood a hundred yards from the very gates of Shane's Castle.

"You'd think Julia Shane would move out of this filthy district," she said. "Sentiment is all right, but there's such a thing as running it into the ground. The smoke and soot is even killing the flowers. They're not half so fine as last year."

Her son William shrugged his narrow, sloping shoulders.

"The ground is worth its weight in gold," he said. "Three railroads—the only site left. She could get her own price."

In the corner saloon a mechanical piano set up a tinny uproar and shattered fragments of The Blue Danube drifted out upon the hot air through the swinging doors into the street, throttling for the moment any further conversation.

The county auditor and his wife drove uncertainly through the gates, for the county auditor had drunk too much and failed to understand that horses driven with crossed reins do not respond according to any preconceived plan. His wife, her face red as a ripe tomato, took them from him and swore.

"She needn't think she's so damned swell," she said. "What's she got to make her so proud? I should think she'd blush at what has happened in that rotten old house. Why, she's got nothing but Hunkies and Dagos for neighbors!"

She cut the horses across the back, dashed forward, and passed the victoria of Mrs. Harrison and her son William at a triumphant gallop.

With a loud, officious bang, Hennery closed the wrought iron gates and the wise, old faces of the alien women pressed once more against the bars. One of the throng—the big boy with the shock of yellow hair, a Ukrainian named Stepan Krylenko—shouted something in Russian as the gates banged together. It was a tongue foreign to Hennery but from the look in the fierce blue eye of the young fellow, the negro understood that what he said was not friendly. The women admonished the boy and fell to whispering in awe among themselves, but the offender in no way modified his manner. When Judge Weissman, fat and perspiring and covered with jewelry, whirled past him in a phaeton a moment later, the boy shouted in Russian, "Jew! Dirty Jew!" Judge Weissman regarded the boy with his pop eyes, wiped his mahogany face and muttered to his companion, Lawyer Briggs, "These foreigners are getting too free in their manners. . . . The Harrisons will have trouble at the Mills one of these days. . . . There ought to be a law against letting them into the country."

The Judge was angry, although his anger was stirred not by the shout of Stepan Krylenko but by the fact that Julia Shane had become suddenly blind as his phaeton swept round the corner of the old house. The shout was something upon which to fasten his anger.

Chapter 3

FROM HER POINT of vantage on the wistaria clad piazza, the old woman watched the little drama at the entrance to the Park, and when the gates had been flung closed once more, she moved back into the cool shadows, still wondering where Lily and Irene and the Governor could have hidden themselves. She settled herself on an iron bench, praying that no one would pass to disturb her, and at the same moment the sound of sobbing reached her ears. It came from the inside of the house, from the library just beyond the tall window. There, in a corner beyond the great silver mounted globe, Irene had flung herself down and was weeping. The half-suppressed sobs shook the girl's frail body. Her muslin dress with the blue sash was crushed and damp. The mother bent over her and drew the girl into a sitting posture against the brocade of the rosewood sofa.

"Come, Irene," said the old woman. "It is no time for tears. There is time enough when this infernal crowd is gone. What is it? What has come over you since yesterday?"

The girl's sobs grew more faint but she did not answer nor raise her head. She was frail and blond with wide blue eyes set far apart. Her thick hair was done low at the back of her neck. She had a small pretty mouth and a rather prominent nose. Her mother must have resembled her before she hardened into a cynical old woman, before the prominent nose became an eagle's beak and the small pretty mouth a thin-lipped sardonic one. The mother, puzzled and silent, sat stiffly beside the sobbing girl, fingering all the while the chain of amethysts set in Spanish silver.

"Are you tired?" she asked presently.

"No."

"Then what is it, Irene? There must be some reason. Girls don't behave like this for nothing. What have you done that has made you miserable?"

"Nothing," sobbed the girl. "Nothing!"

The mother sat up a little straighter and began to trace with her ebony stick the outlines of the roses on the Aubusson carpet. At length she spoke again in a clear, hard voice.

"Then you must pull yourself together and come out. I want you to find Lily and the Governor.—Every one is leaving and they should be here. There's

no use in giving a party for him if he is going to snub the politicians. . . . Here
—sit up! . . . Turn round while I fasten your hair."

With perfect deliberation the mother arranged the girl's hair, smoothed the
crumpled muslin of her dress, patted straight the blue ribbon sash, dried her
eyes, and bade her stand away to be surveyed.

"Now," she said in the same crisp voice, "You look all right . . . I can't
have you behaving like this. . . . You should be out in the garden. Before
I die, Irene, I want to see you married. You never will be if you hide yourself
where no one can see you. . . . I don't worry over Lily—she can take care of
herself. Go and find them and bring them back. . . . Tell them I said to
return at once."

The girl, without a word, went out of the room into the big dark hallway
and thence into the garden. Her mother's voice was one made to command. It
was seldom that any one refused to carry out her orders. When Irene reached
the terrace the guests were making their way back toward the house in little
groups of two or three, ladies in summer dresses very tight at the waists,
shielding their complexions from the June sun with small, bright-colored
parasols . . . Mrs. Mills, the rector's wife, Miss Bird, the Town librarian,
Mrs. Smyth, wife of the Methodist clergyman, Mrs. Miliken, wife of the
sheriff, Miss Abercrombie, Mrs. . . . And behind them, the husbands, and
the stray politicians who treated the little arbor over the punch bowl as though
it were a corner saloon. The punch was gone now and the last of the pink
ices melted. From other parts of the garden more guests made their way toward
the house. Irene passed them, bowing and forcing herself to smile though the
effort brought her a kind of physical pain. Among the rhododendrons she
came upon a little terra-cotta Virgin and Child brought by her father from
Sienna and, remembering her convent training, she paused for a moment and
breathed a prayer.

Lily and the Governor were not among the rhododendrons. She ran on to
the little pavilion beyond the iris walk. It was empty. The arbor, green with
the new leaves of the Concord grapes, was likewise untenanted save by the
shadows of the somber, tall cypresses. The girl ran on and on from one spot
of shelter to another, distracted and terrified, her muslin dress soiled and torn
by the twigs. The little park grew empty and the shadows cast by the setting
sun sprawled across the patches of open grass. Two hiding places remained,
but these Irene avoided. One was the clump of bushes far down by the iron
gates. She dared not go there because the little crowd of aliens peering through
the bars terrified her. Earlier in the afternoon she had wandered there to be
alone and a big towheaded boy shouted at her in broken English, "There are
bones . . . people's bones hidden in your cellar!"

No, she dared not again risk the torment of his shouting.

The other hiding place was the old well behind the stables, a well abandoned
now and almost lost under a tangle of clematis. There was a sheltered seat
by its side. The girl ran as far as the stables and then, summoning her strength
to lie to her mother if the necessity arose, turned back without looking and

hastened across the garden toward the piazza. She had not the courage to
approach the well because she knew that it was there she would find her sister
Lily and the Governor.

When Irene entered the house, she found her mother in the drawing-room
seated alone in the twilight. The guests had all departed and the old woman
was smoking, a pleasure she had denied herself until the last of the visitors
were gone. No one in the Town had ever seen her smoke. It was well enough
to smoke at Biarritz or Monte Carlo; smoking in the Town was another matter.
Julia Shane smoked quietly and with a certain elegance of manner which
removed from the act all trace of vulgarity. She sat in a corner of the big room
near one of the tall windows which stood open a little way admitting ghostly
fragments of scent, now of iris, now of wistaria, now of lilac. Sometimes there
penetrated for a second the acrid tang of soot and gas from the distant furnaces.
The diamonds and amethysts on her thin fingers glittered in the fading light.
She was angry and the unmistakable signs of her anger were present—the
flash in her bright blue eye, the slight trembling of the veined hands. The
ebony stick rested by her side. As Irene entered she did not move or shift for
a second the expression of her face.

"And where are they?—Have you found them?"

The girl's lips grew pale, and when she replied, she trembled with the
awful consciousness of lying to her mother.

"I cannot find them. I have looked everywhere."

The mother frowned. "Bring me an ash tray, Irene, and do not lie to me.
They are in the garden." She crushed out the ember of her cigarette. "That
man is a fool. He has offended a dozen important men after I took the trouble
to invite them here. God knows, I didn't want them!"

While she was speaking, the sound of footsteps arose in the open gallery
that ran along the far side of the drawing-room, and two figures, silhouetted
against the smoky, setting sun, appeared at the windows moving toward the
doorway. They were the missing Lily and the Governor. He followed her at
a little distance as though they had been quarreling and she had forbidden
him to address her. At the sight of them, Irene moved toward the door, but
her mother checked her escape.

"Irene! Where are you going now? What are you afraid of? If this behavior
does not stop, I shall forbid you to go to mass. You are already too pious for
any good on this earth."

The frightened girl returned silently and sat down with her usual air of
submission on the sofa that stood in the shadows by a mantelpiece which
supported a painting of Venice, flamboyant and glowing, executed by the hand
of Turner. At the sound of Lily's voice, she shrank back among the cushions
as if to hide herself. There was in the voice nothing to terrify her. On the
contrary it was a voice, low and warm, indolent and ingratiating—a voice full
of charm, one which inspired affection.

Lily was taller than her sister and two years older; yet there was an enormous
difference between them which had to do less with age than with manner.

There was about Irene something childish and undeveloped. Lily was a woman, a young woman, to be sure, tall and lovely. Her hair was the color of honey. It held bright copper lights; and she wore it, in the fashion of Irene, low on a lovely neck that carried a warning of wilfulness. Her skin was the transparent sort which artists love for its green lights, and her eyes were of a shade of violet which in some lights appeared a clear blue. Her arms were laden with irises, azure and pale yellow, which she had plucked on her way from the old well. She too wore a frock of muslin with a girdle of radiant blue. As she entered, she laid the flowers gently among the crystal and silver bibelots of a rosewood table and rang for Sarah, the mulatto wife of Hennery, guardian of the wrought iron gates.

The Governor followed her, a tall man of perhaps forty, strongly built with a fine chest and broad shoulders. His hair was black and vigorous and he wore it cropped close to a well-shaped head. He had the drooping mustaches of the period. His was a figure which commands the attention of mobs. His manner, when he was not too pompous or condescending, was charming. People said there was no reason why he should not one day be president. He was shrewd in the way of politicians, too shrewd perhaps ever to be anything but one who made other men presidents.

He was angry now with a primitive, boiling anger which threatened to burst the bonds of his restraint. His breath came huskily. It was the anger of a man accustomed to dominate, who has encountered suddenly some one who cares not a fig for his powers.

"Madame," he said, "your daughter has refused to marry me."

The mother took up her ebony stick and placed it squarely before her, at the same time leaning forward upon it. For a moment, she smiled, almost secretly, with a sort of veiled amusement at his pompous speech. She did not speak until the mulatto woman, slipping in noiselessly, had taken the flowers and disappeared again into the vast hall. Then she addressed Lily who stood leaning against the mantelpiece, her lovely body slightly balanced, her manner as calm and as placid as if nothing had gone wrong.

"Is this true, Lily?"

The girl nodded and smiled, so slightly that the play of expression could scarcely have been called a smile. It was as though she kept the smile among her other secrets, not to be shared by people who knew nothing of its meaning.

"It is serious, Madame, I promise you," the Governor interrupted. "I love your daughter. She has told me that she loves me." He had grown a little pompous now, as though he were addressing an assembly of constituents. "What else is there?" He turned to Lily suddenly, "It is true, isn't it?"

The girl nodded. "Yes, I have told you that. . . . But I will not marry you. . . . I am not refusing because I want to be unkind. . . . I can't help it. Believe me, I cannot."

The mother began tracing the design on the carpet, round and round the petals of the faded roses. When she spoke she did not raise her head. She kept on tracing . . . tracing. . . .

"There must be some reason, Lily. . . . It is a match not to be cast aside lightly. . . . It would make me very happy."

She was interrupted by the sound of a closing door. Irene had vanished into the gallery on the far side of the drawing-room. The three of them saw her running past the window back into the garden as though she were pursued. The mother fell once more to tracing the outlines on the carpet. In the growing darkness the scent of the lilac grew more and more strong.

The Governor, who had been standing by the window, turned sharply. "I would like to speak to you, Mrs. Shane . . . alone, if possible. There are some things which I must tell . . . things which are unpleasant but of tremendous importance, both to Lily and to me." He coughed and the blood mounted to his coarse handsome face. "As an honorable man, I must confess them."

At this last statement, a faint sound of mirth came from Lily. She bowed her head suddenly and looked away.

"It would be better if Lily left us," he added savagely.

The girl smiled and smoothed her red hair. "You may speak to mother if you like. It will do you no good. It will only make matters worse. After all, it concerns no one but ourselves."

He shouted at her suddenly. "Please, will you go. Haven't you done enough? There is no need to behave like a devil!"

The girl made no reply. She went out quietly, closing the door behind her, and made her way across the terrace to the rhododendrons where she knew she would find Irene. It was almost dark now and the glow from the furnaces below the hill had begun to turn the whole sky to a murky, glowing red. A locomotive whistled shrilly above the steady pounding of the roller mills. Through a gap in the dying hedge, the signal lights began to show, in festoons of jewels. The wind had turned and the soot and smoke were being swept toward Cypress Hill. It meant the end of the flowers. In the rare times when the wind blew from the south the blossoms were scorched and ruined by the gases.

Among the fireflies Lily hastened along the path to the rhododendrons. There, before the terra-cotta Virgin and Child, she found her sister praying earnestly. Lily knelt down and clasped the younger girl in her arms, speaking affectionately to her and pressing her warm cheek against Irene's pale one.

Chapter 4

THAT NIGHT Irene and Lily had dinner in their own rooms. In the paneled dining-room, a gloomy place decorated with hunting prints and lighted by tall candles in silver holders, Julia Shane and the Governor dined alone, served by the mulatto woman who shuffled in and out noiselessly, and was at last dismissed and told not to enter the room again until she was summoned. There followed a long talk between the Governor and the old lady, during which the handsome Governor pulled his mustaches furiously and sometimes raised his voice until the room shook and Julia Shane was forced to bid him be more cautious. She permitted him to do most of the talking, interrupting him rarely and then only to interject some question or remark of uncanny shrewdness.

At length when he had pushed back his chair and taken to pacing the room, the mother waited silently for a long time, her gaze fixed upon the tiny goblet of chartreuse which glowed pale gold and green in the light from the dying candles. Presently she leaned back in her chair and addressed him.

"It is your career, then, which is your first consideration," she began. "It is that which you place above everything else . . . above everything?"

For a moment the tall Governor halted, standing motionless across the table from her. He made no denial. His face grew more flushed.

"I have told you that I love Lily."

The old woman smiled at this evasion and the sharp look gleamed for a second in her bright blue eyes. Her thin lips contracted into the faintest of smiles, a mere shadow, mocking and cynical. In the face of his anger and excitement, she was calm, cold, with the massive dignity of an iceberg.

"It is I," she said, "who should be offended. You have no cause for anger." She turned the rings on her fingers round and round. The diamonds and amethysts caught the light, shattering it and sending it forth again in a thousand fragments. "Besides," she added softly, "love can be so many things. . . . Believe me, I know."

Slowly she pushed back her chair and drew herself up, supported by the ebony stick. "There is nothing to do now but hear what Lily has to say. . . . It is, after all, her affair."

The library was a square room, high-ceilinged and dark, walled by books and dominated by a full-length portrait of John Shane, builder of Cypress Hill and the first gentleman of the Western Reserve. The picture had been painted in the fifties soon after he came to the Town and a decade before he married Julia MacDougal. In the dark portrait he stood against a table with a white Irish setter at his feet. He was a tall man, slim and wiry, and wore dove gray trousers and a long black coat reaching to the knees. Set rakishly and with an air of defiance on the small well-shaped head was a dove gray top hat. His neckerchief was bright scarlet but the varnishings and dust of years had modified its color to a dull maroon. One hand hung by his side and the other rested on the table, slender, nervous and blue-veined, the hand of an aristocrat. But it was the face that impressed you above all else. It was the face of one possessed, a countenance that somehow was both handsome and ugly, shifting as you regarded it from one phase to the other as though the picture itself mysteriously altered its character before your eyes. It was a lean face, swarthy and flushed with too much drinking, the lips red and sensual yet somehow firm and cruel. The eyes, which followed you about the room, were large and deeply set and of a strange deep blue like cobalt glass with light shining through it. It was the portrait of a gentleman, of a duellist, of a sensitive man, of a creature haunted by a temper verging upon insanity. One moment it was a horrible picture; the next it held great charm. Above all else, it was baffling.

It was in this room that Julia Shane and the Governor waited in silence for Lily, who came down a little while later in response to the message from the mulatto woman. The sound of her footsteps on the long stairs reached them before she arrived; it came lightly, almost tripping, until she appeared all at once at the open door, clad in a black cloak which she had thrown over her peignoir. Her red hair was piled carelessly atop her head and at the moment her eyes were blue and not violet. She carried herself lightly and with a certain defiance, singularly like the dare-devil defiance of the tall man in the darkening portrait. For a moment, she paused in the doorway regarding her mother who sat beneath the picture, and the Governor who stood with his hands clasped behind him, his great chest rising and falling as he watched her. Pulling the cloak higher about her white throat, she stepped into the room, closing the door softly behind her.

"Sit down," said the mother, in a strained colorless voice. "I know everything that has happened. . . . We must talk it over and settle it to-night one way or another, for good and all."

The girl sat down obediently and the Governor came over and stood before her.

"Lily," he said and then halted as though uncertain how to continue. "Lily . . . I don't believe you realize what has happened. I don't believe you understand."

The girl smiled faintly. "Oh, yes . . . I know . . . I am not a child, you know . . . certainly not *now*." All the while she kept her eyes cast down thoughtfully.

The mother leaning forward, interrupted. "I hadn't thought it would end in this fashion," she said. "I had hoped to have him for a son-in-law. You know, Lily, you must consider him too. Don't you love him?"

The girl turned quickly. "I love him. . . . Yes, . . . I love him and I've thought of him. . . . You needn't fear a scandal. There is no need for one. No one would ever have known if he hadn't told you. It was between us alone." The Governor pulled his mustaches furiously and attempted to speak but the girl halted him. "I know . . . I know," she said. "You're afraid I might tell some one. . . . You're afraid there might be a child. . . . Even if there was it would make no difference."

"But why . . . why?" began her mother.

"I can't tell why . . . I don't know myself. I only know that I don't want to marry him, that I want to be as I am. . . ." For a second the shadow of passion entered her voice. "Why can't I be? Why won't you let me? I have money of my own. I can do as I please. It is my affair."

Chapter 5

FOR A LITTLE while the room grew silent save for the distant pounding of the Mills, regular and reverberant, monotonous and unceasing. The wind from the South bore a smell of soot which smothered the scent of wistaria and iris. All at once a cry rang out and the Governor, very red and handsome in his tight coat, fell on his knees before her, his arms about her waist. The girl remained sitting quietly, her face quite white now against the black of her cloak.

"Please . . . please, Lily," the man cried. "I will give up everything . . . I will do as you like. I will be your slave." He became incoherent and muddled, repeating over and over again the arguments he had used in the afternoon by the old well. For a long time he talked, while the girl sat as still as an image carved from marble, regarding him curiously as though the whole scene were a nightmare and not reality at all. At last he stopped talking, kissed her hand and stood up once more. The old woman seated under the portrait said nothing. She regarded the pair silently with wise, narrowed eyes.

It was Lily who spoke. "It is no use. . . . How can I explain to you? I would not be a good wife. I know . . . you see, I know because I know myself. I love you, I suppose, but not better than myself. It is my affair." A note almost of stubbornness entered her voice. "Two days ago I might have married you. I cannot now, because I know. I wanted to know, you see." She looked up suddenly with a strange smile. "Would you have preferred me to take a lover from the streets?"

For the first time the mother stirred in her chair. "Lily . . . Lily . . . How can you say such a thing?"

The girl rose and stood waiting in a respectful attitude. "There is nothing more to be said. . . . May I go?" Then turning to the Governor. "Do you want to kiss me. . . . I think it would please me."

For a second there was a terrific struggle between the desire of the man and his dignity. It was clear then beyond all doubt that he loved her passionately. He trembled. His face grew scarlet. At last, with a terrible effort he turned suddenly from her. He did not even say farewell.

"You see," said the mother, "I can do nothing. There is too much of her father in her." A shade of bitterness crept into her voice, a quality of hardness aroused by a man who no longer existed save in the gray portrait behind her. "If it had been Irene," she continued and then, checking herself, "but what am I thinking of? It could never have been Irene."

Quietly Lily opened the door and stole away, the black cloak trailing behind her across the polished floor, the sound of her footsteps dying slowly away as she ascended the stairs.

At midnight Hennery brought the carriage round from the stables, the

Governor climbed in, and from the shelter of the piazza Julia Shane, leaning on her stick, watched him drive furiously away down the long drive through the iron gates and into the street bordered by the miserable shacks and boarding houses occupied by foreigners. At the corner the jangling music of the mechanical piano drifted through the swinging doors of the saloon where a mob of steel puddlers, in from the night shift, drank away the memories of the hot furnaces.

Thus the long association of the Governor with the old house at Cypress Hill came abruptly to an end.

He left behind him three women. Of these Lily was already asleep in the great Italian bed. In an adjoining room her mother lay awake staring into the darkness, planning how to keep the knowledge of the affair from Irene. It was impossible to predict the reaction which it might have upon the girl. It might drive her, delicate and neurotic, into any one of a score of hysterical paths. The room was gray with the light of dawn before Julia Shane at last fell asleep.

As for the third—Irene—she too lay awake praying to the Blessed Virgin for strength to keep her terrible secret. She closed her eyes; she buried her face in her pillow; but none of these things could destroy the picture of the Governor stealthily opening the door of Lily's room.

Chapter 6

THERE HAD BEEN a time, within the memory of Lily, though not of Irene who was but two years old, when the first transcontinental railroad stretched its ribbons of steel through the northern edge of the Town, when the country surrounding Cypress Hill was open marsh land, a great sea of waving green, of cattails and marsh grasses with a feathery line of willows where a muddy, sluggish brook called the Black Fork threaded a meandering path. In those days Cypress Hill had been isolated from the Town, a country place accessible only by the road which John Shane constructed across the marshes from the Town to the great mound of glacial moraine where he set up his fantastic house. As a young man, he came there out of nowhere in the fifties when the Town was little more than a straggling double row of white wood and brick houses lining a single street. He was rich as riches went in those days, and he purchased a great expanse of land extending along one side of the single street down the hill to the opposite side of the marsh. His purchase included the site of the Cypress Hill house, which raised itself under his direction before the astonished eyes of the county people.

Brickmakers came west over the mountains to mold bricks for him in the kilns of the claybanks along the meandering Black Fork. Town carpenters returned at night with glowing tales of the wonders of the new house. Strange trees and shrubs were brought from the east and a garden was planted to surround the structure and shield it from the hot sun of the rolling, fertile, middle west. Gates of wrought iron were set up and stables were added, and at last John Shane returned from a trip across the mountains to occupy his house. It gained the name of Shane's Castle and, although he called it Cypress Hill, the people of the Town preferred their own name and it was known as Shane's Castle to the very end.

Who John Shane was or whence he came remained a mystery. Some said he was Irish, which might well have been. Others were certain that he was English because he spoke with the clipped accent of an Englishman. There were even some who held that so swarthy a man could only have come from Spain or Italy; and some were convinced that his love of travel was due to an obscure strain of gipsy blood. As to the light which Shane himself cast upon the subject, no one ever penetrated beyond a vague admission that he had lived in London and found the life there too tame.

He set himself up in the house at Cypress Hill to lead the life of a gentleman, a worldly cynical gentleman, perhaps the only gentleman in the archaic sense of the word in all the Western Reserve. In a frontier community where every one toiled, he alone made, beyond the control of his farms, no pretense at working. He had his horses and his dogs, and because there were no hounds to follow and no hunters to ride with him, he set aside on the land bordering the main street of the Town a great field where he rode every day including the Sabbath, and took the most perilous jumps to the amazement of the farmers and townspeople who gathered about the paddock to watch his eccentric behavior.

Among these were a Scotch settler and his son-in-law, Jacob Barr, who owned jointly a great stretch of land to the west of Shane's farm. They kept horses to ride though they were in no sense sporting men. They were honest stock, dignified and hard-working, prosperous and respected throughout the country as men who had wrested from the wilderness a prosperous living. MacDougal was the first abolitionist in the county. He it was who established the first station of the underground railway and organized the plans for helping slaves to escape across the border into Canada. These two sometimes brought their horses into the paddock at Shane's farm and there, under his guidance, taught them to jump.

The abolitionist activities culminated in the Civil War, and the three men joined the colors, Shane as a lieutenant because somewhere in his mysterious background there was a thorough experience in military affairs. His two friends joined the ranks, rising at length to commands. MacDougal lost his life in the campaign of the Wilderness. Jacob Barr returned stricken by fever, and Shane himself received a bullet in the thigh.

Returning as a colonel from the war he found that in place of the dead MacDougal he had as a riding companion the farmer's youngest daughter, a girl of nineteen. She had taken to the saddle with enthusiasm and was a horsewoman after his own heart. She knew no such thing as fear; she joined him recklessly in the most perilous feats and sat his most unruly horses with the ease and grace of an Amazon. She was not a pretty girl. The word "handsome" would have described her more accurately. She was strong, lithe and vigorous, and her features, though large like the honest MacDougal's, were clearly chiseled and beautiful in a large way.

The strange pair rode together in the paddock more and more frequently until, at last, the astonished county learned that John Shane, the greatest gentleman in the state, had taken MacDougal's youngest daughter east over the mountains and quietly made her mistress of Shane's Castle. It also learned that he had taken his bride to Europe, and that his housekeeper, a pretty middle-aged Irish woman who never mingled with the townspeople, had been sent away, thus ending rumors of sin which had long scandalized the county. It appeared, some citizens hinted, that Julia MacDougal had been substituted for the Irish woman.

For two years the couple remained abroad, but during that time they were separated, for Shane, conscious of his bride's rustic simplicity, sent her to a boarding school for English girls kept by a Bonapartist spinster named Violette de Vaux at St. Cloud on the outskirts of Paris. During those two years he did not visit her, choosing instead to absent himself upon some secret business in the south of Europe; and when he returned, his bride found it difficult to recognize in the man with a thick, blue black beard, the husband she had married two years earlier. The adornment gave him an appearance even more alien and sinister.

The two years were for the girl wretched ones, but in some incomprehensible fashion they hardened her and fitted her to begin the career her mysterious husband had planned. When they returned to Cypress Hill, Shane shaved off his beard once more and entered politics. From then on, great people came to stay at Cypress Hill—judges, politicians, lawyers, once even a president. As for Shane he sought no office for himself. It seemed that he preferred in politics to be the power behind the throne, the kingmaker, the man who advised and planned campaigns; he preferred the intrigues without the responsibilities. And so he became a figure in the state, a strange, bizarre, dashing figure which caught somehow the popular imagination. His face became known everywhere, as well as the stories about his private life, of strange brawls in the growing cities of the middle west, of affairs with women, of scandals of every sort save those which concerned his personal honesty. Here he was immune. No one doubted his honesty. And the scandals did him little harm save in a small group of his own townspeople who regarded him as the apotheosis of sin, as a sort of Lucifer dwelling in a great brick house in the center of the Black Fork marshes.

In the great house, his wife, whose life it was whispered was far from happy, bore him two daughters, a circumstance which might have disappointed most men. It pleased the perverse John Shane who remarked that he was glad there was no son to carry on "his accursed name."

As he grew older the unpopularity increased until among the poorer residents of the Town strange stories found their way into circulation, tales of orgies and wickedness in the great brick house. The stories at length grew by repetition until they included the unfortunate wife. But Shane went his proud way driving his handsome horses through the Town, riding like mad in the paddock. The Town grew and spread along the outskirts of his farm, threatening to surround it, but Shane would not sell. He scorned the arguments for progress and prosperity and held on to his land. At last there came a second railroad and then a third which crossed the continent, passing on their way along the banks of the sluggish Black Fork through the waving green swamp. Shane found himself powerless because the state condemned the land and it was his own party which promoted the railroad. He gave way and his land doubled and tripled in value. Factories began to appear and the marsh land became precious because in its midst three railroads crossed in a triangle which surrounded the house at Cypress Hill. Shane became older and more perverse. The tales increased, tales of screams heard in the night and of brutalities committed upon his wife; more scandals about a young servant girl leaked out somehow and were seized by the population of the Town. But throughout the state Shane's name still commanded respect. When the great came to the Town they stopped at Shane's Castle where the drawing-room was thrown open and receptions were held with the rag, tag and bobtail permitted to satisfy their curiosity. They found nothing but a handsome house, strange and beautifully furnished in a style unknown in the Town. John Shane and his wife, her face grown hard now as the jewels on her fingers, stood by this judge or that governor to receive, calm and dignified, distinguished by a worldliness foreign to the rugged, growing community.

And at last the master of Shane's Castle was stricken dead by apoplexy one winter night at the top of the long polished stairway; and the wiry, thin old body rolled all the way to the bottom. Irene, who was a neurotic, timid girl, saw him fall and ran screaming from the house. Lily was in Europe at St. Cloud on the outskirts of Paris, a *pensionnaire* in the boarding school of Mademoiselle Violette de Vaux. The wife quietly raised the body, laid it on a sofa under the portrait in the library and summoned a doctor who made certain that the terrible old man at last was dead.

When the news of his death spread through the Town, Italian workmen passing along the railroad at the foot of Cypress Hill crossed themselves and looked away as though the devil himself lay in state inside the wrought iron gates. Governors, judges and politicians attended the funeral and the widow appeared in deep mourning which she wore for three years. She played the rôle of a wife bereft of a devoted husband. The world whispered tales of her unhappiness, but the world *knew* nothing. When great people came to the Town, they were still entertained at Cypress Hill. The legend of John Shane attained the most fantastic proportions; it became a part of the Town's tradition. The words which Stepan Krylenko, the towheaded Ukrainian, shouted through the wrought iron gates at the terrified Irene were simply an echo of certain grotesque stories.

After the death of her husband, Julia Shane sold off piecemeal at prodigious prices the land in the marshes traversed by the railroads. Factory after factory was erected. Some built farming implements, some manufactured wooden ware, but it was steel which occupied most of the district. Rolling mills came in and blast furnaces raised their bleak towers until Shane's Castle was no longer an island surrounded by marshes but by great furnaces, steel sheds and a glistening maze of railway tracks. New families grew wealthy and came into prominence, the Harrisons among them. Some of the Shane farm land was sold, but out of it the widow kept a wide strip bordering Main Street where she erected buildings which brought her fat rents. The money that remained she invested shrewdly so that it increased at a startling rate. She became a rich woman and the legend of Shane's Castle grew, spurred on by envy.

To the foreigners who lived in the hovels at the gate of Cypress Hill, the house and the park became the symbols of an oppressing wealth, of a crude relentless power no less savage than the old world which they had deserted for this new one. It was true that Julia Shane had nothing to do with the mills and furnaces; her money came from the land she owned. The mills were owned by the Harrisons and Judge Weissman; but Shane's Castle became an easy symbol upon which to fix a hatred. Its fading grandeur arose in the very midst of the hot and overcrowded kennels of the workers.

Chapter 7

SIX WEEKS after the night the Governor drove furiously away from the house at Cypress Hill, Julia Shane gave her last dinner before sending Lily away. It was small, including only Mrs. Julis Harrison, her son William, and Miss Abercrombie, but it served her purpose clearly as a piece of strategy to deceive the Town. Irene was absent, having gone back to the convent in the east where she had been to school as a little girl. A great doctor advised the visit, a doctor who held revolutionary ideas gained in Vienna. It was, he said, the one means of bringing the girl round, since he could drag from her no sane reason for her melancholy and neurasthenic behavior. Her mother could discover nothing; indeed it appeared that the girl had a strange fear of her which struck her dumb. So Julia Shane overcame her distaste for the Roman Catholic Church and permitted the girl to return, thanking Heaven that she had kept from her the truth. This, she believed, would have caused Irene to lose her mind.

In the drawing-room after dinner a discreet battle raged with Julia Shane on one side and Mrs. Julis Harrison and Miss Abercrombie on the other. Lily and William Harrison withdrew to the library. In a curious fashion the drawing-room made an excellent battle-ground for so polite a struggle. It was so old, so mysterious and so delicate. There were no lights save the lamps, three of them, one majolica, one blue faience and one Ming, and the candles in the sconces on each side of the tall mirror and the flaming Venice of Mr. Turner. The only flowers were a bowl of white peonies which Lily had been able to save from the wreck of a garden beaten for three days by a south wind.

"The Governor's visit," observed Mrs. Harrison, "turned out unfortunately. He succeeded in offending almost every one of importance."

"And his sudden going-away," added Miss Abercrombie, eagerly leaning forward.

Julia Shane stirred in her big chair. To-night she wore an old-fashioned gown of black lace, very tight at the waist and very low in the neck, which displayed boldly the boniness of her strong shoulders. "I don't think he intended slighting any one," she said. "He was called away by a telegram. A Governor, you know, has duties. When Colonel Shane was alive . . ." And she launched into an anecdote of twenty years earlier, told amusingly and skilfully, leading Mrs. Julis Harrison and Miss Abercrombie for the time being far away from the behavior of the Governor. She spoke of her husband as she always did, in terms of the most profound devotion.

Mrs. Harrison was a handsome stout woman, a year or two older than Julia Shane but, unlike her, given to following the fashions closely. She preserved an illusion of youth by much lacing and secret recourse to rouge, a vain deception before Julia Shane, who knew rouge in all its degrees in Paris where rouge was used both skilfully and frankly. She moved, the older woman, with a slight pomposity, conscious always of the dignity of her position as the richest woman in the Town; for she was richer by a million or two than Julia Shane, to whom she acceded nothing save the prestige which was Cypress Hill and its tradition.

Miss Abercrombie, a spinster of uncertain age, wore her hair in a pompadour and spoke French, as she believed, perfectly. It was necessary that she believe in her own French, for she it was who instructed the young girls of the Town in French and in history, drawing upon a background derived from a dozen summers spent at one time or another on the continent. Throughout Julia Shane's long anecdote, Miss Abercrombie interrupted from time to time with little fluttering sighs of appreciation, with "Ohs!" and "Ahs!" and sudden observations of how much pleasanter the Town had been in the old days. When the anecdote at last was finished, she it was who brought the conversation by a sudden heroic gesture back to the Governor.

"And tell me, dear Julia," she said. "Is there no news of Lily? . . . Has nothing come of the Governor's devotion?"

There was nothing, Julia replied with a sharp, compressed smile. "Nothing at all, save a flirtation. Lily, you know, is very pretty."

"So beautiful!" remarked Mrs. Harrison. "I was telling my son William so, only to-night. He admires her . . . deeply, you know, deeply." She had taken to fanning herself vigorously for the night was hot. She did it boldly, endeavoring in vain to force some stray zephyr among the rolls of fat inside her tight bodice.

"What I can never understand," continued Miss Abercrombie, "is why

Lily hasn't already married. A girl so pretty and so nice to every one . . .
especially older people."

Mrs. Shane became falsely deprecating of Lily's charms. "She is a good
girl," she said. "But hardly as charming as all that. The trouble is that she's
very fastidious. She isn't easy to suit." In her deprecation there was an
assumption of superiority, as though she could well afford to deprecate because no one could possibly take her seriously.

"She's had plenty of chances. . . . I don't doubt that," observed Miss
Abercrombie. "I can remember that summer when we were all in Aix together.
. . . Do you remember the young Englishman, Julia? The nice one with
yellow hair?" She turned to Mrs. Julis Harrison with an air of arrogant pride
and intimacy. "He was the second son of a peer, you know, and she could
have had him by a turn of her finger."

And the association with the peerage placed for the time being Miss
Abercrombie definitely on the side of Julia Shane in the drawing-room
skirmish.

"And Harvey Biggs was so devoted to her," she babbled on. "Such a nice
boy . . . gone now to the war like so many other brave fellows." Then as
though remembering suddenly that William Harrison was not at the war
but safe in the library across the hall, she veered quickly. "They say the
Spanish atrocities in Cuba are beyond comprehension. I feel that we should
spread them as much as possible to rouse the spirit of the people."

"I've thought since," remarked Mrs. Harrison, "that you should have had
flags for decorations at the garden party, Julia. With a war on and especially
with the Governor here. I only mention it because it has made people talk.
It only adds to the resentment against his behavior."

"I thought the flowers were enough," replied Mrs. Shane, making a wry
face. "They were so beautiful until cinders from your furnaces destroyed them.
Those peonies," she added, indicating the white flowers that showed dimly
in the soft light, "are all that is left." There was a moment's pause and the
distant throb of the Mills filled the room, proclaiming their eternal presence.
It was a sound which never ceased. "The garden party seems to have been a
complete failure. I'm growing too old to entertain properly."

"Nonsense!" declared Mrs. Julis Harrison with great emphasis. "But I
don't see why you persist in living here with the furnaces under your nose."

"I shan't live anywhere else. Cypress Hill was here before the Mills . . .
long before."

Almost unconsciously each woman discovered in the eye of the other a
faint gleam of anger, the merest flash of spirit, a sign of the eternal struggle
between that which is established and that which is forever in a state of flux,
which Mrs. Julis Harrison in her heart called "progress" and Julia Shane in
hers called "desecration."

Chapter 8

THE STRUGGLE ENDED here because at that moment the voice of William Harrison, drawling and colorless, penetrated the room. He came in from the hallway, preceded by Lily, who wore a gown of rose-colored satin draped at the waist and ornamented with a waterfall of lace which descended from the discreet V at the neck. He was an inch or two shorter than Lily, with pale blond hair and blue eyes that protruded a little from beneath a high bald forehead. His nose was long and his mouth narrow and passionless. He held himself very straight, for he was conscious that his lack of stature was inconsistent with the dignity necessary to the heir of the Harrison millions.

"It is late, mother," he said. "And Lily is leaving to-morrow for New York. She is sailing, you know, on Thursday."

His face was flushed and his manner nervous. He fingered his watch chain, slipping the ruby clasp backward and forward restlessly.

"Sailing!" repeated Mrs. Harrison, sitting bold upright in her chair and suspending her fan in mid-air. "Sailing! Why didn't you tell me, Julia? I should have sent you a going-away present, Lily."

"Sailing," echoed Miss Abercrombie, "to France, my dear! I have some commissions you must do for me. Do you mind taking a package or two?"

Lily smiled slowly. "Of course not. Can you send them down in the morning? I'm afraid I won't get up to the Town to-morrow."

She moved aside suddenly to make way for the mulatto woman, Hennery's wife, for whom Julia Shane had rung at the moment of William Harrison's first speech.

"Tell Hennery," she said, "to send round Mrs. Harrison's carriage." The old woman was taking no chances now.

There followed the confusion which surrounds the collecting of female wraps, increased by the twittering of Miss Abercrombie in her excitement over the thought of a voyage to "the continent." The carriage arrived and the guests were driven off down the long drive and out into the squalid street.

When Miss Abercrombie had been dropped at a little old house which, sheltered by lilacs, elms and syringas, stood in the old part of the Town, William Harrison shifted his position in the victoria, fingered his watch chain nervously and lowered his voice lest the coachman hear him above the rumble of the rubber-tires on the cobble-stones.

"She refused me," he said.

For a time the victoria rumbled along in silence with its mistress sitting very straight, breathing deeply. At length she said, "She may come round. . . . You're not clever with women, William."

The son writhed in the darkness. He must sometimes have suspected that his mother's opinion of him was even less flattering than his own. There was no more talk between them that night. For Mrs. Harrison a great hope had been killed—put aside perhaps expressed it more accurately, for she was a powerful woman who did not accept defeat passively. She had hoped that she might unite the two great fortunes of the Town. Irene had been tried and found impossible. She would never marry any one. One thing puzzled the indomitable woman and so dulled a little the keen edge of her disappointment. It was the sudden trip to Paris. A strange incredible suspicion raised itself in her mind. This she considered for a time, turning it over and over with a perverse pleasure. At last, despite all her desire to believe it, she discarded it as too fantastic.

"It couldn't be," she thought. "Julia would never have dared to invite us to meet the girl. Lily herself could not have been so calm and pleasant. No, it's impossible!"

All the same when she went to her room in the great ugly house of red sandstone, she sat down before undressing and wrote a note to a friend who lived in Paris.

Chapter 9

AT CYPRESS HILL, Julia Shane and her elder daughter returned, when the door had closed on their guests, to the drawing-room to discuss after a custom of long standing the entertainment of the evening. They agreed that Mrs. Harrison had grown much too stout, that she was indeed on the verge of apoplexy; that Miss Abercrombie became steadily more fidgety and affected.

"A woman should marry," said Julia Shane, "even if she can do no better than a day laborer."

Two candles by the side of the tall mirror and one by the flaming Venice of Mr. Turner guttered feebly and expired. Now that she was alone, the old woman lighted a cigarette and blew the smoke quietly into the still air. It was Lily who interrupted the silence.

"Willie proposed to me again," she said presently.

The mother made no answer but regarded the girl quietly with a curious questioning look in her tired eyes. Lily, seated in the glow of light from the majolica lamp, must have understood what was passing in her mind.

"No," she said, "if I had wanted to marry, I could have had a man . . . a real man." For a second her eyes grew dark with emotion and her red lips curved as if she remembered suddenly and with a shameless pleasure the embraces of her lover. "No," she continued, "I wouldn't play such a trick, even on a poor thing like Willie."

The old woman knocked the ashes from her cigarette. The rings flashed and glittered in the candle light. "Sometimes," she said softly, "I think you are hopeless . . . altogether abandoned."

There was a note of melancholy in her voice, so poignant that the girl suddenly sprang from her chair, crossed the little space between them and embraced her mother impulsively. "I'm sorry for your sake, Mama," she said. "I'm sorry. . . ." She kissed the hard, handsome face and the mother returned the embrace with a sudden fierce burst of unaccustomed passion.

"It's all right, Lily dear. I'm only thinking of you. I don't think anything can really hurt me any longer. I'm an old warrior, tough and well-armored." For a second she regarded the girl tenderly and then asked, "But aren't you afraid?"

"No!" The answer was quiet and confident.

"You're a strange, strange girl," said the mother.

Chapter 10

MADAME GIGON with Fifi lived in a tiny apartment in the Rue de la Assomption. In the summer she went to live at Germigny l'Evec in a curve of the Marne after it has passed Meaux and Trilport, wandering its soft and amiable way between sedges and wild flags under rows of tall plane trees with bark as green and spotted as the backs of salamanders. Here she occupied the lodge of the château belonging to her cousin, a gentleman who inherited his title from a banker of the First Empire and lent the lodge rent free to Madame Gigon, whose father, also a banker, was ruined by the collapse of the Second Empire. M. Gigon, a scholar and antiquarian, one of the curators of the Cluny Museum, was long since dead—an ineffectual little man with a stoop and a squint, who lived his life gently and faded out of it with so little disturbance that even Madame Gigon sometimes examined her conscience and her respectability because there were long periods when she forgot that he had ever existed at all. Fifi was to her far more of a personality—Fifi with her fat waddle, her black and tan coat, and her habit of yapping for *gâteaux* at tea time.

Although Madame Gigon was not English at all, tea was a fixed rite in her life. She came by the custom at the boarding school of Mademoiselle Violette de Vaux at St. Cloud on the edge of Paris where tea was a regular meal because there was always a score of English girls among Mademoiselle's *pensionnaires*. On the passing of Monsieur Gigon she had taken, under the stress of bitter necessity, a place as instructress in art and history at the establishment of the aging Mademoiselle de Vaux, who, like herself, was a Bonapartist, a *bourgeoise* and deeply respectable. She saved from her small salary a comfortable little fortune, and at length retired with Fifi to the little flat in the Rue de la Assomption to live upon her interest and the bounty of her cousin the Baron. But above even her respectability and her small fortune, she honored her position, an element which she had preserved through a lifetime of adversity. She was respected still as the daughter of a man who had ruined himself to support Napoleon the Little. She still attended the salons of the Bonapartist families in the houses and apartments of Passy, of the Boulevard Flandrin, and the new Paris of the Place de l'Étoile. She was respected still in the circles which moved about the aging figure of the Prince Bonaparte and, greatest of all, she received a card of admission signed by his own hand whenever the Prince addressed the Geographical Society.

Madame Gigon was in the act of closing her tiny apartment in the Rue de la Assomption for the summer when the letter of Julia Shane arrived. At the news it contained, she suspended the operations necessary to her departure for the lodge of Germigny l'Evec and settled herself to await the arrival of pretty Lily Shane, contenting herself meanwhile with taking Fifi for airings in the Bois de Boulogne, a suitable distance away for one of Madame's age and infirmities. And when the day came, she managed to meet Lily in a fiacre at the Gare du Nord.

There was something touching in Madame Gigon's reception of the girl, something even more touching in Lily's reception by the fat and wheezing Fifi. The shrewd old dog remembered her as the girl who had been generous with *gâteaux*, and when Lily, dressed smartly in a purple suit with a large hat covered with plumes, climbed into the fiacre, the plump Fifi shouted and leapt about with all the animation of a puppy.

Throughout the journey to Meaux and on the succeeding trip by carriage along the Marne to Germigny, the pair made no mention of Julia Shane's letter. They talked of the heat, of the beauty of the countryside, of Mademoiselle de Vaux, who was past ninety and very feeble, of the new girls at the school . . . until the peasant coachman drew up his fat horse before the gate of the lodge and carried their luggage into the vine-covered cottage.

Chapter 11

AFTER LILY had rested in the room just beneath the dovecote, the pair, assisted by a red-cheeked farm girl, set themselves to putting the place in order. With the approach of evening, Madame Gigon took off her wig, donned a lace cap, and they were settled until the month of October.

When they had finished a supper of omelette, potatoes and wine, they seated themselves on the terrace and Madame Gigon at length approached the matter, delicately and with circumspection. It was a blue, misty evening of the sort frequent in the Isle de France, when the stillness becomes acute and tangible, when the faintest sound is sharply audible for an amazing distance across the waving fields of wheat. From the opposite side of the river arose the faint tinkling of a bell as a pair of white oxen made their way slowly from the farm to the sedge-bordered river. Overhead among the vines on the roof of the lodge, the pigeons stirred sleepily, cooing and preening themselves. The evening was beautiful, unbelievably calm, with the placidity of a marvelous dream.

After a long silence, Madame Gigon began to gossip once more and presently, she said, "To be sure, it has happened before in this world. It will happen again. The trouble is that you are too pretty, dear Lily, and you lose your head. You are too generous. I always told Mademoiselle you were more like our girls than the English or Americans."

Lily said nothing. It appeared that she heard nothing old Madame Gigon said. Wrapped in her black cloak against the chill of the faint mist which swam above the Marne, she seemed lost in the breathless beauty of the evening.

"Why, in my family, it has happened. There was my cousin . . . a sister of the Baron who lives here in the château. . . ." And Madame Gigon moved from one case to another, justifying Lily's strange behavior. When she had finished with a long series, she shook her head gently and said, "I know, I know . . . ," smiling all the while as though she had known many lovers and been as seductive as Cleopatra. She drank the last of her coffee, drying her mustache when she had finished.

"I brought down some fine lawn and some lace from Paris," she said, "I remember that you always sewed beautifully. We shall be busy this winter in the little flat."

And then Lily stirred for the first time, moving her body indolently with her eyes half-closed, her head resting on the back of the chair. "We shan't live in the little flat, Madame Gigon. . . . We shall have a house. . . . I know just the one, in the Rue Raynouard. You see, I am going to live in Paris always. I am never going back to America to live."

The old Frenchwoman said nothing, either in approval or disagreement, but she grew warm suddenly with pleasure. The house in the Rue Raynouard captured her imagination. It meant that she would have the dignity of surroundings suitable to one who received signed cards from the Prince Bonaparte to his lectures. She could have a salon. She knew that Lily Shane, like all Americans, was very rich.

A little while later they went inside and Lily in her room just under the dovecote lighted a candle and settled herself to writing letters. One she addressed to the convent where Irene was stopping, one to Cypress Hill, and the last, very short and formal, she addressed to the Governor. It was the first line she had written him. Also it was the last.

Chapter 12

IN THE TOWN the tidings of Lily's sudden departure followed the course of all bits of news from Shane's Castle. It created for a time a veritable cloud of gossip. Again when it became gradually known that she intended living in

Paris, heads wagged for a time and stories of her father were revived. Her name became the center of a myriad tales such as accumulate about beautiful women who are also indifferent.

But of one fact the Town learned nothing. It had no knowledge of a cablegram which arrived at Shane's Castle containing simply the words, "John has arrived safely and well." Only the telegraph operator saw it and to him the words could have meant nothing.

It was Mrs. Julis Harrison who kept alive the cloud of rumors that closed over the memory of Lily. When she was not occupied with directing the activities of the Mills through the mouthpiece of her son Willie, she fostered her suspicions. The letter addressed to a friend in Paris bore no fruit. Lily, it seemed, had buried herself. She was unknown to the American colony. But Mrs. Harrison, nothing daunted, managed herself to create a story which in time she came to believe, prefacing it to her choicest friends with the remark that "Shane's Castle has not changed. More things go on there than this world dreams of."

As for the Governor, he visited the Town two years later on the eve of election; but this time he did not stay at Shane's Castle. It was known that he paid old Julia Shane a mysterious visit lasting more than an hour, but what passed between them remained at best a subject for the wildest speculation.

With the departure of Lily, her mother settled slowly into a life of retirement. There were no more receptions and garden parties. With Lily gone, there appeared to be no reasons for gaiety. Irene, as every one knew, hated festivities of every sort.

"I am growing too old," said Julia Shane. "It tires me to entertain. Why should I?"

It was not true that she was old, yet it was true that she was tired. It was clear that she was letting slip all threads of interest, even more apparent that she actually cherished her solitude.

She still condescended to go to an occasional dinner in the Town, driving in her victoria with Hennery on the box, through sweating, smelly Halsted street, across the writhing oily Black Fork and up the Hill to the respectable portion of the Town where lived the people of property. It was impossible to have guessed her thoughts on that infrequent journey. They must have been strange . . . the thoughts of a woman not long past middle-age who had seen within her lifetime the most extraordinary metamorphosis in the Town of her birth. She could remember the days when she rode with John Shane in his paddock, now completely buried beneath massive warehouses. She could remember the days when Halsted street was only a private drive across the marshes to Cypress Hill. Indeed it appeared, as the years passed, that Julia Shane was slipping slowly back across all those years into the simplicity that marked her childhood as a farmer's daughter. She talked less and avoided people. She no longer cared for the elegance of her clothes. As though her gaunt and worldly air had been only a mockery she began to slough it off bit by bit with the passing months. The few women who crossed the threshold of Shane's Castle returned with stories that Julia Shane, having closed the rest of the house, had taken to living in two or three rooms.

People said other things too, of Julia and her two daughters, but mostly of Lily, for Lily somehow captured their imagination. In the midst of the Town, born and bred upon the furnace girt hill, she was an exotic, an orchid appearing suddenly in a prosperous vegetable garden.

People said such things as, "Julia Shane gets no satisfaction out of her daughter Irene. . . . I believe myself that the girl is a little queer."

Or it might be that Mrs. Julis Harrison, with a knowing shake of the head would remark, "It's strange that Lily has never married. They say she is enjoying herself in Paris, although she doesn't see anything of the Americans there. It's like John Shane's daughter to prefer the French."

Chapter 13

MEANWHILE THE TOWN grew. The farm where Julia Shane spent her youth disappeared entirely, broken up into checker board allotments, crossed by a fretwork of crude concrete sidewalks. Houses, uniform and unvaryingly ugly in architecture and cheap in construction, sprang up in clusters like fungi to house the clerks and the petty officials of the Mills. In the Flats, which included all that district taken over by the factories, hundreds of alien workmen drifted in to fill the already overcrowded houses beyond endurance. Croats, Slovenes, Russians, Poles, Italians, Negroes took up their abodes in the unhealthy lowlands, in the shadows of the furnace towers and the resounding steel sheds, under the very hedges of Shane's Castle. In Halsted street, next door to the corner saloon, a handful of worthy citizens, moved by the gravity of conditions in the district, opened an establishment which they gave the sentimental name of Welcome House, using it to aid the few aliens who were not hostile and suspicious of volunteer workers from the Town.

All this, Julia Shane, living in another world, ignored. She saw nothing of what happened beneath her very windows.

It was true that she found no satisfaction in her daughter Irene. On the return of the girl from a long rest at the convent, there took place between mother and daughter a terrible battle which did not end in a sudden, decisive victory but dragged its length across many weeks. Irene returned with her thin pretty face pale and transparent, her ash blond hair drawn back tightly from her forehead in severe nunlike fashion. She wore a suit of black stuff, plainly made and ornamented only by a plain collar of white lawn.

On the first evening at home, the mother and daughter sat until midnight in the library, a room which they used after dinner on evenings when they were alone. The little French clock struck twelve before the girl was able to summon courage to address her mother, and when at last she succeeded, she was forced to interrupt the old woman in the midst of a new book by Collette Willy, sent her by Lily, which she was reading with the aid of a silver mounted glass.

"Mother," began Irene gently. "Mother . . ."

Julia Shane put down the glass and looked up. "What is it?"

"Mother, I've decided to enter the Church."

It was an announcement far from novel, a hope expressed year after year only to be trodden under foot by the will of the old woman. But this time there was a new quality in Irene's voice, a shade of firmness and determination that was not at all in keeping with the girl's usual humility. The mother's face grew stern, almost hard. Cheri slipped gently to the floor where it lay forgotten.

"Is this my reward for letting you go back to the convent?" The voice was cold, dominating, a voice which always brought Irene into a trembling submission. The Church to both meant but one thing—the Roman Catholic Church—which John Shane, a Romanist turned scoffer, had mocked all his life, a church which to his Presbyterian widow was always the Scarlet Woman of Rome.

The girl said nothing but kept her eyes cast down, fingering all the while the carving on the arm of her rosewood chair. She had grown desperately pale. Her thin fingers trembled.

"Has this anything to do with Lily?" asked the mother with a sudden air of suspicion, and Irene answered "No! No!" with such intensity that Julia Shane, convinced that she still knew nothing, tried a new tack.

"You know how I feel," she said. "I am old and I am tired. I have had enough unhappiness, Irene. This would be the last."

Tears came into the eyes of the girl, and the trembling grew and spread until her whole body was shaking. "It is all I have," she cried.

"Don't be morbid!"

The eagle look came into Mrs. Shane's face—the look with which she faced down all the world save her own family.

"I won't hear of it," she added. "I've told you often enough, Irene. . . . I won't have a daughter of mine sell herself to the devil if I can prevent it." She spoke with a rising intensity of feeling that was akin to hatred. "You shall not do it as long as I live and never after I am dead, if I can help it."

The girl tried not to sob. The new defiance in her soul gave her a certain spiritual will to oppose her mother. Never before had she dared even to argue her case. "If it were Lily . . ." she began weakly.

"It would make no difference. Besides, it could never be Lily. That is out of the question. Lily is no fool. . . ."

The accusation of Irene was an old one, secret, cherished always in the depths of a lonely submissive heart. It was born now from the depths of her soul, a cry almost of passion, a protest against a sister whom every one pardoned, whom every one admired, whom all the world loved. It was an accusation directed against the mother who was so sympathetic toward Lily, so uncomprehending toward Irene.

"I suppose they have been talking to you . . . the sisters," continued Julia Shane. And when the girl only buried her face miserably in her arms, she added more gently, "Come here, Irene. . . . Come over here to me."

Quietly the daughter came to her side where she knelt down clasping the fingers covered with rings that were so cold against her delicate, transparent skin. For an instant the mother frowned as if stricken by some physical pain. "My God!" she said, "Why is it so hard to live?" But her weakness passed quickly. She stiffened her tired body, sighed, and began again. "Now," she said gruffly. "We must work this out. . . . We must understand each other better, my dear. If you could manage to confide in me . . . to let me help you. I am your mother. Whatever comes to you comes to me as well . . . everything. There are three of us, you and Lily and me." Her manner grew slowly more tender, more affectionate. "We must keep together. You might say that we stood alone . . . three women with the world against us. When I die, I want to leave you and Lily closer to each other than you and I have been. If there is anything that you want to confess . . . if you have any secret, tell it to me and not to the sisters."

By now Irene was sobbing hysterically, clinging all the while to the hand of her mother. "There is nothing . . . nothing!" she cried, "I don't know why I am so miserable."

"Then promise me one thing . . . that you will do nothing until we have talked the matter out thoroughly." She fell to stroking the girl's blond hair with her thin veined hand, slowly, with a hypnotic gesture.

"Yes. . . . Yes. . . . I promise!" And gradually the sobbing ebbed and the girl became still and calm.

For a time they sat thus listening to the mocking frivolous tick-tick of the little French clock over the fireplace. A greater sound, rumbling and regular like the pounding of giant hammers they did not hear because it had become so much a part of their lives that it was no longer audible. The throb of the Mills, working day and night, had become a part of the very stillness.

At last Julia Shane stirred and said with a sudden passion, "Come, Irene! . . . Come up to my room. There is no peace here." And the pair rose and hurried away, the mother hobbling along with the aid of her ebony stick, never once glancing behind her at the portrait whose handsome malignant eyes appeared to follow them with a wicked delight.

Chapter 14

FOR DAYS a silent struggle between the two continued, a struggle which neither admitted, yet one of which they were always conscious sleeping or waking.

And at last the mother gained from the tormented girl a second promise . . . that she would never enter the Church so long as her mother was alive. Shrewdly she roused the interest of the girl in the families of the mill workers who dwelt at the gates of Cypress Hill. Among these Irene found a place. Like a sister of charity she went into their homes, facing all the deep-rooted hostility and the suspicions of Shane's Castle. She even went by night to teach English to a handful of laborers in the school at Welcome House. For three years she labored thus, and at the end of that time she seemed happy, for there were a few among the aliens who trusted her. There were among them devout and simple souls who even came to believe that there was something saintly in the lady from Shane's Castle.

It was this pale, devout Irene that Lily found when she returned home after four years to visit her mother at Cypress Hill. Without sending word ahead she arrived alone at the sooty brick station in the heart of the Flats, slipping down at midnight from the transcontinental express, unrecognized even by the old station master who had been there for twenty years. She entered the Town like a stranger, handsomely dressed with a thick Parisian veil and heavy furs which hid her face save for a pair of dark eyes. When one is not expected one is not easily recognized, and there were people in the Town who believed that Lily Shane might never return from Paris.

She remained for a moment on the dirty platform, looking about her at the new factory sheds and the rows of workmen's houses which had sprung up since her departure. They appeared dimly through the falling snow as if they were not solid and real at all, but queer structures born out of dreams. Then she entered one of the station cabs, smelling faintly of mold and ammonia, and drove off. Throughout the journey up Halsted street to Shane's Castle, she kept poking her head in and out of the cab window to regard the outlines of new chimneys and new sheds against the glow in the sky. The snow fell in great wet flakes and no sooner did it touch the ground than it became black, and melting, flowed away in a dirty stream along the gutters. At the corner saloon, a crowd of steel workers peered at her in a drunken wonder tinged with hostility, amazed at the sight of a strange woman so richly dressed driving through the Flats at midnight. Whatever else was in doubt, they must have known her destination was the great black house on the hill.

As the cab turned in the long drive, Lily noticed by the glare of the street light that the wrought iron gates had not been painted and were clotted with rust. The gaps in the hedge of arbor vitae had spread until in spots the desolation extended for a dozen yards or more. In the house the windows all were dark save on the library side where a dull light glowed through the falling snow. The house somehow appeared dead, abandoned. In the old days it had blazed with light.

Jerry, the cab driver, lifted down her bags, stamped with the bright labels of Hotels Royale Splendide and Beau Rivage, of Ritz-Carltons and Metropolitans, in St. Moritz, in Cannes, in Sorrento and Firenze, and deposited them on the piazza with the wrought iron columns. The wistaria vines, she discovered suddenly, were gone and only the black outline of the wrought iron supports showed in a hard filigree against the dull glow of the furnaces.

The door was locked and she pulled the bell a half dozen times, listening to the sound of its distant tinkle, before the mulatto woman opened and admitted her to the accompaniment of incoherent mutterings of welcome.

"Mama!" Lily called up the long polished stairway. "Irene! Mama! Where are you?"

She gave her coat and furs to the mulatto woman and as she untied her veil, the sound of her mother's limping step and the tapping of her stick echoed from overhead through the silent house. A moment later, Julia Shane herself appeared at the top of the stairs followed by Irene clad like a deaconess in a dress of gray stuff with a high collar.

Chapter 15

ON THE OCCASION of Lily's first dinner at home, the mulatto woman brought out the heaviest of the silver candelabra and despatched Hennery into the Town for a dozen tall candles and a great bunch of pink roses which filled the silver épergne when the mother and the two daughters came down to dinner; Julia Shane, as usual, wore black with a lace shawl thrown over her gray hair, a custom which she had come to adopt in the evenings and one which gave the Town one more point of evidence in the growing chain of her eccentricities. Irene, still clad in the gray dress with the high collar and looking somehow like a governess or a nurse employed in the house, took her place at the side of the table. As for Lily, her appearance so fascinated the mulatto woman and the black girl who aided her that the dinner was badly served and brought a sharp remonstrance from Mrs. Shane. No longer had Lily any claims to girlhood. Indisputably she was become a woman. A fine figure of a woman, she might have been called, had she been less languid and indolent. Her slimness had given way to a delicate voluptuousness, a certain opulence like the ripeness of a beautiful fruit. Where there had been slimness before there now were curves. She moved slowly and with the same curious dignity of her mother, and she wore no rouge, for her lips were full and red and her cheeks flushed with delicate color. Her beauty was the beauty of a peasant girl from which all coarseness had been eliminated, leaving only a radiant glow of health. She was, after all, the granddaughter of a Scotch farmer; there was nothing thin-blooded about her, nothing of the anemia of Irene. To-night she wore a tea-gown from Venice, the color of water in a limestone pool, liquid, cool, pale green. Her reddish hair, in defiance of the prevailing fashions, she wore bound tightly about her head and fastened by a pin set with brilliants. About her neck on a thin silver cord hung suspended a single pear-shaped emerald which rested between her breasts, so that sometimes it hung outside the gown and sometimes lay concealed against the delicate white skin.

Irene throughout the dinner spoke infrequently and kept her eyes cast down as though the beauty of her sister in some way fascinated and repelled her. When it was finished, she stood up and addressed her mother.

"I must go now. It is my night to teach at Welcome House."

Lily regarded her with a puzzled expression until her mother, turning to explain, said, "She teaches English to a class of foreigners in Halsted street." And then to Irene, "You might have given it up on the first night Lily was home!"

A look of stubbornness came into the pale face of the younger sister. "I can't. They are depending on me. I shall see Lily every day for weeks. This is a duty. To stay would be to yield to pleasure."

"But you're not going alone into Halsted street?" protested Lily. "At night! You must be crazy!"

"I'm perfectly safe. . . . They know me and what I do," the sister answered proudly. "Besides there is one of the men who always sees me home."

She came round to Lily's chair and gave her a kiss, the merest brushing of cool lips against the older sister's warm cheek. "Good-night," she said, "in case you have gone to bed before I return."

When Irene had gone, an instant change took place in the demeanor of the two women. It was as though some invisible barrier, separating the souls of mother and daughter, had been let down suddenly. Lily leaned back and stretched her long limbs. The mulatto woman brought cigarettes and the mother and daughter settled themselves to talking. They were at last alone and free to say what they would.

"How long has Irene been behaving in this fashion?" asked Lily.

"It is more than three years now. I don't interfere because it gives her so much pleasure. It saved her, you know, from entering the Church. Anything is better than that."

Then all at once as though they had suddenly entered another world, they began to talk French, shutting out the mulatto woman from their conversation.

"*Mais elle est déja religieuse*," said Lily, "*tout simplement*. You might as well let her enter the Church. She already behaves like a nun . . . in that ridiculous gray dress. She looks ghastly. You should forbid it. A woman has no right to make herself look hideous. There's something sinful in it."

The mother smiled wearily. "Forbid it? You don't know Irene. I'm thankful to keep her out of the Church. She is becoming fanatic." There was a pause and Mrs. Shane added, "She never goes out now . . . not since a year and more."

"She is like a spinster of forty. . . . It is shameful for a girl of twenty-five to let herself go in that fashion. No man would look at her."

"Irene will never marry. . . . It is no use speaking to her. I have seen the type before, Lily . . . the *religieuse*. It takes the place of love. It is just as ecstatic."

The mulatto woman, who had been clearing away the dishes, came and stood by her mistress' chair to await, after her custom, the orders for the following day. "There will only be three of us . . . as usual. That is all, Sarah!"

The woman turned to go but Lily called after her. "Mama," she said, "can't we open the rest of the house while I'm here? It's horrible, shut up in this fashion. I hate sitting in the library when there is all the drawing-room."

Mrs. Shane did not argue. "Get some one to help you open the drawing-room to-morrow, Sarah. We will use it while Miss Lily is here."

The mulatto woman went out and Lily lighted another cigarette. "You will want it open for the Christmas party," she said. "You can't entertain all the family in the library."

"I had thought of giving up the Christmas party this year," replied the mother.

"No . . . not this year," cried Lily. "It is such fun, and I haven't seen Cousin Hattie and Uncle Jacob and Ellen for years."

Again the mother yielded. "You want gaiety, I see."

"Well, I'm not pious like Irene, and this house is gloomy enough." At the sight of her mother rising from her chair, she said . . . "Let's not go to the library. Let's sit here. I hate it in there."

So there they remained while the tall candles burned lower and lower. Suddenly after a brief pause in the talk, the mother turned to Lily and said, "*Et toi.*"

Lily shrugged her shoulders. "*Moi? Moi? Je suis contente.*"

"*Et Madame Gigon, et le petit Jean.*"

"They are well . . . both of them. I have brought a picture which I've been waiting to show you."

"He is married, you know."

"When?"

"Only three weeks ago. He came here after your letter to offer to do anything he could. He wants the boy to go to school in America."

Here Lily smiled triumphantly. "But Jean is mine. I shall accept nothing from him. He is afraid to recognize Jean because it would ruin him. I shall send the boy where I like." She leaned forward, glowing with a sudden enthusiasm. "You don't know how handsome he is and how clever." She pushed back her chair. "Wait, I'll get his picture."

The mother interrupted her. "Bring me the enameled box from my dressing table. There is something in it that will interest you."

Chapter 16

IN A MOMENT the daughter returned bearing the photograph and the enameled box. It was the picture which interested Julia Shane. Putting aside the box she took it up and gazed at it for a long time in silence while Lily watched her narrowly across the polished table.

"He is a handsome child," she said presently. "He resembles you. There is nothing of his father." Her blue eyes were moist and the tired hard face softened. "Come here," she added almost under her breath, and when the daughter came to her side she kissed her softly, holding her close to her thin breast. When she released Lily from her embrace, she said, "And you? When are you going to marry?"

Lily laughed. "Oh, there is plenty of time. I am only twenty-seven, after all. I am very happy as I am." She picked up the enameled box, smiling. "Show me the secret," she said.

Mrs. Shane opened the box and from a number of yellow clippings drew forth one which was quite new. "There," she said, giving it to the daughter. "It is a picture of him and his new wife, taken at the wedding."

There was a portrait of the Governor, grown a little more stout, but still tall, straight and broad shouldered. His flowing mustache had been clipped; otherwise he was unchanged. In the picture he grinned amiably toward the camera as if he saw political capital even in his own honeymoon. By his side stood a woman of medium height and strong build. Her features were heavy and she too smiled, although there was something superior in her smile as though she felt a disdain for the public. It was a plain face, intelligent, yet somehow lacking in charm. The clipping identified her as the daughter of a wealthy middle-western manufacturer and a graduate of a woman's college. It continued with a short biographical account of the Governor, predicting for him a brilliant future and congratulating him upon a marriage the public had long awaited with interest.

Lily replaced the clipping in the enameled box and closed the lid with a snap. "He had done well," she remarked. "She sounds like a perfect wife for an American politician. I should have been a hopeless failure. As it is we are both happy."

The look of bewilderment returned to her mother's eyes. "The boy," she said, "should have a father. You should marry for his sake, Lily."

"He shall have . . . in time. There is no hurry. Besides, his position is all right. I am Madame Shane, a rich American widow. Madame Gigon has taken care of that. My position is excellent. No woman could be more respected."

Gradually she drifted into an account of her life in Paris. It followed closely the line of pleasant anticipations which Madame Gigon had permitted herself during the stillness of that first evening on the terrace above the Marne. The house in the Rue Raynouard was big and old. It had been built before the Revolution at a time when Passy was a suburb surrounded by open meadows. It had a garden at the back which ran down to the Rue de Passy, once the open highroad to Auteuil. Apartments, shops and houses now covered the open meadows but the old house and the garden remained unchanged, unaltered since the day Lenôtre planned them for the Marquise de Sevillac. The garden had a fine terrace and a pavilion which some day Jean should have for his own quarters. The house itself was well planned for entertaining. It had plenty of space and a large drawing-room which extended along the garden side with tall windows opening outward upon the terrace. At a little distance off was the Seine. One could hear the excursion steamers bound for Sèvres and St. Cloud whistling throughout the day and night.

As for friends, there were plenty of them . . . more than she desired. There were the respectable baronnes and comtesses of Madame Gigon's set, a group which worshiped the Prince Bonaparte and talked a deal of silly nonsense about the Restoration of the Empire. To be sure, they were fuddy-duddy, but their sons and daughters were not so bad. Some of them Lily had known at the school of Mademoiselle de Vaux. Some of them were charming, especially the men. She had been to Compiègne to hunt, though she disliked exercise of so violent a nature. Indeed they had all been very kind to her.

"After all," she concluded, "I am not clever or brilliant. I am content with them. I am really happy. As for Madame Gigon, she is radiant. She has become a great figure in her set. She holds a salon twice a month with such an array of *gâteaux* as would turn you ill simply to look at. I give her a fat allowance but she gets herself up like the devil. I think she is sorry that crinolines are no longer the fashion. She looks like a Christmas tree, but she is the height of respectability." For an instant a thin shade of mockery, almost of bitterness colored her voice.

Julia Shane reached over suddenly and touched her daughter's arm. Something in Lily's voice or manner had alarmed her. "Be careful, Lily. Don't let yourself grow hard. That's the one thing."

Chapter 17

THEY SAT TALKING thus until the candles burnt low, guttered and began to go out, one by one, and at last the distant tinkle of a bell echoed through the house. For a moment they listened, waiting for one of the servants to answer and when the bell rang again and again, Lily at last got up languidly saying, "It must be Irene. I'll open if the servants are in bed."

"She always has a key," said her mother. "She has never forgotten it before."

Lily made her way through the hall and boldly opened the door to discover that she was right. Irene stood outside covered with snow. As she stepped in, her sister caught a glimpse through the mist of falling flakes of a tall man, powerfully built, walking down the long drive toward Halsted street. He walked rapidly, for he wore no overcoat and the night was cold.

In the warm lamplighted hall, Irene shook the snow from her coat and took off her plain ugly black hat. Her pale cheeks were flushed, perhaps from the effort of walking so rapidly up the drive.

"Who is the man?" asked Lily with an inquisitive smile.

Her sister, pulling off her heavy overshoes, answered without looking up. "His name is Krylenko. He is a Ukrainian . . . a mill worker."

An hour later the two sisters sat in Lily's room while she took out gown after gown from the brightly labeled trunks. Something had happened during the course of the evening to soften the younger sister. She showed for the first time traces of an interest in the life of Lily. She even bent over the trunks and felt admiringly of the satins, the brocades, the silks and the furs that Lily lifted out and tossed carelessly upon the big Italian bed. She poked about among the delicate chiffons and laces until at last she came upon a small photograph of a handsome gentleman in the ornate uniform of the cuirassiers. He was swarthy and dark-eyed with a crisp vigorous mustache, waxed and turned up smartly at the ends. For a second she held it under the light of the bed lamp.

"Who is this?" she asked, and Lily, busy with her unpacking, looked up for an instant and then continued her task. "It is the Baron," she replied. "Madame Gigon's cousin . . . the one who supports her."

"He is handsome," observed Irene in a strange shrewd voice.

"He is a friend. . . . We ride together in the country. Naturally I see a great deal of him. We live at his château in the summer."

The younger sister dropped the conversation. She became silent and withdrawn, and the queer frightened look showed itself in her pale blue eyes. Presently she excused herself on the pretense that she was tired and withdrew to the chaste darkness of her own room where she knelt down before a plaster virgin, all pink and gilt and sometimes tawdry, to pray.

Chapter 18

ON THE FOLLOWING night the house, as it appeared from the squalid level of Halsted street, took on in its setting of snow-covered pines and false cypresses the appearance to which the Town had been accustomed in the old days. The drawing-room windows glowed with warm light; wreaths were hung against the small diamond shaped panes, and those who passed the wrought iron gates heard during the occasional pauses in the uproar of the Mills the distant tinkling of a piano played with a wild exuberance by some one who chose the gayest of tunes, waltzes and polkas, which at the same hour were to be heard in a dozen Paris music halls.

Above the Flats in the Town, invitations were received during the course of the week to a dinner party, followed by a ball in the long drawing-room.

"Cypress Hill is becoming gay again," observed Miss Abercrombie.

"It must be the return of Lily," said Mrs. Julis Harrison. "Julia will never entertain again. She is too broken," she added with a kind of triumph.

A night or two after Lily's return Mrs. Harrison again spoke to her son William of Lily's beauty and wealth, subtly to be sure and with carefully concealed purpose, for Willie, who was thirty-five now and still unmarried, grew daily more shy and more deprecatory of his own charms.

It was clear enough that the tradition of Cypress Hill was by no means dead, that it required but a little effort, the merest scribbling of a note, to restore all its slumbering prestige. The dinner and the ball became the event of the year. There was great curiosity concerning Lily. Those who had seen her reported that she looked well and handsome, that her clothes were far in advance of the local fashions. They talked once more of her beauty, her charm, her kindliness. They spoke nothing but good of her, just as they mocked Irene and jeered at her work among the foreigners in the Flats. It was Lily who succeeded to her mother's place as chatelaine of the beautiful gloomy old house at Cypress Hill.

It was also Lily who, some two weeks before Christmas, received Mrs. Julis Harrison and Judge Weissman on the mission which brought them together in a social way for the only time in their lives. The strange pair arrived at Shane's Castle in Mrs. Harrison's victoria, the Jew wrapped in a great fur coat, his face a deep red from too much whiskey; and the dowager, in an imperial purple dress with a dangling gold chain, sitting well away to her side of the carriage as if contact with her companion might in some horrid way contaminate her. Lily, receiving them in the big hall, was unable to control her amazement at their sudden appearance. As the Judge bowed, rather too obsequiously, and Mrs. Harrison fastened her face into a semblance of cordiality, a look of intense mirth spread over Lily's face like water released suddenly from a broken dam. There was something inexpressibly comic in Mrs. Harrison's obvious determination to admit nothing unusual in a call made with Judge Weissman at ten in the morning.

"We have come to see your mother," announced the purple clad Amazon. "Is she able to see us?"

Lily led the pair into the library. "Wait," she replied, "I'll see. She always stays in bed until noon. You know she grows tired easily nowadays."

"I know . . . I know," said Mrs. Harrison. "Will you tell her it is important? A matter of life and death?"

While Lily was gone the pair in the library waited beneath the mocking gaze of John Shane's portrait. They maintained a tomb-like silence, broken only by the faint rustling of Mrs. Harrison's taffeta petticoats and the cat-like step of the Judge on the Aubusson carpet as he prowled from table to table examining the bits of jade or crystal or silver which caught his Oriental fancy. Mrs. Harrison sat bolt upright, a little like a pouter pigeon, with her coat thrown back to permit her to breathe. She drummed the arm of her chair with her fat fingers and followed with her small blue eyes the movements of the elk's tooth charm that hung suspended from the Judge's watch chain and swayed with every movement of his obese body. At the entrance of Julia Shane, so tall, so gaunt, so cold, she rose nervously and permitted a nervous smile to flit across her face. It was the deprecating smile of one prepared to swallow her pride.

Mrs. Shane, leaning on her stick, moved forward, at the same time fastening upon the Judge a glance which conveyed both curiosity and an undisguised avowal of distaste.

"Dear Julia," began Mrs. Harrison, "I hope you're not too weary. We came to see you on business." The Judge bobbed his assent.

"Oh, no, I'm quite all right. But if you've come about buying Cypress Hill, it's no use. I have no intention of selling it as long as I live."

Mrs. Harrison sat down once more. "It's not that," she said. "It's other business." And then turning. "You know Judge Weissman, of course."

The Judge gave an obsequious bow. From the manner of his hostess, it was clear that she did not know him, that indeed thousands of introductions could never induce her to know him.

"Won't you sit down?" she said with a cold politeness, and the Judge settled himself into an easy chair, collapsing vaguely into rolls of fat.

"We should like to talk with you alone," said Mrs. Harrison. "If Lily could leave. . . ." And she finished the speech with a nod of the head and a turn of the eye meant to convey a sense of grave mystery.

"Certainly," replied Lily, and went out closing the door on her mother and the two visitors.

For two hours they remained closeted in the library while Lily wandered about the house, writing notes, playing on the piano; and once, unable to restrain her curiosity, listening on tip-toe outside the library door. At the end of that time, the door opened and there emerged Mrs. Julis Harrison, looking cold and massively dignified, her gold chain swinging more than usual, Judge Weissman, very red and very angry, and last of all, Julia Shane, her old eyes lighted by a strange new spark and her thin lips framed in an ironic smile of triumph.

The carriage appeared and the two visitors climbed in and were driven away on sagging springs across the soot-covered snow. When they had gone, the mother summoned Lily into the library, closed the door and then sat down, her thin smile growing at the same time into a wicked chuckle.

"They've been caught . . . the pair of them," she said. "And Cousin Charlie did it. . . . They've been trying to get me to call him off."

Lily regarded her mother with eyebrows drawn together in a little frown. Plainly she was puzzled. "But how Cousin Charlie?" she asked. "How has he caught them?"

The mother set herself to explaining the whole story. She went back to the very beginning. "Cousin Charlie, you know, is county treasurer. It was Judge Weissman who elected him. The Jew is powerful. Cousin Charlie wouldn't have had a chance but for him. Judge Weissman only backed him because he thought he'd take orders. But he hasn't. That's where the trouble is. That's why they're worried now. He don't do what Judge Weissman tells him to do!"

Here she paused, permitting herself to laugh again at the discomfiture of her early morning callers. So genuine was her mirthful satisfaction that for an instant, the guise of the worldly woman vanished and through the mask showed the farm girl John Shane had married thirty years before.

"You see," she continued, "in going through the books, Cousin Charlie discovered that the Cyclops Mills owe the county about five hundred thousand dollars in back taxes. He's sued to recover the money together with the fines, and he cannot lose. Judge Weissman and Mrs. Harrison have just discovered that and they've come to me to call him off because he is set on recovering the money. He's refused to take orders. You see, it hits their pocket-books. The man who was treasurer before Cousin Charlie has disappeared neatly. There's a pretty scandal somewhere. Even if it doesn't come out, the Harrisons and Judge Weissman will lose a few hundred thousands. The Jew owns a lot of stock, you know."

The old woman pounded the floor with her ebony stick as though the delight was too great to escape expression by any other means. Her blue eyes shone with a wicked gleam. "It's happened at last!" she said. "It's happened at last! I've been waiting for it . . . all these years."

"And what did you tell them?" asked Lily.

"Tell them! Tell them!" cried Julia Shane. "What could I tell them? Only that I could do nothing. I told them they were dealing with an honest man. It is impossible to corrupt Hattie's husband. I could do nothing if I would, and certainly I would do nothing if I could. They'll have to pay . . . just when they're in the midst of building new furnaces." Suddenly her face grew serious and the triumph died out of her voice. "But I'm sorry for Charlie and Hattie, just the same. He'll suffer for it. He has killed himself politically. The Jew is too powerful for him. It'll be hard on Hattie and the children, just when Ellen was planning to go away to study. Judge Weissman will fight him from now on. You've no idea how angry he was. He tried to bellow at me, but I soon stopped him."

And the old woman laughed again at the memory of her triumph.

As for Lily her handsome face grew rosy with indignation. "It can't be as bad as that! That can't happen to a man because he did his duty! The Town can't be as rotten as that!"

"It is though," said her mother. "It is. You've no idea how rotten it is. Why, Cousin Charlie is a lamb among the wolves. Believe me, I know. It's worse than when your father was alive. The mills have made it worse."

Then both of them fell silent and the terrible roar of the Cyclops Mills, triumphant and monstrous, invaded the room once more. Irene came in from a tour of the Flats and looking in at the door noticed that they were occupied with their own thoughts, and so hurried on to her room. At last Mrs. Shane rose.

"We must help the Tollivers somehow," she said. "If only they weren't so damned proud it would be easier."

Lily, her eyes dark and serious, stood at the window now looking across the garden buried beneath blackened snow. "I know," she said. "I was thinking the same thing."

Chapter 19

FOR THIRTY YEARS Christmas dinner had been an event at Shane's Castle. John Shane, who had no family of his own, who was cut off from friends and relatives, adopted in the seventies the family of his wife, and established the custom of inviting every relative and connection to a great feast with wine, a turkey, a goose and a pair of roast pigs. In the old days before the MacDougal Farm was swallowed up by the growing town, New Year's dinner at the farmhouse had also been an event. The family came in sleds and sleighs from all parts of the county to gather round the groaning table of Jacob Barr, Julia Shane's brother-in-law and the companion of John Shane in the paddock now covered by warehouses. But all that was a part of the past. Even the farmhouse no longer existed. Christmas at Cypress Hill was all that remained.

Once there had been as many as thirty gathered about the table, but one by one these had vanished, passing out of this life or migrating to the West when the Mills came and the county grew crowded; for the MacDougals, the Barrs and all their connection were adventurers, true pioneers who became wretched when they were no longer surrounded by a sense of space, by enough air, unclogged by soot and coal gas, for their children to breathe.

On Christmas day there came to Cypress Hill a little remnant of seven. These with Julia Shane and her two daughters were all that remained of a family whose founder had crossed the Appalachians from Maryland to convert the wilderness into fertile farming land. They arrived at the portico with the wrought iron columns in two groups, the first of which was known as The Tolliver Family. It included Cousin Hattie, her husband Charles Tolliver, their daughter Ellen, two sons Fergus and Robert, and Jacob Barr, who made his home with them and shared with Julia Shane the position of Head of the Family.

They drove up in a sleigh drawn by two horses—good horses, for Jacob Barr and Charles Tolliver were judges of horseflesh—and Mrs. Tolliver got down first, a massive woman, large without being fat, with a rosy complexion and a manner of authority. She wore a black feather boa, a hat trimmed with stubby ostrich plumes perched high on her fine black hair, and a short jacket of astrakhan, slightly *démodé* owing to its leg-of-mutton sleeves. After her descended her father, the patriarch Jacob Barr. The carriage rocked beneath his bulk. He stood six feet three in his stocking feet and for all his eighty-two years was bright as a dollar and straight as a poker. A long white beard covered his neckerchief and fell to the third button of his embroidered waistcoat, entangling itself in the heavy watch chain from which hung suspended a nugget of gold, souvenir of his adventure to the Gold Coast in the Forties. He carried a heavy stick of cherry wood and limped, having broken his hip and recovered from it at the age of eighty.

Next Ellen got down, her dark curls transformed into a pompadour as her mother's concession to a recent eighteenth birthday. She was tall, slim, and handsome despite the awkwardness of the girl not yet turned woman. Her eyes were large and blue and her hands long and beautiful. She had the family nose, prominent and proudly curved, which in Julia Shane had become an eagle's beak. After her, Fergus, a tall, shy boy of fourteen, and Robert, two years younger, sullen, wilful, red-haired like his venerable grandfather, who in youth was known in the county as The Red Scot. The boys were squabbling and had to be put in order by their mother before entering Cousin Julia's handsome house. Under her watchful eye there was a prolonged scraping of shoes on the doormat. She managed her family with the air of a field-marshal.

As for Charles Tolliver, he turned over the steaming horses to Hennery, bade the black man blanket them well, talked with him for a moment, and then followed the others into the house. Him Hennery adored, with the adoration of a servant for one who understands servants. In the stables, Hennery put extra zeal into the rubbing down of the animals, his mind carrying all the while the picture of a tall gentleman with graying hair, kindly eyes and a pleasant soft voice.

"Mr. Tolliver," he told the mulatto woman later in the day, "is one of God's gentlemen."

The other group was known as The Barr Family. The passing of years had thinned its ranks until there remained only Eva Barr, the daughter of Samuel Barr and therefore a niece of the vigorous and patriarchal Jacob. Characteristically she made her entrance in a town hack, stopping to haggle with the driver over the fare. Her thin, spinsterish voice rose above the roaring of the Mills until at length she lost the argument, as she always did, and paid reluctantly the prodigious twenty-five cents. She might easily have come by way of the Halsted street trolley for five cents, but this she considered neither safe nor dignified. As she grew older and more eccentric, she had come to exercise extraordinary precautions to safeguard her virginity. She was tall, thin, and dry, with a long nose slightly red at the end, and hair that hung in melancholy little wisps about an equine face; yet she had a double lock put on the door of her room at Haines' boarding house, and nothing would have induced her to venture alone into the squalid Flats. She was poor and very pious. Into her care fell the destitute of her parish. She administered scrupulously with the hard efficiency of a penurious house-keeper.

Dinner began at two and assumed the ceremonial dignity of a tribal rite. It lasted until the winter twilight, descending prematurely because of the smoke from the Mills, made it necessary for the mulatto woman and her black helpers to bring in the silver candlesticks, place them amid the wreckage of the great feast, and light them to illumine the paneled walls of the somber dining-room. When the raisins and nuts and the coffee in little gilt cups had gone the rounds, the room resounded with the scraping of chairs, and the little party wandered out to distribute itself at will through the big house. Every year the distribution followed the same plan. In one corner of the big drawing-room Irene, in her plain gray dress, and Eva Barr, angular and piercing in durable and shiny black serge, foregathered, drawn by their mutual though very different interest in the poor. Each year the two spinsters fell upon the same arguments; for they disagreed about most fundamental things. The attitude of Irene toward the poor was the Roman attitude, full of paternalism, beneficent, pitying. Eva Barr in her Puritan heart had no room for such sentimental slop. "The poor," she said, "must be taught to pull themselves out of the rut. It's sinful to do too much for them."

Two members of the family, the oldest, Jacob Barr, and the youngest, his grandson, disappeared completely, the one to make his round of the stables and park, the other to vanish into the library where, unawed by the sinister portrait of old John Shane, he poked about, stuffing himself with the candy sent by Willie Harrison as a token of a thrice renewed courtship. The grandfather, smoking what he quaintly called a cheroot, surveyed scrupulously the stable and the house, noting those portions which were falling into disrepair. These he later brought to the attention of Julia Shane; and the old woman, leaning on her stick, listened with an air of profound attention to her brother-in-law only to forget everything he had advised the moment the door closed upon him. Each year it was the same. Nothing changed.

In the far end of the drawing-room by the grand piano, Lily drew Ellen Tolliver and the tall shy brother Fergus to her side. Here Mrs. Tolliver joined them, her eyes bright with flooding admiration for her children. The girl was plainly fascinated by her glamorous cousin. She examined boldly Lily's black gown from Worth, her pearls, and her shoes from the Rue de la Paix. She begged for accounts of the Opéra in Paris and of Paderewski's playing with the Colonne Orchestra. There was something pitiful in her eagerness for some contact with the glamorous world beyond the Town.

"I'm going to New York to study, next year," she told Lily. "I would go this year but Momma says I'm too young. Of course, I'm not. If I had money, I'd go anyway." And she cast a sudden defiant glance at her powerful mother.

Lily, her face suddenly grave with the knowledge of Judge Weissman's visit, tried to reassure her. "You'll have plenty of opportunity, Ellen. You're still a young girl . . . only eighteen."

"But there's never any money," the girl replied, with an angry gleam in her wide blue eyes. "Papa's always in debt. I'll never get a chance unless I make it myself."

In the little alcove by the gallery, Julia Shane leaning on her stick, talked business with Charles Tolliver. This too was a yearly custom; her nephew, the county treasurer, gave her bits of advice on investments which she wrote down with a silver pencil and destroyed when he had gone. She listened and begged his advice because the giving of it encouraged him and gave him confidence. He was a gentle, honest fellow, and in her cold way she loved him, better even than she loved his wife who was her niece by blood. The advice he gave was mediocre and uninspired; besides Julia Shane was a shrewd woman and more than a match in business matters for most men.

When they had finished this little ceremony, the old woman turned the conversation to the Cyclops Mill scandal.

"And what's to come of it?" she asked. "Are you going to win?"

Charles Tolliver smiled. "We've won already. The case was settled yesterday. The Mill owes the state some five hundred thousand with fines."

Julia Shane again pounded the floor in delight. "A fine Christmas present!" she chuckled. "A fine Christmas present!" And then she did an unaccountable thing. With her thin ringed hand she slapped her nephew on the back.

"You know they came to me," she said, "to get my influence. I told them to go to the Devil! . . . I suppose they tried to bribe you."

The nephew frowned and the gentleness went out of his face. The fine mouth grew stern. "They tried . . . carefully though, so carefully they couldn't be caught at it."

"It will make you trouble. Judge Weissman is a bad enemy. He's powerful."

"I know that. I've got to fight him. The farmers are with me."

"But the Town is not, and it's the Town which counts nowadays. The day of the farmer is past."

"No, the Town is not."

The face of Charles Tolliver grew serious and the blue eyes grave and worried. Julia Shane saw that he was watching his tall daughter who sat now at the piano, preparing to play.

"If you need money at the next election," she said, "Come to me. I can help you."

Chapter 20

AT THE SOUND of Ellen's music, the conversation in the long drawing-room ceased save for the two women who sat in the far corner—Irene and Eva Barr. They went on talking in an undertone of their work among the poor. The others listened, captivated by the sound, for Ellen played well, far better than any of the little group save Lily and Julia Shane knew. To the others it was simply music; to the old woman and her daughter it was something more. They found in it the fire of genius, the smoldering warmth of a true artist, a quality unreal and transcendental which raised the beautiful old room for a moment out of the monotonous slough of commonplace existence. Ellen, in high-collared shirtwaist and skirt with her dark hair piled high in a ridiculous pompadour, sat very straight bending over the keys from time to time in a caressing fashion. She played first of all a Brahms waltz, a delicate thread of peasant melody raised to the lofty realm of immortality by genius; and from this she swept into a Chopin valse, melancholy but somehow brilliant, and then into a polonaise, so dashing and so thunderous that even Irene and Eva Barr, ignorant of all the beauty of sound that tumbled flood-like into the old room, suspended their peevish talk for a time and sat quite still, caught somehow in the contagious awe of the others.

The thin girl at the piano was not in a drawing-room at all. She sat in some enormous concert hall on a high stage before thousands of people. The faces stretched out before her, row after row, until those who sat far back were misty and blurred, not to be distinguished. When she had finished the polonaise she sat quietly for a moment as though waiting for a storm of applause to arise after a little hush from the great audience. There was a moment of silence and then the voice of Lily was heard, warm and soft, almost caressing,

"It was beautiful, Ellen . . . really beautiful. I had no idea you played so well."

The girl, blushing, turned and smiled at the cousin who lay back so indolently among the cushions of the sofa, so beautiful, so charming in the black gown from Worth. The smile conveyed a world of shy and inarticulate gratitude. The girl was happy because she understood that Lily knew. To the others it was just music.

"Your daughter is an artist, Hattie," remarked Julia Shane. "You should be proud of her."

The mother, her stout figure tightly laced, sat very straight in her stiff chair, her work-stained hands resting awkwardly in her lap. Her face beamed with the pride of a woman who was completely primitive, for whom nothing in this world existed save her children.

"And now, Ellen," she said, "play the McKinley Funeral March. You play it so well."

The girl's young face clouded suddenly. "But it's not McKinley's Funeral March, Mama," she protested. "It's Chopin's. It's not the same thing."

"Well, you know what I mean . . . the one you played at the Memorial Service for McKinley." She turned to Lily, her pride written in every line of her strong face. "You know, Ellen was chosen to play at the services for McKinley. Mark Hanna himself made a speech from the same platform."

Chapter 21

AN IRREPRESSIBLE smile swept Lily's face. "They couldn't have chosen better, I'm sure. Do play it, Ellen."

The girl turned to the piano and a respectful silence fell once more. Slowly she swept into the somber rhythms of the *March Funèbre*, beginning so softly that the music was scarcely audible, climbing steadily toward a climax. From the depths of the old Pleyel she brought such music as is seldom heard. The faces in the drawing-room became grave and thoughtful. Lying among the pillows of the divan, Lily closed her eyes and listened through a wall of darkness. Nearby, her mother, leaning on the ebony stick, bowed her head because her eyes had grown dim with tears, a spectacle which she never permitted this world to witness. Presently the music swung again into a somber retarding rhythm; and then slowly, surely, with a weird, unearthly certainty, it became synchronized with the throbbing of the Mills. The steady beat was identical. Old Julia Shane opened her eyes and stared out of the window into the gathering darkness. The music, all at once, made the pounding of the Mills hideously audible.

When the last note echoing through the old house died away, Eva Barr, fidgeting with her embroidered reticule in search of a handkerchief to wipe her lean red nose, rose and said, "Well, I must go. It's late and the hack is already here. He charges extra for waiting, you know."

That was the inevitable sign. The dinner was ended. Grandpa Barr, very rosy from his promenade about the grounds, and the red-haired Robert, much stuffed with Willie Harrison's courting chocolates, reappeared and the round of farewells was begun.

Before Hennery brought round from the stable the Tolliver's sleigh, Lily placing her arm about Ellen's waist, drew her aside and praised her playing. "You must not throw it away," she said. "It is too great a gift." She whispered. Her manner became that of a conspirator. "Don't let them make you settle into the pattern of the Town. It's what they'll try to do, but don't let them. We only live once, Ellen, don't waste your life. The others . . . the ones who aren't remarkable in any way will try to pull you down from your pedestal to their level. But don't let them. Fitting the pattern is the end of their existence. 'Be like every one else,' is their motto. Don't give in. And when the time comes, if you want to come and study in Paris with the great Philippe, you can live with me."

The girl blushed and regarded the floor silently for a moment. "I won't let them," she managed to say presently. "Thank you, Cousin Lily." At the door, she turned sharply, all her shyness suddenly vanished, an air of defiance in its place. "I won't let them. . . . You needn't worry," she added with a sudden fierceness.

"And next week," said Lily, "come here and spend the night. I want to hear more music. There's no music in this Town but the Mills."

By the fireplace under the flaming Venice of Mr. Turner, Julia Shane talked earnestly with her niece, Mrs. Tolliver, who stood warming her short astrakhan jacket by the gentle blaze.

"And one more thing, Hattie," said the old woman. "I've been planning to give you these for some time but the opportunity never arose. I shan't live many more years and I want you to have them."

With an air of secrecy she took from her thin fingers two rings and slipped them into the red, worn hands of her niece. "Don't tell any one," she added. "It's a matter between us."

Mrs. Tolliver's hand closed on the rings. She could say nothing, but she kissed Aunt Julia affectionately and the tears came into her eyes because the old woman understood so well the intricate conventions of pride in matters of money. The rings were worth thousands. Hattie Tolliver could not have accepted their value in money.

At the door the little party made its departure with a great deal of healthy hubbub, colliding at the same time with a visitor who had driven up unseen. It was Willie Harrison, come to call upon Lily and to propose a visit to the Mills to look over the new furnaces that were building. In the stream of light from the doorway the caller and Charles Tolliver recognized each other and an awkward moment followed. It was Willie Harrison, overcome with confusion, who bowed politely. Charles Tolliver climbed into his sleigh without making any sign of recognition. The feud between the old and the new, concealed for so many years, was emerging slowly into the open.

Chapter 22

THE DAY after Christmas dawned bright and clear, as clear as any day dawned in the Flats where at sunrise the smoke turned the sun into a great copper disk rising indolently toward the zenith of the heavens. The false warmth of the January thaw, precocious that year, brought gentle zephyrs that turned the icicles on the sweeping eaves of the house into streams of water which added their force to the rivulets already coursing down the long drive to leave the gravel bare and eroded, swelling with the upheaval of the escaping frost. But the false warmth brought no beauty; no trees burgeoned forth in clouds of bright green and no crocuses thrust forth their thin green swords and errant blossoms. The January thaw was but a false hope of the northern winter. When the sun of the early afternoon had destroyed all traces of the snow save drifts which hid beneath the rhododendrons or close against the north wall of the stable, it left behind an expanse of black and dessicated lawn, in spots quite bare even of dying grass. The garden stripped of its winter blanket at last stood revealed, a ravaged fragment of what had once been a glory.

Lily, drawn from the house by the warmth of the sun, wandered along the barren paths like a lovely hamadryad enticed by deceitful gods from her winter refuge. She ran from clump to clump of shrubbery, breaking off the tender little twigs in search of the green underbark that was a sign of life. Sometimes she found the green; more often she found only dead, dry wood, bereft of all vitality. In the flower garden she followed the brick path to its beginning in the little arbor covered with wistaria vine. Here too the Mills had taken their toll; the vine was dead save a few thin twining stalks that clung to the arbor. In the border along the walk, she found traces of irises—hardy plants difficult to kill—an occasional thick green leaf of a companula or a foxglove hiding among the shelter of leaves provided by the careful Hennery. But there were great gaps of bare earth where nothing grew, stretches which in her childhood had been buried beneath a lush and flowery growth of sky-blue delphinium, scarlet poppies, fiery tritomas, blushing peonies, foxglove, goosefoot, periwinkle, and cinnamon pinks. . . . All were gone now, blighted by the capricious and fatal south wind with its burden of gas and soot. It was not alone the flowers which suffered. In the niches clipped by Hennery in the dying walls of arbor vitae, the bits of white statuary were streaked with black soot, their pure bodies smudged and defiled. The Apollo Belvedere and the Venus of Cydnos were no longer recognizable.

In the course of her tour about the little park, her red hair became loosened and disheveled and her cheeks flushed with her exertion. When she again re-entered the house, she discovered that her slippers, high-heeled and delicate, were ruined. She called the mulatto woman and bade her throw them away.

On the stairs she encountered her mother, whom she greeted with a little cry of horror. "The garden, Mama, is ruined. . . . Nothing remains!"

The expression on the old woman's face remained unchanged and stony.

"Nothing will grow there any longer," she said. "Besides, it does not matter. When I die, there will be no one to live in the house. Irene hates it. She wants me to take a house in the Town."

Lily, her feet clad only in the thinnest of silk-stockings, continued on her way up the long stairs to her room. If Willie Harrison had ever had a chance, even the faintest hope, the January thaw, revealing the stricken garden a fortnight too soon, destroyed it once and for all.

Chapter 23

AT THREE that afternoon Willie's victoria called to bear Lily and Irene to the Cyclops Mills for the tour which he proposed. Workmen, passing the carriage, regarded the two sisters with curiosity, frowning at the sight of Irene in a carriage they recognized as Harrison's. A stranger might have believed the pair were a great lady and her housekeeper on the way to market, so different and incongruous were the appearances of the two women. Lily, leaning back against the thick mulberry cushions, sat wrapped in a sable stole. She wore a gray tailored suit and the smallest and smartest of black slippers. Around her white throat, which she wore exposed in defiance of fashions which demanded high, boned collars, she had placed a single string of pearls the size of peas. By the side of her opulent beauty Irene possessed the austerity and plainness of a Gothic saint. As usual she wore a badly cut suit, a plain black hat and flat shoes with large, efficient heels. Her thin hands, clad in knitted woolen gloves, lay listlessly in her lap.

Willie Harrison was waiting for them at the window of the superintendent's office just inside the gate. They saw him standing there as the victoria turned across the cinders in through the red-painted entrance. He stood peering out of the window in a near-sighted way, his shoulders slightly stooped, his small hands fumbling as usual the ruby clasp of his watch chain. At the sight of him Lily frowned and bit her fine red lip as though she felt that a man so rich, a man so powerful, a man who owned all these furnaces and steel sheds should have an air more conquering and impressive.

Irene said, "Oh, there's William waiting for us now." And a second later the victoria halted by the concrete steps and Willie himself came out to greet them, hatless, his thin blond hair waving in a breeze which with the sinking of the sun grew rapidly more chilly. The sun itself, hanging over the roseate tops of the furnaces, had become a shield of deep copper red.

"You're just in time," said Willie. "The shifts will be changing in a little while. Shall we start here? I'll show you the offices."

They went inside and Willie, whose manner had become a little more confident at the prospect of such a display, led them into a long room where men sat in uniform rows on high stools at long tables. Over each table hung suspended a half-dozen electric lights hooded by green shades. The lights, so Willie told them, were placed exactly to the sixteenth of an inch eight feet and three inches apart. It was part of his theory of precision and regularity.

"This," said Willie, with a contracted sweep of his arm, "is the bookkeeping department. The files are kept here, the orders and all the paper work."

At the approach of the visitors, the younger men looked up for an instant fascinated by the presence of so lovely a creature as Lily wandering in to shatter so carelessly the sacred routine of their day. There were men of every age and description, old and young, vigorous and exhausted, men in every stage of service to the ponderous mill gods. The younger ones had a restless air and constantly stole glances in the direction of the visitors. The middle-aged ones looked once or twice at Lily and then returned drearily to their columns of figures. The older ones did not notice her at all. They had gone down for the last time in a sea of grinding routine.

Irene, who knew the Town better than Lily, pointed out among the near-sighted, narrow-chested workers men who were grandsons or great-grandsons of original settlers in the county, descendants of the very men who had cleared away the wilderness to make room for banks and lawyers and mills.

"Let's go on," said Lily, "to the Mills. They're more interesting than this, I'm sure. You know I've never been inside a mill-yard." She spoke almost scornfully, as if she thought the counting room were a poor show indeed. A shadow of disappointment crossed Willie's sallow face.

After donning a broadcloth coat with an astrakhan collar and a derby hat, he led the way. For a long time they walked among freight cars labeled with names from every part of North America. . . . Santa Fé, Southern Pacific, Great Northern, Chicago, Milwaukee and St. Paul. . . . They passed between great warehouses and vast piles of rusty pig iron still covered with frost, the dirty snow lying unmelted in the crevasses; and at last they came to an open space where rose a vast, shapeless object in the process of being raised toward the sky.

"Here," said Willie, "are the new furnaces. There are to be six of them. This is the first."

"I like this better," said Lily. "There is spirit here . . . even among the laborers."

The structure bore a strange resemblance to the Tower of Babel. Swarthy workmen, swarming over the mass of concrete and steel, shouted to each other above the din of the Mills in barbaric tongues which carried no meaning to the visitors. Workmen, like ants, pushed wheelbarrows filled with concrete, with fire clay or fire bricks. Overhead a giant crane lifted steel girders with an effortless stride and swung them into place. The figures of the workmen swept toward the tower in a constant stream of movement so that the whole took on a fantastic composition, as if the tower, rushing on its way heavenward, were growing taller and taller before their very eyes, as if before they moved away it might pierce the very clouds.

At the sight of Willie Harrison, the foremen grew more officious in manner and shouted their orders with redoubled vigor, as if the strength of their lungs contributed something toward the speed with which the great tower grew. But the workmen moved no more rapidly. On returning to the mounds of sand and fire brick, they even stopped altogether at times to stare calmly like curious animals at the visitors. One or two nodded in recognition of Irene's "Good-day, Joe," or "How are you, Boris?"—words which appeared to cloud somewhat Willie's proud enjoyment of the spectacle. And every man who passed stared long and hard at Lily, standing wrapped in her furs, a little aloof, her eyes bright nevertheless with the wonder of the sight. Neither Lily nor Irene nor Willie spoke more than was necessary, for in order to be heard above the din they were forced to scream.

From the growing tower the little party turned west toward the sunset, walking slowly over a rough roadway made of cinders and slag. Once a cinder penetrated Lily's frail shoe and she was forced to lean against Willie while she took it off and removed the offending particle. He supported her politely and turned away his face so that he should not offend her by seeing her shapely stockinged foot.

A hundred yards further on they came upon a dozen great vats covered by a single roof of sheet iron. From the vats rose a faint mist, veiling the black bodies of negroes who, shouting as they worked, dipped great plates of steel in and out. An acrid smell filled the air and penetrated the throats of the visitors as they passed rapidly by, causing Lily to take from her handbag a handkerchief of the thinnest linen which she held against her nose until they were once more beyond the zone of the fumes.

"Those are the tempering vats," said Willie. "Only negroes work here."

"But why?" asked Irene.

"Because the other workers won't," he said. "The acid eats into their lungs. The negroes come from South Carolina and Georgia to do it. They are willing!"

As they walked the sound of pounding, which appeared to come from the great iron shed lying before them black against the sunset, grew louder and louder, steadily more distinct. In the fading twilight that now surrounded them the Mill yard became a fantastic world inhabited by monsters of iron and steel. Great cranes swung to and fro against the glow of the sky, lifting and tossing into piles huge plates of steel that fell with an unearthly slithering din when an invisible hand, concealed somewhere high among the black vertebræ of the monsters, released a lever. High in the air lights, red and green, or cold piercing blue-white, like eyes appeared one by one peering down at them wickedly. Beyond the cranes in the adjoining yard the black furnaces raised gigantic towers crowned by halos of red flame that rose and fell, palpitating as the molten iron deep in the bowels of the towers churned and boiled with a white infernal heat. Dancing malignant shadows assailed them on every side.

The three visitors, dwarfed by the monsters of steel, made their way across the slag and cinders, deafened by the unearthly noise.

"Yesterday," shouted William Harrison in his thin voice, "there was a terrible accident yonder in the other yard. A workman fell into a vat of molten iron."

Irene turned to her companion with horror stricken eyes. "I know," she said. "It was an Italian named Rizzo. I heard of it this morning. I have been to see his wife and family. There are nine of them."

William shouted again. "They found nothing of him. He became a part of the iron. He is part of a steel girder by now."

Out of the evil, dancing shadows a man blackened by smoke leapt suddenly at them. "Look out!" he cried, and thrust them against the wall of a neighboring shed so roughly that Irene fell forward upon her knees. A great bundle of steel plates—tons of them—swung viciously out of the darkness, so close to the little party that the warmth of the metal touched their faces. It vanished instantly, drawn high into the air by some invisible hand. It was as if the monster had rebelled suddenly against its master, as if it sought to destroy Willie Harrison as it had destroyed the Italian named Rizzo.

Willie lost all power of speech, all thought of action. Irene, her face deathly white, leaned against the wall calling upon Lily to support her. It was Lily, strangely enough, who alone managed to control herself. She displayed no fear. On the contrary she was quiet, fiercely quiet as if a deadly anger had taken complete possession of her soul.

"Great God!" she exclaimed passionately. "This is a nightmare!" Willie fumbled helplessly by her side, rubbing the wrists of the younger sister until she raised her head and reassured them.

"I'm all right," said Irene. "We can go on now."

But Lily was for taking her home. "You've seen enough. I'm not going to have you faint on my hands."

"I'm all right . . . really," repeated Irene, weakly. "I want to see the rest. I must see it. It's necessary. It is part of my duty."

"Don't be a fool! Don't try to make a martyr of yourself!"

But Irene insisted and Lily, who was neither frightened nor exhausted, yielded at last, weakened by her own curiosity. At the same moment her anger vanished; she became completely amiable once more.

Willie led them across another open space shut in on the far side by the great shed which had loomed before them throughout the tour. They passed through a low, narrow door and stood all at once in an enormous cavern glowing with red flames that poured from the mouths of a score of enormous ovens. From overhead, among the tangle of cranes and steelwork, showers of brilliant cold light descended from hooded globes. The cavern echoed and re-echoed with the sound of a vast hammering, irregular and confused—the very hammering which heard in the house at Cypress Hill took on a throbbing, strongly-marked rhythm. On the floor of the cavern, dwarfed by its very immensity, men stripped to the waist, smooth, hard, glistening and streaked with sweat and smoke, toiled in the red glow from the ovens.

Chapter 24

BEFORE ONE of these the little party halted while Lily, and Irene, who seemed recovered though still deathly pale, listened while Willie described the operation. Into a great box of steel and fire clay were placed block after block of black iron until the box, filled at length, was pushed forward, rolling easily on balls of iron, into the fiery mouth of the oven. After a little time, the box was drawn out again and the blocks of whitehot iron were carried aloft and deposited far off, beside the great machines which rolled and hammered them into smooth steel plates.

While they stood there, workmen of every size and build, of a dozen nationalities, toiled on ignoring them. Lily, it appeared, was not deeply interested in the explanation, for she stood a little apart, her gaze wandering over the interior of the cavern. The adventure—even the breathless escape of a moment before—left her calm and indifferent. In her gaze there was a characteristic indolence, an air of absent-mindedness, which frequently seized her in moments of this sort. Nothing of her apparel was disarranged. Her hat, her furs, her pearls, her suit, were in perfect order. The flying dust and soot had gathered in her long eyelashes, but this only gave her a slightly theatrical appearance; it darkened the lashes and made her violet eyes sparkle the more. Her gaze appraised the bodies of the workmen who stood idle for the moment waiting to withdraw the hot iron from the ovens. They leaned upon the tools of their toil, some on shovels, some on long bars of iron, great chests heaving with the effort of their exertions.

Among them there was one who stood taller than the others, a giant with yellow hair and a massive face with features which were like the features of a heroic bust not yet completed by the sculptor. There was in them something of the unformed quality of youth. The man was young; he could not have been much over twenty, and the muscles of his arm and back stood out beneath his fair skin like the muscles on one of Rodin's bronze men in the Paris salons. Once he raised a great hand to wipe the sweat from his face and, discovering that she was interested in him, he looked at her sharply for an instant and then sullenly turned away leaning on a bar of iron with his powerful back turned to her.

She was still watching the man when Willie approached her and touched her arm gently. It seemed that she was unable to look away from the workman.

"Come over here and sit down," said Willie, leading her to a bench that stood a little distance away in the shadow of the foreman's shack. "Irene wants to speak to one of the men."

Lily followed him and sat down. Her sister, looking pale and tired, began a conversation with a swarthy little Pole who stood near the oven. The man greeted her with a sullen frown and his remarks, inaudible to Lily above the din, appeared to be ill-tempered and sulky as if he were ashamed before his fellows to be seen talking with this lady who came to the cavern accompanied by the master.

"Do you find it a wonderful sight?" began Willie.

Lily smiled. "I've seen nothing like it in all my life. I never knew what lay just beyond the garden hedge."

"It will be bigger than this next year and even bigger the year after." His eyes brightened and for a moment the droop of his shoulders vanished. "We want some day to see the Mills covering all the Flats. The new furnaces are the beginning of the expansion. We hope to grow bigger and bigger." He raised his arms in a sudden gesture. "There's no limit, you know."

But Lily's gaze was wandering again back and forth, up and down, round and round the vast cavern as if she were not the least interested in Willie's excitement over bigness. Irene had left the swarthy little man and was talking now to the towheaded young giant who leaned upon the iron bar. His face was sulky, though it was plain that he was curiously polite to Irene, who seemed by his side less a woman of flesh and blood than one of paper, so frail and wan was her face. He smiled sometimes in a shy, withdrawn fashion.

Politely Lily turned to her companion. "But you are growing richer and richer, Willie. Before long you will own the Town."

He regarded her shyly, his thin lips twisted into a hopeful smile. Once more he began to fumble with the ruby clasp of his watch chain.

"I could give you everything in the world," he said suddenly, as though the words caused him a great effort. "I could give you everything if you would marry me." He paused and bent over Lily who sat silently turning the rings on her fingers round and round. "Would you, Lily?"

"No." The answer came gently as if she were loath to hurt him by her refusal, yet it was firm and certain.

Willie bent lower. "I would see that Mother had nothing to do with us." Lily, staring before her, continued to turn the rings round and round. The young workman with Irene had folded his muscular arms and placed his iron bar against the wall of the oven. He stood rocking back and forth with the easy, balanced grace of great strength. When he smiled, he showed a fine expanse of firm white teeth. Irene laughed in her vague half-hearted way. Lily kept watching . . . watching. . . .

"You could even spend half the time in Europe if you liked," continued Willie. "You could do as you pleased. I would not interfere." He placed one hand gently on her shoulder to claim her attention, so plainly wandering toward the blond and powerful workman. She seemed not even to be conscious of his hand.

The workmen had begun to move toward the oven now, the young fellow with the others. He carried his iron bar as if it were a straw. He moved with a sort of angry defiance, his head thrown back upon his powerful shoulders. He it was who shouted the orders when the great coffin full of hot iron was drawn forth. He it was who thrust his bar beneath the mass of steel and lifting upward shoved it slowly and easily forward on the balls of iron. His great back bent and the muscles rippled beneath the skin as if they too were made of some marvelous flexible steel.

Willie Harrison took Lily's hand and put an end to the turning of the rings. "Tell me, Lily," he said softly, "is it no use? Maybe next year or the year after?"

All at once as though she had heard him for the first time, she turned and placed the other hand gently on top of his, looking up at the same time from beneath the wide brim of her hat. "It's no use, Willie. I'm sorry. I'm really sorry." She laughed softly. "But you were wrong in your method. You shouldn't have given me the promise about Europe. When I marry, it will be a man who will not let me leave his side."

That was all she said to him. The rest, whatever it was, remained hidden, deep within her, behind the dark eyes which found so little interest in Willie Harrison, which saw nothing but the blond giant who moved with such uncanny strength, with such incredibly easy grace about his heroic task. Perhaps if Willie had guessed, even for a moment, what was passing in her mind, he would have blushed, for Willie was, so people said, a nice young man who had led a respectable life. Such things were no doubt incomprehensible to him. Perhaps if she had spoken the truth, if she had bothered herself to explain, she would have said, "I could not marry you. I could give myself to no man but one who caught my fancy, in whom there was strength and the grace of a fine animal. Beauty, Willie, counts for much . . . far more than you guess, living always as you do in the midst of all this savage uproar. I am rich. Your money means nothing. And your power! It is not worth the snap of a finger to me. . . . Ah, if you had a face like that workman . . . a face . . . a real face, and a body . . . a real body like his, then you might ask with hope. It is hopeless, Willie. You do not interest me, though I am not eager to hurt you just the same."

But she said none of these things, for people seldom say them. On the contrary, she was content to put him off with a bare denial. It is doubtful whether such thoughts even occurred to her, however deep they may have been rooted in her soul; for she was certainly not a woman given to reflection. To any one, it was apparent that she did not examine her motives. She was content, no doubt, to be beautiful, to live where there was beauty, to surround herself with beautiful, luxurious things.

She was prevented from saying anything further by the arrival of Irene who had abandoned her workmen to rejoin Willie and her sister. Willie, crimson and still trembling a little with the effort of his proposal, suggested that they leave. It was already a quarter to six. The workmen vanished suddenly into a little shed. Their shift was finished. They were free now to return to their squalid homes, to visit the corner saloon or the dismal, shuttered brothels of Franklin street, free to go where they would in the desolate area of the Flats for twelve brief hours of life.

Chapter 25

THE THREE VISITORS made their way back to the office of the superintendent across a mill yard now bright with the cold glare of a hundred arc lights. On the way, Lily turned suddenly to her sister and asked, "Who was the man you were talking to . . . the tall one with the yellow hair?"

Irene, moving beside her, cast a sudden glance at her sister and the old terrified look entered her pale eyes. "His name is Krylenko," she replied in a voice grown subdued and cold. "He is the one who brought me home from Welcome House the other night. He is a bright boy. I've taught him English."

Willie, who had been walking behind them, quickened his pace and came abreast. "Krylenko?" he said. "Krylenko? Why, that's the fellow who's been making trouble. They've been trying to introduce the union." He addressed Irene. "Your Welcome House is making trouble I'm afraid, Irene. There's no good comes of educating these men. They don't want it."

Lily laughed. "Come now," she said, "that's what your mother says, isn't it? I can hear her saying it."

Willie failed to answer her, but a sheepish, embarrassed look took possession of his sallow face, as if the powerful figure of his mother had joined them unawares. And Irene, walking close to Lily, whispered to her sister, "You shouldn't have said that. It was cruel of you."

At the office of the superintendent they found Willie's victoria waiting, the horses covered with blankets against the swift, piercing chill of the winter night. The coachman shivered on the box. The three of them climbed in and Willie bade the man drive to Halsted street where he would get down, leaving the carriage to the ladies. When Lily protested, he answered, "But I want to walk up the hill to the Town. I need the exercise."

They drove along between two streams of mill workers, one entering, one leaving the Mill yards with the change of shifts. The laborers moved in two columns, automatons without identity save that one column was clean and

the men held their heads high and the other was black with oil and soot and
the heads were bent with a terrible exhaustion. It was a dark narrow street
bordered on one side by the tall blank walls of warehouses and on the other by
the Mill yard. The smells of the Black Fork, coated with oil and refuse, cor-
rupted the damp air. On the Mill side a high fence made of barbed wire strung
from steel posts was in the process of construction. To this Willie called their
attention with pride. "You see," he said, "we are making the Mills impregnable. If the unions come in there will be trouble. It was my idea . . . the fence.
A stitch in time saves nine." And he chuckled softly in the darkness.

At Halsted street Willie got down and, removing his hat, bade the sisters
a dry and polite good-night. But before the carriage drove on, Lily called out
to him, "You're coming to the ball to-night, aren't you? Remember, there's
a quadrille and you can't leave us flat at the last minute."

"I'm coming," said William. "Certainly I'm coming." And he turned away,
setting off in the opposite direction toward the Hill and Mrs. Julis Harrison
who sat in the ugly house of red sandstone awaiting news of the proposal. He
walked neatly, placing his small feet firmly, his hands clasped behind his
back, his head bowed thoughtfully. The umbrella, held in the crook of his
arm, swung mournfully as he walked. His shoulders drooped wearily. He had
shown Lily all his wealth, all his power; and she treated it as if it were nothing
at all. In the brownstone house, Mrs. Harrison sat waiting.

The carriage drove up Halsted street past the corner saloon now thronged
with mill workers, toward the house at Cypress Hill. In a tenement opposite
the wrought iron gates a nostalgic Russian sat on the front stoop squeezing
mournfully at a concertina which filled the winter evening with the somber
music of the steppes.

Irene, leaning back pale and exhausted on the mulberry cushions, said,
"Why did you ask Willie whether he was coming? You know he never misses
anything if he can help it."

"I only wanted to make him feel welcome," her sister replied absently.
"Since this affair over the taxes, Mama and Mrs. Harrison haven't been very
thick. . . . I feel sorry for Willie. He doesn't know what it's all about."

Chapter 26

INSIDE THE old house, Irene went to her room, and Lily, instead of seeking out
her mother for their usual chat, went quietly upstairs. She ignored even the
preparations for the ball. After she had taken off her clothes, she lay for a long
time in a hot bath scented with verbena salts, drowsing languidly until the
hot water had eliminated every soiling trace of the Mills. Returning to her
room, she sat clad in a thin satin wrapper for a long time before the mirror
of her dressing table, polishing her pink nails, examining the tiny lines at the
corners of her lips,—lines which came from smiling too much. Then she

powdered herself all over with scented powder and did up her red hair, fastening it with the pin set in brilliants. And presently, the depression having passed away, she began to sing in her low warm voice, *Je sais que vous êtes gentil*. It was a full-throated joyous song. At times her voice rose in a crescendo that penetrated the walls of the room where Irene lay in the darkness on her narrow white bed.

As she dressed for dinner, she continued to sing one song after another, most of them piquant and racy, songs of the French cuirassiers. She sang *Sur la route á Montauban, Toute la longe de la Tamise* and *Auprés de ma Blonde*. The dressing was the languid performance which required an hour or more, for she took the most minute care with every detail. The chemise must not have a wrinkle; the peacock blue stockings must fit as if they were the skin itself; the corsets were drawn until the result, examined for many minutes before the glass, was absolutely perfect. At the last she put on a gown of peacock blue satin with a long train that swept about her ankles, and rang for one of the black servants to hook it. Before the slavey arrived, Lily had discovered a wrinkle beneath the satin and began all over again the process of dressing, until at the end of the second attempt she stood before the mirror *soignée* and perfect in the soft glow from the open fire by her bed. The tight-fitting gown of peacock blue followed the curves of her figure flawlessly. Then she hung about her fine throat a chain of diamonds set in a necklace of laurel leaves wrought delicately in silver, lighted a cigarette and stood regarding her tall figure by the light of the lamps. Among the old furniture of the dark room she stood superbly dressed, elegant, *mondaine*. A touch to the hair that covered her small head like a burnished helmet, and she smiled with satisfaction, the face in the mirror smiling back with a curious look of elation, of abundant health, of joy; yet there was in it something too of secrecy and triumph.

Chapter 27

IRENE'S ROOM was less vast and shadowy. In place of brocade the windows were curtained with white stuff. In one corner stood a *prie dieu* before a little paint and plaster image of the Virgin and Child—all blue and pink and gilt,— which Lily had sent her sister from Florence. The bed was small and narrow and the white table standing near by was covered with books and papers neatly arranged—the paraphernalia of Irene's work among the people of the Flats. Here Lily discovered her when she came in, flushed and radiant, to sit on the edge of the white bed and talk with her sister until the guests arrived.

She found Irene at the white table, the neat piles of books and papers pushed aside to make room for a white tray laden with food, for Irene was having dinner alone in her room. There had been no question of her coming to the ball. "I couldn't bear it," she told her mother. "I would be miserable. I don't want to come. Why do you want to torture me?" She had fallen, of late, into using the most exaggerating words, out of all proportion with truth or dignity. But Julia Shane, accustomed more and more to yielding to the whims of her younger daughter, permitted her to remain away.

"Have you anything to read?" began Lily. "Because if you haven't, my small trunk is full of books."

"I've plenty, and besides, I'm going out."

"Where?" asked Lily, suddenly curious.

"To Welcome House. It's my night to teach. I should think you would have remembered that." Her voice sounded weary and strained. She turned to her sister with a look of disapproval, so intense that it seemed to accuse Lily of some unspeakable sin.

"I didn't remember," Lily replied. "How should I?" And then rising she went to her sister's side and put one arm about her shoulders, a gesture of affection which appeared to inspire a sudden abhorrence in the woman, for she shivered suddenly at the touch of the warm bare arm. "You shouldn't go out to-night. You are too tired!"

"I must go," Irene replied. "They're counting on me."

"What are you eating? . . ." remarked Lily, picking up a bit of cake from the tray. "Peas, potatoes, rice, dessert, milk. . . . Why you've no meat, Irene. You should eat meat. It is what you need more than anything. You're too pale."

Irene's pale brow knitted into a frown. "I've given it up," she said. "I'm not eating meat any longer."

"And why not?" Lily moved away from her and stood looking down with the faintest of mocking smiles. The transparent cheek of her sister flushed slightly.

"Because I don't believe in it. I believe it's wrong."

"Well, I'm going to speak to Mama about it. It's nonsense. You'll kill yourself with such a diet. Really, Irene . . ." Her voice carried a note of irritation, but she got no further for Irene turned on her suddenly, like a beaten dog which after long abuse snaps suddenly at the offending hand.

"Why can't you leave me in peace? You and Mama treat me like a child. I am a grown woman. I want to do as I please. I am harming no one but myself . . . no one . . . I'm sick of it, I tell you. I'm sick of it!"

And suddenly she began to weep, softly and hysterically, her thin shoulders shaking as the sobs tore her body. "I want to go away," she moaned. "I want to be alone, where I can think and pray. I want to be alone!" Her sobbing was at once pitiful and terrible, the dry, parched sobbing of a misery long pent up. For a moment Lily stood helplessly by her side and then, all at once, she went down on her knees in the peacock blue gown and put her lovely bare arms about her sister, striving to comfort her. The effort failed strangely. Irene only drew away and sobbed the more. "If you would only let me have peace . . . I could find it alone!"

Lily said nothing but knelt by her sister's side kissing and caressing the thin white hands until Irene's sobbing subsided a little and she fell forward among the books and papers, burying her head in her arms. The misery of the soul and spirit in some way appalled Lily. She watched her sister with a look of bewilderment in her eyes as if she had discovered all at once a world of which she had been ignorant up to now. The spectacle stifled quickly the high spirits of a moment before. The bawdy French ballads were forgotten. She had become suddenly grave and serious, the lines in her beautiful face grown hard. She was sitting on the floor, her head in Irene's lap, when a knock and the sound of her name roused her.

"Miss Lily," came the mulatto woman's voice, "Mis' Shane says the guests are a-coming and you must come down."

"All right, Sarah. . . . I'll be down at once."

Lily, struggling with the tight satin dress, rose slowly, kissed her sister and said, "Please, dear, stay home to-night and rest."

But Irene, still sobbing softly as if entranced by the sensual satisfaction of weeping, did not answer her. She remained leaning over the table, her face buried in her arms. But she was more quiet now, with the voluptuous stillness of one who has passed through a great emotional outburst.

Lily, once more before the mirror in her own room, rearranged her ruffled hair listening to the murmur of talk that arose from the well of the stairs. It was not until she had fastened the pin set with brilliants for a second time that she discovered with sudden horror that the peacock blue gown was split and ripped at one side from the arm to the waist. In the sudden outburst of affection for her sister, she had flung herself to her knees abandoning all thought of vanity. The gown was ruined.

From below stairs the murmur grew in volume as carriage after carriage arrived. Lily swore beneath her breath in French, tore off the gown and brought from her closet another of a pale yellow-green, the color of chartreuse. The process of dressing began all over again and in half an hour, after the mulatto woman had called twice and been sent away and the guests had gone in to dinner, Lily stood once more before the mirror, radiant and beautiful. The gown was cut lower than the one she had tossed aside, and the yellow-green blended with the tawny red of her hair so that there was something nude and voluptuous in her appearance. The smile returned to her face, a smile which seemed to say, "The Town will see something the like of which it has never seen before."

Before going down she went to Irene's room once more, only to find it dark and empty. Clad in the gray suit and the plain black hat Irene had made her way silently to the stairs at the back of the house and thence through the gallery that led past the drawing-room windows into the dead park. The austere and empty chamber appeared to rouse a sudden shame in Lily, for she returned to her room before descending the long stairs and took from the trunk a great fan of black ostrich feathers to shield her bare breasts alike from the stares of the impudent and the disapproving.

The ball was a great success. The orchestra, placed in the little alcove by the gallery, played a quadrille followed by waltzes, two-steps and polkas. Until ten o'clock the carriages made their way along Halsted street past the Mills and the squalid houses through the wrought iron gates into the park; and at midnight they began to roll away again carrying the guests to their homes. Lily, all graciousness and charm, moved among the dancers distributing her favors equitably save in the single instance of Willie Harrison, who looked so downcast and prematurely old in his black evening clothes that she danced with him three times and sat out a waltz and a polka. And all the Town, ignorant of the truth, whispered that Willie's chances once more appeared good.

Ellen Tolliver was there, in a dress made at home by her mother, and she spent much of the evening by the side of her aunt Julia who sat in black jet and amethysts at one end of the drawing-room leaning on her stick and looking for all the world like a wicked duchess. At the sound of the music and the sight of the dancers, the old gleam returned for a little time to her tired eyes.

Ellen was younger than the other guests and knew most of them only by sight but she had partners none the less, for she was handsome despite her badly made gown and her absurd pompadour, and she danced with a barbaric and energetic grace. When she was not dancing her demeanor carried no trace of the drooping wall-flower. She regarded the dancers with an expression of defiance and scorn. None could have taken her for a poor relation.

Chapter 28

A LITTLE WHILE before midnight Irene, accompanied by Krylenko, returned from the Flats and hurried quietly as a moth through the gallery past the brightly lighted windows and up the stairway to her room. The mill worker left her at the turn of the drive where he stood for a time in the melting snow fascinated by the sound of music and the sight of the dancers through the tall windows. Among them he caught a sudden glimpse of Irene's sister, the woman who had watched him at work in the mill shed. She danced a waltz with the master of the Mills, laughing as she whirled round and round with a wild exuberance. Amid the others who took their pleasures so seriously, she was a bacchante, pagan, utterly abandoned. The black fan hung from her wrist and the pale yellow-green ball gown left all her breast and throat exposed in a voluptuous glow of beauty. Long after the music stopped and she had disappeared, Krylenko stood in the wet snowbank staring blindly at the window which she had passed again and again. He stood as if hypnotized, as if incapable of action. At length a coachman, passing by, halted for a moment to regard him in astonishment, and so roused him into action. Murmuring something in Russian, he set off down the long drive walking well to one side to keep from under the wheels of the fine carriages which had begun to leave.

The last carriage, containing Willie Harrison and two female cousins, passed through the wrought iron gates a little after one o'clock, leaving Lily, her mother and Ellen Tolliver who, having no carriage of her own, had chosen this night to spend at Cypress Hill, alone amid the wreckage of crumpled flowers and forgotten cotillion favors. With the departure of the last carriage and the finish of the music, the gleam died out of Julia Shane's eyes. She became again an old woman with a tired bent figure, her sharp eyes half closed by dark swellings which seemed to have appeared all at once with the death of the last chord.

"I'm going to bed," she said, bidding the others good-night. "We can discuss the party in the morning."

She tottered up the stairs leaving her daughter and grandniece together in the long drawing-room. When she had gone, Lily rose and put out the lamps and candles one by one until only three candles in a sconce above the piano remained lighted.

"Now," she said, lying back among the cushions of the divan and stretching her long handsome legs, "play for me . . . some Brahms, some Chopin."

The girl must have been weary but the request aroused all her extraordinary young strength. She sat at the piano silhouetted against the candle light . . . the curve of her absurd pompadour, the more ridiculous curve of her corseted figure. From the divan Lily watched her through half-closed eyes. She played first of all two études of Chopin and then a waltz or two of Brahms, superbly and with a fine freedom and spectacular fire, as if she realized that at last she had the audience she desired, a better audience than she would ever have again no matter how celebrated she might become. Above the throbbing of the Mills the thread of music rose triumphant in a sort of eternal beauty, now delicate, restrained, now rising in a tremendous, passionate crescendo. The girl invested it with all the yearnings that are beyond expression, the youth, the passionate resentment and scorn, the blind gropings which swept her baffled young soul. Through the magic of the sound she managed to convey to the woman lying half-buried among the cushions those things which it would have been impossible for her to utter, so high and impregnable was the wall of her shyness and pride. And Lily, watching her, wept silently at the eloquence of the music.

Not once was there a spoken word between them, and at last the girl swung softly and mournfully into the macabre beauties of the *Valse Triste*, strange and mournful music, not great, even a little mediocre, yet superbly beautiful beneath her slim fingers. She peopled the shadowy room with ghostly unreal figures, of tragedy, of romance, of burning, unimagined desires. The dancing shadows cast by the candles among the old furniture became through the mist of Lily's tears fantastic, yet familiar, like memories half-revealed that fade before they can be captured and recognized. The waltz rose in a weird un-earthly ecstasy, swirling and exultant, the zenith of a joy and a completion yearned for but never in this life achieved . . . the something which lies just beyond the reach, sensed but unattainable, something which Ellen sought and came nearest to capturing in her music, which Irene, kneeling on the *prie dieu* before the Sienna Virgin, sought in a mystic exaltation, which Lily sought in her own instinctive, half-realized fashion. It was a quest which must always be a lonely one; somehow the music made the sense of loneliness terribly acute. The waltz grew slower once more and softer, taking on a new and melancholy fire, until at last it died away into stillness leaving only the sound of the Mills to disturb the silence of the old room.

After a little pause, Ellen fell forward wearily upon the piano, her head resting upon her arms, and all at once with a faint rustle she slipped gently to the floor, the home-made ball dress crumpled and soiled beneath her slim body. Lily sprang from among the pillows and gathered the girl against her white, voluptuous breasts, for she had fainted.

Chapter 29

THE VISIT of Ellen was extended from one night to three. The piano was a beautiful one, far better than the harsh-toned upright in the Tolliver parlor in the Town, and Ellen gladly played for hours with only Lily, lying among the cushions, and old Julia Shane, lost in her own fantastic memories, for an audience.

On the third night, long after twelve o'clock, as Lily and her cousin climbed the long stairway, the older woman said, "I have some clothes, Ellen, that you may have if you like. They have been worn only a few times and they are more beautiful than anything you can find in America."

The girl did not answer until they had reached Lily's room and closed the door behind them. Her face was flushed with the silent struggle between a hunger for beautiful things and a fantastic pride, born of respectable poverty. In some way, her cousin sensed the struggle.

"They are yours if you want them," she said. "You can try them on if you like at any rate."

Ellen smiled gratefully. "I'd like to," she said timidly. "Thank you."

While the girl took off her shirtwaist and skirt, Lily busied herself among the shadows of her closet. When she returned she bore across her arms three gowns, one dull red, one black and one yellow. The girl stood waiting shyly, clad only in her cheap underclothing coarsened and yellowed by many launderings.

"You must take those things off," said Lily. "I'll give you others." And she brought out undergarments of white silk which Ellen put on, shivering a little in the chill of the big room.

Then Lily took the pale yellow gown and slipped it over her cousin's head. It belonged to no period of fashion. It hung from the shoulders in loose folds of shining silk, clinging close to the girl's slim body. There was a silver girdle which fastened over the hips. Ellen turned to regard herself in the mirror.

"But wait," said Lily, laughing, "you've only begun. We've got to change your hair and do away with that ridiculous rat. Why do you spoil such beautiful hair with a wad of old wire?"

She took out the pins and let the hair fall in a clear, black shower. It was beautiful hair of the thick, sooty-black color that goes with fair skin and blue eyes. It fell in great coils over the pale yellow gown. Lily, twisting it into loose strands, held it against the light of the lamp.

"Beautiful hair," she said, "like the hair of Rapunzel."

Then she twisted it low about Ellen's head, loosely so that the light, striking the free ends created a kind of halo. With a supreme gesture of scorn, she tossed the "rat" into the scrap basket.

"There," she said, turning her cousin to face the long mirror. "There . . . Behold the great pianist . . . the great artist."

In the magical mirror stood a tall lovely woman. The ridiculous awkward girl had vanished; it was another creature who stood there transfigured and beautiful. And in her frank blue eyes, there was a new look, something of astonishment mingled with determination. The magical mirror had done its work. From that moment the girl became a stranger to the Town. She had come of age and slipped all unconsciously into a new world.

With shining eyes she turned and faced her cousin.

"May I really have the clothes, Lily?"

"Of course, you silly child!"

And Lily smiled because the clothes had never been worn at all. They were completely new.

Chapter 30

AT BREAKFAST on the following morning, the mulatto woman laid before Lily's plate a cablegram. It read simply, "Jean has measles."

Trunks were packed with desperate haste. The entire household was thrown into an uproar, all save old Julia Shane who continued to move about with the same unruffled calm, with the same acceptancy of whatever came to her. At midnight Lily boarded the express for the East. It was not until the middle of the week, when the drawing-room had been wrapped once more in cheese-cloth and scented with camphor, that the Town learned of Lily's sudden return to Paris. It was impossible, people decided, to calculate the whims of her existence.

Three months after her sudden departure, she sat one early spring afternoon on the terrace of her garden in the Rue Raynouard, when old Madame Gigon, in a bizarre gown of maroon poplin, with the fat and aging Fifi at her heels, brought her a letter from Julia Shane.

Tearing it open, Lily began to read,

"Of course the biggest bit of news is Ellen's escapade. She has eloped with a completely commonplace young man named Clarence Murdock, a traveling salesman for an electrical company, who I believe was engaged to May Seton . . . the Setons who own the corset factory east of the Harrison Mills. They have gone to New York to live and now, I suppose, Ellen will have her chance to go on with her music. Knowing Ellen, I am certain she does not love this absurd man. As for Hattie she is distraught and feels that Ellen has committed some terrible sin. Nothing I can say is able to alter her mind. To be sure, the fellow has nothing to commend him, but I'm willing to let Ellen work it out. She's no fool. None of our family is that. Hattie thinks it was the gowns you gave Ellen which turned her head. But I suspect that Ellen saw this young drummer simply as a means of escape . . . a way out of all her troubles. Of course the Town is in a buzz. Miss Abercrombie says nothing so unrespectable has happened in years. More power to Ellen . . . !"

For a moment Lily put down the letter and sat thinking. In the last sentence there was a delicious echo of that wicked chuckle which had marked the departure of the discomfited Judge Weissman and Mrs. Julis Harrison from Cypress Hill . . . the merest echo of triumph over another mark in the long score of the old against the new.

For a time Lily sat listening quietly to the distant sounds from the river . . . the whistling of the steamer bound for St. Cloud, the faint clop-clop of hoofs in the Rue de Passy and the ugly chug-chug of one of the new motor wagons which were to be seen with growing frequency along the boulevards. Whatever she was thinking, her thoughts were interrupted suddenly by a little boy, very handsome and neat, in a sailor suit, who dragged behind him across the flagged terrace a stuffed toy bear. He climbed into her lap and began playing with the warm fur piece she had thrown over her shoulders.

"Mama," he cried. "J'ai faim. . . . Je veux un biscuit!"

Lily gathered him into her arms, pressing his soft face against hers. "Bien, petit . . . va chercher la bonne Madame Gigon."

She seized him more closely and kissed him again and again with all the passion of a savage, miserly possession.

"Je t'aime, Mama . . . tellement," whispered the little fellow, and climbed down to run into the big house in search of kind Madame Gigon and her cakes. The gaze of Lily wandered after his sturdy little body and her dark eyes grew bright with a triumphant love.

When he had disappeared through one of the tall windows, she took up the letter once more and continued her reading.

"Irene," wrote her mother, "seems more content now that you are gone. I confess that I understand her less and less every day. Sometimes I think she must be not quite well . . . a little touched perhaps by a religious mania. She is giving her life, her strength, her soul, to these foreigners in the Flats. What for? Because it brings her peace, I suppose. But still I cannot understand her. There is one man . . . Krylenko, by name, I believe, whom she has made into a sort of disciple. I only hope that news of him won't reach the Town. God knows what sort of a tale they would make out of it. I'm afraid too of her becoming involved in the troubles at the Mills. Some day there will be open warfare in the Flats."

When Lily had finished reading, she tore the letter slowly into bits after a custom of long standing and tossed the torn fragments into one of the stone urns that bordered the terrace. . . . Then she rose and pulling her fur cloak closer about her began to walk up and down restlessly as if some profound and stirring memory had taken possession of her. The rain began to fall gently and darkness to descend upon the garden. In the house behind her the servants lighted the lamps. Still she paced up and down tirelessly.

After a time she went down from the terrace to the gravel path of the garden and there continued her walking until the gate in the garden wall opened suddenly and a man stepped in, his erect soldierly figure black against the lamps of the Rue de Passy. It was the Baron, Madame Gigon's cousin. He came toward her quickly and took her into his arms, embracing her passionately for a long time in silence.

When at last he freed her, a frown crossed his dark face, and he said, "What is it? What is distracting you? Are you troubled about something?"

Lily thrust her arm through his and leaned against him, but she avoided his gaze. "Nothing," she said. "It's nothing."

And thus they walked through the rain until they reached the pavilion designed by Lenôtre which stood at a distance from the house. Here they halted and the Baron, taking from his pocket a key, unlocked the door and they went in silently.

Once inside, he kissed her again and presently he said, "What is it? There is something between us. There is a difference."

"Nothing," she murmured stubbornly. "It is nothing. You must be imagining things."

Chapter 31

ALL THAT Julia Shane had written her daughter was true enough. The escapade of Ellen shocked the Town, not altogether unwillingly however, for it opened a new field for talk and furnished one more evidence of the wildness of a family which had never been content with conformity, a clan which kept bursting its bonds and satisfying in a barbarous fashion its hunger after life.

When Hattie Tolliver, tearful and shaken, came to her aunt for consolation, Julia Shane received her in the vast bedroom she occupied above the Mill yard. The old woman said, "Come, Hattie. You've no reason to feel badly. Ellen is a good girl and a wise one. It's the best thing that could have happened, if you'll only see it in that light."

But Mrs. Tolliver, so large, so energetic, so emotional, was hurt. She kept on sobbing. "If only she had told me! . . . It's as if she deceived me."

At which Julia Shane smiled quietly to herself. "Ah, that's it, Hattie. She couldn't have told you, because she knew you so well. She knew that you couldn't bear to have her leave you. The girl was wise. She chose the better way. It's your pride that's hurt and the feeling that, after all, there was something stronger in Ellen than her love for you." She took the red work-stained hand of her niece in her thin, blue-veined one and went on, "We have to come to that, Hattie . . . all of us. It's only natural that a time comes when children want to be free. It's like the wild animals . . . the foxes and the wolves. We aren't any different. We're just animals too, helpless in the rough hands of Nature. She does with us as She pleases."

But Mrs. Tolliver continued to sob helplessly. It was the first time in her life that she had refused to accept in the end what came to her.

"You don't suppose I wanted Lily to go and live in Paris? You don't suppose I wanted to be left here with Irene who is like a changeling to me? It's only what is bound to come. If Lily did help Ellen it was only because all youth is in conspiracy against old age. All children are in a conspiracy against their parents. When we are old, we are likely to forget the things that counted so much with us when we were young. We take them for granted. We see them as very small troubles after all, but that's because we are looking at them from a long way off. The old are selfish, Hattie . . . more selfish than you imagine. They envy even the life and the hunger of the young."

For a moment the old woman paused, regarding her red-eyed niece silently. "No," she continued presently, "You don't understand what I've been saying, yet it's all true . . . as true as life itself. Besides, life is hard for our children, Hattie. It isn't as simple as it was for us. Their grandfathers were pioneers and the same blood runs in their veins, only they haven't a frontier any longer. They stand . . . these children of ours . . . with their backs toward this rough-hewn middle west and their faces set toward Europe and the East. And they belong to neither. They are lost somewhere between."

But Mrs. Tolliver understood none of this. With her there were no shades of feeling, no variations of duty. To her a mother and child were mother and child whether they existed in the heart of Africa or in the Faubourg St. Germain. After tea she went home, secretly nursing her bruised heart. She told her husband that no woman in the world had ever been called upon to endure so much.

As for Charles Tolliver, his lot was not the happiest. At the next election, despite the money which old Julia Shane poured into his campaign, he was defeated. His ruin became a fact. The Mills were too strong. The day of the farmer was past. After floundering about helplessly in an effort to make ends meet, he took at last a place as clerk in one of the banks controlled by his enemy Judge Weissman . . . a cup of humiliation which he drank for the sake of his wife and children, goaded by the sheer necessity of providing food and shelter for them. So he paid for his error, not of honesty but of judgment. Because he was honest, he was sacrificed to the Mills. He settled himself, a man of forty-five no longer young, behind the brass bars of the Farmer's Commercial Bank, a name which somehow carried a sense of irony because it had swallowed up more than one farm in its day.

In the Town tremendous changes occurred with the passing of years. There was a panic which threatened the banks. There were menacing rumors of violence and discontent in the Flats; and these things affected the Town enormously, as depressions in the market for wheat and cattle had once affected it. No longer was there any public market. On the Square at the top of Main street, the old scales for weighing hay and grain were removed as a useless symbol of a buried past, a stumbling block in the way of progress. Opposite the site once occupied by the scales, the Benevolent and Protective Order of Elks purchased the Grand Western Hotel and made it into a club house with a great elk's head in cast iron over the principal doorway. Through its windows, it was possible in passing to see fat men with red faces, coats off and perspiring, while they talked of progress and prosperity and the rising place of the Town among the cities of the state. One by one the old landmarks of the Square vanished, supplanted by "smokehouses," picture palaces with fronts like frosted pastries, candy shops run by Greeks, a new element in the growing alien population of the Town. On the far side of the square the tower of the courthouse, itself a monument to graft, was at last completed to the enrichment of Judge Weissman and other politicians who had to do with the contract.

In the early evening after the sun had disappeared, the figure of the Judge himself might be seen, ambulating about the square, hugging the shadows; for the heat was bad for a man so red-faced and apoplectic. For all his avoidance of the sun, he walked arrogantly, with the air of one proud of his work. When he had tired of the promenade, it was his custom to return to the Elks' club to squeeze his body between the arms of a rocking chair and sit watching the passers-by and the noisy bustle of trade. At such moments one might hear the sound of money dripping into tills as one heard the distant sound of the Mills which in the evening penetrated as far as the square itself. He gloated openly over the prosperity to which he had contributed so much. He went his way, petty, dishonest, corrupt . . . traits which even his enemies forgave him because he had "done so much to make the Town what it was." Not since the piggish obstinacy of Charles Tolliver had he been thwarted, and even in the matter of the taxes the sympathy of the Town had been on his side, because the decision in the case had delayed the building of new furnaces for more than two years and thus halted the arrival of hundreds of new alien workers who would have made the Town the third largest in the state. Charles Tolliver, most people believed, had been piggish and obstinate. He had put himself between his own Town and its booming prosperity.

Chapter 32

IN THE FLATS, as the years passed, new tides of immigrants swept in, filling the abominable dirty houses to suffocation, adding to the garbage and refuse which already clogged the sluggish waters of the Black Fork. The men worked twelve hours and sometimes longer in the Mills. The women wore shawls over their heads and bore many children, most of whom died amid the smoke and filth. Here the Town overlooked one opportunity. With a little effort it might have saved the lives of these babies to feed to the Mills later on; but it was simpler to import more cheap labor from Europe. Let those die who could not live.

And none of these new residents learned to speak English. They clung to their native tongues. They were simply colonists transplanted, unchanged and unchanging, from Poland, Ukrainia, South Italy and the Balkans—nothing more, nothing less. The Town had nothing to do with them. They were pariahs, outcasts, "Hunkies," "Dagos," and the Town held it against them that they did not learn English and join in the vast chorus of praise to prosperity.

But trouble became more frequent nowadays. Willie Harrison no longer dared take his exercise by walking alone up the hill to the Town. The barricade of barbed wire was complete now. It surrounded the Mills on all sides, impregnable, menacing. It crowded the dead hedges of arbor vitae that enclosed the park at Shane's Castle. There had been no need for it yet. It was merely waiting.

Welcome House, the tentative gesture of a troubled civic conscience, went down beneath the waves of prosperity. Volunteer citizens no longer ventured into the troubled area of the Flats. Money ceased to flow in for its support. It dropped at length from the rank of an institution supported by a community to the rank of a school supported by one woman and one man. The woman was Irene Shane. The man was Stepan Krylenko. The woman was rich. The man was a Mill worker who toiled twelve hours a day and gave six hours more to the education of his fellow workers.

The years and the great progress had been no more kind to Irene than they had been to the Town. She aged . . . dryly, after the fashion of spinsters who have diverted the current of life from its wide course into a single narrow channel of feverish activity. She grew thinner and more pale. There were times when the blue veins showed beneath the transparent skin like the rivers of a schoolboy's map. Her pale blond hair lost its luster and grew thin and straight, because she had not time and even less desire to care for it. Her hands were red and worn with the work she did in helping the babies of the Flats to live. She dressed the same, always in a plain gray suit and ugly black hat, which she replaced when they became worn and shabby. But in replacing them, she ignored the changing styles. The models remained the same, rather outmoded and grotesque, so that in the Town they rewarded her for her work among the poor by regarding her as queer and something of a figure of fun.

Yet she retained a certain virginal look, and in her eye there was a queer exalted light. Since life is impossible without compensations of one sort or another, it is probable that Irene had her share of these. She must have found peace in her work and satisfaction in the leader she molded from the tow-haired boy who years before had shouted insults at her through the wrought iron gates of Shane's Castle.

For Krylenko had grown into a remarkable man. He spoke English perfectly. He worked with Irene, a leader among his own people. He taught the others.

He read Jean Jacques Rousseau, John Stuart Mill, Karl Marx, and even Voltaire . . . books which Irene bought him in ignorance of their flaming contents. At twenty-five Stepan Krylenko was a leader in the district, and in the Town there were men of property who had heard vaguely of him as a disturber, an anarchist, a madman, a Socialist, a criminal.

Although Irene seldom penetrated the Town any longer and her mother never left the confines of Shane's Castle, their affairs still held an interest for those who had known Cypress Hill in the days of its vanished splendor. For women who had long since ceased to take any part in the life of a community, the names of old Julia Shane and her two daughters came up with startling frequency at the dinners and lunches and tea parties in the Town. It may have been that in a community where life was so noisy, so banal, so strenuous, so redolent of prosperity, the Shanes and the old house satisfied some profound and universal hunger for the mysterious, the beautiful, the bizarre, even the mystic. Certainly in the midst of so materialistic a community the Shanes were exotic and worthy of attention. And always in the background there was the tradition of John Shane and the memories of things which it was whispered had happened in Shane's Castle. It was Lily who aroused the most talk, perhaps because she was even more withdrawn and mysterious than her mother and sister, because it was so easy to imagine things about her. . . . Lily who could come back and bring all the Town once more to Shane's Castle; Lily, the generous, the good-natured, the beautiful Lily.

Mrs. Julis Harrison discussed them; and her son, the rejected Willie; and Miss Abercrombie, who with the passing of years had developed an affection of the nerves which made her face twitch constantly so that always, even in the midst of the most solemn conversations, she had the appearance of winking in a lascivious fashion. It was a trial which she bore, with a truly noble fortitude.

Chapter 33

ON THE EVENING of the day that Mrs. Harrison called for the last time at Cypress Hill, Miss Abercrombie was invited to dine with her in the ugly sandstone house on the Hill. The call was Mrs. Harrison's final gesture in an effort to patch up the feud which had grown so furiously since the affair over the taxes. Of its significance Miss Abercrombie had been told in advance, so it must have been with a beating, expectant heart that she arrived at the Harrison mansion.

The two women dined alone in a vast dining-room finished in golden oak, beneath a gigantic brass chandelier fitted with a score of pendant brass globes. They sat at either end of a table so long that shouting was almost a necessity.

"William is absent," explained Mrs. Harrison in a loud, deep voice. "There is a big corporation from the east that wants to buy the Mills. It wants to absorb them at a good price with a large block of stock for William and me. Of course, I oppose it . . . with all my strength. As I told William, the Mills *are* the Harrisons . . . I will never see them out of the family . . . Judge Weissman has gone east with William to see that he does nothing rash. Neither of them ought to be away, I told Willie, with all this trouble brewing in the Flats." Here she paused for a long breath. "Why, only this afternoon, some of those Polish brats threw stones at my victoria, right at the foot of Julia's drive. . . . Imagine that in the old days!"

This long and complicated speech, she made with but a single pause for breath. She had grown even more stout, and her stupendous masculine spirit had suffered a certain weakening. A light stroke of paralysis she had passed over heroically, dismissing it by sheer force of her tremendous will. The misfortune left no trace save a slight limp as she dragged her body across the floor and settled it heavily in the plush covered armchair at one end of the table.

The butler—Mrs. Harrison used a butler as the symbol of her domination in the Town, wearing him as a sort of crest—noiselessly brought the thick mushroom soup, his eye gleaming at the sight of the two women. He was an old man with white hair and the appearance of a gentleman.

"How dreadful!" exclaimed Miss Abercrombie, and then unable longer to restrain herself, she said, "Tell me! Do tell me about Julia!"

Mrs. Harrison drank from her water glass, set it down slowly and then said impressively, "She did not receive me!"

"I feared so," rejoined Miss Abercrombie, winking with nervous impatience.

"It is the end! No one can say that I have not done my part toward a reconciliation." This statement she uttered with all the majesty of an empress declaring war. "And to think," she added mournfully, "that such an old friendship should come to such an end."

"It's just the way I feel," replied Miss Abercrombie. "And you know, my friendship was even older. I knew her before you. Why, I can remember when she was only a farmer girl." Here her illness forced her to wink as if there were something obscene in her simple statement.

"Well," said Mrs. Harrison, "I don't suppose any one in the Town was ever closer to Julia than I was. D'you know? That mulatto woman actually turned me away today, and I must say her manner was insolent. She said Julia was not feeling well enough to see me. Imagine, not well enough to see *me*, her oldest friend!" This statement the sycophantic Miss Abercrombie allowed to pass unchallenged. "Heaven knows," continued Mrs. Harrison. "It was only friendship that prompted me. I certainly would not go prying about for the sake of curiosity. You know that, Pearl. Why, I wasn't allowed to set my foot inside the door. You'd have thought I was diseased."

After this a silence descended during which the room vibrated with unsaid things. At the memory of her reception, Mrs. Harrison's face grew more and more flushed. The gentlemanly butler removed the soup and brought on whitefish nicely browned and swimming in butter.

"It's a queer household," remarked Miss Abercrombie, with an air of hinting at unspeakable things and feeling her way cautiously toward a letting down of all bars. Undoubtedly it was unfortunate that they had disputed the position of "oldest friend." In a way it tied both their hands.

"It has always been queer," replied the hostess. "Even since the house was built."

Again a pregnant silence, and then Miss Abercrombie with another unwilled and obscene wink added, "I must say I can't understand Irene's behavior." About this effort, there was something oblique and yet effective. It marked another step.

"Or Lily's," rejoined Mrs. Harrison, taking a third step.

"They say," said Miss Abercrombie, pulling fishbones from her mouth, "that there is a common mill worker who is very attentive to Irene. Surely she can't be considering marriage with *him*."

"No, from what I hear, she *isn't*," observed Mrs. Harrison. After this dark hint she paused for a moment tottering upon the edge of new revelations with the air of a swimmer about to dive into cold water. At last she plunged.

"They say," she murmured in a lowered voice, "that there is more between them than most people guess . . . more than is proper."

Miss Abercrombie leaned forward. "You know," she said, "that's funny. I've heard the same thing."

"Well, I heard it from Thomas, the coachman. Of course, I reproved him for even hinting at such things. I must say he only hinted . . . very delicately. He was discreet. If I hadn't guessed there was something of the sort going on, I should never have known what he was driving at."

Miss Abercrombie bridled and leaned back for the butler to remove her fish plate. "Imagine!" she said, "Imagine a child of yours being the subject of gossip among servants!"

Her hostess gave a wicked chuckle. "You've forgotten John Shane. When he was alive, his behavior was the talk of every one. But how could you have forgotten the talk that went the rounds? It was common property . . . common property."

Miss Abercombie sighed deeply. "I know . . . I know. Julia's life has not been happy." And into the sigh she put a thousand implications of the superior happiness of virgins.

"Of course," said Mrs. Harrison, "he was insane. There's no doubt about it. People may talk, but facts are facts. John Shane was insane . . . certainly toward the end he was insane."

The butler brought the roast fowl, and until his back was turned once more both women kept silence. When he had gone out of the room, they found themselves striving for first place in the race. Both spoke at once but Mrs. Harrison overwhelmed the sycophantic Abercrombie.

"Of course," she said, "I think Julia herself is a little queer at times. I've noticed it for years . . . ever since . . . well . . . ever since Lily went to Paris to live."

"Yes," observed Miss Abercrombie, moving toward something more definite. "Ever since the Governor's garden party. All that was very queer . . . very queer."

Here again they found themselves halted by the immensity of the unspoken. Mrs. Harrison veered aside.

"The house has gone to ruin. Even the gate is hanging by one hinge. Nothing is kept up any longer."

"Have you seen this lover of Irene's?" asked Miss Abercrombie, calling a spade a spade and endeavoring to keep to one thing at a time.

"I've seen him once . . . William pointed him out to me at the Mills. He's one of the men who have been making trouble there."

"Is he good looking?" asked Miss Abercrombie.

"Yes and no," replied her companion.

"Well, what does that mean?"

"Well, he's tall and has a handsome face . . . a little evil perhaps. The real trouble is that I should call him common. Yes, common is the word I should use, decidedly common."

Miss Abercrombie raised her eyebrows and smiled. "But, my dear, after all he is nothing but a workman."

"Yes," replied Mrs. Harrison, "he *is*." In a manner which put an end to all doubt in the matter.

"Do you really think," asked Miss Abercrombie, "that there is anything in it?"

Mrs. Harrison poised her fork and gave her guest a knowing look. "Well, of course I can't see what he sees in her . . . pale and haggard as she is. Now with him it's different. He's . . . well." She halted suddenly, adding, "This fowl is tough, Pearl . . . I'm sorry it happened when you were dining with me." And then, "I suppose it's money he's after. She must be very rich."

The butler, after bringing more rich food, disappeared again and this time, Miss Abercrombie, casting to the winds all restraint, rose and said, "I'm going to bring my chair nearer, Belle. I can't talk all the way from this end of the table."

And she moved her chair and plate to a more strategic position so that when the butler returned, he found the two women sitting quite close to each other, their heads together, their voices lowered to the most confidential of pitches. Fragments of their talk reached an ear long trained to eavesdropping upon old women.

"But Lily is the one," drifted to the ear. "I'd really like to know the truth about her. Of course blood is thicker than water. They say she . . ." Mrs. Harrison rattled the ice in her glass, thus destroying the remainder of the sentence.

So they sat until near midnight—two old women, one of them at the end of a life barren of love, the other abandoned by love forever and cast aside, a slowly decaying mass of fat—pawing over the affairs of two women for whom the force of love in some manifestation or other was still a radiant reality. They knew nothing; they possessed only suspicions and fragments of gossip, but out of these they succeeded in patching together a mosaic which glowed with all the colors of the most glamorous sin and the most romantic passion.

Chapter 34

AND AT THE same moment in the house at Cypress Hill, Julia Shane lay propped up in her bed reading a French novel. It was an enormous bed with a vast dusty canopy supported by two ironical wood-gilt cupids who hung suspended from the ceiling; and Julia Shane, reading by the light of her night lamp, appeared lost in it like a woman tossing on the waves of the sea. To-night, feeling more ill than usual, she had her dinner in bed, wrapped in a peignoir of mauve ribbon and valenciennes, her bony neck exposed above the linen of her night dress.

She read, as usual, with the aid of a silver mounted reading glass which tossed the sentences in enormous capitals well into the range of her fading vision. On the table beside her stood one of the gilt coffee cups, a mute witness to the old woman's disobedience of the doctor's orders. Beside it lay two paper backed French novels and on the floor in the shadow of the table a half dozen more tossed aside carelessly, some lying properly, others open and sprawled, exposing the ragged edges of the hastily cut pages.

In the fashion of the ill and aging, she lived nowadays in memories . . . memories of her girlhood when she had ridden John Shane's wildest mare Doña Rita recklessly about the paddock of the farm, memories of Mademoiselle Violette de Vaux and the picnics with French and English girls in a neatly kept wood at Sèvres, memories of Cypress Hill in the days immediately after her return when John Shane was still more the passionate lover than the husband. As she grew older, the memories became clearer and more vivid, but they were neither vivid nor diverse enough to occupy all her time. What remained she divided between the game of patience and the French novels which Lily supplied faithfully, shipping them from Paris in lots of a dozen at a time.

The old woman had evolved her own scheme of reading, a plan which Irene condemned by the word "skimming," but which satisfied Julia Shane because it revealed the plot without an unnecessary waste of time over long, involved descriptions of scenery and minute analyses of incomprehensible Gallic passions. Under the skimming system she read a few pages at the beginning and then turned to the end to learn the outcome of the tale. After this, she plunged into the middle of the book and read a page or two here and there until her curiosity was satisfied and her interest flagged. And at last the book was tossed aside to be carried off by the mulatto woman, who never failed to go through each volume carefully as though by looking at the words frequently enough she would be able at length to unlock the secrets of foreign tongues. The books which lay on the floor beside the bed had been "skimmed." They lay prostrate and sprawled like the dead soldiers of an army. The titles served as an index of the old woman's favorite authors. They appeared some in black ink, some in red, some even in blue . . . Paul Marguerite, Marcel Prévost, Pierre Loti, Paul Bourget, Collette Willy and, strange to relate, Anatole France represented by *L'Ile des Penguins* which, it seemed, had baffled the "skimming" system, for of all the lot it was the only volume in which every page had been cut.

After she grew weary, she tossed aside *Les Anges Gardiens* which she had been reading and sat leaning back with her eyes closed. Perhaps she pondered the doings of the four evil governesses in the Prévost tale; perhaps she turned her thoughts to the Town and Mrs. Julis Harrison whom she had sent away because she "was not in a mood to be bored." It is even possible that she knew at this very moment that in the sandstone house of the Harrisons, they were discussing her affairs. She was too wise and too worldly not to have known what Belle Harrison would say of her. Yet she appeared calm and content enough, completely indifferent to the opinions of her acquaintances, of the Town—indeed of all the world. She had reached the time when such things are no longer of any importance.

So great was her indifference that in more than three months she had left the house only once and then to follow the coffin of Jacob Barr to the cemetery on the hill. The old man was dead at last, after an illness which had drained with a bitter, heart-breaking slowness all the vigor of his strong and energetic body. On the day of the funeral the foreign women in Halsted street caught a swift glimpse of the mistress of Cypress Hill as she drove through on her way to the cemetery. They must have guessed that it was an event of great importance which drew her from her seclusion; and indeed it was such an event, for it was the funeral of the oldest member of the family, the last of all his generation save Julia Shane.

And after the funeral Julia Shane returned and shut herself in, resolved to see no one but Irene and her niece, Hattie Tolliver.

Chapter 35

WHATEVER HER THOUGHTS and memories may have been, they were interrupted presently by the knock of the mulatto woman who came to bear away the gilt coffee cup and pile of ravaged novels. The sound of the woman's shuffling approach aroused Julia Shane who opened her eyes and said, "Here, Sarah. Give me a hand. I've slipped down."

Sarah helped lift her once more into a sitting posture. The old woman raised herself scornfully as if there was between her indomitable spirit and her wrecked body no bond of any sort, as if she had only contempt for the body as a thing unworthy of her, a thing which had failed her, over which she had neither control nor responsibility.

The mulatto woman bent to pick up the scattered novels, and as she stood up, her mistress, chuckling, said, "My God. They're tiresome, Sarah. They never write about anything but *l'amour*. You'd think there was nothing else in the world. Even *l'amour* gets to be a bore after a time."

The mulatto woman waited obediently. "Yes, Mis' Shane. I guess you're right," she said presently. At which the old woman smiled.

"And Sarah," the mistress continued. "When Miss Irene comes in, tell her I should like to see her. It's important."

The servant hesitated for an instant. "But Miss Irene don't come in till after midnight, Mis' Shane." She spoke with the manner of concealing something. In her soft voice there was a thin trace of insinuating suspicion, almost of servile accusation. "That foreign fella brings her home," she added.

"It's all right," replied the old woman. "I shall be awake." And then in a cold voice she added, "I'm sure it's good of him to bring her home. I shouldn't want her wandering about alone at that hour of the night. It's very thoughtful of him."

At midnight, true to her word, she was still awake. She had even managed to gain her feet painfully and to make her way with unsteady step across the room to the drawer which held her cigarettes. These too the doctor had forbidden her.

On the way back to her vast bed, she passed by the window and, drawing aside the curtain for a moment, she looked out over the hot panorama of glowing furnaces and tall black chimneys. As she stood there, she saw entering the wrought iron gates two figures sharply outlined against the glare of the white arc light in Halsted street. The woman was Irene. She was accompanied by Krylenko.

Quietly the old woman extinguished the candle on the table beside her. The room became a vault of darkness. Beneath her window at the turn in the drive, the pair halted and stood talking in voices so low that what they said was inaudible even through the open window. After a time Irene seated herself wearily on the horseblock. Her frail body sagged with fatigue. She leaned against the cast iron Cupid who held in one outstretched hand an iron ring. Krylenko bent over her and his hands, with the curious, eloquent gestures of an alien, pantomimed their tale against the distant arc light. Above them in the recessed window the mother, clinging all the while to the heavy curtains for support, watched silently. She could hear nothing. She could only keep watch. At length Irene arose and lifting the ugly black hat from her head, ran her finger through her loose hair all damp with the terrible heat. Now was the moment. The old woman, awaiting proof, leaned against the table by her side.

But there was no proof. There was no embrace, not even the faintest exchange of intimacies. Krylenko chastely took Irene's hand, bade her goodnight and turned with his swinging powerful stride down the long drive.

Irene, passing along the gallery by the drawing room, slipped her key into the lock and entered the house.

Above stairs she found her mother sitting up in bed, lost again in the midst of *Les Anges Gardiens*. Still carrying the worn hat in her hand, the daughter came over to the bed. With the increasing illness of the old woman, Irene's manner had become more gentle. She even smiled a tired smile.

"What?" she said playfully. "Are you still awake? Skimming again, I see."

Yet her manner was not the manner of a daughter with a mother. Rather it was that of a casual friend. It was too playful, too forced. The chasm of thirty years and more was not to be bridged by any amount of strained cordiality.

Julia Shane put down her reading glass. "I couldn't sleep, so I tried to read," she said.

Irene drew up a chair and sat by the bed. She appeared worn and exhausted, as though the August heat had drained to the dregs all her intense, self-inspired vitality.

"How are you feeling?"

"Better . . . much better except for the ache in my back."

Irene's face grew serious. "You've been smoking again," she said, "after the doctor forbade you." The old woman, quite prepared to lie, started to protest, shaking her head in negation. "It's no use, Mama . . . I saw you . . . I saw the glow of your cigarette at the window."

(So Irene knew that she had been watched, and there was no need to protest.) The old woman sat still for a moment twisting the silver reading glass round and round, her brow contracted in an angry frown as though she resented bitterly the decay of body which gave any one authority over her. (That Julia Shane should ever take orders from a doctor or stand reproved by her own daughter!) It was this angry emotion that stood revealed and transparent in every line of her face, in the very defiance of her thin body. At length the frown melted slowly away.

"What sort of a man is he, Irene?" she asked looking straight into her daughter's tired eyes. Irene moved uneasily.

"What man?" she asked, "I don't know who you mean."

"That foreigner . . . I don't remember his name. You've never told me. . . . You might have told your mother." There was a note of peevishness in her voice which sounded queer and alien, almost a portent.

"Oh, Krylenko," said Irene, twisting her black hat with her thin hands. "Krylenko." Then she waited for a moment. "He's a fine man . . . a wonderful man. He has given up everything for his people."

"But they are not *your* people," observed her mother looking at her sharply.

"They are my people," replied Irene softly. "All of them down to the last baby. If they are not my people, who are?"

The old woman, opposed once more by the inevitable wall of Irene's obsessions, frowned. "You are wealthy," she said. "You were born to a position."

In Irene's smile there was a shade of bitterness. "In this Town?" she inquired scornfully. "Oh! No! Position in this Town! That's almost funny." She leaned forward a little, pressing her hand against her forehead. "My people?" she said in a hushed voice. "My people. . . . Why, I don't even know where my father came from."

The mother, half-buried among the heavy pillows raised herself slowly as if a wave of new vigor had taken possession of her worn-out body. "Get me a cigarette, Irene."

The girl opened her lips to protest, but her mother silenced her. "Please, Irene, do as I say. It can't possibly matter what I do now."

"Please, Mama," began Irene once more. "The doctor has forbidden it." Then Julia Shane gave her daughter a terrible look pregnant with all the old arrogance and power.

"Will you do as I say, Irene, or must I send for Sarah? She at least still obeys me."

For a second, authority hung in the balance. It was the authority of a lifetime grounded upon a terrific force of will and sustained by the eternal and certain precedent of obedience. It was the old woman who won the struggle. It was her last victory. The daughter rose and obediently brought the cigarette, even holding the candle to light it. She held the flame at arm's length with a gesture of supreme distaste as if she had been ordered to participate in some unspeakable sin. After she had replaced the candle, her mother puffed thoughtfully for a time.

"Your father," she said presently, "was born in Marseilles. His mother was Spanish and his father Irish. He came to this country because he had to run away. That's all I know. He might have told me more if he had not died suddenly. It's not likely that any of us will ever know his story, no matter how hard we try. Life isn't a story book, you know. In life there are some things that we never know, even about our own friends, our own children. Each man's soul is a secret, which even himself is not able to reveal."

For an instant the light of triumph swept Irene's pale countenance. "You see!" she said. "I am just like the rest . . . like Stepan Krylenko and all the others. My father was a foreigner."

The mother's lips curved in a sudden, scornful smile. "But he was a gentleman, Irene. . . . That is something. And your mother was an American. Her grandfather was the first settler in the wilderness. . . . The Town was named for him. Have you no pride?"

"No," replied Irene, "to be proud is a vice. . . . I have killed it. I am not proud. I am like all the others." And yet there was a fierce pride in her voice, a smug, fierce, pride in not being proud.

"You are perverse," said her mother. "You are beyond me. You talk like a fool. . . ." Irene raised her head to speak but the will of the old woman swept her back. "I know," she continued. "You think it is saintly. Does it ever occur to you that it might only be smugness?"

The old eyes flashed with anger and resentment, emotions which merely shattered themselves against the barrier of Irene's smiling and fanatic sense of righteousness. A look of obstinacy entered her face. (She regarded herself as superior to Julia Shane! Incredible!)

"You amaze me, Irene. Your hardness is beyond belief. If you could be soft for a moment, gentle and generous . . . like Lily."

The daughter's hands tightened about the battered old hat.

"It's always Lily," she said bitterly. "It's always Lily . . . Lily this and Lily that. She's everywhere. Every one praises her . . . even Cousin Hattie." The stubborn look of smugness again descended upon her face. "Well, let them praise her . . . I know that it is I who am right, I who am good in the sight of God." And then for the first time in all the memory of Julia Shane, a look of anger, cold and unrelenting came into the eyes of her daughter. "Lily! Lily!" she cried scornfully, "I hate Lily. . . . May God forgive me!"

Chapter 36

THEN FOR A long time a silence descended upon the room. Julia Shane crushed out the embers of her cigarette and fell once more to turning the silver mounted reading glass round and round, regarding it fixedly with the look of one hypnotized. At last she turned again to her daughter.

"Are you going to marry him?" she asked.

"No, of course not."

"I should be satisfied, if he is as fine as you say he is. I would rather see you married before I die, Irene."

The daughter shook her head stubbornly. "I shall never marry any one."

The old woman smiled shrewdly. "You are wrong, my girl. You are wrong. I haven't had a very happy time, but I wouldn't have given it up. It is a part of life, knowing love and having children. . . . Love can be so many things, but at least it is part of life . . . the greatest part of all. Without it life is nothing."

For a long time Irene remained silent. She kept her eyes cast down and when she spoke again it was without raising them. "But Lily . . ." she began shrewdly. "She has never married." It was the old retort, always Lily. Her mother saw fit to ignore it, perhaps because, knowing what she knew, it was impossible to answer it.

"You've been seeing a great deal of this Krylenko," she said. "It's been going on for years . . . since before Lily was here the last time. That's years ago."

Irene looked up suddenly and a glint of anger lighted her pale eyes. "Who's been talking to you about me? . . . I know. It's Cousin Hattie. She was here to-day. Oh, why can't people let me alone? I harm no one. I want to be left in peace."

Then Julia Shane, perhaps because she already knew too well the antipathy between her coldly virginal daughter and her niece whose whole life was her children, deliberately lied.

"Cousin Hattie did not even mention it." She turned her eyes away from the light. "I would like to see you married, Irene," she repeated. It was clear that for some reason the old hope, forgotten since that tumultuous visit of the Governor, was revived again. It occupied the old woman's mind to the exclusion of all else.

"There is nothing between us, Mama," said Irene. "Nothing at all. Can't you see. We've been friends all along. I taught him to read English. I got him books." Her voice wavered a little and her hands trembled. It was as if she had become a little girl again, the same girl who, in a white muslin dress with a blue sash, sobbed alone on the sofa in the library beneath John Shane's portrait. "I've made him what he is," she continued. "Don't you see. I'm proud of him. When I found him, he was nothing . . . only a stupid Ukrainian boy who was rebellious and rude to me. And now he works with me. He's willing to sacrifice himself for those people. We understand each other. All we want is to be left alone. Don't you understand? I'm just proud of him because I've made him what he is. I'm nothing," she stammered. "I'm nothing to him in that way at all. That would spoil everything . . . like something evil, intruding upon us."

The pale tired face glowed with a kind of religious fervor. For an instant there was something maternal and exalted in her look. All the plainness vanished, replaced suddenly by a feverish beauty. The plain, exhausted old maid had disappeared.

"Why haven't you told me this before?" asked the old woman.

"You never asked me. . . . You never wanted to know what I was doing. You were always interested in Lily. How could you ever have thought I'd marry him? I'm years older." Suddenly she extended her arms with a curious exhibitive gesture like a gesture Lily sometimes made when she was looking her loveliest. "Look at me. I'm old and battered and ugly. How could he ever love me in that way? He is young."

The thin hands dropped listlessly into her lap and lay against the worn black serge. She fell silent, all exhausted by the emotion. Her mother stared at her with the look of one who has just penetrated the soul of a stranger. Irene, it appeared, was suddenly revealed to her.

"Why, you know he's never looked at a woman," Irene continued in a lowered voice. "He's lived in the Flats all these years and he's never looked at a woman. Do you know what that means in the Flats?" Her voice dropped still lower. "Of course, you don't know, because you know nothing about the Flats," she added with a shade of bitterness.

At this her mother smiled. "The rest of the world is not so different, Irene."

But Irene ignored her. "He's worked hard all these years to make himself worth while and to help his people. He's never had time to be bad." Her mother smiled faintly again. Perhaps she smiled at the spinsterish word by which Irene chose to designate fornication.

"He's pure," continued Irene. "He's fine and noble and pure. I want to keep him so."

"You are making of him a saint," observed the old woman dryly.

"He is a saint! That's just what he is," cried Irene. "And you mock him, you and Lily. . . . Oh, I know . . . I know you both. He's been driven from the Mills for what he's done for the people in the Flats. He's been put on a black list so he can never get work in any other Mill. He told me so to-night. That's what he was telling me when you stood watching us." A look of supreme triumph came into her face once more. "But it's too late!" she cried. "It's too late. . . . They've voted to strike. It begins to-morrow. Stepan is the one behind it."

It was as if a terrible war, long hanging in the balance, had suddenly become a reality. Julia Shane, propped among the pillows, turned restlessly and sighed.

"What fools men are!" she said, almost to herself. "What fools!" And then to Irene. "It won't be easy, Irene. It'll be cruel. You'd best go to bed now, dear. You look desperately tired. You'll have plenty of work before you."

Irene pressed a cold, distant kiss on the ivory cheek of her mother and turned to leave.

"Shall I put out the light?"

"Yes, please."

The room subsided into darkness and Irene, opening the door, suddenly heard her mother's voice.

"Oh, Irene." The voice was weary, listless. "I've written for Lily to come home. The doctor told me to-day that I could not possibly live longer than Christmas. I forced it out of him. There was no use in having nonsense. I wanted to know."

And Irene, instead of going to her own room, returned and knelt by the side of her mother's bed. The hardness melted and she sobbed, perhaps because the old woman who faced death with such proud indifference was so far beyond the need of prayer and comfort.

Yet when the smoky dawn appeared at last, it found Irene in her own chaste room still kneeling in prayer before the pink and blue Sienna Virgin.

"Oh, Blessed Virgin," she prayed, from the summit of her complacency. "Forgive my mother her sins of pride and her lack of charity. Forgive my sister her weakness of the flesh. Enter into their hearts and make them good women. Make them worthy to enter the Kingdom of Heaven. Enter into the heart of my sister and cleanse her. Make her a good woman . . . a pure woman, loving only those things which are holy. Cleanse her of the lusts of the flesh!"

Her pale eyes were wet with tears. Although she prayed to a plaster Virgin in pink gilt, she used the sonorous rolling words drawn all unconsciously from the memories of a Presbyterian childhood. And the Lily for whom she prayed . . . the Lily who had been sent for . . . was there in the old house just as she was always in the Town and in the memories of those who knew her beauty, her tolerance and her charm. There were, indeed, times when

Krylenko, caught perhaps in the memory of a night when he stood in the melting snow peering into the windows of Shane's Castle, spoke of her; and these were times when Irene turned away from him, frightened by the shadow of something in his eyes.

Chapter 37

IT BECAME KNOWN as the Great Strike and it served to mark an epoch. Long afterward people in the Town said, "It was the year of the Great Strike" as they said, "It was the year of the Spanish-American War" or "the year that Bryan was a candidate for the first time." Willie Harrison found a use for his enclosures of barbed wire and his heavily barricaded gates. As the strike progressed and the violence increased, other machines of warfare were set up . . . such things as machine guns and searchlights which at night fingered the Flats and the sky above with shafts of white light, rigid and unbending as steel.

In one sense the strike was a Godsend. When the Mills shut down there were no more fires in the ovens and the furnaces; no more soot fell in clouds like infernal snow over the low eminence of Cypress Hill and the squalid expanse of the Flats. For the first time in a score of years the sun became clearly visible. Instead of rising and setting as a ball of hot copper immersed in smoke, it appeared and disappeared quite clear and white, a sun such as God intended it to be. But even more remarkable was the blanket of silence which descended upon all the district. With the banking of the fires, there was no more hammering, and in place of the titanic clamor there was a stillness so profound and so unusual that people noticed it as people notice a sudden clap of loud thunder and remark upon it to each other. The silence became noisy.

In the house at Cypress Hill the world of Julia Shane narrowed from the castle itself to a single room and at last to the vast Italian bed. It was seldom that she gathered sufficient strength to struggle to her feet and make her way, leaning on the ebony and silver stick, to the window where the Mill yards and the Flats lay spread out beneath her gaze. During those last months she knew again the stillness which enveloped the Cypress Hill of her youth. But there was a difference; the green marshes were gone forever, buried beneath the masses of cinders, clay and refuse upon which the Mills raised their sheds and towers and the Flats its flimsy, dirty, matchwood houses, all smoke stained and rotting at the eaves. The lush smell of damp growing things was replaced by the faint odor of crowded, sweating humanity. Not one slim cat-tail, not one feathery willow remained in all the desert of industry. There was, however, a sound which had echoed over the swamps almost a hundred years earlier, a sound which had not been heard since the days when Julia Shane's grandfather built about what was now the public square of the Town a stockade to protect the first settlers from the redskins. It was the sound of guns. Sometimes as she sat at the window, there arose a distant rat-tat-tat like the noise of a typewriter but more staccato and savage, followed by a single crack or two. She discovered at length the origin of the sound. In the Mill yard beneath her window a target had been raised, and at a little distance off men lay on their stomachs pointing rifles mounted upon tripods. Sometimes they fired at rusty buckets and old tin cans because these things did not remain stupid and inanimate like the target, but jumped and whirled about in the most tortured fashion when the bullets struck them, as though they had lives which might be destroyed. It made the game infinitely more fascinating and spirited. The men who indulged in this practise were, she learned from Hennery, the hired guards whom the Harrisons and Judge Weissman had brought in to protect the Mills, riff-raff and off-scourings from the slums of New York, Chicago, Pittsburgh and Cleveland.

There came a day, after the sights and sounds of the Mill yard had become a matter of indifference to the old woman, when the doctor forbade her to leave her bed if she wished to survive the day set for Lily's arrival. It was October, and the park remained unchanged save that the atmosphere was less hot and the sun shone more clearly; for the trees and shrubs on the low hill were long since dead and far beyond the stage of sending out new leaves to fall at the approach of winter. It was bald now and very old. The brick house, dominating all the horizon, stood out day after day gaunt and blackened by soot against the brilliant October sky.

Lily had been delayed. Before leaving Paris she wrote to her mother and Irene that it was necessary for her to take a small boy, the son of a friend, to England. After placing him in school there, she wrote, she would sail at once for America and come straight to Cypress Hill. There were also matters of business which might delay her; but she would not arrive later than the middle of November. So Julia Shane set herself to battling with Death, bent upon beating Him off until she had seen Lily once more.

Chapter 38

IN THOSE DAYS, because it was difficult and dangerous for any one to visit Cypress Hill and because, after all, no one had any particular reason to visit it, there was at the old house, only one caller beside the doctor. This was Hattie Tolliver, whose strength had given way a little to an increasing stoutness but whose pride and spirit flagged not at all. To the police and the hired guards at the Mills, she became as familiar a figure as the doctor himself. She came on foot, since all service on the clanging trolley cars of Halsted street was long since suspended, her large powerful body clad in black clothes of good quality, a basket suspended over one arm and the inevitable umbrella swinging from the other. She walked with a sort of fierce disdain directed with calculated ostentation alike at the Mill guards, the police, and the dwellers of the Flats who viewed her bourgeois approach with a sullen hostility. The basket contained delicacies concocted by her own skilled and housewifely hand . . . the most golden of custards, the most delicate of rennets, fragile biscuits baked without sugar—in short, every sort of thing which might please the palate of an invalid accustomed to excellent food.

In effect, Cypress Hill fell slowly into a state of siege. Surrounded on three sides by the barrier of barbed wire, the sole means of egress was the long drive turning into Halsted street. Here there was danger, for disorders occurred frequently at the very wrought iron gates, now rusted and broken. Stones were hurled by the strikers and shots fired by the police. The wagons of the Town no longer delivered goods at a spot so isolated and dangerous, and the duties of supplying the place with food came gradually to be divided between Irene and Hattie Tolliver, whose lack of friendliness and understanding toward each other approached an open hatred. They alone of the little garrison went in and out of the wrought iron gates; for Hennery and the mulatto woman were far too terrified by the disorders outside ever to venture into the Town.

On the day of Lily's letter Hattie Tolliver, bearing a well-laden basket, arrived and went at once to Aunt Julia's room. She brooked no interference from the mulatto woman.

After bidding Sarah place the contents of the basket in a cool place she swept by the servant with a regal swish of black skirts.

Upstairs in the twilight Julia Shane lay in the enormous bed, flat on her back staring at the ceiling. At the approach of her niece she raised herself a little and asked in a feeble voice to be propped up. It was as though the approach of her vigorous rosy-faced niece endowed her with a sudden energy.

"And how are you?" asked Hattie Tolliver when she had smoothed the pillows with an expert hand and made the old woman more comfortable than she had been in many days.

"The same . . . just the same," was the monotonous answer. "Lily is a long time in coming."

Cousin Hattie went to the windows and flung back the curtains. "Light and air will do you good," she said. "There's nothing like light and air." And then turning, "Why don't you make Sarah keep the windows open?"

Julia Shane sat up more straightly, breathing in the crisp air. "I tell her to . . . but she doesn't like air," she said weakly.

"You let her bully you! She needs some one to manage her. I'm surprised Irene doesn't put her in her place."

The old woman smiled. "Irene," she said. "Irene . . . Why she's too meek ever to get on with servants. It's no use . . . her trying anything."

"I've brought you a custard and some cakes," continued her niece, at the same time flicking bits of dust from the dressing table with her handkerchief and setting the pillows of the chaise longue in order with a series of efficient pats. "There's going to be trouble . . . real trouble before long. The strikers are getting bolder."

"They're getting more hungry too, Irene says," replied the old woman. "Perhaps that's why."

Cousin Hattie came over to the bed now and sat herself down, at the same time taking out a pillow-case which she set herself to hemming. "You know what they're saying in the Town," she remarked. "They're saying that Irene is helping the strike by giving the strikers money."

To this the old woman made no reply and Cousin Hattie continued. "I don't see the sense in that. The sooner every one gets to work, the better. It isn't safe in Halsted street any longer. I'm surprised at Irene helping those foreigners against the Harrisons. I didn't think she had the spirit to take sides in a case like this."

Julia Shane moved her weary body into a more comfortable position. "She doesn't take sides. She only wants to help the women and children. . . . I suppose she's right after all. . . . They are like the rest of us."

At this Cousin Hattie gave a grunt of indignation. "They didn't have to come to this country. I'm sure nobody wants 'em."

"The Mills want them," said her aunt. "The Mills want them and the Mills want more and more all the time."

"But I don't see why we have to suffer because the Mills want foreigners. There ought to be some law against it."

As though there seemed to be no answer to this, Julia Shane turned on her side and remarked, "I had a letter from Lily to-day."

Her niece put down the pillow-case and regarded her with shining eyes. Her heavy body became alive and vibrant. "What did she say? Was there any news of Ellen? Shall I read it?"

"No, go on with your work. If you prop me a little higher and give me my glass, I'll read it."

This operation completed, she read the letter through. It was not until Ellen's name occurred that Cousin Hattie displayed any real interest. At the sound of her daughter's name, the woman put down her sewing and assumed an attitude of passionate listening.

"Ellen," ran the letter, "is doing splendidly. She is contented here and is working hard under Philippe. She plays better than ever . . . if that is possible, and plans to make her début in London next year. She has every reason to make a great success. I am leaving her in my house when I come to America. She gets on beautifully with Madame Gigon. That was my greatest worry, for Madame Gigon has grown worse as she has grown older. But she has taken a fancy to Ellen . . . fortunately, so everything is perfect. Tell Cousin Hattie that one day she will be proud of her daughter."

Julia Shane, when she had finished, put down the letter, and regarded her niece. "You see, Hattie," she said, "there is no need to worry. Everything is going splendidly. Ellen couldn't be in better hands. Lily knows her way about the world a great deal better than most. Some day your daughter will be famous."

There came no response from her niece. Mrs. Tolliver sat upright and thoughtful. Presently she took up the pillow-case and set to work again.

"These débuts," she said. "They cost money, don't they?"

"Yes," replied her aunt.

"Well, where is Ellen to get it? Clarence's life insurance must all be gone by this time."

"I suppose Lily has found a way. Lily is clever. Besides Ellen isn't altogether helpless."

Again there was a thoughtful pause and the old woman said, "I don't think you'd be pleased if Ellen *was* a great success."

"I don't know. I'd be more pleased if I had her nearer to me. I don't like the idea of her being in Paris. It's not a healthy place. It's the wickedest city in the world."

"Come, Hattie. You mustn't forget Ellen was made to live in the world. You brought her up to be successful and famous. It's your fault if you have reason to be proud of her."

Into this single sentence or two Julia Shane managed to condense a whole epic. It was an epic of maternal sacrifices, of a household kept without servants so that the children might profit by the money saved, of plans which had their beginning even before the children were born, of hopes and ambitions aroused skilfully by a woman who now sat deserted, hemming a pillow-case to help dispel her loneliness. She had, in effect, brought about her own sorrow. They were gone now, Ellen to Paris, Fergus and Robert to New York. It was in their very blood. All this was written, after all, in the strong proud face bent low over the pillow-case . . . an epic of passionate maternity.

"We have to expect these things of our children," continued Aunt Julia. "I'm old enough to know that it's no new story, and I've lived long enough to know that we have no right to demand of them the things which seem to us the only ones worth while. Every one of us is different from the others. There are no two in the least alike. And no one ever really knows any one else. There is always a part which remains secret and hidden, concealed in the deepest part of the soul. No husband ever knows his wife, Hattie, and no wife ever really knows her husband. There is always something just beyond that remains aloof and untouched, mysterious and undiscoverable because we ourselves do not know just what it is. Sometimes it is shameful. Sometimes it is too fine, too precious, ever to reveal. It is quite beyond revelation even if we chose to reveal it. . . ."

Chapter 39

AT THE CLOSE of this long speech, the old woman fell into a fit of coughing and her niece rose quickly to bring more medicine and water. If Hattie Tolliver had understood even for a moment these metaphysical theories, they were forgotten in the confusion of the coughing fit. It is more than probable that she understood nothing of the speech and probable that she was too far lost in thoughts of Ellen to have heard it. In any case, she was, like most good mothers and housewives, a pure realist who dealt in terms of the material. At least she gave no sign, and when the coughing fit was over, she returned at once to the main thread of the conversation.

"These careers," she said, "may be all right but I think that Ellen might be happier if she had something more sound . . . like a husband and children and a home."

It was useless to argue with her. Like all women whose domestic life has been happy and successful, she could not be convinced that there was anything in the world more desirable than the love of a good husband and children. With her it was indeed something even stronger—a tribal instinct upon which life itself is founded. She was a fundamental person beside whom Irene and Lily, even her own daughter Ellen, were sports in the biological sense. They were removed by at least two generations from the soil. In them the struggle for life had become transvalued into a pursuit of the arts, of religion, of pleasure itself.

In the gathering twilight, Hattie Tolliver brought a lamp and lighted it to work by. Julia Shane watched her silently for a time, observing the strong neck, the immaculate full curve of her niece's figure, the certainty with which the strong worn fingers moved about their delicate work.

"You remember," she said, "that Lily mentioned a boy . . . a young boy, in her letter?"

"Yes," replied Hattie Tolliver, without glancing from her work. The child of a friend. I thought she might have passed him by to come home to her mother. . . . Funny how children can forget you."

Julia Shane stirred softly in the deep bed. "I thought you might be thinking that," she said. "I thought it would be better to tell you the truth. I wanted you to know anyway. The truth is, Hattie, that the child is her own. She is more interested in him than in me, and that's natural enough and quite proper."

The strong fingers paused abruptly in their work and lay motionless against the white linen. Hattie Tolliver's face betrayed her amazement; yet clearly she was a little amused.

"Charles always said there was something mysterious about Lily," she said. "But I never guessed she'd been secretly married."

The old woman, hesitating, coughed before she replied, as though the supremely respectable innocence of her niece somehow made her inarticulate. At last she summoned strength.

"But she's never been married, Hattie. There never was any ceremony."

"Then how . . ." In Mrs. Tolliver's face the amazement spread until her countenance was one great interrogation.

"Children," interrupted her aunt in a voice filled with tremulous calm, "can be born without marriage certificates. They have nothing to do with legal processes."

For a long time the niece kept silent, fingering the while the half finished pillow-case. It appeared that she found some new and marvelous quality in it. She fingered the stuff as though she were in the act of purchasing it across a counter. At last she raised her head.

"Then it was true . . . that old story?" she asked.

"What story?"

"The one they told in the Town . . . about Lily's *having* to go away to Paris."

"Yes. . . . But no one ever really knew. They only guessed. They knew nothing at all. And they know nothing more to-day." The old woman paused for a second as though to give her words emphasis. "I'm trusting you never to tell, Hattie. I wanted you to know because if ever it was necessary, I wanted Lily to come to you for help. It never will be. It isn't likely."

Hattie Tolliver sat up very stiff and red. "Tell!" she said, "Tell! Who should I ever tell in the Town? Why should I tell any of them?" The tribal instinct rose in triumph. It was a matter of her family against the Mills, the Town, all the world if necessary. Torture could not have dragged from her the truth.

Yet Hattie Tolliver was not unmoved by the confession. It may even have been that she herself long ago had suspicions of the truth which had withered and died since from too much doubt. To a woman of her nature the news of a thousand strikes, of murder and of warfare was as nothing beside the thing Julia Shane revealed. For a long time she said nothing at all, but her strong fingers spoke for her. They worked faster and more skilfully than ever, as if all her agitation was pouring itself out through their tips. The fingers and the flying needle said, "That this should have happened in our family! I can't believe it. Perhaps Aunt Julia is so sick that her mind is weakened. Surely she must imagine this tale. Such things happen only to servant girls. All this is unreal. It cannot be true. Lily could not be so happy, so buoyant if this were true. Sinners can only suffer and be miserable."

All this time she remained silent, breathing heavily, and when at last she spoke, it was to ask, "Who was the man?" in so terrible a voice that the old woman on the bed started for a moment and then averted her face lest her niece see the ghost of a smile which slipped out unwilled.

"It was the Governor," the aunt replied at last.

And then, "Why would he not marry her?" in a voice filled with accumulations of hatred and scorn for the ravishers of women.

This time Julia Shane did not smile. Her pride,—the old fierce and arrogant pride—was touched.

"Oh," she replied, "it was not that. It was Lily who refused to marry him. He begged her . . . on his knees he begged her. I saw him. He would have been glad enough to have her."

And this led only to a "Why?" to which the old woman answered that she did not know except that Lily had said she wished to be herself and go her own way, that she was content and would not marry him even if he became president. "Beyond that, I do not know," she said. "That is where a mother does not know even her own daughter. I don't believe Lily knows herself. Can you tell why it is that Ellen must go on studying and studying, why she cannot help it? Can I know why Irene wants only to be left in peace to go her own way? No, we never really know any one."

All this swept over the head of Hattie Tolliver. She returned to one thing. "It would not have been a bad match. He is a senator now."

It had grown quite dark during their talk and from inside the barrier of the Mills the searchlights began to operate, at first furtively and in jerky fashion and then slowly with greater and greater deliberation, sweeping in gigantic arcs the sky and the squalid area of the Flats. A dozen times in their course the hard white beams swept the walls of the barren old house, penetrating even the room where Julia Shane lay slowly dying. The flashes of light came suddenly, bathing in an unearthly glow and with a dazzling clarity the walls and the furniture. At last, as the beams swept the face of the ormulu clock, Hattie Tolliver, rising, folded her pillow-case and thrust it into the black bag she carried.

"I must go now," she said. "Charlie will be wanting his supper."

The old woman asked her to bend down while she kissed her. It was the first time she had ever made such a request and she passed over the extraordinary event by hastily begging her niece to draw the curtains.

"The lights make me nervous," she said. "I don't know why, but they are worse than the noise the Mills used to make."

And when this opeation was completed she summoned her niece again to her side. "Would you like to see a picture of Lily's boy?"

Hattie Tolliver nodded.

"It is in the top drawer of the chiffonier. Will you fetch it to me?"

Her niece brought the picture and for a time the two women regarded it silently. It was the photograph of a handsome child, singularly like Lily although there was something of the Governor's rather florid good looks, particularly about the high sweeping forehead.

"He is a fine child, isn't he?" the old woman remarked. "I never expected to have a grandchild named Shane."

Still regarding the picture with a sort of fascination, Mrs. Tolliver replied, "He is a darling, isn't he? Does she call him that?"

"Of course. What would she call him?"

"Yes, he is a fine lad. He looks like our family." And then after a long pause she added, "I'm glad you told me all the story. I'm glad Lily did what she did deliberately. I should hate to think that any of us would be weak enough to let a man take advantage of her. That makes a great difference."

After she had put on her small black hat trimmed with worn and stubby ostrich plumes, she turned for the last time. "If you have another of those pictures, Aunt Julia, I would like to have one. I'd like to show it to Charles. He's always admired Lily. It's funny what a way she has with men."

There was no sting in the remark. It was a simple declaration, spoken as though the truth of it had occurred to her for the first time. She was too direct and vigorous to be feline.

As she closed the door the voice of her aunt trailed weakly after. "You needn't worry about Ellen. All her strength and character is your strength and character, Hattie. She can take care of herself."

The niece turned in the doorway, her thick strong figure blocking the shower of dim light from the hall. "No," she said. "It's not as though Lily were bad. She isn't bad. I've always had an idea that she knew what she was about. I suppose she has her own ideas on life. Perhaps she lives up to them. I can't say they're my ideas." For a second she leaned against the frame of the door, searching with an air of physical effort for words to express her thoughts. "No, she isn't bad," she continued. "No one who ever knew her can say she is a bad woman. I can't explain what I mean, but I suppose she believes in what she does."

And with this wise and mysterious observation Mrs. Tolliver returned to the world of the concrete—her own world—swept down the long stairway and into the kitchen where she reclaimed her basket, and left the house without waiting for the hostile mulatto woman to open the door.

Chapter 40

PERHAPS BECAUSE she was so dazed and fascinated by the story which Julia Shane had poured into her astonished ears, she walked in a sort of dream to the foot of the long drive where she found herself suddenly embroiled in a waking nightmare. On all sides of her there rose a great tumult and shouting. Stones were thrown. Cries rang out in barbaric tongues. Men struggled and fought, and above the men on foot rose the figures of the constabulary mounted on wild and terrified horses who charged and curvetted as their masters struck about them with heavy clubs.

Through all this, Hattie Tolliver passed with an air of the most profound detachment and scorn, somewhat in the manner of a great sea-going freighter riding the waves of an insignificant squall. She carried her head high, despising the Irish constabulary as profoundly as she despised the noisy alien rabble. Clearly it was none of her affair. This embroiled rabble had nothing to do with her, nothing to do with her family, nothing to do with her world. The riot was as nothing beside the tale that kept running through her mind, blinding her senses to all the struggle that took place at her very side.

And then, suddenly and without warning, the crack of a pistol tore the air; then another and another, and there fell at the feet of Hattie Tolliver, completely blocking her overwhelming progress, the body of a swarthy man with heavy black mustaches. Before she was able to move, one of the constabulary, rushing up, kicked the prostrate body of the groaning man.

But he did not kick twice, for he was repulsed a second later by the savage thrust in the stomach from the umbrella of Mrs. Tolliver who, rushing to the attack, cried out, "Get away, you filthy brute! . . . You dirty coward!"

And the trooper, seeing no doubt that she was not one of the foreigners, retired sheepishly before the menace of the angry mob to join his fellows.

The basket and umbrella were cast aside and Mrs. Tolliver, bending over the writhing man, searched for the wound. When she looked up again she found, standing over her, the gigantic steel worker who she knew was Irene's friend. She did not know his name.

"Here," she said, with the manner of a field marshal. "Help me get this fellow into the house over there."

Without a word, Krylenko bent down, picked up the stricken workman and bore him, laid across his brawny shoulders, into the corner saloon whither Hattie Tolliver with her recovered basket and umbrella followed him, surrounded by a protecting phalanx of excited and gibbering strikers.

The saloon was empty, for all the hangers-on had drifted long before into the streets to watch the riot from a safe distance. But the electrical piano kept up its uncanny uproar playing over and over again, Bon-Bon Buddy, the Chocolate Drop and I'm Afraid to go Home in the Dark.

There on the bar, among the empty glasses, Krylenko laid the unconscious striker and Hattie Tolliver, with the scissors she had used but a moment before in hemstitching a pillow-case, cut away the soiled shirt and dressed the wound. When her work was done she ordered Krylenko to take down one of the swinging doors and on this the strikers bore the wounded man to his own house.

When the little procession had vanished around a corner, Mrs. Tolliver brushed her black clothes, gathered up her basket and umbrella and set out up the hill to the Town. It was the first time she had ever set foot inside an establishment which sold intoxicating liquors.

Behind her in the darkened room at Cypress Hill, the sound of shots and cries came distantly to Julia Shane as through a high impenetrable wall, out of another world. At the moment she was alive in a world of memories, a world as real and as tangible as the world of the Mills and the Flats, for the past may be quite as real as the present. It is a vast country full of trees and houses, animals and friends, where people may go on having adventures as long as they live. And the sounds she heard in her world bore no relation to the sounds in sordid Halsted street. They were the sounds of pounding hoofs on hard green turf, and the cries of admiration from a little group of farmers and townspeople who leaned on the rail of John Shane's paddock while his wife, with a skilful hand sent his sleek hunter Doña Rita over the bars—first five, then six and last of all and marvelous to relate, a clean seven!

A stained and dusty photograph slipped from her thin fingers and lost itself among the mountainous bedclothing which she found impossible to keep in order. It was the portrait of a youngish man with a full black beard and eyes that were wild, passionate, adventurous . . . the portrait of John Shane, the lover, as he returned to his wife at the school of Mademoiselle Violette de Vaux at St. Cloud on the outskirts of Paris.

Chapter 41

As JULIA SHANE grew weaker, it was Cousin Hattie Tolliver who "took hold" of the establishment at Shane's Castle. It was always Mrs. Tolliver, capable and housewifely, who "took hold" in a family crisis. She managed funerals, weddings and christenings. Cousins came to die at her shabby house in the Town. She gathered into her large strong hands the threads of life and death that stretched themselves through a family scattered from Paris to Australia. Her relatives embroiled themselves in scrapes, they grew ill, they lost or made fortunes, they succumbed to all the weaknesses to which the human flesh is prone; and always, at the definitive moment, they turned to Hattie Tolliver as to a house built upon a rock.

Irene, so capable in succoring the miserable inhabitants of the Flats, grew helpless when death peered in at the tall windows of Shane's Castle. Besides, she had her own work to do. As the strike progressed she came to spend days and nights in the squalid houses of Halsted street, returning at midnight to inquire after her mother. She knew nothing of managing a house and Hattie Tolliver knew these things intimately. More than that, Mrs. Tolliver enjoyed "taking hold"; and she extracted, beyond all doubt, a certain faintly malicious satisfaction in taking over the duties which should have fallen upon Irene, while Irene spent her strength, her very life, in helping people unrelated to her, people who were not even Americans.

So it was Hattie Tolliver, wearing a spotless apron and bearing a dustcloth, who opened the door when Hennery, returning from his solitary and heroic venture outside the gates, drove Lily up from the dirty red brick station, bringing this time no great trunks covered with gay labels of Firenze and Sorrento but a pair of black handbags and a small trunk neatly strapped. It may have been that Hennery, as Irene hinted bitterly, made that perilous journey through the riots of Halsted street only because it was Mis' Lily who was returning. Certainly no other cause had induced him to venture outside the barren park.

The encounter, for Hattie Tolliver, was no ordinary one. From her manner it was clear that she was opening the door to a woman . . . her own cousin . . . who had lived in sin, who had borne a child out of wedlock. Indeed the woman might still be living in sin. Paris was a Babylon where it was impossible to know any one's manner of living. Like all the others, Mrs. Tolliver had lived all her life secure in the belief that she knew Lily. She remembered the day of her cousin's birth . . . a snowy blustering day. She knew Lily throughout her childhood. She knew her as a woman. "Lily," she undoubtedly told herself, "was thus and so. If any one knows Lily, I know her." And then all this knowledge had been upset suddenly by a single word from Lily's mother. It was necessary to create a whole new pattern. The woman who stood on the other side of the door was not Lily at all—at least not the old Lily—but a new woman, a stranger, whom she did not know. There might be, after all, something in what Aunt Julia said about never really knowing any one.

All this her manner declared unmistakably during the few strained seconds that she stood in the doorway facing her cousin. For an instant, while the two women, the worldly and the provincial, faced each other, the making of family history hung in the balance. It was Mrs. Tolliver who decided the issue. Suddenly she took her beautiful cousin into her arms, encircling her in an embrace so warm and so filled with defiance of all the world that Lily's black hat, trimmed with camelias, was knocked awry.

"Your poor mother!" were Cousin Hattie's first words. "She is very low indeed. She has been asking for you."

And so Lily won another victory in her long line of conquests, a victory which she must have known was a real triumph in which to take a profound pride.

Then while Lily took off her hat and set her fine hair in order, her cousin poured out the news of the last few days. It was news of a sort that warmed the heart of Mrs. Tolliver . . . news of Julia Shane's illness delivered gravely with a vast embroidery of detail, a long account of the mulatto woman's insolence and derelictions which increased as the old woman grew weaker; and, last of all, an eloquent and denunciatory account of Irene's behavior.

"She behaves," said Mrs. Tolliver, "as though a daughter had no obligations toward her own mother." Her face grew scarlet with indignation at this flouting of family ties. "She spends all her time in the Flats among those foreigners and never sees her own mother more than a minute or two a day. There she lies, a sick and dying woman, grieving because her daughter neglects her. You'd think Irene loved the strikers more . . . especially one young fellow who is the leader," she added darkly.

Lily, knowing her mother, must have guessed that Cousin Hattie's account suffered from a certain emotional exaggeration. The picture of old Julia Shane, grieving because her daughter neglected her, was not a convincing one. The old woman was too self reliant for that sort of behavior. She expected too little from the world.

But Lily said nothing. She unstrapped her bag and brought out a fresh handkerchief and a bottle of scent. Then she raised her lovely head and looked sharply at her cousin. "I suppose it's this same Krylenko," she said. "D'you think she's in love with him?"

"No," replied Mrs. Tolliver shrewdly, "I don't think she loves anybody or anything but her own soul. She's like a machine. She has an idea she loves the strikers but that's only because she thinks she's saving her soul by good works. I suppose it makes her happy. Only yesterday I told her, thinking it would be a hint, that charity begins at home." For a moment Mrs. Tolliver waited thoughtfully, and then she added, "You know, sometimes Irene looks at her mother as if she wanted her to make haste with her dying. I've noticed the look—more than once."

And so they talked for a time, as people always talked of Irene, as if she were a stranger, a curiosity, something which stood outside the realm of human understanding. And out of the ruin of Irene's character, Hattie Tolliver rose phoenix-like, triumphant, as the heroine who had seen Irene's duty and taken it upon herself.

"You know, I'm nursing your mother," she continued. "She wouldn't have a nurse because she couldn't bear to have a stranger in the house. She has that one idea now . . . seeing no one but the doctor and her own family. Now that you've come, I suppose she won't even see the doctor any more. She's asleep now, so I came down-stairs to put the house into some sort of order. Heaven knows what it would have been like if the drawing-room had been open too. That mulatto woman," she added bitterly, "hasn't touched a thing in weeks."

Silently, thoughtfully, Lily pushed open the double doors into the drawing-room.

"It's not been opened since you left," continued Mrs. Tolliver. "Not even for the Christmas party. But that wasn't necessary because there aren't many of us left. You could put all of us into the library. There's only Eva Barr and Charles and me. The old ones are all dead and the young ones have gone away." For a moment she paused, for Lily appeared not to be listening. Then she added softly, "But I guess you know all that. I'd forgotten Ellen was living with you."

For the time being, the conversation ended while the two women, Lily in her smart suit from the Rue de la Paix and Hattie Tolliver in shiny black alpaca with apron and dustcloth, stood in the doorway reverently surveying the vast old room, so dead now and so full of memories. The rosewood chairs, shrouded like ghosts, appeared dimly in the light that filtered through the curtained windows. In the far end, before the long mirror, the piano with its shapeless covering resembled some crouching, prehistoric animal. Above the mantelpiece, the flaming Venice of Mr. Turner glowed vaguely beneath layers of dust. Cobwebs hung from the crystal chandeliers and festooned the wall sconces; and beneath the piano the Aubusson carpet, rolled into a long coil, waited like a python. The room was the mute symbol of something departed from the Town.

Silently the two women regarded the spectacle and when Lily at length turned away, her dark eyes were shining with tears. She was inexpressibly lovely, all softened now by the melancholy sight.

"I suppose it will never be opened again," observed Mrs. Tolliver in a solemn voice. "But I mean to clean it thoroughly the first time I have an opportunity. Just look at the dust." And with her competent finger she traced her initials on the top of a lacquer table.

For a moment Lily made no reply. At last she said, "No. I suppose it is closed for good."

"You wouldn't come back here to live?" probed her cousin with an air of hopefulness.

"No. Why should I?" And a second later Lily added, "But how quiet it is. You can almost hear the stillness."

Mrs. Tolliver closed the door, seizing at the same time the opportunity to polish the knobs on the hallway side. "Yes, it's a relief not to hear the Mills. But there are other noises now . . . riots and machine guns, and at night there are searchlights. Only last night the police clubbed an old woman to death at the foot of the drive. She was a Polish woman . . . hadn't been harming any one. I wonder you didn't see the blood. It's smeared on the gates. Irene can tell you all about it." For a moment she polished thoughtfully; then she straightened her vigorous body and said, "But I got back at them. I gave one of the hired policemen a poke he won't soon forget. It's a crime the way they behave. . . . It's murder. No decent community would allow it." And she told Lily the story of the rescue at the corner saloon.

As Lily made her way up the long stairway, Mrs. Tolliver paused in her work to watch the ascending figure until it reached the top. Her large honest face was alive with interest, her eyes shining as if she now really saw Lily for the first time, as if the old Lily had been simply an illusion. The beautiful stranger climbed the stairs languidly, the long, lovely lines of her body showing through the trim black suit. Her red hair glowed in the dim light of the hallway. She was incredibly young and happy, so unbelievably fresh and lovely that Mrs. Tolliver, after Lily had disappeared at the turn of the stair, moved away shaking her head and making the clucking sound which primitive women use to indicate a disturbance of their suspicions.

And when she returned to dusting the library under the handsome, malignant face of John Shane she worked in silence, abandoning her usual habit of humming snatches of old ballads. After the Ball was Over and The Baggage Coach Ahead were forgotten. Presently, when she had finished polishing the little ornaments of jade and crystal, she fell to regarding the portrait with a profound interest. She stood thus, with her arms akimbo, for many minutes regarding the man in the picture as if he too had become a stranger to her. She discovered, it appeared, something more than a temperamental and clever old reprobate who had been indulgent toward her. Her manner was that of a person who stands before a suddenly opened door in the presence of magnificent and incomprehensible wonders.

Lily found her there when she came down-stairs.

"You know," observed Mrs. Tolliver, "I must be getting old. I have such funny thoughts lately . . . the kind of thoughts a normal healthy woman doesn't have."

Chapter 42

Room by room, closet by closet, Mrs. Tolliver and Lily put the big house in order. They even set Hennery to cleaning the cellar, and themselves went into the attic where they poked about among old boxes and trunks filled with clothing and photographs, bits of yellow lace and brocade for which no use had ever been found. There were photographs of Lily and Irene as little girls in tarlatan dresses much ornamented with artificial pansies and daisies; pictures of John Shane on the wrought iron piazza, surrounded by men who were leaders in state politics; dim photographs of Julia Shane in an extremely tight riding habit with a bustle, and a hat set well forward over the eyes; pictures of the annual family gatherings at Christmas time with all its robust members standing in the snow outside the house at Cypress Hill. There were even pictures of Mrs. Tolliver's father, Jacob Barr, on the heavy hack he sometimes rode, and one of him surrounded by his eight vigorous children.

From the sentimental Mrs. Tolliver, this collection wrenched a tempest of sighs. To Lily she said, "It's like raising the dead. I just can't believe the changes that have occurred."

The arrival of Lily brought a certain repose to the household. The mulatto woman who behaved so sulkily under the shifting dominations of the powerful Mrs. Tolliver and the anemic Irene, began slowly to regain her old respectful attitude. It appeared that she honored Miss Lily with the respect which servants have for those who understand them. Where the complaints of Irene and the stormy commands of Mrs. Tolliver had wrought nothing, the amiable smiles and the interested queries of Lily accomplished miracles. For a time the household regained the air of order and dignity which it had known in the days of Julia Shane's domination. Lily was unable to explain her success. After all, there was nothing new in the process. Servants had always obeyed her in the same fashion. She charmed them whether they were her own or not.

Although her arrival worked many a pleasant change in the house and appeared to check for a time the inward sweeping waves of melancholy, there was one thing which she was unable, either consciously or unconsciously, to alter in any way. This was the position of Irene. The sister remained an outsider. It was as if the old dwelling were a rooming house and she were simply a roomer, detached, aloof . . . a roomer in whom no one was especially interested. She was, in fact, altogether incomprehensible. Lily, to be sure, made every effort to change the condition of affairs; but her efforts; it appeared, only drove her sister more deeply into the shell of taciturnity and indifference. The first encounter of the two sisters, for all the kisses and warmth of Lily, was an awkward and soulless affair to which Irene submitted listlessly. So apparent was the strain of the encounter that Mrs. Tolliver, during the course of the morning's work, found occasion to refer to it.

"You mustn't mind Irene's behavior," she said. "She has been growing queerer and queerer." And raising her eyebrows significantly she continued, "You know, sometimes I think she's a little cracked. Religion sometimes affects people in that way, especially the sort of popery Irene practises."

And then she told of finding Irene, quite by accident, prostrate before the pink-gilt image of the Virgin, her hair all disheveled, her eyes streaming with tears.

Once Mrs. Tolliver had reconciled herself to Lily's secret, her entire manner toward her cousin suffered a change. The awe which had once colored her behavior disappeared completely. She was no longer the provincial, ignorant of life outside the Town, face to face with an experienced woman of the world. She was one mother with an understanding for another. Before many days had passed the pair worked and gossiped side by side, not only as old friends might have gossiped but as old friends who are quite the same age, whose interests are identical. In her manner there was no evidence of any strangeness save in the occasional moments when she would cease working abruptly to regard her lovely cousin with an expression of complete bewilderment, which did not vanish until Lily, attracted by her cousin's steady gaze, looked up and caused Mrs. Tolliver to blush as if it were herself who had sinned.

Chapter 43

IT WAS LILY who in the end mentioned the affair. She spoke of it as they sat at lunch in the paneled dining-room.

"Mama," she said suddenly, "tells me that you know all about Jean."

"Yes," replied Mrs. Tolliver, in a queer unearthly voice. "She told me."

"I'm glad, because I wanted to tell you before, only she wouldn't let me. She said you wouldn't understand."

There was an awesome little pause and Mrs. Tolliver, her fork poised, said, "I don't quite understand, Lily. I must say it's puzzling. But I guessed you knew what you were doing. It wasn't as if you were a common woman who took lovers." She must have seen the faint tinge of color that swept over Lily's face, but she continued in the manner of a virtuous woman doing her duty, seeing a thing in the proper light, being fair and honest. "I guessed there was some reason. Of course, I wouldn't want a daughter of mine to do such a thing. I would rather see her in her grave."

Her manner was emphatic and profound. It was clear that however she might forgive Lily in the eyes of the world, she had her own opinions which none should ever know but herself and Lily.

Lily blushed, the color spreading over her lovely face to the soft fringe of her hair. "You needn't worry, Cousin Hattie," she said. "Ellen would never do such a thing. You see, Ellen is complete. She doesn't need anything but herself. She's not like me at all. She isn't weak. She would never do anything because she lost her head."

Ellen's mother, who had stopped eating, regarded her with a look of astonishment. "But your mother said you hadn't lost your head. She said it was you who wouldn't marry the Governor."

Lily's smile persisted. She leaned over to touch her cousin's hand, gently as though pleading with her to be tolerant.

"It's true," she said. "Some of what mother told you. It's true about my refusing to marry him. You see the trouble is that I'm not afraid when I should be. I'm not afraid of the things I should be afraid of. When there is danger, I can't run away. If I could run away I'd be saved, but I can't. Something makes me see it through. It's something that betrays me . . . something that is stronger than myself. That's what happened with the Governor. It was I who was more guilty than he. It is I who played with fire. If I was not unwilling, what could you expect of him . . . a man. Men love the strength of women as a refuge from their own weakness." She paused and her face grew serious. "When it was done, I was afraid . . . not afraid, you understand of bearing a child or even afraid of what people would say of me. I was afraid of losing myself, because I knew I couldn't always love him. . . . I knew it. I knew it. I knew that something had betrayed me. I couldn't give up all my life to a man because I'd given an hour of it to him. I was afraid of what he would become. Can you understand that? That was the only thing I was afraid of . . . nothing else but that. It was I who was wrong in the very beginning."

But Mrs. Tolliver's expression of bewilderment failed to dissolve before this disjointed explanation. "No," she said, "I don't understand. . . . I should think you would have wanted a home and children and a successful husband. He's been elected senator, you know, and they talk of making him president."

Lily's red lip curved in a furtive, secret, smile. "And what's that to me?" she asked. "They can make him what they like. A successful husband isn't always the best. I could see what they would make him. That's why I couldn't face being his wife. I wasn't a girl when it happened. I was twenty-four and I knew a great many things. I wasn't a poor innocent seduced creature. But it wasn't so much that I thought it out. I couldn't help myself. I couldn't marry him. Something inside me wouldn't let me. A part of me was wise. You see, only half of me loved him . . . my body, shall we say, desired him. That is not enough for a lifetime. The body changes." For a second she cast down her eyes as if in shame and Mrs. Tolliver, who never before had heard such talk, looked away, out of the tall window across the snow covered park.

"Besides," Lily continued, after a little silence, "I have a home and I have a child. Both of them are perfect. I am a very happy woman, Cousin Hattie . . . much happier than if I had married him. I know that from what he taught me . . . in that one hour."

Mrs. Tolliver regarded her now with a curious, prying, look. Plainly it was a miracle she had found in a woman who had sinned and still was happy. "But you have no husband," she said presently, with the air of presenting a final argument.

"No," replied Lily, "I have no husband."

"But that must mean something."

"Yes, I suppose it does mean something."

And then the approach of the mulatto woman put an end to the talk for the time being. When she had disappeared once more, it was Mrs. Tolliver who spoke. "You know," she said, "I sometimes think Irene would be better off if such a thing had happened to her. It isn't natural, the way she carries on. It's morbid. I've told her so often enough."

"But it couldn't have happened to Irene. She will never marry. You see Irene's afraid of men . . . in that way. Such a thing I'm sure would drive her mad." And Lily bowed her lovely head for a moment. "We must be good to Irene. She can't help being as she is. You see she believes all love is a kind of sin. Love, I mean, of the sort you and I have known."

At this speech Mrs. Tolliver grew suddenly tense. Her large, honest face became scarlet with indignation. "But it isn't the same," she protested. "What I knew and what you knew. They're very different things. My love was consecrated."

Lily's dark eyes grew thoughtful. "It would have been the same if I had married the Governor. People would have said that we loved each other as you and Cousin Charles love each other. They wouldn't have known the truth. One doesn't wash one's dirty linen in public."

Her cousin interrupted her abruptly. "It is not the same. I could not have had children by Charlie until I was married to him. I mean there could have been nothing like that between us beforehand."

"That's only because you were stronger than me," said Lily. "You see I was born as I am. That much I could not help. There are times when I cannot save myself. You are more fortunate. Irene is like me. That is the reason she behaves as she does. After all, it is the same thing in us both."

But Mrs. Tolliver, it was plain to be seen, understood none of this. It was quite beyond her simple code of conduct. Her life bore witness to her faith in the creed that breaking the rules meant disaster.

"I know," continued Lily, "that I was lucky to have been rich. If I had been poor it would have been another matter. I should have married him. But because I was rich, I was free. I was independent to do as I wished, independent . . . like a man, you understand. Free to do as I pleased." All at once she leaned forward impulsively. "Tell me, Cousin Hattie . . . it has not made me hard, has it? It has not made me old and evil? It has not made people dislike me?"

Mrs. Tolliver regarded her for a moment as if weighing arguments, seeking reasons, why Lily seemed content and happy despite everything. At length, finding no better retort, she said weakly, "How could they dislike you? No one ever knew anything about it."

A look of triumph shone in Lily's dark eyes. "Ah, that's it!" she cried. "That's it! They didn't know anything, so they don't dislike me. If they had known they would have found all sorts of disagreeable things in me. They would have said, 'We cannot speak to Lily Shane. She is an immoral woman.' They would have made me into a hard and unhappy creature. They would have created the traits which they believed I should possess. It is the knowing that counts and not the act itself. It is the old story. It is worse to be found out in a little sin than to commit secretly a big one. There is only one thing that puzzles them." She raised her slim, soft hands in a little gesture of badinage. "Do you know what it is? They can't understand why I have never married and why I am not old and rattly as a spinster should be. It puzzles them that I am young and fresh."

For a time Mrs. Tolliver considered the dark implications of this speech. But she was not to be downed. "Just the same, I don't approve, Lily," she said. "I don't want you to think for a minute that I approve. If my daughter had done it, it would have killed me. It's not right. One day you will pay for it, in this world or the next."

At this threat Lily grew serious once more and the smoldering light of rebellion came into her eyes. She was leaning back in her old indolent manner. It was true that there was about her something inexpressibly voluptuous and beautiful which alarmed her cousin. It was a dangerous, flaunting beauty, undoubtedly wicked to the Presbyterian eyes of Mrs. Tolliver. And she was young too. At that moment she might have been taken for a woman in her early twenties.

After a time she raised her head. "But I am happy," she said, defiantly, "completely happy."

"I wish," said Mrs. Tolliver with a frown, "that you wouldn't say such things. I can't bear to hear you."

And presently the talk turned once more to Irene. "She is interested in this young fellow called Krylenko," said Mrs. Tolliver. "And your mother is willing to have her marry him, though I can't see why. I would rather see her die an old maid than be married to a foreigner."

"He is clever, isn't he?" asked Lily.

"I don't know about that. He made all this trouble about the strike. Everything would be peaceful still if he hadn't stirred up trouble. Maybe that's being clever. I don't know."

"But he must be clever if he could do all that. He must be able to lead the workers. I'm glad he did it, myself. The Harrison crowd has ruled the roost long enough. It'll do them good to have a jolt . . . especially when it touches their pocketbooks. I saw him once, myself. He looks like a powerful fellow. I should say that some day you will hear great things of him."

Mrs. Tolliver sniffed scornfully. "Perhaps . . . perhaps. If he is, it will be because Irene made him great. All the same I can't see her marrying him . . . a common immigrant . . . a Russian!"

"You needn't worry. She won't. She could never marry him. To her he isn't a man at all. He's a sort of idea . . . a plaster saint!" And for the first time in all her discussion of Irene a shade of hard scorn colored her voice.

Chapter 44

For AN HOUR longer they sat talking over the coffee while Lily smoked indolently cigarette after cigarette beneath the disapproving eye of her cousin. They discussed the affairs of the household, the news in the papers of Mrs. Julis Harrison's second stroke, of Ellen, and Jean from whom Lily had a letter only that morning.

"Has the Governor ever asked for him?" inquired Mrs. Tolliver, with the passionate look of a woman interested in details.

"No," said Lily, "I have not heard from him in years. He has never seen the boy. You see Jean is mine alone because even if the Governor wanted him he dares not risk a scandal. He is as much my own as if I had created him alone out of my own body. He belongs to me and to me alone, do you see? I can make him into what I will. I shall make him into a man who will know everything and be everything. He shall be stronger than I and cleverer. He is handsome enough. He is everything to me. A queen would be proud to have him for her son."

As she spoke a light kindled in her eyes and a look of exultation spread over her face. It was an expression of passionate triumph.

"You see," she added, "it is a wonderful thing to have some one who belongs to you alone, who loves you alone and no one else. He owns me and I own him. There is no one else who counts. If we were left alone on a desert island, we would be content." The look faded slowly and gave place to a mocking smile that arched the corners of her red lips. "If I had married the Governor, the boy might have become anything. . . . I should have seen him becoming crude and common under my very eyes. I should have hated his father and I could have done nothing. As it is, his father is only a memory . . . pleasant enough, a handsome man who loved me, but never owned me . . . even for an instant . . . not even the instant of my child's conception!"

During this speech the manner of Mrs. Tolliver became more and more agitated. With each bold word a new wave of color swept her large face, until at the climax of Lily's confession she was struck mute, rendered incapable of either thought or action. It was a long time before she recovered even a faint degree of her usual composure. At last she managed to articulate, "I don't see, Lily, how you can say such things. I really don't. The words would burn my throat!"

Her cousin's smile was defiant, almost brazen. "You see, Cousin Hattie, I have lived among the French. With them such things are no more than food and drink . . . except perhaps that they prefer love to everything else," she added, with a mischievous twinkle in her dark eyes.

"And besides," continued Mrs. Tolliver, "I don't know what you mean. I'm sure Charles has never *owned* me."

"No, my dear," said Lily, "He never has. On the contrary it is you who have always owned him. It is always one thing or the other. The trouble is that at first women like to be owned." She raised her hand. "Oh, I know. The Governor would have owned me sooner or later. There are some men who are like that. You know them at once. I know how my father owned my mother and you know as well as I that she was never a weak, clinging woman. If she had been as rich as I, she would have left him . . . long ago. She could not because he owned her."

"But that was different," parried Mrs. Tolliver. "He was a foreigner."

They were treading now upon that which in the family had been forbidden ground. No one discussed John Shane with his wife or children because they had kept alive for more than thirty years a lie, a pretense. John Shane had been accepted silently and unquestioningly as all that a husband should be. Now the manner of Mrs. Tolliver brightened visibly at the approach of an opening for which she had waited more years than she was able to count.

"But he was a man and she was a woman," persisted Lily. "I know that most American women own their husbands, but the strange thing is that I could never have married a man whom I could own. You see that is the trouble with marriage. It is difficult to be rid of a husband."

Mrs. Tolliver shifted nervously and put down her coffee cup. "Really, Lily," she said, "I don't understand you. You talk as though being married was wrong." Her manner, for the first time, had become completely cold and disapproving. She behaved as though at any moment she might rise and turn her back forever upon Lily.

"Oh, don't think, Cousin Hattie, that people get married because they like being tied together by law. Most people get married because it is the only way they can live together and still be respected by the community. Most people would like to change now and then. It's true. They're like that in their deepest hearts . . . far down where no one ever sees."

She said this so passionately that Mrs. Tolliver was swept into silence. Books the good woman never read because there was no time; and even now with her children gone, she did not read because it was too late in life to develop a love for books. Immersed always in respectability, such thoughts as these had never occurred to her; and certainly no one had ever talked thus in her presence.

"I don't understand," she was able to articulate weakly after a long pause. "I don't understand." And then as if she saw opportunity escaping from her into spaces from which it might never be recovered, she said, "Tell me, Lily. Have you ever had any idea from where your father came?"

The faint glint of amusement vanished from her cousin's eyes and her face grew thoughtful. "No. Nothing save that his mother was Spanish and his father Irish. He was born in Marseilles."

"And where's that?" asked Mrs. Tolliver, aglow with interest.

"It's in the south of France. It's a great city and an evil one . . . one of the worst in the world. Mamma says we'll never know the truth. I think perhaps she is right."

After this the conversation returned to the minutiae of the household for a time and, at length, as the bronze clock struck three the two women rose and left the room to make their way upstairs to the chamber of the dying old woman. In the hall, Lily turned, "I've never talked like this to any one," she said. "I'd never really thought it all out before. I've told you more than I've ever told any one, Cousin Hattie . . . even my mother."

Upstairs Mrs. Tolliver opened the door of the darkened room, Lily followed her on tiptoe. In the gray winter light, old Julia Shane lay back among the pillows sleeping peacefully.

"Will you wake her for her medicine?" whispered Lily.

"Of course," replied her cousin, moving to the bedside, where she shook the old woman gently and softly called her name.

"Aunt Julia! Aunt Julia!" she called again and again. But there was no answer as Mrs. Tolliver's powerful figure bent over the bed. She felt for the weakened pulse and then passed her vigorous hand over the face, so white now and so transparent. Then she stood back and regarded the bony, relentless old countenance and Lily drew nearer until her warm full breasts brushed her cousin's shoulder. The hands of the two women clasped silently in a sort of fearful awe.

"She has gone away," said Mrs. Tolliver, "in her sleep. It could not have been better."

And together the two women set about preparing Julia Shane for the grave, forgetful of all the passionate talk of an hour before. In the face of death, it counted for nothing.

Chapter 45

A LITTLE WHILE later, Lily herself went down the snow covered drive and summoned a passing boy whom she sent into the Flats in search of Irene, since she herself dared not venture among the sullen strikers. After two hours, he returned to say he could find no trace of the sister. So it was not until Irene returned at midnight that she learned her mother was dead. She received the news coldly enough, perhaps because in those days death and suffering meant so little to her; but even Lily must have seen the faint glimmer of triumph that entered her sister's pale, red-rimmed eyes at the news that she was free at last.

Just before dawn when the searchlights, swinging their gigantic arcs over the Flats, pierced the guiet solitude of Lily's room and wakened her, she heard through the mist of sleep the voice of Irene praying in her room for mercy upon the soul of their mother. For a second, she raised her head in an attitude of listening and then sank back and quickly fell asleep, her rosy face pillowed on her white bare arm, her bright hair all loose and shining in the sudden flashes of reflected light.

The Town newspapers published long obituaries of Julia Shane, whole columns which gave the history of her family, the history of John Shane, so far as it was known, and the history of Cypress Hill. In death it seemed that Julia Shane reflected credit in some way upon the Town. She gave it a kind of distinction just as the Cyclops Mills or any other remarkable institution gave it distinction. The newspapers treated her as if she were good advertising copy. The obituaries included lists of celebrated people who had been guests at Cypress Hill. Presidents were mentioned, an ambassador, and the Governor who was now a senator. They remarked that Julia Shane was the granddaughter of the man who gave the Town its name. For a single day Cypress Hill regained its lost and splendid prestige. Newcomers in the Town, superintendents and clerks from the idle Mills, learned for the first time the history of Shane's Castle, all but the scandalous stories about John Shane which were omitted as unsuitable material for an obituary. Besides no one really knew whether they were true or not.

And despite all this vulgar fanfare, it was clear that a great lady had passed, one who in her day had been a sovereign, but one whose day had passed with the coming of the Mills and the vulgar, noisy aristocracy of progress and prosperity.

The obituaries ended with the sentence, "Mrs. Shane is survived by two unmarried daughters, Irene, who resides at Cypress Hill, and Lily who for some ten years has made her home in Paris. Both were with their mother at the time of her passing."

It was this last sentence which interested the older residents. *Lily, who for some ten years has made her home in Paris. Both were with their mother at the time of her passing.* How much lay hidden and mysterious in those two lines. Until the publishing of the obituary, the Town had known nothing of Lily's return.

At five o'clock on the afternoon of the funeral Willie Harrison sat in his mother's bedroom in the sandstone house giving her a detailed account of the funeral. Outside the snow fell in drifting clouds, driven before a wind which howled wildly among the ornamental cupolas and projections of the ugly house. Inside the air hung warm and stifling, touched by the pallid odor of the sickroom. It was a large square room constructed with a great effect of solidity, and furnished with heavy, expensive furniture upholstered in dark red plush. The walls were tan and the woodwork of birch stained a deep mahogany color. Above the ornate mantelpiece hung an engraved portrait of the founder of the Mills and of the Harrison fortune . . . Julis Harrison, coarse, powerful, beetle-browed, his heavy countenance half-buried beneath a thick chin beard. The engraving was surrounded by a wide frame of bright German gilt; it looked down upon the room with the gaze of one who has wrought a great success out of nothing by the sweat of his brow and labor of bulging muscles, as once he had hammered crude metal into links and links into chains in the blacksmith shop which stood upon the spot now occupied by the oldest of the furnaces. It was a massive awkward room, as much like a warehouse as like a boudoir or a bedroom. It suited admirably the face in the portrait and the heavy body of the old woman who lay in the mahogany bed, helpless and ill-tempered beneath a second stroke of paralysis.

The son sat awkwardly on the edge of the red plush sofa near the mother. As he grew older, his manner became more and more uneasy in the presence of the old woman. His hair had grown thinner and on the temples there were new streaks of gray. There was something withered about him, something incomplete and unfinished like an apple that has begun to shrink before it has reached maturity. In the massive room, beneath the gaze of the overwhelming portrait, beside the elephantine bed in which he was conceived and born of the heavy old woman, Willie Harrison was a curiosity, a mouse born of a mountain in labor. He was the son of parents who were both quite masculine.

In a strange fit of forgetfulness he had worn his heavy overshoes into the sacred precincts of his mother's bedroom and they now lay beside him on the floor where he had placed them timidly when his mother commanded him to remove them lest his feet become overheated and tender, thus rendering him liable to sudden colds. Indeed, since the very beginning of the strike Willie had not been well. The struggle appeared to weigh him down. Day by day he grew paler and more nervous. He rarely smiled, and a host of new fine lines appeared upon his already withered countenance. Yet he had gone through the blowing snow and the bitter cold to the cemetery, partly at the command of his mother who was unable to go and partly because he had hoped to see Lily once more, if only for a moment by the side of an open grave.

And now Mrs. Julis Harrison, lying helpless upon her broad back, waited to hear the account of the funeral. She lay with her head oddly cocked on one side in order to see her son. Her speech came forth mumbled and broken by the paralysis.

"Were there many there?" she asked.

"Only a handful," replied her son in his thin voice. "Old William Baines . . . you know, the old man, the Shanes' family lawyer. . . ."

"Yes," interrupted his mother. "An old fogy . . . who ought to have died ten years ago."

William Harrison must have been used to interruptions of this sort from his mother. He continued, "One or two church people and the two girls. It was frightfully cold on top of that bald hill. The coffin was covered with snow the moment it was lowered into the grave."

"Poor Julia," muttered the woman on the bed. "She lived too long. She lost interest in life." This remark she uttered with the most mournful of intonations. On the verge of the grave herself, she still maintained a lively interest in deaths and funerals.

"I'm glad you went," she added presently. "It shows there was no feeling, no matter how bad Julia treated me. It shows that I forgave her. People knew I couldn't go."

There was a long pause punctuated by the loud monotonous ticking of the brass clock. Outside the wind whistled among the cornices.

"She must have left a great deal of money," observed Mrs. Harrison. "More than a couple of millions, I shouldn't wonder. They haven't spent anything in the last ten years."

Willie Harrison lighted a cigarette. "Except Irene," he said. "She has been giving money to the strikers. Everybody knows that."

"But that's her own," said his mother. "It has nothing to do with what Julia left." She stirred restlessly. "Please, Willie, will you not smoke in here. I can't bear the smell of tobacco."

Willie extinguished the cigarette and finding no place in the whole room where he might dispose of the remains, he thrust them silently into his pocket.

"I asked her at the funeral if it was true," he said. "And she told me it was none of my business . . . that she would give everything she possessed if she saw fit."

Mrs. Harrison grunted. "It's that Krylenko," she observed. "That's who it is. Don't tell me she'd give away her money for love of the strikers. No Shane ever gave his fortune to the poor."

The clock again ticked violently and without interruption for a long time.

"And Lily," said Mrs. Harrison presently.

Willie began fumbling with the ruby clasp on his watch chain, slipping it backward and forward nervously.

"She's just the same," he said. "Just the same. . . . Younger if anything. It's surprising how she keeps so young. I asked her to come and see you and she wanted to know if you had asked her to. I said you had and then she smiled a little and asked, 'Is it for curiosity? You can tell her how I look. You can tell her I'm happy.' That was all. I don't suppose she'll ever come back to the Town again after this time."

This Mrs. Harrison pondered for a time. At last she said, "I guess it's just as well she wouldn't have you. There's something bad about her. She couldn't be so young and happy if she was just an old maid. I guess after all you're better off. They have bad blood in 'em. It comes from old John Shane."

Willie winced at the bluntness of his mother's speech and attempted to lead her into other paths. "There was no trouble in the Flats to-day. None of the strikers came into Halsted street. Everything was quiet all day. The superintendent says it was on account of the old woman's funeral."

"You see," said Mrs. Harrison. "It's that Krylenko. I can't understand it . . . how a frumpish old maid like Irene can twist him around her finger."

Willie stopped fumbling with his chain. "She's made a weapon of him to fight us."

Mrs. Harrison shook her massive head with a negative gesture.

"Oh, no," she said, speaking slowly and painfully. "It may look like that, but she never thought it out. She isn't smart enough. Neither of them is,

Irene or Lily. I've known them since they were little girls. They both do what they can't help doing. Julia might have done such a thing but I'm certain it never occurred to her. Besides," she added after a little pause, "she's dead and buried now."

"She came to hate us before she died," persisted Willie.

"Yes . . . that's true enough. I guess she did hate us . . . ever since that affair over the taxes."

Willie clung to his idea. "But don't you see. It's all worked out just the same, just as if they had planned it on purpose. It's the second time they have cost the Mills thousands of dollars."

This, somehow, Mrs. Harrison found herself unable to deny.

"Tell me," she said presently. "How did they appear to take it? . . . Lily and Irene?"

Willie was once more fumbling with the ruby clasp. "I don't know. Irene wasn't even dressed in mourning. She had on the same old gray suit and black hat. She looked like a crow. As for Lily, she was able to smile when she spoke to me. But you can't tell how she feels about anything. She always smiles."

After this little speech Willie rose and began to move about the room, fingering nervously the sparsely placed ornaments—a picture of himself as an anemic child with long, yellow curls, a heavy brass inkwell, a small copy in marble of the tomb of Scipio Africanus, the single memento of a voyage to Rome. He drifted over toward the window and drew aside the curtain to look out into the storm.

Chapter 46

ALL THIS TIME his mother, her vast bulk immovable beneath the mountainous sheets, followed him with her eyes. She must have recognized the symptoms, for presently she broke the way.

"Have you anything you want to say?" she asked.

Willie moved back to the bed and for a time stood in silence fingering the carving of the footboard. He cleared his throat as if to speak but only fell silent again. When at last he was able to say what was in his mind, he did so without looking up. He behaved as though the carving held for him the most profound interest.

"Yes," he said gently, "I want to say that I'm going to get out of the Mills. I hate them. I've always hated them. I'm no good at it!" To forestall her interruptions he rushed on with his speech. The sight of his mother lying helpless appeared to endow him with a sudden desperate courage. She was unable to stop him. He even raised his head and faced her squarely. "I don't like this strike. I don't like the fighting. I want to be an ordinary, simple man who could walk through Halsted street in safety. I want to be left alone."

Mrs. Harrison did not raise her head, but all the violent emotion, pent up and stifled by her helplessness, rose and flashed in her eyes. The scorn was thunderous but somehow it failed to overwhelm the faded, middle-aged man at the foot of the gigantic bed.

"I thank God your father cannot hear those words! He would strike you down!"

Still Willie did not flinch. "My father is dead," he observed quietly. But his smile carried implications and a malice of its own. "My father is dead," said the smile. "And my mother is helpless. Before long I shall be free . . . for the first time in my life . . . free . . . to do as I please . . . the slave of no one."

The smile wavered and clung to his face. Of course he said none of this. What he said was, "It is a dirty business. And I want nothing to do with it . . . not even any stock. If it hadn't been for the Mills, Lily might have married me."

From the bed arose the scornful sound of a hoarse chuckle, "Oh no, she wouldn't. You don't know her! She wouldn't marry you because you were such a poor thing."

At this Willie began to tremble. His face became as white as the spotless coverlet, and he grasped the bed rail with such intensity that his thin knuckles showed blue against his skin. It was the old taunt of a mother toward a child whose gentleness and indecision were to her both incomprehensible and worthy only of contempt, a child who had never suited her gigantic ideas of power and wealth.

"And pray tell me what you *do* intend to do," she asked with rich sarcasm.

A tremulous quality entered Willie's voice as he replied, "I want to have a farm where I can raise chickens and ducks and rabbits."

"Great God!" replied his mother in her deep voice. It was all she said. Moving her head with a terrible effort, she turned her face to the wall away from her son. But Willie, though he still trembled a little in the presence of the old woman and the glowering portrait above his head, had a look of triumph in his pale eyes. It said, "I have won! I have won! I have achieved a a victory. I am free at last from the monster which I have always hated. . . . I am through with the Mills. I am through with Judge Weissman. . . . I can be bullied no more!"

Outside the wind howled and tore at the eaves and presently there came a suave knock at the door . . . the knock of the worldly, white haired butler. "Miss Abercrombie is here to see Mrs. Harrison," came a suave voice, and before Willie could answer, his mother's crony, her nose very red from the cold, had pushed her way like a wriggling ferret into the room.

At the sight of Willie, she halted for a moment winking at him in a purely involuntary fashion.

"Your mother is so much better," she said bridling. "Aren't you delighted?"

Willie's answer was an inarticulate grunt.

"I've come to hear all about the funeral," she continued in her bustling manner. "I would have gone myself except for the weather. Now sit down like a good boy and tell me all about." She too treated him as an anemic child still wearing curls.

Willie shook her hand politely. "My mother will tell you," he said. "I have told her everything."

And he slipped from the room leaving the two women, the ferret and the mountain, to put the finishing touches upon the obsequies of Julia Shane.

Chapter 47

IN THE HOUSE at Cypress Hill the two sisters stayed on to await the settlement of the will proceedings.

The state of siege continued unrelieved, and as the winter advanced, as if Nature herself were hostile to the strikers, there came that year no January thaw at all. There was only more snow and unbroken cold so that Irene, instead of finding freedom with the death of her mother, encountered only more duties among the wretched inhabitants of Halsted street. The Harrisons and Judge Weissman evicted a score of families from houses owned by the Mills. Bag and baggage, women and children, were thrust out into the frozen street to find refuge in other squalid houses already far too crowded.

Judge Weissman also saw to it that the strikers were unable to secure a hall in which to meet. When the men attempted to congregate in the streets, they were charged and clubbed by the constabulary. When they sought to meet in vacant lots, Judge Weissman saw to it that the owners ordered them off. When there was a fire, the strikers were charged by the Town papers with having set it. When there was a riot, it was always the strikers who caused it. But there was one charge which the Town found, above all others, unforgivable. The editors accused the workmen of obstructing progress. They charged the strikers with menacing prosperity and injuring the "boom spirit." The Rotary Club and the Benevolent Order of Elks, the Chamber of Commerce, even the Episcopal church (very high and much given to incense and genuflexions) espoused the cause of prosperity.

The strikers had no newspapers, no money, no voice. They might starve as slowly as they pleased. Krylenko himself was powerless.

Of what took place in the Town itself the two sisters knew nothing. During the day while Irene was absent Lily, clad in a peignoir of black silk, wandered aimlessly about the house in search of ways to divert herself. She suffered profoundly from boredom. In the course of her ramblings she discovered one morning a great wooden box piled high with the yellow backed French novels "skimmed" and cast away by her mother. These occupied her for a time and when she grew tired of reading, she sought to pass the time by writing letters—addressed always to one of three people, Jean, Madame Gigon or Madame Gigon's cousin, the Baron. Wrapped in her mother's old-fashioned cloak of sealskin, she made her way to the foot of the drive and paid a passing boy to post them for her. She was careful always that none of them fell in the way of Irene.

She had the mulatto woman lay a fire in the drawing-room and, opening the grand piano which had fallen sadly out of tune, she spent hours in playing fragments of Chopin, Bach and a new composer called Debussy. Mingled with these were odd snatches of music hall waltzes and the bawdy, piquant ballads of the cuirassiers. Once at the suggestion of Irene she took up knitting socks and mufflers for the families of the strikers, but the work progressed so slowly that at last she gave up in despair and, making a solitary excursion up the hill to the Town, she purchased an enormous bundle of socks and sweaters which she turned over to her sister to distribute among the suffering laborers and their families.

She slept a great deal too, until her opulent beauty showed signs of plumpness and this led her into the habit of walking each morning a dozen times around the border of the barren, deserted park. These perambulations wore a deep path in the snow, and the Mill guards, coming to expect her at a certain hour each day, took up positions inside the barrier to watch the beautiful stranger as she passed, wrapped in the antiquated sealskin coat with leg of mutton sleeves, her eyes cast down modestly. As the month advanced, they grew bolder and stared quite openly. One or two even ventured to whistle at her, but their demonstrations aroused not the slightest response, nor did they interrupt the regular hour of her exercise. They might have been owls hooting among the branches of the dead trees.

The only visitors were Hattie Tolliver and William Baines, the "old fogy" lawyer, who paid a round half-dozen calls bearing a little black bag filled with papers. With Mrs. Tolliver, he shared an attitude of supreme indifference alike toward the strikers and the guards. It appeared that he still lived in a day when there were no mills and no strikers. He was a tall withered old man with drooping white mustaches and a thick mass of vigorous white hair. He went about his business gruffly, wasting no time over details, and no emotion over sentiment. He treated both sisters in the same cold, legal manner.

The will was brief and concocted shrewdly by Julia Shane and old Mr. Baines. Nor was it complicated. The house and all the old woman's jewels were left to her daughter Lily. There was also a sizable gift for Hattie Tolliver and a strange bequest which came as a surprise to all but old Mr. Baines. It was added in a codicil, so he said, a short time before her death. It provided for a trust fund to support Welcome House and provide a visiting nurse until Mr. Baines and the two daughters deemed these things no longer necessary.

"That," observed the cynical Mr. Baines dryly, as he read the will, "will be as long as the human race exists. I tried to persuade her against it but she would not listen. She always knew what she was doing and just what she wanted, right to the very end."

Thus Julia Shane placed herself for all time among the enemies of the Mills.

Otherwise the property was divided evenly with an allowance made to Irene for the value of the Cypress Hill holdings.

Then Mr. Baines delivered with considerable ceremony and advice two letters, one addressed to Lily and one to Irene, which had been left in his keeping.

The letter addressed to Lily read, "I am leaving the house to you because Irene hates it. I know that she would only dispose of it at once and give the money to the church. Likewise I am leaving my jewels to you, with the exception of two rings which I gave Hattie Tolliver years ago—the emerald set with diamonds and the single big emerald. No doubt you remember them. There is no use in leaving such things to Irene. She would only sell them and spend the money to buy candles for a saint. And that is not the purpose for which God made jewels. He meant them to adorn beautiful women. Therefore I give them to you."

And thus the amethysts set in Spanish silver, two emerald rings, seven rings set with diamonds, a ruby necklace, a festoon of pearls, a quantity of earrings of onyx, diamonds, emeralds, and rubies and a long diamond chain passed into the possession of the elder daughter.

"In worldly possessions," the letter continued, "I have left you both wealthy. There are other possessions over which I had no control. They were left to you by your father and by me—the possessions which one cannot sell nor throw away, the possessions which are a part of you, possessions good and evil, bad and indifferent, the possessions which in the end are you yourself.

"There are some things which it is difficult to discuss, even between a mother and her daughter. I am gone now. I shall not be forced to look at you and feel shame at what you know. Yet I have always wanted to tell you, to explain to you that, after all, I was never so hard, so invincible, so hopelessly brittle as I must have seemed. You see, my dear, there are some things which one cannot control and one of these is the unconscious control over self-control—the thing which does not permit you to speak. Another is pride.

"You see there was never anything in common between your father and me, unless it was love of horses and that, after all, is not much. Before he ever saw me, he must have known more of life than I ever knew. But those things were secret and because of them, perhaps, I fell in love with him—after a fashion. I say 'after a fashion' because that is what it was. I was a country girl, the daughter of a farmer . . . nothing else, you understand. And you cannot know what that meant in the days when the Town was a village and no one in it ever went outside the state and seldom outside the county. He was fascinating . . . more fascinating than you can ever know. I married him on account of that. It was a great match. He was a wonderful lover . . . not a lover like the men of the county who make such good husbands, but a lover out of another world. But that, my dear, did not make him a good husband, and in a little while it became clear that I was little more to him than a convenience. Even sending me to France didn't help matters.

"It was a bad affair, but in my day when one married there was no thought of anything but staying married. So what was done was done. There was no unmaking a mistake, even less chance after you and Irene were born. He came of one race and I of another. And never once in our life together did we touch in our sympathies. It was, in short, a marriage founded upon passion alone—a despicable state of affairs which is frequently worse than a *marriage de convenance*, for in that there is no desire to burn itself out. . . . You see, I understood the affair of the Governor far better than you ever imagined.

"And so there are things descended to both of you over which I have no control. I can only ask God to be merciful. Be gentle with Irene and thank God that you are made so that life cannot hurt you. She cannot help that which she is. You see I have known and understood more than any one guessed."

That was all. The ending was as abrupt as the manner of Julia Shane while she lived. Indeed to Lily, reading the letter, it must have seemed that her mother was still alive. She sat thoughtfully for a long time and at last tearing the letter slowly into bits, she tossed it into the drawing-room fire. Of its contents she said nothing to Irene.

The letter to Irene was brief. It read, "I leave you your money outright with no string to it, because the dead have no rights which the living are bound to respect. You may do with it as you like. . . . You may give it all to your beloved church, though it will be without my approval. You may do anything with it which will bring you happiness. I have prayed to God to make you happy. If you can find happiness by burying yourself, do it before you are an hour older, for life is too short to waste even an hour of happiness. But do not believe that it is such an easy thing to find.

"I have loved you, Irene, always, though I have never been able to understand you. I have suffered for you, silently and alone. I, who am dead, may tell you these things which in life I could not tell you. Only know that I cherished you always even if I did not know how to reach you. There are some things that one cannot say. At least I—even I, your own mother—could not make you understand because I never really knew you at all. But remember always that I loved you in spite of all the wretched walls which separated even a mother from her daughter. God be with you and guide you."

Irene, in the stillness of her bare, austere room, wept silently, the tears streaming down her battered, aging face. When she had finished reading she thrust the letter inside her dress against her thin breasts, and a little later when she descended and found the drawing-room empty she tore it into tiny bits to be consumed by the same fire which had secretly destroyed Lily's letter a little while before.

Chapter 48

SHE MADE no mention of this letter to Lily, but before she left the house late the same afternoon she went to Lily's room, a thing which she had never done before. She found her sister lying on the bed in her darkened room.

"What is it, Irene?"

Irene standing in the doorway, hesitated for an instant.

"Nothing," she said presently. "I just stopped to see if you were all right." Again there was a little pause. "You aren't afraid . . . alone here in the evenings, are you?"

Out of the darkness came the sound of Lily's laughter.

"Afraid? Lord, no! What is there to be afraid of? I'm all right." And Irene went away, down the long drive into Halsted street which lay in thick blackness because the strikers had cut the wires of the street lights.

On the same evening Lily had dinner on a lacquer table before the fire in the drawing-room. She ate languidly, leaning back in her rosewood arm-chair, dividing her attention between the food and the pages of Henri Bordeaux. Save for a chair or two and the great piano, the room was still in camphor, the furniture swathed in linen coverings, the Aubusson carpet rolled up in its corner. Dawdling between the food and the book, she managed to consume an hour and a half before she finished her coffee and cigarette. Despite the aspect of the room there was something pleasant about it, a certain indefinable warmth and sense of space which the library lacked utterly.

The business of the will was virtually settled. She had announced her intention of leaving within a day or two. Two of her bags were already packed. One of them she had not troubled herself to unpack because she had not the faintest need of clothes unless she wished to dress each night for her lonely dinner as if she expected a dozen guests. And being indolent she preferred to lounge about comfortably in the black kimono embroidered in silver with a design of wistaria. Yet in her lounging there was nothing of sloppiness. She was too much a woman of taste. She was comfortable; but she was trim and smart, from her bronze hair so well done, to the end of her neat silver-slippered toe.

When she had finished her cigarette she rose and went to the piano where she played for a long time, rather sentimentally and without her usual ecstatic dash. She played as if a yearning sadness had descended upon her. It may have been the thought of quitting the old house which had come to the end of the road. In another week its only occupants would be Sarah and Hennery. The others would have vanished. . . . Irene, Lily, even the black servants. There was no such thing as age or tradition. The Town had no time for such things. There was no longer room for Cypress Hill. It stood in the way of progress. The Town council was eager to buy and destroy it in order to raise on its site a new railway station, more vast and pretentious than any in the state.

It may have been this which made her sad.

Certainly her mood drove her to the depths, for she played such music as the *Liebesträume* and a pair of sentimental German waltzes. And gradually she played more and more softly until at length her hands slipped from the keyboard to her lap and she sat with bowed head regarding the pink tips of her polished finger-nails.

The curtains were drawn across the windows so that no sound penetrated from the outside. In the grate the fire of cannel coal crackled softly and new flames leapt up.

Presently she returned to her chair and novel, but she did not read. She remained staring into the fire in the same distracted fashion.

Chapter 49

SHE WAS SITTING thus when she turned at the sound of shuffling footsteps and saw Sarah coming softly toward her. The countenance of the mulatto carried a vague, indefinable expression of fear. It was gray with terror.

"What is it, Sarah?" asked Lily. "In the name of Heaven what is the matter?"

The woman trembled. "There's trouble a-brewin', Miss Lily," she said. "The park is full of men. They've been comin' in at the gate and they're all over the place." The woman hesitated again. "Hennery's watching now. He sent me to ask if he was to send for the police?"

Lily stood up and fastened the black and silver kimono higher about her throat.

"Who are they?"

"I don't know, Miss Lily. Hennery thinks mebbe they're strikers. He's put out the light at the back, so he can watch 'em without bein' seen."

For a moment Lily remained silent and thoughtful. Presently she said, "Put out the lights in here, Sarah. I'll go and look myself."

And she went out, leaving the frightened servant to extinguish the lamps.

A moment later, groping her way through the dark hallway to the servants' quarters, she stumbled suddenly upon the terrified figure of Hennery kneeling down by a window, keeping watch.

"It's Miss Lily, Hennery," she said. "Don't be frightened."

The window was a blue rectangle against the wall of the hallway. It was a clear night but moonless, although the bright, cold sky was all powdered with glistening stars. Outside in the park, among the dead trunks of the trees, moved scores of figures black against the blue gray snow. Some of them carried lanterns of one sort or another. There were even women among them, women with shawls over their heads, wearing short heavy skirts which cleared the top of the deep snow. Behind them, the searchlights from the mill yard fingered the blue dome of the sky nervously, sweeping now up and down, now across striking the black chimneys and furnace towers, cutting them cleanly in two as if the cold rays of light were knives.

In the hallway the nervous breathing of Hennery became noisy. It was clear that something about the scene . . . something which had to do with the silent, cold furnaces, the dead trees and the blackness of the moving figures aroused all the superstitious terror of the negro.

Outside the number of men increased. They appeared to be congregating now, in a spot near the deserted kennels. The lanterns moved among the trees like dancing lights above a swamp.

"It's all right, Hennery," said Lily presently. "It's all right. The police would only make matters worse. I suppose Miss Irene told them to meet here in the park. The police won't let them meet anywhere else. It's the last place they have."

"Mebbe," Hennery muttered, doubtfully. "Mebbe."

The figure of the mulatto woman appeared shuffling her way along the wall of the corridor.

"The best thing to do," said Lily softly, "is for you to go to bed and forget about it. Nothing will happen. Just don't interfere. Forget about it. I'll go up to my own room. . . . You might see that all the doors are locked."

And with that she left the two negroes crouching on the floor of the corridor gazing with a sort of fascination at the spectacle in the barren park.

Upstairs in her own room, she drew up the chaise longue and pulled aside the curtains from the window. The glass ran to the floor so that she was able, lying down, to watch everything that took place in the park. The room was in darkness and the French traveling clock, as if to comfort her, chimed out ten as she flung herself down, covering her long limbs with a silk comforter against the chill that crept in everywhere.

Outside the strange pageant continued to grow in size and animation. Sometimes the searchlight, swinging low in its course, flashed swiftly across the park, revealing for an instant a hundred swarthy faces and as many figures wrapped in heavy coats, bits of old blanket, rags . . . anything to shut out the bitter cold. Above each figure hung a little cloud of steaming breath, a soul hovering above a body. There were negroes among them,—the negroes doubtless, whom she had seen working in the choking fumes of the acid vats.

Yet none of the figures held any individuality. They might have been automatons. Figures in a single mob, none of them possessed a distinct personality. All this was welded into one vague mass, which carried a threat of anger and violence. The terror of Hennery was not altogether beyond conception. They kept moving about too in a restless uncertain fashion among the dead trees and deserted borders. In the niches of the dead hedge the figures of the Venus of Cydnos and the Apollo Belvedere gleamed darkly.

And as Lily watched, the light in her dark eyes brightened slowly and steadily. She became like one hypnotized. She began to breathe more quickly as if the old excitement, against which she was so powerless, had entered her blood. The soft white hand holding the back of the chaise longue trembled a little.

Slowly the moving figures gathered into a black throng at the side of the kennels. Somewhere in their midst a light began to glow, increasing slowly in volume until the tongues of red flame showed above the black heads of the mob. They had built a great fire for warmth, and near it some one had set up a barrel for the speakers to stand on. By the light of the flames she was able to see that the first speaker was a little man, rather thin and wiry like a bearded gnome, who danced about a great deal, waving his arms and legs. His manner was explosive. It was impossible to hear above the flames through the heavy glass of the window what he was saying, but clearly it produced an effect. The mob began to churn about and wave its lanterns. Sometimes the sound of shouts and cries vaguely penetrated the darkened room.

At last the little man finished and was lifted down by a score of hands. More wood was thrown on the fire and the red flames hungrily chased a shower of sparks high up among the dead branches of the trees. A moment later a second man climbed to the top of the barrel. He was an enormous fellow, a veritable giant who towered far above the mob. At the sight of him the strikers cheered wildly. Lily, from her point of vantage, must have recognized in him something vaguely familiar . . . the merest suggestion of memory in the sudden, eloquent gestures, the easy powerful grace with which he balanced himself as he spoke, the same grace she had seen one afternoon in the great shed beneath the hill. More wood was thrown upon the fire. The flames leaped higher and in the wild light, doubt was no longer possible. It was Krylenko who harangued, feverishly and desperately, the threatening sullen mob.

Chapter 50

INSIDE THE warm room, Lily raised herself slowly and felt her way to the closet where she took down the old sealskin coat with the leg of mutton sleeves. With this thrown about her shoulders, she went back to the window, cautiously unfastened the clasp and stepped out upon the snow covered roof of the wrought iron piazza. The snow was deep and the silver slippered feet sank to the ankles. But of this she seemed to take no notice. As if fascinated, she leaned close against the bricks, sheltering herself from the wind, and stood listening.

Krylenko addressed the strikers in some foreign tongue which might have been Russian or Polish. He spoke in a clear strong voice that rose and fell with the sincerity of an overpowering emotion. It was impossible to know what he was saying, yet the effect was tremendous. The man was a born leader. In that moment he could have led the mob where he would.

And presently he began to speak Italian . . . rather haltingly and with an air of desperate frustration. This Lily was able to understand in part. He urged them not to yield. He plead with them to fight to the end. The victory, he said, was within. . . .

Above the crackling of the fire and the voice of the speaker the air was ripped suddenly by a solitary rifle shot. Then another and another in quick succession, until the air became alive and vibrant with the sound of guns. From the throng rose a solitary scream, followed by a groan or two and the confused, animal cries of a mob suddenly stricken by a panic. The figure on the barrel disappeared, engulfed by a swarming mass of terrified humanity. Lanterns were flung to the ground and trampled. One or two exploded in bursts of red flame. The little park was alive with running figures, women in shawls, men in rags. On the gray blue snow by the deserted kennels lay a solitary black figure. By the arbor where the wistaria had once flourished was another which stirred faintly.

Lily, leaning against the dead vines on the house, understood what had happened. The Mill guards, from the security of the barrier, had fired upon the helpless mob. The innocent plan of Irene had been, after all, nothing but a trap.

Something struck the bricks above her head with a sharp spatter and bits of mortar fell into her hair. Quickly she slipped through the tall window back into the room and waited.

The little park was empty now, so empty that if it had not been for the embers in the snow and black still figure lying near by, one might have believed that there had been no mob at all, no fire and no savage cries of terror. Lily remained standing inside the window as if she were unable to move. The dying embers appeared to exert an overpowering fascination . . . the dying embers and the still black figure in the snow.

Presently there crept out from the shelter of the kennels a man, bending low to the ground as he moved. Cautiously he made his way to the figure in the snow, halting there for a moment to fumble with the ragged coat for some sign of life, risking his life in full sight of the guards. Another shot rang out and then another, and the man still crouching low to the ground ran toward the shelter of the big house. He came nearer and nearer until, as he crossed the drive, he was no longer a unit in the mob. He became an individual. It was Krylenko.

A second later he disappeared beneath the edge of piazza roof and Lily lay down once more on the chaise longue. She was still trembling. It may have been the cold.

Outside the night once more settled back into a dreadful stillness. The searchlights fingered the sky with a new agitation. The house itself grew still as death. The only sound was the faint, irregular, untraceable creaking which afflicts old houses in the midst of the night. The French traveling clock struck eleven and at the same time a new sound, not at all like the distant unearthly creaking, came faintly through the open door of Lily's room. It was an indistinct scraping sound as if some one were trying a key in a lock.

Chapter 51

LILY SAT UP, listening. The sound was repeated and presently there followed the noise of a door being opened slowly and cautiously. Lily rose and made her way to the dressing table where she pulled the bell. Once she pulled, and then again and again. There was no response. Either the servants were asleep or too terrified to answer. She gave the bell a final pull and when the only answer was silence, she took from the dressing table an electric torch and from the drawer of her carved desk a tiny pistol with a handle of mother of pearl which had been her mother's. Then she made her way quietly into the hall until she reached the top of the stairway where she leaned over the rail and flashed the light.

The glare illuminated all the lower hall, lighting up the familiar carved chest, the straight-backed chair, the crystal chandelier, the mirror. Everything was the same save that on the chest with his head bowed and resting on his hands in an attitude of despair, sat Krylenko, hatless, his coat all torn, the blood streaming down the side of his face.

It appeared that he was weak and dazed, for he remained in this same position for a long time, failing to notice even the bright shower of light which, without warning, drenched the hall. When at last he stirred, it was to lean back wearily against the wall and say in a low voice, "I have used the key, Miss Irene."

At the sound Lily ran down the long stairs, more rapidly than she had descended them in all the years she had lived in the house. She soared above the polished wood, until she stood suddenly by his side. She bent over him and touched his shoulder.

"It is not Miss Irene . . . I am Lily," she said. "Lily . . . Miss Irene's sister."

With one arm Krylenko wiped the blood from his eyes.

"Then you don't know me," he said weakly. "I am not a thief . . . breaking in."

The little revolver Lily placed beside him on the chest. "I know you," she said. "I have seen you . . . you are Krylenko." She placed one arm beneath his. "Come," she said, "this is no place for you. There is a divan in the drawing-room. Come and lie down there. I'll fetch some whiskey."

With an air of great weariness the man managed to gain his feet and, leaning upon her, he made his way preceded by the little circle of white light from Lily's torch across the polished floor into the drawing-room. Lily was tall but Krylenko towered above her like a giant.

She made him comfortable, piling the brocade pillows carelessly beneath his bloody head. Then she went out and as she left, there rose behind her the sound of a heart breaking sigh, like the cry of a defeated, sobbing child.

After a little while she returned bearing a white basin filled with water, a pair of linen pillow-cases and a small silver flask. Presently he sat up.

It was the first time she had seen him since that afternoon in the Mill shed when Willie Harrison, fumbling with the ruby clasp of his watch chain, proposed to her for the last time. He had changed. He was older. Experience had traced its record in the fine lines about his eyes and mouth. The crudeness of the massive head had likewise undergone a change, giving place to a more certain modeling and a new dignity. Where there had once been a

certain shapelessness of feature, there was now a firmness of line, a determination in the fine mouth, the strong nose and the high massive forehead.

Lily, tearing the linen pillow-cases into long strips, watched him narrowly.

The wavy blond hair, where it was not stained with blood, clung against
the damp forehead. Where the coat was torn and the dark flannel shirt
ripped from the throat, the powerful muscles of the arm and shoulder lay
exposed. The fair skin was as white as Lily's own soft body. The man's whole
figure carried an air of freedom, of a certain fierce desire to burst through the
shabby, stained clothing.

All at once he raised his head and looked about him. The color returned
a little way into his face.

"The blinds," he said, "are they shut?"

"Yes," said Lily. "You are safe here."

She had thrown off the old sealskin coat and sat by him clad in the black
and silver kimono, seductive, beautiful, perfect, save for the tips of her silver
slippers all soaked by the melted snow. The kimono had come open at the
neck and left her white soft throat exposed. Krylenko was watching her now
in a puzzled fashion. He behaved almost as if she terrified him in some new
and indefinable way.

"I let myself in with a key," he told her. "A key Miss Irene gave me. She
told me to use it if ever I had to hide." He paused for a moment and took a
second drink from the flask. "You see, I am safe here because it is the last
place they would look for me. They would never look for me in the house of
a rich man. They wouldn't expect to find me in the house of an American,
a wealthy lady."

He looked up at her in a singularly straightforward fashion.

"I suppose," he said, "you too are on our side."

Lily dipping a bit of linen into the basin did not reply for a moment. At
last she said, "I'd never thought about it one way or another until now. It
doesn't matter, I suppose. But you needn't fear what I'll do. I'd rather have
you here than the police."

"If they caught me now," he continued weakly, "they'd hang me. I wouldn't
have a chance with Judge Weissman and the rest. Any jury in the Town would
hang me. You see there were men killed out there in the park . . . men on both
sides. That fellow over by the fire . . . he's dead. I stopped to make certain.
I didn't kill anybody myself, but that makes no difference. It's me they're
after. They've been waiting for a chance like this."

He spoke English with a curious lack of accent, for the chaste Irene as
a teacher was thorough. He spoke it deliberately and rather carefully to be
sure, but without serious faults. His manner was neither shy nor awkward.
It was the manner of a man unused to women's company, of a man who had
never before addressed a great lady; for Irene could not properly be called
either a woman or a great lady. She was, rather, the embodiment of an idea.

"You're safe," said Lily. "You may depend on it. I, myself, will see to it.
I don't love the police or the Harrisons or Judge Weissman . . . I don't love

any of them." She drew her chair nearer. "Now lie down and I'll bathe your head."

He lay down and instantly sat up again. "My head!" he protested. "It's all bloody. . . . It'll spoil everything." He picked up one of the pillows. "See, I've done it already. They're covered with blood."

Lily smiled at him in her charming fashion, an imperceptible, secret smile. She behaved as if she were entertaining a great man, an ambassador or a rich banker, as if she were intent only upon making him comfortable, at ease.

"It makes no difference," she said. "In a few days there will be no one to use the pillows. There are times, you know, when such things don't matter. Lie down," she commanded. "One must know when such things are of no account. It is part of knowing how to live."

Protesting, Krylenko laid his great body back gently and she bent over him, first removing the rings from her finger and placing them in a glittering heap upon the lacquer table. He closed his eyes with a sigh and she washed away with great gentleness the blood from his hair, from the side of his face. Her soft white fingers swept across the tanned face, then lower to where the throat became white and across the smooth, hard muscles of the shoulder until at last there was in her touch more of the caress of a woman than the ministering of a nurse.

"It is not serious," she said in a low voice. "The bullet only cut the skin."

She took the strips of linen and bound them with the same gentle, caressing fingers round and round his head. And presently she discovered that he was still watching her in a curious embarrassed fashion. When she had finished the dressing, she bathed the deep cut on his shoulder and bound it carefully.

At length he sat up once more. A sudden change came over him. His blue eyes grew dark, almost clouded.

"You are a good nurse," he said, and took another drink from the silver flask.

Lily moved about, clearing away the blood stained cloths and the bowl of reddish water. The soft glow of the lamp captured the silver of her kimono and fixed it as she moved with a flashing light. And all the time Krylenko regarded her with a strange look of awe, as if he had never before seen a woman.

"Strange," she said presently, "that we should meet like this. You, who have never seen me before."

Krylenko stirred and ran one strong hand awkwardly over the back of the other. "I've seen you before . . . twice . . . No . . . three times. Once on that day you came to the Mills, once in the street in your carriage and once"—he looked up—"once in this room, right here. You were with the boss that time . . . dancing with him."

Lily laughed softly. She must have remembered the shameless gown of chartreuse green. "I'll never be dancing with him again. I doubt if I'll ever see him."

Krylenko regarded her quizzically. "But he is rich. . . . Don't rich women marry rich men?" And he finished with a puzzled grunt of inquiry.

"Yes," replied Lily. "It's because I'm rich that I wouldn't marry him." It must have occurred to her then how wide was the chasm which separated her world from Krylenko's. Still he failed to understand.

"That's no reason," she continued, "for marrying him . . . a poor thing like that."

She sat down and drew her chair quite close to the rosewood sofa, laughing at the same time. Clearly the whole adventure struck her as bizarre, ridiculous . . . even unreal. Yet she trembled as if she were shivering with cold, and her laugh carried a vague hint of hysteria. She leaned forward and began to stroke his aching head gently.

After a long awkward pause, she said, "Miss Irene will be home any time now."

"Yes." And Krylenko gave a sort of grunt. Unmistakably there was a crudeness about him. He was gauche, awkward; yet there was in his manner a quality of power, of domination which had its origin somewhere in the dim ages, when there were no drawing-rooms and no books of etiquette. He had a manifest self-possession. He did not become obsequious before this great lady as Judge Weissman and other men in stations beneath her had done. He treated her, after all, as his equal. He was even a little arrogant; a trifle scornful of her wealth.

"Miss Irene," he observed presently, "is a noble woman. You understand she gives up her life to my people. Do you know where she is now?" His voice was raised, his manner excited. "She's looking after the fellows that got hurt. There was a woman, too. I saw her . . . shot through the arm . . . Ah, Miss Irene is a saint. You know she could go anywhere in the Flats. No one would touch her."

The whole speech was touched with a tone of simple adoration. The essence of him was a great, a really profound simplicity.

"She works hard," said Lily. "She works hard. She cares for nothing else." By the watch on her white wrist it was midnight. "So that is why she is late," she added.

"There will be much work for her to-night," said Krylenko. He kept watching Lily in the same furtive fashion, his gaze wandering to the lovely line of her bare white throat.

Again there was an awkward pause. "You don't know how much she does," he said presently. "You don't know what life is in the Flats. You sit here in a warm house . . . with silk and pillows and good food. You don't know," he said bitterly. "You don't know!"

Until now their conversation had been broken, disjointed, awkward, as if circumstance compelled them to talk about something. Now for the first time, a certain fire entered the Russian's voice. Lily kept silent, watching him with her great burning eyes. She still trembled.

"Maybe you think I like working twelve hours a day in that hot shed like you saw me. Maybe you think I don't want time to read and think." The man was working himself into a kind of frenzy. "You don't know. . . . You don't know. . . . And then they shoot us down like pigs." He leaned forward and raised at Lily a strong finger. "I come here from Russia. I come here because I could not live in Russia. . . . My father . . . My father . . . He was shot by the Cossacks. I come here because they tell me that in America you are free and have a good life. And what do they give me? They make me work twelve hours in a hot shed. They put me into a filthy house. They say, you must not complain. You must do as we say. We will not pay you more. We will not let you live like a man. You are Hunkies! . . . You are dirt! You did not have to come here. But all the same, they want us. They send men to Russia to tell us great things about America so we will come here because they need men for the Mills . . . men to feed to the furnaces like coal . . . to make a few men rich." He sighed bitterly and buried his face in his hands. "And now they shoot us like the Cossacks shot my father in Russia. . . . I came here full of hope and peace . . . only to be shot like my father in Russia!"

In his excitement he forgot the perfect English Irene had taught him. His blue eyes flashed and his face grew pale once more.

"No. . . . They can take me. . . . They can hang me. . . . Let them! I will not go away. . . . It is not America or Russia that counts. . . . It is all humanity! . . . Christians. . . . Bah!" He spat suddenly upon the polished floor. And all at once he pitched back again among the pillows, weak and fainting. The bandage slipped from his wounded head over one eye.

Quickly Lily bent over him. She poured more whiskey between his lips and refastened the bandage. Then she settled herself to chafing his strong wrists and rubbing his forehead in the old caressing motion with a delicate, white hand that trembled beyond control. A queer light came into her dark eyes.

Presently he sighed and looked up at her. "I am sorry," he said, "to bother a fine lady like you. If it had been Miss Irene." He closed his eyes suddenly. "I have been hungry, you know. We haven't even enough food in the Flats." Then he took her hand and pressed it in a naive, grateful fashion. "I am sorry, you know . . ." he murmured gently.

She did not move. She remained there stroking his head. "I know. . . . I understand. . . . You must lie still. Be quiet," she said softly. For a long time they remained thus, and presently Krylenko, opening his eyes looked up at her with a puzzled expression. "You are not the same as Miss Irene," he said in a low voice. "You are different . . . very different."

To this she made no reply. Gently the motion of her hand ceased. A pool of silence enveloped them. *You are not the same as Miss Irene.*

Chapter 52

THE MINUTES PASSED and then suddenly, sharply, there arose a loud uproar, the sound of angry knocking and a hand rattling the big outer door. Krylenko sat up white and still. Neither of them moved. The knocking continued, punctuated now by shouts.

"It's the police!" said Lily, and stood up. "Come with me. Bring the bowl . . . the bandages!"

Krylenko stood by helplessly. It was Lily who arranged everything with a sudden clairvoyance which seemed to have overtaken her at the instant of the knocking. She turned the brocade cushions so that the bloody side was concealed and, gathering up the bandages, she led the way through the hall into the corridor where an hour earlier Hennery and the mulatto woman had crouched in fascinated terror. At last she turned into a store room piled high with boxes. Here she led him to a great box in the corner where she halted.

"I'll hide you here," she said. "They'll never find you. It is full of books." And together, with flying hands, they emptied the box. Krylenko climbed in and assumed a crouching position. He was buried beneath the books which Lily hurled into the box in bunches of three or four, in armfuls. At last he lay completely hidden beneath a great heap of yellow backed novels . . . the novels of Paul Marguerite, Marcel Prévost, Paul Bourget, Collette Willy . . . the novels that Julia Shane had "skimmed" and cast aside, the novels which to her covenanting blood *l'amour* made so tiresome.

As Lily ran through the corridor the knocking increased in violence, punctuated by shouts of "Hello, in there!" and "Open the door," uttered in a gruff bass voice. As she ran she wrapped the kimono high about her throat, and as she passed the carved chest she picked up the tiny pearl handled pistol. Then she turned the key quickly and opened the door standing with the pistol in one hand and the yellow backed *Les Anges Gardiens* in the other.

Outside on the snow covered piazza stood a half dozen men in the uniforms of the constabulary. At the apparition of the beautiful woman in the doorway they remained for an instant silent, startled.

"What is it you want?" she asked.

One of the men, a burly fellow with a brutal jaw stepped forward. "We want to search the house. We're looking for a man."

"What man?" asked Lily.

"Never mind," came the gruff answer. "You wouldn't know him. He's nothing to you. His name is Krylenko."

"There's no one in the house but me and the servants." Her voice trembled a little before the menacing group on the piazza.

"That's all right," said the man. "We're going to see for ourselves. We saw him come in here."

He began to edge his way slowly toward the open door and as he moved the pearl handled pistol raised slowly, menacingly, in an even tempo with his slow insolent advance.

"You cannot come in," said Lily in a slow, firm voice. The pistol was level now with the heart of the intruder. "I've told you there is no one here. You might, it seems to me, take the word of a lady. I've been here all the evening and I would know. . . ." She raised the yellow backed novel in a brief little gesture. "I've been reading. There is no one here but myself."

The man growled. "That's all right but we want to look for ourselves." There was a painful pause. "We're going to have a look," he added with determination.

When Lily spoke again there was a new note in her voice, a sudden timbre of determination, a hint of unreasonable, angry, feminine stubbornness which appeared to awe the intruder.

"Oh, no, you're not," she said. "It is my house. You have no right to enter it. You have no warrant. It is mine. You cannot enter it." And then, as if by an afterthought she added, "Even my sister is not here. I don't know this Krylenko. I never saw him."

The man, it seemed, was baffled. If the woman in the doorway had been the wife of a workman, a simple Italian or Slovak, he undoubtedly would have brushed her aside, shot her if necessary, trampled her under foot the way his comrades had trampled to death the old Polish woman in Halsted street at the foot of the drive. But the woman in the doorway was a lady. She was not a poor foreigner. She was more American than himself. Behind her in the shadows gleamed dully a silver mounted mirror, a chandelier of sparkling crystal. Her fine, beautiful body was clad in a garment of black and silver. On her fingers glittered rings. All these things meant wealth, and wealth meant power. The man, after all, had only the soul of a policeman, a soul at once bullying and servile. For him these symbols might spell ruin. Besides, the woman was hysterically stubborn, strangely unafraid . . . so unafraid that her courage carried a hint of suspicious origin. He did not brush her aside nor did he shoot her.

"It's no use," she said. "If you return with a warrant, all right. I can do nothing. For the present, it is my house."

The man turned away and began a low conversation with his companions. He had a sheepish air, and as he talked the door was closed suddenly and locked, shutting him out in the darkness, leaving him no choice in the matter. For a time the little group of men conversed angrily, and presently they went away in defeat down the long drive.

So Lily had placed herself on the side of the strikers . . . against the Town, against the Mills. She stood now with all her family, with Irene, with the dead Julia Shane, with Hattie Tolliver and her savage umbrella.

Chapter 53

INSIDE THE HOUSE, she listened until the creak of boots on the snow died away. Then she moved off along the hall toward the corridor. She walked uncertainly and from time to time leaned against the wall for support. The spot of light from the electric torch preceded her slippered feet, a bright moving circle which seemed to devour and destroy the streak of flooring which it crossed on its way to the storeroom. Weakly she opened the door and stepped inside.

"It's all right, now. I've sent them away."

The books in the great box stirred with a heaving motion and out of them presently emerged Krylenko, pale and shaken. He climbed out and as his foot struck the floor, Lily gave a little cry and pitched forward so that he caught her suddenly. The electric torch dropped to the floor. The glass shattered with a faint pop and the room swam in a thick, soft darkness.

She did not faint. In a moment she recovered herself and managed to stand upright, but she did not move away from Krylenko. She stood there, waiting. Slowly his powerful arms closed about her with the vague gesture of a man wakening slowly from a profound sleep.

"It's all right," she whispered faintly. "I've saved you."

He made no other answer than a faint crooning sound. He stroked her hair gently with his strong, calloused hand, and tried to quiet the violent trembling which once more had taken possession of her. Again the house was silent save for the distant, ghostly creaking.

Perhaps he was seized by an overwhelming sense of awe which until that moment he had never experienced . . . an awe for some unknown and terrific force against which he was helpless, like a little child. It may have been that, as Irene believed, he had never known any woman, that he had been pure as a saint. If these things had not been, it is impossible to say what might have happened. He stood holding Lily close to him, kissing with a strange, awed gentleness the white line of her bare throat.

He discovered presently that she was sobbing. . . . Lily, who never wept. It was a terrible heartbreaking sound as if, all at once, she had sensed the tragedy of a whole lifetime, as if she stood in a vast and barren plain surrounded only by loneliness.

Krylenko's hands and arms became unaccountably gentle. His cheek brushed against her white forehead with a comforting, caressing motion. And presently he lifted her as easily and as gently as he had lifted the wounded striker at Mrs. Tolliver's command, and bore her from the room and down the dark corridor. She lay quietly, still sobbing in the same heartbroken fashion.

Thus he carried her into the long drawing-room and placed her among the brocade cushions of the divan, her amber hair all disheveled, her eyes bright with tears. For a moment he stood by her side awkwardly, silent and incoherent, overwhelmed by some new and profound emotion. The fire of cannel coal had died down. In the grate there was nothing now but ashes. Silently he knelt beside the sofa and rested his blond head on her breasts. Neither of them spoke a word, but Lily's hand returned once more to the old gentle caressing motion across his tired eyes.

The minutes slipped away, one by one in a quick stream as if they were no more than the trickle of clear spring water which is beyond all peril of drought, as if time itself were nothing and eternity even less.

So engulfed were they by the mood that even the sound of a key turning distantly in a clumsy lock and the echo of a light footfall in the hallway failed to disturb them. They were, it seemed, oblivious to everything until suddenly there stepped through the doorway the thin figure of Irene in the worn gray suit and battered black hat. At the sight of them she halted, an apparition with a tired white face, drawn and quivering. It was not until she gave a low convulsive cry that Lily and Krylenko discovered she was watching them. Krylenko remained on his knees, only straightening his body to look at her. Lily turned her head a little, gently, listlessly, almost with indifference.

Irene had become hideous. In her eyes was the light of fury. When she spoke her voice was cold with an insane, unearthly hatred.

"So," she said bitterly, "it has happened!" The worn hat fell from her grasp. Her fingers intertwined with a strangling gesture. "I might have known it. . . . I should have guessed. . . ." And then her voice rose to a suppressed scream. "You are no better than a street walker! You are damned forever! I have prayed. . . . I have prayed but God himself could not save you. . . . He would not want you . . . a vile creature . . . a strumpet! . . . to destroy all that I have spent my life to create." She began to sob wildly. "To destroy in a night what cost me years."

Slowly, silently, Krylenko rose to his feet. He watched Irene with a look of bewilderment, as if he found himself in a wild nightmare. Lily turned away silently and buried her face in the pillows. A Fury had descended upon them unawares.

Irene continued to cry. "I have known always. . . . I have known from the beginning. . . . I knew about the Governor. . . . I saw him go into your room. . . . Only God knows how many men you have had. . . . You are lost, damned, forever!" The terrible sound of her weeping echoed and reëchoed through the silent old house.

Lily raised her body from the cushions and sat with her silver slippers touching the floor. "What are you saying, Irene?" she asked. "You are mad. There has been nothing . . . nothing . . . nothing. You are mad!"

It was true that for the moment Irene was quite insane, yet her madness endowed her with the clairvoyance that is beyond sanity. She rushed toward Lily. She would have strangled her but Krylenko stepped between them and held her as if she had been an angry bad-tempered little child.

"Ah, don't lie to me," she cried. "I'm no fool. I can see. It is written in your eyes. Both of you. . . . I know. I know! . . . It is there! I see it!"

She struggled fiercely in the powerful grasp of Krylenko. "Let me go. . . . You . . . You are no better than the others . . . a common beast, a swine like the others . . . a swine like all men, lying to me all these years. And on a night like this. May God damn you both in Hell forever and ever!"

She freed herself and sank to the floor at Krylenko's feet. The tirade gave way to a torrent of wild hysterical sobbing. Her pale, battered face was all distorted, her thin hair disarrayed. She collapsed suddenly into a barren shattered old woman, abandoned by life. She had lost in her battle against something which was far stronger than herself, stronger even than Lily and Krylenko. She was broken, pitiful.

Lily sat by helplessly, her own tears dried now. She turned the rings round and round on her fingers and in the gesture there was a concentrated agony.

"You must not mind her," she said presently. "She is not well." Then she rose slowly and moved toward her sister. "Irene," she said softly. "Irene."

But Irene shuddered and drew away from her. "Don't touch me . . . evil one! Don't touch me!" she cried monotonously.

"Perhaps if she had rest," said Krylenko. "Perhaps if she slept."

Irene kept up moaning and rocking. "In the Flats they're dying. . . . In the Flats they're dying . . . and you two up here, like beasts all that time . . . like beasts!"

Lily began to walk up and down the long shadowy room in a wild distracted manner, as if the contagion of her sister's hysteria had touched her too. "There is nothing I can do," she kept saying. "There is nothing. . . . Perhaps if we left her . . ."

It was Krylenko who solved the difficulty. He bent over Irene and picked her up despite her protests. She screamed. She wept. She would have scratched and bitten him if his arms had been less powerful and his grip less certain. He turned to Lily. "Where is her bed?"

He spoke with a curious, intimate understanding. In an hour he had come nearer to Lily than ten years had brought him to the chaste fanatic sister.

Silently Lily led the way up the long stairs while he followed bearing Irene who moaned like a wounded animal. At the door of the room with the white bed and the pink-gilt image of the Virgin, he halted as if fearful of desecrating its purity. But Lily led the way boldly and together they laid the sister upon the narrow white bed. When they had gone out, closing the door behind them, the sound of her faint moaning haunted the dark hallway.

At the door of her own room Lily halted. "Wait," she said, and left him, returning in a moment, her arms burdened with blankets.

"Take these," she said. "It will be cold in the drawing-room." In all the confusion, she had not forgotten his wounds, his comfort.

Krylenko smiled vaguely. "It will be hard to sleep anywhere to-night," he said softly.

"But it is spoiled now . . ." replied Lily. "Everything."

And Krylenko turned away and went silently down the stairs.

It is true that no one slept until the dawn. Irene and Lily did not sleep at all. The one lay awake sobbing and praying, the other lay with her head buried in the pillows keeping her body rigid to still its wild trembling. Krylenko was the only one who slept. With the coming of dawn he sank into a deadening thick slumber among the stained brocade pillows of the rosewood sofa.

There he slept undisturbed until midday, for with the curtains tightly drawn there was no light to waken him. When at last he did waken, he found on the lacquer table beside him a note, which read;

"There are some things in this world which are impossible, things fate herself will not permit. This you will understand, I am sure. I have gone away. Irene has gone too. Where she has gone I do not know. Perhaps it does not matter. There is small chance of our ever meeting again. Our paths lie too far apart. . . . I have arranged for you to remain in the house . . . as long as it is necessary. As long even as you desire it. There is no one but yourself and the two black servants. They have been told. It is my house. It would please me to think of you there. It would please me . . . and my mother too . . . to know that you were safe inside it still leading the strike. It is a good place, for you can keep in hiding and still lead the fight. My blessings are with you and your cause."

The note was signed with Lily's name, and underneath it in the same sprawling hand was written, "O God! I love you. Good-by."

She had come in some time between the dawn and the broad daylight to leave the note by his side. She had passed him and gone away without a word, whither he could not possibly know. Nothing remained save a confused memory of her and this short, enigmatic, note which avowed nothing and yet everything.

For a long time Krylenko held the bit of paper between his strong heavy fingers, staring dully all the while at the generous impetuous writing. At last he took out a battered cigarette, put a match to it, and at the same moment set fire to the wisp of paper which he tossed among the cold ashes of the dead fire. . . . *There are some things in this world which are impossible.*

He got up and began pacing the floor angrily, up and down, up and down, scarring the polished floor at each step. It made no difference now. There was no one there any longer to use the floor. Presently he began muttering to himself. "They are no different than the others. They are all alike. When they are tired they run away because they are rich. Damn them and their money!"

And then all at once he went down upon his knees before the sofa and seizing one of the stained cushions in his arms, he kissed it again and again as if it were Lily instead of a feather-stuffed bit of brocade which he held in his arms.

Chapter 54

HE DID NOT quit the old house. He remained there in hiding to direct the strike. He was still there when Hennery packed the glowing Venice of Mr. Turner and the handsome malignant portrait of John Shane to be shipped to Lily in Paris. From the old house he sent out to the strikers message after message of encouragement and exhortation, until, at last, the strike was lost and there was no longer either need or place for him in the Mills or in the Town. No one knew when he went away or whither it was he went.

And the greatest of all the stories of Shane's Castle remained a secret. The Town knew nothing of the greatest sacrifice ever made within its walls.

Chapter 55

THE DRAWING-ROOM of the house in the Rue Raynouard was a long, high-ceilinged room with tall windows opening upon a terrace and a sloping lawn which ran down to the high wall that shut out the dust and the noise of the Rue de Passy. It was curiously like the muffled, shuttered drawing-room in the old house in Cypress Hill, not because the furnishings were the same; they were not. From Shane's Castle Lily brought only two things . . . the glowing Venice and the portrait of her father. Mr. Turner's flamboyant painting hung above the black marble mantelpiece in the Rue Raynouard. The portrait of John Shane hung against the satinwood paneling opposite the row of tall windows. The similarity was not an easy thing to define, for its roots lay in nothing more tangible than the bond between old Julia Shane and her daughter Lily, in a subtle sense of values which the one had passed on to the other.

The cold, impersonal hand of a decorator had nothing to do with either room. There was no striving toward a museum accuracy of period. The effect was much warmer, much more personal than that. The distinction was achieved by the collection, bit by bit, of beautiful things each chosen for some quality which warmed the heart of the purchaser . . . carpets, bits of crystal and carved jade on ebony stands, books, cushions, chairs, pictures, sconces, candelabra, brocades and old Italian damasks, footstools, and mirrors which coldly reflected the warm bodies of beautiful women. Even in a city where taste and beauty were the rule, the drawing-room in the Rue Raynouard was a marvel of these qualities. It was more beautiful than the rooms of Madame Gigon's respectable friends; for these women were French *bourgeoises* and neither wealth nor decorators could endow them with a quality that descends from Heaven only upon the few and the blessed. These women admired Madame Shane's drawing-room and envied it . . . all of them, Madame de Cyon, the Comptesse de Turba, Madame Marchand, the mysterious old Madame Blaise, who people said had been a famous beauty in her youth; Geneviève Malbour, who wrote novels as dowdy as herself and struck the literary note; even the rich Duchesse de Gand, who frequented the royalist *soirées* and the parties given by the *chic* Jews, and only came occasionally to Madame Gigon to placate her husband whose title was created by the first Napoleon. They attempted to imitate the seductive, quiet beauty of Numero Dix but they failed somehow, perhaps because they could not resist introducing a pillow of just the wrong, violent shade or a pair of rubber plants, or some monstrous piece of furniture from the period of the Second Empire.

"This American" had outdone them, quite without striving or effort. Indeed if the success of Lily's drawing-room had depended upon either of these things it would have remained forever as ugly as on the day she moved into it, to succeed a chocolate manufacturer whose growing prosperity led him to a small palace in the new German style on the Avenue de Jena. She was incapable of effort. If she had been poor, if she had been forced to work, she would have become sloven; even her beauty would have deteriorated and grown sloppy through neglect. It was money which stood between her and these disasters . . . money which permitted her to enter a shop and say, "I will have this and this and this for my drawing-room," money which permitted her to enter any *salon* of the Rue de la Paix and say, "I will have this gown, or this one, or this," money which permitted her to go to the hairdresser, Augustine, and say, "I will have my hair waved and my complexion treated." And having been born with taste, she made no errors.

Although the friends of Madame Gigon spoke of her as "the American," it is seldom that they thought of her as a foreigner. Only her indolence and her extravagance could have betrayed to a stranger the fact that she was not a true Frenchwoman. In the seven years that followed the death of her mother, Lily abandoned forever all thought of returning to America. She spoke French to perfection, indolently and gracefully, with a fine smooth accent. Her son, for all his American parentage and British schooling, was French; or at least, not American. He had a taste for music, for pictures, even for poetry.

"Fancy that," she remarked to Ellen. "Fancy that, and think what his father has become."

And she held up a newspaper photograph of the Governor . . . now the Senator . . . clipped from one of the American newspapers which Ellen brought to Numero Dix. It portrayed him in the act of addressing the Benevolent Order of Camels in Detroit. The pose was in itself flamboyant. Everything about him flowed. His loose black cravat flowed in the breeze. His hair, worn rather long, waved behind him. His alpaca suit ballooned about his heavy figure. His stomach rested upon a flag-draped railing, and his face wore a smile that was old and familiar, the smile of one who patronized his audience. In the background there was a vague suggestion of a square, solid figure in a richly flowered costume, wearing a pince-nez and a cloud of flowing veils . . . obviously the figure of the Senatoress.

Though Lily sometimes mocked the Governor, she never mentioned him as the source of Jean's restless vitality and intelligence. But it did not matter, since no one in her world and, least of all Ellen, was interested in the Governor or eager to defend him.

The women who came to her drawing-room were, first of all, "Madame Gigon's friends." Toward Lily, for all her good-nature and her submission to their world, their attitude was never more than that of acquaintances. She saw them many times a month but there remained always an insurmountable

barrier. It existed perhaps because she was too indolent to make those over-
tures necessary to friendship, perhaps because deep down in the heart of their
bourgeois respectability they detected in the American traces of the wanton.
They came to the "salons" of Madame Gigon and Lily went in turn to theirs.
But she never entertained in the evening save at small dinners of four and
six, and she never went to balls. Her hunger for gaiety she satisfied in the midst
of crowds, at the Opéra, in the music halls, at the races. And always she was
accompanied by Jean or Ellen or Madame Gigon so that no one was able
to say that she was indiscreet. If she went out frequently with the Baron, he
was after all the cousin and protector of the old woman who accompanied
them. If the Baron came frequently to her house it was to see Madame Gigon
who was flattered by his attentions and his gifts of money.

Yet it could not be said that she was more friendly with men than with
women. The men admired her. Indeed men from the world of fashion, from
the world of the Duchesse de Guermantes' *soirées*, sometimes mingled with
the dowdy Bonapartists of Madame Gigon's salon, brought there by friends
who moved in the circle closest to "the American." They were pleasantly
received and sent on their way, having accomplished nothing. If they became
a trifle ardent she called Madame Gigon or the Baron to her side and the
incident ended without difficulty. The visits came to nothing, for Lily
appeared to have no ambitions. She was bafflingly content. She might have
had great success in a score of ways, for her flamboyant beauty was a sort
rarely seen among French women and it attracted notice wherever she appeared. But she had no ambitions; she was both wealthy and content. People
remarked her at the Opéra but it was seldom that any one was able to identify
her, for none knew her. Her circle was small, dowdy and infinitely respectable.
She lived quietly with old Madame Gigon, now almost blind, and a charming
son. It seemed that she was even content to forego a second marriage. And
among those who admired her, because she was so good-natured and lovely
to look upon, was the wife of the Baron, a pretty blond woman, rich and
stupid, the daughter of a manufacturer from Lyons.

Madame Gigon adored her in two quite distinct fashions. The first because
Lily was pleasant, kindly and generous. The second adoration, less commendable perhaps but none the less thorough, was the adoration of a woman
pinched all her life by poverty for a fellow creature who secured her declining
years with every possible luxury. Madame Gigon could not possibly forget
that it was Lily who had set her up in a situation worthy of a woman whose
father had been ruined by his loyalty to Napoleon the Little. The widow of
the curator of the Cluny Museum had grown very small and dry. Her face
resembled a withered pomegranate both in texture and color. Her dog Fifi
had long since been laid to rest in the dog's cemetery on a little island in the
Seine where Madame Shane had kindly raised a tombstone with Fifi in marble
sitting on a bronze cushion, "*tout á fait comme dans la vie.*" Fifi had not one
successor but two, both provided by Madame Shane to console "her poor
old Louise." One was a black and tan, for all the world like the departed

Fifi, and bore the name of Criquette. The other, a perky black Scotty brought back from England as a surprise, bore the name of Michou. They slept in Madame Gigon's room overlooking the garden and had their own corner in the Louis Seize dining-room, where they ate when the rest of the household sat down at an enormous table lighted by tall candles. Like Fifi they had gone the way of *gâteaux* and were stout and short of breath.

Chapter 56

THESE FOUR . . . Lily, Madame Gigon, Criquette and Michou . . . were the permanent tenants of Numero Dix. There were two others who came and went, spending now a week's holiday, now a whole month or more. They even paid visits frequently to the lodge at Germigny l'Evec in the park of the Baron, where Lily spent the spring and the autumn of every year, taking a house during the summer at Houlgate where she lived as a Frenchwoman in the very heart of the small American colony. The transients in the establishment of Madame Shane were her son Jean and her cousin Ellen Tolliver. They flitted in and out like birds of passage, less regular in their arrival and departure, though no less spirited and noisy.

The Ellen Tolliver of the pompadour and starched shirt waists had become the Lilli Barr whom crowds packed concert halls to see and hear, whom music critics found themselves bound to commend—the same Lilli Barr whose photograph seated beside a great composer appeared in the Sunday supplements of American newspapers. This of course, the public never knew. It knew only that she was a fine pianist with a sensational presence and a vitality which reached out and engulfed them through the medium of surging music. It knew nothing of her past. Indeed there were few who knew she was an American. Her name might have been Russian or Austrian, Hungarian or German. It carried with it the glamor sought by the public which will receive the most sublime artist with indifference if her name happened to be Mary Smith and her origin Evanston, Indiana. This she realized. She shrewdly explained to Lily the evolution of her name.

"Barr," she said, "is the name of my grandfather. I have a perfect right to it. Alone and unadorned it is not thrilling. Therefore I have chosen Lilli. That, my dear, is a tribute to you, because if it had not been for you I should probably be an old maid giving music lessons at fifty cents an hour to the daughters of mill clerks." She laughed noisily. "Lilli Barr. . . . A great name, don't you think? It will suit everybody. It will suit those who believe American musicians should be encouraged and it will suit those who must have a little exotic European sauce with their fowl. Lilli Barr. . . . It might be anything at all."

"Lilli Barr" was a name which betrayed nothing of a rather materialistic elopement with a traveling salesman called Clarence Murdock. It betrayed nothing of Clarence's quiet passing out of this life from a weakened heart too greatly tried by life with a robust and ambitious wife. It had nothing to do with a father, ruined by honesty, who wore away his middle age as clerk in an industrial bank. It gave no hint of a mother who, in an effort to follow her ambitious, migratory offspring, had kept a Manhattan rooming house for five years past. Decidedly, emphatically, it was an exotic name. There were even people who believed that she was the protégée of a German Baron named Unschaff (they had his name and the history of his amours) whom she repaid in the usual way. And this story Ellen would have been the last to deny, for she knew its value. She understood that the people who paid money for concerts must have something besides music. And she understood the value of money in a fashion never imagined by Lily. The critics might call her playing sensational, bordering even upon charlatanism, she would not deny it. The public liked an artist who understood the value of a gesture, who came upon the concert stage with the air of a queen, who played with gusto and the sweep of a hurricane. She understood all that. It was not that she was insincere. There were those for whom she played exquisitely and with all the distilled beauty of a sensitive artist, with the same curious passion which had engulfed her music on that last night in the drawing-room at Cypress Hill. She was a clever woman, far more intelligent than Lily, and having been nourished in the midst of poverty and failure, her one god was success, a sort - of embittered success which played upon the silliness and affectation of the world.

Certainly she had kept the promise made to Lily. She fitted no pattern, least of all the pattern of the Town. She had her own ruthless law, founded upon consideration for friends alone. She had her own thoughts and beliefs. Indeed she hated the pattern bitterly, so bitterly that she made a vow never to play in the Town no matter what the fee offered her. In appearance she resembled curiously her grandaunt, Lily's mother. About her features there was the same bold carving. Her face was too long and her eyes a shade too green. Her figure held none of the voluptuous curves that softened her cousin's beauty; on the contrary it was slim and strong. She walked with a fine free swing that carried in it a hint of masculinity. Beside Lily she was not beautiful at all; yet on the concert stage under the glow of the lights her beauty was infinitely more effective than Lily's would have been. . . . Her energy was the energy descended directly from Hattie Tolliver. It crackled through her whole being. She was not like Lily, a woman of the world; there was a quality of directness and naïvete, a breeziness springing from her background and her ancestry, which all the courts of Europe might never overcome. She was, above all else, herself, incapable of affectation or pretense. And this, she also understood, was a thing of great value because one expected it of the artistic temperament. An artist made no compromises.

Chapter 57

ONE LATE AFTERNOON in April, nineteen thirteen, when the trees in the garden were all feathery and soft with the first green of the Gallic springtime, Madame Gigon sat in her chair by the door of the long drawing-room bidding her guests good-by, one by one, as they left her usual Thursday *salon*. The drawing-room, owing to the sharp slope of the ground upon which the house was built, lay below the surface of the Rue Raynouard on the garden side of the house so that the guests leaving were forced to climb a long flight of stairs that led up to the street door. The stairway, opening directly into the drawing-room, provided a long, high vista leading up to a door, itself noticeable by its very insignificance. It was one of the charming features of the house that on the street side it was but one story high with a single door and a row of high windows which betrayed no hint of the beauty and space within its walls. On the garden side, however, the house presented a beautiful façade some three stories high, constructed of Caen stone and designed in the best manner of the eighteenth century. Lenôtre himself was said to have had a hand in the planning of the terraces and the pavilion that stood at a little distance completely embowered by shrubs and covered by a canopy made of the broad green leaves of plane trees. The house, after a fashion, turned its back upon the world, concealing its beauties from the eye of the random passerby, preserving them for the few who were admitted by the humble and unpretentious door that swung open upon the cobble stones of the Rue Raynouard. To the world it showed the face of a *petite bourgeoise*. To its friends it revealed the countenance of an eighteenth century marquise. And this fact had influenced for more than a century and a half the character of its tenants. The prosperous chocolate manufacturer abandoned it for the German palace in the Avenue de Jena for the very reason that Lily Shane seized it the moment it fell vacant. It was no sort of a house for one who desired the world to recognize his success and the character of his life, but it was an excellent house in which to live quietly, even secretly. It stood isolated in the very midst of Paris.

Madame Gigon sat in a high-backed chair, her small, withered body propped among cushions, her feet resting on a footstool. Since her eyes had grown dim she used her ears as a means of watching her guests; and these, after the fashion of such organs, had become sharper and sharper with the failure of her sight.

A fat and dowdy woman dressed all in white and wearing an extravagant white veil moved up to her.

"Good-by, Madame Gigon," she said. "You come to me on Friday. Don't forget. The Prince himself will be there."

Madame Gigon, instead of peering at the white lady, leaned back. "Ah, it's you, Héloise. . . . Yes, I will be there on Friday. But you are leaving early."

"No," replied the white lady, who was a countess and possessed a fine collection of armor. "No. Others have gone before me. I am dining out in the Boulevard St. Germain."

Madame Gigon smiled. "With your Jewish friends?"

"Yes. It is a long way."

"They say her eldest daughter is to marry a rich American . . . millions. He is called Blumenthal."

"*Oui* . . . a very nice gentleman and the Good God alone knows how rich."

"Well, money is a great thing . . . the foundation of everything, Héloise."

"Yes . . . Good-by . . . On Friday then. And fetch Madame Shane if she cares to come."

And the plump white lady made her way with effort up the long polished stairway to the unpretentious doorway.

Madame Gigon, holding Michou on her lap, began fondling the dog's ears. She leaned back and listened. Most of the guests had gone. Her sharp ears constructed the scene for her. A shrill and peevish voice in the far corner betrayed Madame de Cyon. The old woman saw her, fat, with dyed black hair and a round face well made up to conceal the ravages of time. A Russian woman, married to a French diplomat . . . Bonapartist of course. She translated American novels into French to amuse herself and to help keep up the household in Neuilly. Yet she was rich, for her fat pig's hands were covered with rings and the sable of her cloak was the best.

A man's voice, ill-tempered and gruff, rose through the shadowy room. Captain Marchand, who did not get on with his wife. Tactless of Madame de Cyon to have led them to the bridge table to play with each other. Bridge-mad . . . was Madame de Cyon . . . bridge-mad, and she hated like the Devil to lose. To lose five francs was like losing one of her fat legs. Strange game . . . this bridge. It put every one into a bad temper. Not at all like piquet.

"*Deux pique!*" announced Madame de Cyon.

"*Passe!*" . . . "*Passe!*" . . . "*Passe!*"

From the dining-room issued the sound of two voices in dispute, the one high-pitched, old and somewhat shrill, and the other rather deep and gentle, almost conciliatory. They drifted to Madame Gigon across the murmurous spaces of the drawing-room. Madame Blaise and "Mees Ellen's" friend, Schneidermann. Madame Blaise was a Gasconne, old, shrill and vituperatory, yet somehow amusing and stimulating . . . a little cracked perhaps but still full of spirit, and mysterious in the fashion of those whose existence has its foundations in a world of fanciful, half-mad unreality. She was tall and thin, with a mass of dyed red hair (it must have gone gray ten years earlier) under an old-fashioned purple bonnet trimmed with purple plumes and perched high on her head in the fashion of the eighties. Madame Gigon knew she was by the *gâteaux* . . . eating . . . eating . . . eating . . . as if she starved herself at home. Yet she too was rich.

"Ah, you don't know the Germans as I do!" came the high-pitched voice. "My fine young fellow! I tell you I have lived with them. I have been on business for the government. They are capable of anything. You will see . . ."

And then the voice of Schneidermann, mild and a little amused by the old lady. "Ah . . . ," gently. "Perhaps . . . perhaps. But I do not think that war is any longer possible."

"Nevertheless," persisted the voice. "One fine day you will go marching away like the rest."

Chapter 58

SCHNEIDERMANN WAS Alsatian, and Jew on his father's side, rich, for his family owned steel mills at Toul and Nancy and in the very environs of Paris, as well as coal mines in the neighborhood of St. Quentin and La Bassée. Schneidermann, tall, handsome, swarthy . . . was beautiful in an austere, sensual fashion as only Jews can be beautiful. He came sometimes to play the 'cello with "Mees Ellen," choosing queer music they called "modern" that had none of the beauty and melody of Offenbach and Gounod.

The voice of "Mees Ellen" joining the pair in the dining-room. . . . "War! . . . War! . . . Nonsense! There can't be any war. I must play in Berlin and Munich next season." Her voice rang with genuine conviction, as if she really believed that war itself dared not interfere with still more amazing successes. Madame Blaise' cynical laugh answered her.

"Ah, you young people . . . you young people. What do you know of war and politics? I have been through wars, through revolutions, you understand. I know about these things. I am as old as time."

The old woman was talking in her most fantastic vein. It was her habit to talk thus as if she were wise beyond all people. She was, as Madame Gigon said, a little cracked on this side of her.

"I know . . . I know," she continued to mutter in the most sinister fashion until an unusually large madeleine put an end to her talk.

"How much did you say . . . eight francs?" It was the peevish voice of Madame de Cyon settling her bridge debts.

"Eight francs," came the gruff reply of Captain Marchand. "Eight francs, I tell you." And then the tinkling of the Russian woman's innumerable gold bangles as she thrust her fat bejeweled hand into a small purse to wrench loose from it the precious eight francs. "I had no luck to-day . . . no luck at all," she observed in the same irritable voice. "No cards at all. What can one do without cards? Now last week I won. . . ." And she fell to recounting past victories while Captain Marchand's chair scraped the floor savagely.

And then the voice of Madame Blaise quite close at hand, bidding Madame Gigon good-by.

"On Tuesday, then, Louise. I shall expect you."

"On Tuesday," repeated Madame Gigon.

"And bring Madame Shane if she wishes to come. But not 'Mees Tolliver.'"

I can't bear her and her American ways." The old harridan bent lower, her reticule shaking with the aged trembling of her thin body. "That Schneidermann!" she observed scornfully. "He is a fool! The men I knew when I was young were interested in revolutions and politics . . . not music. Music! Bah!" And to show her disgust she spat on the bare floor. . . . Then she made a hissing noise and swept up the long dim stairway, her boots squeaking as she walked.

Then the confusion of farewells as the last guests departed, Madame de Cyon passing by, still in bad humor over her losses.

"On Friday, Madame Gigon," she said. "My husband will be there. He is home from the Balkans and full of news."

"Of the wars I suppose. . . . On Friday, Madame."

"And tell Madame Shane she is expected also."

Then Captain Marchand and Madame Marchand, also in a bad humor because they got on badly. Madame Marchand's day fell on Monday and she too asked the old woman to bring Madame Shane. Her invitation was made in the same oblique fashion as the other. "Bring Madame Shane if she cares to come."

At last there remained no one save those whom Lily, in her vague, lazy fashion called "the family." These were old Madame Gigon, Ellen Tolliver, Jean, herself and the Baron.

As the blond little Captain Marchand, pompously clanking his spurs as he walked, disappeared up the darkening reaches of the long stairway, Jean, who had been reading in a corner reserved for himself, sprang up with the bound of a young animal and ran across to Ellen and Schneidermann.

"*Alors! Viens donc . . . la musique!*" he cried, seizing her by the hand while she struggled against his youthful strength, and Schneidermann laughed at his exuberance. She resisted, bracing her strong slim body and indulging in a mock struggle.

"Not a sound from me," she replied. "Unless we talk English. I can make no more effort with this waiter's chatter."

It was a price which she exacted frequently, for she spoke French badly, though with great vigor, and with an accent so atrocious that it seemed quite beyond hope of improvement. Her English carried the drawling tang of the middle west. She called "dog" *dawg* and "water" *watter*.

Jean resembled his mother. His hair, like hers, was red though less soft and more carroty. His nose was short, straight, and conveyed an impression of good humor and high spirits. He was tall for his age and strongly built with a slim figure which gave every promise of one day growing into the bulky strength of the Governor. He possessed a restless, noisy, energy quite incomprehensible to Lily. To-day he wore the uniform of a cadet at the cavalry school at St. Cyr. It was the idea of the Baron, himself a cuirassier, that Jean should be trained for the cavalry. "If he does not like it, he may quit," he told Lily. As for Jean, he appeared to like it well enough. He was as eager for a war as Madame Blaise had been certain of one.

"Come along, Nell," he cried. "Be a good cousin, and play that four-handed stuff with me."

Madame Gigon, with Michou and Criquette waddling amiably after her, stole quietly away to her room to lock her door against the hideous sounds which Ellen, Schneidermann and Jean made when they played what they called "modern" music.

From the shelter of a divan placed between two of the tall windows, Lily and the Baron watched the three noisy musicians. On the verge of middle-age, her beauty appeared to have reached its height. There are those who would have preferred her as a young girl, fresher, more gentle and more naive. But likewise there are those who find the greatest beauty in the opulent women of Titian, and it was this beauty which Lily now possessed. She wore a black tea-gown, loosely and curiously made with a collar which came high about her throat and emphasized the ivory green tint of her skin and the copper red of her hair. She lay back among the cushions watching Jean with the triumphant, possessive look which strayed into her dark eyes whenever her son was with her. It was an expression so intense as to be almost tragic.

The Baron smiled too, but his smile was concealed somewhat by the fierce black military mustaches that adorned his face. They were the mustaches of the French army, very long, very luxurious, and purposely rather ill-kempt. There was nothing silky about them. On the contrary they were the mustaches of an *homme de guerre*—stiff, bristling and full of vitality. He was a dark, wiry Frenchman, with strong, nervous hands and very bright black eyes which clouded easily with anger. He was perhaps four or five years older than Lily and did not look his age. Indeed his figure was youthful and muscular with the hard, fierce masculinity which belongs to some men of the Latin race.

Whenever he regarded Ellen, it was with a stern glance that was almost hostile. They did not get on well. Even Lily, indifferent and unobservant, must have seen the hidden clash of their two strong natures. It appeared that he resented Ellen's wilfulness and even the masculine simplicity of her clothes. On this evening she was at her best. Her dark hair she no longer wore in the manner of Lily. It was drawn straight back from her high forehead with an uncompromising severity and done in a knot low on the back of her strong, well-shaped neck. Jean dragged her by sheer force of strength to the piano where the two sat down noisily, the boy searching through the music while Ellen played the most amazing, delicate and agile roulades and cascades of notes on the polished ivory keyboard. Schneidermann, thrown a little into the background by the wild exuberance of the pair, drew up a chair and waited quietly until it was time for him to turn the pages.

And during these preliminaries Lily and the Baron rose and made their way silently through one of the tall windows on to the terrace and thence into the garden. Lily herself confessed that she could not abide the new music.

"I do not understand it," she told her cousin. "And I do not find it beautiful. It is beyond me, I confess. I cannot see what you and Jean find in it. I suppose it is because I am growing old. You and Jean belong to the same generation.

I am too old for new ideas." And for the first time her laugh was not all geniality and warmth. It carried a fine edge of bitterness, scarcely to be discerned but none the less unmistakable.

And now in the soft spring twilight of the garden she and the Baron walked along the neat gravel paths until they reached the wall shutting out the Rue de Passy. Here they sat for a time on a stone bench saying nothing, remaining quite still and silent. And at last as the darkness grew more heavy they rose and wandered off again, aimlessly and slowly, until in the shadow of a laburnum tree, the man seized her suddenly and kissed her, long and passionately. And after a little while when it was quite dark they entered the pavilion hidden by shrubbery where Jean lived when he was home on a holiday.

The garden lay breathless and silent. Even the rumbling noises from the street beyond the wall had died away with the coming of darkness. From the distant Seine arose the faint whistle of the St. Cloud steamer, and through the tall window drifted in wild fragments the savage, barbaric chords of Stravinsky's music.

Chapter 59

DAY IN AND day out Lily's life followed its easy, happy course. Always there were diversions, always gaiety, always people. Yet there were times now—indeed they seemed to have begun upon her return from America following her mother's death—when a cloud of sadness descended upon her, times when she would withdraw suddenly to her own room as if some tiny thing, a word, a gesture, an intonation, had set fire to a train of secret memories. Frequently she kept to her room for the rest of the day, seeing no one, lunching and dining alone on a gilt table placed before her chaise longue by the window.

These sudden fits of melancholy disturbed Ellen who remarked on them gravely to old Madame Gigon.

"She was never like that before. I can't see what it is that disturbs her."

Madame Gigon saw no cause for alarm. "It's true," she said. "She was never like that before. But it may be that she grows tired. You see she is growing older, my dear Mees Ellen. All of us, as we grow older, like moments of solitude and quiet. It gives one time to reflect on life. You don't understand that yet. You're too young. But some day you will understand. As you get older you begin to wonder what it's all about . . . (*pourquoi le combat*)."

"Perhaps," replied Ellen with a vigorous shrug. "I'm sure it can't be her mother. It might, of course, be Irene."

And they fell to discussing for the hundredth time the case of Irene, whom Madame Gigon had not seen since she was a little girl. They talked of her strange behavior, Madame Gigon wagging her old head, staring before her with sightless eyes.

"It is tragic . . . a life like that," she would say. "A life wasted. You know she was a pretty little girl. . . . She could have married."

They spoke of her as if she were dead. It was true that to them . . . to Ellen, to Madame Gigon, she was forever lost. Perhaps they were right, with that instinctive knowledge which underlies the consciousness of women chattering together over the strangeness of human behavior. Perhaps Irene *was* dead. . . . Perhaps she had been dead since a certain night when the last traces of her faith in humanity were throttled. It was true that she had left the world and turned her faith toward God alone, as if she were already dead and in purgatory.

"She was always queer," Ellen would say.

And then Madame Gigon, as if she were conscious of toying with thoughts of blasphemy, would say piously:

"But she is a good woman, who has given her life to good work and prayer."

But she spoke as if trying to convince herself, as if she did not quite believe what she said.

And Lily, all the while, kept her secret. Undoubtedly she was no longer in her first youth. This may have depressed her, for she was a woman to whom beauty and youth were the beginning and the end. Yet the fits of melancholy had something to do with a more definite and tangible thing. They were associated in some way with a little enameled box in which she kept a growing bundle of clippings from the American newspapers which Ellen brought into the house at Numero Dix.

In the solitude of her room, she opened the box and reread them many times, over and over again until the edges became frayed and the print blurred from much fingering. They had to do with the career of a certain labor leader, a man named Krylenko who seemed a strange person to excite the interest of a woman like Madame Shane. The clippings marked the progress of the man. Whenever there was a strike, Krylenko appeared to take a hand in it. Slowly, clipping by clipping, the battle he fought was being won. The unions penetrated now this steel town, now that one. There were battles, brutalities, deaths, fires in his trail, but the trail led steadily upward toward a goal. He was winning slowly. That he was strong there could be no doubt. He was so strong that great newspapers printed editorials against him and his cause. They called him an "anarchist," "an alien disturber," "a peril to the great American nation" and, most frequently of all, "a menace to prosperity and the inalienable rights of property."

Lily kept the enameled box locked in a drawer of her writing desk. No one had ever seen it. No one would see it until she died. It had been there for seven years.

It was on the morning after one of these attacks of melancholy, a few days after Jean's visit, that the Town suddenly intruded once more upon the house in the Rue Raynouard.

Lily sat on the sunlit terrace of the garden before a late breakfast of chocolate and buttered rolls, opposite Ellen whose habit it was to arise early and pursue some form of violent exercise while her cousin still slept. This morning she had been riding in the Bois de Bologne. As a little girl she learned to ride under the instruction of her grandfather, old Jacob Barr, and she rode well and easily with the air and the skill of one who has grown up with horses. The languid Schneidermann accompanied her on these early morning jaunts. She owned her horse because in the long run it was more economical and, as she said, "No pennies slip through my fingers."

She wore a tight black riding habit with a white stock and a low derby hat. The riding crop lay across her strong, slim knees as she smoked and watched Lily devour too many rolls and a too large bowl of rich chocolate.

Between them on the table lay the morning's letters. In Ellen's little heap there were three or four notes from struggling music students, begging help or advice from her, one from a manager proposing an interview with regard to an American tour, a bill from Durand the publisher. Lily's pile was altogether different. It consisted almost entirely of bills, from Coty, from Worth, from Henri the florist, from Augustine the hairdresser, from Lanvin . . . from . . . on and on endlessly and at the bottom a letter from the lawyers who succeeded on the death of William Baines, "the old fogy," to the management of Lily's holdings in the Town.

The last letter she read through twice with so deep an interest that the chocolate grew cold and she was forced to send for a hot cup and more hot rolls. When she had finished she leaned back in the wicker chair, buried beneath the silk, the lace ruffles and the pale tiny bows of her peignoir.

"D'you know, Ellen," she remarked, "I am growing too rich. I've no idea what to do with all my money."

Ellen put down her letter abruptly and knocked the ash from her cigarette. "There are plenty of places for it." She slapped the envelope against her slim thigh. "I've had two letters this morning asking me for money . . . from two music students. Heaven knows I've got nothing to spare. All that's left over I send to Ma. What is it now? A gold mine or an oil well?"

"Neither," said Lily. "It's just the Town making me richer and richer. It's from Folsom and Jones . . . I guess they're since your time. They're lawyers and they handle Irene's and my estate. They want me to sell the rest of the property we own."

Ellen pursed her lips reflectively. "How much are they offered?"

"Something over five hundred thousand. They say they can get six in a pinch."

She whistled softly. "Take it . . . take it. Those old shacks can't be worth that."

"It isn't the shacks," said Lily. "It's the land itself they want. The shacks aren't even worth repair. Why, they were built, most of them, while Father was still living. The lawyers hint that the Town is ashamed of them, that they are a disgrace to the Town."

"I suppose it has changed," remarked Ellen.

"The population has doubled," said her cousin. "There aren't enough houses for the people. Why, last summer people who came to work at the Mills had to live in tents for a time. Even the people on Park avenue let out rooms. The Chamber of Commerce asked them to. They appealed to their pride not to stop the tremendous growth. There's been a tremendous . . ."

Ellen interrupted her. "I know . . . I know. . . . 'Watch us grow. The biggest city in the state in ten years.' Well, it's money in your pocket. You've no kick coming."

The chocolate and rolls arrived and Lily began once more to eat.

"I don't see how you can eat all that and keep your figure," observed Ellen.

"Massage," said Lily. "Massage . . . and luckily the time is coming when I can eat all I want and be as fat as I like. In another fifteen years I'll be an old woman and it won't matter what I do." The faint bitterness again drifted through the speech, evasive and imperceptible.

"What does Irene say to your selling?" inquired Ellen.

"The lawyers say she wants to sell. You know I haven't had a line from her in years. She's in France now, you know."

"In France!" said Ellen, her eyebrows rising in surprise.

"Yes, at Lisieux."

"I should think you'd go and see her."

"She wouldn't see me if I went. What good would it do?"

Chapter 60

THERE WAS a sudden silence while Ellen beat her riding crop against her leg. "I must say she's very queer. I never understood her. You know when I was a girl, she gave me the creeps . . . the way she had of looking at you with those pale eyes."

"I know," replied Lily. And then after a pause. "You know they want to buy Cypress Hill too. The Lord alone knows how many times they tried. They began before Mama died. Irene hasn't any share in it. It belongs outright to me."

"I suppose it's the Mills."

"No, not this time. The Town wants it now." She paused while she buttered another roll. "They want it for a new railway station . . . a union station, you know, for all three roads. It's perfect for that. And each time they increase the offer. Now they write me that they've made a last offer. If I won't sell, they'll undertake proceedings to condemn it."

During this speech the countenance of Ellen Tolliver underwent a complete metamorphosis. The devil-may-care look vanished slowly, replaced by a certain hardness, a squaring of the handsome jaw, a slight hardening of the firm lips. It may have been that while Lily talked her cousin was swept by a torrent of memories—memories of hurt pride, of poverty and indignities endured because she was helpless, memories of patronizing women and young girls who spoke of "poor Ellen Tolliver," memories of her father's defeats and disappointments, of Judge Weissman's dishonesty and corruption, of her mother's agonizing and endless struggle to keep up appearances. As sometimes occurs with individuals of strong personality, a whole life, a complete philosophy stood revealed for an instant in her intelligent face. She had run off with Clarence Murdock "to show the Town." She had become famous and successful because, deep down in her heart, she was resolved always to show the Town how little it counted in her life, how great was the contempt she felt for it. It was always this thought—this more than everything else—which had driven her forward. And now came this new opportunity, perhaps the best of all, to block the Town, to thwart its most cherished desire. It was a chance to prevent a new and flamboyant effort to advertise its wealth, its prosperity, its bigness.

"As if," she said aloud, " 'bigness' was something to be proud of. Let them try and condemn it, Lily. I doubt if they can. Anyway I'd keep it just to spite them. It's a chance to show your power." She leaned earnestly across the table, striking it with her riding crop to emphasize her words. "You hate the place as much as I do. Why, it isn't even the same Town we grew up in. It's another place built upon filth and soot. It's not that we're fouling our own nest. Why, Lily, the Town your mother and my grandfather loved wasn't that sort of place at all. It was a pleasant place where people lived quietly and peacefully, where they had horses and dogs and were decent to each other. And now that's all buried under those damned filthy Mills, under a pile of muck and corruption with Judge Weissman and his crowd enthroned on the very top." She stood up, her blue eyes flashing. "It's changed the very people in it. It's made them noisy, common, cheap. Damn it! I hate them all!" She struck the table a violent blow with her riding crop. "Don't sell it. You don't need the money. It's nothing to you . . . not even if they offered you a million!" And then she laughed savagely. "That's the best part of it. The longer you hold it, the more they'll have to pay you. The more prosperous they are, the more it will cost them to have a new railway station. You're the one who has the power now. Don't you see what power there is in money? . . . the power that grows out of just owning a thing?"

Lily, it appeared, was amazed by the passion of the sudden outburst. For a time she lay back in the wicker chair, regarding her cousin with a thoughtful look. At last, she said, "I had no idea that you felt that way about it. It's the way Mama used to feel. I suppose I never had enough of the place to really hate it."

Ellen again interrupted her passionately. "If you'd had as much as I had, you'd have hated it all right."

"I just ran away from it as soon as I could," continued Lily. "Besides," she added after a pause, "Mama left a letter asking me to keep Cypress Hill. She always felt that way about the Town."

Ellen, persistent, bent over the table toward her cousin. The riding crop fell to the gravel terrace. "Promise me you won't sell it, Lily. . . . Promise me you'll keep it. It's a chance to hit back. . . . Promise!"

And Lily, who after all was indifferent in matters of business, promised, perhaps because the violent revelations made by her cousin astounded her so completely that she was unable to think of any argument. Doubtless she had reasons of her own . . . secret reasons which had to do with the worn clippings in the enameled box.

"I'll keep it," she replied. "They can wait until Hell freezes over. And besides you put the idea so that it amuses me. I'll sell the other stuff and invest the money."

Ellen interrupted her with a bitter laugh. "It's funny, you know, that all this time they've been pouring money into your pocket. That's the joke of it. In a way, it was all this booming and prosperity that helped me too. If you hadn't been so rich, I suppose I'd never have made a success of it."

Lily languidly finished the last of her chocolate. "I'd never thought of it in that way. It's an amusing idea."

Ellen was satisfied. Gathering up her letters she went into the house, changed her clothes, and in a little while, seated under the flaming Venice of Mr. Turner, she was working stormily at her music, filling the house with glorious sound until it overflowed and spilled its rhapsodies over the terrace into the garden where the first bright irises were abloom.

Chapter 61

UPSTAIRS LILY made her way, after a toilette which occupied two hours, to the room of Madame Gigon. It was, amid the elegance of the house, a black-sheep of a room, its walls covered with books, its corners cluttered with broken fragments of Gothic saints and virgins, the sole legacy of the distant and obscure M. Gigon, curator at the Cluny Museum. In the center stood a table covered with dark red rep, heavily embroidered and cluttered with ink-pots, pens and all the paraphernalia of writing. Bits of faded brocade ornamented the wall save for a space opposite the door where hung an immense engraving of the First Napoleon, dominating a smaller portrait of Napoleon the Little in all the glory of his mustaches and imperial. An engraving of the Eugènie by Winterhalter stood over the washstand, a convenience to which Madame Gigon clung even after Lily's installation of the most elaborate American plumbing.

Madame Gigon huddled like a benevolent old witch among the bedclothes of her diminutive bed. At the foot, in a bright patch of sunlight, lay Criquette and Michou amiably close to each other and both quite stuffed with toasted rolls and hot chocolate.

Lily came in looking fresh and radiant in a severe suit and smart hat. They exchanged greetings.

"How are you this morning, Tante Louise?" she inquired of the old woman.

"Not so well . . . not so well. I slept badly. The pain in my hip."

Lily went and sat on the bed, taking the old woman's hand which she caressed as she felt her pulse.

"You have everything you want?" she inquired.

"Oui . . . everything." There was a little pause and Madame Gigon peered at her with dim eyes. "I've been thinking how lucky I am."

Lily smiled.

"I mean that I'm not left poor and alone. You've been good to me."

Lily's smile expanded into a laugh. "Nonsense. . . . Nonsense. It's given me enough pleasure. . . ."

"It seems like the hand of God," said the old woman very piously.

"It may be," said Lily. "Mees Ellen has been telling me it's the hand of man."

And Madame Gigon, not having heard the talk on the terrace, was puzzled. Secretly she disapproved Mees Ellen's lack of piety.

"Mees Ellen plays well this morning . . . beautifully," said Madame Gigon. "She is an artist . . . a true artist. Will you ask her a favor?"

Lily nodded.

"Will you ask her to play something of Offenbach? I've been hungry for it." She looked feeble and appealing, somewhat confused by violence of the life with which she found herself surrounded since the advent of Mees Ellen and the grown-up Jean.

"Of course," said Lily.

"And one more thing," said Madame Gigon. "This I must ask of you. . . . I'm too ill to go to Madame Blaise this afternoon. I want you to go and explain why I have not come. Tell her I am too ill." A slight frown crossed Lily's brow. Madame Gigon, with her dim eyes could not possibly have seen it, yet she said, "Madame Blaise admires you. . . . She thinks you are all that a woman should be . . . a perfect woman."

If Lily had felt any genuine hesitation, the faint flattery destroyed it, for she replied, "I'll go, certainly. I'm lunching out and I'll go there late and tell her."

"Not too late. . . . She is easily offended," said Madame Gigon. "You know she is a little . . ." She made a comic gesture indicating that Madame Blaise was a little cracked.

Then Lily read to her for a time out of Faure's History of Art which undoubtedly bored her but gave Madame Gigon the greatest pleasure; and at last she left for her mysterious lunch. A little while later there arose from below stairs the tinkling melodies of the overture to Orpheus in the Underworld. Somewhere among the piles of old music in the drawing-room closet, Ellen had discovered the whole score and she played it now in a wild good humor. Sometimes the music became actually noisy in its triumphant violence. It was the playing of a woman who had achieved a victory.

Chapter 62

IT IS POSSIBLE that Madame Blaise felt for Lily the admiration which Madame Gigon attributed to her, but she was such a queer old thing that it was impossible ever to know for a certainty. It could not be said that she revealed these sentiments by any open demonstration, or even by an occasional word of approval. There are women whose manner of showing their devotion assumes an inverted character; it takes to displaying itself in sharp criticisms of the object they love or admire. There are women who nag their lovers, who deprecate the charms of their own children, who sharply denounce the behavior of their dearest friends. And if there be any truth in this theory of inverted demonstration, it could be said that Madame Blaise admired Lily. Indeed judging from her behavior it could be said that she experienced a profound affection for the younger woman.

The old woman seldom addressed Lily, yet when Lily politely assumed the initiative and inquired after the health of Madame Blaise or her plans for the summer, Madame Blaise was flattered and smiled with all the warmth of an August sun. To Madame Gigon she criticized Lily unmercifully. She called her indolent, without ambition. She accused her of having wasted her life and permitted her beauty to fade without using its power. It was not true that Lily had faded, yet Madame Blaise was convinced of it. To have heard her talk, one would have thought Lily was a withered old harridan.

"I understand these things," she told Madame Gigon confidentially, "because I was a beauty myself . . . a famous beauty." And the memory of her triumphs led her to bridle and cast a glance at the nearest mirror. Yet she never spoke of these things to Lily, whose greater youth, already turning into middle-age, seemed to inspire the old woman with an awe tinged by actual worship.

"Why does she bury herself among these old women?" she would say. "Has she no energy . . . no zest for life? If only she could capture some of Mees Tolliver's *élan*. Mees Tolliver could spare her a great deal and be the more charming for it."

And to all this, Madame Gigon had one answer which it was her habit to repeat over and over again. "Madame Shane is content. Is not that enough? What more can any of us wish upon this earth?"

So it ran, this perpetual and carping interest of Madame Blaise. Although she avoided Lily, she could not resist discussing her. And Madame Gigon, believing firmly that Madame Blaise was a little cracked, never mentioned these things to Lily.

There hung about Madame Blaise something of the mystery which envelops people suffering from delusions. Not only was it impossible to know when she was lying and when she was speaking the truth . . . it was impossible even to say, "Madame Blaise is thus and so. She is mean or she is benevolent. She is hostile or she is friendly." It was impossible to reach any sensible opinion concerning her. She was subject to the most absurd whims which rendered impossible any anticipation of her actions. Besides, she lived in a world of her own which resembled in no way the world of her friends, so bound up in shopkeepers, food, laundry, housekeeping, etc. Her world was inhabited by all sorts of fantastic and imaginary creatures. She believed passionately that she was still a fine figure of a woman. Not even a mirror could persuade her otherwise. She asserted with a challenging pugnacity that she had once played a prominent part in European politics, and hinted that she was the last of the women who would go down in history as creatures who ruled kings; but what it was she had done or when she had done it, no one could discover. The tragedy was that no one took her seriously. When one spoke of her, there was always a suspicion in the speech of that comic gesture which Madame Gigon used to indicate that her friend was a little cracked. Yet they were kind to her. No one allowed her to suspect that she was accepted generally as a mere pack of highly animated hallucinations. Indeed her *faiblesse* gave her the whip hand over her friends. People humored her. They submitted to her insults with a calm good-nature.

When she began one of her long tales, people smiled and feigned interest and remarked, "How wonderful! Who would have thought it?" Or with mock protests, they would say, "But my dear Madame Blaise, you are still a fine figure of a woman." And she would go off home delighted that she had managed to preserve her figure and her youthful complexion, even if a bit of rouge was at times necessary. Her delight was always apparent. It was visible in every line of her seamed old face.

There were all sorts of stories concerning Madame Blaise, stories of the most fantastic and incredible nature, stories that she was well known in the generation which she had outlived, stories even that she had been the mistress of this or that politician. Indeed some of the most fantastic tales were contributed slyly by Madame Blaise herself. But no one really knew anything of her youth; and although every one repeated the stories with a certain relish, there was no one who really believed them.

The old women who came to Madame Gigon's salon knew that she had come to Paris some twenty years earlier as the widow of a merchant from Marseilles. She was rich, respected, and at that time seemed wholly in her right mind, save for an overfondness to surround herself with mystery. A respectable Bonapartist, the uncle of Captain Marchand, acted as her sponsor. She settled herself presently into the respectable circle. She had her *salon* and all went well. By now she had been accepted for so long a time that she seemed always to have been a part of that neat little society, so neat, so compact and so circumspect. She was a figure. Madame Blaise? Why, of course, every one knew Madame Blaise . . . always. What had gone before became quickly veiled in the mists of the past, and Madame Blaise, whose life may have been after all one of the most romantic and exciting, found herself a part of a singularly dull and prosaic society.

Lily could have known no more than this concerning the old woman. Indeed it is probable that she knew even less, for her good nature and her tolerant indifference had long since stifled all her curiosity concerning people. She went to Madame Blaise on that Tuesday afternoon to please Madame Gigon, because she had no other engagement, and because she was accustomed to obliging her friends. She may even have suspected that the visit would give pleasure to Madame Blaise herself. She arrived very late as usual (it was impossible for Lily to be punctual) having lingered a long time over lunch and made an expensive tour of the shops in the Rue de la Paix.

In a little enclosure shaded by old trees and high, neglected shrubbery in Passy, five minutes' walk from the Trocadero, Madame Blaise had her house. The enclosure was shared by two other houses, less pretentious, which stood respectfully apart at a little distance. The dwelling was built of wood in imitation of a Swiss chalet, and ornamented with little carved balconies and fantastic ornaments in bizarre exaggeration of some cowherd's house on the mountains above Lucerne. A wall ran about the enclosure with an opening which was barred at night by a massive iron gate. Here Lily stepped down from the fiacre, passing, on her way through the gate, Madame de Cyon and the Marchands, who were leaving.

"You are late," observed Madame de Cyon, taking in Lily's costume with her small green eyes.

"I have been hurrying all the way," replied Lily. "I was kept by business."

Captain Marchand and his wife bowed gravely.

"Every one has gone," observed Madame de Cyon, waiting as though curious to see what Lily would do.

"Well, I must go in. . . . Madame Gigon was too ill to come. She asked me to convey her compliments."

Madame de Cyon brightened. "Nothing serious, I hope."

"No," said Lily. "Madame is an old woman. . . ." And then politely, "She tells me Monsieur de Cyon is back from the Balkans."

"Yes. He is full of wars and intrigues. You must come to me on Thursday. He has asked for you."

Lily smiled. "Please remember me to him. I find him very interesting." She turned suddenly. "But I must hurry on. It is disgusting to be so late. Good-by until Thursday."

Madame de Cyon laid a hand on her arm. "Madame Blaise was eager that you should come. She has been asking for you."

"It is good of her," said Lily politely, at the same time moving away.

"Good-by until Thursday," said Madame de Cyon, and as Lily hurried into the shadows of the enclosure the Russian woman turned and looked after her, her small green eyes alight with an interest in which there was a shade of malice and envy. It was well known that de Cyon admired Madame Shane.

When Lily had disappeared in the thick shrubbery surrounding the house,

Madame de Cyon made a clucking noise and passed through the gate into the street on her way to the Metro. She had lost money again to the Marchands. She was planning to economize.

Chapter 63

AT THE DOOR Lily was admitted by a fat Bretonne maidservant who ushered her through a dark hall and up a dark stairway where the light was so bad that she was unable to distinguish any of the furnishings. It might have been a tunnel for all the impression it made upon a visitor. At a turn of the stairs she was forced to press her body against the wall in order to allow to pass two strangers whom she had never seen at Madame Gigon's salon. At the top she was led through another hall lighted by a sort of chalice, with a gas flame burning inside a red globe suspended by Moorish chains from the low ceiling. Here it was possible to discern the most enormous quantity of furniture and decorations, bronze ornaments, bits of chinoiserie, pictures of all sizes in enormous gilt frames, umbrellas, cloaks, chairs, pillows and what not. At the end of the hall the maidservant opened the door of a large square room and silently indicated Madame Blaise who was seated before a gentle charcoal fire. Lily entered and the servant closed the door behind her.

Madame Blaise, dressed in an old-fashioned gown of some thick black stuff, sat on the edge of her chair like a crow upon a wall. Her cheeks and lips were rouged and this, together with the red glow from the fire and the thick mass of dyed red hair, gave her an appearance completely bizarre and inhuman. She could not have heard Lily enter, for she did not look up until the younger woman came quite close to her and said, "Madame Blaise!"

"Ah!" said the old woman suddenly, as if waking from a dream. "It's you."

Lily was smiling and apologetic. She lied about being detained on business. She explained Madame Gigon's indisposition. Altogether she made herself charming, agreeable and insincere.

"Yes," said Madame Blaise. "Madame Gigon is old," in a tone which implied "much older than I shall ever be."

"I shan't stay but a moment," said Lily, sitting in a chair on the opposite side of the fire.

"No, I suppose not."

And then a silence fell during which it seemed that Madame Blaise returned again to her dream. Lily took off her gloves, straightened her hat and fell to regarding the room. It was an amazing room, full of shadows and indefinable and shapeless objects which danced in the dim gaslight. Gradually these things began to take shape. There were all sorts of chairs and tables and cushions of every fashion and period. The room fairly crawled with furniture. Near the fire stood a red lacquer table, exquisitely made, laden with the remnants of tea—a chocolate pot, a tea urn with the lamp extinguished and the tea growing cold, plates with sandwiches and *gâteaux*. The windows were covered by thick curtains of some brocaded stuff which were drawn now to shut out the twilight. But the most remarkable feature of the room was the number of pictures. They hung in every conceivable nook and corner, standing upright in little frames of gilt bronze, tortoiseshell or ebony, leaning against the walls and against the mirror over the fireplace. Some, judging from the flamboyance and heroic note of the poses, were pictures of actresses and opera singers. Others from the pomposity of the subject were undoubtedly politicians. There were pictures of ladies in crinolines and gentlemen with beards or flowing mustaches. Some were photographs, faded and worn; others were sketches or prints clipped out of journals. There were at least a half dozen portraits in oil of varying degrees of excellence.

Lily occupied herself for a time in studying the room. At last Madame Blaise said, "I am glad the others have gone. They weary me—inexpressibly." She leaned forward a little in her chair. "You understand I have had an interesting life. These others . . ." She made a stiff gesture of contempt. "What have they known of life? They go round and round like squirrels in a cage . . . always the same little circle. Always the same dull people."

Lily smiled agreeably. She was remarkably beautiful in the soft light. "I understand," she said, with the air of humoring the old woman.

Madame Blaise rose suddenly. "But I forgot. . . . You must forgive me for not asking you sooner. Will you have some tea or some chocolate?"

"Nothing," said Lily. "I must think of my figure."

Madame Blaise sat down again. "I am glad you have come. . . ." And after a little pause, she added, "Alone." A frown contracted her brow beneath a neatly clipped bang. "You understand. . . . I think we have some things in common . . . you and I."

Lily still sat complacently. "I'm sure we have!" she said, purely to oblige her companion.

"But not what you suppose," said Madame Blaise looking at her sharply. "Not at all what you suppose. I am not speaking of the youth which we share . . . you and I. I am speaking rather of the qualities which have nothing to do with youth. I mean the capacity to love." This sentiment she uttered with a look of profound mystery. In spite of her eccentricity, there gleamed now and then through the cloud of mystery traces of a grand manner, a certain elusive distinction. It showed in a turn of the head, a gesture, an intonation . . . nothing very tangible, indeed, little more than a fleeting illusion.

Lily's eye began to wander once more, round and round the room to this picture and that, hesitating for a moment on one or another of the amazing collection which caught her fancy. When Madame Blaise fell silent once more for a long interval, she remarked,

"But have you no picture of yourself among all these?"

"No," replied the old woman. "I am coming to that later." And without pausing, she added, "You have had lovers of course." And when Lily, astounded by this sudden observation, stirred nervously in her chair, Madame Blaise raised her hand. "Oh, I know. I am not going to reproach you. I approve, you understand. It is what beautiful women are made for." Her eyes took on an uncanny look of shrewdness.

"Don't fancy that I am ignorant. Some people of course say that I am crazy. I am not. It's the others who are crazy, so they think that I am. But I understand. You have a lover now. . . . He is Madame Gigon's cousin." She looked fiercely into Lily's face which had grown deathly pale at the crazy outburst of the old woman. She appeared frightened now. She did not even protest.

"I have watched," continued Madame Blaise, in the most intimate manner possible. "I understand these things. I know what a glance can mean . . . a gesture, a sudden unguarded word. You, my dear, have not always been as cautious, as discreet, as you might have been. You needn't fear. I shall say nothing. I shall not betray you." She reached over and touched Lily's hand with an air of great confidence. "You see, we are alike. We are as one. It is necessary for us to fight these other women . . . like de Cyon. She is a cat, you understand."

Lily, all her complacency vanished now, glanced at the watch on her wrist. She stood up and walked to the fireplace in an effort to break the way toward escape. She was, it appeared, unable to collect her wits so that she might deal with Madame Blaise.

"You must not go yet," continued the harridan. "I have so much to tell you." She pursed her withered lips reflectively and put her head a little on one side. "When I was a young girl, I was very like you. You can see that my hair is still the same. People notice and remark how beautifully it has kept its color. Oh yes, many have spoken to me of it. There is nothing like preserving your beauty." And at this she chuckled a little wildly with an air of savage triumph.

Chapter 64

So SHE TALKED for what must have seemed to Lily hour upon hour. When the younger woman betrayed any sign of leaving, Madame Blaise thrust her tall thin body between her and the door. Even if Lily had desired to speak she would have found small opportunity, for Madame Blaise never once stopped talking. It was as if all the talk of years, repressed and hidden, was suddenly rushing forth in a torrent. The room became intolerably stuffy from the burning gas. Lily's head began to ache and her face to grow more and more pale. If she had been less pleasant by nature she would have made her way by force past the old woman and out into the open air. As it was, she kept hoping, no doubt, that Madame Blaise would come to an end of her talk, that some one would come in and interrupt her . . . the maid perhaps . . . any one.

She no longer heard what Madame Blaise was saying. The talk came to her in fragments, the inexpressibly boring chatter of a cracked old woman. To break the monotony she took up the pictures on the mantelpiece and began to examine them. During a brief pause, she observed, "Your pictures are interesting, Madame Blaise. I should like to call again when I have more time, in order to see them all."

"Ah, yes," said the old woman. "So they are . . . so they are. The men . . . they were not all lovers you understand. But I might have had them for lovers by the raising of my finger."

"This one," said Lily, holding up the portrait of a heavily built man wearing the mustachios of a dragoon. "He is interesting."

"Yes . . . yes. He was a Spaniard . . . a nobleman, very aristocratic. Dead now. . . . Extraordinary how many of them are dead!"

Then all at once the attention of Madame Blaise was arrested by the most extraordinary change in her companion. So remarkable was the change that the old woman actually stopped talking and fell to observing the face of Madame Shane.

Lily held in her hand a small photograph, very faded and soiled, of a man in a black coat with sharp eyes, a high brow and a full black beard. It bore in one corner the stamp of a well-known photographer of the seventies, a gentleman with an establishment in the Galerie des Panoramas. It was a handsome face, fascinating, fanatic, which at once arrested the attention. Beyond all doubt it was the mate of a photograph which Julia Shane, dying, had left to her daughter. Across the face of the one Lily held in her hand was written, "À la Reine de la Nuit de son Cavalier Irlandais." The ink was faded, almost illegible.

"You find that gentleman especially interesting?" asked Madame Blaise in a tone of unbearable curiosity.

For a moment Lily did not reply. She regarded the photograph closely, turning it this way and that under the gaslight.

"Yes," she said at last in a low, hushed voice. "Who is he?"

Madame Blaise bridled. "He was a gentleman . . . very interesting," she said. "He admired me . . . greatly. The inscription? It was a joke between us. He was full of deviltry and fun (un vrai diable . . . tout gamin). I have forgotten what the joke was. . . . He was forced to leave the country by some unpleasantness. . . . I too went away for a time." And again her eyes narrowed in a mysterious look, invoking romantic, glamorous things. Lily, the picture still clasped in her hand, sat down weakly.

Above all else, old photographs have the power of calling up dead memories. It is so perhaps because they are so terribly, so cruelly, realistic. Those things which the memory, desiring to forget, succeeds in losing among the shadows of time, remain in a photograph so long as it exists . . . the posture of a head, the betraying affected gesture of a hand, the manner of carrying oneself, the arrogance of countenance, the habit of dress . . . all these things survive on a bit of paper no larger perhaps than the palm of one's hand.

The photograph with "À *la Reine de la Nuit*" written across it must have invoked forgotten things . . . memories of John Shane's savage temper and whimsical kindnesses, of terrible scenes between him and his proud wife, of his contempt for the anemic Irene and his admiration for the glowing Lily, of a thousand things distant yet appallingly vivid.

While Lily sat thoughtful and silent, Madame Blaise kept up a stream of hysterical chatter, turning crazily from one subject to another, from personalities to anecdotes, from advice to warning. Lily heard none of it. When she had recovered a little, she said, "This gentleman interests me. I wish you could tell me more of him."

But Madame Blaise shook her head ruefully. "I have forgotten so much," she said. "It is terrible how one forgets. Do you know?" And again the look of mad confidence came into her face. "I have forgotten his name. What is it he calls himself in the inscription?"

She took the photograph from Lily's hand and thrust it under the circle of light, holding it at arm's length and squinting in order to discern it properly. "Ah, yes," she said. "*Cavalier Irlandais*. . . . That was his name. I don't remember his other name, though I believe he had one." She paused, thoughtful, as if trying by a tremendous force of will to recapture the thing which had escaped her. "His father was Irish, you understand. . . . Strange I can't remember his name." So she talked on crazily, answering Lily's questions madly, tangling the answers hopelessly in a flood of insane philosophy and distorted observation. The look of mystery and the remnants of a grand manner persisted. Lily watched her with a look of intense curiosity as if she believed that, after all, the queer old creature might once have been young, —young, mysterious and lovely. But she learned little of the gentleman in the portrait. It was impossible for Madame Blaise to concentrate upon her subject. Lily learned only that the gentleman had been forced to leave the country following some unpleasantness arising out of a duel in which he had killed a relative . . . a cousin perhaps. She did not remember. He had been in politics too. That played a part in his flight. He returned once, Madame Blaise believed, but she did not remember why he had come back.

Altogether it was hopeless. Lily replaced the photograph on the high mantel, powdered her nose and drew on her gloves. Presently there came an opening in the flood of Madame Blaise' talk and Lily seized it sharply.

"I must really go, Madame Blaise. I have stayed much too long. It has been so interesting."

She rose and began to move slowly backward in the direction of the door, as if she feared to rouse the old woman to fresh outbursts. She made her departure gently, vanishing noiselessly; but she got no further than the inlaid music box when Madame Blaise, detecting her plan, sprang up and seized her arm fiercely with her thin old hands.

"Wait!" she cried. "There is one more thing I must show you . . . only one. It will take but a second."

The patient Lily acquiesced, though she kept up a mild protest. Madame

Blaise scurried away, rather sidewise as a crab moves, into a dark corner of the room where she disappeared for an instant through a door. When she returned, she bore two dusty paintings in oil. Each was surrounded by a heavy gilt frame and together the pair burdened the strength of the old woman. Her whole manner reeked of secrecy. With an air of triumph she smiled to herself as she took from the chair where she had been sitting a red silk handkerchief with which she dusted the faces of the two paintings. All this time she kept them turned from Lily. At last she stiffened her thin body suddenly and said sharply, "Now, look!"

Lily, bending low, discerned in the light from the fire the character of the two pictures. Each was the portrait of a woman, painted in the smooth, skilful, slightly hard manner of Ingres. Yet there was a difference, which the connoisseur's eye of Lily must have detected. They were cleverly done with a too great facility. But for that one might almost have said they were the work of a genius. Clearly the same woman had posed for both. In one she wore an enormous drooping hat, tilted a little over one eye. In the other she wore a barbaric crown and robes of Byzantine splendor.

Madame Blaise stood by with the air of a great art collector displaying his treasures. "They are beautiful, aren't they?" she said. "Superb! You know I understand these things. I have never shown them to any one in years. I am showing them to you because I know you understand these things. I have seen your house. I have seen your beautiful things. You see it is the same woman who posed for both. . . . The one is called 'The Girl in the Hat' . . . the other is 'The Byzantine Empress.' Theodora, you know, who was born a slave girl."

Chapter 65

LILY, IT SEEMED, had scarcely heard her. She had taken one of the pictures on her lap and was examining it minutely. She held it close to her and then at a little distance. Madame Blaise stood surveying her treasures proudly, her face lighted by a look of satisfaction at Lily's profound interest.

"I wonder," said the old woman presently, "if you see what I see."

For a moment Lily did not answer. She was still fascinated by the pictures. At last she looked up. "Do you mean the woman is like me? Did you see it too?"

Madame Blaise assumed a secretive expression. "Yes," she said. "I have known it all along . . . ever since I saw you. But I never told any one. I kept it as a secret for you." And she spread her skinny hands in an exhibitive gesture, full of satisfaction, of pride, even of triumph.

The likeness was unmistakable. Indeed, upon closer examination it was nothing short of extraordinary. It might have been the Lily of ten years earlier, when she was less heavy and opulent. The Byzantine Empress had the same soft bronze hair, the same green-white skin, the same sensuous red lips.

"It is like me when I was younger."

"Very much," observed Madame Blaise, and then with the air of an empress bestowing a dazzling favor, she added, "I am going to give them to you."

"But they are valuable," protested Lily. "I can see that. They are no ordinary paintings." She spoke without raising her eyes, continuing all the while to examine the pictures, first one and then the other as she frequently examined with infinite care the reflection in her mirror in the Rue Raynouard.

"I realize that you could not carry them home alone," continued Madame Blaise, ignoring her protests. "You might appear ridiculous. You might even be arrested on suspicion. But I shall have them sent round. I must give them to you. What would you have me do? When I die they will be sold. I have no relatives . . . no one. My sister is dead these ten years. I have no child . . . nothing. I am alone, you understand, absolutely alone. Would you have my pictures knocking about some art dealer's place?"

She shook her head savagely. "No, you must have them. You cannot refuse. It is the hand of God in the matter. I understand these things because there is in me something of the woman of all time. The pictures are for you. Nothing can dissuade me."

Again the good-natured Lily was forced to yield, simply by the force of the old woman's crazy will. She must have sensed the fantastic, uncanny quality of the entire affair, for she stirred uneasily and put The Byzantine Empress on the floor, face down. The Girl in the Hat lay across her knees, forgotten for the moment.

Madame Blaise had begun to walk up and down the room in a crazy fashion, muttering to herself. All at once she halted again before Lily.

"It was a famous woman who sat for those pictures," she said. "You could never imagine who she really was."

Vaguely, as if she had been absent from the room for a long time, Lily replied. "No. I'm sure I have no idea. How could I? She was evidently a great beauty."

A look of delight swept the countenance of the old woman. "Wait!" she cried. "Wait! I will make it easy for you. In one moment you will understand!" And she scurried away once more into the dusty closet from which she had brought the pictures. While she was absent Lily leaned back in her chair closing her eyes and pressing a hand against her forehead. For some time she remained thus and when, at last, she opened her eyes at the sharp command of Madame Blaise she found the old woman standing before her with the big hat of the girl in the picture drooped over one eye.

The effect was grotesque, even horrible. Madame Blaise had arranged the dress of black stuff so that her breasts and shoulders were exposed in the fashion of The Girl in the Hat; but the ripe full breasts of the girl in the picture were in the old woman sunken and withered, the color of dusty paper; the gentle soft curve of the throat was shrunken and flabby, and the soft glow of the face and the fresh carmine of the caressing, sensuous lips were grotesquely simulated with hard rouge, and powder which had caked in little channels on the wrinkled face of the old woman. Even the bit of hair which showed beneath the big hat was travestied horribly by dye. Madame Blaise simpered weakly in imitation of the mysterious, youthful smile which curved the lips of the girl in the picture.

There could be no mistake. The features were there, the same modeling, the same indefinable spirit. Madame Blaise was The Byzantine Empress and The Girl in the Hat. The caricature was cruel, relentless, bitter beyond the power of imagination. Lily's eyes widened with the horror of one who has seen an unspeakable ghost. She trembled and The Girl in the Hat slipped from her knee and fell with a clatter face downward upon The Byzantine Empress.

Madame Blaise had begun to walk up and down the room with the languid air of a mannequin. The big hat flopped as she moved. Turning her head coyly, she said, "I have not changed. You see, I am almost the same."

And then she fell to talking rapidly to herself, holding unearthly conversations with men and women who stood in the dark corners of the room among the innumerable pictures and bits of decaying bric-a-brac. Crossing the room she passed near Lily's chair where, halting for a second, she bent down until her painted cheek touched Lily's soft hair. "You see," she cried, pointing toward the dusty closet, "that one over there. . . . He would give his life to have me." She laughed a crazy laugh. "But no . . . not I. Never yield too easily and yield only for love. Live only for love." And she moved off again on her mad promenade, gibbering, bowing and smiling into the dusty corners.

In the midst of a tête-à-tête which the old woman held with an invisible beau whom she addressed as "Your Highness," Lily sprang up and ran toward the door. Opening it, she rushed through the upper hall down the stairway into the dark tunnel below. As the outer door slammed behind her, it shut in the sound of Madame Blaise' cracked singing, punctuated by peals of crazy laughter.

Lily did not stop running until she passed the gate of the little enclosure and stood, breathless and fainting with terror, beneath the lights of the Rue de l'Assomption.

Chapter 66

THEY PASSED the summer at Germigny l'Evec in the lodge on the terrace above the winding Marne. The little house at Houlgate kept its shutters up all through the hot months. It is true that the health of Madame Gigon was none too good. It is true that she might have benefited by the sea air. Although Lily mentioned the migration once or twice as the summer advanced she did not insist upon it. Madame Gigon, it appeared, preferred the house where she had always passed her summers, and Lily was content to remain there as the weeks passed through June and into a hot and breathless July. It seemed that, for the first time, she was tired. Indolent by nature, she had reserves of energy which could be roused when the occasion arose. But it appeared that this occasion was not one of sufficient importance; so she remained quietly, reading, walking by the Marne; sometimes in the early morning when the weather was not too hot, she even rode one of the Baron's horses along the paths of the wood on the opposite side of the river near Trilport.

For diversion the pair were visited by Jean who came romping down from St. Cyr for a brief holiday now and then, always looking handsome and behaving with the ferocity appropriate to a budding cavalryman. Ellen came too, but her visits tired her cousin, especially during the hot months. While she was there Lily pretended that she did not ride because Ellen made riding impossible for her. Ellen insisted upon riding at top speed. She searched for stone walls to jump. She even swam her horse through the Marne on one hot morning in July. Unlike Lily she made no effort to preserve her complexion. She became as tanned as an Indian and as hard as an athlete. Jean admired her enormously, and together they careered wildly across country; for Ellen sat her saddle lightly and as well as any man. Indeed she was as good as a boy for a companion. She even enjoyed the risqué barracks jokes which Jean told her. She listened to the ballads he sang, the bawdy ballads of the cavalry, old songs filled with the traditions of Napoleon's army . . . the same ballads which Lily sang to herself as she dressed for the last ball ever given at Cypress Hill.

Ellen could swear too, in English or in bad French. They became great friends. Lily saw them off in the mornings from her window, looking after them with an expression of mingled envy and regret in her dusky blue eyes. She must have envied the pair their youth. She was jealous of Ellen as she was always jealous of any one for whom Jean showed affection.

But an end came to the early morning excursions when Ellen in August sailed for New York to spend a month with her mother and father. They lived in a little house on Long Island; for Hattie Tolliver, since her children had become successful, no longer kept a rooming house in Manhattan.

"Pa is content now," Ellen said. "He's got a horse and a garden and chickens. That's what he always wanted. Ma is too. But it's different with her. She ought to have another complete family of children. She's never gotten over being a mother. She wants us to stay with her always. She can't bear having us grown up."

It was true. The more successful her children became, the less Hattie Tolliver saw of them.

"It is a warning," said Ellen, "never to be too fond of your children." She laughed ironically. "And yet, if it hadn't been for Ma, I don't suppose I'd be where I am . . . or Fergus or Robert either. She brought us up well. She made us ambitious." And she concluded the speech with the remark that "it was a damned funny world anyway." She had never seen any one who was content.

There had been a time, even a little while before, when she might have said that Lily was the supreme example of contentment, but that time seemed to have passed. Lily was clearly unhappy during that summer. She became more grave and quiet. She was content only when the Baron came down to stay for a week or two and rode with her through the mists of the early summer mornings. When he had gone again, the vague restlessness returned.

Madame Gigon grew to be more and more of a care; and added to the calamities, Criquette on short notice gave birth to a family of puppies of which it appeared the black and tan at the farm was the father. Somehow Madame Gigon took this as a betrayal on the part of the hitherto virginal Criquette. She complained of it as if Criquette had been her own daughter, as indeed she might well have been for the affection and care lavished upon her by the blind old woman. She succumbed completely to her arthritis and lay most of the day in a chair under the clipped linden trees, wearing an injured, fretful air when Lily was not by her side to talk or read to her. Indeed it appeared that between the riotous visits of Jean and Nellie a grayness had descended upon the lodge.

Chapter 67

IT MAY HAVE been that Madame Blaise played her part in the depression. After the night that Lily ran out of her house, she never saw the crazy old woman again, for a day or two later Madame Blaise, in a purple hat and a bright Venetian shawl, was led away on the promise of a wonderful adventure to a house in Versailles where well-to-do lunatics were cared for and allowed to indulge to the utmost their idiosyncrasies. Her guardian was none other than the handsome and distinguished M. de Cyon, who with his brother, a lawyer, looked after the old woman's property. She seemed completely happy in the new establishment, so M. de Cyon reported, because she found there an elderly wine merchant who believed himself descended from Henri Quatre and Diane de Poitiers, and therefore the rightful heir to the French throne. Together they spent their days plotting intrigues and revolutions by which he was to be set upon the throne with Madame Blaise as his consort. So there was no opportunity for Lily to wring from the old woman any further information regarding the photograph of the handsome gentleman in the black beard. The photograph together with the hundreds of other pictures, was packed away in a cavernous storehouse in Montparnasse when the furniture was cleared out of the chalet in the enclosure near the Trocadero and it was let to an Englishwoman interested in art. Life, as old Julia Shane said, was after all no story book in which everything was revealed. Every man had secrets which he carried into the grave.

But before Madame Blaise was led away, she kept her threat and sent round to the house in the Rue Raynouard The Byzantine Empress and The Girl in the Hat. The pictures were left there by the driver of a battered fiacre who went off immediately. To Lily, the pictures had become objects of horror. She would not see them. She bade the housekeeper put them away in the top room of the house where she could not possibly find them. When they arrived she was still in bed, suffering from a wild headache that did not leave her for days after the experience with Madame Blaise.

"It was horrible," she told Ellen. "More horrible than you can imagine, to see that old devil dancing before me like an omen . . . . a warning of old age. If you had seen her . . . so like me in the pictures . . . so like me even in the reality, like me as I might easily be some day. It was horrible . . . horrible!" And she buried her face in her hands.

Ellen, as usual, consulted Madame Gigon.

"She is really ill, this time," she said. "It isn't that she's just tired. She's frightened by something. She's much worse than she's ever been before."

And they sent for a physician, a great bearded man, recommended by Madame de Cyon, who diagnosed the case as a *crise de nerfs* and bade her go at once to the lodge in the country. The servants remarked that Madame seemed ill and tired for the first time in her life.

After a time she appeared to forget the mysterious photograph. It was clear that her father was destined to remain, as he had always been, a solitary, fascinating, malevolent figure translated by some turn of circumstance from the intrigues of the old world into the frontier life of the new. What lay in the past—murder, disgrace, conspiracy—must remain hidden, the secret of the dead and of a mad old woman who in her youth and beauty had been his mistress at the very moment that his bride struggled in the school at St. Cloud to learn the tricks of a great lady. Out of all the mystery only one thing seemed clear—that Lily was his favorite child; and now the reason seemed clear enough. By some whim of Fate she was like The Girl in the Hat, the lovely creature who was now Madame Blaise.

So the *crise de nerfs* persisted throughout the summer. Indeed there were times when it appeared that Lily was on the verge of a settled melancholia, times when she would walk in solitude for hours along the towpaths beneath the mottled limbs of the plane trees. Yet her beauty persisted. She might have been a goddess . . . Ceres . . . as she walked along the green path, bordered on one side by the Marne and on the other by waving fields of yellow grain.

As the weeks passed she suffered increasing annoyance through the persistent efforts of the Town to acquire the property at Cypress Hill. A dozen times a month letters arrived from Folsom and Jones, pressing letters that carried threats which Folsom and Jones passed along smoothly with all the suavity of true lawyers playing both ends against the middle. Indeed, from the tone of certain of the communications it appeared that they too, although they were Lily's agents and paid by her, believed that the interests of the Town surmounted those of their client. Its growth, they wrote, was stupendous. It was rapidly becoming one of the greatest steel centers in the world. If she could only be induced to return for a visit, she would understand the anxiety of the Town council to acquire the holdings at Cypress Hill. Surely she could understand that while sentiment was a commendable thing, it had its place. One could be too sentimental about a situation. The price offered was excellent. ("But not so excellent as it will be in another five years," thought Lily with a certain malice.) The house brought her no return. She only paid taxes on it. And so on, for page after page, letter after letter.

All this, no doubt, sounded reasonable enough, but Lily reading those letters aloud to Madame Gigon, who desired to be read aloud to no matter what the material, would murmur irritably, "Why the devil can't they leave me in peace? Go back and visit that place? My God! What for?" And then sarcastically, "To see Eva Barr, I suppose. I'm sure I'm not interested in their prosperity."

And she would write again that she had no intention of selling and that the more they annoyed her the less she was likely to alter her decision.

It may have been that she enjoyed the sense of power with which the possession of Cypress Hill endowed her . . . a feature she had not realized until it was shown her by Ellen. It may have been that she was simply tired and a little perverse and ill-natured. And it was true that she had not the slightest interest in the money involved. Indeed she had no idea how rich she was. Each year she spent what she desired to spend, and never did she come to the end of her income. What more could she desire? What could she do with more money?

But it is also more than probable that somewhere far back in the dark recesses of her consciousness, there were memories which kindled as she grew older, new fires of resentment against the Mills and the Town and all the things they stood for . . . memories of her mother's open hatred for the Harrisons and Judge Weissman, memories of a terrible night when men and women were shot down under the dead trees of the park, memories of an heroic, unattainable figure, wounded and bloody, but undefeated . . . a figure which doubtless grew in fascination as it receded into the past. It is true, too, that there is sometimes greater peace, even greater happiness, in renunciation than in fulfilment. What has never been a reality, may remain a fine dream. Krylenko had never been more than this.

And so the affair ran on until one evening in September Eustache, the farmer's boy, brought back from Meaux a small envelope bearing the post mark of the Town and addressed in the scrawled, illiterate handwriting of old Hennery. It recounted briefly the end of the house of Cypress Hill. It had caught fire mysteriously in the night and before dawn nothing remained save a hole in the ground filled with the scorched and blackened fragments of fine old carpets, mirrors, jade, crystals, carved chests and old chairs, all the beautiful things which encumbered the site of the proposed railroad station.

The mulatto woman, Hennery wrote with difficulty and the most atrocious spelling, swore that she saw two men running away from the house after the fire began. The police, he added, had been able to find no trace of them.

And the following day Lily received a polite letter from Folsom and Jones giving her a brief account of the catastrophe. They also mentioned the story told by the mulatto woman. They believed, however, that it was simply the crazy imagining of a demented old woman.

"Perhaps now," the letter concluded, "Miss Shane would desire to rid herself of a property that could no longer hold her even by ties of sentiment."

Chapter 68

LILY DID NOT sell and for a time the letters of Folsom and Jones ceased to arrive regularly. Since all her property in the Town was sold save the site of the house at Cypress Hill, there remained no cause for correspondence. Her money she invested through the American banks in Paris. She heard nothing more of the Town until November when she returned to the city. The prospect of a winter in Paris appeared to revive her spirits, and she went, as usual, to hear Ellen play her first concert of the season. That year Lilli Barr played a new Poem with the Colonne Orchestra under the bâton of the elegant Gabriel Pierné. The performance was not a great success. There was too little sympathy between the scholarly soul of the conductor and the vigorous, barbaric temperament of the pianist. Yet it was Ellen who came off best, bearing all the laurels, with all the simpering critics trotting attendance. "Mlle. Barr," they said, "has the perfect temperament for it . . . the superb adjustment of soul and intellect indispensable to the interpretation of such febrile music. It is music which requires a certain coldness of brain, a perception delicate and piercing . . . a thing of the nerves." And so they ran on, wallowing in their delight for the *mot juste*, praising more extravagantly than was either honest or in good taste. One or two saw an opportunity in the praise of hitting a back handed slap at the conductor and his orchestra.

It was M. Galivant, critic of the *Journal des Arts Modernes*, who hit upon the phrases "febrile music" and "delicate perception." He showed Lilli Barr the article in the salon after the concert, with the keys of the great piano barely cool from her hot fingers.

"Pish! Tosh!" she remarked to Lily who waited for her in the dressing room. "Did you see what Galivant has written? It's too exquisite for me. To hear them talk, you'd think I took the veil for months at a time just to meditate what my music is all about. I know what it's about and I don't want praise that's written before they hear me play, just because I help their modern music along. Nerves! Nerves! I haven't got such things!"

Yet she was, as always after a concert, tense and nervous, filled with a terrible energy which would not let her sleep until dawn. To-night she wore a long tight gown of cloth of silver, without sleeves and girdled by a single chain of rhinestones. With her dark hair drawn tightly back, she resembled a fine greyhound—lean, muscular, quivering.

"At least they liked it," said Lily, "judging from the applause." She sat waiting in a long cloak of black velvet, held together with silver clasps.

There was a sudden knock at the door and Lily murmured "Come in." It was the porter, a lean, sallow man with a stoop and enormous black mustaches.

"There is a gentleman to see Madame l'artiste," he said.

Ellen turned. "Who is it?"

The man grimaced. "How should I know? He says he knows you."

A shadow of irritation crossed Ellen's smooth brow. "If he wants to see me, tell him to send in his name." And then to Lily as the porter withdrew, "You see what fame is. The porter doesn't even know my name. He calls me Madame l'artiste . . . Madame indeed! He hasn't even bothered to read the bills."

The fellow returned again, this time opening the door without the courtesy of a knock.

"His name, Madame, is 'arrisong."

Ellen pursed her lips thoughtfully and struck a match on the sole of her slipper, holding the flame to the cigarette in her strong slim fingers.

"Harrison? . . . Harrison?" she repeated, holding the cigarette between her lips and the lighted match poised. "I don't know any Harrison. . . . Tell him to come in."

The stranger must have been waiting just outside the door, for at the word he stepped timidly inside. He was dressed in black and wore a derby hat set well on the back of his head. Over one arm hung an umbrella. He was rather sallow and macabre despite his plumpness. There was the faint air of an undertaker about him. He might have been any age.

As he advanced he smiled and, observing Lily, his countenance assumed an expression of surprise. Ellen gave no sign of recognition. It was Lily who stirred suddenly and stood up, her face glowing with a genuine spontaneous pleasure.

"Willie Harrison!" she cried. "Where have *you* come from?"

At the sound of his name Ellen's smooth brow wrinkled in a slight frown. "Willie Harrison," she murmured, and then joined Lily in welcoming him.

For a moment he stood awkwardly regarding the two women. Then he said, "I came to your concert, Ellen. . . . I saw it advertised in the *Herald*. I knew you were Lilli Barr." He chortled nervously. "Funny how famous you are now! Nobody ever would have thought it!"

The sight of Willie appeared suddenly to loosen all Ellen's taut nerves. She sat down, leaned back in the chair, and laughed. "Yes. I fooled them, didn't I?" she said. "I fooled them." And a sort of grim satisfaction entered her voice.

Lily was smiling now, out of sheer pleasure at the sight of Willie. It amused her probably more than anything that could have happened to her at that moment.

"But what on earth are you doing in Paris?"

From the tone of her voice, it was clear that she regarded his presence as a sort of miracle. . . . That Willie Harrison should have had the energy to cross the Atlantic and wander about alone in Paris.

Willie sat down, rather stiffly, and told his story. He was with a Cook's party. His tour included London, Paris, the château country and Switzerland. He was leaving shortly.

"It's been a wonderful trip," he remarked, his plump face all aglow. "I'd no idea how much country there was over here."

"Yes," said Ellen, "there's a good deal, taking it all in all." She said this with an undisguised air of patronizing him. It was she who was great now, she who held the whip hand. She was no longer an awkward girl in a home-made ball gown so unpretentious that men like Willie Harrison failed to notice her.

But Willie failed to understand. He was childishly excited over Paris. "It's a great city!" he observed, fingering nervously the ruby clasp of his watch chain. "A great city!"

Lily stood up suddenly.

"Willie," she said, "come home and have supper with us." And turning to Ellen she added, "Paul will be waiting for us. He must be there already." And to Willie, "Paul is Monsieur Schneidermann, a friend of Ellen's and mine."

Willie rose. "I don't know," he said timidly. "Maybe you aren't prepared for me. Maybe I'd be in the way. I didn't mean to force my way in on anything when I called. It was just for the sake of old times."

Lily moved toward the door trailing the magnificent cloak of black and silver. She thrust her arm through his. "Come along, Willie," she said. "No nonsense. Why, we grew up together."

And they went out, Ellen following them in her plum-colored wrap, to the motor which bore on its polished door the crest of the Baron.

Throughout the journey Willie kept poking his head in and out of the closed motor, drinking in the sights along the way . . . the hushed, shadowy mass of the Madeleine, the warm glow before Maxims', the ghostly spaces of the Place de la Concorde, the white palaces of the Champs Élysées. Ellen in her corner remained sulky and taciturn, smoking savagely. Lily talked merrily, pointing out from time to time sights which she deemed worthy of Willie's appreciation. He seemed not to be listening.

"It's a wonderful place," he kept saying over and over again. "It's a wonderful place." And a kind of pathetic and beautiful awe crept into his thin voice. It seemed that he had no other words than "wonderful." He kept repeating it again and again like a drunken man holding a conversation with himself.

At Numero Dix, Rue Raynouard, Willie underwent the experience of every stranger. He entered by the unpretentious door and found himself suddenly at the top of a long, amazing stairway which led down to a drawing-room all rosy with the glow of warm light. Half-way down the stairs candles burned in sconces against the dull paneling. From below drifted the faint sound of music . . . a Debussy nocturne being played with caressing fingers in the shadowy, dim-lit spaces of the drawing-room.

"Paul is here," observed Ellen and led the way down the long stairs.

Lily followed and close at her silver heels Willie Harrison, divested now of his derby and umbrella. Half-way down, he paused for a moment and Lily, conscious that he had ceased to follow her, waited too. As she turned she saw that he was listening. There was a strange blurred look in his pale eyes . . . the look of one awaking from a long sleep.

"It's beautiful," he said reverently. "My God! It's beautiful!" A kind of dignity seized him. He was no longer gauche and timid. He stared at Lily who stood with her back to a mirror, the black and silver cloak thrown carelessly back from her voluptuous white shoulders, her handsome head crowned with gold bronze hair. And then all at once the tears shone in his eyes. He leaned against the paneling.

"I understand now," he said softly. "I understand . . . everything. I know now how little I must have counted. . . . me and all the Mills together."

And in Lily's eyes there was mirrored another picture . . . that of a vast resounding shed bright with flames and thick with the odor of soot and half-naked bodies . . . Willie, eternally fingering the ruby clasp of his watch chain, herself turning the rings round and round on her slim fingers, and in the distance the white, stalwart body of a young Ukrainian steel worker . . . a mere boy . . . but beautiful. Krylenko was his name . . . Krylenko . . . Krylenko . . . It was a long time ago, more than fourteen years. How time flew!

Lily's dusky blue eyes darkened suddenly and the tears brimmed over. Perhaps it came to her then for the first time . . . a sense of life, of a beautiful yet tragic unity, of a force which swept both of them along helplessly.

All at once she held her handkerchief, quite shamelessly, to her eyes. "We are beginning to be old, Willie," she said softly. "Do you feel it too?"

And she turned and led the way downwards. The music had ceased and the voices of Ellen and Paul Schneidermann rose in dispute. They were arguing with a youthful fire over the merits of the new concerto.

"Here," came Ellen's voice. "This part. It is superb!" And then the sound of a wild, ecstatic sweep of music, terrifying and beautiful. "You understand the strings help a great deal. Part of it lies in the accompaniment." And she began singing the accompaniment as she played.

But Lily with her companion trooping along behind her, did not interrupt the discussion. They made their way, enveloped in a peaceful silence, into the dining-room where supper waited them—some sort of hot stuff in a silver dish with an alcohol flame burning beneath it, an urn steaming with hot chocolate, a bowl of whipped cream, a few sandwiches—superlatively French sandwiches, very thin and crustless with the faintest edge of buff-colored paté showing between the transparent slices of white bread. It was all exquisite, perfect, flawless.

"Sit down," said Lily, as she flung off the black and silver cloak. "Sit down and tell me all about yourself."

Willie drew up a chair. "I shan't be able to stay very late," he said. "You see, I'm leaving early in the morning." He watched Lily fumbling with the lamp beneath the urn. She was plumper than he had expected. Indeed she was almost fat. There was a faint air of middle-age about her, indiscernible but unmistakably present.

"What about yourself?" he asked politely. "What has your life been?"

Lily kept on turning and pushing at the silver burner. "My life?" she said. "Well, you see it all about you, Willie." She made a little gesture to include the long, softly glittering rooms, Ellen, the piano, Paul Schneidermann. "It's just been this," she said. "Nothing more . . . nothing less. Not much has happened." For a moment she stopped her fumbling and sat thoughtful. "Not much has happened," and then after another pause, "No, scarcely anything."

There was a sudden, sharp silence, filled by the sound of Ellen's music. She had become absorbed in it, utterly. It was impossible to say when she would come in to supper.

Then Willie, in an attempt at courtliness, strained the truth somewhat. "You don't look a day older, Lily . . . not a day. . . . Just the same. It's remarkable."

His companion lifted the lid of the chafing dish. "Some hot chicken, Willie?" she asked, and when he nodded, "I must say you look younger . . . ten years younger than the last time I saw you. Why, you look as though you'd forgotten the Mills . . . completely."

Willie laughed. It was a curious elated laugh, a little wild for all its softness.

"I have," he said. "You see I'm out of the Mills for good. I've been out of them for almost seven years."

Lily looked at him. "Seven years," she said, "seven years! Why that's since the strike. You must have gotten out at the same time."

"I did," he replied, "I own some stock. That's all. Judge Weissman is dead, you know. When mother died, the old crowd went out of it for good. All the Mills are now a part of the Amalgamated."

Chapter 69

THUS IN A few words, he sketched the passing of one epoch and its succession by another. The day of the small private enterprise in the Town had passed, succeeded by the day of the great corporation. Everything was owned now by capitalists, by stockholders who never saw the Mills, to whom the workers of the Flats were little more than mythical creatures, animated engines without minds or souls, whose only symbol of existence was the dividend twice a year. Machines they were . . . machines . . . dim machines . . . not in the least real or human.

Most of the tale Willie omitted. He did not tell of the monkey-faced little man who came to the Town representing the Amalgamated. Nor did he tell of the monkey-faced man's address to the Chamber of Commerce in which he talked a great deal of Jesus and declared that religion was what the world most needed, religion and a sense of fellowship between men. He did not tell of how the Amalgamated broke the strike by buying all the wretched houses and turning out the strikers, men, women and children. He omitted the blacklisting, the means by which the strikers were prevented from obtaining work elsewhere. He did not observe that the power which money gave Judge Weissman, himself and his mother, was as nothing compared to the power of the Amalgamated—a vast incalculable power founded upon gold and the possession of property. Nor did he say that the passing of the Mills had killed Mrs. Julis Harrison . . . a thing which was as true as truth. These things were to him of no importance. He was now simply "an average citizen" minding his own business.

All Willie said was, "When mother died, the old crowd went out of it for good."

In the drawing-room Ellen had been completely captured by the concerto. She was playing it all over again, from beginning to end, rapturously, savagely. Schneidermann lay among the cushions of the divan, his lean figure sprawled languidly, his dark eyes closed.

"And what do you do now?" asked Lily. "You must do something to occupy yourself."

Willie's plump face brightened. "I have a farm," he said. "I raise ducks and chickens." A slow smile crept over Lily's face. "It's a success too," he continued. "You needn't laugh at it. I make it pay. Why, I made this trip on last year's profits. And I have a great deal of fun out of it." He smiled again with an air of supreme contentment. "It's the first time I've ever done what I wanted to do."

Lily regarded him with a faint air of surprise. It may have been that she guessed then for the first time, that he was not after all a complete fool. He, too, like Ellen, like herself, even like Irene, had escaped in spite of everything.

They had been talking thus for half an hour when Ellen, followed by Paul Schneidermann, joined them. Willie stood up nervously.

"Paul," said Lily, "Mr. Harrison—Mr. Harrison, Monsieur Schneidermann." They bowed. "You are both steel manufacturers," she added with a touch of irony, "You will find much in common."

Willie protested. "No longer," he said. "Now I am a farmer."

"And I," said Schneidermann, "have never been. I am a musician. . . ." Ellen laughed scornfully and he turned to her with a curious blushing look of self-effacement, "Perhaps," he said, "dilettante is a better word."

For a time they talked—the stupid, polite conversation that occurs between strangers; and then, the proprieties satisfied, Ellen and Paul drifted quickly back into the realm of music. Lily devoted herself to Willie Harrison.

"It was too bad," he remarked, "about the house at Cypress Hill."

Lily leaned forward on the table holding up one white wrist to shield her eyes from the light of the candles. "Yes," she said. "I'm sorry . . . sentimentally, I suppose. I should never have gone back to it. It was perfectly useless to me. But I'm sorry it's gone. I suppose it, too, was changed."

"You would never have known it," said Willie. "It was completely black . . . even the white trimmings." He leaned forward confidentially. "Do you know what they say? They say in the Town that some one was hired to burn it, so that you would be willing to sell."

For a moment Lily remained silent. Her hand trembled a little. She looked across at Ellen to see whether she had been listening. Her cousin was plainly absorbed in her argument.

"They can have it now," said Lily, with an intense bitterness. "I begrudge them even the taxes I have to pay on it. But they'll have to pay a good price," she added quietly. "I'll squeeze the last cent out of them."

It was the end of their conversation, for Willie glancing at his watch, announced that he must leave. Lily accompanied him up the long stairs to the unpretentious door. There he hesitated for a moment on bidding her good night.

"You have changed," he said. "I can see it now."

Lily smiled vaguely, "How?"

He fell to fumbling with the ruby clasp. "I don't know. More calm, I think. . . . You're not so impatient. And you're like a Frenchwoman. . . . Why, you even speak English with an accent."

"Oh, no, Willie . . . I'm not like a Frenchwoman. I'm still American. There's a good deal of my mother in me. I've realized it lately. It's that desire to run things. You understand what I mean. . . . Perhaps it's because I'm getting to the age where one can't live upon the food of youth." She laughed suddenly. "We Americans don't change. What I mean is that I'm growing old."

Willie shook hands politely and went out, leaving Lily in the doorway to watch his neat figure, silhouetted against the glow of light from the Café des Tourelles, until he reached the corner and disappeared.

It was the last time she ever saw him so it was impossible for her to have known the vagaries of his progress after he left the door of Numero Dix. Yet this progress held a certain interest. At the corner of the Rue Franklin, Willie hailed with his umbrella a passing taxicab and bade the driver take him to an address in the Rue du Bac. It was not the address of the American Hotel; on the contrary it designated a three story house with a café on the first floor and lodgings above. In one of these lived a discreet lady who frequented the Louvre by day and employed Art as a means of making the acquaintance of quiet gentlemen hanging about the fringes of tourist parties.

Indeed, she could have written an interesting compendium on the effect of art and Paris upon the behavior of soberly dressed, mousy gentlemen.

For Willie, with the death of his mother and the passing of the Mills, had begun to live . . . in his own awkward timid fashion, to be sure . . . but none the less he had begun to live.

As he sped on his way in the crazy taxicab, it became more and more evident that his mood was changed by the encounter with Lily. He sat well back in the cab, quietly, immersed in the thought. The dim white squares, empty and deserted now; the flamboyant houses of the section near the Étoile, the light-bordered Seine, the tall black skeleton of the Eiffel Tower . . . all these things now left him, for some strange reason, unmoved. They swept by the windows of the cab unnoticed. Willie was thinking of something else.

As the taxi turned into the ghostly spaces of the Place de la Concorde, Willie stirred himself suddenly and thrust his head out of the window.

"*Cocher! Cocher! Chauffeur!*" he cried suddenly in atrocious French. "*Allez a l'hotel Americain.*"

The mustachioed driver grunted, turned his cab, and sped away once more as if pursued by the devil; and presently he pulled up before the American Hotel, a respectable hostelry frequented by school teachers and temperance workers.

An hour later he lay chastely in his own bed, awake and restless in the dark, but still innocent. And in the Rue du Bac the sophisticated lady waited until long after midnight. At length, after cursing all Americans, she took her lamp from the window and went angrily to bed.

Chapter 70

AT TWO O'CLOCK in the house in the Rue Raynouard, Ellen came in to sit on the edge of her cousin's bed and discuss the happenings of the day.

"I guess," she observed, "Willie will be able to tell them a good story when he gets back to the Town. His mouth fairly hung open all the time when he was here."

Lily smiled. "I don't know," she replied, braiding her heavy bronze hair. "From what he tells me, he's in the backwater now. There are a lot of people there who have never heard of us. I suppose Willie and you and I are just back numbers so far as the Town is concerned."

After Ellen had gone to her own room, Lily settled herself on the chaise longue and, wrapped in a peignoir of pale blue chiffon all frothy with old lace the color of ivory, she took from her desk the enameled box, opened it and read the worn clippings. The pile had grown mightily. There were a score of new clippings. The headlines had increased in size and the editorials were an inch or two longer. The man was progressing. He was denounced with a steadily increasing hatred and bitterness. It was clear that he had become a national figure, that he was a leader in the battle against the roaring furnaces.

For a long time she lay with her eyes closed . . . thinking. And at last, hours after the rest of the rest of the house had grown still and dark, she sighed, replaced the clippings in the box and locked them once more into her desk. Then she settled herself to writing a letter over which she spent a long time, biting the end of the silver penholder from time to time with her firm white teeth. When at last the effort satisfied her, she placed it in an envelope and addressed it to Sister Monica in the Carmelite Convent at Lisieux. It was the hundredth letter she had written, letters in which she abased herself and begged forgiveness, letters to which there was never any reply save an unforgiving and relentless silence. It was like dropping the pale gray envelopes into a bottomless crevasse.

In the following May, Ellen went to Munich. It was the first step in a grand tour of the German cities. She would visit Salzburg, Cologne, Vienna, Leipsic. She would call upon Schönberg, Busoni, Richard Strauss, Pfitzner, von Schilling. . . . If the spirit moved her, she might even penetrate Russia. And certainly she would go to the festival at Weimar. All this was included in the plan she set forth to Lily. There was no schedule. She would simply progress from one place to another as her fancy dictated. She knew no German but she would learn it, as she had learned French, by living among the people. She went alone. Therefore she would have to learn the language.

The expedition was singularly characteristic of all her life. When she found that the Town was unendurable she had reversed the plan of her pioneer ancestors and turned east instead of west, to seek a new world which to her was far more strange than the rolling prairies of the west had been to her great-grandfather. When the traveling salesman, whom she used as a stepping stone, fell by the wayside and departed this life she was free to go unhindered on her own roving way, fortified by the experience of a few years of married life. She owned no fixed home. On the contrary, she moved about restlessly . . . exploring, conquering, exhausting now this city, now that one. She was, it seemed, possessed of a veritable demon of restlessness, of energy, of a sharp inquiring intelligence. It was this quality, stimulated constantly by an overpowering curiosity, which sent her pioneering into the world of new music which Lily disliked so intensely. She explored those regions which musicians of a more contemplative and less restless nature dared not enter. It was as if she were possessed by a Gargantuan desire to devour all the world within a single lifetime.

Once in Paris she said to Lily, "You know, I am obsessed by a terrible sense of the shortness of life. It is impossible to know and experience all that I wish to know."

But this was as near as she came to a contemplative philosophy. She had no time for reflection. The hours she spent with the indolent Lily inevitably fired her with a fierce and resentful unrest. It was then that she grew impatient, bad-tempered, unendurable. It was the descent of one of these black moods which drove her from the peaceful solitude of the house at Germigny upon a new voyage of exploration.

And so it happened that Lily and Madame Gigon were alone on the peaceful summer evening when Eustache, the red-cheeked farmer's boy, returning on his bicycle through the rain from Meaux, brought the final edition of the *Figaro* containing a short paragraph of the most enormous importance to all the world.

Madame Gigon had been installed days before on the first floor of the lodge, because she was no longer able to leave her bed and insisted upon being placed where her ears would serve her to the greatest advantage. The door of her room opened outward upon the terrace above the Marne and here, just inside the door, sat Lily when Eustache arrived.

She opened the *Figaro* and spread it across her knees.

Madame Gigon, hearing the rustle of the paper, stirred and said peevishly, "What is new to-day?"

"Not much of importance," said Lily, and after a pause. "The Archduke of Austria has been assassinated. Shall I read you that?"

"Certainly," replied the old woman with a fierce impatience. "Certainly!"

It was only part of a daily game . . . this asking Madame Gigon what she would have read to her; because in the end the entire journal was read aloud by Lily—the daily progress of the celebrated case of Madame Caillaux, the signed articles by this or that politician, the news of the watering places . . . Deauville, Vichy, Aix, Biarritz, the accounts of the summer charity fêtes, the annual ball at the Opéra, the military news . . . everything was read to the old woman. For Madame Gigon found a keen delight in the recognition of a name among those who had been present at this fête or were stopping at that watering-place. After her own fashion, the blind old woman reduced all France to the proportions of a village. To her, the Caillaux trial became simply an old wives' tale, a village scandal.

So Lily read of the Archduke's assassination and Madame Gigon listened, thoughtfully, interrupting her occasionally with a clucking sound to indicate how terrible the affair really was. She understood these things, being a Bonapartist. It was as if the Prince himself had been shot down. It was the natural result of the Republican movement, of socialism, which was, after all, the same thing. Just another example of what these wild ideas might lead to.

"These are sad times," remarked Madame Gigon when Lily had finished reading. "There is no such thing as law and order . . . no such thing as respect and regard for rank. A wild confusion (*une melée sauvage*) to see who can gain the most wealth and make the greatest display. Money!" the old woman muttered. "That's it. Money! If you make a fortune out of chocolate or soap, that is enough to put you into the government. Good God! What times are ahead!"

To this harangue, Lily listened absently. It was all monotonously familiar to her. Madame Gigon had said it a thousand times. Every evil she attributed to "these dirty times." She concluded by saying, "Crazy Madame Blaise is right after all. There will be a war . . . She was right. . . . There will be."

While she was speaking, Lily tore open the only interesting letter among the dozen. Quietly she read it to herself. When she had finished she interrupted Madame Gigon.

"I have a letter from M. de Cyon," she said, "about some furniture I was selling. He writes that Madame is ill again with indigestion . . . quite seriously this time."

Madame Gigon made a little grunting noise. "Nadine eats too much . . . I have told her so a dozen times but she will not listen. A woman as fat as that. . . ."

And from the superior pinnacle of her great age, Madame allowed the sentence to trail off into unspeakable vistas of Madame de Cyon's folly. At the end of a long time during which they both sat silently in the dripping quiet of the summer evening Madame Gigon said explosively, "She will go off suddenly one of these days . . . like that," and she snapped her fingers weakly.

At the sound Criquette and Michou got up lazily, stretched themselves, and waddled close to her chair. For a moment she scratched their heads with groping fingers and then turning to Lily said, "It is time for their milk. . . . And see to it, my child, that they have a little cream in it."

Lily rose and called the dogs inside the lodge. Across the river in the tiny church, the old curé, M. Dupont, rang the vesper bell. Behind the cropped willows along the Marne the last glow faded above the rolling fields of wheat. Inside the house Lily was singing softly, "O, *le coeur de ma mie est petit, tous p'tit, p'tit.*" There was no other sound.

Presently, Madame Gigon leaned back in her bed and called to Lily. "To-morrow," she said, "you might ask M. Dupont to call on me. It has been two days since he was here."

Chapter 71

UPON GERMIGNY L'EVEC, removed from the highroad and the railway, the war descended at first slowly, with the unreality of a vague dream, and then with a gathering, ponderous ferocity of an appalling nightmare. In the beginning even the farmer and his men, familiar with the army and with military service, could not believe it. Still there was the memory of 1870, said the pessimists. It was not impossible.

"Ah, but war is unthinkable," said Lily to Madame Gigon. "The days of war are over. It could not happen. They would not dare to permit it."

But Madame Gigon, again from the pinnacle of her superior age, replied, "My child. You have never seen a war. You know nothing of it. It is not at all impossible. You see, I can remember well 1870."

All the talk, it seemed, turned back at once to 1870. Sooner or later every one returned to it—M. Dupont, the curé, who had served at Metz with Mac-Mahon, the farmer and his wife, even Eustache. 1870 was no longer a half-century away. It became only yesterday, an event which was just finished the evening before at sunset. And slowly it became clear that war was not at all an impossibility. The order for mobilization made it a reality so hideous, so monstrous, as to be utterly lacking in reality. In the château and at the farm, there were no longer any barriers. The cook and the farmer's wife, came and sat on the terrace, red-faced and weeping. In the quiet of the evening there drifted across the wheatfields the ominous whistling of trains which followed no schedule, and from the distant high-road the faint sound of an unceasing procession of taxicabs and omnibuses rushing east and north through Pantin, through Meaux, on to La Ferté-sous-Jouarre.

From Paris came three letters, two by messenger, and orderly of the Baron, the other by post. One was from the Baron himself and one was from M. de Cyon.

"It is all more grave than any of us suspect," wrote the Baron. "Unhappily, Dear Lily, it is impossible for me to see you. I cannot leave my regiment. You cannot come to Vincennes. We must try to endure all this in the fashion of philosophers. It is not, you understand, as if it had been unexpected. It has been slow—more slow than any one hoped—in arriving.

"As for what may come of it, to me or to Jean. What is there to do? We are all helpless as if caught in a web. May God be with us all! Jean will be with me. Your heart can be assured that I shall do all it is possible to do for him. The rest remains with the good God. I would give . . . What would I give? Ten years or more of my life to have seen you before going away. But that, it seems, is impossible. So we must wait until it is possible.

"We are leaving to-night. I have sent old Pierre to see to it that you and Madame Gigon are brought safely back to Paris. Germigny is safe from the Germans, but there is always a chance. Who can say what will happen? Good God! The suddenness of it!

"Au revoir, dear Lily, in haste. A thousand kisses from thy Césaire."

It was the first time that there had been in all their correspondence even the faintest note of anything more compromising than a proper friendship between the Baron and the woman who had made his old cousin, Madame Gigon, comfortable for life. It was this which somehow gave the letter a gravity more terrible than any hint of foreboding contained in its crisp white pages. It was as if the barriers of convention had suddenly been destroyed, as if they had gone down in ruin to reveal life in all the primitive directness of unfettered nature. It seemed to say, "Nothing matters any longer save those things which have to do with life, death and love."

"The letter from M. de Cyon was more calm and dignified, the proper letter of a diplomat. It was the letter of a distinguished, white-haired gentle-man.

"You must leave Germigny as soon as it is possible. I write you this in confidence and beg you not to arouse a panic among the peasants and the citizens of Meaux. It is war, Madame, and no one can say what will happen. Your security is of the deepest concern to me. I beg you to waste no time. Go on foot, by ox-cart, by train—however it is possible, but go. A battle is no place for so beautiful a woman."

That was all, yet it contained hints and innuendoes of things too terrible for the imagination. M. de Cyon undoubtedly knew more than he chose to reveal in his circumspect note. He was, to be sure, near to the Ministry of War.

There was a letter too from Jean, breathless and full of spirit, the letter of a young warrior eager for battle, forgetful of all else, of God, of his mother, of everything save the prospect of fighting.

"Dear Mama," he wrote, "we are leaving to-night for the front. I shall return perhaps a captain. Think of it! Thy Jean a captain! Do not worry. Our troops are in excellent condition. I fancy the war will be over in a fortnight. I am in Césaire's company. I think of you, of course.

"Thy Jean."

With the three letters in her hand Lily left Madame Gigon and set out to walk the white towpath at the edge of the river. On the far side the farm appeared deserted as if suddenly its occupants had been overcome by a sleep of enchantment. The oxen were nowhere to be seen. The fowls were gone. The house lay shuttered and empty as a house of the dead. Above the towpath, the château likewise stood silent and empty. In all the landscape there was no sign of life, no dogs, no chickens, no crying children. And as she walked she turned her head presently and saw, leaving the far side of the farm, a lumbering two-wheeled cart piled high with furniture,—mattresses, a sewing machine, a few chairs, and swinging underneath, little cages of osier in which were crowded the barnyard fowls. Tied to the wheels, three goats followed the gentle motion of the cart. Fat Madame Borgue, the farmer's wife, trudged by the side guiding the slow-gaited oxen with a long wand, and high up, perched on a truss of straw, sat her mother, an immensely old and wrinkled woman, with Madame Borgue's baby in her arms. They were deserting, driven before the straggling columns of refugees which had appeared like magic during the early morning along the high-roads from La Ferté to Meaux. There could be no doubt. The farm and the château were empty. At Germigny only Lily and Madame Gigon remained behind.

Chapter 72

It appeared that the discovery made no impression upon Lily, for she continued on her way along the deserted river path without stopping, without even checking the mad speed at which she walked. Her manner was that of one fleeing before a terror from which there is no escape. When she had reached a spot opposite the little island that divided the waters of the river, she halted suddenly by a clump of hazel bushes and flung herself down upon the thick grass in the shadow of the plane trees. She began to weep, soundlessly with long, racking, silent sobs which shook her whole body as if she had been stricken by some frightful pain.

Far off a train whistled distantly. The bright red kepis of the soldiers showed in rows like poppies at the windows of the coaches. On the white solid bridge at Trilport there appeared a double procession; one column, hot, dusty, bedraggled, full of crying, exhausted women and children, moved toward Paris. The other was gay and bright. The men wore bright red trousers and bright red caps. It moved briskly forward. The guns were like a field of wheat come suddenly to life, moving gallantly to throw itself upon the reaper.

After a time, Lily sat up, her hair all blown and disheveled, her dark eyes bright from weeping. She read the letters over and over absorbing the same phrases . . . May God be with us all! . . . It is all more grave than any of us suspect . . . A thousand kisses from thy Césaire . . . It is war, Madame, and no one can say what will happen . . . A battle is no place for a beautiful woman . . . Perhaps I shall return . . . Perhaps I shall return a captain . . . Think of it! Thy Jean a captain! . . . Thy Jean! . . . Thy Jean . . . Thy Césaire! . . . Thy Jean! Thy precious Jean!

Slowly she refolded the letters and thrust them into the bosom of her dress and then, as if her emotion were too strong for silence, she said aloud. . . . "Me . . . myself . . . Why do they worry about me? . . . Do they think that I am afraid?" She laughed suddenly. "Afraid of what?"

Besides it was impossible to flee with a sick old woman and no means of conveyance. She laughed again and said bitterly, "What do they think . . . that I am a magician?"

Lying there in the deep grass, it must have occurred to her all at once that her whole life had been pillaged and destroyed because an Austrian archduke was shot in a little hole called Serajevo. Madame Gigon dying. Césaire and Jean on their way to destruction. Who remained? What remained? De Cyon, perhaps. No one else. No one in all the world. The years of her life come to an end like this . . . that everything she loved, everything she cherished, might be swept away overnight like so much rubbish into a dustbin. As if she were no more than a poor forsaken flower vender or charwoman! What was money now? What were beautiful things? What was all her life?

And she flung herself down once more, sobbing wildly as she had sobbed another time in the old house at Cypress Hill, when all at once, she had sensed the tragedy of a whole lifetime, as if she stood in a vast plain surrounded only by loneliness.

At dusk she arose slowly and, from long habit put her hair in order, smoothed her dress, and set out upon her homeward journey, walking slowly, with feet from which all youth had gone. When she arrived at the lodge, the traces of her weeping had disappeared and she entered proudly and in silence.

For a moment there came into her pale lovely face a fleeting likeness to her mother, a certain determination that was inseparable from the rugged countenance of the stoic Julia Shane.

The house was still because old Madame Gigon had slipped out of her bed and was lying asleep on the floor. When Lily attempted to rouse the old woman, she discovered that she was not sleeping at all but unconscious, and suddenly Lily too slipped to the floor, buried her face in her hands and wept noisily and without restraint. The sound of her sobbing penetrated the breathless garden and the distant empty rooms of the château, but there was no one to answer it. The only sound was the triumphant, ironic whistle of a steel locomotive, its belly hot with red flames, its nostrils breathing fire and smoke.

At last she lifted Madame Gigon into the bed by the window and, lying by the side of the unconscious old woman, she fell into a profound sleep.

Chapter 73

IT WAS DARK when she awoke and rose wearily to light a lamp. The first flame of the match illuminated the room. It revealed all the familiar furniture . . . the chintz covered chairs, the bright curtains of *toile de Juouy*, the bowl of ghostly white phloxes by the window. Everything was the same save that Madame Gigon . . . old Tante Louise . . . lay unconscious upon the bed, and the house was so still that the silence was suffocating.

She went into the kitchen and prepared a mixture of egg, milk and brandy which she fed the old woman through a tube. She understood the care of Madame Gigon. The old woman had been like this before. Lily, herself, ate nothing, but took from the cupboard by the window a bottle of port and drank a brimming glass. And after a time she went outside to listen to the silence.

With her black cloak wrapped about her she sat there for a long time. The farm, the tiny inn, the houses of the village were black and silent. There hung in the atmosphere the ghostly feeling of a house suddenly deserted by its inhabitants, standing empty and alone. The mournfulness was overwhelming. After a time she lighted a cigarette and smoked it, holding the ember away from her and regarding it at a little distance as if the faint light in some way dissipated the loneliness.

For a time she regarded the distant horizon and the queer flashes of color like heat lightning which appeared at intervals. Sometimes the rising night wind bore toward her a faint sound like that of distant thunder. And then all at once, there appeared in the house by the village church a bright light. It was a lamp placed close to the open window so that the rays piercing the darkness traversed the river, penetrated the low branches of the plane trees and enveloped Lily herself in a faint glow.

She watched it for a time with a breathless curiosity. The cigarette, untouched, burned low and dropped from her fingers, and then behind the light appeared the figure of the curé in his rusty black clothes. He had stayed behind to guard his church. He was there, moving about his little house, as if nothing had happened. Presently he took down from a shelf above the table a heavy book, laid it before him, took out his steel rimmed spectacles, and began to read.

After an hour of silence during which she lay motionless in her chair, Lily rose and went inside to look at Madame Gigon. The old woman lay on her back, snoring peacefully. She felt her pulse. It was weak and irregular. Then she brought more brandy and milk, fed it to Madame Gigon, and wrapping the black cloak about herself, set off down the terrace to the iron bridge that led across the Marne to the house of the curé.

Away to the north the flashes in the sky became more frequent and the distant thunder less broken and more distinct. On the way to the bridge the alder branches stirring softly in the breeze, whispered together in a vague, ghostly fashion. She walked slowly in the same tired fashion until she reached the little white house by the church.

Chapter 74

INSIDE, the old priest at the sound of her knock looked up from his reading and took off his spectacles.

"Come in," he said, and Lily stepped uncertainly through the door, her eyes blinded by the bright flame of the petrol light. M. Dupont, regarding her with an expression of amazement, rose from his chair.

"It is I, Madame Shane," said Lily. "The friend of Madame Gigon."

"Ah, yes, I remember you well."

Before this night there had passed between them occasional greetings when he came to the lodge to play piquet with Madame Gigon, when he passed Lily riding through the wood in the early morning.

"Won't you sit down?" and then, "Why are you here? You know the Germans may come any time now. Surely before morning."

"As soon as that?" asked Lily indifferently. She had not thought of the Germans. Perhaps they would come. It did not matter greatly.

The old man bent his head over the table and began to turn the pages of the book. "Our soldiers are brave, Madame," he said. "But there is too much against them. They were not ready. In the end we will win. . . . For the present . . ." He finished with a gesture implying that the matter lay in the hands of the good God. He was a simple man, a peasant trained for the priest-hood by devout and adoring parents.

"It would be better if you would go away," he said after a sudden pause. "I imagine it will not be pleasant."

Lily laughed softly. For a moment something of her old gay indifference appeared to return, even a shade of the spirit with which she had met another adventure years before in the park at Cypress Hill.

"There is Madame Gigon," she said. M. Dupont again bent over the table silently. It was a gesture of assent, of resignation, of agreement.

"Besides," continued Lily, "I am not afraid. I think I may even enjoy the experience. . . . I should like to know what war is like." And then, as if she feared that he did not understand her, she added, "Not, of course, because I like war. Oh! not at all! But you understand what it means for the men. . . . I have men in it." She shivered a little and drew the black cape more closely about her. "I think it might be easier for the women if they could go into battle as well. It would be easier than waiting . . . at home . . . alone."

The man closed his book. "Madame is a beautiful woman," he said, softly.

Again Lily smiled faintly. "Oh, I understand what you mean . . . perfectly." A thoughtful expression entered her dark eyes. She seemed suddenly to be listening to the faint and distant thunder. "Yes," she said with a sigh, "I understand. Fortunately I have no temptation to run away. I could not go if I chose. Madame Gigon, you understand, has given up her life to me. . . . It would be impossible to desert her now."

She sat now with her back to the whitewashed wall of the little room; her black cape and her red hair carried the quality of a beautiful painting. All the color was gone from her face and beneath her eyes hung dark circles which somehow increased the brilliance of her eyes and the whiteness of her skin. She looked old but it was the oldness of beauty, possessing a clear refinement and delicacy.

"She is a good woman . . . Madame Gigon," said the priest.

M. Dupont spoke in a low voice, respectful, scarcely audible, but the words exerted upon his visitor an extraordinary effect. All at once she leaned forward resting her elbows on the table. The cloak slipped to the floor. She began to talk passionately with a kind of fierce melancholy in her voice.

"Ah, she *is* a good woman," she said. "She has given her life to me. She has lived with me for twenty years. She has been everything to me. You understand . . . a friend . . . a companion . . . even a mother."

And then, without warning, she poured out the whole story of her life, incident by incident, chapter by chapter, reserving nothing, disguising nothing. Before the eyes of the astonished old priest she recreated the house at Cypress Hill, the Mills, the Town, the figures of her bizarre father, her cynical mother, the hysterical Irene, all the kaleidoscopic picture of a wandering, aimless life. She told him of Jean. She even related bit by bit the long tale of her love for the Baron. She told him that in her heart she had even sinned for the sake of a common laborer . . . Krylenko.

"And yet," she said, "he was not exactly that. He was a great deal more. He was, you understand, something of a martyr. He gave up everything for his people. He would have given his life had it been necessary. . . . It hurts me, even now, to think of him. He was a powerful man . . . a good man . . . a noble man."

It was of him that she talked for a long time, wildly, passionately invoking him in her enthusiasm before the stricken eyes of the old priest. He stood there for a long time in the bare, whitewashed room, powerful, austere, suffering, as he had been on the night of the slaughter in the park at Cypress Hill.

"He was a good man. . . . He still is," she said. She talked breathlessly with a bright exalted light in her eyes. "I have never told this to any one. . . . There was no sin between us . . . nothing unless to love deeply is a sin."

As if turned to stone, M. Dupont sat listening quietly. Only once did he speak and that was when she mentioned the Baron. Then he stirred uneasily and peered at her closely as if he suspected her of lying.

"Incredible!" he murmured to himself. "Incredible!" And after a little pause. "Only God can know what lies in the darkness of men's hearts. Only God. . . . It is impossible to know. . . . It is impossible to know!"

But Lily swept past the interruption. The torrent of her revelations flowed on. She talked eagerly, with a kind of wild delight; yet what she said lacked the quality of a confession. She seemed to have no profound consciousness of sin. She was even unrepentant. She told the story breathlessly with a kind of wonder at herself, at the tragedy of her own soul, that she loved so easily. Instead of confessing, she appeared to be pouring out to the trembling old man secrets, too long confined, which she found herself driven to reveal.

At last she drew to a conclusion. "You understand now," she said, "why to me the war is inexpressibly tragic. You understand what Madame Gigon has been to me."

She picked up the fallen cloak and, shivering, wrapped it about her and sank back in the stiff little chair with a weary air of finality and resignation. "You see, it is not only the war . . . Madame Gigon is dying. The war has taken everything. You understand I shall be alone . . . completely alone."

M. Dupont made no reply. He kept his head bowed. He was repeating a prayer as Irene had done in the old days. They prayed for Lily, who had not been inside a church in more than seven years.

"I came to fetch you to her," continued Lily, "She is dying now. . . . I am certain she cannot live much longer."

When the priest at last raised his head, it was to say, "Come. If she is dying we must waste no time," in so gentle a voice that the tears welled in Lily's eyes. She took out her handkerchief, already wet.

"I thought," she said, "that I was through with weeping. I must have a great many tears." (Lily who never wept.)

Chapter 75

M. Dupont, after collecting those things which are necessary in the administration of the last rites, put on his shovel hat and took up a lantern.

"Come," he said, "we must hurry." And together they set out along the white road, between the whispering alders and over the iron bridge. The lantern swung feebly in his grasp. They walked in complete silence until they reached the terrace when Lily, looking up suddenly, saw that the sky behind the lodge was filled with a cloudy whiteness as if gray smoke were drifting across the sky.

"There is a fire somewhere," she said placing a hand on the arm of her companion.

M. Dupont halted and regarded the sky for a moment, holding his lantern high so that the rays might penetrate the darkness beyond the vine-covered lodge.

"It is not smoke," he said suddenly. "It is dust. The cavalry is passing along the road."

And then for the first time the small revealing noises reached Lily's ear . . . the clanking of spurs, the creaking of girths, the muffled sound of hoofs striking the white road, and then the solitary whicker of a horse.

Chapter 76

Inside the lodge, Lily left Madame Gigon to the curé. He assured her that she was right. It was impossible for the old woman to live much longer. It would have been useless to have secured a physician even if one had been available.

"She has been dying a long while," said the old man. "I fancy she would prefer not to be hindered in her going."

As Lily closed the door upon the two old friends, she saw M. Dupont kneel down in the lamplight and begin to pray.

Wearily she climbed the narrow winding stairway which led to the upper floor and, finding herself unable to sleep, she went to the window above the gateway and sat down to watch the column of cavalry on its way into battle. The men had been riding for hours and now they rode silently, white with dust, the black plumes of horsehair swaying as the horses moved. It was impossible to distinguish one from another. They were simply black figures, units of a body, mysterious and without personality. There was not even the sound of a voice, nothing but the faint rattle of sabers and the ghostly breathing of the horses. Jean might have been among them . . . even Césaire him-self. It was impossible to say. They were each like the other, no longer in-dividuals, now only units, cogs in a vast machine. No one of them counted any longer for anything.

Presently the column came to an end and a battery of artillery, caissons rattling, men upright upon the cartridge boxes, followed in its place. And at last it too passed, swallowed up by the questioning darkness. The silence became unreal, terrifying. From below stairs arose the droning sound of M. Dupont's voice conducting the service that would lead Madame Gigon safely into the world beyond . . . the world beyond. To-night in all the lonely breathless quiet, the world beyond was very near. One might almost enter it simply by closing one's eyes, by stepping through a doorway into the night.

Lily sat motionless and upright, watching. A second column passed and then a third; and at last, a man riding a black horse whose chest was white with froth turned in at the gateway. He was a man like the others . . . a unit, a being without individuality save that he rode alone a little in the rear of the other horsemen. Under the archway he dismounted from his horse, and in the next moment he performed an act which at once restored to him his identity. He walked directly to the iron ring which hung concealed among the ivy leaves and there fastened the black horse. Thus he betrayed himself. Only one person could have known the exact place where the ring lay hidden among the leaves. There could be no longer any doubt.

When he had fastened the black horse, he stepped out a little way from the house and called softly, "Lily . . . Lily."

Chapter 77

THERE WAS no answer, but before he called again a tall figure in a black cloak ran from the doorway and hurried toward him.

"Césaire! . . . Césaire!" were the only words she spoke. She clung against him, the metal of his bright cuirass pressing her lovely, soft body. For a time Césaire kissed her passionately and at length, without a word, she led him away from the house to the pleached walk that led from the château garden down to the river. They walked sadly with arms encircling each other's waists.

"I have but a moment," said the Baron. "At most, ten minutes. I have no right even to that."

She told him that Madame Gigon was dying. She explained that old Pierre had not appeared to help them to escape and that he would have been of no use since it was impossible to move her companion. And when she had wasted three precious minutes in these explanations, she said, "You need not worry for me . . . I shall be quite safe. . . . If only I could be as certain of you."

At this he laughed softly, reassuring her and pulling his fierce mustachios in warlike fashion.

"You need not fear for me," he said. "I have had such great luck . . . always." And he looked at her closely with shining eyes.

Then they sat for a time in silence, clinging closely to each other. Presently he took off his helmet and rested it in her lap allowing her to twist her fingers in and out among the long black hair of the plume.

"And Jean," she said, after a time. "He is with you?"

"He is with me. He passed with the others beneath your window. He sent you his love. He would have come too, but he knew it was unsoldierly to break the ranks. . . . He is a good soldier," he added softly. "A valiant fellow. With me it is different. I am an old fellow. I have learned that there are times when one must break the ranks. There are times when even breaking ranks does not matter."

In the darkness Lily's eyes closed as if she felt a sharp, sudden pain. "Ellen advised me," she said, "never to be too fond of my child."

Her lover kissed her and answered, "Come, you must not think of it like that. You must understand he is a boy . . . an ardent boy."

And then he fell again to talking of her danger. He urged her not to remain.

"I have the curé here . . . M. Dupont," she said.

"Leave him with Madame Gigon."

"No. That I will not do. . . . Besides the Germans may never arrive here after all."

"No," he said, gravely. "Perhaps not. We shall try to prevent them."

Then they walked back again to the gateway. The house was silent now and the voice of M. Dupont no longer to be heard. The Baron replaced his helmet, untied his horse and swung himself on the back of the animal. Leaning down, he kissed her again and then turned through the gateway into the road. She listened to the sound of the black horse's hoofs as he galloped past the moving columns, and at last when the echo was no longer audible she re-entered the house and flung herself down upon the bed. Throughout the brief visit, she had restrained herself. Now she wept quietly, almost in peace, as if she were enveloped already by a great resignation.

Chapter 78

MADAME GIGON lived through the night, sleeping peacefully in her high bed near the door that opened upon the terrace. But Lily did not sleep at all. She kept watch, sometimes sitting at the bedside, sometimes lying wrapped in her cloak in the long chair beneath the plane trees. She watched the flashes on the horizon beyond the wood, until the dawn rising slowly absorbed them and rendered them invisible in a faint glow which grew and grew until it enveloped all the dome of the sky and transformed, suddenly and without warning, the dark wood from a low black wall extending across the sky into a grove of slender trunks silhouetted against the rising light.

At dawn the troops no longer passed the house. The dusty white road lay deserted between the rows of chestnut trees. But in the dust were the prints of a thousand hoofs and the tracks of the wide wheeled caissons. The little procession on the distant bridge at Trilport had vanished. There were no soldiers going forward; and coming back, there was now only an occasional, straggling cart or the figure of a shopkeeper pushing before him in a wooden wheelbarrow all that he had salvaged of his little shop.

At noon there appeared out of the wood a rolling kitchen drawn by tired horses and driven by weary soldiers all white with dust. It came nearer and nearer until it arrived at the farm where, in the shadow of the big gray barns, it halted and the men ate. A little while later soldiers began to appear among the trees, tiny figures in red trousers and red caps, no longer bright like the poppies, but all stained and dust covered. The red marked them against the wall of greenery as if it had been planned that they should serve as targets.

Singly and in little groups of two or three the soldiers straggled across the fields toward the kitchen set up against the gray wall of the barn. The sun shone brilliantly, and in the clear white light the red tiles, the white walls, and the green of the trees appeared gay and bright. Some of the men carried arms suspended in slings. One or two wore about their close-cropped heads bandages that were stained with spots of red as if the color had come loose from their tragic little caps and stained their skins. There was one dandified young officer, with fine waxed mustaches, who dragged a shattered leg and still wore the bedraggled remnants of the spotless white gloves he had carried into the battle.

When they had eaten and drunk, the soldiers made their way across the iron bridge and turning along the towpath at the foot of the garden kept on their way, moving in a thin, trickling stream in the direction of Paris.

At length Lily, rousing herself, went to the foot of the garden, opened the gate and stood on the path. She carried wine which she gave them to drink as they passed.

"And how does it go?" she asked now and then.

The respectful answer was always the same. "Badly, Madame. . . . Badly. It would be better if you did not remain."

Or a shrug and "What can we do, Madame? They have better guns . . . better shells. One cannot see them. They are dressed so that they look like the trees themselves. And we . . . we." A gesture indicating the fatal red trousers and kepi.

Early in the afternoon the sound of the guns became audible again, not distant this time and indistinct like thunder, but sharp and clear . . . the barking "ping" of the seventy-fives.

When the wine was all gone, Lily returned again to the terrace to wait. She had not been sitting there long when there arose all at once the sound of a terrific explosion. Turning her head she saw above the river at Trilport a great cloud of white dust and black smoke. They had destroyed the solid white bridge. It was the French themselves who had destroyed it. The Germans must be very near.

Madame Gigon slept peacefully just inside the doorway, all undisturbed by the explosion.

As for Lily, lying in the low chair, the explosion appeared to have worked a miracle. The color had begun to return to her white face. It showed itself in bright spots as if she had been seized by a fever. And presently she arose and began to walk about, up and down the garden, going at last into the château itself from which she returned in a little while carrying a pair of the Baron's binoculars. With these she climbed to the little turret which rose above the vine-covered dovecote. There she settled herself to watching.

In a little while the men about the kitchen gathered themselves into a group, put the horses once more into the harness and drove away, carrying with them a boy of the last class whose strength had given out. M. Dupont followed them until he reached the edge of the iron bridge where he halted and stood looking after them, his hands shading his old eyes against the long rays of the setting sun, until they disappeared around a turn of the river. Then he went quietly indoors.

A little while later a battery of guns appeared among the trees, halted on the edge of the wood, and began firing in the direction of La Ferté where a cloud of smoke from the burning houses hung low upon the horizon. It was a pretty picture. The men worked the guns rapidly. The cannon spat forth little curls of white smoke followed by sudden angry barks, not in the least deafening. In the clear evening light it was all like one of Meissonier's battle pictures, rather clear and pretty and bright-colored.

But in a little while the battery stopped firing, the horses leaned forward once more into the harness and the guns drew away down the lane, past the white farm and across the iron bridge. The planks reverberated with a thunderous sound under the hoofs of the galloping horses. The little cavalcade turned along the towpath and vanished. Out of the wood there appeared suddenly three gray-green figures on horseback who halted and surveyed the landscape. They were the first of the Uhlans.

Chapter 79

WITH THE FALLING of night, the Germans were in possession of the château and the gardens. In bands of twenty or thirty they pushed beyond across the field and through the copses in the direction of Meaux. A few remained behind, and these occupied the château, using the best linen of the Baroness, taking down from the wall of the kitchen the cook's great battery of spotless copper kettles in which to cook their beans and soup.

Lily, sitting quietly inside the darkened lodge by the side of Madame Gigon, heard their shouts and the stamping of their horses in the stables. Dark figures moved about among the trees of the garden, the figures of her enemies, the men who would kill if it were possible Césaire and Jean. In the excitement, no one ventured as far from the château as the lodge, and for a time she remained safe and in peace.

The cannon were no longer to be heard. For a little while there arose the distant crackling of rifles like the sound of brush fires made by the foresters in August; but this too died away after a time.

She bathed her head, fed Madame Gigon once more and sat down again to wait, and at last, overcome by exhaustion she sank quietly into sleep.

In the château the weary Germans slept and in the stables the horses ceased their stamping. A deep unbroken stillness settled again over the garden and the wheatfields beyond, so peaceful that the firing and the shouting of a little while before might have been wholly an illusion, a nightmare which had nothing to do with reality.

Thus passed three hours.

It was the sound of knocking which aroused Lily, a violent imperious sort of knocking which wakened her sharply and brought her quickly to her feet. As if by force of habit, she opened the door and said in French, "Gently . . . please. . . . Gently. It is not necessary to break down the door. There is a sick woman here."

As it swung open she was enveloped by the sudden bright glare of an electric torch. At the same moment a voice speaking the most excellent French said, "I am sorry, Madame. I ask your pardon. I did not know the lodge was occupied."

The voice was not gruff. It was rather cold and smooth and carried a hint of weariness. "I found the door locked. I always knock upon locked doors," continued the voice. "May I come in?"

All this time Lily, blinded by the sudden light, stood leaning against the door, emerging slowly from the effects of her deep slumber. For a moment she was silent.

"I prefer to come outside," she replied. "There is a sick woman here. . . . If you will turn your light inside, you will see that I am not lying. She is there."

The light flashed across the high bed of Madame Gigon. "I believe you, Madame."

Lily closed the door and stood leaning against it. From the one of the lower windows of the château streamed a path of light which illuminated faintly the terrace, the front of the lodge and the Uhlan officer. He was not tall and was not in the least savage in appearance. On the contrary his face was smooth shaven and narrow, rather the face of a scholar than a soldier. Yet he carried himself very erect. There was something about him that was cold, stiff, almost brittle.

"What do you want of me?" asked Lily in a voice expressionless and free of all emotion.

For a moment her companion hesitated. He switched off the electric torch which until now he had kept turned full upon her. "Were you sleeping?" he asked.

"Yes." Again in the same dead tone.

"Extraordinary. You must be a woman of great nerve."

"No . . . not at all. I had not slept in thirty-six hours."

Again he hesitated. "I . . . I have been riding for that length of time . . . and still I cannot sleep. I have tried. . . . My nerves are too much on edge." She waited silently.

"Tell me . . . why did you remain behind?" he began presently.

She made a gesture indicating the window behind which lay Madame Gigon. "You have seen the reason," she said. "It was impossible to go away." The man whistled softly. "Aren't you in the least afraid?"

For a time there was no sound except a deep sigh. "There was nothing to be done," she answered presently in the same dead voice. "When there is nothing to be done, it is foolish to fret. It is best to make the most of it. What would you have me do?" For a moment a trace of life, almost of humor entered her voice. "Would you have me lie down and scream?" Again she sighed. "What good would it do? What would come of it? I do not believe in scenes."

The Uhlan laughed. "Unlike most women," he said. "But you are right. Afterwards, scenes are ridiculous. Nothing really matters much. . . . I've learned that in two days," he added with a sort of pride.

To this she made no reply but her very silence carried its own gesture of assent. She did not deny his statement.

"I suppose you hate me," he began, "like a good Frenchwoman."

For the first time she raised her head and looked squarely at the stranger. "What do you want?" she asked. "Why are you talking in this fashion? You understand I am helpless. I must talk with you if you choose." In the darkness she frowned. "I suppose that is war." And then, "Besides, I am not a Frenchwoman at all. I am an American."

At this the stranger gave a sudden start, in the darkness more audible than visible by the sudden click of metal on some part of his uniform.

"Then you must hate me even more. . . . I have lived in Paris. The Americans there are more French than the French."

This remark, it appeared, angered her for she answered quickly. "I know no Americans in Paris. I know nothing about them."

The Uhlan laughed. "Madame, I have no intention of injuring you . . . in any way."

To this she replied, "I suppose you do not mind if I sit down. I am a little weary."

The stranger's manner changed abruptly. He became courteous, almost courtly.

"I am sorry. I did not know there were chairs. You see I am a stranger here. Sit down if you prefer it, by all means. . . . I am not one to work hardships for a woman." She moved toward the long chair under the lindens and lay down, wrapping the cloak about her and closing her eyes.

"Perhaps," said the stranger, "you would prefer to sleep."

"No," she replied quietly, "I could not sleep now." And as if the idea amused her she added, "I might as well talk with you . . . since you too suffer from insomnia."

"As you will . . . if you do not hate me too much."

He sat in the chair by her side and slipped from his waist the belt in which hung his black Luger pistol. Thus they remained for some time, silently and peacefully, as if they were old friends between whom there was no necessity for speech. The German sat with his elbows resting on his knees, his head buried in his hands. There was a smoothness and angularity about his thin figure so trimly clad in a uniform that now carried the stains of battle.

At last he took out a cigarette and said, "I suppose you smoke, Madame?"

To which Lily replied without opening her eyes, "No."

He was so polite, so scrupulously polite. And presently he sighed, "Ah, this civilization . . . this world of monkeys. (*Monde de singes.*)" And once more the night stillness descended, for Lily made no effort at speech now. She lay motionless, so still that she might have been dead. Her silence appeared to reproach him for he turned suddenly and said, "Do you fancy I like this . . . this living like a burglar in a château . . . your château?"

"It is not mine," Lily murmured.

"Do you fancy I like this war. . . . I am not pleased with killing men. Why should I? I do not hate them. How is it possible? How can you even hate me?"

She stirred impatiently. "No. It is impossible to hate genuinely . . . without a reason one can put one's finger on. All the same you are my enemy," she added stubbornly.

The Uhlan laughed. "Who has made me so, Madame? Not myself, surely." And then after a little pause, he added with a kind of desperation, "No, I am like all the others. I have nothing to do with it. We are all caught, Madame, . . . hopelessly caught in one great web spun by a monster. Ah, what a monster!"

In the distant stable arose suddenly the sound of two horses quarreling. There was a violent kicking . . . a squealing that was savage and implacable.

"We are not even like that," he said. "It is not even that we bite and kick. . . . We shoot each other at a distance. You, Madame, perhaps have friends among the men I am fighting. I kill them and they me only because the first who shoots is the safest. You know the artillerymen kill men they never even see." He spat suddenly. "Bah! It is mechanics . . . all mechanics . . . machinery, you understand, which they make in great roaring factories. They kill men in factories in order to kill more men on the battlefield. What is there in that?"

Again she made no answer to his question. The quarreling horses had been separated and their squealing silenced. There was only the overpowering stillness once more, a stillness unearthly in quality which lifted all that it enveloped upon a new plane, determined by new values. Life, death, reality, dreams—all these things were confused and yet amazingly clear, as if the whole had been pierced by a single beam of cold white light.

Chapter 80

IT MUST have occurred to Lily that the man was talking in an hysterical fashion with all the frenzy of a neurasthenic. "Madame, you should see one of our towns where there are great furnaces . . . Essen, Madame, or Saarbrucken . . . black, incredibly vile, a wallow of roaring fire and white hot steel . . . I know them, Madame, I have lived in them."

Then for the first time Lily stirred. She even laughed, faintly yet with unmistakable bitterness. "Know them? I know them. We have them in America."

The stranger paid no heed to her interruption. "Look, Madame," he commanded, pointing to the north where the horizon was lighted by the glow of a burning town. "Look, Madame. You see that fire in the sky. The ladles have overflowed. The white hot steel has spread across Europe. There is gold in it too . . . red hot gold. . . . Melted Gods . . . idols which we worship to-day."

His voice rose until he was shouting. When he finished, he leaned back in his chair, the fine uniform suddenly crumpled and limp. And after a time he began to speak again, softly as if the torrent of emotion had exhausted him. "And where have we to go? If we sought to escape where have we to go? There is no place. Because the monkeys . . . the fools have civilized all the world, so that they might sell their cheap cotton and tin trays. They have created a monster which is destroying them. There is no longer any peace . . . any solitude. They have even wrenched the peasant from his plow . . . the shepherd from his hillside." Again he pointed toward the burning horizon. "They have driven them out upon the plains where the cauldrons have overflowed across all Europe. It is the monsters, Madame, who are at the bottom of all this. Ah, commerce, industry, wealth, power." He tossed away his cigarette and lighted another. "When this is over, who do you think will have gained? Not the peasant, Madame. Not the shepherd, not the poet. Ah, no! They will be shoveled under the earth . . . whole bodies and pieces of bodies because they are no longer of any use. Not the worker, Madame, whom the monster devours. Ah, no." His voice rose suddenly. "It is the monster who will have gained . . . the monster and the men whose pockets he fills with gold . . . the monster of material, of industry. He will destroy us. He will devour us. What can we do? You see, I know. I have lived in

France. I have lived in England. . . . My grandmother, you understand, was English. I would prefer to live in England. But No! I was in England three weeks ago. And suddenly I must go home to join my regiment, to set out upon the expedition that has brought me here into this trampled garden. What for? Who can say? Why? Who knows? Not surely because it gives me pleasure. Not surely because I care a fig whether the German empire lives or dies. That is merely an excuse to drag us into battle." His head dropped wearily again. "You see, this is why I have not been able to sleep. I have been thinking of these things. They are not the sort that lull a man to sleep. There is blood on my hands. I killed to-day . . . by shooting and stabbing. I assure you it gave me no pleasure. I should doubtless have loved the men I killed. I am helpless. I cannot fight against it. No, there is only one thing to be done. I must kill as many men as possible. I must destroy all that it is possible to destroy because if we destroy enough the monster will have nothing to feed upon. He, too, will die . . . and with him this civilization . . . banal, ugly, materialistic, unchristian . . . this greed-ridden world."

The Uhlan fell forward upon the table, burying his face in his arms. At the sight Lily raised herself gently and watched her strange companion in a wondering silence. At last she said softly, "Why do you tell me this? Is it because you are afraid?"

The man made a chuckling, confused sound and sat up once more. "Ah, no! Madame. You fancy I am hysterical. Well, so I am. I don't deny it. You see it is not easy for me to be a warrior. I am a little mad. No, I talk like this because . . ." For a moment he hesitated as if groping for some explanation of an emotional crisis which in a soldier was not logical at all. His manner seemed to imply that he should have accepted the affair without question. "Because . . . Well, there is a time when fear does not matter, when terror does not exist, when one is enveloped by a despair so great that what happens to one's body is of no concern. You understand that. You have answered it yourself a little time before, when you said there came a time when it was useless to be afraid." He leaned back and made a little gesture of negation. "It does not matter," he concluded. In the faint light from the lower windows of the château it was plain that he was smiling in a bitter, despairing fashion. "No, I shall go on killing until I am killed. It will not be a long affair. It is absurd to hope that I shall live many more days." He whistled softly. "I might even be killed to-night . . . after I have left you. I shall kill as many men as possible. I can only submit. There is nothing I can do. I am not a boy full of playing soldier."

At this Lily winced suddenly as if he had struck her. Then she raised herself slowly. The black cloak fell from her shoulders.

"I have in the war a son and a lover," she said. "If you met them, you would kill them. Is it not so?"

The Uhlan bowed his head in silent assent.

"And yet you do not believe in it?"

"No, Madame."

"Then that is wrong. It is sinful."

The stranger leaned toward her. "It is not I who would kill them. I am only a chance, a little dagger in the hand of fate . . . one of a billion chances that have to do with their deaths. I myself would not be killing them. . . . It would be a strange . . . even an impossible accident, if I killed one of them with my own hands. You understand, we are talking facts now . . . hard facts. There is no room for sentimentality at a time like this. . . ." He smiled ironically. "I can understand that it is difficult for a woman to talk facts. It is simply a matter of chances . . . like roulette shall we say?"

For a time Lily remained thoughtful and silent. At last she said, "They are in the cavalry like yourself. You would kill them. You are one of the chances." The calmness of her manner stood in terrible contrast to the hysterical outburst of the soldier.

"I can see you are a philosopher . . . a *femme savant*," mocked the stranger.

"You might choose a better time to jeer."

The man coughed. "Forgive me. . . . I am sorry. . . . I was wrong. If you were a *femme savant*, I would not be talking to you like this. . . . You are a woman . . . a beautiful woman. One cannot help talking to you."

"I am only a woman living by what she believes. That is simple enough."

"It requires courage, Madame . . . and indifference, far more of both than I have." He coughed again, nervously. "Perhaps I am too rational. . . . Perhaps I do not think resistance worth the trouble . . . especially now, at a time when the mob . . . the politicians rule absolutely."

"You are one of the chances," Lily repeated stubbornly.

Chapter 81

THE GERMAN laughed softly. "You are a primitive woman, Madame. It refreshes me to find a woman so charmingly direct, so completely feminine. There are not many left. It is a quality which should always accompany beauty. If a woman is not beautiful, it does not matter." He paused waiting for her to speak and when she said nothing, he continued. "I envy your lover. He is a fortunate man."

At this Lily stirred once more. It was a faint movement, yet it carried a warning of anger.

"Of course, you may say and do what you please," she said. "I am completely helpless."

The Uhlan rattled his spurs in the darkness. "Come . . . come, now. I have no intention of harming you. I told you that before. It seems to me that this once . . . on a night such as this . . . we might talk honestly . . . as if there was no nonsense in the world. I do not know your name and you do not know mine. We shall never meet again, for I, no doubt, will be dead before many days. You have admitted that you have a lover." He leaned across the table with a curious pleading gesture. "You see, I am tired. I mean to say that I am wearied of keeping up deceits. Has it ever occurred to you how many barriers surround us all . . . even those friends whom we know very well. The countless secrets which lie behind them . . . the things which we never know, even about our dearest friends. For once . . . just once, it would be a delight to talk without pretense . . . to speak as if each one of us were free, quite free, to do as he pleased . . . to answer to no one, to fear no one. There is no more freedom in the world. There are too many people in the world. And the life of no one is any longer his own." He paused and passed a thin, nervous hand across his brow as if he would clear away some entanglement which had entrapped his thoughts. "I cannot say what I mean. I, like all the others, have kept my secrets hidden for too long a time. You see, if it were possible for us to talk thus with freedom . . . we might separate, you knowing me and I knowing you, better than any one else in the world." He laughed and his mood changed quickly from a resigned weariness back to the old mocking flippancy. "It is an interesting idea, but impossible of course . . . because we no longer know even ourselves. We have sacrificed ourselves to those who crowd in upon us, who dare not share our secrets . . . because the crowd is too stupid . . . too cowardly . . . too weak . . . too bereft of understanding. The crowd is like sheep. They must be protected by little shepherd laws . . . against themselves. And so the strong are sacrificed to the weak. That will put an end to us all some day . . . an end to all this blessed civilization. Ah, if you knew how stupid sheep can be. I have a farm in Silesia, Madame. I can tell you all about sheep." For an instant he paused, considering the imbecility of sheep. "And socialism! It's no better, Madame. It simply buries the individual deeper under layers of muck. No, it is all wrong from the bottom up. We must kill . . . kill . . . you understand . . . until there is room to breathe! Until the earth is freed of the sheep! Then we can be free! Then we can find solitude!"

Again his voice rang with subdued frenzy. Inside the house the frivolous gilt traveling clock struck midnight, and far away in the direction of Trilport there arose again the faint crackling sound like the brush fires. It rose and fell, tossed about at the caprice of the night wind.

"They have begun again," said the Uhlan. "In a little while I shall be forced to leave. You see, we cannot remain here. We have pushed in too far." He leaned forward and drew with his lighted cigarette upon the top of the table between them a V shaped line. "You see," he said, indicating the point of the V. "We have been pushed in here. . . . We cannot possibly remain. It is as far as we shall advance. We have come too far already. Any fool could see it. Any fool but Von Kluck. . . . Why, my boot boy would know it." He laughed again. "But my boot boy is not a general. He is not stupid enough."

He kept wriggling, wriggling helplessly, like a butterfly impaled by a pin . . . an individualist, a lonely man, caught by the savage rush of the mob.

Chapter 82

WHAT HE SAID appeared to pass ignored by Lily, for when he had finished she began to talk once more. "I can understand the bravery of fighting for that which you believe," she said. "I cannot understand yielding without a fight to the monster you despise. I knew a man. . . ." For a second she hesitated. "He fought for what he believed. He gave up everything for the fight . . . his health, his friends, his work, his money. He was beaten and bloody and wounded. He would have given his life if it had been necessary. He was a poor, ignorant Ukrainian peasant . . . a Russian who could barely read. Yet he fought. He fought and learned . . . up from nothing." Again she paused and the distant crackling sound filled in the silence, this time more distinct and sharp, nearer at hand. "You see, I am telling you this because it is the very monster that you hate which he too fought. He is still fighting it. In the end he will win. . . . If one could not believe such things, one could not live. He will go on fighting because there is inside him something which will not let him stop. But there are not many like him. There are too many like you."

Her voice carried the ring of supreme scorn. There was a quality of iciness in it, penetrating, contemptuous, acid.

Suddenly she covered her face with her hands. "In times like this," she said, "I think of him. It helps one to live." And after a moment, she added bitterly. "He would not have gone off to kill!"

"I can see, Madame," said the stranger, "that you despise me."

"It is more than that," answered Lily, her face still covered by her white hands. "I am certain now that I hate you."

The Uhlan frowned. "I am sorry," he said, "I thought you were sympathetic."

The only answer was a laugh, incredibly cold and savage from so beautiful a woman.

Within the château more lights appeared, and in the courtyard there rose the sound of hoofs striking the cobblestones and of orders being shouted back and forth in guttural German. Far away to the east a solitary cannon barked. The noise ripped the blue stillness with the sound of a tapestry being torn.

"You have forgotten," said Lily, "that I have a son and a lover in the war. You understand, they too are in the cavalry."

She had scarcely finished speaking when the air was shattered by the terrific rattle of a dozen rifles fired simultaneously below the terrace somewhere among the buildings of the farm. A faint glare trembled above the iron bridge and then a second volley, terrifying and abrupt, and a second brief glare.

The Uhlan did not move but Lily sat up suddenly. They remained thus for some time, the woman in an attitude of listening. It appeared that she was straining every nerve, every muscle, lest the faintest sound escape her. When the volley was not repeated she turned her head, slowly and scornfully, in the direction of her companion. In her eyes there was a look of terrible accusation, a look charged with contempt and hatred. The stranger watched her as if fascinated and unable to remove his eyes from her face. At last she spoke, slowly and distinctly, in an awed, breathless whisper.

"What was that?"

The face of the Uhlan remained smooth and empty of all expression, as clean of all emotion as a bit of smooth white paper. In the flickering light from the lanterns which moved among the trees, the countenance appeared vague and lineless, almost imbecile in its negation. Then slowly his lips moved.

"It is the curé, Madame. . . . They have shot the curé." The voice was as smooth as the face. It carried the hard, mocking cruelty of indifference. "They caught him signaling with his lantern from the steeple of the church."

Without a sound Lily lay back once more and buried her face in her cloak. Her body shook silently.

"I could do nothing else," continued the smooth voice. It came out from the thin lipped mouth as a serpent from a crevice in a rock. "It was not I who killed. I had nothing to say in the matter. I did what I could not help doing. *Enfin*, it was the monster!"

Across the fields of wheat from the direction of Meaux the faint crackling sound came nearer and nearer. It was as if the grain had caught fire and the flames were rushing toward them. Lily still lay with her eyes covered as if to shut out the picture which had risen in her imagination. M. Dupont . . . the friend of dying Madame Gigon, the priest to whom she had told her life . . . M. Dupont dead among the dungheaps of the farmyard!

Somewhere in the direction of the Trilport bridge, the solitary cannon fired again and as though it had summoned Madame Gigon back to life, they heard her speaking suddenly inside the lodge. She was talking rapidly in a low voice.

"You need not worry, Henri. To-morrow there will be fresh vegetables in from the barrier. At dark, a balloon with two passengers will be released at the Gare St. Lazare. Gabriel himself told me." And then for a time she muttered incoherently and when her speech became clear again, she was saying, "There is a notice on the Rue de Rivoli that they are selling animals in the Jardin de Plantes. For food you understand . . . I hear at ten sous the pound." Again more mumbling and then, "Ah, that one was close. Yesterday a shell exploded in the Boulevard Montparnasse. We must place our faith in God. . . . Yes, we must pray, Henri. There is not enough God in the world."

Then she became silent for a time and the Uhlan said, "Madame is delirious. She is living through 1870. . . . You see we have not progressed at all. It is merely turn about, first the French, and then we take a turn." He laughed a nervous laugh devoid of mirth. "Ah, it is a pretty business, Madame . . . a pretty business. The sooner we are all killed off the better. The animals could manage this world better than we have done."

He had not finished speaking when a sudden rattle of rifles sounded somewhere near at hand, a little to the east by the copse in the long meadow. At the same time the confusion in the stables and the little park redoubled. A horse whinneyed. Men shouted. Water pails were overturned. Out of the darkness a man in rough gray uniform appeared and addressed the Captain in excited, guttural German. The Uhlans had begun to leave the stable. They were making their way through the black trees over the neatly ordered flowers to the gate in the garden wall.

The stranger talked for a moment with the soldier and then rising, he said, "Good-by, Madame. It is not likely that we shall ever meet again. I thank you for the conversation. It saved the night for an insomniac. It is more stimulating to talk with a beautiful woman than with common soldiers."

Lily lay buried in her cloak. She did not even uncover her face, but the Uhlan bowed in a polite ironic fashion and slipped away through the trees, vanishing at once like a shadow. The uproar in the château gardens and in the stable increased. It swallowed the stranger.

As the sound of his footsteps died away, she raised herself cautiously and looked about her. The sound of firing continued. The air was full of an unearthly red glow. Supporting herself on one elbow she saw that the light came from the opposite side of the river. The farm had been fired by the departing troops. For a time she watched the flames, eating their way slowly at the windows and along the eaves, growing always in intensity. The iron bridge was filled with retreating Uhlans, all black against the red haze. The thunder of hoofs on the planks again filled the air.

Chapter 83

THUS SHE REMAINED as if under a spell, ignoring the uproar that had arisen all about her, in the fields, in the château garden and along the towpath. When at last she moved, it was to sit up and place her feet upon the ground where they struck some hard object that made a clicking, metallic sound as it grated against the stone. Reaching down, her fingers closed over the cold metal of a Luger pistol. In the confusion and the shouting it had slipped from its holster. The stranger had forgotten it. Slowly she raised the weapon and held it up in the glow of the burning farm. For a long time she regarded the pistol as if it held some sinister fascination and presently, leaning upon the back of her chair, she rose slowly and concealed it in the folds of her cloak. When she had gained a full sense of her balance, she moved off from the terrace through the black trees in the direction of the iron bridge.

The firing had increased. There were cries in French and in guttural German, and from the shrubbery along the garden wall the low moan of a wounded soldier. With the long cloak trailing across the dewy grass she continued to move in an unswerving line to the garden gate. As she passed through it a stray bullet, striking the wall beside her, chipped the ancient mortar into her face and her thick, disordered hair. Outside on the towpath she walked until she stood on the little knoll above the iron bridge.

In the center of the structure could be discerned the figures of three men silhouetted against the flames of the burning farm. Two were kneeling at work on some object which absorbed all their attention. The third stood upright shielding his eyes from the glow, keeping watch and urging them to hurry. He was slim and very neat, and carried himself with a singular air of scorn. Unmistakably he was the visitor, the stranger upon the terrace. At the far end of the bridge, three horses, held in check by the rider of a fourth horse, curvetted and neighed in terror at the leaping flames.

All this Lily saw from the eminence of the low knoll. And when she had watched it for some time she raised her arm, holding the Luger pistol, and slowly took careful aim. The cloak slipped from her shoulders into the grass. Once she fired and then again and again. The slim, neat man stumbled suddenly, struck his head against an iron girder of the bridge and slipped struggling into the river. There was a faint splash and he disappeared. Of the other two men, one fell upon his face, struggled up again and, aided by his companion, crawled painfully toward the terrified horses. The flames roared wildly. The horses leapt and curvetted for a moment and then disappeared with their riders, followed by the horse whose rider lay at the bottom of the Marne.

On the low knoll the pistol dropped from Lily's hand and slipped quietly into the river. A party of three French infantrymen coming suddenly out of the sedges along the river discovered her lying in the thick wet grass. Bending over her they talked volubly for a time and at last carried her back through the gate into the lodge. They could wring from her no sort of rational speech. She kept talking in the strangest manner, repeating over and over again, "It is simply a matter of chance . . . like roulette . . . but one of a million chances . . . but one . . . but one. . . . Still one chance is too many."

Inside the lodge, one of the soldiers struck a sulphur match and discovered in the bed by the window the body of an old woman. He summoned his companions and they too leaned over the body. Beyond all doubt the old woman was dead.

Chapter 84

FROM THAT NIGHT on the sound of firing grew steadily more faint and the glow in the sky more dim. There were times when Lily, lying delirious in the lodge under the care of Madame Borgue, the farmer's wife, behaved in the wildest manner. When the wind blew from the north, it carried the sound of the guns across forests and wheatfields into the park at Germigny and the barrage, no longer confused and close at hand, took on a pulsing regular throb like the beating of surf upon a beach of hard shingle. At such times Lily would sit up and talk wildly in a mixture of French and English of Mills and monsters, of cauldrons, of white hot metal that absorbed the very bodies of men. The distant rumbling was for all the world like the pounding which had enveloped Cypress Hill in the days of Lily's youth. But Madame Borgue, knowing nothing of all this, could make no sense of the ravings of her patient.

She remained a long time ill. While she lay unconscious with the fever, Madame Gigon was buried among the beaded *couronnes* of the cemetery at Trilport between her obscure husband, the curator, and the father who had been ruined by his loyalty to Napoleon the Little.

It happened that on the very day of the lonely funeral, Madame de Cyon died in Paris of indigestion brought on by overeating and the loss of twenty francs at bridge, played secretly to be sure, for in those days no one played bridge in Paris. So Madame Gigon, by dying first, was cheated out of her triumphant, "I told you so!" Of course, it may have been that in another world she knew this satisfaction; for it was true that Nadine "went off just like that."

And in early October, on the first day that Lily ventured from the lodge out upon the green terrace, she read in the *Figaro* that she had been decorated with the Croix de Guerre. The citation appeared in the midst of the military news.

"*Shane, Madame Lily. Widow. American by birth. Decorated for valor at Germigny l'Evec during the Battle of the Marne, when she prevented a detachment of Uhlans from destroying an iron bridge of the utmost importance to our troops.*"

This she read aloud to Madame Borgue. It was a tiny paragraph, printed in very small black type, and it caused Lily to laugh, bitterly, mirthlessly. Letting fall the *Figaro* by the side of her chair, she lay back.

"As if," she said, "I had ever thought of the bridge! As if I even knew that they were trying to destroy it!"

And when Madame Borgue, alarmed by this outburst, sought to lead her back into the house, Lily said, "I am not delirious. . . . Truly . . . I am not. It is so absurdly funny!" And she laughed again and again.

She never knew that it was M. de Cyon who brought the affair to the attention of the Ministry of War and secured her the distinction.

Slowly it became clear that fate had not allotted to the dead Uhlan the chance of Césaire's death. She received no news of him. Even M. de Cyon, in the government at Paris, could discover nothing. The hours grew into days and the days into months until, at last, she was able to leave the lodge and visit Jean in the hospital at Neuilly. There came at length a day when there was no longer any doubt. The Baron was simply among the missing . . . the great number concerning whom there was no news. It was as if he had bade her farewell at the vine-covered gate and galloped off on the black horse into a darkness which swallowed him forever.

In Paris, the house in the Rue Raynouard acquired an air of complete desolation. There was no one, not even Jean who lay at the hospital in Neuilly with his right leg amputated at the knee, to share it with Lily. The mirrors reflected nothing save the figures of the mistress, the servants and M. de Cyon who appeared to find consolation for his recent loss in visits to the big house at Numero Dix.

Ellen, escaped at last from Central Europe, had returned to America. Madame Gigon was dead. Of her friends none remained. Madame de Cyon was in her grave. Madame Blaise still lived in a polite madhouse, convinced that the war was only a revolution which would place her friend, the wine merchant, upon the throne of a glorified and triumphant France. The others? Some had gone into the provinces, and of those who remained, all were interested in their own families. They had sons, brothers, nephews, cousins, at the front. . . . There were no more *salons*. It was impossible to go alone to the theater. There remained nothing to do but visit Jean (a sad business though he seemed cheerful enough) and sit in the big empty house, so silent now, so empty of chatter, of music, of laughter. Even the great piano under the glowing Venice of Mr. Turner remained closed and silent save in the rare moments when Lily, as if unable any longer to endure the silence, opened it and played with only half a heart the tunes which once had filled the house and overflowed into the garden. It was clear that it required more than mirrors, jades, pictures and old carpets to make a dwelling endurable. As Lily remarked to M. de Cyon at tea one afternoon in early November, these things, each one the reminder of some precious association, only rendered Numero Dix the more unbearable.

"I can understand," she said, "that sometimes my mother must have died of loneliness in the house at Cypress Hill."

She told M. de Cyon the history of the burned house, bit by bit, from the day it was built until the day it was destroyed. Indeed she told him all the story of her father, of her own childhood, of the Mills and the Town. She even told him something of Irene's story, though not enough to be sure for him to evolve the whole truth, for there were certain barriers beyond which she allowed no one to penetrate; no one save an old village priest who was, after all, not a man but an agent of God himself. And he was dead now.

In those days the pair drew more closely to each other, as if they found in the friendship a consolation for the melancholy and overwhelming loneliness. And it is true that Lily had grown more sympathetic. The old carefree gaiety had given place to a new and more gentle understanding. The indolence, it seemed, had vanished before a new determination to dominate her own aimless existence. She had grown more calm. Indeed there were times now when she became wholly grave and serious, even pensive, as she sat quietly with the pleasant, white-haired Frenchman who found her company so agreeable that he seldom permitted a day to pass without calling at Numero Dix on his way from the Ministry of War. She became, as she had observed to Willie Harrison, more and more like her mother.

Each day was like the one before, and this monotony to Lily must have been a new and painful experience. The only variation occurred when Paul Schneidermann, returning from a hospital in Cannes, arrived in Paris and became a second visitor at the house in the Rue Raynouard. But even in this there was an inexpressible sadness, for the bullet which had wounded Schneidermann paralyzed forever his left arm. He was never again able to play the piano in the long drawing-room nor the cello he had brought to the house when Ellen was there.

With Ellen gone, the American newspapers no longer found their way into the house. Indeed it seemed impossible to obtain them anywhere in Paris, even if Lily had been capable of such an effort. So there were no more clippings for the enameled box. The last one bore the date of the first month of the war. Since then there had been nothing. It was as if Krylenko, too, —the Krylenko whose progress Lily watched from so great a distance—had died or gone away like all the others. There remained only the wreckage of a life which had once been complete, content, even magnificent in its quiet way.

When at last Jean was able to leave the hospital, he secured through M. de Cyon an appointment at the Ministry of War. As for Lily, she undertook presently the establishment of a soup kitchen for soldiers who passed through Paris on leave. But at this diversion she was no more successful than she had been at knitting socks for the strikers; and after a few months she abandoned it completely to the care of women less wealthy and more capable. She continued, however, until the end to supply it lavishly with money. In her enthusiasm for the charities of the war she succeeded in exhausting for the first time her annual income. She even dipped into her principal. The two hundred thousand dollars which the Town paid her for Cypress Hill she used to provide food and comfort for the soldiers of another nation.

Chapter 85

IN THE TOWN no new railway station raised its splendors because in those years the Town and the Mills were too busy making money. In all the haste even the new railway station was forgotten. The deserted park became a storing place for the shells which the Mills turned out in amazing numbers. Gas shells, high explosives, shrapnel cases . . . all these things were piled high along the brick paths where delphiniums and irises once flourished. Even the Venus of Cydnos and the Apollo Belvedere, cracked and smudged in the niches of the dead hedge, were completely buried beneath munitions.

Because somewhere in the world men were being killed, the Mills did an enormous business. The Town grew as it had never before grown. Prices were tremendous. The place reeked with prosperity and progress. People even said that the war would finish Germany, that no longer would she be able to compete in the great steel markets of the world. And that, of course, meant more prosperity, more riches.

The flames leapt high above the furnaces. The great sheds echoed with such a pounding as had never before been heard upon this earth. Girls in gas masks worked long hours filling shells with corroding acids which turned their faces haggard, and yellow as the aprons they wore. Little clerks acquired automobiles. Men who dealt in real estate grew rich. Every one would have been content, save for an insatiable appetite for even greater wealth.

Once, to be sure, there occurred an explosion which was for all the world like the end of everything. Forty-seven blackened bodies were carried out under white sheets which clung to the scorched flesh. Of seventeen others nothing at all was found save a few bones, a hand or a foot, a bit of blackened skin; and from these it was impossible to construct any thing. So they were dumped into great trenches, and when the earth had covered them, the world rushed merrily on. The flames leapt higher and redder than ever. The sheds fairly split with the sound of hammering. The little clerks dashed about madly in the sudden luxury of their motors. Every one had money. The Town was prosperous. It grew until it was the biggest in the state. Progress rattled on like everything, so nothing else mattered.

In Paris the war came to an end. One or two statesmen and a whole flock of politicians, after swooping about for a time, descended upon the peace.

In those days Paris acquired an insane and desperate gaiety such as it knew neither before nor since. The bright boulevards swarmed with the soldiers of fourteen nations clad in ten times as many gay uniforms. It became gay and frantic with the neurotic excitement of a madhouse. Street walkers from the provinces, even from Italy and England and Spain, rushed to Paris because business there was so good. In dives and cabarets a barbaric abandon reigned. Every one learned new vices and depravities. Brutes, vulgarians, savages stalked the avenues. Overnight boys became old men, burdened with a corroding wisdom which otherwise they might never have known.

And in the Town people shook their heads sagely and said that war was a great thing when it was fought in a just cause. "It purifies!" they said. "It brings out the finest side of men!"

What was prosperous was right. Wasn't success its own vindication? About this there could be no argument. Money talks, my boy! Money talks! What is successful is right. Germany, the bully among nations! Germany, the greedy materialistic Germany, was done in forever.

Of course it may have been that when they spoke of War as the Great Purifier, they were thinking of the vast army of the Dead.

Chapter 86

WHEN POLITICIANS gather it is necessary to have conventions, receptions, or some sort of a congregation where they may talk or at least make of themselves a spectacle. And so it happened that Paris, where most of the politicians in the world had congregated, began to break out as if suffering from a disease with receptions at this hotel, or that embassy or this palace. It was important that every one should see every one else. It was an opportunity not to be overlooked.

And so it happened that Lily Shane, one gray afternoon in the late winter, found herself for the first time in years surrounded by her countrymen. Rather weary, confused, and a little breathless, she discovered a refuge from the throng in a little alcove of the Hotel Crillon by a window which gave out upon the wide spaces of the Place de la Concorde. The white square was filled now with trophies. High on the terrace of the Tuileries gardens lay a row of shattered aeroplanes—hawklike Gothas, Fokkers like chimney swifts, all torn and battered now, their bright wings bedraggled by the mud and grease of victory. At intervals along the parapet rose great pyramids of German helmets, empty, ghastly, like the heaps of skulls strewn by Ghengis Khan to mark his triumphant progress across the face of Europe. Near the obelisk—so ancient, so withdrawn, so aloof, survivor of a dozen civilizations—the captured guns crouched together pointing their steel muzzles mutely toward the low gray sky. Some came from the great furnaces of the Krupps, some from the celebrated Skoda mills. In the circle marked by the seven proud cities of France, the statues of Lille and Strasbourg, no longer veiled in crêpe, stood impassive, buried beneath heaps of wreaths and flowers. The whole square appeared dimly through the mists that rose from the Seine. The fog hung low and gray, clinging in torn veils about the silent guns, settling low upon the pyramids of empty, skull-like helmets, caressing the hard, smooth granite of the eternal obelisk that stood aloof, mocking, ironic, silent.

Lily sat alone watching the spectacle of the square, as if conscious that in that moment she was at the very heart of the world. Behind her at a little distance moved a procession of figures, confused, grotesque, in the long crystal-hung corridors. It circulated restlessly through the big rooms, moving about the gilt furniture, past the gilt framed mirrors, brushing the heavy curtains. There were British, French, Belgians, Italians, Portuguese, triumphant Japanese, smiling secretly perhaps at the spectacle in the misty Place de la Concorde. There was, of course, a vast number of Americans, . . . politicians, senators, congressmen, mere meddlers, some in neat cutaways, some in gray or blue suits. There were women among them . . . a great many women, brave in mannish clothes, dominating and active in manner.

In all the crowd, so merry, so talkative over the victory, the figure of Lily, withdrawn and silent, carried an inexpressible air of loneliness. It was as if she imitated the obelisk and turned a scornful back upon the restless, gaudy spectacle. She was dressed all in black in a neat suit and a close fitting hat that covered all but a narrow band of amber hair. About her full white throat she wore a tight collar of big pearls. She was no longer young. The voluptuous curves had vanished. She was thinner and, despite the rouge on her lips and cheeks, appeared old. The youthful sparkle of her dark eyes had given place to a curious, hard brilliance. The old indolence appeared to have vanished forever. She sat upright, and at the moment the poise of her body carried a curious sense of likeness to the defiance which had been her mother's. Yet despite all these things she was beautiful. It was impossible to deny her beauty, even though its quality of flamboyance was gone forever. The new beauty was serene, distinguished, worldly—above all else calm. Even the weariness of her face could not destroy a beauty which had to do as much with spirit as with body. She was, after all, no pretty blond thing of the sort which fades into a haggard old age. She was a fine woman, a magnificent woman, not to be overlooked even with youth gone forever.

After a time she turned away from the window and fell to watching the procession of figures. Her rouged lips were curved in the faintest of mocking smiles,—a smile which conveyed a hint of scoffing at some colossal futility, a smile above all else of sophistication and weariness, as if she were at once amused and saddened by the spectacle. Yet it was a kindly smile, tolerant, sympathetic, colored by a hint of some secret, profound, and instinctive wisdom. Motionless, she sat thus for a long time stirring only to fumble with the clasp of the silver bag that lay in her lap. No one noticed her, for she took no part in the spectacle. She sat apart, a little in the shadow, in a backwater, while the noisy tempestuous throng pushed its way through the long vista of gilded, rococo rooms.

Chapter 87

SHE MUST have been sitting there for half an hour when the smile vanished suddenly and the fingers fumbling with the silver bag grew still. Her face assumed an expression of rigidity, the look of one who has seen something in which he is not quite able to believe.

Moving toward her down the long vista of crystal and brocade curtains came a man. He was a big man, tall, massive, handsome in a florid way. He must have been in his middle fifties, although there was but little gray in the thick black hair which he wore rather long in a fashion calculated to attract the notice of passersby. He wore horn-rimmed spectacles and a flowing black tie in striking contrast to the gray neatness of his cutaway and checkered waistcoat. Unmistakably he was an American. His manner carried the same freedom, the identical naive simplicity which characterized the figure of the vigorous Ellen. He possessed the same overflowing vitality. Even as Lily stood, silently, with her back to the tragic spectacle of the square, the vitality overflowed suddenly in a great explosive laugh and a slap on the back of a friend he had encountered in the throng. Above the subdued murmur, the sound of his booming voice reached her.

"Well, well, well! . . . And what are you doing in wicked Paris? Come to fix up the peace, I suppose!"

The answer of the stranger was not audible. The pair withdrew from the path of the procession and talked for a moment. The conversation was punctuated from time to time by the sudden bursts of laughter from the man in the checkered waistcoat.

In her corner Lily leaned forward a little in order to see more clearly the figure which had fascinated her. Presently he turned, bade his friend goodby and moved away again, coming directly down the vista toward Lily. He walked with a swinging stride, and as he approached his large face beamed with satisfaction. He turned his head from side to side with a patronizing air, an air which to Lily must have been startlingly familiar. Even twenty years could not have dissipated the memory of it. It was this which identified him beyond all doubt. He beamed to right and to left. His whole figure betrayed an enormous self-satisfaction. It was impossible any longer to doubt. The man was the Governor. His success was written upon a face now grown heavy and dark.

When he had advanced to within a few paces of Lily's corner, she rose and moved toward him. Only once did she hesitate and then at the very moment he passed by her. Putting out her hand in a furtive movement, she withdrew it hastily. He passed and was on his way to disappearing once more in the throng. For a second she leaned against the wall and then, as if she could no longer resist the temptation, she moved quickly forward and touched his shoulder.

"Henry," she said softly and waited.

The Governor turned and for an instant his face was clouded by a look of bewilderment. Then slowly, almost breathlessly, he recovered himself. The beaming look vanished completely, replaced by an expression of the greatest gravity.

"Lily . . . !" he said. "Lily Shane. . . . For the love of God!"

She drew him aside out of the path of the procession.

"Then you remember me?" she said with a faint, amused smile. "Twenty years is not such a long time."

Again he looked at her. "Lily . . . Lily Shane!" he said. And he took her hand and pressed it with a savage, startled warmth.

"I knew you," she said. "I knew you at once. . . . There are some things about a person which never change . . . little things which *are* the person . . . not much . . . a gesture perhaps. . . . You were unmistakable."

And when he had recovered a little from his astonishment, he managed to say, "It's the last place I'd expect to see you."

Lily laughed at him, in a fashion which must have destroyed suddenly the wall of twenty years. It was a fashion of laughing which belonged to her alone. It was provocative, faintly mocking. Willie Harrison knew it well. "I've lived in Paris for the last twenty years," she retorted with an amused grimace, "and I'm still here. I will be until I die."

Spontaneity does not come easily to a conversation between persons reunited unexpectedly after twenty years; and it was plain that the circumstances surrounding the separation contributed nothing to the facility of the conversation. Lily appeared to have forgotten, or at least to have disregarded the night following the garden party at Cypress Hill. Her manner was that of an old friend, nothing more, nothing less. If she knew any shame, she concealed it admirably. Plainly it was not so easy for her companion. The sudden pallor which had attacked his florid face gave place to a blushing scarlet. He was like a little boy caught in a shameful act.

"You haven't changed much," she said as if to clear the way, "I mean you yourself have not changed . . . not your figure."

He laughed. "I'm fatter . . . much fatter."

It was true.

What had once been clearly a barrel-like chest was sunk to the low estate of a stomach. "But you," he continued, "You haven't changed at all. You're as young as ever."

"You still say the right thing, Henry. But it isn't the truth. I use rouge now. . . . I even dye my hair a little. We can't pretend we're not growing old. It's no use. It's written. . . . It's in our faces."

The Governor thrust a hand into his pocket and fell to jingling a few francs and a key ring. With the other hand he took out his watch. "Couldn't we find some place to sit?" he said. "We might talk for a little while." He coughed nervously. "I haven't much time."

At this she again laughed at him. Her laugh had not grown old. It remained unchanged, still ringing with the same good humor.

"I've no intention of keeping you," she said. "You may go whenever you like." For an instant she cast down her eyes. "When I saw you, I couldn't resist. . . . I had to speak to you. Nothing could have prevented it. I felt, you see, as if I were possessed."

And then she led him back to the corner by the tall window overlooking the misty square. It had grown darker and the cold fog now veiled completely the buildings on the far side of the river. There was only the great square filled with cannon and helmets and shattered planes and above the mass of trophies the rigid, eternal obelisk piercing the mist like a sword.

There they settled themselves to talk, lost in a throng which paid no heed to the middle-aged couple in the alcove. The Governor remained ill at ease, sitting forward upon the edge of his chair as if prepared to spring up and escape at the first opportunity. Lily, so calm, so placid, appeared only to inspire him with confusion. It may have been that she aroused a whole train of memories which he had succeeded in forgetting.

For a time, the conversation flowed along the most stiff and conventional of channels. There were polite inquiries after each other's health. Lily told him of her mother's death, of the fire at Cypress Hill, of the fact that she had severed the last tie with the Town and would never return to it.

"Never?" asked the Governor. "Never?"

"No. Why should I? It is not the same. I have nothing there to call me back. My life is here now. I shall probably die here. The Town is nothing to me."

The Governor's face lighted suddenly. He struck his thigh—a thigh which had once been so handsome and now was flabby with fat—a sharp blow.

"No, it is not the same. You've no idea how it has grown. I was there about six months ago. It's twice as big as in the old days. You know, it's now one of the greatest steel towns in the world. You've a right to be proud of it."

But Lily said nothing. She was looking out of the tall window into the white square.

"And Ellen," the Governor continued, "I hear she has become famous." He laughed. "Who would have thought it? I remember her as a bad-tempered little girl with pigtails. Of course I know nothing about music. It's not in my line. But they say she's great."

When she did not answer him, he regarded her silently for a time and presently he coughed as if to attract her attention. At last he leaned forward a little and said, "What are you thinking?"

For an instant, an unexpected note of tenderness entered his voice. He peered at her closely, examining her soft white skin, the soft hair that escaped from beneath her toque, the exquisite poise of her throat and head. To this scrutiny Lily put an end by turning with a smile to say, "Thinking? I was thinking that there is something hopelessly sad about having no happy realities in the place where you spent your childhood. You see, if I were to go back, I should find nothing. Cypress Hill burned. . . . My Uncle Jacob's farm buried under new houses, each one like its neighbor, in ugly cheap rows . . . the brook ruined by oil and filth. Why, even the people aren't the same. There's no one I should like to see except perhaps Willie Harrison, and it's a long way to go just to see one person. I was thinking that if I'd been born in France, I would have had memories of a village and green country and pleasant stone houses. The people would be the same always. . . . I couldn't go back to the Town now. I couldn't. . . . I have memories of it. I wouldn't want them spoiled." For an instant the tears appeared in her eyes. She leaned toward him and touched his hand. "It's not that I'm disloyal, Henry. Don't think that. It's that I have nothing to be loyal to . . . nothing that I can cherish but memories. I couldn't be happy there because there's nothing but noise and ugliness. I suppose that somewhere in America there are towns full of realities that one could love, but they aren't in my part of the country. There's nothing there." There was a little pause and she added, "It's all happened so quickly. Think of it—it's all happened since I was a little girl."

All this the Governor, it seemed, failed to understand. He looked at her with a hopeless expression of bewilderment. But he said, "Yes, I understand." And again an awkward silence enveloped them.

At last Lily turned to him. "Tell me," she said, "you've been successful. Tell me about yourself."

The Governor leaned back a little in his chair. "But you must have heard all that," he said with astonishment. "It's been in the newspapers. If you're in politics you can't keep out of the press." The beaming look returned to his eyes and with it the old manner of condescension.

"But you forget," replied Lily. "I haven't read American newspapers. I've been away from America for a long time."

"To be sure . . . to be sure." He coughed nervously. "There isn't much to tell. I've been elected senator now for five terms running. I guess I can go on being elected as long as I live. I've gotten what I've set out for. . . . I'm a success in my party. I helped to frame the tariff bill that protected American industry and gave the Town a bigger boom than it ever had before. Oh, I've done my share! . . . Perhaps more than my share! We have a good life in Washington, my wife and I. She's prominent, you know. She's chairman of the State Woman's Republican Committee. Oh, she's very prominent . . . a born leader and a splendid politician. You should hear her make a speech."

Lily listened with an air of profound interest. She was smiling again. As Willie Harrison said, "It was impossible to know what Lily thought. She was always smiling."

The Governor was over-zealous; somehow it seemed that he protested too much.

"Isn't that fine?" she said. "You see, Henry, it has worked out as I told you it would. I should have made you a wretched wife. I would have been no good in politics."

This, it seemed, made him nervous again. He sat forward on the edge of his chair. It was clear that he became terrified when the conversation turned too abruptly toward certain incidents of his youth. It was impossible for him to talk simply and easily. Something kept intruding. Lily may have guessed what it was, for she was a woman of experience in such things. Her companion was merely uncomfortable. He stood up and looked out into the misty square where the lights had begun to show through the fog in little globes of indefinite yellow.

"Extraordinary," he said, "the number of motors in the square." He turned toward her with a sudden enthusiasm. "There you have it! There's America for you . . . motor upon motor! There are more motors with the American High Commission than with any other two combined. We're a rich country, Lily. The war has made us powerful. We can rule the world and do as we please. It's ours from now on. . . . The future is ours if these fools on the American commission don't spoil everything."

Lily smiled again. "Yes. It's quite wonderful. We ought to be proud."

"But you are, aren't you?" he asked severely.

"Yes."

"That's one reason I came over here . . . to put an end to this league of nations nonsense. We won the war and now they're trying to wriggle out. There's no reason we should be mixed up in their troubles. . . . There's no reason we should suffer for it. It's none of our affair."

He drew himself up until his stomach came near to regaining its old place as a chest. His manner became pompous. It was the identical manner Julia Shane had greeted with derision more than twenty years before in the paneled dining-room at Cypress Hill. It was astounding how little the years had softened him. They had, it seemed, brought him nothing of gentleness, nothing of humor, nothing of wisdom . . . only a certain vulgar shrewdness.

"No," he continued, shaking a finger at her, "I've no intention of letting this nonsense pass. There's no reason why we should help them out of what they themselves created."

Lily's eyes grew large and bright. The smile, mysterious, faintly mocking, persisted. "You're wonderful, Henry," she said. "I always knew what you would be like. Do you remember? I told you once. You are just like that . . . just like my prediction."

From her voice or her manner it was impossible to discover what she meant by this cryptic statement. The Governor interpreted it in his own fashion.

"Well," he said, "I have no intention of seeing the American nation being made a dupe just because we're rich and prosperous and the others have ruined themselves. My wife believes I am quite right. She too expects to make a speaking tour." He became enthusiastic again. "You should hear her speak. She has an excellent voice, and great power."

"Yes," said Lily softly. "I would never be able to do all that. I would have been such a failure. . . ."

"She's here with me now . . . in Paris," continued the Governor. "She'd never been abroad. I thought she would enjoy the sights, too, so I brought her along."

"Is she here to-day?" asked Lily. Again the Governor betrayed signs of an overwhelming confusion.

"Yes," he said, "Yes." And suddenly became silent.

For a moment Lily watched him as if the sight of his confusion provided her with some secret amusement. At length she said, "I'd like to see her. I don't ask to meet her, of course. That would be questionable taste. Besides, why should we meet? We could mean nothing to each other."

"No, perhaps not."

Again he began staring out of the window. Lily glanced at the watch on her wrist.

"I shall be forced to leave soon myself," she said. "My husband will be waiting for me."

With a start her companion turned from the window toward her.

"So you're married," he said. "And you never told me."

"You never asked me about myself. I didn't think you were interested in what my life had been."

He thrust out a great hand. "I must congratulate you!" he said with an overflowing enthusiasm. "I must congratulate you! I knew you'd marry some day. How long has it been?" The news appeared to furnish him with a genuine delight. Perhaps he felt more secure now, less frightened of Lily.

She shook hands with him quietly.

"Not for long. . . . Since three months."

"And what is his name?"

"De Cyon . . . René de Cyon. He is in the new ministry. . . . You see I married a politician after all."

She laughed again in that same mysterious, half-mocking, half-cynical fashion. It was impossible to penetrate the barrier of her composure. She was invulnerable. One could not hazard the faintest guess at what she was thinking.

"That is why I am here to-day." And then for the space of an instant she betrayed herself. "Think of it," she said. "What a long way from Cypress Hill to being the wife of a French cabinet minister. We've both traveled a long way since we last met, Henry. A great deal has happened to both of us. On my side, I wouldn't change a thing. There are lives and lives, of course. Some like one sort and some another. I know you've been thinking what a lot I've missed by not marrying you." He moved as if to interrupt her. "Oh, I know you didn't say so openly. It's good of you to be so generous . . . to want me to have shared it." She cast down her eyes suddenly and her voice grew more gentle although it still carried that same devilish note of raillery. "I appreciate all that. . . . But I wouldn't have changed anything. I wouldn't have married you anyway."

Again the Governor coughed and looked out of the window.

"We all come to it sooner or later," he said. "It's a good thing to be married."

"Yes . . . a lonely old age isn't pleasant."

And here a deadlock arose once more in the conversation.

The crowd had begun to thin a little. Down the long vista of rooms it was possible now to distinguish a figure here and there in the throng. Outside the darkness had descended, veiling completely the white square. There was nothing now but the faint globes of light and the dim shooting rays of the passing motors.

The Governor turned suddenly and opened his mouth to speak. Then he closed it again sharply. It was clear that he had intended to say something and had lost his courage. He spoke at last, evading clearly what he had intended to say.

"Tell me . . . Where's Irene?"

"She's buried. . . . She's been buried these eleven years."

The Governor frowned.

"I'd no idea," he stammered. "I wouldn't have asked if I had known."
He was sinking deeper in his confusion. There was something almost pitiful
in his manner, so empty now of pompousness, so devoid of complacency.

Lily smiled. "Oh, she's not dead. She's a nun. She's in the Carmelite
convent at Lisieux . . . I meant that she was buried so far as life is concerned.
She's lost to the world. She never leaves the convent, you know. It's part of
her vow. She's buried there . . . alive! It's a living death." All at once she
cast down her eyes and shuddered. "Perhaps she is dead. . . . When one's
faith is killed one is not alive any more. You see, I killed her faith in this
world. That's all I meant. She's really buried, . . . alive, you understand."

The Governor made a low whistling sound. "I'm not surprised."

As if she did not hear him, Lily said, "I used to think that it was possible
to live by one's self, alone . . . without touching the lives of others. It isn't
possible, is it? Life is far too complicated."

The Governor flushed slowly. He turned the speech nervously once more
to Irene. "You don't forget how she acted on the night . . ." Suddenly he
choked. It was too late now and he finished the speech, inarticulately. "On
the night of the garden party!"

Chapter 88

IT WAS DONE now. He had betrayed himself. The wall was down, and before
them both there must have arisen once more the painful scene in the library
under the malignant portrait of John Shane. (Lily, a young girl, smiling and
saying, "I love you, I suppose, but not better than myself. I might have
married you once. I cannot now, because I know." Julia Shane, so long dead
now, leaning on her ebony stick, hard, unflinching, in the face of everything.
"You see, I can do nothing. There is too much of her father in her.")

It stood before them now, the crisis of two lives, naked, stripped of all
forgetfulness. The Governor, his face scarlet and apoplectic, remained silent,
unable to speak. Lily said softly, "I'm sorry . . . I'm sorry. I should never
have mentioned it. I did not guess it would pain you so."

The new gentleness, the new sympathy revealed itself for the first time
in all their talk together. It showed in her dark, lustrous eyes. There could be
no doubt of it. She was no longer mocking. She was sorry for the lover, grown
old, confused now by the memory of a youthful, overwhelming passion.
She even touched his hand gently.

"It does not matter now," she said. "After all, it was simply a part of life.
I'm not sorry, myself . . . and the world would say that it was I who
suffered most. I didn't suffer . . . Believe me, I didn't suffer." She smiled.
"Besides what could regrets possibly accomplish? It is the future in which

one must live . . . not the past. The longer I live the more certain I am of that."

Still he remained silent. He had become humble, subdued, wilted before the memory of something which had happened more than twenty years before. She must have guessed then, for the first time, what in the unwitting cruelty of her youth she had never known . . . that he had really suffered, far more deeply than she had ever imagined. It may have been hurt pride, for he was a proud man. It may have been that he had loved her passionately. He was, after all, a crude, unsubtle man who must have regarded the whole affair as dishonorable and wretched. It was clear that the wound had never healed, that it still had the power to cause him pain.

"I'm sorry," she repeated. "I'm sorry. . . . There was never any question of forgiveness. I was not injured. . . . Besides it was more my fault than yours."

And then the Governor did a fantastic thing. He bent over his own fat stomach and raised her hand gently to his lips. There was in the gesture a a curious absence of sentimentality. It was not even theatrically self-conscious, as well might have been expected. It was the simple gesture of a man who made speeches before thousands and became helpless and mute before one woman. It was eloquent. It spoke more than whole volumes of words. And somehow it released his tongue.

"The boy?" he said, "What about the boy?"

For a moment Lily did not answer him. She turned away, looking out of the window. She trembled a little and when at last she spoke, it was with averted face, for she lied to him, coldly and with deliberation.

"He is dead," she said gently. "He was killed in the war . . . the very first year, at the beginning." And then she turned with a sudden air of domination over herself and her ravaged, saddened lover. "I must go now," she said. "Good-by, Henry. I wish you luck. I know now that what I respected in you is not dead. It has survived everything. It is not completely destroyed. Until just now, I was afraid."

"Good-by, Lily."

In a moment she was gone, down the long corridor to the spot where M. de Cyon awaited her. Halfway to her destination she turned and saw that the Governor was still watching her. She saw that he watched her despite the fact that he was talking now to a woman, a large woman who was unmistakably his wife. She was deep-bosomed, of the type which becomes masculine with the approach of middle age. She wore flat-heeled shoes and a picture hat with a series of flowing veils. Her gown was of dark blue foulard, figured with an enormous white pattern. Far out upon her massive bosom hung a gold pince-nez suspended from a little hook fashioned in the shape of an elaborate fleur-de-lis. Her manner was commanding, a manner appropriate to the chairman of the State Woman's Republican Committee. She could, no doubt, make wonderful speeches. Doubtless she had a powerful voice. Certainly her manner with the Governor was executive. It is easy to see that in the world of politics she had contributed much to the success of the husband she worshiped. What energy she had! What an appalling power!

As Lily turned away, she saw that he was still watching her, slyly, wistfully, with his head bent a little.

Chapter 89

IT WAS NOT until the spring of 1920 that work was at last begun on the new railway station in the Town. Months before the actual building was undertaken, the Town Council raised on each side of the triangular and barren park at Cypress Hill enormous signs with lettering three feet high. The signs faced the tracks of three great transcontinental railroads. Above the squalor and filth of the Flats they raised their explosive legends. Each read the same.

MAKE YOUR HOME HERE!!!!!
THE HIGHEST, HEALTHIEST, LIVEST, BIGGEST
CITY IN THE STATE
EIGHT STEEL MILLS
AND
SIXTY-SEVEN OTHER INDUSTRIES
WATCH US GROW!!!!

In the deserted park at Cypress Hill workmen appeared who cut down the remaining dead trees. The Venus of Cydnos and the Apollo Belvedere were pulled down from their pedestals in the dead hedge. One of the workmen, a Calabrian, carted them off, scrubbed them clean of the corroding soot and set them up in the back yard of his little house in the Flats. They came to a good end, for the workman cherished them earnestly. In the little garden behind his house, which by some miracle of devotion he managed to fill with green things, he placed the two statues on pedestals which he himself constructed of bricks and concrete. At the base he planted ivy which flourished and spread over the cracked marble and the adjoining fence. So in all the desert of the great mill town there was one corner at least where beauty was worshiped in a humble setting of cabbages and tomato vines. In the evening when the light was not too bright, the little corner looked for all the world like a bit of a Florentine garden.

The steam shovels set to work on a bright April morning with a terrific sound of hissing steam, of grinding cables and clattering chains. In great gulps they tore up the earth which had lain undisturbed since the passing of the second great glacier. For the Town was not satisfied with the destruction of the house at Cypress Hill; it was not content until the Hill itself was scooped up and carted away. It was a wonderful feat and brought the Town a vast amount of advertisement. Pictures of the hill's destruction found their way into the illustrated papers. They were shown in movie palaces in every part of the country.

It happened that on the very day the steam shovels set to work Eva Barr died in the boarding house where she had lived for more than a decade upon the pension provided by her cousin, Lily Shane. Of the family which had founded the Town, she was the last.

On the hill there remained a few people who remembered Cypress Hill in the days of its glory. But most persons had never heard of Shane's Castle and knew nothing of Lily and Irene Shane. When their names were mentioned, the old residents would say, "Yes . . . Lily and Irene. Of course, you never knew them. They belonged to the old Town. Lily was very beautiful and a little fast, so the stories ran, although no one ever knew for certain. Or course, they may be dead by now. I believe Lily was living in Paris the last that was heard of her."

That was all. Within a century Shane's Castle had risen and disappeared. Within a century the old life was gone, and with it the memory of a great, respectable family which had made the history of the county. It survived only in the name of the Town; and that it would have been unprofitable to change since the Town was known round the world as one of the greatest of industrial centers.

Chapter 90

WITH LILY'S MARRIAGE and the end of the war, the house in Rue Raynouard regained something of its old life and gaiety. For M. de Cyon, the match was one surrounded by advantages. His wife was rich and beautiful. She had superb taste. She spoke excellent French and yet she was an American and thus provided a bond with the powerful nation whose favor was invaluable to every nation of Europe. His friends were charmed by her, for she had a way of listening to them, of drinking in their talk with a breathless air. Therefore they declared her not only beautiful but clever, a distinction which even Lily had never claimed. The world knew only that she was an American widow, wealthy, distinguished, beautiful, who had lived very quietly in Paris for more than twenty years. None knew anything against her. Indeed the only person who knew her story was dead, shot in the dungheaps of a French barnyard.

Yet there was, as people said, something about Lily de Cyon that aroused curiosity, even a tenuous suspicion. Somehow she did not fit the story of a quiet existence among the dowdy friends of Madame Gigon. She appeared to have mysterious resources, of instinct, of knowledge, of mystery. *Enfin!* She was a fascinating woman.

The strange gift of the crazy Madame Blaise appeared no longer to fill
her with horror; for The Girl in the Hat and The Byzantine Empress were
brought down from their hiding place in the dusty garret of Numero Dix
and hung on either side of the flaming Venice of Mr. Turner. They were
greatly admired by the painters whom Paul Schneidermann brought to the
house. Some attributed them to Ingres, but none was certain. It was impossible
to say who had painted them for they bore no signature. There were some who
believed that they were the only great pictures of an obscure artist whose
solitary rise from mediocrity came through the inspiration of a woman, a
marvelously beautiful woman with dark amber hair and green white skin.

In the spring of 1920, the postman left with the concierge of Numero Dix
a thin letter bordered in black bearing the postmark of Lisieux. It contained
only a line or two, the mere mention of the death of Sister Monica. She
was buried within the walls of the convent which she had not left in more
than thirteen years.

Chapter 91

THE PAVILON in the garden Lily gave to M. de Cyon for a study. Here it was
her habit to meet him daily on his return from the Ministry when his motor,
a gift from her, left him at the gate on the Rue de Passy.

One bright October day of the same year, she went as usual to the pavilion
to amuse herself until he arrived by reading the newspapers which were placed
upon his table. They lay in a neat pile . . . Le Journal de Genève, Il Seccolo
of Milan, La Tribuna of Roma, the London Post, the London Times, Le
Figaro, L'Echo de Paris, Le Petit Parisien, Le Matin, L'Oeuvre.

She skimmed through them, reading snatches of news, of the opera, and
the theater, of society, of politics, of races, the personals in the London Times
. . . this or that, whatever caught her fancy.

In the drawing-room Ellen and Jean, with his crutches by his side, sat
at the piano playing with four hands snatches of music from the operettas
of the moment, from Phi-Phi and La Reine Joyeuse. They sang and laughed
as they played. The sound of their gaiety drifted out across the garden.

Lily read the journals until she grew bored. Something had delayed M.
de Cyon. Already he was late by half an hour. She came at last, languidly, to
the bottom of the pile, to L'Oeuvre which lay buried beneath the more
pompous and expensive papers. This she never read because it was a socialist
daily and therefore dull. Doubtless she would have passed it by again for
the hundredth time but a name, buried in one corner in the smallest of print,
caught her attention. It must have struck her suddenly with all the force of
a blow in the face, for she closed her eyes and leaned back in her chair. The
paper slipped to the floor forgotten.

It was a brief paragraph, not more than three or four lines. It recounted the death of one Stepan Krylenko, a man well known as a leader in international labor circles. He died, according to the despatch, of typhus in Moscow whither he had been deported by the American government.

(Perhaps, after all, the Uhlan was right. The Monster would devour them all in the end.)

After a time Lily rose and went out of the pavilion into the garden where she walked slowly up and down for a long time, seating herself at last on the bench under the laburnum tree.

Inside the house the wild merriment persisted. Ellen was singing now in a rich contralto voice a valse which she played with an exaggerated sweep of sentimentality. From the peak of her hard and cynical intelligence, she mocked the song. She sang,

> "O, la troublante volupté
> de la première etreinte
> qu'on risque avec timidité
> et presque avec contrainte
> Le contact vous fait frisonner. . . ."

In a wild burst of mocking laughter, the song came abruptly to an end. The shattered chords floated out into the garden where Lily sat leaning against the laburnum tree, silent and thoughtful, her eyes filled with sorrow and wonder. She was in that moment more beautiful than she had ever been before . . . a symbol of that which is above all else eternal, which knows no bonds, which survives cities and mills and even nations, which is in itself the beginning and end of all things, without which the world itself must fail.

And presently, far down among the plane trees, the gate in the high wall swung gently open and, against the distant lights of the Rue de Passy, the figure of the white-haired M. de Cyon came into the garden.

THE END

EARLY AUTUMN

Chapter 1

THERE WAS a ball in the old Pentland house because for the first time in nearly forty years there was a young girl in the family to be introduced to the polite world of Boston and to the elect who had been asked to come on from New York and Philadelphia. So the old house was all bedizened with lanterns and bunches of late spring flowers, and in the bare, white-painted, dignified hallway a negro band, hidden discreetly by flowers, sat making noisy, obscene music.

Sybil Pentland was eighteen and lately returned from school in Paris, whither she had been sent against the advice of the conservative members of her own family, which, it might have been said, included in its connections most of Boston. Already her great-aunt, Mrs. Cassandra Struthers, a formidable woman, had gone through the list of eligible young men—the cousins and connections who were presentable and possessed of fortunes worthy of consideration by a family so solidly rich as the Pentlands. It was toward this end that the ball had been launched and the whole countryside invited, young and old, spry and infirm, middle-aged and dowdy—toward this end and with the idea of showing the world that the family had lost none of its prestige for all the lack of young people in its ranks. For this prestige had once been of national proportions, though now it had shrunk until the Pentland name was little known outside New England. Rather, it might have been said that the nation had run away from New England and the Pentland family, leaving it stranded and almost forgotten by the side of the path which marked an unruly, almost barbaric progress away from all that the Pentland family and the old house represented.

Sybil's grandfather had seen to it that there was plenty of champagne; and there were tables piled with salads and cold lobster and sandwiches and hot chicken in chafing-dishes. It was as if a family whose whole history had been marked by thrift and caution had suddenly cast to the winds all semblance of restraint in a heroic gesture toward splendor.

But in some way, the gesture seemed to be failing. The negro music sounded wild and spirited, but also indiscreet and out of place in a house so old and solemn. A few men and one or two women known for their fondness for drink consumed a great deal of champagne, but only dulness came of it, dulness and a kind of dead despair. The rich, the splendorous, the gorgeous, the barbaric, had no place in rooms where the kind Mr. Longfellow and the immortal Messrs. Emerson and Lowell had once sat and talked of life. In a hallway, beneath the gaze of a row of ancestors remarkable for the grimness of their faces, the music appeared to lose its quality of abandon; it did not belong in this genteel world. On the fringes of the party there was some drunkenness among the undergraduates imported from Cambridge, but there was very little gaiety. The champagne fell upon barren ground. The party drooped.

Though the affair was given primarily to place Sybil Pentland upon the matrimonial market of this compact world, it served, too, as an introduction for Thérèse Callendar, who had come to spend the summer at Brook Cottage across the stony meadows on the other side of the river from Pentlands; and as a reintroduction of her mother, a far more vivid and remarkable person. Durham and the countryside thereabouts was familiar enough to her, for she had been born there and passed her childhood within sight of the spire of the Durham town meeting-house. And now, after an absence of twenty years, she had come back out of a world which her own people—the people of her childhood—considered strange and ungenteel. Her world was one filled with queer people, a world remote from the quiet old house at Pentlands and the great brownstone houses of Commonwealth Avenue and Beacon Street. Indeed, it was this woman, Sabine Callendar, who seemed to have stolen all the thunder at the ball; beside her, neither of the young girls, her own daughter nor Sybil Pentland, appeared to attract any great interest. It was Sabine whom every one noticed, acquaintances of her childhood because they were devoured by curiosity concerning those missing twenty years, and strangers because she was the most picturesque and arresting figure at the ball.

It was not that she surrounded herself by adoring young men eager to dance with her. She was, after all, a woman of forty-six, and she had no tolerance for mooning boys whose conversation was limited to bootlegging and college clubs. It was a success of a singular sort, a triumph of indifference.

People like Aunt Cassie Struthers remembered her as a shy and awkward young girl with a plain face, a good figure and brick-red hair which twenty years ago had been spoken of as "Poor Sabine's ugly red hair." She was a girl in those days who suffered miserably at balls and dinners, who shrank from all social life and preferred solitude. And now, here she was—returned—a tall woman of forty-six, with the same splendid figure, the same long nose and green eyes set a trifle too near each other, but a woman so striking in appearance and the confidence of her bearing that she managed somehow to dim the success even of younger, prettier women and virtually to extinguish the embryonic young things in pink-and-white tulle. Moving about indolently from room to room, greeting the people who had known her as a girl, addressing here and there an acquaintance which she had made in the course of the queer, independent, nomadic life she had led since divorcing her husband, there was an arrogance in her very walk that frightened the young and produced in the older members of Durham community (all the cousins and connections and indefinable relatives), a sense of profound irritation. Once she had been one of them, and now she seemed completely independent of them all, a traitress who had flung to the winds all the little rules of life drilled into her by Aunt Cassie and other aunts and cousins in the days when she had been an awkward, homely little girl with shocking red hair. Once she had belonged to this tight little world, and now she had returned—a woman who should have been defeated and a little declassée and somehow, irritatingly, was not. Instead, she was a "figure" much sought after in the world, enveloped by the mysterious cloud of esteem which surrounds such persons—a woman, in short, who was able to pick her friends from the ranks of distinguished and even celebrated people. It was not only because this was true, but because people like Aunt Cassie *knew* it was true, that she aroused interest and even indignation. She had turned her back upon them all and no awful fate had overtaken her; instead, she had taken a firm hold upon life and made of it a fine, even a glittering, success; and this is a thing which is not easily forgiven.

As she moved through the big rooms—complete and perfect from her superbly done, burnished red hair to the tips of her silver slippers—there was about her an assurance and an air of confidence in her own perfection that bordered upon insolence. There was a hard radiance and beauty in the brilliant green dress and the thin chain of diamonds that dimmed all of the others, that made most of the women seem dowdy and put together with pins. Undoubtedly her presence also served to dampen the gaiety. One knew from the look in the disdainful green eyes and the faint mocking smile on the frankly painted red mouth that she was aware of the effect she made and was delighted with her triumph. Wherever she went, always escorted by some man she had chosen with the air of conferring a favor, a little stir preceded her. She was indeed very disagreeable. . . .

If she had a rival in all the crowd that filled the echoing old house, it was Olivia Pentland—Sybil's mother—who moved about, alone most of the time, watching her guests, acutely conscious that the ball was not all it should have been. There was about her nothing flamboyant and arresting, nothing which glittered with the worldly hardness of the green dress and the diamonds and burnished red hair of Sabine Callendar; she was, rather, a soft woman, of gentleness and poise, whose dark beauty conquered in a slower, more subtle fashion. You did not notice her at once among all the guests; you became aware of her slowly, as if her presence had the effect of stealing over you with the vagueness of a perfume. Suddenly you marked her from among all the others . . . with a sense of faint excitement . . . a pale white face, framed by smooth black hair drawn back low over the brows in a small knot at the back of her head. You noticed the clear, frank blue eyes, that in some lights seemed almost black, and most of all you noticed when she spoke that her voice was low, warm, and in a way irresistible, a voice with a hundred shades of color. She had a way, too, of laughing, when she was struck by the absurdity of something, that was like a child. One knew her at once for a great lady. It was impossible to believe that she was nearly forty and the mother of Sybil and a boy of fifteen.

Circumstance and a wisdom of her own had made of her a woman who

seemed inactive and self-effacing. She had a manner of doing things effort-
lessly, with a great quietness, and yet, after one came to know her, one felt
that she missed little which took place within sight or hearing—not only the
obvious things which any stupid person might have noticed, but the subtle,
indefinite currents which passed from one person to another. She possessed,
it seemed, a marvelous gift for smoothing out troubles. A security, of the
sort which often marks those who suffer from a too great awareness, enveloped and preceded her, turning to calm all the troubled world about her.
Yet she was disturbing, too, in an odd, indefinable way. There was always a
remoteness and a mystery, a sense almost of the *fey*. It was only after one had
known her for a long time, enveloped in the quietness of her pleasant presence, that a faint sense of uneasiness was born. It would occur to you, with
the surprise almost of a shock, that the woman you saw before you, the
woman who was so gentle and serene, was not Olivia Pentland at all, but a
kind of lay figure which concealed, far beneath the veneer of charm, a
woman you did not know at all, who was remote and sad and perhaps lonely.
In the end, she disturbed the person of discernment far more profoundly
than the glittering, disagreeable Sabine Callendar.

In the midst of the noise and confusion of the ball, she had been moving
about, now in this big room, now in that one, talking quietly to her guests,
watching them, seeing that all went well; and, like all the others, she was
fascinated at the spectacle of Sabine's rebellion and triumph, perhaps even a
little amused at the childishness of such defiance in a woman of forty-six who
was clever, independent and even distinguished, who need not have troubled
to flaunt her success.

Watching Sabine, whom she knew intimately enough, she had guessed that
underneath the shell made so superbly by hairdresser, couturier and jeweler
there lay hidden an awkward, red-haired little girl who was having her revenge now, walking roughshod over all the prejudices and traditions of such
people as Aunt Cassie and John Pentland and Cousin Struthers Smallwood, D.D., whom Sabine always called "the Apostle to the Genteel." It was
almost, thought Olivia, as if Sabine, even after an exile of twenty years, was
still afraid of them and that curious, undefeatable power which they represented.

But Sabine, she knew, was observing the party at the same time. She had
watched her all the evening in the act of "absorbing" it; she knew that when
Sabine walked across from Brook Cottage the next day, she would know
everything that had happened at the ball, for she had a passion for inspecting
life. Beneath the stony mask of indifference there boiled a perpetual and
passionate interest in the intricacies of human affairs. Sabine herself had
once described it as "the curse of analysis which took all the zest out of life."

She was fond of Sabine as a creature unique in the realm of her experience,
one who was amusing and actually made fetishes of truth and reality. She
had a way of turning her intellect (for it was really a great intellect) upon
some tangled, hopeless situation to dissolve it somehow into its proper ele-

ments and make it appear suddenly clear, uncomplicated and, more often than not, unpleasant; because the truth was not always a sweet and pleasant thing.

2

No one suffered more keenly from Sabine's triumphant return than the invincible Aunt Cassie. In a way, she had always looked upon Sabine, even in the long years of her voluntary exile from the delights of Durham, as her own property, much as she might have looked upon a dog, if, indeed, the old lady had been able to bear the society of anything so untidy as a dog. Childless herself, she had exercised all her theories of upbringing upon the unfortunate orphaned little daughter of her husband's brother.

At the moment, the old lady sat half-way down the white stairs, her sharp black eyes surveying the ball with a faint air of disapproval. The noisy music made her nervous and uneasy, and the way young girls had of using paint and powder seemed to her cheap and common. "One might as well brush one's teeth at the dinner-table." Secretly, she kept comparing everything with the ball given for herself forty years earlier, an event which had resulted at length in the capture of Mr. Struthers. Dressed economically (for she made it a point of honor to live on the income of her income), and in mourning for a husband dead eight years earlier, she resembled a dignified but slightly uneasy crow perched on a fence.

It was Sabine who observed that Aunt Cassie and her "lady companion," Miss Peavey, sitting on the steps together, resembled a crow and a pouter pigeon. Miss Peavey was not only fat, she was actually bulbous—one of those women inclined by nature toward "flesh," who would have been fat on a diet of sawdust and distilled water; and she had come into the family life thirty years earlier as a companion, a kind of slave, to divert Aunt Cassie during the long period of her invalidism. She had remained there ever since, taking the place of a husband who was dead and children who had never been born.

There was something childlike about Miss Peavey—some people said that she was not quite bright—but she suited Aunt Cassie to a T, for she was as submissive as a child and wholly dependent in a financial sense. Aunt Cassie even gave her enough to make up for the losses she incurred by keeping a small shop in Boston devoted to the sale of "artistic" pottery. Miss Peavey was a lady, and though penniless, was "well connected" in Boston. At sixty she had grown too heavy for her birdlike little feet and so took very little exercise. To-night she was dressed in a very fancy gown covered with lace and sequins and passementerie, rather in the mode which some one had told her was her style in the far-off days of her girlhood. Her hair was streaked with gray and cut short in a shaggy, uneven fashion; not, however, because short hair was *chic*, but because she had cut it ten years before short hair had been heard of, in a sudden futile gesture of freedom at the terrible moment she made her one feeble attempt to escape Aunt Cassie and lead her own life. She had come back in the end, when her poor savings gave out and bankruptcy faced her, to be received by Aunt Cassie with dignified sighs and flutters as a returned and repentant prodigal. In this rôle she had lived ever since in a state of complete subjection. She was Aunt Cassie's creature now, to go where Aunt Cassie ordered, to do as she was bid, to be an ear-piece when there was at hand no one more worthy of address.

At the sight of Sabine's green dress and red hair moving through the big hall below them, Aunt Cassie said, with a gleam in her eye: "Sabine seems to be worried about her daughter. The poor child doesn't seem to be having a success, but I suppose it's no wonder. The poor thing is very plain. I suppose she got the sallow skin from her father. He was part Greek and French. . . . Sabine was never popular as a young girl herself."

And she fell to speculating for the hundredth time on the little-known circumstances of Sabine's unhappy marriage and divorce, turning the morsels over and over again with a variety of speculation and the interjection of much pious phraseology; for in Aunt Cassie's speech God seemed to have a hand in everything. He had a way of delivering trials and blessings indiscriminately, and so in the end became responsible for everything.

Indeed, she grew a bit spiteful about Sabine, for there was in the back of her mind the memory of an encounter, a day or two earlier, when she had been put completely to rout. It was seldom that Aunt Cassie met any one who was a match for her, and when such an encounter took place the memory of it rankled until she found some means of subduing the offender. With Miss Peavey she was completely frank, for through long service this plump, elderly virgin had come to be a sort of confessor in whose presence Aunt Cassie wore no mask. She was always saying, "Don't mind Miss Peavey. She doesn't matter."

"I find Sabine extremely hard and worldly," she was saying. "I would never know her for the same modest young girl she was on leaving me." She sighed abysmally and continued, "But, then, we mustn't judge. I suppose the poor girl has had a great deal of misery. I pity her to the depths of my heart!"

In Aunt Cassie's speeches, in every phrase, there was always a certain mild theatrical overtone as if she sought constantly to cast a sort of melodramatic haze over all she said. Nothing was ever stated simply. Everything from the sight of a pot of sour cream to the death of her husband affected her extravagantly, to the depths of her soul.

But this brought no response from Miss Peavey, who seemed lost in the excitement of watching the young people, her round candid eyes shining through her pince-nez with the eagerness of one who has spent her whole life as a "lady companion." At moments like this, Aunt Cassie felt that Miss Peavey was not quite bright, and sometimes said so.

Undiscouraged, she went on. "Olivia looks bad, too, to-night . . . very tired and worn. I don't like those circles under her eyes. . . . I've thought for a long time that she was unhappy about something."

But Miss Peavey's volatile nature continued to lose itself completely in the spectacle of young girls who were so different from the girls of her day; and in the fascinating sight of Mr. Hoskins, a fat, sentimental, middle-aged neighbor who had taken a glass too much champagne and was talking archly to the patient Olivia. Miss Peavey had quite forgotten herself in the midst of so much gaiety. She did not even see the glances of Aunt Cassie in her direction—glances which plainly said, "Wait until I get you alone!"

For a long time Aunt Cassie had been brooding over what she called "Olivia's strange behavior." It was a thing which she had noticed for the first time a month or two earlier when Olivia, in the midst of one of Aunt Cassie's morning calls, had begun suddenly, quietly, to weep and had left the room without a word of explanation. It had gone from bad to worse lately; she felt Olivia slipping away from all control directly in opposition to her own benevolent advice. There was the matter of this very ball. Olivia had ignored her counsels of economy and thrift, and now Aunt Cassie was suffering, as if the champagne which flowed so freely were blood drawn from her own veins. Not for a century, since Savina Pentland purchased a parure of pearls and emeralds, had so much Pentland money been expended at one time on mere pleasure.

She disapproved, too, of the youthfulness of Olivia and of Sabine. Women of their ages ought not to look so fresh and young. There was something vulgar, even a little improper, in a woman like Sabine who at forty-six looked thirty-five. At thirty, Aunt Cassie herself had settled down as a middle-aged woman, and since then she had not changed greatly. At sixty-five, "childless and alone in the world" (save, of course, for Miss Peavey), she was much the same as she had been at thirty in the rôle of wife to the "trying Mr. Struthers." The only change had been her recovery from a state of semi-invalidism, a miracle occurring simultaneously with the passing of Mr. Struthers.

She had never quite forgiven Olivia for being an outsider who had come into the intricate web of life at Pentlands out of (of all places) Chicago. Wisps of mystery and a faint sense of the alien had clung to her ever since. Of course, it wasn't to be expected that Olivia could understand entirely what it meant to marry into a family whose history was so closely woven into that of the Massachusetts Bay Colony and the life of Boston. What could it mean to Olivia that Mr. Longfellow and Mr. Lowell and Dr. Holmes had often spent weeks at Pentlands? That Mr. Emerson himself had come there for week-ends? Still (Aunt Cassie admitted to herself), Olivia had done remarkably well. She had been wise enough to watch and wait and not go ahead strewing her path with blunders.

Into the midst of these thoughts the figure of Olivia herself appeared, moving toward the stairway, walking beside Sabine. They were laughing over something, Sabine in the sly, mocking way she had, and Olivia mischievously, with a suspicious twinkle in her eyes. Aunt Cassie was filled with an awful feeling that they were sharing some joke about the people at the ball, perhaps even about herself and Miss Peavey. Since Sabine had returned, she felt that Olivia had grown even more strange and rebellious; nevertheless, she admitted to herself that there was a distinction about them both. She preferred the quiet distinction of Olivia to the violence of the impression made by the glittering Sabine. The old lady sensed the distinction, but, belonging to a generation which lived upon emotion rather than analysis, she did not get to the root of it. She did not see that one felt at once on seeing Olivia, "Here is a lady!"—perhaps, in the true sense of the word, the only lady in the room. There was a gentleness about her and a softness and a proud sort of poise—all qualities of which Aunt Cassie approved; it was the air of mystery which upset the old lady. One never knew quite what Olivia was thinking. She was so gentle and soft-spoken. Sometimes of late, when pressing Olivia too hotly, Aunt Cassie, aware of rousing something indefinably perilous in the nature of the younger woman, drew back in alarm.

Rising stiffly, the old lady groaned a little and, moving down the stairs, said, "I must go, Olivia dear," and, turning, "Miss Peavey will go with me."

Miss Peavey would have stayed, because she was enjoying herself, looking down on all those young people, but she had obeyed the commands of Aunt Cassie for too long, and now she rose, complaining faintly, and made ready to leave.

Olivia urged them to stay, and Sabine, looking at the old lady out of green eyes that held a faint glitter of hatred, said abruptly: "I always thought you stayed until the bitter end, Aunt Cassie."

A sigh answered her . . . a sigh filled with implications regarding Aunt Cassie's position as a lonely, ill, bereft, widowed creature for whom life was finished long ago. "I am not young any longer, Sabine," she said. "And I feel that the old ought to give way to the young. There comes a time. . . ."

Sabine gave an unearthly chuckle. "Ah," she said, in her hard voice, "I haven't begun to give up yet. I am still good for years."

"You're not a child any more, Sabine," the old lady said sharply.

"No, certainly I'm not a child any more." And the remark silenced Aunt Cassie, for it struck home at the memory of that wretched scene in which she had been put to rout so skilfully.

There was a great bustle about getting the two old ladies under way, a great search for cloaks and scarfs and impedimenta; but at last they went off, Aunt Cassie saying over her thin, high shoulder, "Will you say good-by to your dear father-in-law, Olivia? I suppose he's playing bridge with Mrs. Soames."

"Yes," replied Olivia from the terrace, "he's playing bridge with Mrs. Soames."

Aunt Cassie merely cleared her throat, forcibly, and with a deep significance. In her look, as in the sound of her voice, she managed to launch a flood of disapproval upon the behavior of old John Pentland and old Mrs. Soames.

Bidding the driver to go very slowly, she climbed into her shabby, antiquated motor, followed respectfully by Miss Peavey, and drove off down the long elm-bordered drive between the lines of waiting motors.

Olivia's "dear father-in-law" was Aunt Cassie's own brother, but she chose always to relate him to Olivia, as if in some way it bound Olivia more closely, more hopelessly, into the fabric of the family.

As the two younger women re-entered the house, Olivia asked, "Where's Thérèse? I haven't seen her for more than an hour."

"She's gone home."

"Thérèse . . . gone home . . . from a ball given for her!"

Olivia halted in astonishment and stood leaning against the wall, looking so charming and lovely that Sabine thought, "It's a sin for a woman so beautiful to have such a life."

Aloud Sabine said, "I caught her stealing away. She walked across to the cottage. She said she hated it and was miserable and bored and would rather be in bed." Sabine shrugged her handsome shoulders and added, "So I let her go. What difference does it make?"

"None, I suppose."

"I never force her to do things of this sort. I had too much forcing when I was young; Thérèse is to do exactly as she likes and be independent. The trouble is, she's been spoilt by knowing older men and men who talk intelligently." She laughed and added, "I was wrong about coming back here. I'll never marry her off in this part of the world. The men are all afraid of her."

Olivia kept seeing the absurd figure of Sabine's daughter, small and dark, with large burning eyes and an air of sulky independence, striding off on foot through the dust of the lane that led back to Brook Cottage. She was so different from her own daughter, the quiet, well-mannered Sybil.

"I don't think she's properly impressed by Durham," said Olivia, with a sudden mischievous smile.

"No . . . she's bored by it."

Olivia paused to say good-night to a little procession of guests . . . the Pingree girls dressed alike in pink tulle; the plump Miss Perkins, who had the finest collection of samplers in New England; Rodney Phillips, whose life was devoted to breeding springers and behaving like a perfect English gentleman; old Mr. Tilney, whose fortune rested on the mills of Durham and Lynn and Salem; and Bishop Smallwood, a cousin of the Pentlands and Sabine (whom Sabine called the Apostle of the Genteel). The Bishop complimented Olivia on the beauty of her daughter and coquetted heavily with Sabine. Motors rushed out from among the lilacs and syringas and bore them away one by one.

When they had gone Sabine said abruptly, "What sort of man is this Higgins. . . . I mean your head stableman?"

"A good sort," replied Olivia. "The children are very fond of him. Why?"

"Oh . . . no reason at all. I happened to think of him to-night because I noticed him standing on the terrace just now looking in at the ball."

"He was a jockey once . . . a good one, I believe, until he got too heavy.

He's been with us ten years. He's good and reliable and sometimes very funny. Old Mr. Pentland depends on him for everything. . . . Only he has a way of getting into scrapes with the girls from the village. He seems irresistible to them . . . and he's an immoral scamp."

Sabine's face lighted up suddenly, as if she had made a great discovery. "I thought so," she observed, and wandered away abruptly to continue the business of "absorbing" the ball.

She had asked about Higgins because the man was stuck there in her brain, set in the midst of a strange, confused impression that disturbed a mind usually marked by precision and clarity. She did not understand why it was that he remained the most vivid of all the kaleidoscopic procession of the ball. He had been an outsider, a servant, looking in upon it, and yet there he was—a man whom she had never noticed before—vivid and clear-cut, dominating the whole evening.

It had happened a little earlier when, standing in the windowed alcove of the old red-paneled writing-room, she had turned her back for a moment on the ball, to look out upon the distant marshes and the sea, across meadows where every stone and tree and hedge was thrown into a brilliant relief by the clarity of the moonlight and the thin New England air. And trapped suddenly by the still and breathless beauty of the meadows and marshes and distant white dunes, lost in memories more than twenty years old, she had found herself thinking: "It was always like this . . . rather beautiful and hard and cold and a little barren, only I never saw it before. It's only now, when I've come back after twenty years, that I see my own country exactly as it is."

And then, standing there quite alone, she had become aware slowly that she was being watched by some one. There was a sudden movement among the lilacs that stood a little way off wrapped in thick black shadows . . . the faintest stirring of the leaves that drew her sharply back to a consciousness of where she was and why she was there; and, focusing all her attention, she was able to make out presently a short, stocky little figure, and a white face peering out from among the branches, watching the dancers who moved about inside the house. The sight produced in her suddenly a sensation of uneasiness and a faint prickling of the skin, which slipped away presently when she recognized the odd, prematurely wrinkled face of Higgins, the Pentland groom. She must have seen him a dozen times before, barely noticing him, but now she saw him with a kind of illuminating clarity, in a way which made his face and figure unforgettable.

He was clad in the eternal riding-breeches and a sleeveless cotton shirt that exposed the short, hairy, muscular arms. Standing there he seemed, with his arched, firmly planted legs, like some creature rooted into the soil . . . like the old apple-tree which stood in the moonlight showering the last of its white petals on the black lawn. There was something unpleasant in the sight, as if (she thought afterwards) she had been watched without knowing it by some animal of an uncanny intelligence.

And then abruptly he had slipped away again, shyly, among the branches of the lilacs . . . like a faun.

Olivia, looking after Sabine as she walked away, smiled at the knowledge of where she was bound. Sabine would go into the old writing-room and there, sitting in a corner, would pretend that she was interested in the latest number of the *Mercure de France* or some fashion paper, and all the time she would be watching, listening, while old John Pentland and poor battered old Mrs. Soames sat playing bridge with a pair of contemporaries. Sabine, she knew, wanted to probe the lives of the two old people. She wasn't content like the others at Pentlands to go on pretending that there had never been anything between them. She wanted to get to the root of the story, to know the truth. It was the truth, always the truth, which fascinated Sabine.

And Olivia felt a sudden, swift, almost poignant wave of affection for the abrupt, grim woman, an affection which it was impossible to express because Sabine was too scornful of all sentiment and too shut in ever to receive gracefully a demonstration; yet she fancied that Sabine knew she was fond of her, in the same shy, silent way that old John Pentland knew she was fond of him. It was impossible for either of them ever to speak of such simple things as affection.

Since Sabine had come to Durham, it seemed to Olivia that life was a little less barren and not quite so hopeless. There was in Sabine a curious hard, solid strength which the others, save only the old man, lacked completely. Sabine had made some discovery in life that had set her free . . . of everything but that terrible barrier of false coldness.

In the midst of these thoughts came another procession of retreating guests, and the sadness, slipping away from Olivia's face, gave way to a perfect, artificial sort of gaiety. She smiled, she murmured, "Good-night, must you go," and, "Good-night, I'm so glad that you liked the ball." She was arch with silly old men and kind to the shy young ones and repeated the same phrases over and over again monotonously. People went away saying, "What a charming woman Olivia Pentland is!"

Yet immediately afterward she did not remember who had passed by her.

One by one the guests departed, and presently the black musicians packed up their instruments and went away, and at last Sybil appeared, shy and dark, looking a little pale and tired in her clinging gown of pale green. At sight of her daughter a little thrill of pride ran through Olivia. She was the loveliest of all the girls at the ball, not the most flamboyant, but the gentlest and really the most beautiful. She possessed the same slow beauty of her mother, which enveloped one in a kind of mist that lingered long after she herself had gone away. She was neither loud and mannish and vulgar like the "horsey" women nor common like the girls who used too much paint and tried to behave like women of the world. There was already about her the timelessness that envelops a lady no matter the generation in which she appears; there was a mystery, a sophistication and knowledge of life which put to rout all the cheap flashiness of the others. And yet, somehow, that same cool, shy poise and beauty frightened people. Boys who were used to calling young girls "Good old So-and-so" found themselves helpless before the dignity of a young girl who looked in her green gown a little like a cool wood-nymph. It troubled Olivia profoundly, not for herself, but because she wanted the girl to be happy—more than that, to know the depths of happiness which she herself had sensed but never found. It was in a way as if she saw herself again in Sybil, as if looking back now from the pinnacle of her own experience she could guide this younger self, standing on the brink of life, along paths less barren than those trod by her own feet. It was so necessary that Sybil should fall in love with a man who would make her happy. With most girls it would make little difference one way or another, so long as they had money; if they were unhappy or bored they would divorce their husbands and try again because that was the rule in their world. But with Sybil, marriage would be either an immense, incalculable happiness or a profound and hopeless tragedy.

She thought suddenly of what Sabine had said of Thérèse a little while before. "I was wrong about coming back here. I'll never marry her off in this part of the world."

It was true somehow of Sybil. The girl, in some mysterious fashion, knew what it was she wanted; and this was not a life which was safe and assured, running smoothly in a rigid groove fixed by tradition and circumstance. It was not marriage with a man who was like all the other men in his world. It went deeper than all that. She wanted somehow to get far down beneath the surface of that life all about her, deep down where there was a savor to all she did. It was a hunger which Olivia understood well enough.

The girl approached her mother and, slipping her arm about her waist, stood there, looking for all the world like Olivia's sister.

"Have you enjoyed it?" asked Olivia.

"Yes. . . . It's been fun."

Olivia smiled. "But not too much?"

"No, not too much." Sybil laughed abruptly, as if some humorous memory had suddenly come to life.

"Thérèse ran away," said her mother.

"I know . . . she told me she was going to."

"She didn't like it."

"No . . . she thought the boys stupid."

"They're very much like all boys of their age. It's not an interesting time."

Sybil frowned a little. "Thérèse doesn't think so. She says all they have to talk about is their clubs and drinking . . . neither subject is of very much interest."

"They might have been, if you'd lived here always . . . like the other girls. You and Thérèse see it from the outside." The girl didn't answer, and Olivia asked: "You don't think I was wrong in sending you to France to school?"

Quickly Sybil looked up. "Oh, no . . . no," she said, and then added with smoldering eagerness, "I wouldn't have changed it for anything in the world."

"I thought you might enjoy life more if you saw a little more than one corner of it. . . . I wanted you to be away from here for a little time." (She did not say what she thought—"because I wanted you to escape the blight that touches everything at Pentlands.")

"I'm glad," the girl replied. "I'm glad because it makes everything different. . . . I can't explain it. . . . Only as if everything had more meaning than it would have otherwise."

Suddenly Olivia kissed her daughter and said: "You're a clever girl; things aren't wasted on you. And now go along to bed. I'll stop in to say good-night."

She watched the girl as she moved away through the big empty hall past the long procession of Pentland family portraits, thinking all the while that beside them Sybil seemed so fresh and full of warm eager life; and when at last she turned, she encountered her father-in-law and old Mrs. Soames moving along the narrow passage that led from the writing-room. It struck her sharply that the gaunt, handsome old John Pentland seemed really old tonight, in a way he had never been before, old and a little bent, with purplish circles under his bright black eyes.

Old Mrs. Soames, with her funny, intricate, dyed-black coiffure and rouged cheeks and sagging chin supported by a collar of pearls, leaned on his arm—the wreck of a handsome woman who had fallen back upon such silly, obvious tricks as rouge and dye—a vain, tragic old woman who never knew that she was a figure of fun. At sight of her, there rose in Olivia's mind a whole vista of memories—assembly after assembly with Mrs. Soames in stomacher and tiara standing in the reception line bowing and smirking over rites that had survived in a provincial fashion some darker, more barbaric, social age.

And the sight of the old man walking gently and slowly, out of deference to Mrs. Soames' infirmities, filled Olivia with a sudden desire to weep.

John Pentland said, "I'm going to drive over with Mrs. Soames, Olivia dear. You can leave the door open for me." And giving his daughter-in-law a quick look of affection he led Mrs. Soames away across the terrace to his motor.

It was only after they had gone that Olivia discovered Sabine standing in the corridor in her brilliant green dress watching the two old people from the shadow of one of the deep-set windows. For a moment, absorbed in the sight of John Pentland helping Mrs. Soames with a grim courtliness into the motor, neither of them spoke, but as the motor drove away down the long drive under the moon-silvered elms, Sabine sighed and said, "I can remember her as a great beauty . . . a really great beauty. There aren't any more like her, who make their beauty a profession. I used to see her when I was a little girl. She was beautiful—like Diana in the hunting-field. They've been like that for . . . for how long. . . . It must be forty years, I suppose."

"I don't know," said Olivia quietly. "They've been like that ever since I came to Pentlands." (And as she spoke she was overcome by a terrible feeling of sadness, of an abysmal futility. It had come to her more and more often of late, so often that at times it alarmed her lest she was growing morbid.)

Sabine was speaking again in her familiar, precise, metallic voice. "I wonder," she said, "if there has ever been anything. . . ."

Olivia, divining the rest of the question, answered it quickly, interrupting the speech. "No . . . I'm sure there's never been anything more than we've seen. . . . I know him well enough to know that."

For a long time Sabine remained thoughtful, and at last she said: "No . . . I suppose you're right. There couldn't have been anything. He's the last of the Puritans. . . . The others don't count. They go on pretending, but they don't believe any more. They've no vitality left. They're only hypocrites and shadows. . . . He's the last of the royal line."

She picked up her silver cloak and, flinging it about her fine white shoulders, said abruptly: "It's almost morning. I must get some sleep. The time's coming when I have to think about such things. We're not as young as we once were, Olivia."

On the moonlit terrace she turned and asked: "Where was O'Hara? I didn't see him."

"No . . . he was asked. I think he didn't come on account of Anson and Aunt Cassie."

The only reply made by Sabine was a kind of scornful grunt. She turned away and entered her motor. The ball was over now and the last guest gone, and she had missed nothing—Aunt Cassie, nor old John Pentland, nor O'Hara's absence, nor even Higgins watching them all in the moonlight from the shadow of the lilacs.

The night had turned cold as the morning approached and Olivia, standing in the doorway, shivered a little as she watched Sabine enter her motor and drive away. Far across the meadows she saw the lights of John Pentland's motor racing along the lane on the way to the house of old Mrs. Soames; she watched them as they swept out of sight behind the birch thicket and reappeared once more beyond the turnpike, and as she turned away at last it occurred to her that the life at Pentlands had undergone some subtle change since the return of Sabine.

Chapter 2

It was Olivia's habit (and in some way every small action at Pentlands came inevitably to be a habit) to go about the house each night before climbing the paneled stairs, to see that all was in order, and by instinct she made the little tour as usual after Sabine had disappeared, stopping here and there to speak to the servants, bidding them to go to bed and clear away in the morning. On her way she found that the door of the drawing-room, which had been open all the evening, was now, for some reason, closed.

It was a big square room belonging to the old part of the house that had been built by the Pentland who made a fortune out of equipping privateers and practising a sort of piracy upon British merchantmen—a room which in the passing of years had come to be a museum filled with the relics and souvenirs of a family which could trace its ancestry back three hundred years to a small dissenting shopkeeper who had stepped ashore on the bleak New England coast very soon after Miles Standish and Priscilla Alden. It was a room much used by all the family and had a worn, pleasant look that compensated for the monstrous and incongruous collection of pictures and furniture. There were two or three Sheraton and Hepplewhite chairs and a handsome old mahogany table, and there were a plush sofa and a vast rocking-chair of uncertain ancestry, and a hideous bronze lamp that had been the gift of Mr. Longfellow to old John Pentland's mother. There were two execrable water-colors—one of the Tiber and the Castle San Angelo and one of an Italian village—made by Miss Maria Pentland during a tour of Italy in 1846, and a stuffed chair with tassels, a gift from old Colonel Higginson, a frigid steel engraving of the Signing of the Declaration which hung over the white mantelpiece, and a complete set of Woodrow Wilson's History of the United States given by Senator Lodge (whom Aunt Cassie always referred to as "dear Mr. Lodge"). In this room were collected mementoes of long visits paid by Mr. Lowell and Mr. Emerson and General Curtis and other good New Englanders, all souvenirs which Olivia had left exactly as she found them when she came to the big house as the bride of Anson Pentland; and to those who knew the room and the family there was nothing unbeautiful or absurd about it. The effect was historical. On entering it one almost expected a guide to step forward and say, "Mr. Longfellow once wrote at this desk," and, "This was Senator Lodge's favorite chair." Olivia knew each tiny thing in the room with a sharp sense of intimacy.

She opened the door softly and found that the lights were still burning and, strangest of all, that her husband was sitting at the old desk surrounded by the musty books and yellowed letters and papers from which he was compiling laboriously a book known as "The Pentland Family and the Massachusetts Bay Colony." The sight of him surprised her, for it was his habit to retire punctually at eleven every night, even on such an occasion as this. He had disappeared hours earlier from the ball, and he still sat here in his dinner coat, though it was long after midnight.

She had entered the room so softly that he did not hear her and for a moment she remained silently looking down at him, as if undetermined whether to speak or to go quietly away. He sat with his back to her so that the sloping shoulders and the thin, ridged neck and partly bald head stood outlined against the white of the paneling. Suddenly, as if conscious of being watched, he turned and looked at her. He was a man of forty-nine who looked older, with a long horse-face like Aunt Cassie's—a face that was handsome in a tired, yellow sort of way—and small, round eyes the color of pale-blue porcelain. At the sight of Olivia the face took on a pouting expression of sourness . . . a look which she knew well as one that he wore when he meant to complain of something.

"You are sitting up very late," she observed quietly, with a deliberate air of having noticed nothing unusual.

"I was waiting to speak to you. I want to talk with you. Please sit down for a moment."

There was an odd sense of strangeness in their manner toward each other, as if there had never been, even years before when the children were babies, any great intimacy between them. On his part there was, too, a sort of stiff and nervous formality, rather quaint and Victorian, and touched by an odd air of timidity. He was a man who would always do not perhaps the proper thing, but the thing accepted by his world as "proper."

It was the first time since morning that the conversation between them had emerged from the set pattern which it had followed day after day for so many years. When he said that he wanted to speak to her, it meant usually that there was some complaint to be made against the servants, more often than not against Higgins, whom he disliked with an odd, inexplicable intensity.

Olivia sat down, irritated that he should have chosen this hour when she was tired, to make some petty comment on the workings of the house. Half without thinking and half with a sudden warm knowledge that it would annoy him to see her smoking, she lighted a cigarette; and as she sat there, waiting until he had blotted with scrupulous care the page on which he had been writing, she became conscious slowly of a strange, unaccustomed desire to be disagreeable, to create in some way an excitement that would shatter for a moment the overwhelming sense of monotony and so relieve her nerves. She thought, "What has come over me? Am I one of those women who enjoys working up scenes?"

He rose from his chair and stood, very tall and thin, with drooping shoulders, looking down at her out of the pale eyes. "It's about Sybil," he said. "I understand that she goes riding every morning with this fellow O'Hara."

"That's true," replied Olivia quietly. "They go every morning before breakfast, before the rest of us are out."

He frowned and assumed almost mechanically a manner of severe dignity. "And you mean to say that you have known about it all along?"

"They meet down in the meadows by the old gravel-pit because he doesn't care to come up to the house."

"He knows, perhaps, that he wouldn't be welcome."

Olivia smiled a little ironically. "I'm sure that's the reason. That's why he didn't come to-night, though I asked him. You must know, Anson, that I don't feel as you do about him."

"No, I suppose not. You rarely do."

"There's no need to be unpleasant," she said quietly.

"You seem to know a great deal about it."

"Sybil tells me everything she does. It is much better to have it that way, I think."

Watching him, it gave her a faint, warm sense of satisfaction to see that Anson was annoyed by her calmness, and yet she was a little ashamed, too, for wanting the excitement of a small scene, just a tiny scene, to make life seem a little more exciting. He said, "But you know how Aunt Cassie and my father feel about O'Hara."

Then, for the first time, Olivia began to see light in the darkness. "Your father knows all about it, Anson. He has gone with them himself on the red mare, once or twice."

"Are you sure of that?"

"Why should I make up such a ridiculous lie? Besides, your father and I get on very well. You know that." It was a mild thrust which had its success, for Anson turned away angrily. She had really said to him, "Your father comes to *me* about everything, not to *you*. He is not the one who objects or I should have known." Aloud she said, "Besides, I have seen him with my own eyes."

"Then I will take it on my own responsibility. I don't like it and I want it stopped."

At this speech Olivia's brows arched ever so slightly with a look which might have been interpreted either as one of surprise or one of mockery or perhaps a little of both. For a moment she sat quite still, thinking, and at last she said, "Am I right in supposing that Aunt Cassie is at the bottom of this?" When he made no reply she continued, "Aunt Cassie must have gotten up very early to see them off." Again a silence, and the dark little devil in Olivia urged her to say, "Or perhaps she got her information from the servants. She often does, you know."

Slowly, while she was speaking, her husband's face had grown more and more sour. The very color of the skin seemed to have changed so that it appeared faintly green in the light from the Victorian luster just above his narrow head.

"Olivia, you have no right to speak of my aunt in that way."

"We needn't go into that. I think you know that what I said was the truth." And a slow warmth began to steal over her. She was getting beneath his skin. After all those long years, he was finding that she was not entirely gentle.

He was exasperated now and astonished. In a more gentle voice he said, "Olivia, I don't understand what has come over you lately."

She found herself thinking, wildly, "Perhaps he is going to soften. Perhaps there is still a chance of warmth in him. Perhaps even now, after so long, he is going to be pleasant and kind and perhaps . . . perhaps . . . more."

"You're very queer," he was saying. "I'm not the only one who finds you so."

"No," said Olivia, a little sadly. "Aunt Cassie does, too. She's been telling all the neighborhood that I seem to be unhappy. Perhaps it's because I'm a little tired. I've not had much rest for a long time now . . . from Jack, from Aunt Cassie, from your father . . . and . . . from *her*." At the last word she made a curious little half-gesture in the direction of the dark north wing of the big house.

She watched him, conscious that he was shocked and startled by her mentioning in a single breath so many things which they never discussed at Pentlands, things which they buried in silence and tried to destroy by pretending that they did not exist.

"We ought to speak of those things, sometimes," she continued sadly. "Sometimes when we are entirely alone with no one about to hear, when it doesn't make any difference. We can't pretend forever that they don't exist."

For a time he was silent, groping obviously, in a kind of desperation for something to answer. At last he said feebly, "And yet you sit up all night playing bridge with Sabine and old Mrs. Soames and Father."

"That does me good. You must admit that it is a change at least."

But he only answered, "I don't understand you," and began to pace up and down in agitation while she sat there waiting, actually waiting, for the thing to work itself up to a climax. She had a sudden feeling of victory, of intoxication such as she had not known in years, not since she was a young girl; and at the same time she wanted to laugh, wildly, hysterically, at the sight of Anson, so tall and thin, prancing up and down.

Opposite her he halted abruptly and said, "And I can see no good in inviting Mrs. Soames here so often."

She saw now that the tension, the excitement between them, was greater even than she had imagined, for Anson had spoken of Mrs. Soames and his father, a thing which in the family no one ever mentioned. He had done it quite openly, of his own free will.

"What harm can it do now? What difference can it make?" she asked. "It is the only pleasure left to the poor battered old thing, and one of the few left to your father."

Anson began to mutter in disgust. "It is a silly affair . . . two old . . . old. . . ." He did not finish the sentence, for there was only one word that could have finished it and that was a word which no gentleman and certainly no Pentland ever used in referring to his own father.

"Perhaps," said Olivia, "it is a silly affair now. . . . I'm not so sure that it always was."

"What do you mean by that? Do you mean. . . ." Again he fumbled for words, groping to avoid using the words that clearly came into his mind. It was strange to see him brought face to face with realities, to see him grow so helpless and muddled. "Do you mean," he stammered, "that my father has ever behaved . . ." he choked and then added, "dishonorably."

"Anson . . . I feel strangely like being honest to-night . . . just for once . . . just for once."

"You are succeeding only in being perverse."

"No . . ." and she found herself smiling sadly, "unless you mean that in this house . . . in this room . . ." She made a gesture which swept within the circle of her white arm all that collection of Victorian souvenirs, all the mementoes of a once sturdy and powerful Puritan family, ". . . in this room to be truthful and honest is to be perverse."

He would have interrupted her here, angrily, but she raised her hand and continued, "No, Anson; I shall tell you honestly what I think . . . whether you want to hear it or not. I don't hope that it will do any good. . . . I do not know whether, as you put it, your father has behaved dishonorably or not. I hope he has. . . . I hope he was Mrs. Soames' lover in the days when love could have meant something to them. . . . Yes . . . something fleshly is exactly what I mean. . . . I think it would have been better. I think they might have been happy . . . really happy for a little time . . . not just living in a state of enchantment when one day is exactly like the next. . . . I think your father, of all men, has deserved that happiness. . . ." She sighed and added in a low voice, "There, now you know!"

For a long time he simply stood staring at the floor with the round, silly blue eyes which sometimes filled her with terror because they were so like the eyes of that old woman who never left the dark north wing and was known in the family simply as *she*, as if there was very little that was human left in her. At last he muttered through the drooping mustache, as if speaking to himself, "I can't imagine what has happened to you."

"Nothing," said Olivia. "Nothing. I am the same as I have always been, only to-night I have come to the end of saying 'yes, yes' to everything, of always pretending, so that all of us here may go on living undisturbed in our dream . . . believing always that we are superior to every one else on the earth, that because we are rich we are powerful and righteous, that because . . . oh, there is no use in talking. . . . I am just the same as I have always been, only to-night I have spoken out. We all live in a dream here . . . a dream that some day will turn sharply into a nightmare. And then what will we do? What will you do . . . and Aunt Cassie and all the rest?"

In her excitement her cheeks grew flushed and she stood up, very tall and beautiful, leaning against the mantelpiece; but her husband did not notice her. He appeared to be lost in deep thought, his face contorted with a kind of grim concentration.

"I know what has happened," he said presently. "It is Sabine. She should never have come back here. She was like that always . . . stirring up trouble . . . even as a little girl. She used to break up our games by saying: 'I won't play house. Who can be so foolish as to pretend muddy water is claret! It's a silly game.'"

"Do you mean that she is saying it again now . . . that it's a silly game to pretend muddy water is claret?"

He turned away without answering and began again to pace up and down over the enormous faded roses of the old Victorian carpet. "I don't know what you're driving at. All I know is that Sabine . . . Sabine . . . is an evil woman."

"Do you hate Sabine because she is a friend of mine?"

She had watched him for so many years disliking the people who were her friends, managing somehow to get rid of them, to keep her from seeing them, to force her into those endless dinners at the houses of the safe men he knew, the men who had gone to his college and belonged to his club, the men who would never do anything that was unexpected. And in the end she had always done as he wanted her to do. It was perhaps a manifestation of his resentment toward all those whom he could not understand and even (she thought) feared a little—the attitude of a man who will not allow others to enjoy what he could not take for himself. It was the first time she had ever spoken of this dog-in-the-manger game, but she found herself unable to keep silent. It was as if some power outside her had taken possession of her body. She had a strange sensation of shame at the very moment she spoke, of shame at the sound of her own voice, a little strained and hysterical.

There was something preposterous, too, in the sight of Anson prancing up and down the old room filled with all the souvenirs of that decayed respectability in which he wrapped himself . . . prancing up and down with all his prejudices and superstitions bristling. And now Olivia had dragged the truth uncomfortably into the light.

"What an absurd thing to say!" he said bitterly.

Olivia sighed. "No, I don't think so. . . . I think you know exactly what I mean." (She knew the family game of pretending never to understand a truthful, unpleasant statement.)

But this, too, he refused to answer. Instead, he turned to her, more savage and excited than she had ever seen him, so moved that he seemed for a second to attain a pale flash of power and dignity. "And I don't like that Fiji Islander of a daughter of hers, who has been dragged all over the world and had her head filled with barbaric ideas."

At the sight of him and the sound of his voice Olivia experienced a sudden blinding flash of intuition that illuminated the whole train of their conversation, indeed, the whole procession of the years she had spent here at Pentlands or in the huge brownstone house in Beacon Street. She knew suddenly what it was that frightened Anson and Aunt Cassie and all that intricate world of family. They were terrified lest the walls, the very foundations, of their existence be swept away leaving them helpless with all their little prides and vanities exposed, stripped of all the laws and prejudices which they had made to protect them. It was why they hated O'Hara, an Irishman and a Roman Catholic. He had menaced their security. To be exposed thus would be a calamity, for in any other world save their own, in a world where they stood unprotected by all that money laid away in solid trust funds, they would have no existence whatever. They would suddenly *be* what they *really* were.

She saw sharply, clearly, for the first time, and she said quietly, "I think you dislike Thérèse for reasons that are not fair to the girl. You distrust her because she is different from all the others . . . from the sort of girls that you were trained to believe perfect. Heaven knows there are enough of them about here . . . girls as like as peas in a pod."

"And what about this boy who is coming to stay with Sabine and her daughter . . . this American boy with a French name who has never seen his own country until now? I suppose he'll be as queer as all the others. Who knows anything about him?"

"Sabine," began Olivia.

"Sabine!" he interrupted. "Sabine! What does she care who he is or where he comes from? She's given up decent people long ago, when she went away from here and married that Levantine blackguard of a husband. Sabine! . . . Sabine would only like to bring trouble to us . . . the people to whom she belongs. She hates us. . . . She can barely speak to me in a civil fashion."

Olivia smiled quietly and tossed her cigarette into the ashes beneath the cold steel engraving of the Signing. "You are beginning to talk nonsense, Anson. Let's stick to facts, for once. I've met the boy in Paris. . . . Sybil knew him there. He is intelligent and handsome and treats women as if they were something more than stable-boys. There are still a few of us left who like to be treated thus . . . as women . . . a few of us even here in Durham. No, I don't imagine you'll care for him. He won't belong to your club or to your college, and he'll see life in a different way. He won't have had his opinions all ready made, waiting for him."

"It's my children I'm thinking of. . . . I don't want them picking up with any one, with the first person who comes along."

Olivia did not smile. She turned away now and said softly, "If it's Jack you're worrying about, you needn't fuss any longer. He won't marry Thérèse. I don't think you know how ill he is. . . . I don't think, sometimes, that you really know anything about him at all."

"I always talk with the doctors."

"Then you ought to know that they're silly . . . the things you're saying."

"All the same, Sabine ought never to have come back here. . . ."

She saw now that the talk was turning back into the inevitable channel of futility where they would go round and round, like squirrels in a cage, arriving nowhere. It had happened this way so many times. Turning with an air of putting an end to the discussion, she walked over to the fireplace . . . pale once more, with faint, mauve circles under her dark eyes. There was a fragility about her, as if this strange spirit which had flamed up so suddenly were too violent for the body.

"Anson," she said in a low voice, "please let's be sensible. I shall look into this affair of Sybil and O'Hara and try to discover whether there is anything serious going on. If necessary, I shall speak directly to both of them. I don't approve, either, but not for the same reason. He is too old for her. You won't have any trouble. You will have to do nothing. . . . As to Sabine, I shall continue to see as much of her as I like."

In the midst of the speech she had grown suddenly, perilously, calm in the way which sometimes alarmed her husband and Aunt Cassie. Sighing a little, she continued, "I have been good and gentle, Anson, for years and years, and now, to-night . . . to-night I feel as if I were coming to the end of it. . . . I only say this to let you know that it can't go on forever."

Picking up her scarf, she did not wait for him to answer her, but moved away toward the door, still enveloped in the same perilous calm. In the doorway she turned. "I suppose we can call the affair settled for the moment?"

He had been standing there all the while watching her out of the round cold blue eyes with a look of astonishment as if after all those years he had seen his wife for the first time; and then slowly the look of astonishment melted into one of slyness, almost of hatred, as if he thought, "So this is what you really are! So you have been thinking these things all these years and have never belonged to us at all. You have been hating us all the while. You have always been an outsider—a common, vulgar outsider."

His thin, discontented lips had turned faintly gray, and when he spoke it was nervously, with a kind of desperation, like a small animal trapped in a corner. The words came out from the thin lips in a sharp, quick torrent, like the rush of white-hot steel released from a cauldron . . . words spoken in a voice that was cold and shaken with hatred.

"In any case," he said, "in any case . . . I will not have my daughter marry a shanty Irishman. . . . There is enough of that in the family."

For a moment Olivia leaned against the door-sill, her dark eyes wide with astonishment, as if she found it impossible to believe what she had heard. And then quietly, with a terrible sadness and serenity in her voice, she murmured almost to herself, "What a rotten thing to say!" And after a little pause, as if still speaking to herself, "So that is what you have been thinking for twenty years!" and again, "There is a terrible answer to that. . . . It's so terrible that I shan't say it, but I think you . . . you and Aunt Cassie know well enough what it is."

Closing the door quickly, she left him there, startled and exasperated, among all the Pentland souvenirs, and slowly, in a kind of nightmare, she made her way toward the stairs, past the long procession of Pentland ancestors—the shopkeeping immigrant, the witch-burner, the professional evangelist, the owner of clipper ships, and the tragic, beautiful Savina Pentland —and up the darkened stairway to the room where her husband had not followed her in more than fifteen years.

Once in her own room she closed the door softly and stood in the darkness, listening, listening, listening. . . . There was at first no sound save the blurred distant roar of the surf eating its way into the white dunes and the far-off howling of a beagle somewhere in the direction of the kennels, and then presently, there came to her the faint sound of soft, easy breathing from the adjoining room. It was regular, easy and quiet, almost as if her son had been as strong as O'Hara or Higgins or that vigorous young de Cyon whom she had met once for a little while at Sabine's house in Paris.

The sound filled her with a wild happiness, so that she forgot even what had happened in the drawing-room a little while before. As she undressed in the darkness she stopped now and then to listen again in a kind of fierce tension, as if by wishing it she could keep the sound from ever dying away. For more than three years she had never once entered this room free from the terror that there might only be silence to welcome her. And at last, after she had gone to bed and was falling asleep, she was wakened sharply by another sound, quite different, the sound of a wild, almost human cry . . . savage and wicked, and followed by the thud thud of hoofs beating savagely against the walls of a stall, and then the voice of Higgins, the groom, cursing wickedly. She had heard it before—the sound of old John Pentland's evil, beautiful red mare kicking the walls of her stall and screaming wildly. There was an unearthly, implacable hatred between her and the little apelike man . . . and yet a sort of fascination, too.

As she sat up in her bed, listening, and still startled by the wild sound, she heard her son saying:

"Mama, are you there?"

"Yes."

She rose and went into the other room, where, in the dim light from the night-lamp, the boy was sitting up in bed, his pale blond hair all rumpled, his eyes wide open and staring a little.

"You're all right, Jack?" she whispered. "There's nothing the matter?"

"No—nothing. I had a bad dream and then I heard the red mare."

He looked pale and ill, with the blue veins showing on his temples; yet she knew that he was stronger than he had been for months. He was fifteen, and he looked younger than his age, rather like a boy of thirteen or fourteen, but he was old, too, in the timeless fashion of those who have always been ill.

"Is the party over? . . . Have they all gone?" he asked.

"Yes, Jack. . . . It's almost daylight. You'd better try to sleep again."

He lay down without answering her, and as she bent to kiss him good-night, she heard him say softly, "I wish I could have gone to the party."

"You will, Jack, some day—before very long. You're growing stronger every day."

Again a silence, while Olivia thought bitterly, "He knows that I'm lying. He knows that what I've said is not the truth."

Aloud she said, "You'll go to sleep now—like a good boy."

"I wish you'd tell me about the party."

Olivia sighed. "Then I must close Nannie's door, so we won't waken her." And she closed the door leading to the room where the old nurse slept, and seating herself on the foot of her son's bed, she began a recital of who had been at the ball, and what had happened there, bit by bit, carefully and with all the skill she was able to summon. She wanted to give him, who had so little chance of living, all the sense of life she was able to evoke.

She talked on and on, until presently she noticed that the boy had fallen asleep and that the sky beyond the marshes had begun to turn gray and rose and yellow with the rising day.

Chapter 3

1

WHEN OLIVIA first came to the old house as the wife of Anson Pentland, the village of Durham, which lay inland from Pentlands and the sea, had been invisible, lying concealed in a fold of the land which marked the faint beginnings of the New Hampshire mountains. There had been in the view a certain sleepy peacefulness: one knew that in the distant fold of land surmounted by a single white spire there lay a quiet village of white wooden houses built along a single street called High Street that was dappled in summer with the shadows of old elm-trees. In those days it had been a country village, half asleep, with empty shuttered houses here and there falling into slow decay—a village with fewer people in it than there had been a hundred years before. It had stayed thus sleeping for nearly seventy-five years, since the day when a great migration of citizens had robbed it of its sturdiest young people. In the thick grass that surrounded the old meeting-house there lay a marble slab recording the event with an inscription which read:

FROM THIS SPOT ON THE FOURTEENTH DAY OF AUGUST, EIGHTEEN HUN-
DRED AND EIGHTEEN, THE REVEREND JOSIAH MILFORD, PASTOR OF THIS
CHURCH, WITH ONE HUNDRED AND NINETY MEMBERS OF HIS CONGREGA-
TION—MEN, WOMEN AND CHILDREN—SET OUT, SECURE IN THEIR FAITH IN
ALMIGHTY GOD, TO ESTABLISH HIS WILL AND POWER IN THE WILDER-
NESS OF THE WESTERN RESERVE.

Beneath the inscription were cut the names of those families who had made the journey to found a new town which had since surpassed sleepy Durham a hundred times in wealth and prosperity. There was no Pentland name among them, for the Pentlands had been rich even in the year eighteen hundred and eighteen, and lived in winter in Boston and in summer at Durham, on the land claimed from the wilderness by the first of the family.

From that day until the mills came to Durham the village sank slowly into a kind of lethargy, and the church itself, robbed of its strength, died presently and was changed into a dusty museum filled with homely early American furniture and spinning-wheels—a place seldom visited by any one and painted grudgingly every five years by the town council because it was popularly considered an historical monument. The Pentland family long ago

had filtered away into the cold faith of the Unitarians or the more compromising and easy creeds of the Episcopal church.

But now, nearly twenty years after Olivia had come to Pentlands, the
village was alive again, so alive that it had overflowed its little fold in the
land and was streaming down the hill on the side next to the sea in straight,
plain columns of ugly stucco bungalows, each filled with its little family of
Polish mill-workers. And in the town, across High Street from the white-
spired old meeting-house, there stood a new church, built of stucco and
green-painted wood and dedicated to the great Church of Rome. In the old
wooden houses along High Street there still lingered remnants of the old
families . . . old Mrs. Featherstone, who did washing to support four sickly
grandchildren who ought never to have been born; Miss Haddon, a queer old
woman who wore a black cape and lived on a dole from old John Pentland as a
remote cousin of the family; Harry Peckham, the village carpenter; old Mrs.
Malson, living alone in a damp, gaunt and beautiful old house filled with
bits of jade and ivory brought back from China by her grandfather's clippers;
Miss Murgatroyd, who had long since turned her bullfinch house into a
shabby tea-room. They remained here and there, a few worn and shabby-
genteel descendants of those first settlers who had come into the country
with the Pentlands.

But the mills had changed everything, the mills which poured wealth
into the pockets of a dozen rich families who lived in summer within a few
miles of Durham.

Even the countryside itself had changed. There were no longer any of the
old New Englanders in possession of the land. Sometimes in riding along
the lanes one encountered a thin, silly-faced remnant of the race sitting on a
stone wall chewing a bit of grass; but that was all: the others had been
swallowed up long ago in the mills of Salem and Lynn or died away, from
too much inbreeding and too little nourishment. The few farms that remained fell into the hands of Poles and Czechs, solid, square people who
were a little pagan in their closeness to the earth and the animals which
surrounded them, sturdy people, not too moral, who wrought wonders with
the barren, stony earth of New England and stood behind their walls staring
wide-eyed while the grand people like the Pentlands rode by in pink coats
surrounded by the waving nervous tails of foxhounds. And, one by one, other
old farms were being turned back into a wilderness once more so that there
would be plenty of room for the horses and hounds to run after foxes and
bags of aniseed.

It had all changed enormously. From the upper windows of the big
Georgian brick house where the Pentlands lived, one could see the record of
all the changes. The windows commanded a wide view of a landscape composed of grubby meadows and stone walls, thickets of pine and white birches,
marshes, and a winding sluggish brown river. Sometimes in the late autumn
the deer wandered down from the mountains of New Hampshire to spoil the

fox-hunting by leading the hounds astray after game that was far too fleet for them.

And nearer at hand, nestled within a turn of the river, lay the land where Sabine Callendar had been born and had lived until she was a grown woman—the land which she had sold carelessly to O'Hara, an Irish politician and a Roman Catholic, come up from nowhere to take possession of it, to clip its hedges, repair its sagging walls, paint its old buildings and put up gates and fences that were too shiny and new. Indeed, he had done it so thoroughly and so well that the whole place had a little the air of a suburban real estate development. And now Sabine had returned to spend the summer in one of his houses and to be very friendly with him in the face of Aunt Cassie and Anson Pentland, and a score of others like them.

Olivia knew this wide and somberly beautiful landscape, every stick and stone of it, from the perilous gravel-pit, half-hidden by its fringe of elder-bushes, to the black pine copse where Higgins had discovered only a day or two before a new litter of foxes. She knew it on gray days when it was cold and depressing, on those bright, terribly clear New England days when every twig and leaf seemed outlined by light, and on those damp, cold days when a gray fog swept in across the marshes from the sea to envelop all the country-side in gray darkness. It was a hard, uncompromising, stony country that was never too cheerful.

It was a country, too, which gave her an old feeling of loneliness . . . a feeling which, strangely enough, seemed to increase rather than diminish as the years passed. She had never accustomed herself to its occasional dreari-ness. In the beginning, a long while ago, it had seemed to her green and peaceful and full of quiet, a place where she might find rest and peace . . . but she had come long since to see it as it was, as Sabine had seen it while she stood in the window of the writing-room, frightened by the sudden queer apparition of the little groom—a country beautiful, hard and cold, and a little barren.

2

There were times when the memories of Olivia's youth seemed to sharpen suddenly and sweep in upon her, overwhelming all sense of the present, times when she wanted suddenly and fiercely to step back into that far-off past which had seemed then an unhappy thing; and these were the times when she felt most lonely, the times when she knew how completely, with the passing of years, she had drawn into herself; it was a process of protection like a tortoise drawing in its head. And all the while, in spite of the smiles and the politeness and the too facile amiability, she felt that she was really a stranger at Pentlands, that there were certain walls and barriers which she could never break down, past which she could never penetrate, certain faiths in which it was impossible for her to believe.

It was difficult now for her to remember very clearly what had happened before she came to Durham; it all seemed lost, confused, buried beneath the weight of her devotion to the vast family monument of the Pentlands. She had forgotten the names of people and places and confused the days and the years. At times it was difficult for her to remember the endless confusing voyages back and forth across the Atlantic and the vast, impersonal, vacuous hotels which had followed each other in the bleak and unreal procession of her childhood.

She could remember with a certain pitiful clarity two happy years spent at the school in Saint-Cloud, where for months at a time she had lived in a single room which she might call her own, where she had rested, free from the terror of hearing her mother say, "We must pack to-day. We are leaving to-morrow for St. Petersburg or London or San Remo or Cairo. . . ."

She could scarcely remember at all the immense house of chocolate-colored stone fitted with fantastic turrets and balconies that overlooked Lake Michigan. It had been sold and torn down long ago, destroyed like all else that belonged to the far-off past. She could not remember the father who had died when she was three; but of him there remained at least a yellowing photograph of a great, handsome, brawny man with a humorous Scotch-Irish face, who had died at the moment when his name was coming to be known everywhere as a power in Washington. No, nothing remained of him save the old photograph, and the tenuous, mocking little smile which had come down to her, the way she had of saying, "Yes! Yes!" pleasantly when she meant to act in quite the contrary fashion.

There were times when the memory of her own mother became vague and fantastic, as if she had been no more than a figure out of some absurd photograph of the early nineteen hundreds . . . the figure of a pretty woman, dressed fashionably in clothes that flowed away in both directions, from a wasp waist. It was like a figure out of one of those old photographs which one views with a kind of melancholy amusement. She remembered a vain, rather selfish and pretty woman, fond of flattery, who had been shrewd enough never to marry any one of those gallant dark gentlemen with high-sounding titles who came to call at the eternal changeless hotel sitting-room, to take her out to garden parties and fêtes and races. And always in the background of the memory there was the figure of a dark little girl, overflowing with spirits and a hunger for friends, who was left behind to amuse herself by walking out with the Swiss governess, to make friends among the children she encountered in the parks or on the beaches and the boulevards of whatever European city her mother was visiting at the moment . . . friends whom she saw to-day and who were vanished to-morrow never to be seen again. Her mother, she saw now, belonged to the America of the nineties. She saw her now less as a real person than a character out of a novel by Mrs. Wharton.

But she had never remarried; she had remained the rich, pretty Mrs. Mc-Connel of Chicago until that tragic day (the clearest of all Olivia's memories and the most terrible) when she had died of fever abruptly in a remote and squalid Italian village, with only her daughter (a girl of seventeen), a quack doctor and the Russian driver of her motor to care for her.

The procession of confused and not-too-cheerful memories came to a climax in a gloomy, red brick house off Washington Square, where she had gone as an orphan to live with a rigid, bejetted, maternal aunt who had believed that the whole world revolved about Lenox, the Hudson River Valley and Washington Square—an aunt who had never spoken to Olivia's father because she, like Anson and Aunt Cassie, had a prejudice against Irishmen who appeared out of nowhere, engaging, full of life and high spirits.

So at eighteen she had found herself alone in the world save for one bejetted aunt, with no friends save those she had picked up as a child on beaches and promenades, whose names she could no longer even remember. And the only fixed world she knew was the world of the aunt who talked incessantly of the plush, camphor-smelling splendor of a New York which no longer existed.

Olivia saw it all clearly now. She saw why it was that when Anson Pentland came one night to call upon her aunt she had thought him an elegant and fascinating man whose presence at dinner had the power of transforming the solid walnut and mahogany dining-room into a brilliant place. He was what girls called "an older man," and he had flattered her by his politeness and attentions. He had even taken her, chaperoned by the aunt, to see a performance of "The City," little knowing that the indecorousness to be unfolded there would force them to leave before the play was over. They had gone on a Thursday evening (she could even remember the very day) and she still smiled at the memory of their belief that a girl who had spent all her life in the corridors of European hotels should not know what the play was about.

And then it had all ended by her being asked to Pentlands for a visit . . . to Pentlands, where she had come upon a world such as she had never known before, a world green and peaceful and secure, where every one was elaborately kind to her for reasons that she never learned until long afterward. They never even told her the truth about Anson's mother, the old woman who lived in solitude in the north wing. She was, they said, too ill at the moment to see any one. Pentlands, in that far-off day, had seemed to the tired, friendless girl like some vast, soft green bed where she could fling herself down and rest forever, a world where she could make friends and send down roots that would hold her secure for all time. To a hotel child Pentlands was a paradise; so when Anson Pentland asked her to marry him, she accepted him because she did not find him actually repulsive.

And now, after all those years, it was spring again . . . spring as when she had come to Pentlands for the first time, and she was thirty-nine years old and still young; only everything had changed.

Bit by bit, in the years that followed the birth of Sybil and then of Jack, the whole picture of the life at Pentlands and in the brownstone house on

Beacon Street had come to assume a pattern, to take form out of the first confused and misty impressions, so that, looking back upon it, she was beginning to understand it all with the chill clarity of disillusion.

She saw herself as a shy young girl to whom they had all been elaborately kind because it was so necessary for Anson to have a wife and produce an heir. . . . Anson, the last male descendant of such a glorious family. ("The Pentland Family and the Massachusetts Bay Colony.") She saw herself as they must have seen her . . . a pretty young girl, disarmed by their kindness, who was not known in their world but was at least charming and a lady and quite rich. (She knew now how much the money must have counted with Aunt Cassie.) And she saw Anson now, across all the expanse of years, not as a Prince Charming come to rescue her from an ogre aunt, but as he had really been . . . a rather anemic man, past thirty, of an appalling propriety. (There was a bitter humor in the memories of his timid advances toward her, of all the distaste with which he approached the details of marriage . . . a humor which she had come to understand fully only as she grew older and wiser in the ways of the world.) Looking back, she saw him as a man who had tried again and again to marry young women he had known all his life and who had failed because somehow he had gained a mysterious reputation for being a bore . . . a young man who, left to himself, would never have approached any woman, and gone to the grave as virginal as he had been born.

She saw now that he had never been even in the slightest in love with her. He had married her only because he got no peace from all the others, both the living and the dead, who in such a strange fashion seemed also to live at Pentlands. It was Aunt Cassie and even poor silly Miss Peavey and powerful old John Pentland and the cousins and all those dead hanging in neat rows in the hall who had married her. Anson had only been an instrument; and even in the most bitter moments she felt strangely sorry for him, because he, too, had had all his life ruined.

And so, slowly during all those long years, the pretty, shy, unknown Olivia McConnel, whose father was a Democratic politician out of Chicago, had turned into this puzzled, sometimes unhappy woman, the outsider, who had come in some mysterious fashion to be the one upon whom all of them leaned for strength.

She was glad now that she had stood forth boldly at last and faced Anson and all those who stood behind him there in the drawing-room, both the living and the dead, peering over his shoulder, urging him on. The unpleasant argument, though it had wounded her, had cleared the air a little. It had laid bare for a second the reality which she had been seeking for so long a time. Anson had been right about Sabine: in the clear bright air of the New England morning she knew that it was the sense of Sabine's nearness which had given her the strength to be unpleasant. Sabine, like herself, had known the great world, and so she was able to see their world here in Durham with a clarity that the others never approached. She was strong, too, in her knowledge that whatever happened she (Olivia) was the one person whom they could not afford to lose, because they had depended on her for too long.

But she was hurt. She kept thinking again and again of what Anson had said. . . . *"In any case, I will not have my daughter marry a shanty Irishman. There is enough of that in the family."*

She knew that Anson would suffer from shame for what he had said, but she knew, too, that he would pretend nothing had happened, that he had never made such a speech, because it was unworthy of a gentleman and a Pentland. He would pretend, as he always did, that the scene had never occurred.

When he had made the speech he had meant that she ought to have been thankful that they allowed her to marry into the Pentland family. There was a buried something in them all, a conviction that was a part of their very flesh, which made them believe in such a privilege. And for her who knew so much more than the world knew, who saw so much more than any of them of the truth, there was only one answer, to be wrung from her with a tragic intensity . . . "Oh, my God! . . ."

3

The dining-room was large and square, and having been redecorated in a period later than the rest of the house, was done in heavy mahogany, with a vast shiny table in the center which when reduced to its smallest possible circumference still left those who seated themselves about it formally remote from one another.

It was a well-used table, for since circumstance had kept John Pentland from going into the world, he had brought a part of it into his own home with a hospitality and a warmth that rather upset his sister Cassie. She, herself, like most of the family, had never cared very profoundly for food, looking upon it almost as a necessity. A prune to her palate shared importance as a delicacy with a truffle. In the secrecy of her own house, moved by her passion for economy, she more often than not assuaged her own birdlike appetite with scraps from the cupboard, though at such times the simple but full-blooded Miss Peavey suffered keenly. "A pick-up meal" was a byword with Aunt Cassie, and so she frowned upon the rich food furnished by old John Pentland and his daughter-in-law, Olivia.

Nevertheless, she took a great many meals at the mahogany table and even managed to insinuate within its circle the plump figure of Miss Peavey, whose silly laugh and servile echoes of his sister's opinions the old man detested.

Anson never lunched at home, for he went up to Boston each morning at nine o'clock, like a man of affairs, with much business to care for. He kept an office in Water Street and went to it with a passionate regularity, to spend the day in the petty affairs of club committees and societies for the improvement of this or that; for he was a man who fortified his own soul by arranging the lives of others. He was chairman of a committee which "aired" young girls who had fallen into trouble, and contributed as much as he was able out of his own rather slender income to the activities of the Watch and Ward Society. And a large part of the day was spent in correspondence with genealogists on the subject of "The Pentland Family and the Massachusetts Bay Colony." He did not in a whole year earn enough money to pay the office rent for one month, but he had no patience with the many cases of poverty and destitution which came to his notice. The stocks and bonds of the Pentland estate had been kept carefully out of his reach, by a father who distrusted activities such as Anson's, and even now, when he was nearly fifty, Anson had only a small income left by his grandfather and an allowance, paid him each month by his father, as if he were still a boy in college.

So when Olivia came down to lunch on the day after the ball she was not forced to face Anson and his shame over the scene of the night before. There were only the grandfather and Sybil and Jack—who was well enough to come down.

The old man sat at the head, in the place which he had never relinquished as the dictator, the ruler of all the family. Tall and muscular, he had grown leathery from exposure during the years he had lived in the country, riding day after day in rains and blizzards, in sunlight and in storms, as if there were in him some atavistic hunger for the hardy life led by the first Pentlands to come to Durham. He always rode the vicious and unruly beautiful red mare . . . a grim old man who was a match for her famous bad temper. He was rather like his sister Cassie in appearance—one of the black Pentlands who had appeared mysteriously in the line nearly a hundred years earlier, and he had burning black eyes that looked out from shaggy brows . . . a man as different in appearance and vigor from his son as it was possible to imagine. (For Anson was a typical Pentland—blond, with round blue eyes and an inclination when in health toward ruddiness.) One stood in awe of the old man: there was a grimness about the strong, rough-cut face and contracted lips, and a curious, indefinable air of disapproval which one was never able to pin down or analyze.

He was silent to-day, in one of the black moods which Olivia knew well meant that he was troubled. She knew that this time it had nothing to do with Jack's illness, for the boy sat there opposite them, looking stronger than he had looked in months . . . blond and pale and thin, with the blue veins showing at his pathetic wrists and on his thin, handsome temples.

Olivia had lived through bad times over Jack and she had lived through them always together with John Pentland, so there had grown up between them—the mother and the grandfather—a sense of understanding which was quite beyond speech. Together they had spent so many nights by the side of the boy, keeping him alive almost by the strength of their united wills, forcing him to live when, gasping for life, he would have slipped away easily into death. Together they had kept him in life, because they both loved him and because he was the last son of the family.

Olivia felt sometimes that Sybil, too, played a part in the never-ending struggle against death. The girl, like her grandfather, never spoke of such things, but one could read them in the troubled depths of her violet eyes. That long, weary struggle was one of the tragedies they never spoke of at Pentlands, leaving it buried in silence. One said, "Jack looks well to-day," smiling, and, "Perhaps the doctors are wrong." Sybil was watching her brother now, in that quiet, mysterious way she had, watching him cautiously lest he discover that she was watching; for he discovered troubles easily, with the kind of clairvoyance which comes to people who have always been ill.

They barely talked at all during the lunch. Sybil planned to take her brother in the trap to ride over the farm and down to the white dunes.

"Higgins is going with us," she said. "He's going to show us the new litter of foxes in the black thicket."

And Jack said, "It's a funny thing about Higgins. He always discovers such things before any one else. He knows when it will be a good day for fishing and just when it is going to rain. He's never wrong."

"No . . ." said the grandfather suddenly. "It's a funny thing. He's never wrong . . . not in all the years I've known him."

It was the only time he said anything during the meal, and Olivia, trying to fill in the gaps in the conversation, found it difficult, with the boy sitting opposite her looking so pale and ill. It seemed to her sometimes that he had never really been born, that he had always remained in some way a part of herself. When he was out of her sight, she had no peace because there was always a gnawing terror that she might never see him again. And she knew that deep inside the frail body there was a spirit, a flame, descended from the old man and from herself, which burned passionately with a desire for life, for riding, for swimming, for running across the open meadows . . . a flame that must always be smothered. If only he had been like Anson, his father, who never knew that hunger for life. . . .

"Olivia, my dear . . ." The old man was speaking. "Will you have your coffee with me in the library? There is something I want to discuss with you."

She knew it then. She had been right. There *was* something which troubled him. He always said the same thing when he was faced by some problem too heavy for his old shoulders. He always said, "Olivia, my dear. . . . Will you come into the library?" He never summoned his own son, or his sister Cassie . . . no one but Olivia. Between them they shared secrets which the others never dreamed of; and when he died, all the troubles would be hers . . . they would be passed on for her to deal with . . . those troubles which existed in a family which the world would have said was rich and respected and quite without troubles.

4

As she left the room to follow him she stopped for a moment to say to Sybil, "Are you happy, my dear? You're not sorry that you aren't going back to school in Saint-Cloud?"

"No, Mama; why shouldn't I be happy here? I love it, more than anything in the world."

The girl thrust her hands into the pockets of her riding-coat.

"You don't think I was wrong to send you to France to school . . . away from every one here?"

Sybil laughed and looked at her mother in the frank, half-mocking way she had when she fancied she had uncovered a plot.

"Are you worrying about marrying me off? I'm only eighteen. I've lots of time."

"I'm worrying because I think you'll be so hard to please."

Again she laughed. "That's true. That's why I'm going to take my time."

"And you're glad to have Thérèse here?"

"Of course. You know I like Thérèse awfully, Mama."

"Very well . . . run along now. I must speak to your grandfather."

And the girl went out onto the terrace where Jack stood waiting in the sun for the trap. He always followed the sun, choosing to sit in it even in midsummer, as if he were never quite warm enough.

She *was* worried over Sybil. She had begun to think that perhaps Aunt Cassie was right when she said that Sybil ought to go to a boarding-school with the girls she had always known, to grow loud and noisy and awkward and play hockey and exchange silly notes with the boys in the boarding-school in the next village. Perhaps it was wrong to have sent Sybil away to a school where she would meet girls from France and England and Russia and South America . . . half the countries of the world; a school where, as Aunt Cassie had said bitterly, she would be forced to associate with the "daughters of dancers and opera singers." She knew now that Sybil hadn't liked the ball any more than Thérèse, who had run away from it without a word of explanation. Only with Thérèse it didn't matter so much, because the dark stubborn head was filled with all sorts of wild notions about science and painting and weird books on psychology. There was a loneliness about Thérèse and her mother, Sabine Callendar, only with them it didn't matter. They had, too, a hardness, a sense of derision and scorn which protected them. Sybil hadn't any such protections. Perhaps she was even wrong in having made of Sybil a lady—a lady in the old sense of the word—because there seemed to be no place for a lady in the scheme of life as it had existed at the dance the night before. It was perilous, having a lady on one's hands, especially a lady who was certain to take life as passionately as Sybil.

She wanted the girl to be happy, without quite understanding that it was because Sybil seemed the girl she had once been herself, a very part of herself, the part which had never lived at all.

She found her father-in-law seated at his great mahogany desk in the high narrow room walled with books which was kept sacred to him, at the desk from which he managed the farm and watched over a fortune, built up bit by bit shrewdly, thriftily over three hundred years, a fortune which he had never brought himself to trust in the hands of his son. It was, in its gloomy, cold way, a pleasant room, smelling of dogs and apples and wood-smoke, and sometimes of whisky, for it was here that the old man retired when, in a kind of baffled frenzy, he drank himself to insensibility. It was here that he would sometimes sit for a day and a night, even sleeping in his leather chair, refusing to see any one save Higgins, who watched over him, and Olivia. And so it was Olivia and Higgins who alone knew the spectacle of this solitary drinking. The world and even the family knew very little of it— only the little which sometimes leaked out from the gossip of servants straying at night along the dark lanes and hedges about Durham.

He sat with his coffee and a glass of Courvoisier before him while he smoked, with an air of being lost in some profound worry, for he did not look up at once when she entered, but sat staring before him in an odd, enchanted fashion. It was not until she had taken a cigarette from the silver box and lighted it that he looked up at the sound of the striking match and, focusing the burning black eyes, said to her, "Jack seems very well to-day."

"Yes, better than he has been in a long time."

"Perhaps, after all, the doctors are wrong."

Olivia sighed and said quietly, "If we had believed the doctors we should have lost him long ago."

"Yes, that's true."

She poured her coffee and he murmured, "It's about Horace Pentland I wanted to speak. He's dead. I got the news this morning. He died in Mentone and now it's a question whether we shall bring him home here to be buried in Durham with the rest of the family."

Olivia was silent for a moment and then, looking up, said, "What do you think? How long has it been that he has lived in Mentone?"

"It's nearly thirty years now that I've been sending him money to stay there. He's only a cousin. Still, we had the same grandfather and he'd be the first of the family in three hundred years who isn't buried here."

"There was Savina Pentland. . . ."

"Yes. . . . But she's buried out there, and she would have been buried here if it had been possible."

And he made a gesture in the direction of the sea, beyond the marshes where the beautiful Savina Pentland, almost a legend now, lay, somewhere deep down in the soft white sand at the bottom of the ocean.

"Would he want to be buried here?" asked Olivia.

"He wrote and asked me . . . a month or two before he died. It seemed to be on his mind. He put it in a strange way. He wrote that he wanted to come home."

Again Olivia was thoughtful for a time. "Strange . . ." she murmured presently, "when people were so cruel to him."

The lips of the old man stiffened a little.

"It was his own fault. . . ."

"Still . . . thirty years is a long time."

He knocked the ash from his cigar and looked at her sharply. "You mean that everything may have been forgotten by now?"

Olivia made a little gesture with her white, ringless hands. "Why not?"

"Because people don't forget things like that . . . not in our world, at any rate."

Quietly, far back in her mind, Olivia kept trying to imagine this Horace Pentland whom she had never seen, this shadowy old man, dead now, who had been exiled for thirty years.

"You have no reason for not wanting him here among all the others?"

"No . . . Horace is dead now. . . . It can't matter much whether what's left of him is buried here or in France."

"Except, of course, that they may have been kinder to him over there. . . . They're not so harsh."

A silence fell over them, as if in some way the spirit of Horace Pentland, the sinner whose name was never spoken in the family save between Olivia and the old man, had returned and stood between them, waiting to hear what was to be done with all that remained of him on this earth. It was one of those silences which, descending upon the old house, sometimes filled Olivia with a vague uneasiness. They had a way of descending upon the household in the long evenings when all the family sat reading in the old drawing-room—as if there were figures unseen who stood watching.

"If he wanted to be buried here," said Olivia, "I can see no reason why he should not be."

"Cassie will object to raking up an old scandal that has been forgotten."

"Surely that can't matter now . . . when the poor old man is dead. We can be kind to him now . . . surely we can be kind to him now."

John Pentland sighed abruptly, a curious, heart-breaking sigh that seemed to have escaped even his power of steely control; and presently he said, "I think you are right, Olivia. . . . I will do as you say . . . only we'll keep it a secret between us until the time comes when it's necessary to speak. And then . . . then we'll have a quiet funeral."

She would have left him then save that she knew from his manner that there were other things he wanted to say. He had a way of letting you know his will without speaking. Somehow, in his presence you felt that it was impossible to leave until he had dismissed you. He still treated his own son, who was nearly fifty, as if he were a little boy.

Olivia waited, busying herself by rearranging the late lilacs which stood in a tall silver vase on the polished mahogany desk.

"They smell good," he said abruptly. "They're the last, aren't they?"

"The last until next spring."

"Next spring . . ." he repeated with an air of speaking to himself. "Next spring. . . ." And then abruptly, "The other thing was about Sabine. The nurse tells me *she* has discovered that Sabine is here." He made the family gesture toward the old north wing. "She has asked to see Sabine."

"Who told her that Sabine had returned? How could she have discovered it?"

"The nurse doesn't know. She must have heard some one speaking the name under her window. The nurse says that people in her condition have curious ways of discovering such things . . . like a sixth sense."

"Do you want me to ask Sabine? She'd come if I asked her."

"It would be unpleasant. Besides, I think it might do harm in some way."

Olivia was silent for a moment. "How? She probably wouldn't remember Sabine. When she saw her last, Sabine was a young girl."

"She's gotten the idea now that we're all against her, that we're persecuting her in some way." He coughed and blew a cloud of smoke out of his thin-drawn lips. "It's difficult to explain what I mean. . . . I mean that Sabine might encourage that feeling . . . quite without meaning to, that Sabine might give her the impression that she was an ally. There's something disturbing about Sabine."

"Anson thinks so, too," said Olivia softly. "He's been talking to me about it."

"She ought never to have come back here. It's difficult . . . what I am trying to say. Only I feel that she's up to some mischief. I think she hates us all."

"Not all of us. . . ."

"Not perhaps you. You never belonged here. It's only those of us who have always been here."

"But she's fond of you. . . ."

"Her father and I were good friends. He was very like her . . . disagreeable and given to speaking unpleasant truths. . . . He wasn't a popular man. Perhaps that's why she's friendly toward me . . . on account of him."

"No, it's more than that. . . ."

Slowly Olivia felt herself slipping back into that state of confused enchantment which had overwhelmed her more and more often of late. It seemed that life grew more and more tenuous and complicated, more blurred and indistinct, until at times it became simply a morass of minute problems in which she found herself mired and unable to act. No one spoke directly any more. It was like living in a world of shadows. And this old man, her father-in-law, was the greatest puzzle of all, because it was impossible ever to know how much he understood of what went on about him, how much he chose to ignore in the belief that by denying its existence it would cease to exist.

Sitting there, puzzled, she began to pull a leaf from the cluster of lilacs into tiny bits.

"Sometimes," she said, "I think Sabine is unhappy. . . ."

"No . . . not that. . . . She's beyond happiness or unhappiness. There's something hard in her and unrelenting . . . as hard as a cut diamond. She's a clever woman and a queer one. She's one of those strange creatures that are thrown off now and then by people like us. There's nothing else quite like them in the world. They go to strange extremes. Horace was the same . . . in a different, less creditable fashion."

Olivia looked at him suddenly, astonished by the sudden flash of penetration in the old man, one of those sudden, quick gleams which led her to believe that far down, in the depths of his soul, he was far more profound, far more intelligent, unruly and defiant of tradition than he ever allowed the world to suppose. It was always the old question. How much did he know? How much did he not know . . . far back, behind the lined, severe, leathery old face? Or was it a sort of clairvoyance, not of eternal illness, like Jack's, but of old age?

"I shall ask Sabine," she began.

"It's not necessary at the moment. She appears to have forgotten the matter temporarily. But she'll remember it again and then I think it will be best to humor her, whatever comes. She may not think of it again for months . . . until Sabine has gone. . . . I only wanted to ask you . . . to consult you, Olivia. I thought you could arrange it."

She rose and, turning to go, she heard him saying, "*She* might like some lilacs in her room." He hesitated and in a flat, dead voice, added, "She used to be very fond of flowers."

Olivia, avoiding the dark eyes, thought, "She used to be very fond of flowers. . . . That means forty years ago . . . forty long years. Oh, my God!" But after a second she said simply, "She has taken a dislike to flowers. She fancies they take up the air and stifle her. The sight of them is very bad for her."

"I should have known you'd already thought of it."

For an instant the old man stood facing her with a fixed and searching expression which made her feel shy and led her to turn away from him a little; and then all at once, with an air strangely timid and frightened in a man so grim in appearance, he took her hand and kissing her on the forehead murmured, "You're a good girl, Olivia. They're right in what they say of you. You're a good girl. I don't know how I should have managed without you all these years."

Smiling, she looked at him, and then, touching his hand affectionately, she went out without speaking again, thinking, as she had thought a thousand times, what a terrible thing it must be to have been born so inarticulate and so terrified of feeling as John Pentland. It must be, she thought, like living forever imprisoned in a shell of steel from which one might look out and see friends but never touch or know them.

From the doorway she heard a voice behind her, saying almost joyfully: "The doctors must have been wrong about Jack. You and I together, Olivia, have defeated them."

She said, "Yes," and smiled at him, but when she had turned away again there was in her mind a strange, almost gruesome thought.

"If only Jack lives until his grandfather is dead, the old man will die happy. If only he can be kept alive until then. . . ."

She had a strange way of seeing things in the hard light of reality, and an unreal, lonely childhood had fostered the trait. She had been born thus, and now as a woman she found that in a way it was less a curse than a blessing. In a world which survived only by deceiving itself, she found that seeing the truth and knowing it made her strong. Here, perhaps, lay the reason why all of them had come to depend upon her. But there were times, too, when she wanted passionately to be a poor weak feminine creature, a woman who might turn to her husband and find in him some one stronger than herself. She had a curious feeling of envy for Savina Pentland, who was dead before she was born. . . . Savina Pentland who had been the beauty of the family, extravagant, reckless, feminine, who bought strings of pearls and was given to weeping and fainting.

But she (Olivia) had only Anson to lean upon.

After she had gone away the old man sat for a long time smoking and drinking his brandy, enveloped by a loneliness scarcely more profound than it had been a little while before when he sat talking with Olivia. It was his habit to sit thus sometimes for an hour at a time, unconscious, it seemed, of all the world about him; Olivia had come in more than once at such moments and gone away again, unwilling to shatter the enchantment by so much as a single word.

At last, when the cigar had burned to an end, he crushed out the ember with a short, fierce gesture and, rising, went out of the tall narrow room and along the corridor that led to the dark stairway in the old north wing. These steps he had climbed every day since it had become necessary to keep *her* in the country the year round . . . every day, at the same hour, step by step his big heavy-shod boots had trod the same worn stair carpet. It was a journey begun years ago as a kind of pleasure colored by hope, which for a long time now, bereft of all hope, had become merely a monotonous dreary duty. It was like a journey of penance made by some pilgrim on his knees up endless flights of stairs.

For more than twenty years, as far back as Olivia could remember, he had been absent from the house for a night but twice, and then only on occasions of life and death. In all that time he had been twice to New York and never once to the Europe he had not seen since, as a boy, he had made the grand tour on a plan laid out by old General Curtis . . . a time so remote now that it must have seemed part of another life. In all those years he had never once escaped from the world which his family found so perfect and complete and which to him must have seemed always a little cramped and inadequate. Fate and blood and circumstance, one might have said, had worn him down bit by bit until in the end he had come to worship the same gods they worshiped. Now and then he contrived to escape them for a little while by drinking himself into insensibility, but always he awakened again to find that nothing had changed, to discover that his prison was the same. And so, slowly, hope must have died.

But no one knew, even Olivia, whether he was happy or unhappy; and no one would ever really know what had happened to him, deep inside, behind the gray, leathery old face.

The world said, when it thought of him: "There never was such a devoted husband as John Pentland."

Slowly and firmly he walked along the narrow hall to the end and there halted to knock on the white door. He always knocked, for there were times when the sight of him, entering suddenly, affected her so that she became hysterical and beyond all control.

In response to the knock, the door was opened gently and professionally by Miss Egan, an automaton of a nurse—neat, efficient, inhuman and incredibly starched, whose very smile seemed to come and go by some mechanical process, like the sounds made by squeezing a mechanical doll. Only it was impossible to imagine squeezing anything so starched and jagged as the red-faced Miss Egan. It was a smile which sprang into existence upon sight of any member of the family, a smile of false humility which said, "I know very well that you cannot do without me"—the smile of a woman well enough content to be paid three times the wages of an ordinary nurse. In three or four more years she would have enough saved to start a sanatorium of her own.

Fixing her smile, she faced the old man, saying, "She seems quite well to-day . . . very quiet."

The whole hallway had been flooded at the opening of the door by a thick and complicated odor arising from innumerable medicines that stood row upon row in the obscurity of the dark room. The old man stepped inside, closing the door quickly behind him, for she was affected by too much light. She could not bear to have a door or a window open near her; even on this bright day the drawn shades kept the room in darkness.

She had got the idea somehow that there were people outside who waited to leer at her . . . hundreds of them all pressing their faces against the panes to peep into her bedroom. There were days when she could not be quieted until the window-shades were covered by thick layers of black cloth. She would not rise from her bed until nightfall lest the faces outside might see her standing there in her nightdress.

It was only when darkness had fallen that the nurse was able by means of trickery and wheedling to air the room, and so it smelled horribly of the medicines she never took, but kept ranged about her, row upon row, like the fetishes of witch-doctors. In this they humored her as they had humored her in shutting out the sunlight, because it was the only way they could keep her quiet and avoid sending her away to some place where she would have been shut behind bars. And this John Pentland would not even consider.

When he entered she was lying in the bed, her thin, frail body barely outlined beneath the bedclothes . . . the mere shadow of a woman who must once have been pretty in a delicate way. But nothing remained now of the beauty save the fine modeling of the chin and nose and brow. She lay there, a queer, unreal old woman, with thin white hair, skin like parchment and a silly, vacant face as unwrinkled as that of a child. As he seated himself beside her, the empty, round blue eyes opened a little and stared at him without any sign of recognition. He took one of the thin, blue-veined hands in his, but it only lay there, lifeless, while he sat, silent and gentle, watching her.

Once he spoke, calling her wistfully by name, "Agnes"; but there was no sign of an answer, not so much as a faint flickering of the white, transparent lids.

And so for an eternity he sat thus in the thick darkness, enveloped by the sickly odor of medicines, until he was roused by a knock at the door and the sudden glare of daylight as it opened and Miss Egan, fixing her flashing and teethy smile, came in and said: "The fifteen minutes is up, Mr. Pentland."

When the door had closed behind him he went away again, slowly, thoughtfully, down the worn stairs and out into the painfully brilliant sunlight of the bright New England spring. Crossing the green terrace, bordered with great clumps of iris and peonies and a few late tulips, he made his way to the stable-yard, where Higgins had left the red mare in charge of a Polish boy who did odd tasks about the farm. The mare, as beautiful and delicate as a fine steel spring, stood nervously pawing the gravel and tossing her handsome head. The boy, a great lout with a shock of yellow hair, stood far away from her holding the reins at arm's length.

At the sight of the two the old man laughed and said, "You mustn't let her know you're afraid of her, Ignaz."

The boy gave up the reins and retired to a little distance, still watching the mare resentfully. "Well, she tried to bite me!" he said sullenly.

Quickly, with a youthful agility, John Pentland swung himself to her back . . . quickly enough to keep her from sidling away from him. There was a short, fierce struggle between the rider and the horse, and in a shower of stones they sped away down the lane that led across the meadows, past the thicket of black pines and the abandoned gravel-pit, toward the house of Mrs. Soames.

Chapter 4

IN THE SOLID CORNER of the world which surrounded Durham, Aunt Cassie played the rôle of an unofficial courier who passed from house to house, from piazza to piazza, collecting and passing on the latest bits of news. When one saw a low cloud of dust moving across the brilliant New England sky above the hedges and stone walls of the countryside, one could be certain that it masked the progress of Cassie Struthers on her daily round of calls. She went always on foot, because she detested motors and was terrified of horses; one might see her coming from a great distance, dressed always in dingy black, tottering along very briskly (for a woman of her age and well-advertised infirmities). One came to expect her arrival at a certain hour, for she was, unless there arose in her path some calamity or piece of news of unusual interest, a punctual woman whose life was as carefully ordered as the vast house in which she lived with the queer Aunt Bella.

It was a great box of a dwelling built by the late Mr. Struthers in the days of cupolas and gazebos on land given him by Aunt Cassie's grandfather on the day of her wedding. Inside it was furnished with a great profusion of plush tassels and antimacassars, all kept with the neatness and rigidity of a museum. There were never any cigar ashes on the floor, nor any dust in the corners, for Aunt Cassie followed her servants about with the eye of a fussy old sergeant inspecting his barracks. Poor Miss Peavey, who grew more and more dowdy and careless as old age began to settle over her, led a life of constant peril, and was forced to build a little house near the stables to house her Pomeranians and her Siamese cats. For Aunt Cassie could not abide the thought of "the animals dirtying up the house." Even the "retiring room" of the late Mr. Struthers had been converted since his death into a museum, spotless and purified of tobacco and whisky, where his chair sat before his desk, turned away from it a little, as if his spirit were still seated there. On the desk lay his pipe (as he had left it) and the neat piles of paper (carefully dusted each day but otherwise undisturbed) which he had put there with his own hand on the morning they found him seated on the chair, his head fallen back a little, as if asleep. And in the center of the desk lay two handsomely bound volumes—"Cornices of Old Boston Houses" and "Walks and Talks in New England Churchyards"—which he had written in these last sad years when his life seemed slowly to fade from him . . . the years in which Aunt Cassie seemed rapidly to recover the wiry strength and health for which she had been famous as a girl.

The house, people said, had been built by Mr. Struthers in the expectation of a large family, but it had remained great and silent of children's voices as a tomb since the day it was finished, for Aunt Cassie had never been strong until it was too late for her to bear him heirs.

Sabine Callendar had a whole set of theories about the house and about the married life of Aunt Cassie, but they were theories which she kept, in her way, entirely to herself, waiting and watching until she was certain of them. There was a hatred between the two women that was implacable and difficult to define, an emotion almost of savagery which concealed itself beneath polite phrases and casual observations of an acid character. They encountered each other more frequently than Aunt Cassie would have wished, for Sabine, upon her return to Durham, took up Aunt Cassie's habit of going from house to house on foot in search of news and entertainment. They met in drawing-rooms, on piazzas, and sometimes in the very dusty lanes, greeting each other with smiles and vicious looks. They had become rather like two hostile cats watching each other for days at a time, stealthily. Sabine, Aunt Cassie confided in Olivia, made her nervous.

Still, it was Aunt Cassie who had been the first caller at Brook Cottage after the arrival of Sabine. The younger woman had seen her approach, enveloped in a faint cloud of dust, from the windows of Brook Cottage, and the sight filled her with an inexpressible delight. The spare old lady had come along so briskly, almost with impatience, filled with delight (Sabine believed) at having an excuse now to trespass on O'Hara's land and see what he had done to the old cottage. And Sabine believed, too, that she came to discover what life had done to "dear Mr. Struthers' niece, Sabine Callendar." She came as the Official Welcomer of the Community, with hope in her heart that she would find Sabine a returned prodigal, a wrecked woman, ravaged by time and experience, who for twenty years had ignored them all and now returned, a broken and humbled creature, hungry for kindness.

The sight set fire to a whole train of memories in Sabine . . . memories which penetrated deep into her childhood when with her father she had lived in the old house that once stood where O'Hara's new one raised its bright chimneys; memories of days when she had run off by herself to play in the tangled orchard grass among the bleeding-hearts and irises that surrounded this same Brook Cottage where she stood watching the approach of Aunt Cassie. Only, in those days Brook Cottage had been a ruin of a place, with empty windows and sagging doors, ghostly and half-hidden by a shaggy tangle of lilacs and syringas, and now it stood glistening with new paint, the lilacs all neatly clipped and pruned.

There was something in the sight of the old woman's nervous, active figure that struck deep down into a past which Sabine, with the passing of years, had almost succeeded in forgetting; and now it all came back again, sharply and with a kind of stabbing pain, so that she had a sudden odd feeling of having become a little girl again . . . plain, red-haired, freckled and timid, who stood in terror of Aunt Cassie and was always being pulled here and there by a thousand aunts and uncles and cousins because she *would* not be turned into their idea of what a nice little girl ought to be. It was as if the whole past were concentrated in the black figure of the old lady who had been the ring-leader, the viceroy, of all a far-flung tribe, an old woman who had been old even twenty years earlier, lying always on a sofa under a shawl, issuing her edicts, pouring out her ample sympathies, her bitter criticisms. And here she was, approaching briskly, as if the death of Mr. Struthers had somehow released her from bonds which had chafed for too long.

Watching her, one incident after another flashed through the quick, hard brain of Sabine, all recreated with a swift, astounding clarity—the day when she had run off to escape into the world and been found by old John Pentland hiding in the thicket of white birches happily eating blueberries. (She could see his countenance now, stern with its disapproval of such wild behavior, but softening, too, at the sight of the grubby, freckled plain face stained with blueberry juice.) And the return of the captive, when she was surrounded by aunts who dressed her in a clean frock and forced her to sit in the funereal spare bedroom with a New Testament on her knees until she "felt that she could come out and behave like a nice, well-brought-up little girl." She could see the aunts pulling and fussing at her and saying, "What a shame she didn't take after her mother in looks!" and, "She'll have a hard time with such plain, straight red hair."

And there was, too, the memory of that day when Anson Pentland, a timid, spiritless little Lord Fauntleroy of a boy, fell into the river and would have been drowned save for his cousin Sabine, who dragged him out, screaming and drenched, only to receive for herself all the scolding for having led him into mischief. And the times when she had been punished for having asked frank and simple questions which she ought not to have asked.

It was difficult to remember any happiness until the day when her father died and she was sent to New York, a girl of twenty, knowing very little of anything and nothing whatever of such things as love and marriage, to live with an uncle in a tall narrow house on Murray Hill. It was on that day (she saw it now with a devastating clarity as she stood watching the approach of Aunt Cassie) that her life had really begun. Until then her existence had been only a confused and tormented affair in which there was very little happiness. It was only later that reality had come to her, painfully, even tragically, in a whole procession of events which had made her slowly into this hard, worldly, cynical woman who found herself, without quite knowing why, back in a world she hated, standing at the window of Brook Cottage, a woman tormented by an immense and acutely living curiosity about people and the strange tangles which their lives sometimes assumed.

She had been standing by the window thinking back into the past with such a fierce intensity that she quite forgot the approach of Aunt Cassie and started suddenly at the sound of the curious, familiar thin voice, amazingly unchanged, calling from the hallway, "Sabine! Sabine dear! It's your Aunt Cassie! Where are you?" as if she had never left Durham at all, as if nothing had changed in twenty years.

At sight of her, the old lady came forward with little fluttering cries to fling her arms about her late husband's niece. Her manner was that of a shepherd receiving a lost sheep, a manner filled with forgiveness and pity and condescension. The tears welled easily into her eyes and streamed down her face.

Sabine permitted herself, frigidly, to be embraced, and said, "But you don't look a day older, Aunt Cassie. You look stronger than ever." It was a remark which somehow set the whole tone of the relationship between them, a remark which, though it sounded sympathetic and even complimentary, was a harsh thing to say to a woman who had cherished all her life the tradition of invalidism. It was harsh, too, because it was true. Aunt Cassie at forty-seven had been as shriveled and dried as she was now, twenty years later.

The old woman said, "My dear girl, I am miserable . . . miserable." And drying the tears that streamed down her face, she added, "It won't be long now until I go to join dear Mr. Struthers."

Sabine wanted suddenly to laugh, at the picture of Aunt Cassie entering Paradise to rejoin a husband whom she had always called, even in the intimacy of married life, "Mr. Struthers." She kept thinking that Mr. Struthers might not find the reunion so pleasant as his wife anticipated. She had always held a strange belief that Mr. Struthers had chosen death as the best way out.

And she felt a sudden almost warm sense of returning memories, roused by Aunt Cassie's passion for overstatement. Aunt Cassie could never bring herself to say simply, "I'm going to die" which was not at all true. She must say, "I go to join dear Mr. Struthers."

Sabine said, "Oh, no. . . . Oh, no. . . . Don't say that."

"I don't sleep any more. I barely close my eyes at night."

She had seated herself now and was looking about her, absorbing everything in the room, the changes made by the dreadful O'Hara, the furniture he had bought for the house. But most of all she was studying Sabine, devouring her with sidelong, furtive glances; and Sabine, knowing her so well, saw that the old woman had been given a violent shock. She had come prepared to find a broken, unhappy Sabine and she had found instead this smooth, rather hard and self-contained woman, superbly dressed and poised, from the burnished red hair (that straight red hair the aunts had once thought so hopeless) to the lizard-skin slippers—a woman who had obviously taken hold of life with a firm hand and subdued it, who was in a way complete.

"Your dear uncle never forgot you for a moment, Sabine, in all the years you were away. He died, leaving me to watch over you." And again the easy tears welled up.

("Oh," thought Sabine, "you don't catch me that way. You won't put me back where I once was. You won't even have a chance to meddle in my life.")

Aloud she said, "It's a pity I've always been so far away."

"But I've thought of you, my dear. . . . I've thought of you. Scarcely a night passes when I don't say to myself before going to sleep, 'There is poor Sabine out in the world, turning her back on all of us who love her.'" She sighed abysmally. "I have thought of you, dear. I've prayed for you in the long nights when I have never closed an eye."

And Sabine, talking on half-mechanically, discovered slowly that, in spite of everything, she was no longer afraid of Aunt Cassie. She was no longer a shy, frightened, plain little girl; she even began to sense a challenge, a combat which filled her with a faint sense of warmth. She kept thinking, "She really hasn't changed at all. She still wants to reach out and take possession of me and my life. She's like an octopus reaching out and seizing each member of the family, arranging everything." And she saw Aunt Cassie now, after so many years, in a new light. It seemed to her that there was something glittering and hard and a little sinister beneath all the sighing and tears and easy sympathy. Perhaps she (Sabine) was the only one in all the family who had escaped the reach of those subtle, insinuating tentacles. . . . She had run away.

Meanwhile Aunt Cassie had swept from a vivid and detailed description of the passing of Mr. Struthers into a catalogue of neighborhood and family calamities, of deaths, of broken troths, financial disasters, and the appearance on the horizon of the "dreadful O'Hara." She reproached Sabine for having sold her land to such an outsider. And as she talked on and on she grew less and less human and more and more like some disembodied, impersonal force of nature. Sabine, watching her with piercing green eyes, found her a little terrifying. She had sharpened and hardened with age.

She discussed the divorces which had occurred in Boston, and at length, leaning forward and touching Sabine's hand with her thin, nervous one, she said brokenly: "I felt for you in your trouble, Sabine. I never wrote you because it would have been so painful. I see now that I evaded my duty. But I felt for you. . . . I tried to put myself in your place. I tried to imagine dear Mr. Struthers being unfaithful to me . . . but, of course, I couldn't. He was a saint." She blew her nose and repeated with passion, as if to herself, "A saint!"

("Yes," thought Sabine, "a saint . . . if ever there was one.") She saw that Aunt Cassie was attacking her now from a new point. She was trying to pity her. By being full of pity the old woman would try to break down her defenses and gain possession of her.

Sabine's green eyes took one hard, glinting look. "Did you ever see my husband?" she asked.

"No," said Aunt Cassie, "but I've heard a great deal of him. I've been told how you suffered."

Sabine looked at her with a queer, mocking expression. "Then you've been told wrongly. He is a fascinating man. I did not suffer. I assure you that I would rather have shared him with fifty other women than have had any one of the men about here all to myself."

There was a frank immorality in this statement which put Aunt Cassie to rout, bag and baggage. She merely stared, finding nothing to say in reply to such a speech. Clearly, in all her life she had never heard any one say a thing so bald and so frank, so completely naked of all pretense of gentility.

Sabine went on coldly, pushing her assault to the very end. "I divorced him at last, not because he was unfaithful to me, but because there was another woman who wanted to marry him . . . a woman whom I respect and like . . . a woman who is still my friend. Understand that I loved him passionately . . . in a very fleshly way. One couldn't help it. I wasn't the only woman. . . . He was a kind of devil, but a very fascinating one."

The old woman was a little stunned but not by any means defeated. Sabine saw a look come into her eyes, a look which clearly said, "So this is what the world has done to my poor, dear, innocent little Sabine!" At last she said with a sigh, "I find it an amazing world. I don't know what it is coming to."

"Nor I," replied Sabine with an air of complete agreement and sympathy. She understood that the struggle was not yet finished, for Aunt Cassie had a way of putting herself always in an impregnable position, of wrapping herself in layer after layer of sighs and sympathy, of charity and forgiveness, of meekness and tears, so that in the end there was no way of suddenly tearing them aside and saying, "There you are . . . naked at last, a horrible meddling old woman!" And Sabine kept thinking, too, that if Aunt Cassie had lived in the days of her witch-baiting ancestor, Preserved Pentland, she would have been burned for a witch.

And all the while Sabine had been suffering, quietly, deep inside, behind the frankly painted face . . . suffering in a way which no one in the world had ever suspected; for it was like tearing out her heart, to talk thus of Richard Callendar, even to speak his name.

Aloud she said, "And how is Mrs. Pentland. . . . I mean Olivia . . . not my cousin. . . . I know how *she* is . . . no better."

"No better. . . . It is one of those things which I can never understand. . . . Why God should have sent such a calamity to a good man like my brother."

"But Olivia . . ." began Sabine, putting an end abruptly to what was clearly the prelude to a pious monologue.

"Oh! . . . Olivia," replied Aunt Cassie, launching into an account of the young Mrs. Pentland. "Olivia is an angel . . . an angel, a blessing of God sent to my poor brother. But she's not been well lately. She's been rather sharp with me . . . even with poor Miss Peavey, who is so sensitive. I can't imagine what has come over her."

It seemed that the strong, handsome Olivia was suffering from nerves. She was, Aunt Cassie said, unhappy about something, although she could not see why Olivia shouldn't be happy . . . a woman with everything in the world.

"Everything?" echoed Sabine. "Has any one in the world got everything?"

"It is Olivia's fault if she hasn't everything. All the materials are there. She has a good husband . . . a husband who never looks at other women."

"Nor at his own wife either," interrupted Sabine. "I know all about Anson. I grew up with him."

Aunt Cassie saw fit to ignore this. "She's rich," she said, resuming the catalogue of Olivia's blessings.

And again Sabine interrupted, "But what does money mean, Aunt Cassie? In our world one is rich and that's the end of it. One takes it for granted. When one isn't rich any longer, one simply slips out of it. It has very little to do with happiness. . . ."

The strain was beginning to show on Aunt Cassie. "You'd find out if you weren't rich," she observed with asperity, "if your father and great-grandfather hadn't taken care of their money." She recovered herself and made a deprecating gesture. "But don't think I'm criticizing dear Olivia. She is the best, the most wonderful woman." She began to wrap herself once more in kindliness and charity and forgiveness. "Only she seems to me to be a little queer lately."

Sabine's artificially crimson mouth took on a slow smile. "It would be too bad if the Pentland family drove two wives insane—one after the other."

Again Aunt Cassie came near to defeat by losing her composure. She snorted, and Sabine helped her out by asking: "And Anson?" ironically. "What is dear Anson doing?"

She told her of Anson's great work, "The Pentland Family and the Massachusetts Bay Colony" and of its immense value as a contribution to the history of the nation; and when she had finished with that, she turned to Jack's wretched health, saying in a low, melancholy voice, "It's only a matter of time, you know. . . . At least, so the doctors say. . . . With a heart like that it's only a matter of time." The tears came again.

"And yet," Sabine said slowly, "you say that Olivia has everything."

"Well," replied Aunt Cassie, "perhaps not everything."

Before she left she inquired for Sabine's daughter and was told that she had gone over to Pentlands to see Sybil.

"They went to the same school in France," said Sabine. "They were friends there."

"Yes," said Aunt Cassie. "I was against Sybil's going abroad to school. It fills a girl's head with queer ideas . . . especially a school like that where any one could go. Since she's home, Sybil behaves very queerly. . . . I think it'll stand in the way of her success in Boston. The boys don't like girls who are different."

"Perhaps," said Sabine, "she may marry outside of Boston. Men aren't the same everywhere. Even in Boston there must be one or two who don't refer to women as 'Good old So-and-so.' Even in Boston there must be men who like women who are well dressed . . . women who are ladies. . . ."

Aunt Cassie began to grow angry again, but Sabine swept over her. "Don't be insulted, Aunt Cassie. I only mean ladies in the old-fashioned, glamorous sense. . . . Besides," she continued, "whom could she marry who wouldn't be a cousin or a connection of some sort?"

"She ought to marry here . . . among the people she's always known.

There's a Mannering boy who would be a good match, and James Thorne's youngest son."

Sabine smiled. "So you have plans for her already. You've settled it?"

"Of course, nothing is settled. I'm only thinking of it with Sybil's welfare in view. If she married one of those boys she'd know what she was getting. She'd know that she was marrying a gentleman."

"Perhaps . . ." said Sabine. "Perhaps." Somehow a devil had taken possession of her and she added softly, "There was, of course, Horace Pentland. . . . One can never be quite sure." (She never forgot anything, Sabine.)

And at the same moment she saw, standing outside the door that opened on the terrace next to the marshes, a solid, dark, heavy figure which she recognized with a sudden feeling of delight as O'Hara. He had been walking across the fields with the wiry little Higgins, who had left him and continued on his way down the lane in the direction of Pentlands. At the sight of him, Aunt Cassie made every sign of an attempt to escape quickly, but Sabine said in a voice ominous with sweetness, "You must meet Mr. O'Hara. I think you've never met him. He's a charming man." And she placed herself in such a position that it was impossible for the old woman to escape without losing every vestige of dignity.

Then Sabine called gently, "Come in, Mr. O'Hara. . . . Mrs. Struthers is here and wants so much to meet her new neighbor."

The door opened and O'Hara stepped in, a swarthy, rather solidly built man of perhaps thirty-five, with a shapely head on which the vigorous black hair was cropped close, and with blue eyes that betrayed his Irish origin by the half-hidden sparkle of amusement at this move of Sabine's. He had a strong jaw and full, rather sensual, lips and a curious sense of great physical strength, as if all his clothes were with difficulty modeled to the muscles that lay underneath. He wore no hat, and his skin was a dark tan, touched at the cheek-bones by the dull flush of health and good blood.

He was, one would have said at first sight, a common, vulgar man in that narrow-jawed world about Durham, a man, perhaps, who had come by his muscles as a dock-laborer. Sabine had thought him vulgar in the beginning, only to succumb in the end to a crude sort of power which placed him above the realm of such distinctions. And she was a shrewd woman, too, devoted passionately to the business of getting at the essence of people; she knew that vulgarity had nothing to do with a man who had eyes so shrewd and full of mockery.

He came forward quietly and with a charming air of deference in which there was a faint suspicion of nonsense, a curious shadow of vulgarity, only one could not be certain whether he was not being vulgar by deliberation.

"It is a great pleasure," he said. "Of course, I have seen Mrs. Struthers many times . . . at the horse shows . . . the whippet races."

Aunt Cassie was drawn up, stiff as a poker, with an air of having found herself unexpectedly face to face with a rattlesnake.

"I have had the same experience," she said. "And of course I've seen all the improvements you have made here on the farm." The word "improvements" she spoke with a sort of venom in it, as if it had been instead a word like "arson."

"We'll have some tea," observed Sabine. "Sit down, Aunt Cassie."

But Aunt Cassie did not unbend. "I promised Olivia to be back at Pentlands for tea," she said. "And I am late already." Pulling on her black gloves, she made a sudden dip in the direction of O'Hara. "We shall probably see each other again, Mr. O'Hara, since we are neighbors."

"Indeed, I hope so. . . ."

Then she kissed Sabine again and murmured, "I hope, my dear, that you will come often to see me, now that you've come back to us. Make my house your own home." She turned to O'Hara, finding a use for him suddenly in her warfare against Sabine. "You know, Mr. O'Hara, she is a traitor, in her way. She was raised among us and then went away for twenty years. She hasn't any loyalty in her."

She made the speech with a stiff air of playfulness, as if, of course, she were only making a joke and the speech meant nothing at all. Yet the air was filled with a cloud of implications. It was the sort of tactics in which she excelled.

Sabine went with her to the door, and when she returned she discovered O'Hara standing by the window, watching the figure of Aunt Cassie as she moved indignantly down the road in the direction of Pentlands. Sabine stood there for a moment, studying the straight, strong figure outlined against the light, and she got suddenly a curious sense of the enmity between him and the old woman. They stood, the two of them, in a strange way as the symbols of two great forces—the one negative, the other intensely positive; the one the old, the other, the new; the one of decay, the other of vigorous, almost too lush growth. Nothing could ever reconcile them. According to the scheme of things, they would be implacable enemies to the end. But Sabine had no doubts as to the final victor; the same scheme of things showed small respect for all that Aunt Cassie stood for. That was one of the wisdoms Sabine had learned since she had escaped from Durham into the uncompromising realities of the great world.

When she spoke, she said in a noncommittal sort of voice, "Mrs. Struthers is a remarkable woman."

And O'Hara, turning, looked at her with a sudden glint of humor in his blue eyes. "Extraordinary . . . I'm sure of it."

"And a powerful woman," said Sabine. "Wise as a serpent and gentle as a dove. It is never good to underestimate such strength. And now. . . . How do you like your tea?"

He took no tea but contented himself with munching a bit of toast and afterward smoking a cigar, clearly pleased with himself in a naïve way in the rôle of landlord coming to inquire of his tenant whether everything was satisfactory. He had a liking for this hard, clever woman who was now only a tenant of the land—his land—which she had once owned. When he thought of it—that he, Michael O'Hara, had come to own this farm in the midst of the fashionable and dignified world of Durham—there was something incredible in the knowledge, something which never ceased to warm him with a strong sense of satisfaction. By merely turning his head, he could see in the mirror the reflection of the long scar on his temple, marked there by a broken bottle in the midst of a youthful fight along the India Wharf. He, Michael O'Hara, without education save that which he had given himself, without money, without influence, had raised himself to this position before his thirty-sixth birthday. In the autumn he would be a candidate for Congress, certain of election in the back Irish districts. He, Michael O'Hara, was on his way to being one of the great men of New England, a country which had once been the tight little paradise of people like the Pentlands.

Only no one must ever suspect the depth of that great satisfaction.

Yes, he had a liking for this strange woman, who ought to have been his enemy and, oddly enough, was not. He liked the shrewd directness of her mind and the way she had of sitting there opposite him, turning him over and over while he talked, as if he had been a small bug under a microscope. She was finding out all about him; and he understood that, for it was a trick in which he, himself, was well-practised. It was by such methods that he had got ahead in the world. It puzzled him, too, that she should have come out of that Boston-Durham world and yet could be so utterly different from it. He had a feeling that somewhere in the course of her life something had happened to her, something terrible which in the end had given her a great understanding and clarity of mind. He knew, too, almost at once, on the day she had driven up to the door of the cottage, that she had made a discovery about life which he himself had made long since . . . that there is nothing of such force as the power of a person content merely to be himself, nothing so invincible as the power of simply honesty, nothing so successful as the life of one who runs alone. Somewhere she had learned all this. She was like a woman to whom nothing could ever again happen.

They talked for a time, idly and pleasantly, with a sense of understanding unusual in two people who had known each other for so short a time; they spoke of the farm, of Pentlands, of the mills and the Poles in Durham, of the country as it had been in the days when Sabine was a child. And all the while he had that sense of her weighing and watching him, of feeling out the faint echo of a brogue in his speech and the rather hard, nasal quality that remained from those days along India Wharf and the memories of a ne'er-do-well, superstitious Irish father.

He could not have known that she was a woman who included among her friends men and women of a dozen nationalities, who lived a life among the clever, successful people of the world . . . the architects, the painters, the politicians, the scientists. He could not have known the ruthless rule she put up against tolerating any but people who were "complete." He could have known nothing of her other life in Paris, and London, and New York, which had nothing to do with the life in Durham and Boston. And yet he did know. . . . He saw that, despite the great difference in their worlds, there was a certain kinship between them, that they had both come to look upon the world as a pie from which any plum might be drawn if one only knew the knack.

And Sabine, on her side, not yet quite certain about casting aside all barriers, was slowly reaching the same understanding. There was no love or sentimentality in the spark that flashed between them. She was more than ten years older than O'Hara and had done with such things long ago. It was merely a recognition of one strong person by another.

It was O'Hara who first took advantage of the bond. In the midst of the conversation, he had turned the talk rather abruptly to Pentlands.

"I've never been there and I know very little of the life," he said, "but I've watched it from a distance and it interests me. It's like something out of a dream, completely dead . . . dead all save for young Mrs. Pentland and Sybil."

Sabine smiled. "You know Sybil, then?"

"We ride together every morning. . . . We met one morning by chance along the path by the river and since then we've gone nearly every day."

"She's a charming girl. . . . She went to school in France with my daughter, Thérèse. I saw a great deal of her then."

Far back in her mind the thought occurred to her that there would be something very amusing in the prospect of Sybil married to O'Hara. It would produce such an uproar with Anson and Aunt Cassie and the other relatives. . . . A Pentland married to an Irish Roman Catholic politician!

"She is like her mother, isn't she?" asked O'Hara, sitting forward a bit on his chair. He had a way of sitting thus, in the tense, quiet alertness of a cat.

"Very like her mother. . . . Her mother is a remarkable woman . . . a charming woman . . . also, I might say, what is the rarest of all things, a really good and generous woman."

"I've thought that. . . . I've seen her a half-dozen times. I asked her to help me in planting the garden here at the cottage because I knew she had a passion for gardens. And she didn't refuse . . . though she scarcely knew me. She came over and helped me with it. I saw her then and came to know her. But when that was finished, she went back to Pentlands and I haven't seen her since. It's almost as if she meant to avoid me. Sometimes I feel sorry for her. . . . It must be a queer life for a woman like that . . . young and beautiful."

"She has a great deal to occupy her at Pentlands. And it's true that it's not a very fascinating life. Still, I'm sure she couldn't bear being pitied. . . . She's the last woman in the world to want pity."

Curiously, O'Hara flushed, the red mounting slowly beneath the dark-tanned skin.

"I thought," he said a little sadly, "that her husband or Mrs. Struthers might have raised objections. . . . I know how they feel toward me. There's no use pretending not to know."

"It is quite possible," said Sabine.

There was a sudden embarrassing silence, which gave Sabine time to pull her wits together and organize a thousand sudden thoughts and impressions. She was beginning to understand, bit by bit, the real reasons of their hatred for O'Hara, the reasons which lay deep down underneath, perhaps so deep that none of them ever saw them for what they were.

And then out of the silence she heard the voice of O'Hara saying, in a queer, hushed way, "I mean to ask something of you . . . something that may sound ridiculous. I don't pretend that it isn't, but I mean to ask it anyway."

For a moment he hesitated and then, rising quickly, he stood looking away from her out of the door, toward the distant blue marshes and the open sea. She fancied that he was trembling a little, but she could not be certain. What she did know was that he made an immense and heroic effort, that for a moment he, a man who never did such things, placed himself in a position where he would be defenseless and open to being cruelly hurt; and for the moment all the recklessness seemed to flow out of him and in its place there came a queer sadness, almost as if he felt himself defeated in some way. . . .

He said, "What I mean to ask you is this. . . . Will you ask me sometimes here to the cottage when she will be here too?" He turned toward her suddenly and added, "It will mean a great deal to me . . . more than you can imagine."

She did not answer him at once, but sat watching him with a poorly concealed intensity; and presently, flicking the cigarette ashes casually from her gown, she asked, "And do you think it would be quite moral of me?"

He shrugged his shoulders and looked at her in astonishment, as if he had expected her, least of all people in the world, to ask such a thing.

"It might," he said, "make us both a great deal happier."

"Perhaps . . . perhaps not. It's not so simple as that. Besides, it isn't happiness that one places first at Pentlands."

"No. . . . Still. . . ." He made a sudden vigorous gesture, as if to sweep aside all objections.

"You're a queer man. . . . I'll see what can be done."

He thanked her and went out shyly without another word, to stride across the meadows, his black head bent thoughtfully, in the direction of his new bright chimneys. At his heels trotted the springer, which had lain waiting for him outside the door. There was something about the robust figure, crossing the old meadow through the blue twilight, that carried a note of lonely sadness. The self-confidence, the assurance, seemed to have melted away in some mysterious fashion. It was almost as if one man had entered the cottage a little while before and another, a quite different man, had left it just now. Only one thing, Sabine saw, could have made the difference, and that was the name of Olivia.

When he had disappeared Sabine went up to her room overlooking the sea and lay there for a long time thinking. She was by nature an indolent woman, especially at times when her brain worked with a fierce activity. It was working thus now, in a kind of fever, confused and yet tremendously clear; for the visits from Aunt Cassie and O'Hara had ignited her almost morbid passion for vicarious experience. She had a sense of being on the brink of some calamity which, beginning long ago in a hopeless tangle of origins and motives, was ready now to break forth with the accumulated force of years.

It was only now that she began to understand a little what it was that had drawn her back to a place which held memories so unhappy as those haunting the whole countryside of Durham. She saw that it must have been all the while a desire for vindication, a hunger to show them that, in spite of everything, of the straight red hair and the plain face, the silly ideas with which they had filled her head, in spite even of her unhappiness over her husband, she had made of her life a successful, even a brilliant, affair. She had wanted to show them that she stood aloof now and impregnable, quite beyond their power to curb or to injure her. And for a moment she suspected that the half-discerned motive was an even stronger thing, akin perhaps to a desire for vengeance; for she held this world about Durham responsible for the ruin of her happiness. She knew now, as a worldly woman of forty-six, that if she had been brought up knowing life for what it was, she might never have lost the one man who had ever roused a genuine passion in a nature so hard and dry.

It was all confused and tormented and vague, yet the visit of Aunt Cassie, filled with implications and veiled attempts to humble her, had cleared the air enormously.

And behind the closed lids, the green eyes began to see a whole procession of calamities which lay perhaps within her power to create. She began to see how it might even be possible to bring the whole world of Pentlands down about their heads in a collapse which could create only freedom and happiness to Olivia and her daughter. And it was these two alone for whom she had any affection; the others might be damned, gloriously damned, while she stood by without raising a finger.

She began to see where the pieces of the puzzle lay, the wedges which might force open the solid security of the familiar, unchanging world that once more surrounded her.

Lying there in the twilight, she saw the whole thing in the process of being fitted together and she experienced a sudden intoxicating sense of power, of having all the tools at hand, of being the *dea ex machinâ* of the calamity.

She was beginning to see, too, how the force, the power that had lain behind all the family, was coming slowly to an end in a pale, futile weakness. There would always be money to bolster up their world, for the family had never lost its shopkeeping tradition of thrift; but in the end even money could not save them. There came a time when a great fortune might be only a shell without a desiccated rottenness inside.

She was still lying there when Thérèse came in—a short, plain, rather stocky, dark girl with a low straight black bang across her forehead. She was hot and soiled by the mud of the marshes, as the red-haired unhappy little girl had been so many times in that far-off, half-forgotten childhood.

"Where have you been?" she asked indifferently, for there was always a curious sense of strangeness between Sabine and her daughter.

"Catching frogs to dissect," said Thérèse. "They're damned scarce and I slipped into the river."

Sabine, looking at her daughter, knew well enough there was no chance of marrying off a girl so queer, and wilful and untidy, in Durham. She saw that it had been a silly idea from the beginning; but she found satisfaction in the knowledge that she had molded Thérèse's life so that no one could ever hurt her as they had hurt her mother. Out of the queer nomadic life they had led together, meeting all sorts of men and women who were, in Sabine's curious sense of the word, "complete," the girl had pierced her way somehow to the bottom of things. She was building her young life upon a rock, so that she could afford to feel contempt for the very forces which long ago had hurt her mother. She might, like O'Hara, be suddenly humbled by love; but that, Sabine knew, was a glorious thing well worth suffering.

She knew it each time that she looked at her child and saw the clear gray eyes of the girl's father looking out of the dark face with the same proud look of indifferent confidence which had fascinated her twenty years ago. So long as Thérèse was alive, she would never be able wholly to forget him.

"Go wash yourself," she said. "Old Mr. Pentland and Olivia and Mrs. Soames are coming to dine and play bridge."

As she dressed for dinner she no longer asked herself, "Why did I ever imagine Thérèse might find a husband here? What ever induced me to come back here to be bored all summer long?"

She had forgotten all that. She began to see that the summer held prospects of diversion. It might even turn into a fascinating game. She knew that her return had nothing to do with Thérèse's future; she had been drawn back into Durham by some vague but overwhelming desire for mischief.

Chapter 5

1

WHEN ANSON PENTLAND came down from the city in the evening, Olivia was always there to meet him dutifully and inquire about the day. The answers were always the same: "No, there was not much doing in town," and, "It was very hot," or, "I made a discovery to-day that will be of great use to me in the book."

Then after a bath he would appear in tweeds to take his exercise in the garden, pottering about mildly and peering closely with his near-sighted blue eyes at little tags labeled "General Pershing" or "Caroline Testout" or "Poincaré" or "George Washington" which he tied carefully on the new dahlias and roses and smaller shrubs. And, more often than not, the gardener would spend half the next morning removing the tags and placing them on the proper plants, for Anson really had no interest in flowers and knew very little about them. The tagging was only a part of his passion for labeling things; it made the garden at Pentlands seem a more subdued and ordered place. Sometimes it seemed to Olivia that he went through life ticketing and pigeonholing everything that came his way: manners, emotions, thoughts, everything. It was a habit that was growing on him in middle-age.

Dinner was usually late because Anson liked to take advantage of the long summer twilights, and after dinner it was the habit of all the family, save Jack, who went to bed immediately afterward, to sit in the Victorian drawing-room, reading and writing letters or sometimes playing patience, with Anson in his corner at Mr. Lowell's desk working over "The Pentland Family and the Massachusetts Bay Colony," and keeping up a prodigious correspondence with librarians and old men and women of a genealogical bent. The routine of the evening rarely changed, for Anson disliked going out and Olivia preferred not to go alone. It was only with the beginning of the summer, when Sybil was grown and had begun to go out occasionally to dinners and balls, and the disturbing Sabine, with her passion for playing bridge, had come into the neighborhood, that the routine was beginning to break up. There were fewer evenings now with Olivia and Sybil playing patience and old John Pentland sitting by the light of Mr. Longfellow's lamp reading or simply staring silently before him, lost in thought.

There were times in those long evenings when Olivia, looking up suddenly and for no reason at all, would discover that Sybil was sitting in the same fashion watching her, and both of them would know that they, like old John Pentland, had been sitting there all the while holding books in their hands without knowing a word of what they had read. It was as if a kind of enchantment descended upon them, as if they were waiting for something. Once or twice the silence had been broken sharply by the unbearable sound of groans coming from the north wing when *she* had been seized suddenly by one of her fits of violence.

Anson's occasional comment and Olivia's visits to Jack's room to see that nothing had happened to him were the only interruptions. They spoke always in low voices when they played double patience in order not to disturb Anson at his work. Sometimes he encountered a bit of information for which he had been searching for a long time and then he would turn and tell them of it.

There was the night when he made his discovery about Savina Pentland. . . .

"I was right about Savina Pentland," he said. "She *was* a first cousin and not a second cousin of Toby Cane."

Olivia displayed an interest by saying, "Was that what you wrote to the *Transcript* about?"

"Yes . . . and I was sure that the genealogical editor was wrong. See . . . here it is in one of Jared Pentland's letters at the time she was drowned. . . . Jared was her husband. . . . He refers to Toby Cane as her only male first cousin."

"That will help you a great deal," said Olivia, "won't it?"

"It will help clear up the chapter about the origins of her family." And then, after a little pause, "I wish that I could get some trace of the correspondence between Savina Pentland and Cane. I'm sure it would be full of things . . . but it seems not to exist . . . only one or two letters which tell nothing."

And then he relapsed again into a complete and passionate silence, lost in the rustle of old books and yellowed letters, leaving the legend of Savina Pentland to take possession of the others in the room.

The memory of this woman had a way of stealing in upon the family unaware, quite without their willing it. She was always there in the house, more lively than any of the more sober ancestors, perhaps because of them all she alone had been touched by splendor; she alone had been in her reckless way a great lady. There was a power in her recklessness and extravagance which came, in the end, to obscure all those other plain, solemn-faced, thrifty wives whose portraits adorned the hall of Pentlands, much as a rising sun extinguishes the feeble light of the stars. And about her obscure origin there clung a perpetual aura of romance, since there was no one to know just who her mother was or exactly whence she came. The mother was born perhaps of stock no humbler than the first shopkeeping Pentland to land on the Cape, but there was in her the dark taint of Portuguese blood; some said that she was the daughter of a fisherman. And Savina herself had possessed enough of fascination to lure a cautious Pentland into eloping with her against the scruples that were a very fiber of the Pentland bones and flesh.

The portrait of Savina Pentland stood forth among the others in the white hall, fascinating and beautiful not only because the subject was a dark, handsome woman, but because it had been done by Ingres in Rome during the years when he made portraits of tourists to save himself from starvation. It was the likeness of a small but voluptuous woman with great wanton dark eyes and smooth black hair pulled back from a camellia-white brow and done in a little knot on the nape of the white neck—a woman who looked out of the old picture with the flashing, spirited glance of one who lived boldly and passionately. She wore a gown of peach-colored velvet ornamented with the famous parure of pearls and emeralds given her, to the scandal of a thrifty family, by the infatuated Jared Pentland. Passing the long gallery of portraits in the hallway it was always Savina Pentland whom one noticed. She reigned there as she must have reigned in life, so bold and splendorous as to seem a bit vulgar, especially in a world of such sober folk, yet so beautiful and so spirited that she made all the others seem scarcely worth consideration.

Even in death she had remained an "outsider," for she was the only one of the family who did not rest quietly among the stunted trees at the top of the bald hill where the first Pentlands had laid their dead. All that was left of the warm, soft body lay in the white sand at the bottom of the ocean within sight of Pentlands. It was as if fate had delivered her in death into a grave as tempestuous and violent as she had been in life. And somewhere near her in the restless white sand lay Toby Cane, with whom she had gone sailing one bright summer day when a sudden squall turned a gay excursion into a tragedy.

Even Aunt Cassie, who distrusted any woman with gaze so bold and free as that set down by the brush of Ingres—even Aunt Cassie could not annihilate the glamour of Savina's legend. For her there was, too, another, more painful, memory hidden in the knowledge that the parure of pearls and emeralds and all the other jewels which Savina Pentland had wrung from her thrifty husband, lay buried somewhere in the white sand between her bones and those of her cousin. To Aunt Cassie Savina Pentland seemed more than merely a reckless, extravagant creature. She was an enemy of the Pentland fortune and of all the virtues of the family.

The family portraits were of great value to Anson in compiling his book, for they represented the most complete collection of ancestors existing in all America. From the portrait of the emigrating Pentland, painted in a wooden manner by some traveling painter of tavern signs, to the rather handsome one of John Pentland, painted at middle-age in a pink coat by Sargent, and the rather bad and liverish one of Anson, also by Mr. Sargent, the collection was complete save for two—the weak Jared Pentland who had married Savina, and the Pentland between old John's father and the clipper-ship owner, who had died at twenty-three, a disgraceful thing for any Pentland to have done.

The pictures hung in a neat double row in the lofty hall, arranged chronologically and without respect for lighting, so that the good ones like those by Ingres and Sargent's picture of old John Pentland and the unfinished Gilbert Stuart of Ashur Pentland hung in obscure shadows, and the bad ones like the tavern-sign portrait of the first Pentland were exposed in a glare of brilliant light.

This father of all the family had been painted at the great age of eighty-nine and looked out from his wooden background, a grim, hard-mouthed old fellow with white hair and shrewd eyes set very close together. It was a face such as one might find to-day among the Plymouth Brethren of some remote, half-forgotten Sussex village, the face of a man notable only for the toughness of his body and the rigidity of a mind which dissented from everything. At the age of eighty-four, he had been cast out for dissension from the church which he had come to regard as his own property.

Next to him hung the portrait of a Pentland who had been a mediocrity and left not even a shadowy legend; and then appeared the insolent, disagreeable face of the Pentland who had ducked eccentric old women for witches and cut off the ears of peace-loving Quakers in the colony founded in "freedom to worship God."

The third Pentland had been the greatest evangelist of his time, a man who went through New England holding high the torch, exhorting rude village audiences by the coarsest of language to such a pitch of excitement that old women died of apoplexy and young women gave birth to premature children. The sermons which still existed showed him to be a man uncultivated and at times almost illiterate, yet his vast energy had founded a university and his fame as an exhorter and "the flaming sword of the Lord" had traveled to the ignorant and simple-minded brethren of the English back country.

The next Pentland was the eldest of the exhorter's twenty children (by four wives), a man who clearly had departed from his father's counsels and appeared in his portrait a sensual, fleshly specimen, very fat and almost good-natured, with thick red lips. It was this Pentland who had founded the fortune which gave the family its first step upward in the direction of the gentility which had ended with the figure of Anson bending over "The Pentland Family and the Massachusetts Bay Colony." He had made a large fortune by equipping privateers and practising a near-piracy on British merchantmen; and there was, too, a dark rumor (which Anson intended to overlook) that he had made as much as three hundred per cent profit on a single shipload of negroes in the African slave trade.

After him there were portraits of two Pentlands who had taken part in the Revolution and then another hiatus of mediocrity, including the gap represented by the missing Jared; and then appeared the Anthony Pentland who increased the fortune enormously in the clipper trade. It was the portrait of a swarthy, powerful man (the first of the dark Pentlands, who could all be traced directly to Savina's Portuguese blood), painted by a second-rate artist devoted to realism, who had depicted skilfully the warts which marred the distinguished old gentleman. In the picture he stood in the garden before the Pentland house at Durham with marshes in the background and his prize clipper *Semiramis* riding, with all sail up, the distant ocean.

Next to him appeared the portrait of old John Pentland's father—a man of pious expression, dressed all in black, with a high black stock and a wave of luxuriant black hair, the one who had raised the family to really great wealth by contracts for shoes and blankets for the soldiers at Gettysburg and Bull Run and Richmond. After him, gentility had conquered completely, and the Sargent portrait of old John Pentland at middle-age showed a man who was master of hounds and led the life of a country gentleman, a man clearly of power and character, whose strength of feature had turned slowly into the bitter hardness of the old man who sat now in the light of Mr. Longfellow's lamp reading or staring before him into space while his son set down the long history of the family.

The gallery was fascinating to strangers, as the visual record of a family which had never lost any money (save for the extravagance of Savina Pentland's jewels), a family which had been the backbone of a community, a family in which the men married wives for thrift and housewifely virtues rather than for beauty, a family solid and respectable and full of honor. It was a tribe magnificent in its virtue and its strength, even at times in its intolerance and hypocrisy. It stood represented now by old John Pentland and Anson, and the boy who lay abovestairs in the room next Olivia's, dying slowly.

At ten o'clock each night John Pentland bade them good-night and went off to bed, and at eleven Anson, after arranging his desk neatly and placing his papers in their respective files, and saying to Olivia, "I wouldn't sit up too late, if I were you, when you are so tired," left them and disappeared. Soon after him, Sybil kissed her mother and climbed the stairs past all the ancestors.

It was only then, after they had all left her, that a kind of peace settled over Olivia. The burdens lifted, and the cares, the worries, the thoughts that were always troubling her, faded into the distance and for a time she sat leaning back in the winged armchair with her eyes closed, listening to the sounds of the night—the faint murmur of the breeze in the faded lilacs outside the window, the creaking that afflicts very old houses in the night, and sometimes the ominous sound of Miss Egan's step traversing distantly the old north wing. And then one night she heard again the distant sound of Higgins' voice swearing at the red mare as he made his round of the stables before going to bed.

And after they had all gone she opened her book and fell to reading. "*Madame de Clèves ne répondit rien, et elle pensoit avec honte qu'elle auroit pris tout ce que l'on disoit du changement de ce prince pour des marques de sa passion, si elle n'avoit point été détrompée. Elle se sentoit quelque aigreur contre Madame la Dauphine. . . .*" This was a world in which she felt somehow strangely at peace, as if she had once lived in it and returned in the silence of the night.

At midnight she closed the book, and making a round of the lower rooms, put out the lights and went up the long stairway to listen at the doorway of her son's room for the weak, uncertain sound of his breathing.

2

Olivia was right in her belief that Anson was ashamed of his behavior on the night of the ball. It was not that he made an apology or even mentioned the affair. He simply never spoke of it again. For weeks after the scene he did not mention the name of O'Hara, perhaps because the name brought up inevitably the memory of his sudden, insulting speech; but his sense of shame prevented him from harassing her on the subject. What he never knew was that Olivia, while hating him for the insult aimed at her father, was also pleased in a perverse, feminine way because he had displayed for a moment a sudden fit of genuine anger. For a moment he had come very near to being a husband who might interest his wife.

But in the end he only sank back again into a sea of indifference so profound that even Aunt Cassie's campaign of insinuations and veiled proposals could not stir him into action. The old woman managed to see him alone once or twice, saying to him, "Anson, your father is growing old and can't manage everything much longer. You must begin to take a stand yourself. The family can't rest on the shoulders of a woman. Besides, Olivia is an outsider, really. She's never understood our world." And then, shaking her head sadly, she would murmur, "There'll be trouble, Anson, when your father dies, if you don't show some backbone. You'll have trouble with Sybil; she's very queer and pig-headed in her quiet way, just as Olivia was in the matter of sending her to school in Paris."

And after a pause, "I am the last person in the world to interfere; it's only for your own good and Olivia's and all the family's."

And Anson, to be rid of her, would make promises, facing her with averted eyes in some corner of the garden or the old house where she had skilfully run him to earth beyond the possibility of escape. And he would leave her, troubled and disturbed because the world and this family which had been saddled unwillingly upon him, would permit him no peace to go on with his writing. He really hated Aunt Cassie because she had never given him any peace, never since the days when she had kept him in the velvet trousers and Fauntleroy curls which spurred the jeers of the plain, red-haired little Sabine. She had never ceased to reproach him for "not being a man and standing up for his rights." It seemed to him that Aunt Cassie was always hovering near, like a dark persistent fury, always harassing him; and yet he knew, more by instinct than by any process of reasoning, that she was his ally against the others, even his own wife and father and children. He and Aunt Cassie prayed to the same gods.

So he did nothing, and Olivia, keeping her word, spoke of O'Hara to Sybil one day as they sat alone at breakfast.

The girl had been riding with him that very morning and she sat in her riding-clothes, her face flushed by the early morning exercise, telling her mother of the beauties of the country back of Durham, of the new beagle puppies, and of the death of "Hardhead" Smith, who was the last farmer of old New England blood in the county. His half-witted son, she said, was being taken away to an asylum. O'Hara, she said, was buying his little stony patch of ground.

When she had finished, her mother said, "And O'Hara? You like him, don't you?"

Sybil had a way of looking piercingly at a person, as if her violet eyes tried to bore quite through all pretense and unveil the truth. She had a power of honesty and simplicity that was completely disarming, and she used it now, smiling at her mother, candidly.

"Yes, I like him very much. . . . But . . . but . . ." She laughed softly.

"Are you worrying about my marrying him, my falling in love—because you needn't. I am fond of him because he's the one person around here who likes the things I like. He loves riding in the early morning when the dew is still on the grass and he likes racing with me across the lower meadow by the gravel-pit, and well—he's an interesting man. When he talks, he makes sense. But don't worry; I shan't marry him."

"I *was* interested," said Olivia, "because you do see him more than any one about here."

Again Sybil laughed. "But he's old, Mama. He's more than thirty-five. He's middle-aged. I know what sort of man I want to marry. I know exactly. He's going to be my own age."

"One can't always tell. It's not so easy as that."

"I'm sure I can tell." Her face took on an expression of gravity. "I've devoted a good deal of thought to it and I've watched a great many others."

Olivia wanted to smile, but she knew she dared not if she were to keep her hold upon confidences so charming and naïve.

"And I'm sure that I'll know the man when I see him, right away, at once. It'll be like a spark, like my friendship with O'Hara, only deeper than that."

"Did you ever talk to Thérèse about love?" asked Olivia.

"No; you can't talk to her about such things. She wouldn't understand. With Thérèse everything is scientific, biological. When Thérèse marries, I think it will be some man she has picked out as the proper father, scientifically, for her children."

"That's not a bad idea."

"She might just have children by him without marrying him, the way she breeds frogs. I think that's horrible."

Again Olivia was seized with an irresistible impulse to laugh, and controlled herself heroically. She kept thinking of how silly, how ignorant, she had been at Sybil's age, silly and ignorant despite the unclean sort of sophistication she had picked up in the corridors of Continental hotels. She kept thinking how much better a chance Sybil had for happiness. . . . Sybil, sitting there gravely, defending her warm ideas of romance against the scientific onslaughts of the swarthy, passionate Thérèse.

"It will be some one like O'Hara," continued Sybil. "Some one who is very much alive—only not middle-aged like O'Hara."

(So Sybil thought of O'Hara as middle-aged, and he was four years younger than Olivia, who felt and looked so young. The girl kept talking of O'Hara as if his life were over; but that perhaps was only because she herself was so young.)

Olivia sighed now, despite herself. "You mustn't expect too much from the world, Sybil. Nothing is perfect, not even marriage. One always has to make compromises."

"Oh, I know that; I've thought a great deal about it. All the same, I'm sure I'll know the man when I see him." She leaned forward and said earnestly, "Couldn't you tell when you were a girl?"

"Yes," said Olivia softly. "I could tell."

And then, inevitably, Sybil asked what Olivia kept praying she would not ask. She could hear the girl asking it before the words were spoken. She knew exactly what she would say.

"Didn't you know at once when you met Father?"

And in spite of every effort, the faint echo of a sigh escaped Olivia. "Yes, I knew."

She saw Sybil give her one of those quick, piercing looks of inquiry and then bow her head abruptly, as if pretending to study the pattern on her plate.

When she spoke again, she changed the subject abruptly, so that Olivia knew she suspected the truth, a thing which she had guarded with a fierce secrecy for so long.

"Why don't you take up riding again, Mother?" she asked. "I'd love to have you go with me. We would go with O'Hara in the mornings, and then Aunt Cassie couldn't have anything to say about my getting involved with him." She looked up. "You'd like him. You couldn't help it."

She saw that Sybil was trying to help her in some way, to divert her and drive away the unhappiness.

"I like him already," said Olivia, "very much."

Then she rose, saying, "I promised Sabine to motor into Boston with her to-day. We're leaving in twenty minutes."

She went quickly away because she knew it was perilous to sit there any longer talking of such things while Sybil watched her, eager with the freshness of youth which has all life before it.

Out of all their talk two things remained distinct in her mind: one that Sybil thought of O'Hara as middle-aged—almost an old man, for whom there was no longer any chance of romance; the other the immense possibility for tragedy that lay before a girl who was so certain that love would be a glorious romantic affair, so certain of the ideal man whom she would find one day. What was she to do with Sybil? Where was she to find that man? And when she found him, what difficulties would she have to face with John Pentland and Anson and Aunt Cassie and the host of cousins and connections who would be marshaled to defeat her?

For she saw clearly enough that this youth for whom Sybil was waiting would never be their idea of a proper match. It would be a man with qualities which O'Hara possessed, and even Higgins, the groom. She saw perfectly why Sybil had a fondness for these two outsiders; she had come to see it more and more clearly of late. It was because they possessed a curious, indefinable solidity that the others at Pentlands all lacked, and a certain fire and vitality. Neither blood, nor circumstance, nor tradition, nor wealth, had made life for them an atrophied, empty affair, in which there was no need for effort, for struggle, for combat. They had not been lost in a haze of transcendental maunderings. O'Hara, with his career and his energy, and Higgins, with his rabbitlike love-affairs and his nearness to all that was earthy, still carried about them a sense of the great zest in life. They reached down somehow into the roots of things where there was still savor and fertility.

And as she walked along the hallway, she found herself laughing aloud over the titles of the only three books which the Pentland family had ever produced—"The Pentland Family and the Massachusetts Bay Colony" and Mr. Struthers' two books, "Cornices of Old Boston Houses" and "Walks and Talks in New England Churchyards." She thought suddenly of what Sabine had once said acidly of New England—that it was a place where thoughts were likely to grow "higher and fewer."

But she was frightened, too, because in the life of enchantment which surrounded her, the virtues of O'Hara and Higgins seemed to her the only things in the world worth possessing. She wanted desperately to be alive, as she had never been, and she knew that this, too, was what Sybil sought in all her groping, half-blind romantic youth. It was something which the girl sensed and had never clearly understood, something which she knew existed and was awaiting her.

3

Sabine, watching O'Hara as he crossed the fields through the twilight, had penetrated in a sudden flash of intuition the depths of his character. His profound loneliness was, perhaps, the key which unlocked the whole of his soul, a key which Sabine knew well enough, for there had never been a time in all her existence, save for a sudden passionate moment or two in the course of her life with Callendar, when she was free of a painful feeling that she was alone. Even with her own daughter, the odd Thérèse, she was lonely. Watching life with the same passionate intensity with which she had watched the distant figure of O'Hara moving away against the horizon, she had come long ago to understand that loneliness was the curse of those who were free, even of all those who rose a little above the level of ordinary humanity. Looking about her she saw that old John Pentland was lonely, and Olivia, and even her own daughter Thérèse, rambling off independently across the marshes in search of bugs and queer plants. She saw that Anson Pentland was never lonely, for he had his friends who were so like him as to be very nearly indistinguishable, and he had all the traditions and fetishes which he shared with Aunt Cassie. They were part of a fabric, a small corner in the whole tapestry of life, from which they were inseparable.

Of them all, it seemed to her, as she came to see more and more of O'Hara, that he was the most lonely. He had friends, scores, even hundreds of them, in a dozen circles, ranging from the docks where he had spent his boyhood to the world about Durham where there were others who treated him less coldly than the Pentland family had done. He had friends because there was a quality about him which was irresistible. It lurked somewhere in the depths of the humorous blue eyes and at the corners of the full, rather sensual mouth—a kind of universal sympathy which made him understand the fears, the hopes, the ambitions, the weaknesses of other people. It was that quality, so invaluable in politics, which led enemies unjustly to call him all things to all people. He must have had the gift of friendship, for there were whole sections of Boston which would have followed him anywhere; and yet behind these easy, warm ties there was always a sort of veil shutting him away from them. He had a way of being at home in a barroom or at a hunt breakfast with equal ease, but there was a part of him—the part which was really O'Hara—which the world never saw at all, a strangely warm, romantic, impractical, passionate, headlong, rather unscrupulous Irishman, who lay shut away where none could penetrate. Sabine knew this O'Hara; he had been revealed to her swiftly in a sudden flash at the mention of Olivia Pentland. And afterward when she thought of it, she (Sabine Callendar), who was so hard, so bitter, so unbelieving, surrendered to him as so many had done before her.

Standing there in her sitting-room, so big and powerful and self-reliant, he had seemed suddenly like a little boy, like the little boy whom she had found once late at night long ago, sitting alone and quite still on the curb in front of her house in the Rue de Tilsitt. She had stopped for a moment and watched him, and presently she had approached and asked, "What are you doing here on the curb at this hour of the night?" And the little boy, looking up, had said gravely, "I'm playing."

It had happened years ago—the little boy must have grown into a young man by now—but she remembered him suddenly during the moment when O'Hara had turned and said to her, "It will mean a great deal to me, more than you can imagine."

O'Hara was like that, she knew—sad and a little lonely, as if in the midst of all his success, with his career and his big new house and his dogs and horses and all the other shiny accoutrements of a gentleman, he had looked up at her and said gravely, "I'm playing."

Long ago Sabine had come to understand that one got a savor out of life by casting overboard all the little rules which clutter up existence, all the ties, and beliefs and traditions in which she had been given a training so intense and severe that in the end she had turned a rebel. Behind all the indifference of countenance and the intricacy of brain, there lay a foundation of immense candor which had driven her to seek her companions, with the directness of an arrow, only among the persons whom she had come to designate as "complete." It was a label which she did not trouble to define to any one, doubting perhaps that any one save herself would find any interest in it; even for herself, it was a label lacking in definiteness. Vaguely she meant by "complete" the persons who stood on their own, who had an existence sufficiently strong to survive the assault or the collapse of any environment, persons who might exist independent of any concrete world, who possessed a proud sense of individuality, who might take root and work out a successful destiny wherever fate chanced to drop them. They were rare, she had come to discover, and yet they existed everywhere, such persons as John Pentland and O'Hara, Olivia and Higgins.

So she had come to seek her life among them, drawing them quietly about her wherever in the world she happened to pause for a time. She did it quietly and without loud cries of "Freedom" and "Free Love" and "The Right to Lead One's Life," for she was enough civilized to understand the absurdity of making a spectacle in the market-place, and she was too intense an individualist ever to turn missionary. Here perhaps lay her quiet strength and the source of that vague distrust and uneasiness which her presence created in people like Anson and Aunt Cassie. It was unbearable for Aunt Cassie to suspect that Sabine really did not trouble even to scorn her, unbearable to an old woman who had spent all her life in arranging the lives of others to find that a chit of a woman like Sabine could discover in her only a subject of mingled mirth and pity. It was unbearable not to have the power of jolting Sabine out of her serene and insolent indifference, unbearable to know that she was always watching you out of those green eyes, turning you over and over as if you were a bug and finding you in the end an inferior sort of insect. Those who had shared the discovery of her secret were fond of her, and those who had not were bitter against her. And it was, after all, a very simple secret, that one has only to be simple and friendly and human and "complete." She had no patience with sentimentality, and affectation and false piety.

And so the presence of Sabine began slowly to create a vaguely defined rift in a world hitherto set and complacent and even proud of itself. Something in the sight of her cold green eyes, in the sound of her metallic voice, in the sudden shrewd, disillusioning observations which she had a way of making at disconcerting moments, filled people like Aunt Cassie with uneasiness and people like Olivia with a smoldering sense of restlessness and rebellion. Olivia herself became more and more conscious of the difference with the passing of each day into the next and there were times when she suspected that that fierce old man, her father-in-law, was aware of it. It was potent because Sabine was no outsider; the mockery of an outsider would have slipped off the back of the Durham world like arrows off the back of an armadillo. But Sabine was one of them: it was that which made the difference: she was always inside the shell.

4

One hot, breathless night in June Sabine overcame her sense of bored indolence enough to give a dinner at Brook Cottage—a dinner well served, with delicious food, which it might have been said she flung at her guests with a superb air of indifference from the seat at the head of the table, where she sat painted, ugly and magnificently dressed, watching them all in a perverse sort of pleasure. It was a failure as an entertainment, for it had been years since Sabine had given a dinner where the guests were not clever enough to entertain themselves, and now that she was back again in a world where people were invited for every sort of reason save that you really wanted their company, she declined to make any effort. It was a failure, too, because Thérèse, for whom it was given, behaved exactly as she had behaved on the night of the ball. There was an uneasiness and a strain, a sense of awkwardness among the callow young men and a sense of weariness in Sabine and Olivia. O'Hara was there, for Sabine had kept her half-promise; but even he sat quietly, all his boldness and dash vanished before a boyish shyness. The whole affair seemed to be drowned in the lassitude, the enchantment that enveloped the old house on the other bank of the river.

Olivia had come, almost against her will, reduced to a state of exhaustion after a long call from Aunt Cassie on the subject of the rumored affair between Sybil and their Irish neighbor. And when they rose, she slipped quietly away into the garden, because she could not bear the thought of making strained and artificial conversation. She wanted, horribly, to be left in peace.

It was a superb night—hot, as a summer night should be—but clear, too, so that the whole sky was like a sapphire dome studded with diamonds. At the front of the cottage, beyond the borders of the little terraced garden, the marshes spread their dark carpet toward the distant dunes, which with the descent of darkness had turned dim and blue against the purer white of the line made by the foaming surf. The feel of the damp thick grass against the sole of her silver slippers led her to stop for a moment, breathing deeply, and filled her with a mild, half-mystical desire to blend herself into all the beauty that surrounded her, into the hot richness of the air, the scents of the opening blossoms and of pushing green stems, into the grass and the sea and the rich-smelling marshes, to slip away into a state which was nothing and yet everything, to float into eternity. She had abruptly an odd, confused sense of the timelessness of all these forces and sensations, of the sea and the marshes, the pushing green stems and the sapphire dome powdered with diamonds above her head. She saw for the first time in all her existence the power of something which went on and on, ignoring pitiful small creatures like herself and all those others in the cottage behind her, a power which ignored cities and armies and nations, which would go on and on long after the grass had blanketed the ruins of the old house at Pentlands. It was sweeping past her, leaving her stranded somewhere in the dull backwaters. She wanted suddenly, fiercely, to take part in all the great spectacle of eternal fertility, a mystery which was stronger than any of them or all of them together, a force which in the end would crush all their transient little prides and beliefs and traditions.

And then she thought, as if she were conscious of it for the first time, "I am tired, tired to death, and a little mad."

Moving across the damp grass she seated herself on a stone bench which O'Hara had placed beneath one of the ancient apple-trees left standing from the orchard which had covered all the land about Brook Cottage in the days when Savina Pentland was still alive; and for a long time (she never knew how long) she remained there lost in one of those strange lapses of consciousness when one is neither awake nor asleep but in the vague borderland where there is no thought, no care, no troubles. And then slowly she became aware of some one standing there quite near her, beneath the ancient, gnarled tree. As if the presence were materialized somehow out of a dream, she noticed first the faint, insinuating masculine odor of cigar-smoke blending itself with the scent of the growing flowers in Sabine's garden, and then turning she saw a black figure which she recognized at once as that of O'Hara. There was no surprise in the sight of him; it seemed in a queer way as if she had been expecting him.

As she turned, he moved toward her and spoke. "Our garden has flourished, hasn't it?" he asked. "You'd never think it was only a year old."

"Yes," she said. "It has flourished marvelously." And then, after a little pause, "How long have you been standing there?"

"Only a moment. I saw you come out of the house." They listened for a time to the distant melancholy pounding of the surf, and presently he said softly, with a kind of awe in his voice: "It is a marvelous night . . . a night full of splendor."

She made an effort to answer him, but somehow she could think of nothing to say. The remark, uttered so quietly, astonished her, because she had never thought of O'Hara as one who would be sensitive to the beauty of a night. It was too dark to distinguish his face, but she kept seeing him as she remembered him, seeing him, too, as the others thought of him—rough and vigorous but a little common, with the scar on his temple and the intelligent blue eyes, and the springy walk, so unexpectedly easy and full of grace for a man of his size. No, one might as well have expected little Higgins the groom to say: "It is a night full of splendor." The men she knew—Anson's friends—never said such things. She doubted whether they would ever notice such a night, and if they did notice it, they would be a little ashamed of having done anything so unusual.

"The party is not a great success," he was saying.

"No."

"No one seems to be getting on with any one else. Mrs. Callendar ought not to have asked me. I thought she was shrewder than that."

Olivia laughed softly. "She may have done it on purpose. You can never tell why she does anything."

For a time he remained silent, as if pondering the speech, and then he said, "You aren't cold out here?"

"No, not on a night like this."

There was a silence so long and so vaguely perilous that she felt the need of making some speech, politely and with banality, as if they were two strangers seated in a drawing-room after dinner instead of in the garden which together they had made beneath the ancient apple-trees.

"I keep wondering," she said, "how long it will be until the bungalows of Durham creep down and cover all this land."

"They won't, not so long as I own land between Durham and the sea."

In the darkness she smiled at the thought of an Irish Roman Catholic politician as the protector of this old New England countryside, and aloud she said, "You're growing to be like all the others. You want to make the world stand still."

"Yes, I can see that it must seem funny to you." There was no bitterness in his voice, but only a sort of hurt, which again astonished her, because it was impossible to think of O'Hara as one who could be hurt.

"There will always be the Pentland house, but, of course, all of us will die some day and then what?"

"There will always be our children."

She was aware slowly of slipping back into that world of cares and troubles behind her from which she had escaped a little while before. She said, "You are looking a long way into the future."

"Perhaps, but I mean to have children one day. And at Pentlands there is always Sybil, who will fight for it fiercely. She'll never give it up."

"But it's Jack who will own it, and I'm not so sure about him."

Unconsciously she sighed, knowing now that she was pretending again, being dishonest. She was pretending again that Jack would live to have Pentlands for his own, that he would one day have children who would carry it on. She kept saying to herself, "It is only the truth that can save us all." And she knew that O'Hara understood her feeble game of pretending. She knew because he stood there silently, as if Jack were already dead, as if he understood the reason for the faint bitter sigh and respected it.

"You see a great deal of Sybil, don't you?" she asked.

"Yes, she is a good girl. One can depend on her."

"Perhaps if she had a little of Thérèse or Mrs. Callendar in her, she'd be safer from being hurt."

He did not answer her at once, but she knew that in the darkness he was standing there, watching her.

"But that was a silly thing to say," she murmured. "I don't suppose you know what I mean."

He answered her quickly. "I do know exactly. I know and I'm sure Mrs. Callendar knows. We've both learned to save ourselves—not in the same school, but the same lesson, nevertheless. But as to Sybil, I think that depends upon whom she marries."

("So now," thought Olivia, "it is coming. It is Sybil whom he loves. He wants to marry her. That is why he has followed me out here.") She was back again now, solidly enmeshed in all the intricacies of living. She had a sudden, shameful, twinge of jealousy for Sybil, who was so young, who had pushed her so completely into the past along with all the others at Pentlands.

"I was wondering," she said, "whether she was not seeing too much of you, whether she might not be a bother."

"No, she'll never be that." And then in a voice which carried a faint echo of humor, he added, "I know that in a moment you are going to ask my intentions."

"No," she said, "no"; but she could think of nothing else to say. She felt suddenly shy and awkward and a little idiotic, like a young girl at her first dance.

"I shall tell you what my intentions are," he was saying, and then he broke off suddenly. "Why is it so impossible to be honest in this world, when we live such a little while? It would be such a different place if we were all honest wouldn't it?"

He hesitated, waiting for her to answer, and she said, "Yes," almost mechanically, "very different."

When he replied there was a faint note of excitement in his voice. It was pitched a little lower and he spoke more quickly. In the darkness she could not see him, and yet she was sharply conscious of the change.

"I'll tell you, then," he was saying. "I've been seeing a great deal of Sybil in the hope that I should see a little of her mother."

She did not answer him. She simply sat there, speechless, overcome by confusion, as if she had been a young girl with her first lover. She was even made a little dizzy by the sound of his voice.

"I have offended you. I'm sorry. I only spoke the truth. There is no harm in that."

With a heroic effort to speak intelligently, she succeeded in saying, "No, I am not offended." (It all seemed such a silly, helpless, pleasant feeling.) "No, I'm not offended. I don't know. . . ."

Of only one thing was she certain; that this strange, dizzy, intoxicated state was like nothing she had ever experienced. It was sinister and overwhelming in a bitter-sweet fashion. She kept thinking, "I can begin to understand how a young girl can be seduced, how she cannot know what she is doing."

"I suppose," he was saying, "that you think me presumptuous."

"No, I only think everything is impossible, insane."

"You think me a kind of ruffian, a bum, an Irishman, a Roman Catholic, some one you have never heard of." He waited, and then added: "I *am* all that, from one point of view."

"No, I don't think that; I don't think that."

He sat down beside her quietly on the stone bench. "You have every right to think it," he continued softly. "Every right in the world, and still things like that make no difference, nothing makes any difference."

"My father," she said softly, "was a man very like you. His enemies sometimes used to call him 'shanty Irish.' . . ."

She knew all the while that she should have risen and sought indignant refuge in the house. She knew that perhaps she was being absurd, and yet she stayed there quietly. She was so tired and she had waited for so long (she only knew it now in a sudden flash) to have some one talk to her in just this way, as if she were a woman. She needed some one to lean upon, so desperately.

"How can you know me?" she asked out of a vague sense of helplessness. "How can you know anything about me?"

He did not touch her. He only sat there in the darkness, making her feel by a sort of power which was too strong for her, that all he said was terribly the truth.

"I know, I know, all about you, everything. I've watched you. I've understood you, even better than the others. A man whose life has been like mine sees and understands a great deal that others never notice because for him everything depends upon a kind of second sight. It's the one great weapon of the opportunist." There was a silence and he asked, "Can you understand that? It may be hard, because your life has been so different."

"Not so different, as you might think, only perhaps I've made more of a mess of it." And straightening her body, she murmured, "It is foolish of me to let you talk this way."

He interrupted her with a quick burst of almost boyish eagerness. "But you're glad, aren't you? You're glad, all the same, whether you care anything for me or not. You've deserved it for a long time."

She began to cry softly, helplessly, without a sound, the tears running down her cheeks, and she thought, "Now I'm being a supreme fool. I'm pitying myself." But she could not stop.

It appeared that even in the darkness he was aware of her tears, for he chose not to interrupt them. They sat thus for a long time in silence, Olivia conscious with a terrible aching acuteness, of the beauty of the night and finding it all strange and unreal and confused.

"I wanted you to know," he said quietly, "that there was some one near you, some one who worships you, who would give up everything for you." And after a time, "Perhaps we had better go in now. You can go in through the piazza and powder your nose. I'll go in through the door from the garden."

And as they walked across the damp, scented grass, he said, "It would be pleasant if you would join Sybil and me riding in the morning."

"But I haven't been on a horse in years," said Olivia.

Throughout the rest of the evening, while she sat playing bridge with Sabine and O'Hara and the Mannering boy, her mind kept straying from the game into unaccustomed byways. It was not, she told herself, that she was even remotely in love with O'Hara; it was only that some one—a man who was no creature of ordinary attractions—had confessed his admiration for her, and so she felt young and giddy and elated. The whole affair was silly . . . and yet, yet, in a strange way, it was not silly at all. She kept thinking of Anson's remarks about his father and old Mrs. Soames, "It's a silly affair"— and of Sybil saying gravely, "Only not middle-aged, like O'Hara," and it occurred to her at the same time that in all her life she felt really young for the first time. She had been young as she sat on the stone bench under the ancient apple-tree, young in spite of everything.

And aloud she would say, "Four spades," and know at once that she should have made no such bid.

She was unnerved, too, by the knowledge that there were, all the while, two pairs of eyes far more absorbed in her than in the game of bridge—the green ones of Sabine and the bright blue ones of O'Hara. She could not look up without encountering the gaze of one or the other; and to protect herself she faced them with a hard, banal little smile which she put in place in the mechanical way used by Miss Egan. It was the sort of smile which made her face feel very tired, and for the first time she had a half-comic flash of pity for Miss Egan. The face of the nurse must at times have grown horribly tired.

The giddiness still clung to her as she climbed into the motor beside Sybil and they drove off down the lane which led from Brook Cottage to Pentlands. The road was a part of a whole tracery of lanes, bordered by hedges and old trees, which bound together the houses of the countryside, and at night they served as a promenade and meeting-place for the servants of the same big houses. One came upon them in little groups of three or four, standing by gates or stone walls, gossiping and giggling together in the darkness, exchanging tales of the life that passed in the houses of their masters, stories of what the old man did yesterday, and how Mrs. So-and-so only took one bath a week. There was a whole world which lay beneath the solid, smooth, monotonous surface that shielded the life of the wealthy, a world which in its way was full of mockery and dark secrets and petty gossip, a world perhaps fuller of truth because it lay hidden away where none—save perhaps Aunt Cassie, who knew how many fascinating secrets servants had—ever looked, and where there was small need for the sort of pretense which Olivia found so tragic. It circulated the dark lanes at night after the dinners of the neighborhood were finished, and sometimes the noisy echoes of its irreverent mockery rose in wild Irish laughter that echoed back and forth across the mist-hung meadows.

The same lanes were frequented, too, by lovers, who went in pairs instead of groups of three or four, and at times there were echoes of a different sort of merriment—the wild, half-hysterical laughter of some kitchen-maid being wooed roughly and passionately in some dark corner by a groom or a house-servant. It was a world which blossomed forth only at nightfall. Sometimes in the darkness the masters, motoring home from a ball or a dinner, would come upon an amorous couple, bathed in the sudden brilliant glare of motor-lights, sitting with their arms about each other against a tree, or lying half-hidden among a tangle of hawthorn and elder-bushes.

To-night, as Olivia and Sybil drove in silence along the road, the hot air was filled with the thick scent of the hawthorn-blossoms and the rich, dark odor of cattle, blown toward them across the meadows by the faint salt breeze from the marshes. It was late and the lights of the motor encountered no strayed lovers until at the foot of the hill by the old bridge the glare illuminated suddenly the figures of a man and a woman seated together against the stone wall. At their approach the woman slipped quickly over the wall, and the man, following, leaped lightly as a goat to the top and into the field beyond. Sybil laughed and murmured, "It's Higgins again."

It *was* Higgins. There was no mistaking the stocky, agile figure clad in riding-breeches and sleeveless cotton shirt, and as he leaped the wall the sight of him aroused in Olivia a nebulous, fleeting impression that was like a half-forgotten memory. A startled fawn, she thought, must have scuttled off into the bushes in the same fashion. And she had suddenly that same strange, prickly feeling of terror that had affected Sabine on the night she discovered him hidden in the lilacs watching the ball.

She shivered, and Sybil asked, "You're not cold?"

"No."

She was thinking of Higgins and hoping that this was not the beginning of some new scrape. Once before a girl had come to her in trouble—a Polish girl, whom she helped and sent away because she could not see that forcing Higgins to marry her would have brought anything but misery for both of them. It never ceased to amaze her that a man so gnarled and ugly, such a savage, hairy little man as Higgins, should have half the girls of the country-side running after him.

In her own room she listened in the darkness until she heard the sound of Jack's gentle breathing and then, after undressing, she sat for a long time at the window looking out across the meadows toward the marshes. There was a subdued excitement which seemed to run through all her body and would not let her sleep. She no longer felt the weariness of spirit which had let her slip during these last few months into a kind of lethargy. She was alive, more alive than she had ever been, even as a young girl; her cheeks were hot and flushed, so that she placed her white hands against them to feel a coolness that was missing from the night air; but they, too, were hot with life.

And as she sat there, the sounds from Sybil's room across the hall died away and at last the night grew still save for the sound of her son's slow breathing and the familiar ghostly creakings of the old house. She was alone now, the only one who was not sleeping; and sitting above the mist-hung meadows she grew more quiet. The warm rich scents of the night drifted in at the window, and again she became aware of a kind of voluptuousness which she had sensed in the air as she sat, hours earlier, on Sabine's terrace above the sea. It had assailed her again as they drove through the lane across the low, marshy pastures by the river. And then in the figure of Higgins, leaping the wall like a goat, it had come with a shock to a sudden climax of feeling, with a sudden acuteness which even terrified her. It still persisted a little, the odd feeling of some tremendous, powerful force at work all about her, moving swiftly and quietly, thrusting aside and annihilating those who opposed it.

She thought again, "I am a little mad to-night. What has come over me?" And she grew frightened, though it was a different sort of terror from that which afflicted her at the odd moments when she felt all about her the presence of the dead who lived on and on at Pentlands. What she knew now was no terror of the dead; it was rather a terror of warm, passionate life. She thought, "This is what must have happened to the others. This is how they must have felt before they died."

It was not physical death that she meant, but a death somehow of the soul, a death which left behind it such withered people as Aunt Cassie and Anson, the old woman in the north wing, and even a man so rugged and powerful as John Pentland, who had struggled so much more fiercely than the others. And she got a sudden sense of being caught between two dark, struggling forces in fierce combat. It was confused and vague, yet it made her feel suddenly ill in a physical sense. The warm feeling of life and excitement flowed away, leaving her chilled and relaxed, weary all at once, and filled with a soft lassitude, still looking out into the night, still smelling the thick odor of cattle and hawthorn-blossoms.

She never knew whether or not she had fallen asleep in the bergère by the window, but she did know that she was roused abruptly by the sound of footsteps. Outside the door of her room, in the long hallway, there was some one walking, gently, cautiously. It was not this time merely the creaking of the old house; it was the sound of footfalls, regular, measured, inevitable, those of some person of almost no weight at all. She listened, and slowly, cautiously, almost as if the person were blind and groping his way in the darkness, the step advanced until presently it came opposite her and thin slivers of light outlined the door that led into the hall. Quietly she rose and, still lost in a vague sense of moving in a nightmare, she went over to the door and opened it. Far down the long hall, at the door which opened into the stairway leading to the attic of the house, there was a small circle of light cast by an electric torch. It threw into a black silhouette the figure of an old woman with white hair whom Olivia recognized at once. It was the old woman escaped from the north wing. While she stood watching her, the figure, fumbling at the door, opened it and disappeared quickly into the stairway.

There was no time to be lost, not time even to go in search of the starched Miss Egan. The poor creature might fling herself from the upper windows. So, without stopping even to throw a dressing-gown about her, Olivia went quickly along the dark hall and up the stairway where the fantastic creature in the flowered wrapper had vanished.

The attic was an enormous, unfinished room that covered the whole of the house, a vast cavern of a place, empty save for a few old trunks and pieces of broken furniture. The flotsam and jetsam of Pentland life had been stowed away there, lost and forgotten in the depths of the big room, for more than a century. No one entered it. Since Sybil and Jack had grown, it remained half-forgotten. They had played there on rainy days as small children, and before them Sabine and Anson had played in the same dark, mysterious corners among broken old trunks and sofas and chairs.

Olivia found the place in darkness save for the patches of blue light where the luminous night came in at the double row of dormer windows, and at the far end, by a group of old trunks, the circle of light from the torch that moved this way and that, as if old Mrs. Pentland were searching for something. In the haste of her escape and flight, her thin white hair had come undone and fell about her shoulders. A sickly smell of medicine hung about her.

Olivia touched her gently and said, "What have you lost, Mrs. Pentland? Can I help you?"

The old woman turned and, throwing the light of the torch full into Olivia's face, stared at her with the round blue eyes, murmuring, "Oh, it's you, Olivia. Then it's all right. Perhaps you can help me."

"What was it you lost? We might look for it in the morning."

"I've forgotten what it was now. You startled me, and you know my poor brain isn't very good, at best. It never has been since I married." Sharply she looked at Olivia. "It didn't affect you that way, did it? You don't ever drift away and feel yourself growing dimmer and dimmer, do you? It's odd. Perhaps it's different with your husband."

Olivia saw that the old woman was having one of those isolated moments of clarity and reason which were more horrible than her insanity because for a time she made you see that, after all, she was like yourself, human and capable of thought. To Olivia these moments were almost as if she witnessed the rising of the dead.

"No," said Olivia. "Perhaps if we went to bed now, you'd remember in the morning."

Old Mrs. Pentland shook her head violently. "No, no, I must find them now. It may be all different in the morning and I won't know anything and that Irish woman won't let me out. Say over the names of a few things like prunes, prisms, persimmons. That's what Mr. Dickens used to have his children do when he couldn't think of a word."

"Let me have the light," said Olivia; "perhaps I can find what it is you want."

With the meekness of a child, the old woman gave her the electric torch and Olivia, turning it this way and that, among the trunks and old rubbish, made a mock search among the doll-houses and the toy dishes left scattered in the corner of the attic where the children had played house for the last time.

While she searched, the old woman kept up a running comment, half to herself: "It's something I wanted to find very much. It'll make a great difference here in the lives of all of us. I thought I might find Sabine here to help me. She was here yesterday morning, playing with Anson. It rained all day and they couldn't go out. I hid it here yesterday when I came up to see them."

Olivia again attempted wheedling.

"It's late now, Mrs. Pentland. We ought both to be in bed. You try to remember what it is you want, and in the morning I'll come up and find it for you."

For a moment the old woman considered this, and at last she said, "You wouldn't give it to me if you found it. I'm sure you wouldn't. You're too afraid of them all."

"I promise you I will. You can trust me, can't you?"

"Yes, yes, you're the only one who doesn't treat me as if I wasn't quite bright. Yes, I think I can trust you." Another thought occurred to her abruptly. "But I wouldn't remember again. I might forget. Besides, I don't think Miss Egan would let me."

Olivia took one of the thin old hands in hers and said, as if she were talking to a little child, "I know what we'll do. To-morrow you write it out on a bit of paper and then I'll find it and bring it to you."

"I'm sure little Sabine could find it," said the old woman. "She's very good at such things. She's such a clever child."

"I'll go over and fetch Sabine to have her help me."

The old woman looked at her sharply. "You'll promise that?" she asked. "You'll promise?"

"Of course, surely."

"Because all the others are always deceiving me."

And then quite gently she allowed herself to be led across the moonlit patches of the dusty floor, down the stairs and back to her room. In the hall of the north wing they came suddenly upon the starched Miss Egan, all her starch rather melted and subdued now, her red face purple with alarm.

"I've been looking for her everywhere, Mrs. Pentland," she told Olivia. "I don't know how she escaped. She was asleep when I left. I went down to the kitchen for her orange-juice, and while I was gone she disappeared."

It was the old woman who answered. Looking gravely at Olivia, she said, with an air of confidence, "You know I never speak to her at all. She's common. She's a common Irish servant. They can shut me up with her, but they can't make me speak to her." And then she began to drift back again into the hopeless state that was so much more familiar. She began to mumble over and over again a chain of words and names which had no coherence.

Olivia and Miss Egan ignored her, as if part of her—the vaguely *rational* old woman—had disappeared, leaving in her place this pitiful chattering creature who was a stranger.

Olivia explained where it was she found the old woman and why she had gone there.

"She's been talking on the subject for days," said Miss Egan. "I think it's letters that she's looking for, but it may be nothing at all. She mixes everything terribly."

Olivia was shivering now in her nightdress, more from weariness and nerves than from the chill of the night.

"I wouldn't speak of it to any of the others, Miss Egan," she said. "It will only trouble them. And we must be more careful about her in the future."

The old woman had gone past them now, back into the dark room where she spent her whole life, and the nurse had begun to recover a little of her defiant confidence. She even smiled, the hard, glittering smile which always said, "You cannot do without me, whatever happens."

Aloud she said, "I can't imagine what happened, Mrs. Pentland."

"It was an accident, never mind," said Olivia. "Good-night. Only I think it's better not to speak of what has happened. It will only alarm the others."

But she was puzzled, Olivia, because underneath the dressing-gown Miss Egan had thrown about her shoulders she saw that the nurse was dressed neither in night-clothes nor in her uniform, but in the suit of blue serge that she wore on the rare occasions when she went into the city.

5

She spoke to no one of what had happened, either on the terrace or in the lane or in the depths of the old attic, and the days came to resume again their old monotonous round, as if the strange, hot, disturbing night had had no more existence than a dream. She did not see O'Hara, yet she heard of him, constantly, from Sybil, from Sabine, even from Jack, who seemed stronger than he had ever been and able for a time to go about the farm with his grandfather in the trap drawn by an old white horse. There were moments when it seemed to Olivia that the boy might one day be really well, and yet there was never any real joy in those moments, because always in the back of her mind stood the truth. She knew it would never be, despite all that fierce struggle which she and the old man kept up perpetually against the thing which was stronger than either of them. Indeed, she even found a new sort of sadness in the sight of the pale thin boy and the rugged old man driving along the lanes in the trap, the eyes of the grandfather bright with a look of deluding hope. It was a look which she found unbearable because it was the first time in years, almost since that first day when Jack, as a tiny baby who did not cry enough, came into the world, that the expression of the old man had changed from one of grave and uncomplaining resignation.

Sometimes when she watched them together she was filled with a fierce desire to go to John Pentland and tell him that it was not her fault that there were not more children, other heirs to take the place of Jack. She wanted to tell him that she would have had ten children if it were possible, that even now she was still young enough to have more children. She wanted to pour out to him something of that hunger of life which had swept over her on the night in Sabine's garden beneath the apple-tree, a spot abounding in fertility. But she knew, too, how impossible it was to discuss a matter which old John Pentland, in the depths of his soul believed to be "indelicate." Such things were all hidden behind a veil which shut out so much of truth from all their lives. There were times when she fancied he understood it all, those times when he took her hand and kissed her affectionately. She fancied that he understood and that the knowledge lay somehow at the root of the old man's quiet contempt for his own son.

But she saw well enough the tragedy that lay deep down at the root of the whole matter. She understood that it was not Anson who was to blame. It was that they had all been caught in the toils of something stronger than any of them, a force which with a cruel injustice compelled her to live a dry, monotonous, barren existence when she would have embraced life passionately, which compelled her to watch her own son dying slowly before her eyes.

Always she came back to the same thought, that the boy must be kept alive until his grandfather was dead; and sometimes, standing on the terrace, looking out across the fields, Olivia saw that old Mrs. Soames, dressed absurdly in pink, with a large picture-hat, was riding in the trap with the old man and his grandson, as if in reality she were the grandmother of Jack instead of the mad old woman abovestairs.

The days came to resume their round of dull monotony, and yet there was a difference, odd and indefinable, as if in some way the sun were brighter than it had been, as if those days, when even in the bright sunlight the house had seemed a dull gray place, were gone now. She could no longer look across the meadows toward the bright new chimneys of O'Hara's house without a sudden quickening of breath, a warm pleasant sensation of no longer standing quite alone.

She was not even annoyed any longer by the tiresome daily visits of Aunt Cassie, nor by the old woman's passion for pitying her and making wild insinuations against Sabine and O'Hara and complaining of Sybil riding with him in the mornings over the dew-covered fields. She was able now simply to sit there politely as she had once done, listening while the old woman talked on and on; only now she did not even listen with attention. It seemed to her at times that Aunt Cassie was like some insect beating itself frantically against a pane of glass, trying over and over again with an unflagging futility to enter where it was impossible to enter.

It was Sabine who gave her a sudden glimpse of penetration into this instinct about Aunt Cassie, Sabine who spent all her time finding out about people. It happened one morning that the two clouds of dust, the one made by Aunt Cassie and the other by Sabine, met at the very foot of the long drive leading up to Pentlands, and together the two women—one dressed severely in shabby black, without so much as a fleck of powder on her nose, the other dressed expensively in what some Paris dressmaker chose to call a *costume de sport,* with her face made up like a Parisian—arrived together to sit on the piazza of Pentlands insulting each other subtly for an hour. When at last Sabine managed to outstay Aunt Cassie (it was always a contest between them, for each knew that the other would attack her as soon as she was out of hearing) she turned to Olivia and said abruptly, "I've been thinking about Aunt Cassie, and I'm sure now of one thing. Aunt Cassie is a virgin!"

There was something so cold-blooded and sudden in the statement that Olivia laughed.

"I'm sure of it," persisted Sabine with quiet seriousness. "Look at her. She's always talking about the tragedy of her being too frail ever to have had children. She never tried. That's the answer. She never tired." Sabine tossed away what remained of the cigarette she had lighted to annoy Aunt Cassie, and continued, "You never knew my Uncle Ned Struthers when he was young. You only knew him as an old man with no spirit left. But he wasn't that way always. It's what she did to him. She destroyed him. He was a full-blooded kind of man who liked drinking and horses and he must have liked women, too, but she cured him of that. He would have liked children, but instead of a wife he only got a woman who couldn't bear the thought of not being married and yet couldn't bear what marriage meant. He got a creature who fainted and wept and lay on a sofa all day, who got the better of him because he was a nice, stupid, chivalrous fellow."

Sabine was launched now with all the passion which seized her when she had laid bare a little patch of life and examined it minutely.

"He didn't even dare to be unfaithful to her. If he looked at another woman she fainted and became deathly ill and made terrible scenes. I can remember some of them. I remember that once he called on Mrs. Soames when she was young and beautiful, and when he came home Aunt Cassie met him in hysterics and told him that if it ever happened again she would go out, 'frail and miserable as she was,' and commit adultery. I remember the story because I overheard my father telling it when I was a child and I was miserable until I found out what 'committing adultery' meant. In the end she destroyed him. I'm sure of it."

Sabine sat there, with a face like stone, following with her eyes the cloud of dust that moved along the lane as Aunt Cassie progressed on her morning round of visits, a symbol in a way of all the forces that had warped her own existence.

"It's possible," murmured Olivia.

Sabine turned toward her with a quick, sudden movement. "That's why she is always so concerned with the lives of other people. She has never had any life of her own, never. She's always been afraid. It's why she loves the calamities of other people, because she's never had any of her own. Not even her husband's death was a calamity. It left her free, completely free of troubles as she had always wanted to be."

And then a strange thing happened to Olivia. It was as if a new Aunt

Cassie had been born, as if the old one, so full of tears and easy sympathy who always appeared miraculously when there was a calamity in the neighborhood, the Aunt Cassie who was famous for her good works and her tears and words of religious counsel, had gone down the lane for the last time, never to return again. To-morrow morning a new Aunt Cassie would arrive, one who outwardly would be the same; only to Olivia she would be different, a woman stripped of all those veils of pretense and emotions with which she wrapped herself, an old woman naked in her ugliness who, Olivia understood in a blinding flash of clarity, was like an insect battering itself against a pane of glass in a futile attempt to enter where it was impossible for her ever to enter. And she was no longer afraid of Aunt Cassie now. She did not even dislike her; she only pitied the old woman because she had missed so much, because she would die without ever having lived. And she must have been young and handsome once, and very amusing. There were still moments when the old lady's charm and humor and sharp tongue were completely disarming.

Sabine was talking again, in a cold, unrelenting voice. "She lay there all those years on the sofa covered with a shawl, trying to arrange the lives of every one about her. She killed Anson's independence and ruined my happiness. She terrorized her husband until in the end he died to escape her. He was a good-natured man, horrified of scenes and scandals." Sabine lighted a cigarette and flung away the match with a sudden savage gesture. "And now she goes about like an angel of pity, a very brisk angel of pity, a harpy in angel's clothing. She has played her rôle well. Every one believes in her as a frail, good, unhappy woman. Some of the saints must have been very like her. Some of them must have been trying old maids."

She rose and, winding the chiffon scarf about her throat, opened her yellow parasol, saying, "I know I'm right. She's a virgin. At least," she added, "in the technical sense, she's a virgin. I know nothing about her mind."

And then, changing abruptly, she said, "Will you go up to Boston with me to-morrow? I'm going to do something about my hair. There's gray beginning to come into it."

Olivia did not answer her at once, but when she did speak it was to say, "Yes; I'm going to take up riding again and I want to order clothes. My old ones would look ridiculous now. It's been years since I was on a horse."

Sabine looked at her sharply and, looking away again, said, "I'll stop for you about ten o'clock."

Chapter 6

HEAT, DAMP AND OVERWHELMING, and thick with the scent of fresh-cut hay and the half-fetid odor of the salt marshes, settled over Durham, reducing all life to a state of tropical relaxation. Even in the mornings when Sybil rode with O'Hara across the meadows, there was no coolness and no dew on the grass. Only Aunt Cassie, thin and wiry, and Anson, guided perpetually by a sense of duty which took no reckoning of such things as weather, resisted the muggy warmth. Aunt Cassie, alike indifferent to heat and cold, storm or calm, continued her indefatigable rounds. Sabine, remarking that she had always known that New England was the hottest place this side of Sheol, settled into a state of complete inertia, not stirring from the house until after the sun had disappeared. Even then her only action was to come to Pentlands to sit in the writing-room playing bridge languidly with Olivia and John Pentland and old Mrs. Soames.

The old lady grew daily more dazed and forgetful and irritating as a fourth at bridge. John Pentland always insisted upon playing with her, saying that they understood each other's game; but he deceived no one, save Mrs. Soames, whose wits were at best a little dim; the others knew that it was to protect her. They saw him sit calmly and patiently while she bid suits she could not possibly make, while she trumped his tricks and excused herself on the ground of bad eyesight. She had been a great beauty once and she was still, with all her paint and powder, a vain woman. She would not wear spectacles and so played by looking through lorgnettes, which lowered the whole tempo of the game and added to the confusion. At times, in the midst of the old lady's blunders, a look of murder came into the green eyes of Sabine, but Olivia managed somehow to prevent any outburst; she even managed to force Sabine into playing on, night after night. The patience and tenderness of the old man towards Mrs. Soames moved her profoundly, and she fancied that Sabine, too,—hard, cynical, intolerant Sabine—was touched by it. There was a curious, unsuspected soft spot in Sabine, as if in some way she understood the bond between the two old people. Sabine, who allowed herself to be bored by no one, presently became willing to sit there night after night bearing this special boredom patiently.

Once when Olivia said to her, "We'll all be old some day. Perhaps we'll be worse than old Mrs. Soames," Sabine replied with a shrug of bitterness, "Old age is a bore. That's the trouble with us, Olivia. We'll never give up and become old ladies. It used to be the beauties who clung to youth, and now all of us do it. We'll probably be painted old horrors . . . like her."

"Perhaps," replied Olivia, and a kind of terror took possession of her at the thought that she would be forty on her next birthday and that nothing lay before her, even in the immediate future, save evenings like these, playing bridge with old people until presently she herself was old, always in the melancholy atmosphere of the big house at Pentlands.

"But I shan't take to drugs," said Sabine. "At least I shan't do that."

Olivia looked at her sharply. "Who takes drugs?" she asked.

"Why, she does . . . old Mrs. Soames. She's taken drugs for years. I thought every one knew it."

"No," said Olivia sadly. "I never knew it."

Sabine laughed. "You are an innocent," she answered.

And after Sabine had gone home, the cloud of melancholy clung to her for hours. She felt suddenly that Anson and Aunt Cassie might be right, after all. There was something dangerous in a woman like Sabine, who tore aside every veil, who sacrificed everything to her passion for the truth. Somehow it riddled a world which at its best was not too cheerful.

There were evenings when Mrs. Soames sent word that she was feeling too ill to play, and on those occasions John Pentland drove over to see her, and the bridge was played instead at Brook Cottage with O'Hara and a fourth recruited impersonally from the countryside. To Sabine, the choice was a matter of indifference so long as the chosen one could play well.

It happened on these occasions that O'Hara and Olivia came to play together, making a sort of team, which worked admirably. He played as she knew he would play, aggressively and brilliantly, with a fierce concentration and a determination to win. It fascinated her that a man who had spent most of his life in circles where bridge played no part, should have mastered the intricate game so completely. She fancied him taking lessons with the same passionate application which he had given to his career.

He did not speak to her again of the things he had touched upon during that first hot night on the terrace, and she was careful never to find herself alone with him. She was ashamed at the game she played—of seeing him always with Sabine or riding with Sybil and giving him no chance to speak; it seemed to her that such behavior was cheap and dishonest. Yet she could not bring herself to refuse seeing him, partly because to refuse would have aroused the suspicions of the already interested Sabine, but more because she *wanted* to see him. She found a kind of delight in the way he looked at her, in the perfection with which they came to understand each other's game; and though he did not see her alone, he kept telling her in a hundred subtle ways that he was a man in love, who adored her.

She told herself that she was behaving like a silly schoolgirl, but she could not bring herself to give him up altogether. It seemed to her unbearable that she should lose these rare happy evenings. And she was afraid, too, that Sabine would call her a fool.

As early summer turned into July, old Mrs. Soames came less and less frequently to play bridge and there were times when Sabine, dining out or retiring early, left them without any game at all and the old familiar stillness came to settle over the drawing-room at Pentlands . . . evenings when Olivia and Sybil played double patience and Anson worked at Mr. Lowell's desk over the mazes of the Pentland Family history.

On one of these evenings, when Olivia's eyes had grown weary of reading, she closed her book and, turning toward her husband, called his name. When he did not answer her at once she spoke to him again, and waited until he looked up. Then she said, "Anson, I have taken up riding again. I think it is doing me good."

But Anson, lost somewhere in the chapter about Savina Pentland and her friendship with Ingres, was not interested and made no answer.

"I go in the mornings," she repeated, "before breakfast, with Sybil."

Anson said, "Yes," again, and then, "I think it an excellent idea—your color is better," and went back to his work.

So she succeeded in telling him that it was all right about Sybil and O'Hara. She managed to tell him without actually saying it that she would go with them and prevent any entanglement. She had told him, too, without once alluding to the scene of which he was ashamed. And she knew, of course, now, that there was no danger of any entanglement, at least not one which involved Sybil.

Sitting with the book closed in her lap, she remained for a time watching the back of her husband's head—the thin gray hair, the cords that stood out weakly under the desiccated skin, the too small ears set too close against the skull; and in reality, all the while she was seeing another head set upon a full muscular neck, the skin tanned and glowing with the flush of health, the thick hair short and vigorous; and she felt an odd, inexplicable desire to weep, thinking at the same time, "I am a wicked woman. I must be really bad." For she had never known before what it was to be in love and she had lived for nearly twenty years in a family where love had occupied a poor forgotten niche.

She was sitting thus when John Pentland came in at last, looking more yellow and haggard than he had been in days. She asked him quietly, so as not to disturb Anson, whether Mrs. Soames was really ill. "No," said the old man, "I don't think so; she seems all right, a little tired, that's all. We're all growing old."

He seated himself and began to read like the others, pretending clearly an interest which he did not feel, for Olivia caught him suddenly staring before him in a line beyond the printed page. She saw that he was not reading at all, and in the back of her mind a little cluster of words kept repeating themselves—"*a little tired, that's all, we're all growing old; a little tired, that's all, we're all growing old*"—over and over again monotonously, as if she were hypnotizing herself. She found herself, too, staring into space in the same enchanted fashion as the old man. And then, all at once, she became aware of a figure standing in the doorway beckoning to her, and, focusing her gaze, she saw that it was Nannie, clad in a dressing-gown, her old face screwed up in an expression of anxiety. She had some reason for not disturbing the others, for she did not speak. Standing in the shadow, she beckoned; and Olivia, rising quietly, went out into the hall, closing the door behind her.

There, in the dim light, she saw that the old woman had been crying and was shaking in fright. She said, "Something has happened to Jack, something dreadful."

She had known what it was before Nannie spoke. It seemed to her that she had known all along, and now there was no sense of shock but only a hard, dead numbness of all feeling.

"Call up Doctor Jenkins," she said, with a kind of dreadful calm, and turning away she went quickly up the long stairs.

In the darkness of her own room she did not wait now to listen for the sound of breathing. It had come at last—the moment when she would enter the room and, listening for the sound, encounter only the stillness of the night. Beyond, in the room which he had occupied ever since he was a tiny baby, there was the usual dim night-light burning in the corner, and by its dull glow she was able to make out the narrow bed and his figure lying there as it had always lain, asleep. He must have been asleep, she thought, for it was impossible to have died so quietly, without moving. But she knew, of course, that he *was* dead, and she saw how near to death he had always been, how it was only a matter of slipping over, quite simply and gently.

He had escaped them at last—his grandfather and herself—in a moment when they had not been there watching; and belowstairs in the drawing-room John Pentland was sitting with a book in his lap by Mr. Longfellow's lamp, staring into space, still knowing nothing. And Anson's pen scratched away at the history of the Pentland Family and the Massachusetts Bay Colony, while here in the room where she stood the Pentland family had come to an end.

She did not weep. She knew that weeping would come later, after the doctor had made his silly futile call to tell her what she already knew. And now that this thing which she had fought for so long had happened, she was aware of a profound peace. It seemed to her even, that the boy, her own son, was happier now; for she had a fear, bordering upon remorse, that they had kept him alive all those years against his will. He looked quiet and still now and not at all as he had looked on those long, terrible nights when she had sat in this same chair by the same bed while, propped among pillows because he could not breathe lying down, he fought for breath and life, more to please her and his grandfather than because he wanted to live. She saw that there could be a great beauty in death. It was not as if he had died alone. He had simply gone to sleep.

She experienced, too, an odd and satisfying feeling of reality, of truth, as if in some way the air all about her had become cleared and freshened. Death was not a thing one could deny by pretense. Death was real. It marked the end of something, definitely and clearly for all time. There could be no deceptions about death.

She wished now that she had told Nannie not to speak to the others. She wanted to stay there alone in the dimly lighted room until the sky turned gray beyond the marshes.

They did not leave her in peace with her son. There came first of all a knock which admitted old Nannie, still trembling and hysterical, followed by the starched and efficient Miss Egan, who bustled about with a hard, professional manner, and then the rattling, noisy sounds of Doctor Jenkins' Ford as he arrived from the village, and the far-off hoot of a strange motor-horn and a brilliant glare of light as a big motor rounded the corner of the lane at the foot of the drive and swept away toward Brook Cottage. The hall seemed suddenly alive with people, whispering and murmuring together, and there was a sound of hysterical sobbing from some frightened servant. Death, which ought to occur in the quiet beauty of solitude, was being robbed of all its dignity. They would behave like this for days. She knew that it was only now, in the midst of all that pitiful hubbub, that she had lost her son. He had been hers still, after a fashion, while she was alone there in the room.

Abruptly, in the midst of the flurry, she remembered that there were others besides herself. There was Sybil, who had come in and stood beside her, grave and sympathetic, pressing her mother's hand in silence; and Anson, who stood helplessly in the corner, more awkward and useless and timid than ever in the face of death. But most of all, there was John Pentland. He was not in the room. He was nowhere to be seen.

She went to search for him, because she knew that he would never come there to face all the others; instead, he would hide himself away like a wounded animal. She knew that there was only one person whom he could bear to see. Together they had fought for the life of the boy and together they must face the cold, hard fact of his death.

She found him standing on the terrace, outside the tall windows that opened into the drawing-room, and as she approached, she saw that he was so lost in his sorrow that he did not even notice her. He was like a man in a state of enchantment. He simply stood there, tall and stiff and austere, staring across the marshes in the direction of the sea, alone as he had always been, surrounded by the tragic armor of loneliness that none of them, not even herself, had ever succeeded in piercing. She saw then that there was a grief more terrible than her own. She had lost her son but for John Pentland it was the end of everything. She saw that the whole world had collapsed about him. It was as if he, too, had died.

She did not speak to him at first, but simply stood beside him, taking his huge, bony hand in hers, aware that he did not look at her, but kept staring on and on across the marshes in the direction of the sea. And at last she said softly, "It has happened, at last."

Still he did not look at her, but he did answer, saying, "I knew," in a whisper that was barely audible. There were tears on his leathery old cheeks. He had come out into the darkness of the scented garden to weep. It was the only time that she had ever seen tears in the burning black eyes.

Not until long after midnight did all the subdued and vulgar hubbub that surrounds death fade away once more into silence, leaving Olivia alone in the room with Sybil. They did not speak to each other, for they knew well enough the poverty of words, and there was between them no need for speech.

At last Olivia said, "You had best get some sleep, darling; to-morrow will be a troublesome day."

And then, like a little girl, Sybil came over and seating herself on her mother's lap put her arms about her neck and kissed her.

The girl said softly, "You are wonderful, Mother. I know that I'll never be so wonderful a woman. We should have spared you to-night, all of us, and instead of that, it was you who managed everything." Olivia only kissed her and even smiled a little at Sybil. "I think he's happier. He'll never be tired again as he used to be."

She had risen to leave when both of them heard, far away, somewhere in the distance, the sound of music. It came to them vaguely and in snatches borne in by the breeze from the sea, music that was filled with a wild, barbaric beat, that rose and fell with a passionate sense of life. It seemed to Olivia that there was in the sound of it some dark power which, penetrating the stillness of the old house, shattered the awesome silence that had settled down at last with the approach of death. It was as if life were celebrating its victory over death, in a savage, wild, exultant triumph.

It was music, too, that sounded strange and passionate in the thin, clear air of the New England night, such music as none of them had ever heard there before; and slowly, as it rose to a wild crescendo of sound, Olivia recognized it—the glowing barbaric music of the tribal dances in *Prince Igor*, being played brilliantly with a sense of abandoned joy.

At the same moment Sybil looked at her mother and said, "It's Jean de Cyon. . . . I'd forgotten that he was arriving to-night." And then sadly, "Of course he doesn't know."

There was a sudden light in the girl's eye, the merest flicker, dying out again quickly, which had a strange, intimate relation to the passionate music. Again it was life triumphing in death. Long afterward Olivia remembered it well . . . the light of something which went on and on.

Chapter 7

1

THE NEWS REACHED Aunt Cassie only the next morning at ten and it brought her, full of reproaches and tears, over the dusty lanes to Pentlands. She was hurt, she said, because they had not let her know at once. "I should have risen from my bed and come over immediately," she repeated. "I was sleeping very badly, in any case. I could have managed everything. You should have sent for Aunt Cassie at once."

And Olivia could not tell her that they had kept her in ignorance for that very reason—because they knew she *would* rise from her bed and come over at once.

Aunt Cassie it was who took the burden of the grief upon her narrow shoulders. She wept in the manner of a professional mourner. She drew the shades in the drawing-room, because in her mind death was not respectable unless the rooms were darkened, and sat there in a corner receiving callers, as if she were the one most bereft, as if indeed she were the only one who suffered at all. She returned to her own cupolaed dwelling only late at night and took all her meals at Pentlands, to the annoyance of her brother, who on the second day in the midst of lunch turned to her abruptly and said: "Cassie, if you can't stop this eternal blubbering, I wish you'd eat at home. It doesn't help anything."

At which she had risen from the table, in a sudden climax of grief and persecution, to flee, sobbing and hurt, from the room. But she was not insulted sufficiently to take her meals at home. She stayed on at Pentlands because, she said, "They needed some one like me to help out. . . ." And to the trembling, inefficient Miss Peavey, who came and went like a frightened rabbit on errands for her, she confided her astonishment that her brother and Olivia should treat death with such indifference. They did not weep; they showed no signs of grief. She was certain that they lacked sensibility. They did not feel the tragedy. And, weeping again, she would launch into memories of the days when the boy had come as a little fellow to sit, pale and listless, on the floor of her big, empty drawing-room, turning the pages of the Doré Bible.

And to Miss Peavey she also said, "It's at times like this that one's breeding comes out. Olivia has failed for the first time. She doesn't understand the things one must do at a time like this. If she had been brought up properly, here among us. . . ."

For with Aunt Cassie death was a mechanical, formalized affair which one observed by a series of traditional gestures.

It was a remarkable bit of luck, she said, that Bishop Smallwood (Sabine's Apostle to the Genteel) was still in the neighborhood and could conduct the funeral services. It was proper that one of Pentland blood should bury a Pentland (as if no one else were quite worthy of such an honor). And she went to see the Bishop to discuss the matter of the services. She planned that immensely intricate affair, the seating of relations and connections—all the Canes and Struthers and Mannerings and Sutherlands and Pentlands—at the church. She called on Sabine to tell her that whatever her feelings about funerals might be, it was her duty to attend this one. Sabine must remember that she was back again in a world of civilized people who behaved as ladies and gentlemen. And to each caller whom she received in the darkened drawing-room, she confided the fact that Sabine must be an unfeeling, inhuman creature, because she had not even paid a visit to Pentlands.

But she did not know what Olivia and John Pentland knew—that Sabine had written a short, abrupt, almost incoherent note, with all the worn, tattered, pious old phrases missing, which had meant more to them than any of the cries and whispering and confusion that went on belowstairs, where the whole countryside passed in and out in an endless procession.

When Miss Peavey was not at hand to run errands for her, she made Anson her messenger. . . . Anson, who wandered about helpless and lost and troubled because death had interrupted the easy, eventless flow of a life in which usually all moved according to a set plan. Death had upset the whole household. It was impossible to know how Anson Pentland felt over the death of his son. He did not speak at all, and now that "The Pentland Family and the Massachusetts Bay Colony" had been laid aside in the midst of the confusion and Mr. Lowell's desk stood buried beneath floral offerings, there was nothing to do but wander about getting in the way of every one and drawing upon his head the sharp reproofs of Aunt Cassie.

It was Aunt Cassie and Anson who opened the great box of roses that came from O'Hara. It was Aunt Cassie's thin, blue-veined hand that tore open the envelope addressed plainly to "Mrs. Anson Pentland." It was Aunt Cassie who forced Anson to read what was written inside:

"Dear Mrs. Pentland,
  You know what I feel. There is no need to say anything more.
                                        Michael O'Hara."

And it was Aunt Cassie who said, "Impertinent! Why should he send flowers at all?" And Aunt Cassie who read the note again and again, as if she might find in some way a veiled meaning behind the two cryptic sentences. It was Aunt Cassie who carried the note to Olivia and watched her while she read it and laid it quietly aside on her dressing-table. And when she had discovered nothing she said to Olivia, "It seems to me impertinent of him to send flowers and write such a note. What is he to us here at Pentlands?"

Olivia looked at her a little wearily and said, "What does it matter whether he is impertinent or not? Besides, he was a great friend of Jack's." And then, straightening her tired body, she looked at Aunt Cassie and said slowly, "He is also a friend of mine."

It was the first time that the division of forces had stood revealed, even for a second, the first time that Olivia had shown any feeling for O'Hara, and there was something ominous in the quietness of a speech made so casually. She ended any possible discussion by leaving the room in search of Anson, leaving Aunt Cassie disturbed by the sensation of alarm which attacked her when she found herself suddenly face to face with the mysterious and perilous calm that sometimes took possession of Olivia. Left alone in the room, she took up the note again from the dressing-table and read it through for the twentieth time. There was nothing in it . . . nothing on which one could properly even pin a suspicion.

So, in the midst of death, enveloped by the odor of tuberoses, the old lady rose triumphant, a phoenix from ashes. In some way she found in tragedy her proper rôle and she managed to draw most of the light from the other actors to herself. She must have known that people went away from the house saying, "Cassie rises to such occasions beautifully. She has taken everything on her own shoulders." She succeeded in conveying the double impression that she suffered far more than any of the others and that none of the others could possibly have done without her.

And then into the midst of her triumph came the worst that could have happened. Olivia was the first to learn of the calamity as she always came to know before any of the others knowledge which old John Pentland possessed; and the others would never have known until the sad business of the funeral was over save for Aunt Cassie's implacable curiosity.

On the second day, Olivia, summoned by her father-in-law to come to the library, found him there as she had found him so many times before, grim and silent and repressed, only this time there was something inexpressibly tragic and broken in his manner.

She did not speak to him; she simply waited until, looking up at last, he said almost in a whisper, "Horace Pentland's body is at the Durham station."

And he looked at her with the quick, pitiful helplessness of a strong man who has suddenly grown weak and old, as if at last he had come to the end of his strength and was turning now to her. It was then for the first time that she began to see how she was in a way a prisoner, that from now on, as one day passed into another, the whole life at Pentlands would come to be more and more her affair. There was no one to take the place of the old man . . . no one, save herself.

"What shall we do?" he asked in the same low voice. "I don't know. I am nearly at the end of things."

"We could bury them together," said Olivia softly. "We could have a double funeral."

He looked at her in astonishment. "You wouldn't mind that?" and when she shook her head in answer, he replied: "But we can't do it. There seems to me something wrong in such an idea. . . . I can't explain what I mean. . . . It oughtn't to be done. . . . A boy like Jack and an old reprobate like Horace."

They would have settled it quietly between them as they had settled so many troubles in the last years when John Pentland had come to her for strength, but at that moment the door opened suddenly and, without knocking, Aunt Cassie appeared, her eyes really blazing with an angry, hysterical light, her hair all hanging in little iron-gray wisps about her narrow face.

"What is it?" she asked. "What has gone wrong? I know there's something, and you've no right to keep it from me." She was shrill and brittle, as if in those two days all the pleasure and activity surrounding death had driven her into an orgy of excitement. At the sound of her voice, both Olivia and John Pentland started abruptly. She had touched them on nerves raw and worn.

The thin, high-pitched voice went on. "I've given up all my time to arranging things. I've barely slept. I sacrifice myself to you all day and night and I've a right to know." It was as if she had sensed the slow breaking up of the old man and sought now to hurl him aside, to depose him as head of the family, in one great *coup d'état*, setting herself up there in his place, a thin, fiercely intolerant tyrant; as if at last she had given up her old subtle way of trying to gain her ends by intrigue through the men of the family. She stood ready now to set up a matriarchy, the last refuge of a family whose strength was gone. She had risen thus in the same way once before within the memory of Olivia, in those long months when Mr. Struthers, fading slowly into death, yielded her the victory.

John Pentland sighed, profoundly, wearily, and murmured, "It's nothing, Cassie. It would only trouble you. Olivia and I are settling it."

But she did not retreat. Standing there, she held her ground and continued the tirade, working herself up to a pitch of hysteria. "I won't be put aside. No one ever tells me anything. For years now I've been shut out as if I were half-witted. Frail as I am, I work myself to the bone for the family and don't even get a word of thanks. . . . Why is Olivia always preferred to your own sister?" And tears of luxurious, sensual, self-pity began to stream down her withered face. She began even to mumble and mix her words, and she abandoned herself completely to the fleshly pleasure of hysterics.

Olivia, watching her quietly, saw that this was no usual occasion. This was, in truth, the new Aunt Cassie whom Sabine had revealed to her a few days before . . . the aggressively virginal Aunt Cassie who had been born in that moment on the terrace to take the place of the old Aunt Cassie who had existed always in an aura of tears and good works and sympathy. She understood now what she had never understood before—that Aunt Cassie was not merely an irrational hypochondriac, a harmless, pitiful creature, but a ruthless and unscrupulous force. She knew that behind this emotional debauch there lay some deeply conceived plan. Vaguely she suspected that the plan was aimed at subduing herself, or bringing her (Olivia) completely under the will of the old woman. It was the insect again beating its wings frantically against the windows of a world which she could never enter. . . .

And softly Olivia said, "Surely, Aunt Cassie, there is no need to make a scene . . . there's no need to be vulgar . . . at a time like this."

The old woman, suddenly speechless, looked at her brother, but from him there came no sign of aid or succor; she must have seen, plainly, that he had placed himself on the side of Olivia . . . the outsider, who had dared to accuse a Pentland of being vulgar.

"You heard what she said, John. . . . You heard what she said! She called your sister vulgar!" But her hysterical mood began to abate suddenly, as if she saw that she had chosen, after all, the wrong plan of attack. Olivia did not answer her. She only sat there, looking pale and patient and beautiful in her black clothes, waiting. It was a moment unfair to Aunt Cassie. No man, even Anson, would have placed himself against Olivia just then.

"If you must know, Cassie . . ." the old man said slowly. "It's a thing you won't want to hear. But if you must know, it is simply that Horace Pentland's body is at the station in Durham."

Olivia had a quick sense of the whited sepulcher beginning to crack, to fall slowly into bits.

At first Aunt Cassie only stared at them, snuffling and wiping her red eyes, and then she said, in an amazingly calm voice, "You see. . . . You never tell me anything. I never knew he was dead." There was a touch of triumph and vindication in her manner.

"There was no need of telling you, Cassie," said the old man. "You wouldn't let his name be spoken in the family for years. It was you—you and Anson—who made me threaten him into living abroad. Why should you care when he died?"

Aunt Cassie showed signs of breaking down once more. "You see, I'm always blamed for everything. I was thinking of the family all these years. We couldn't have Horace running around loose in Boston." She broke off with a sudden, fastidious gesture of disgust, as if she were washing her hands of the whole affair. "I could have managed it better myself. He ought never to have been brought home . . . to stir it all up again."

Still Olivia kept silent and it was the old man who answered Aunt Cassie. "He wanted to be buried here. . . . He wrote to ask me, when he was dying."

"He had no right to make such a request. He forfeited all rights by his behavior. I say it again and I'll keep on saying it. He ought never to have been brought back here . . . after people even forgot whether he was alive or dead."

The perilous calm had settled over Olivia. . . . She had been looking out of the window across the marshes into the distance, and when she turned she spoke with a terrible quietness. She said: "You may do with Horace Pentland's body what you like. It is more your affair than mine, for I never saw him in my life. But it is *my* son who is dead . . . *my* son, who belongs to *me* more than to any of you. You may bury Horace Pentland on the same day . . . at the same service, even in the same grave. Things like that can't matter very much after death. You can't go on pretending forever. . . . Death is too strong for that. It's stronger than any of us puny creatures because it's the one truth we can't avoid. It's got nothing to do with prejudices and pride and respectability. In a hundred years—even in a year, in a month, what will it matter what we've done with Horace Pentland's body?"

She rose, still enveloped in the perilous calm, and said: "I'll leave Horace Pentland to you two. There is none of his blood in my veins. Whatever you do, I shall not object . . . only I wouldn't be too shabby in dealing with death."

She went out, leaving Aunt Cassie exhausted and breathless and confused. The old woman had won her battle about the burial of Horace Pentland, yet she had suffered a great defeat. She must have seen that she had really lost everything, for Olivia somehow had gone to the root of things, in the

presence of John Pentland, who was himself so near to death. (Olivia daring
to say proudly, as if she actually scorned the Pentland name, "There is none
of his blood in my veins.")

But it was a defeat which Olivia knew she would never admit: that was
one of the qualities which made it impossible to deal with Aunt Cassie. Perhaps, even as she sat there dabbing at her eyes, she was choosing new weapons
for a struggle which had come at last into the open because it was impossible
any longer to do battle through so weak and shifting an ally as Anson.

She was a natural martyr, Aunt Cassie. Martyrdom was the great feminine
weapon of her Victorian day and she was practised in it; she had learned all
its subtleties in the years she had lain wrapped in a shawl on a sofa subduing
the full-blooded Mr. Struthers.

And Olivia knew as she left the room that in the future she would have to
deal with a poor, abused, invalid aunt who gave all her strength in doing good
works and received in return only cruelty and heartlessness from an outsider, from an intruder, a kind of adventuress who had wormed her way into
the heart of the Pentland family. Aunt Cassie, by a kind of art of which she
possessed the secret, would somehow make it all seem so.

2

The heat did not go away. It hung in a quivering cloud over the whole
countryside, enveloping the black procession which moved through the lanes
into the highroad and thence through the clusters of ugly stucco bungalows
inhabited by the mill-workers, on its way past the deserted meeting-house
where Preserved Pentland had once harangued a tough and sturdy congregation and the Rev. Josiah Milford had set out with his flock for the Western
Reserve. . . . It enveloped the black, slow-moving procession to the very
doors of the cool, ivy-covered stone church (built like a stage piece to imitate
some English country church) where the Pentlands worshiped the more
polite, compromising gods scorned and berated by the witch-burner. On the
way, beneath the elms of High Street, Polish women and children stopped
to stare and cross themselves at the sight of the grand procession.

The little church seemed peaceful after the heat and the stir of the
Durham street, peaceful and hushed and crowded to the doors by the relatives and connections of the family. Even the back pews were filled by the
poor half-forgotten remnants of the family who had no wealth to carry them
smoothly along the stream of life. Old Mrs. Featherstone (who did washing)
was there sobbing because she sobbed at all funerals, and old Miss Haddon,
the genteel Pentland cousin, dressed even in the midst of summer in her
inevitable cape of thick black broadcloth, and Mrs. Malson, shabby-genteel in
her foulards and high-pitched bonnet, and Miss Murgatroyd whose bullfinch
house was now "Ye Witch's Broome" where one got bad tea and melancholy
sandwiches. . . .

Together Bishop Smallwood and Aunt Cassie had planned a service calculated skilfully to harrow the feelings and give full scope to the vast emotional capacities of their generation and background.

They chose the most emotional of hymns, and Bishop Smallwood, renowned for his effect upon pious and sentimental old ladies, said a few insincere and pompous words which threw Aunt Cassie and poor old Mrs. Featherstone into fresh excesses of grief. The services for the boy became a barbaric rite dedicated not to his brief and pathetic existence but to a glorification of the name he bore and of all those traits—the narrowness, the snobbery, the lower middle-class respect for property—which had culminated in the lingering tragedy of his sickly life. In their respective pews Anson and Aunt Cassie swelled with pride at the mention of the Pentland ancestry. Even the sight of the vigorous, practical, stocky Polish women staring round-eyed at the funeral procession a little before, returned to them now in a wave of pride and secret elation. The same emotion in some way filtered back through the little church from the pulpit where Bishop Smallwood(with the sob in his voice which had won him prizes at the seminary) stood surrounded by midsummer flowers, through all the relatives and connections, until far in the back among the more obscure and remote ones it became simply a pride in their relation to New England and the ancient dying village that was fast disappearing beneath the inroads of a more vigorous world. Something of the Pentland enchantment engulfed them all, even old Mrs. Featherstone, with her poor back bent from washing to support the four defective grandchildren who ought never to have been born. Through her facile tears (she wept because it was the only pleasure left her) there shone the light of a pride in belonging to these people who had persecuted witches and evolved transcendentalism and Mr. Lowell and Doctor Holmes and the good, kind Mr. Longfellow. It raised her somehow above the level of those hardy foreigners who worshiped the Scarlet Woman of Rome and jostled her on the sidewalks of High Street.

In all the little church there were only two or three, perhaps, who escaped that sudden mystical surge of self-satisfaction. . . . O'Hara, who was forever outside the caste, and Olivia and old John Pentland, sitting there side by side so filled with sorrow that they did not even resent the antics of Bishop Smallwood. Sabine (who had come, after all, to the services) sensed the intensity of the engulfing emotion. It filled her with a sense of slow, cold, impotent rage.

As the little procession left the church, wiping its eyes and murmuring in lugubrious tones, the clouds which a little earlier had sprung up against the distant horizon began to darken the whole sky. The air became so still that the leaves on the tall, drooping elms hung as motionless as leaves in a painted picture, and far away, gently at first, and then with a slow, increasing menace, rose the sound of distant echoing thunder. Ill at ease, the mourners gathered in little groups about the steps, regarding alternately the threatening sky and the waiting hearse, and presently, one by one, the more timorous ones began to drift sheepishly away. Others followed them slowly

until by the time the coffin was borne out, they had all melted away save
for the members of the "immediate family" and one or two others. Sabine
remained, and O'Hara and old Mrs. Soames (leaning on John Pentland's
arm as if it were her grandson who was dead), and old Miss Haddon in her
black cape, and the pall-bearers, and of course Bishop Smallwood and the
country rector who, in the presence of this august and saintly pillar of the
church, had faded to insignificance. Besides these there were one or two other
relatives, like Struthers Pentland, a fussy little bald man (cousin of John
Pentland and of the disgraceful Horace), who had never married but devoted
himself instead to fathering the boys of his classes at Harvard.

It was this little group which entered the motors and hurried off after
the hearse in its shameless race with the oncoming storm.

The town burial-ground lay at the top of a high, bald hill where the first
settlers of Durham had chosen to dispose of their dead, and the ancient
roadway that led up to it was far too steep and stony to permit the passing
of motors, so that part way up the hill the party was forced to descend and
make the remainder of the journey on foot. As they assembled, silently but
in haste, about the open, waiting grave, the sound of the thunder accompanied now by wild flashes of lightning, drew nearer and nearer, and the
leaves of the stunted trees and shrubs which a moment before had been so
still, began to dance and shake madly in the green light that preceded the
storm.

Bishop Smallwood, by nature a timorous man, stood beside the grave opening his jewel-encrusted Prayer Book (he was very High Church and fond of
incense and precious stones) and fingering the pages nervously, now looking
down at them, now regarding the stolid Polish grave-diggers who stood about
waiting to bury the last of the Pentlands. There were irritating small delays,
but at last everything was ready and the Bishop, reading as hastily as he
dared, began the service in a voice less rich and theatrical than usual.

"I am the Resurrection and the Life, saith the Lord. . . ."

And what followed was lost in a violent crash of thunder so that the Bishop
was able to omit a line or two without being discovered. The few trees on
the bald hill began to sway and rock, bending low toward the earth, and
the crape veils of the women performed wild black writhings. In the uproar
of wind and thunder only a sentence or two of the service became
audible. . . .

"For a thousand years in Thy sight are but as yesterday, seeing that the past
is as a watch in the night. . . ."

And then again a wild, angry Nature took possession of the services, drowning out the anxious voice of the Bishop and the loud theatrical sobs of Aunt
Cassie, and again there was a sudden breathless hush and the sound of the
Bishop's voice, so pitiful and insignificant in the midst of the storm, reading. . . .

"*O teach us to number our days that we may apply our hearts unto wisdom.*"

And again:

"*For as much as it hath pleased Almighty God in His Providence to take out of the world the soul of our deceased brother.*"

And at last, with relief, the feeble, reedlike voice, repeating with less monotony than usual: "*The Grace of our Lord Jesus Christ and the Love of God and the Fellowship of the Holy Ghost be with us all evermore. Amen.*"

Sabine, in whose hard nature there lay some hidden thing which exulted in storms, barely heard the service. She stood there watching the wild beauty of the sky and the distant sea and the marshes and thinking how different a thing the burial of the first Pentland must have been from the timorous, hurried rite that marked the passing of the last. She kept seeing those first fanatical, hard-faced, rugged Puritans standing above their tombs like ghosts watching ironically the genteel figure of the Apostle to the Genteel and his jeweled Prayer Book. . . .

The Polish grave-diggers set about their work stolidly indifferent to the storm, and before the first motor had started down the steep and stony path, the rain came with the wild, insane violence, sweeping inward in a wall across the sea and the black marshes. Sabine, at the door of her motor, raised her head and breathed deeply, as if the savage, destructive force of the storm filled her with a kind of ecstasy.

On the following day, cool after the storm and bright and clear, a second procession made its way up the stony path to the top of the bald hill, only this time Bishop Smallwood was not there, nor Cousin Struthers Pentland, for they had both been called away suddenly and mysteriously. And Anson Pentland was not there because he would have nothing to do with a blackguard like Horace Pentland, even in death. In the little group about the open grave stood Olivia and John Pentland and Aunt Cassie, who had come because, after all, the dead man's name was Pentland, and Miss Haddon (in her heavy broadcloth cape), who never missed any funeral and had learned about this one from her friend, the undertaker, who kept her perpetually *au courant*. There were not even any friends to carry the coffin to the grave, and so this labor was divided between the undertaker's men and the grave-diggers. . . .

And the service began again, read this time by the rector, who since the departure of the Bishop seemed to have grown a foot in stature. . . .

"*I am the Resurrection and the Life, saith the Lord. . . .*"

"*For a thousand years in Thy sight are but as yesterday, seeing that is past as a watch in the night. . . .*"

"*O teach us to number our days that we may apply our hearts unto wisdom.*"

Aunt Cassie wept again, though the performance was less good than on

the day before, but Olivia and John Pentland stood in silence while Horace
Pentland was buried at last in the midst of that little colony of grim and
respectable dead.

Sabine was there, too, standing at a little distance, as if she had a contempt for all funerals. She had known Horace Pentland in life and she had
gone to see him in his long exile whenever her wanderings led her to the
south of France, less from affection than because it irritated the others in
the family. (He must have been happier in that warm, rich country than he
could ever have been in this cold, stony land.) But she had come to-day less
for sentimental reasons than because it gave her the opportunity of a triumph
over Aunt Cassie. She could watch Aunt Cassie out of her cold green eyes
while they all stood about to bury the family skeleton. Sabine, who had not
been to a funeral in the twenty-five years since her father's death, had
climbed the stony hill to the Durham town burial-ground twice in as many
days. . . .

The rector was speaking again. . . .

"*The Grace of our Lord Jesus Christ and the Love of God and the Fellowship of the Holy Ghost be with us all evermore. Amen.*"

The little group turned away in silence, and in silence disappeared over
the rim of the hill down the steep path. The secret burial was finished
and Horace Pentland was left alone with the Polish grave-diggers, come home
at last.

3

The peace which had taken possession of Olivia as she sat alone by the
side of her dead son, returned to her slowly with the passing of the excitement over the funeral. Indeed, she was for once thankful for the listless, futile
enchantment which invested the quiet old world. It soothed her at a moment when, all interest having departed from life, she wanted merely to be
left in peace. She came to see for a certainty that there was no tragedy in
her son's death; the only tragedy had been that he had ever lived at all such
a baffled, painful, hopeless existence. And now, after so many years of anxiety,
there was peace and a relaxation that seemed strange and in a way delicious
. . . moments when, lying in the chaise longue by the window overlooking
the marshes, she was enveloped by deep and healing solitude. Even the visits
of Aunt Cassie, who would have forced her way into Olivia's room in the
interests of "duty," made only a vague, dreamlike impression. The old lady
became more and more a droning, busy insect, the sound of whose buzzing
grew daily more distant and vague, like the sound of a fly against a window-
pane heard through veils of sleep.

From her window she sometimes had a distant view of the old man, riding
alone now, in the trap across the fields behind the old white horse, and sometimes she caught a glimpse of his lean figure riding the savage red mare along
the lanes. He no longer went alone with the mare; he had yielded to Higgins'

insistent warnings of her bad temper and permitted the groom to go with him, always at his side or a little behind to guard him, riding a polo pony with an ease and grace which made horse and man seem a single creature . . . a kind of centaur. On a horse the ugliness of the robust, animal little man seemed to flow away. It was as if he had been born thus, on a horse, and was awkward and ill at ease with his feet on the earth.

And Olivia knew the thought that was always in the mind of her father-in-law as he rode across the stony, barren fields. He was thinking all the while that all this land, all this fortune, even Aunt Cassie's carefully tended pile, would one day belong to a family of some other name, perhaps a name which he had never even heard.

There were no more Pentlands. Sybil and her husband would be rich, enormously so, with the Pentland money and Olivia's money . . . but there would never be any more Pentlands. It had all come to an end in this . . . futility and oblivion. In another hundred years the name would exist, if it existed at all, only as a memory, embalmed within the pages of Anson's book.

The new melancholy which settled over the house came in the end even to touch the spirit of Sybil, so young and so eager for experience, like a noxious mildew. Olivia noticed it first in a certain shadowy listlessness that seemed to touch every action of the girl, and then in an occasional faint sigh of weariness, and in the visits the girl paid her in her room, and in the way she gave up willingly evenings at Brook Cottage to stay at home with her mother. She saw that Sybil, who had always been so eager, was touched by the sense of futility which she (Olivia) had battled for so long. And Sybil, Sybil of them all, alone possessed the chance of being saved.

She thought, "I must not come to lean on her. I must not be the sort of mother who spoils the life of her child."

And when John Pentland came to sit listlessly by her side, sometimes in silence, sometimes making empty speeches that meant nothing in an effort to cover his despair, she saw that he, too, had come to her for the strength which she alone could give him. Even old Mrs. Soames had failed him, for she lay ill again and able to see him only for a few minutes each day. (It was Sabine's opinion, uttered during one of her morning visits, that these strange sudden illnesses came from overdoses of drugs.)

So she came to see that she was being a coward to abandon the struggle now, and she rose one morning almost at dawn to put on her riding-clothes and set out with Sybil across the wet meadows to meet O'Hara. She returned with something of her pallor gone and a manner almost of gaiety, her spirit heightened by the air, the contact with O'Hara and the sense of having taken up the struggle once more.

Sabine, always watchful, noticed the difference and put it down to the presence of O'Hara alone, and in this she was not far wrong, for set down there in Durham, he affected Olivia powerfully as one who had no past but only a future. With him she could talk of things which lay ahead—of his plans for the farm he had bought, of Sybil's future, of his own reckless, irresistible career.

O'Hara himself had come to a dangerous state of mind. He was one of those men who seek fame and success less for the actual rewards than for the satisfaction of the struggle, the fierce pleasure of winning with all the chances against one. He had won successes already. He had his house, his horses, his motor, his well-tailored clothes, and he knew the value of these things, not only in the world of Durham, but in the slums and along the wharves of Boston. He had no illusions about the imperfect workings of democracy. He knew (perhaps because, having begun at the very bottom, he had fought his way very near to the top) that the poor man expects a politician to be something of a splendorous affair, especially when he has begun his career as a very common and ordinary sort of poor man. O'Hara was not playing his game foolishly or recklessly. When he visited the slums or sat in at political meetings, he was a sort of universal common man, a brother to all. When he addressed a large meeting or presided at an assembly, he arrived in a glittering motor and appeared in the elegant clothes suitable to a representative of the government, of power; and so he reflected credit on those men who had played with him as boys along India Wharf and satisfied the universal hunger in man for something more splendorous than the machinery of a perfect democracy.

He understood the game perfectly and made no mistakes, for he had had the best of all training—that of knowing all sorts of people in all sorts of conditions. In himself, he embodied them all, if the simple and wholly kindly and honest were omitted; for he was really not a simple man nor a wholly honest one and he was too ruthless to be kindly. He understood people (as Sabine had guessed), with their little prides and vanities and failings and ambitions.

Aunt Cassie and Anson in the rigidity of their minds had been unjust in thinking that their world was the goal of his ambitions. They had, in the way of those who depend on their environment as a justification for their own existence, placed upon it a value out of all proportion in the case of a man like O'Hara. To them it was everything, the ultimate to be sought on this earth, and so they supposed it must seem to O'Hara. It would have been impossible for them to believe that he considered it only as a small part of his large scheme of life and laid siege to it principally for the pleasure that he found in the battle; for it was true that O'Hara, once he had won, would not know what to do with the fruits of his victory.

Already he himself had begun to see this. He had begun to understand that the victory was so easy that the battle held little savor for him. Moments of satisfaction such as that which had overtaken him as he sat talking to Sabine were growing more and more rare . . . moments when he would stop and think, "Here am I, Michael O'Hara, a nobody . . . son of a laborer and a housemaid, settled in the midst of such a world as Durham, talking to such a woman as Mrs. Richard Callendar."

No, the savor was beginning to fail, to go out of the struggle. He was beginning to be bored, and as he grew bored he grew also restless and unhappy.

Born in the Roman Catholic church, he was really neither a very religious nor a very superstitious man. He was skeptic enough not to believe all the faiths the church sought to impose upon him, yet he was not skeptic enough to find peace of mind in an artificial will to believe. For so long a time he had relied wholly upon himself that the idea of leaning for support, even in lonely, restless moments, upon a God or a church, never even occurred to him. He remained outwardly a Roman Catholic because by denying the faith he would have incurred the enmity of the church and many thousands of devout Irish and Italians. The problem simply did not concern him deeply one way or the other.

And so he had come, guided for the moment by no very strong passion, into the doldrums of confusion and boredom. Even his fellow-politicians in Boston saw the change in him and complained that he displayed no very great interest in the campaign to send him to Congress. He behaved at times as if it made not the slightest difference to him whether he was elected to Congress or not . . . he, this Michael O'Hara who was so valuable to his party, so engaging and shrewd, who could win for it almost anything he chose.

And though he took care that no one should divine it, this strange state of mind troubled him more deeply than any of his friends. He was assailed by the certainty that there was something lacking from his life, something very close to the foundations. Now that he was inactive and bored, he had begun to think of himself for the first time. The fine, glorious burst of first youth, when everything seemed part of a splendid game, was over and done now, and he felt himself slipping away toward the borderland of middle-age. Because he was a man of energy and passion, who loved life, he felt the change with a keen sense of sadness. There was a kind of horror for him in the idea of a lowered tempo of life—a fear that filled him at times with a passionately satisfactory sort of Gaelic melancholy.

In such moments, he had quite honestly taken stock of all he possessed, and found the amassed result bitterly unsatisfactory. He had a good enough record. He was decidedly more honorable than most men in such a dirty business as politics—indeed, far more honorable and freer from spites and nastinesses than many of those who had come out of this very sacred Durham world. He had made enough money in the course of his career, and he was winning his battle in Durham. Yet at thirty-five life had begun to slacken, to lose some of that zest which once had led him to rise every morning bursting with animal spirits, his brain all a-glitter with fascinating schemes.

And then, in the very midst of this perilous state of mind, he discovered one morning that the old sensation of delight at rising had returned to him, only it was not because his brain was filled with fascinating schemes. He arose with an interest in life because he knew that in a little while he would see Olivia Pentland. He arose, eager to fling himself on his horse and, riding across the meadows, to wait by the abandoned gravel-pit until he saw her coming over the dew-covered fields, radiant, it seemed to him, as the morning itself. On the days when she did not come it was as if the bottom had dropped out of his whole existence.

It was not that he was a man encountering the idea of woman for the first time. There had been women in his life always, since the very first bedraggled Italian girl he had met as a boy among the piles of lumber along the whárves. There had been women always because it was impossible for a man so vigorous and full of zest, so ruthless and so scornful, to have lived thirty-five years without them, and because he was an attractive man, filled when he chose to be, with guile and charm, whom women found it difficult to resist. There had been plenty of women, kept always in the background, treated as a necessity and prevented skilfully from interfering with the more important business of making a career.

But with Olivia Pentland, something new and disturbing had happened to him . . . something which, in his eagerness to encompass all life and experience, possessed an overwhelming sensuous fascination. She was not simply another woman in a procession of considerable length. Olivia Pentland, he found, was different from any of the others . . . a woman of maturity, poised, beautiful, charming and intelligent, and besides all these things she possessed for him a kind of fresh and iridescent bloom, the same freshness, only a little saddened, that touched her young daughter.

In the beginning, when they had talked together while she planned the garden at Brook Cottage, he had found himself watching her, lost in a kind of wonder, so that he scarcely understood what she was saying. And all the while he kept thinking, "Here is a wonderful woman . . . the most wonderful I've ever seen or will ever see again . . . a woman who could make life a different affair for me, who would make of love something which people say it is."

She had affected him thus in a way that swept aside all the vulgar and cynical coarseness with which a man of such experience is likely to invest the whole idea of woman. Until now women had seemed to him made to entertain men or to provide children for them, and now he saw that there was, after all, something in this sentiment with which people surrounded a love affair. For a long time he searched for a word to describe Olivia and in the end he fell back upon the old well-worn one which she always brought to mind. She was a "lady"—and as such she had an overwhelming effect upon his imagination.

He had said to himself that here was a woman who could understand him, not in the aloof, analytical fashion of a clever woman like Sabine Callendar, but in quite another way. She was a woman to whom he could say, "I am thus and so. My life has been of this kind. My motives are of this sort," and she would understand, the bad with the good. She would be the one person in the world to whom he could pour out the whole burden of secrets, the one woman who could ever destroy the weary sense of loneliness which sometimes afflicted him. She made him feel that, for all his shrewdness and hard-headed scheming, she was far wiser than he would ever be, that in a way he was a small boy who might come to her and, burying his head in her lap, have her stroke his thick black hair. She would understand that there were times when a man wanted to be treated thus. In her quiet way she was a strong woman, unselfish, too, who did not feed upon flattery and perpetual attention, the sort of woman who is precious to a man bent upon a career. The thought of her filled him with a poignant feeling of sadness, but in his less romantic moments he saw, too, that she held the power of catching him up out of his growing boredom. She would be of great value to him.

And so Sabine had not been far wrong when she thought of him as the small boy sitting on the curbstone who had looked up at her gravely and said, "I'm playing." He was at times very like such an image.

But in the end he was always brought up abruptly against the hard reality of the fact that she was already married to a man who did not want her himself but who would never set her free, a man who perhaps would have sacrificed everything in the world to save a scandal in his family. And beyond these hard, tangible difficulties he discerned, too, the whole dark decaying web, less obvious but none the less potent, in which she had become enmeshed.

Yet these obstacles only created a fascination to a mind so complex, so perverse, for in the solitude of his mind and in the bitterness of the long struggle he had known, he came to hold the whole world in contempt and saw no reason why he should not take what he wanted from this Durham world. Obstacles such as these provided the material for a new battle, a new source of interest in the turbulent stream of his existence; only this time there was a difference . . . that he coveted the prize itself more than the struggle. He wanted Olivia Pentland, strangely enough, not for a moment or even for a month or a year, but for always.

He waited because he understood, in the shrewdness of his long experience, that to be insistent would only startle such a woman and cause him to lose her entirely, and because he knew of no plan of action which could overcome the obstacles which kept them apart. He waited, as he had done many times in his career, for circumstances to solve themselves. And while he waited, with each time that he saw her she grew more and more desirable, and his own invincible sense of caution became weaker and weaker.

4

In those long days spent in her room, Olivia had come slowly to be aware of the presence of the newcomer at Brook Cottage. It had begun on the night of Jack's death with the sound of his music drifting across the marshes, and after the funeral Sabine had talked of him to Olivia with an enthusiasm

curiously foreign to her. Once or twice she had caught a glimpse of him
crossing the meadows toward O'Hara's shining chimneys or going down the
road that led through the marshes to the sea—a tall, red-haired young man
who walked with a slight limp. Sybil, she found, was strangely silent about
him, but when she questioned the girl about her plans for the day she found,
more often then not, that they had to do with him. When she spoke of him,
Sybil had a way of blushing and saying, "He's very nice, Mother. I'll bring
him over when you want to see people. . . . I used to know him in Paris."

And Olivia, wisely, did not press her questions. Besides, Sabine had told
her almost all there was to know . . . perhaps more than Sybil herself knew.

Sabine said, "He belongs to a rather remarkable family . . . wilful, reckless
and full of spirit. His mother is probably the most remarkable of them all.
She's a charming woman who has lived luxuriously in Paris most of her life
. . . not one of the American colony. She doesn't ape any one and she's
incapable of pretense of any sort. She's lived, rather alone, over there on
money . . . quite a lot of money . . . which seems to come out of steel-mills
in some dirty town of the Middle West. She's one of my great friends . . . a
woman of no intellect, but very beautiful and blessed with a devastating
charm. She is one of the women who was born for men. . . . She's irresistible to them, and I imagine there have been men in her life always. She was
made for men, but her taste is perfect, so her morals don't matter."

The woman . . . indeed all Jean de Cyon's family . . . seemed to fasci-
nate Sabine as she sat having tea with Olivia, for she went on and on, talking
far more than usual, describing the house of Jean's mother, her friends, the
people whom one met at her dinners, all there was to tell about her.

"She's the sort of woman who has existed since the beginning of time.
There's some mystery about her early life. It has something to do with Jean's
father. I don't think she was happy with him. He's never mentioned. Of
course, she's married again now to a Frenchman . . . much older than herself . . . a man, very distinguished, who has been in three cabinets. That's
where the boy gets his French name. The old man has adopted him and
treats him like his own son. De Cyon is a good name in France, one of the
best; but of course Jean hasn't any French blood. He's pure American, but
he's never seen his own country until now."

Sabine finished her tea and putting her cup back on the Regence table
(which had come from Olivia's mother and so found its graceful way into a
house filled with stiff early American things), she added, "It's a remarkable
family . . . wild and restless. Jean had an aunt who died in the Carmelite
convent at Lisieux, and his cousin is Lilli Barr . . . a really great musician."
She looked out of the window and after a moment said in a low voice, "Lilli
Barr is the woman whom my husband married . . . but she divorced him,
too, and now we are friends . . . she and I." The familiar hard, metallic
laugh returned and she added, "I imagine our experience with him made us
sympathetic. . . . You see, I know the family very well. It's the sort of blood
which produces people with a genius for life . . . for living in the moment."

She did not say that Jean and his mother and the ruthless cousin Lilli Barr fascinated her because they stood in a way for the freedom toward which she had been struggling through all the years since she escaped from Durham. They were free in a way from countries, from towns, from laws, from prejudices, even in a way from nationality. She had hoped once that Jean might interest himself in her own sullen, independent, clever Thérèse, but in her knowledge of the world she had long ago abandoned that hope, knowing that a boy so violent and romantic, so influenced by an upbringing among Frenchmen, a youth so completely masculine, was certain to seek a girl more soft and gentle and feminine than Thérèse. She knew it was inevitable that he should fall in love with a girl like Sybil, and in a way she was content because it fell in admirably with her own indolent plans. The Pentlands were certain to look upon Jean de Cyon as a sort of gipsy, and when they knew the whole truth. . . .

The speculation fascinated her. The summer in Durham, even with the shadow of Jack's death flung across it, was not proving as dreadful as she had feared; and this new development interested her as something she had never before observed . . . an idyllic love affair between two young people who each seemed to her a perfect, charming creature.

5

It had all begun on the day nearly a year earlier when all Paris was celebrating the anniversary of the Armistice, and in the morning Sybil had gone with Thérèse and Sabine to lay a wreath beside the flame at the Arc de Triomphe (for the war was one of the unaccountable things about which Sabine chose to make a display of sentiment). And afterward she played in the garden with the dogs which they would not let her keep at the school in Saint-Cloud, and then she had gone into the house to find there a fascinating and beautiful woman of perhaps fifty—a Madame de Cyon, who had come to lunch, with her son, a young man of twenty-four, tall, straight and slender, with red hair and dark blue eyes and a deep, pleasant voice. On account of the day he was dressed in his cuirassier's uniform of black and silver, and because of an old wound he walked with a slight limp. Almost at once (she remembered this when she thought of him) he had looked at her in a frank, admiring way which gave her a sense of pleasurable excitement wholly new in her experience.

Something in the sight of the uniform, or perhaps in the feel of the air, the sound of the military music, the echoes of the *Marseillaise* and the *Sambre et Meuse*, the sight of the soldiers in the street and the great Arc with the flame burning there . . . something in the feel of Paris, something which she loved passionately, had taken possession of her. It was something which, gathering in that moment, had settled upon the strange young man who regarded her with such admiring eyes.

She knew vaguely that she must have fallen in love in the moment she stood there in Sabine Callendar's salon bowing to Lily de Cyon. The experience had grown in intensity when, after lunch, she took him into the garden to show him her dogs and watched him rubbing the ears of the Doberman "Imp" and talking to the dog softly in a way which made her know that he felt about animals as she did. He had been so pleasant in his manner, so gentle in his bigness, so easy to talk to, as if they had always been friends.

And then almost at once he had gone away to the Argentine, without even seeing her again, on a trip to learn the business of cattle-raising because he had the idea that one day he might settle himself as a rancher. But he left behind him a vivid image which with the passing of time grew more and more intense in the depths of a romantic nature which revolted at the idea of Thérèse choosing a father scientifically for her child. It was an image by which she had come, almost unconsciously, to measure other men, even to such small details as the set of their shoulders and the way they used their hands and the timbre of their voices. It was this she had really meant when she said to her mother, "I know what sort of man I want to marry. I know exactly." She had meant, quite without knowing it, that it must be a man like Jean de Cyon . . . charming, romantic and a little wild.

She had not forgotten him, though there were moments at the school in Saint-Cloud when she had believed she would never see him again—moments when she was swept by a delicious sense of hopeless melancholy in which she believed that her whole life had been blighted, and which led her to make long and romantic entries in the diary that was kept hidden beneath her mattress. And so as she grew more hopeless, the aura of romance surrounding him took on colors deeper and more varied and intense. She had grown so pale that Mademoiselle Vernueil took to dosing her, and Thérèse accused her abruptly of having fallen in love, a thing she denied vaguely and with overtones of romantic mystery.

And then with the return to Pentlands (a return advised by her mother on account of Jack's health) the image dimmed a little in the belief that even by the wildest flights of imagination there was no chance of her seeing him again. It became a hopeless passion; she prepared herself to forget him and, in the wisdom of her young mind, grow accustomed to the idea of marrying one of the tame young men who were so much more suitable and whom her family had always known. She had watched her admirers carefully, weighing them always against the image of the young man with red hair, dressed in the black and silver of the cuirassiers, and beside that image they had seemed to her—even the blond, good-looking Mannering boy—like little boys, rather naughty and not half so old and wise as herself. She had reconciled herself secretly and with gravity to the idea of making one of the matches common in her world—a marriage determined by property and the fact that her fiancé would be "the right sort of person."

And so the whole affair had come to take on the color of a tragic romance, to be guarded secretly. Perhaps when she was an old woman she would tell the story to her grandchildren. She believed that whomever she married, she would be thinking always of Jean de Cyon. It was one of those half-comic illusions of youth in which there is more than a grain of melancholy truth. And then abruptly had come the news of his visit to Brook Cottage. She still kept her secret, but not well enough to prevent her mother and Sabine from suspecting it. She had betrayed herself first on the very night of Jack's death when she had said, with a sudden light in her eye, "It's Jean de Cyon. . . . I'd forgotten he was arriving to-night." Olivia had noticed the light because it was something which went on and on.

And at Brook Cottage young de Cyon, upset by the delay caused by the funeral and the necessity of respecting the mourning at Pentlands, had sulked and behaved in such a way that he would have been a nuisance to any one save Sabine, who found amusement in the spectacle. Used to rushing head-long toward anything he desired (as he had rushed into the French army at seventeen and off to the Argentine nine months ago), he turned ill-tempered and spent his days out of doors, rowing on the river and bathing in the soli-tude of the great white beach. He quarreled with Thérèse, whom he had known since she was a little girl, and tried to be as civil as possible toward the amused Sabine.

She knew by now that he had not come to Durham through any great interest in herself or Thérèse. She knew now how wise she had been (for the purposes of her plan) to have included in her invitation to him the line . . . "Sybil Pentland lives on the next farm to us. You may remember her. She lunched with us last Armistice Day."

She saw that he rather fancied himself as a man of the world who was being very clever in keeping his secret. He asked her about Sybil Pentland in a casual way that was transparently artificial, and consulted her on the lapse of time decently necessary before he broke in upon the mourning at Pent-lands, and had Miss Pentland shown any admiration for the young men about Durham? If he had not been so charming and impatient he would have bored Sabine to death.

The young man was afraid of only one thing . . . that perhaps she had changed in some way, that perhaps she was not in the reality as charming as she had seemed to him in the long months of his absence. He was not without experience (indeed, Sabine believed that he had gone to the Argentine to escape from some Parisian complication) and he knew that such calamitous disappointments could happen. Perhaps when he came to know her better the glamour would fade. Perhaps she did not remember him at all. But she seemed to him, after months of romantic brooding, the most desirable woman he had ever seen.

It was a new world in which he discovered himself, in some way a newer and more different world than the vast grass-covered plains from which he had just come. People about Durham, he learned, had a way of saying that

Boston and Durham were like England, but this he put down quietly as a kind of snobbery, because Boston and Durham weren't like England at all, so far as he could see; in spots Boston and Durham seemed old, but there wasn't the same richness, the same glamour about them. They should have been romantic and yet they were not; they were more, it seemed to him, like the illustrations in a school history. They were dry . . . *sec*, he thought, considering the French word better in this case on account of its sound.

And it wasn't the likeness to England that he found interesting, but rather the difference . . . the bleak rawness of the countryside and the sight of whole colonies of peoples as strange and foreign as the Czechs and Poles providing a sort of alien background to the whole picture.

He had gone about the business of becoming acquainted with his own country in a thorough, energetic fashion, and being a sensuous youth, filled with a taste for colors and sounds and all the emanations of the spectacle of life, he was acutely conscious of it.

To Sabine, he said, "You know the funny thing is that it seems to me like coming home. It makes me feel that I belong in America . . . not in Durham, but in New York or some of those big roaring towns I've passed through."

He spoke, naturally enough, not at all like an American but in the clipped English fashion, rather swallowing his words, and now and then with a faint trace of French intonation. His voice was deeper and richer than the New England voices, with their way of calling Charles Street "Challs Street" and sacred Harvard . . . "Havaad."

It was the spectacle of New York which had fascinated him more than any other because it surpassed all his dreams of it and all the descriptions people had given him of its immense force and barbaric splendor and the incredible variety of tongues and people. New York, Sabine told him with a consciousness of uttering treason, *was* America, far more than the sort of life he would encounter in Durham.

As he talked to Sabine of New York, he would rise to that pitch of excitement and enthusiasm which comes to people keenly alive. He even confided in her that he had left Europe never to return there to live.

"It's old country," he said, "and if one has been brought up there, as I've been, there's no reason for going back there to live. In a way it's a dead world . . . dead surely in comparison to the Americas. And it's the future that interests me . . . not the past. I want to be where the most is going on . . . in the center of things."

When he was not playing the piano wildly, or talking to Sabine, or fussing about with Thérèse among the frogs and insects of the laboratory she had rigged up on the glass-enclosed piazza, he was walking about the garden in a state of suppressed excitement, turning over and over in his young mind his own problem and the plans he had for adjusting himself in this vigorous country. To discover it now, at the age of twenty-five, was an exciting experience. He was beginning to understand those young Americans he had encountered occasionally in Europe (like his cousin Fergus Tolliver, who died in the war), who seemed so alive, so filled with a reckless sense of adventure . . . young men irresistible in such an old, tired world, because Nature itself was on their side.

To ease his impatience he sought refuge in a furious physical activity, rowing, swimming and driving with Sabine about the Durham countryside. He could not walk far, on account of the trouble caused by his old wound, but he got as far as O'Hara's house, where he met the Irishman and they became friends. O'Hara turned over to him a canoe and a rowing-scull and told him that whenever his leg was better he might have a horse from his stables.

One morning as he pulled his canoe up the muddy bank of the river after his early exercise, he heard the sound of hoofs in the thick mud near at hand and, turning, he saw Sybil Pentland on her mare Andromache coming out of the thicket almost at his side.

It was a superb morning—cool for Durham in mid-August—and on the lazy river the nympheas spread their waxy white blossoms in starlike clusters against a carpet of green pads. It was a morning made for delights, with the long rays of the rising sun striking to silver the dew-hung spider-webs that bound together the tangled masses of wild-grape vines; and young de Cyon, standing on the edge of the path, flushed with health and the early morning exercise, his thick red hair all rumpled, was overcome swiftly by a sense of tremendous physical well-being and strength. A whole world lay before him waiting to be conquered; and into it, out of the tangled thicket, had come Sybil Pentland, more charming in the flesh than she had seemed to him even on the long starlit nights when he lay awake on the pampas thinking of her.

For a second neither of them said anything. The girl, startled and blushing a little, but touched, too, by a quiet sense of dignity, drew in her mare; and Jean, looking up at her, said in a falsely casual way (for his veins were throbbing with excitement), "Oh! Hello! You're Miss Pentland."

"Yes." But she looked suddenly disappointed, as if she *really* believed that he had almost forgotten her.

Standing clad only in trousers and a rowing-shirt, he looked down at his costume and said, grinning, "I'm not dressed to receive visitors."

Somehow this served to break the sense of restraint, and they fell into conversation, exchanging a few banal remarks on the beauty of the morning, and Jean, standing by Andromache, rubbing her nose with the same tenderness he had shown toward Sybil's dogs, looked at her out of the candid blue eyes and said, "I should have come to see you sooner, only I thought you mightn't want to see me."

A quivering note of warmth colored his voice.

"It would have made no difference," she said. "And now you must come often . . . as often as you like. How long are you staying at Brook Cottage?"

For a second he hesitated. "A fortnight . . . perhaps. Perhaps . . . longer."

And looking down at him, she thought, "I must make him stay. If I lose him again now. . . . I must make him stay. I like him more than any one in the world. I can't lose him now."

And she began to reason with herself that Fate was on her side, that destiny had delivered him again into her hands. It was like a thing ordained, and life with him would be exciting, a thrilling affair. The quiet stubbornness, come down to her from Olivia, began to rise and take possession of her. She was determined not to lose him.

They moved away up the river, still talking in a rather stiff fashion, while Jean walked beside Andromache, limping a little. One banality followed another as they groped toward each other, each proud and fearful of showing his feelings, each timid and yet eager and impatient. It was the excitement of being near to each other that made the conversation itself take on a sense of importance. Neither of them really knew what they were saying. In one sense they seemed strange and exciting to each other, but in another they were not strange at all because there lay between them that old feeling, which Sybil had recognized in the garden of the Rue de Tilsitt, that they had known each other always. There were no hesitations or doubts or suspicions.

The sky was brilliant; the scent of the mucky river and growing weeds was overwhelming. There came to both of them a quickening of the senses, a sort of heightened ecstasy, which shut out all the world. It was a kind of enchantment, but different from the enchantment which enveloped the dead house at Pentlands.

6

Each time that Olivia rose at dawn to ride out with Sybil and meet O'Hara at the old gravel-pit, the simple excursion became more glamorous to her. There was a youth in the contact with Sybil and the Irishman which she had almost forgotten, a feeling of strength for which she had long been hungering. It was, she found, a splendid way to begin the day—in the cool of the morning, riding away over the drenched grass; it made a freshening contrast to the rest of a day occupied largely by such old people as her father-in-law and Anson (who was really an old man) and the old woman in the north wing and by the persistent fluttering attacks of Aunt Cassie. And Olivia, who was not without a secret vanity, began to notice herself in the mirror . . . that her eyes were brighter and her skin was more clear. She saw that she was even perhaps beautiful, and that the riding-habit became her in a romantic fashion.

She knew, too, riding across the fields between Sybil and O'Hara, that he sometimes watched her with a curious bright light in his blue eyes. He said nothing; he betrayed in no way the feeling behind all that sudden, quiet declaration on the terrace of Brook Cottage. She began to see that he was (as Sabine had discovered almost at once) a very clever and dangerous man. It was not alone because of the strange, almost physical, effect he had upon people—an effect which was almost as if his presence took possession of you completely—but because he had patience and knew how to be silent. If he had rushed in, recklessly and clumsily, everything would have been precipitated and ruined at once. There would have been a scene ending with his dismissal and Olivia, perhaps, would have been free; but he had never touched her. It was simply that he was always there, assuring her in some mysterious way that his emotions had not changed, that he still wanted her more than anything in all the world. And to a woman who was romantic by nature and had never known any romance, it was a dangerous method.

There came a morning when, waiting by the gravel-pit, O'Hara saw that there was only one rider coming toward him across the fields from Pentlands. At first it occurred to him that it must be Sybil coming alone, without her mother, and the old boredom and despair engulfed him swiftly. It was only when the rider came nearer and he saw the white star in the forehead of her horse that he knew it was Olivia herself. That she came alone, knowing what he had already told her, he took as a sign of immense importance.

This time he did not wait or ride slowly toward her. He galloped impatiently as a boy across the wet fields to meet her.

She had the old look of radiance about her and a shyness, too, that made her seem at first a trifle cool and withdrawn. She told him quietly, "Sybil didn't come this morning. She went out very early to fish with Jean de Cyon. The mackerel are beginning to run in the open water off the marshes."

There was an odd, strained silence and O'Hara said, "He's a nice boy . . . de Cyon." And then, with a heroic effort to overcome the shyness which she always managed to impose upon him, he said in a low voice, "But I'm glad she didn't come. I've wanted it to be like this all along."

She did not say archly that he must not talk in this vein. It was a part of her fascination that she was too honest and intelligent not to dispense with such coquetry. He had had enough of coquetry from cheap women and had wearied of it long ago. Besides, she had wanted it "like this" herself and she knew that with O'Hara it was silly to pretend, because sooner or later he always found her out. They were not children, either of them. They both knew what they were doing, that it was a dangerous, even a reckless thing; and yet the very sense of excitement made the adventure as irresistible to the one as to the other.

For a little time they rode in silence, watching the dark hoofs of the horses as they sent up little showers of glittering dew from the knee-deep grass and clover, and presently as they turned out of the fields into the path that led into the birch woods, he laughed and said, "A penny for your thoughts."

Smiling, she replied, "I wouldn't sell them for millions."

"They must be very precious."

"Perhaps . . . precious to me, and to no one else."

"Not to any one at all. . . ."

"No. . . . I don't think they'd interest any one. They're not too cheerful."

At this he fell silent again, with an air of brooding and disappointment. For a time she watched him, and presently she said, "You mustn't sulk on a morning like this."

"I'm not sulking. . . . I was only . . . thinking."

She laughed. "A penny for your thoughts."

He did not laugh. He spoke with a sudden intensity. "They, too, are worth a million . . . more than that . . . only I'll share them with you. I wouldn't share them with any one else."

At the sound of his voice, a silly wave of happiness swept through Olivia. She thought, "I'm being young and ridiculous and enjoying myself."

Aloud she said, "I haven't a penny, but if you'll trust me until to-morrow?"

And then he turned to her abruptly, the shyness gone and in its place an emotion close to irritation and anger. "Why buy them?" he asked. "You know well enough what they are. You haven't forgotten what I told you on the terrace at Brook Cottage. . . . It's grown more true every day . . . all of it." When he saw that she had become suddenly grave, he said, "And what about you?"

"You know how impossible it is."

"Nothing is impossible . . . nothing. Besides, I don't mean the difficulties. Those will come later. . . . I only mean your own feelings."

"Can't you see that I like you? . . . I must like you else I wouldn't have come alone this morning."

"Like me," he echoed with bitterness. "I'm not interested in having you like me!" And when she made no reply, he added, almost savagely, "Why do you keep me away from you? Why do you always put a little wall about yourself?"

"Do I?" she asked, stupidly, and with a sense of pain.

"You are cool and remote even when you laugh."

"I don't want to be—I hate cold people."

For a moment she caught a quick flash of the sudden bad temper which sometimes betrayed him. "It's because you're so damned ladylike. Sometimes I wish you were a servant or a scrub-woman."

"And then I wouldn't be the same—would I?"

He looked up quickly, as if to make a sudden retort, and then, checking himself, rode on in silence. Stealing a glance at him, Olivia caught against the wall of green a swift image of the dark, stubborn tanned head—almost, she thought, like the head of a handsome bull—bent a little, thoughtfully, almost sadly; and again a faint, weak feeling attacked her—the same sensation that had overcome her on the night of her son's death when she sat regarding the back of Anson's head and not seeing it at all. She thought, "Why is it that this man—a stranger—seems nearer to me than Anson has ever been? Why is it that I talk to him in a way I never talked to Anson?" And a curious feeling of pity seized her at the sight of the dark head. In a quick flash of understanding she saw him as a little boy searching awkwardly for something which he did not understand; she wanted to stroke the thick, dark hair in a comforting fashion.

He was talking again. "You know nothing about me," he was saying. "And sometimes I think you ought to know it all." Looking at her quickly he asked, "Could you bear to hear it . . . a little of it?"

She smiled at him, certain that in some mysterious, clairvoyant fashion she had penetrated the very heart of his mood, and she thought, "How sentimental I'm being . . . how sickeningly sentimental!" Yet it was a rich, luxuriant mood in which her whole being relaxed and bathed itself. She thought again, "Why should I not enjoy this? I've been cautious all my life."

And seeing her smile, he began to talk, telling her, as they rode toward the rising sun, the story of his humble origin and of those early bitter days along India Wharf, and from time to time she said, "I understand. My own childhood wasn't happy," or, "Go on, please. It fascinates me . . . more than you can imagine."

So he went on, telling her the story of the long scar on his temple, telling her as he had known he would, of his climb to success, confessing everything, even the things of which he had come to be a little ashamed, and betraying from time to time the bitterness which afflicts those who have made their own way against great odds. The shrewd, complex man became as naïve as a little boy; and she understood, as he had known she would. It was miraculous how right he had been about her.

Lost in this mood, they rode on and on as the day rose and grew warm, enveloped all the while in the odor of the dark, rich, growing thicket and the acrid smell of the tall marsh-ferns, until Olivia, glancing at her watch, said, "It is very late. I shall have missed the family breakfast." She meant really that Anson would have gone up to Boston by now and that she was glad—only it was impossible to say a thing like that.

At the gravel-pit, she bade him good-by, and turning her mare toward Pentlands she felt the curious effect of his nearness slipping away from her with each new step; it was as if the hot August morning were turning cold. And when she came in sight of the big red brick house sitting so solidly among the ancient elms, she thought, "I must never do this again. I have been foolish." And again, "Why should I not do it? Why should I not be happy? They have no right to any claim upon me."

But there was one claim, she knew; there was Sybil. She must not make a fool of herself for the sake of Sybil. She must do nothing to interfere with what had been taking place this very morning in the small fishing-boat far out beyond the marshes somewhere near the spot where Savina Pentland had been drowned. She knew well enough why Sybil had chosen to go fishing instead of riding; it was so easy to look at the girl and at young de Cyon and know what was happening there. She herself had no right to stand in the way of this other thing which was so much younger and fresher, so much more nearly perfect.

As she put her mare over the low wall by the stables she looked up and chanced to see a familiar figure in rusty black standing in the garden, as if she had been there all the while looking out over the meadows, watching them. As she drew near, Aunt Cassie came forward with an expression of anxiety on her face, saying in a thin, hushed voice, as if she might be overheard, "I thought you'd never come back, Olivia dear. I've been looking everywhere for you."

Aware from the intense air of mystery that some new calamity had occurred, Olivia replied, "I was riding with O'Hara. We went too far and it was too hot to hurry the horses."

"I know," said Aunt Cassie. "I saw you." ("Of course she would," thought Olivia. "Does anything ever escape her?") "It's about *her*. She's been violent again this morning and Miss Egan says you may be able to do something. She keeps raving about something to do with the attic and Sabine."

"Yes, I know what it is. I'll go right up."

Higgins appeared, grinning and with a bright birdlike look in his sharp eyes, as if he knew all that had been happening and wanted to say, "Ah, you were out with O'Hara this morning . . . alone. . . . Well, you can't do better, Ma'am. I hope it brings you happiness. You ought to have a man like that."

As he took the bridle, he said, "That's a fine animal Mr. O'Hara rides, Ma'am. I wish we had him in our stables. . . ."

She murmured something in reply and without even waiting for coffee hastened up the dark stairs to the north wing. On the way past the row of tall deep-set windows she caught a swift glimpse of Sabine, superbly dressed and holding a bright yellow parasol over her head, moving indolently up the long drive toward the house, and again she had a sudden unaccountable sense of something melancholy, perhaps even tragic, a little way off. It was one of those quick, inexplicable waves of depression that sweeps over one like a shadow. She said to herself, "I'm depressed now because an hour ago I was too happy."

And immediately she thought, "But it was like Aunt Cassie to have such a thought as that. I must take care or I'll be getting to be a true Pentland . . . believing that if I'm happy a calamity is soon to follow."

She had moments of late when it seemed to her that something in the air, some power hidden in the old house itself, was changing her slowly, imperceptibly, in spite of herself.

Miss Egan met her outside the door, with the fixed eternal smile which to-day seemed to Olivia the sort of smile that the countenance of Fate itself might wear.

"The old lady is more quiet," she said. "Higgins helped me and we managed to bind her in the bed so that she couldn't harm herself. It's surprising how much strength she has in her poor thin body." She explained that old

Mrs. Pentland kept screaming, "Sabine! Sabine!" for Mrs. Callendar and that she kept insisting on being allowed to go into the attic.

"It's the old idea that she's lost something up there," said Miss Egan. "But it's probably only something she's imagined." Olivia was silent for a moment. "I'll go and search," she said. "It might be there is something and if I could find it, it would put an end to these spells."

She found them easily, almost at once, now that there was daylight streaming in at the windows of the cavernous attic. They lay stuffed away beneath one of the great beams . . . a small bundle of ancient yellowed letters which had been once tied together with a bit of mauve ribbon since torn in haste by some one who thrust them in this place of concealment. They had been opened carelessly and in haste, for the moldering paper was all cracked and torn along the edges. The ink, violet once, had turned to a dirty shade of brown.

Standing among the scattered toys left by Jack and Sybil the last time they had played house, Olivia held the letters one by one up to the light. There were eleven in all and each one was addressed to Mrs. J. Pentland, at Pentlands. Eight of them had been sent through the Boston post-office and the other three bore no stamps of any kind, as if they had been sent by messengers or in a bouquet or between the leaves of a book. The handwriting was that of a man, large, impetuous, sprawling, which showed a tendency to blur the letters together in a headlong, impatient way.

She thought at once, "They are addressed to Mrs. J. Pentland, which means Mrs. Jared Pentland. Anson will be delighted, for these must be the letters which passed between Savina Pentland and her cousin, Toby Cane. Anson needed them to complete the book."

And then it occurred to her that there was something strange about the letters—in their having been hidden and perhaps found by the old lady belowstairs and then hidden away a second time. Old Mrs. Pentland must have found them there nearly forty years ago, when they still allowed her to wander about the house. Perhaps it had been on one of those rainy days when Anson and Sabine had come into the attic to play in this very corner with these same old toys—the days when Sabine refused to pretend that muddy water was claret. And now the old lady was remembering the discovery after all these years because the return of Sabine and the sound of her name had lighted some train of long-forgotten memories.

Seating herself on a broken, battered old trunk, she opened the first of the letters reverently so as not to dislodge the bits of violet sealing-wax that still clung to the edges, and almost at once she read with a swift sense of shock:

Carissima,

I waited last night in the cottage until eleven and when you didn't come I knew he had not gone to Salem, after all, and was still there at Pentlands with you. . . .

She stopped reading. She understood it now. . . . The scamp Toby Cane had been more than merely a cousin to Savina Pentland; he had been her lover and that was why she had hidden the letters away beneath the beams of the vast unfinished attic, intending perhaps to destroy them one day. And then she had been drowned before there was time and the letters lay in their hiding-place until John Pentland's wife had discovered them one day by chance, only to hide them again, forgetting in the poor shocked mazes of her mind what they were or where they were hidden. They were the letters which Anson had been searching for.

But she saw at once that Anson would never use the letters in his book, for he would never bring into the open a scandal in the Pentland family, even though it was a scandal which had come to an end, tragically, nearly a century earlier and was now almost pure romance. She saw, of course, that a love affair between so radiant a creature as Savina Pentland and a scamp like Toby Cane would seem rather odd in a book called "The Pentland Family and the Massachusetts Bay Colony." Perhaps it was better not to speak of the letters at all. Anson would manage somehow to destroy all the value there was in them; he would sacrifice truth to the gods of Respectability and Pretense.

Thrusting the letters into her pocket, she descended the dark stairway, and in the north wing Miss Egan met her to ask, almost with an air of impatience, "I suppose you didn't find anything?"

"No," said Olivia quickly, "nothing which could possibly have interested her."

"It's some queer idea she's hatched up," replied Miss Egan, and looked at Olivia as if she doubted the truth of what she had said.

She did not go downstairs at once. Instead, she went to her own room and after bathing, seated herself in the chaise longue by the open window above the terrace, prepared to read the letters one by one. From below there arose a murmur of voices, one metallic and hard, the other nervous, thin, and high-pitched—Sabine's and Aunt Cassie's—as they sat on the terrace in acid conversation, each trying to outstay the other. Listening, Olivia decided that she was a little weary of them both this morning; it was the first time it had ever occurred to her that in a strange way there was a likeness between two women who seemed so different. That curious pair, who hated each other so heartily, had the same way of trying to pry into her life.

None of the letters bore any dates, so she fell to reading them in the order in which they had been found, beginning with the one which read:

Carissima,

I waited last night in the cottage until eleven and when you didn't come I knew he had not gone to Salem, after all, and was still there at Pentlands with you. . . .

She read on:

It's the thought of his being there beside you, even taking possession of you sometimes, that I can't bear. I see him sitting there in the drawing-room, looking at you—eating you with his eyes and pretending all the while that he is above the lusts of the flesh. The flesh! The flesh! You and I, dearest, know the glories of the flesh. Sometimes I think I'm a coward not to kill him at once.

For God's sake, get rid of him somehow to-night. I can't pass another evening alone in the dark gloomy cottage waiting in vain. It is more than I can bear to sit there knowing that every minute, every second, may bring the sound of your step. Be merciful to me. Get rid of him somehow.

I have not touched a drop of anything since I last saw you. Are you satisfied with that?

I am sending this in a book by black Hannah. She will wait for an answer.

Slowly, as she read on and on through the mazes of the impetuous, passionate writing, the voices from the terrace below, the one raised now and a little angry, the other still metallic, hard and indifferent, grew more and more distant until presently she did not hear them at all and in the place of the sound her senses received another impression—that of a curious physical glow, stealing slowly through her whole body. It was as if there lay in that faded brown writing a smoldering fire that had never wholly died out and would never be extinguished until the letters themselves had been burned into ashes.

Word by word, line by line, page by page, the whole tragic, passionate legend came to recreate itself, until near the end she was able to see the three principal actors in it with the reality of life, as if they had never died at all but had gone on living in this old house, perhaps in this very room where she sat . . . the very room which once must have belonged to Savina Pentland.

She saw the husband, that Jared Pentland of whom no portrait existed because he would never spend money on such a luxury, as he must have been in life—a sly man, shrewd and pious and avaricious save when the strange dark passion for his wife made of him an unbalanced creature. And Savina Pentland herself was there, as she looked out of the Ingres portrait —dark, voluptuous, reckless, with her bad enticing eyes—a woman who might easily be the ruin of a man like Jared Pentland. And somehow she was able to get a clear and vivid picture of the writer of those smoldering letters— a handsome scamp of a lover, dark like his cousin Savina, and given to drinking and gambling. But most of all she was aware of that direct, unashamed and burning passion that never had its roots in this stony New England soil beyond the windows of Pentlands. A man who frankly glorified the flesh! A waster! A seducer! And yet a man capable of this magnificent fire which leaped up from the yellow pages and warmed her through and through. It occurred to her then for the first time that there was something heroic and noble and beautiful in a passion so intense. For a moment she was even seized by the feeling that reading these letters was a kind of desecration.

They revealed, too, how Jared Pentland had looked upon his beautiful wife as a fine piece of property, an investment which gave him a sensual satisfaction and also glorified his house and dinner-table. (What Sabine called the "lower middle-class sense of property.") He must have loved her and hated her at once, in the way Higgins loved and hated the handsome red mare. He must have been proud of her and yet hated her because she possessed so completely the power of making a fool of him. The whole story moved against a background of family . . . the Pentland family. There were constant references to cousins and uncles and aunts and their suspicions and interference.

"It must have begun," thought Olivia, "even in those days."

Out of the letters she learned that the passion had begun in Rome when Savina Pentland was sitting for her portrait by Ingres. Toby Cane had been there with her and afterwards she had gone with him to his lodgings: and when they had returned to the house at Durham (almost new then and the biggest country seat in all New England) they had met in the cottage—Brook Cottage, which still stood there within sight of Olivia's window—Brook Cottage, which after the drowning had been bought by Sabine's grandfather and then fallen into ruins and been restored again by the too-bright, vulgar, resplendent touch of O'Hara. It was an immensely complicated and intricate story which went back, back into the past and seemed to touch them all here in Durham.

"The roots of life at Pentlands," thought Olivia, "go down, down into the past. There are no new branches, no young, vigorous shoots."

She came at length to the last of the letters, which had buried in its midst the terrible revealing lines—

If you knew what delight it gives me to have you write that the child is ours beyond any doubt, that there cannot be the slightest doubt of it! The baby belongs to us . . . to us alone! It has nothing to do with him. I could not bear the idea of his thinking that the child is his if it was not that it makes your position secure. The thought tortures me but I am able to bear it because it leaves you safe and above suspicion.

Slowly, thoughtfully, as if unable to believe her eyes, she reread the lines through again, and then placed her hands against her head with a gesture of feeling suddenly weak and out of her mind.

She tried to think clearly. "Savina Pentland never had but one child, so far as I know . . . never but one. And that must have been Toby Cane's child."

There could be no doubt. It was all there, in writing. The child was the child of Toby Cane and a woman who was born Savina Dalgedo. He was not a Pentland and none of his descendants had been Pentlands . . . not one.

They were not Pentlands at all save as the descendants of Savina and her lover had married among the Brahmins where Pentland blood was in every family. They were not Pentlands by blood and yet they were Pentlands beyond any question, in conduct, in point of view, in tradition. It occurred to Olivia for the first time how immense and terrible a thing was that environment, that air which held them all enchanted . . . all the cloud of prejudices and traditions and prides and small anxieties. It was a world so set, so powerful, so iron-bound that it had made Pentlands of people like Anson and Aunt Cassie, even like her father-in-law. It made Pentlands of people who were not Pentlands at all. She saw it now as an overwhelming, terrifying power that was a part of the old house. It stood rooted in the very soil of all the landscape that spread itself beyond her windows.

And in the midst of this realization she had a swift impulse to laugh, hysterically, for the picture of Anson had come to her suddenly . . . Anson pouring his whole soul into that immense glorification to be known as "The Pentland Family and the Massachusetts Bay Colony."

Slowly, as the first shock melted away a little, she began to believe that the yellowed bits of paper were a sort of infernal machine, an instrument with the power of shattering a whole world. What was she to do with this thing—this curious symbol of a power that always won every struggle in one way or another, directly as in the case of Savina and her lover, or by taking its vengeance upon body or soul as it had done in the case of Aunt Cassie's poor, prying, scheming mind? And there was, too, the dark story of Horace Pentland, and the madness of the old woman in the north wing, and even those sudden terrible bouts of drinking which made so fine a man as John Pentland into something very near to a beast.

It was as if a light of blinding clarity had been turned upon all the long procession of ancestors. She saw now that if "The Pentland Family and the Massachusetts Bay Colony" was to have any value at all as truth it must be rewritten in the light of the struggle between the forces glorified by that drunken scamp Toby Cane and this other terrible force which seemed to be all about her everywhere, pressing even herself slowly into its own mold. It was an old struggle between those who chose to find their pleasure in this world and those who looked for the vague promise of a glorified future existence.

She could see Anson writing in his book, "In the present generation (192-) there exists Cassandra Pentland Struthers (Mrs. Edward Cane Struthers), a widow who has distinguished herself by her devotion to the Episcopal Church and to charity and good works. She resides in winter in Boston and in summer at her country house near Durham on the land claimed from the wilderness by the first Pentland, distinguished founder of the American family."

Yes, Anson would write just those words in his book. He would describe thus the old woman who sat belowstairs hoping all the while that Olivia would descend bearing the news of some new tragedy . . . that virginal old woman who had ruined the whole life of her husband and kept poor half-witted Miss Peavey a prisoner for nearly thirty years.

The murmur of voices died away presently and Olivia, looking out of the window, saw that it was Aunt Cassie who had won this time. She was standing in the garden looking down the drive with that malignant expression which sometimes appeared on her face in moments when she thought herself alone. Far down the shadow-speckled drive, the figure of Sabine moved indolently away in the direction of Brook Cottage. Sabine, too, belonged in a way to the family; she had grown up enveloped in the powerful tradition which made Pentlands of people who were not Pentlands at all. Perhaps (thought Olivia) the key to Sabine's restless, unhappy existence also lay in the same dark struggle. Perhaps if one could penetrate deeply enough in the long family history one would find there the reasons for Sabine's hatred of this Durham world and the reasons why she had returned to a people she disliked with all the bitter, almost fanatic passion of her nature. There was in Sabine an element of cold cruelty.

At the sight of Olivia coming down the steps into the garden, Aunt Cassie turned and moved forward quickly with a look of expectancy, asking, "And how is the poor thing?"

And at Olivia's answer, "She's quiet now . . . sleeping. It's all passed," the look changed to one of disappointment.

She said, with an abysmal sigh, "Ah, she will go on forever. She'll be alive long after I've gone to join dear Mr. Struthers."

"Invalids are like that," replied Olivia, by way of saying something. "They take such care of themselves." And almost at once, she thought, "Here I am playing the family game, pretending that she's not mad but only an invalid."

She had no feeling of resentment against the busy old woman; indeed it seemed to her at times that she had almost an affection for Aunt Cassie —the sort of affection one has for an animal or a bit of furniture which has been about almost as long as one can remember. And at the moment the figure of Aunt Cassie, the distant sight of Sabine, the bright garden full of flowers . . . all these things seemed to her melodramatic and unreal, for she was still living in the Pentlands of Savina and Toby Cane. It was impossible to fix her attention on Aunt Cassie and her flutterings.

The old lady was saying, "You all seem to have grown very fond of this man O'Hara."

(What was she driving at now?) Aloud, Olivia said, "Why not? He's agreeable, intelligent . . . even distinguished in his way."

"Yes," said Aunt Cassie. "I've been discussing him with Sabine, and I've come to the conclusion that I may have been wrong about him. She thinks him a clever man with a great future." There was a pause and she added with an air of making a casual observation, "But what about his past? I mean where does he come from."

"I know all about it. He's been telling me. That's why I was late this morning."

For a time Aunt Cassie was silent, as if weighing some deep problem.

At last she said, "I was wondering about seeing too much of him. He has a bad reputation with women. . . . At least, so I'm told."

Olivia laughed. "After all, Aunt Cassie, I'm a grown woman. I can look out for myself."

"Yes. . . . I know." She turned with a disarming smile of Christian sweetness. "I don't want you to think that I'm interfering, Olivia. It's the last thing I'd think of doing. But I was considering your own good. It's harmless enough, I'm sure. No one would ever think otherwise, knowing you, my dear. But it's what people will say. There was a scandal I believe about eight years ago . . . a road-house scandal!" She said this with an air of great suffering, as if the words "road-house scandal" seared her lips.

"I suppose so. Most men . . . politicians, I mean . . . have scandals connected with their names. It's part of the business, Aunt Cassie."

And she kept thinking with amazement of the industry of the old lady— that she should have taken the trouble of going far back into O'Hara's past to find some definite thing against him. She did not doubt the ultimate truth of Aunt Cassie's insinuation. Aunt Cassie did not lie deliberately; there was always a grain of truth in her implications, though sometimes the poor grain lay buried so deeply beneath exaggerations that it was almost impossible to discover it. And a thing like that might easily be true about O'Hara. With a man like him you couldn't expect women to play the rôle they played with a man like Anson.

"It's only on account of what people will say," repeated Aunt Cassie.

"I've almost come to the conclusion that what people say doesn't really matter any longer. . . ."

Aunt Cassie began suddenly to pick a bouquet from the border beside her. "Oh, it's not you I'm worrying about, Olivia dear. But we have to consider others sometimes. . . . There's Sybil and Anson, and even the very name of Pentland. There's never been any such suspicion attached to it . . . ever."

It was incredible (thought Olivia) that any one would make such a statement, incredible anywhere else in the world. She wanted to ask, "What about your brother and old Mrs. Soames?" And in view of those letters that lay locked in her dressing-table. . . .

At that moment lunch was announced by Peters' appearance in the doorway. Olivia turned to Aunt Cassie, "You're staying, of course."

"No, I must go. You weren't expecting me."

So Olivia began the ancient game, played for so many years, of pressing Aunt Cassie to stay to lunch.

"It makes no difference," she said, "only another plate." And so on through a whole list of arguments that she had memorized long ago. And at last Aunt Cassie, with the air of having been pressed beyond her endurance, yielded, and to Peters, who had also played the game for years, Olivia said, "Lay another place for Mrs. Struthers."

She had meant to stay all along. Lunching out saved both money and trouble, for Miss Peavey ate no more than a bird, at least not openly; and, besides, there were things she must find out at Pentlands, and other things which she must plan. In truth, wild horses could not have dragged her away.

As they entered the house, Aunt Cassie, carrying the bouquet she had plucked, said casually, "I met the Mannering boy on the road this morning and told him to come in to-night. I thought you wouldn't mind. He's very fond of Sybil, you know."

"No, of course not," replied Olivia. "I don't mind. But I'm afraid Sybil isn't very interested in him."

Chapter 8

1

THE DEATH of Horace Pentland was not an event to be kept quiet by so simple a means as a funeral that was almost secret; news of it leaked out and was carried here and there by ladies eager to rake up an old Pentland scandal in vengeance upon Aunt Cassie, the community's principal disseminator of calamities. It even penetrated at last the offices of the *Transcript*, which sent a request for an obituary of the dead man, for he was, after all, a member of one of Boston's proudest families. And then, without warning, the ghost of Horace Pentland reappeared suddenly in the most disconcerting of all quarters—Brook Cottage.

The ghost accompanied Sabine up the long drive one hot morning while Olivia sat listening to Aunt Cassie. Olivia noticed that Sabine approached them with an unaccustomed briskness, that all trace of the familiar indolence had vanished. As she reached the edge of the terrace, she called out with a bright look in her eyes, "I have news . . . of Cousin Horace."

She was enjoying the moment keenly, and the sight of her enjoyment must have filled Aunt Cassie, who knew her so well, with uneasiness. She took her own time about revealing the news, inquiring first after Aunt Cassie's health, and settling herself comfortably in one of the wicker chairs. She was an artist in the business of tormenting the old lady and she waited now to squeeze every drop of effect out of her announcement. She was not to be hurried even by the expression which Aunt Cassie's face inevitably assumed at the mention of Horace Pentland—the expression of one who finds himself in the vicinity of a bad smell and is unable to escape.

At last, after lighting a cigarette and moving her chair out of the sun, Sabine announced in a flat voice, "Cousin Horace has left everything he possesses to me."

A look of passionate relief swept Aunt Cassie's face, a look which said, "Pooh! Pooh! Is that all?" She laughed—it was almost a titter, colored by mockery—and said, "Is that all? I imagine it doesn't make you a great heiress."

("Aunt Cassie," thought Olivia, "ought not to have given Sabine such an opportunity; she has said just what Sabine wanted her to say.")

Sabine answered her: "But you're wrong there, Aunt Cassie. It's not money that he's left, but furniture . . . furniture and bibelots . . . and it's a wonderful collection. I've seen it myself when I visited him at Mentone."

"You ought never to have gone. . . . You certainly have lost all moral sense, Sabine. You've forgotten all that I taught you as a little girl."

Sabine ignored her. "You see, he worshiped such things, and he spent twenty years of his life collecting them."

"It seems improbable that they could be worth much . . . with as little money as Horace Pentland had . . . only what we let him have to live on."

Sabine smiled again, sardonically, perhaps because the tilt with Aunt Cassie proved so successful. "You're wrong again, Aunt Cassie. . . . They're worth a great deal . . . far more than he paid for them, because there are things in his collection which you couldn't buy elsewhere for any amount of money. He took to trading pieces off until his collection became nearly perfect." She paused for a moment, allowing the knife to rest in the wound. "It's an immensely valuable collection. You see, I know about it because I used to see Cousin Horace every winter when I went to Rome. I knew more about him than any of you. He was a man of perfect taste in such things. He really knew."

Olivia sat all the while watching the scene with a quiet amusement. The triumph on this occasion was clearly Sabine's, and Sabine knew it. She sat there enjoying every moment of it, watching Aunt Cassie writhe at the thought of so valuable a heritage going out of the direct family, to so remote and hostile a connection. It was clearly a disaster ranking in importance with the historic loss of Savina Pentland's parure of pearls and emeralds at the bottom of the Atlantic Ocean. It was property lost forever that should have gone into the family fortune.

Sabine was opening the letter slowly, allowing the paper to crackle ominously, as if she knew that every crackle ran painfully up and down the spine of the old lady.

"It's the invoice from the Custom House," she said, lifting each of the five long sheets separately. "Five pages long . . . total value perhaps as much as seventy-five thousand dollars. . . . Of course there's not even any duty to pay, as they're all old things."

Aunt Cassie started, as if seized by a sudden pain, and Sabine continued. "He even left provision for shipping it . . . all save four or five big pieces which are being held at Mentone. There are eighteen cases in all."

She began to read the items one by one . . . cabinets, commodes, chairs, lusters, tables, pictures, bits of bronze, crystal and jade . . . all the long list of things which Horace Pentland had gathered with the loving care of a connoisseur during the long years of his exile; and in the midst of the reading, Aunt Cassie, unable any longer to control herself, interrupted, saying,

"It seems to me he was an ungrateful, disgusting man. It ought to have gone to my dear brother, who supported him all these years. I don't see why he left it all to a remote cousin like you."

Sabine delved again into the envelope. "Wait," she said. "He explains that point himself . . . in his own will." She opened a copy of this document and, searching for a moment, read, "To my cousin, Sabine Callendar (Mrs. Cane Callendar), of—Rue de Tilsitt, Paris, France, and Newport, Rhode Island, I leave all my collections of furniture, tapestries, bibelots, etc., in gratitude for her kindness to me over a period of many years and in return for her faith and understanding at a time when the rest of my family treated me as an outcast."

Aunt Cassie was beside herself. "And how should he have been treated if not as an outcast? He was an ungrateful, horrible wretch! It was Pentland money which supported him all his miserable life." She paused a moment for breath. "I always told my dear brother that twenty-five hundred a year was far more than Horace Pentland needed. And that is how he has spent it, to insult the very people who were kind to him."

Sabine put the papers back in the envelope and, looking up, said in her hard, metallic voice: "Money's not everything, as I told you once before, Aunt Cassie. I've always said that the trouble with the Pentlands . . . with most of Boston, for that matter . . . lies in the fact that they were lower middle-class shopkeepers to begin with and they've never lost any of the lower middle-class virtues . . . especially about money. They've been proud of living off the income of their incomes. . . . No, it wasn't money that Horace Pentland wanted. It was a little decency and kindness and intelligence. I fancy you got your money's worth out of the poor twenty-five hundred dollars you sent him every year. It was worth a great deal more than that to keep the truth under a bushel."

A long and painful silence followed this speech and Olivia, turning toward Sabine, tried to reproach her with a glance for speaking thus to the old lady. Aunt Cassie was being put to rout so pitifully, not only by Sabine, but by Horace Pentland, who had taken his vengeance shrewdly, long after he was dead, by striking at the Pentland sense of possessions, of property.

The light of triumph glittered in the green eyes of Sabine. She was paying back, bit by bit, the long account of her unhappy childhood; and she had not yet finished.

Olivia, watching the conflict with disinterest, was swept suddenly by a feeling of pity for the old lady. She broke the painful silence by asking them both to stay for lunch, but this time Aunt Cassie refused, in all sincerity, and Olivia did not press her, knowing that she could not bear to face the ironic grin of Sabine until she had rested and composed her face. Aunt Cassie seemed suddenly tired and old this morning. The indefatigable, meddling spirit seemed to droop, no longer flying proudly in the wind.

The queer, stuffy motor appeared suddenly on the drive, the back seat filled by the rotund form of Miss Peavey surrounded by four yapping Pekinese. The intricate veils which she wore on entering a motor streamed behind her. Aunt Cassie rose and, kissing Olivia with ostentation, turned to Sabine and went back again to the root of the matter. "I always told my dear brother," she repeated, "that twenty-five hundred a year was far too much for Horace Pentland."

The motor rattled off, and Sabine, laying the letter on the table beside her, said, "Of course, I don't want all this stuff of Cousin Horace's, but I'm determined it shan't go to her. If she had it the poor old man wouldn't rest in his grave. Besides, she wouldn't know what to do with it in a house filled with tassels and antimacassars and souvenirs of Uncle Ned. She'd only sell it and invest the money in invincible securities."

"She's not well . . . the poor old thing," said Olivia. "She wouldn't have had the motor come for her if she'd been well. She's pretended all her life, and now she's really ill—she's terrified at the idea of death. She can't bear it."

The old relentless, cruel smile lighted Sabine's face. "No, now that the time has come she hasn't much faith in the Heaven she's preached all her life." There was a brief silence and Sabine added grimly, "She will certainly be a nuisance to Saint Peter."

But there was only sadness in Olivia's dark eyes, because she kept thinking what a shallow, futile life Aunt Cassie's had been. She had turned her back upon life from the beginning, even with the husband whom she married as a convenience. She kept thinking what a poor barren thing that life had been; how little of richness, of memories, it held, now that it was coming to an end.

Sabine was speaking again. "I know you're thinking that I'm heartless, but you don't know how cruel she was to me . . . what things she did to me as a child." Her voice softened a little, but in pity for herself and not for Aunt Cassie. It was as if the ghost of the queer, unhappy, red-haired little girl of her childhood had come suddenly to stand there beside them where the ghost of Horace Pentland had stood a little while before. The old ghosts were crowding about once more, even there on the terrace in the hot August sunlight in the beauty of Olivia's flowery garden.

"She sent me into the world," continued Sabine's hard voice, "knowing nothing but what was false, believing—the little I believed in anything—in false gods, thinking that marriage was no more than a business contract between two young people with fortunes. She called ignorance by the name of innocence and quoted the Bible and that milk-and-water philosopher Emerson . . . 'dear Mr. Emerson' . . . whenever I asked her a direct, sensible question. . . . And all she accomplished was to give me a hunger for facts—hard, unvarnished facts—pleasant or unpleasant."

A kind of hot passion entered the metallic voice, so that it took on an unaccustomed warmth and beauty. "You don't know how much she is responsible for in my life. She . . . and all the others like her . . . killed my chance of happiness, of satisfaction. She cost me my husband. . . . What chance had I with a man who came from an older, wiser world . . . a world in which things were looked at squarely, and honestly as truth . . . a man who expected women to be women and not timid icebergs? No, I don't think I shall ever forgive her." She paused for a moment, thoughtfully, and then added, "And whatever she did, whatever cruelties she practised, whatever nonsense she preached, was always done in the name of duty and always 'for your own good, my dear.'"

Then abruptly, with a bitter smile, her whole manner changed and took on once more the old air of indolent, almost despairing, boredom. "I couldn't begin to tell you all, my dear. . . . It goes back too far. We're all rotten here . . . not so much rotten as desiccated, for there was never much blood in us to rot. . . . The roots go deep. . . . But I shan't bore you again with all this, I promise."

Olivia, listening, wanted to say, "You don't know how much blood there is in the Pentlands. . . . You don't know that they aren't Pentlands at all, but the children of Savina Dalgedo and Toby Cane. . . . But even that hasn't mattered. . . . The very air, the very earth of New England, has changed them, dried them up."

But she could not say it, for she knew that the story of those letters must never fall into the hands of the unscrupulous Sabine.

"It doesn't bore me," said Olivia quietly. "It doesn't bore me. I understand it much too well."

"In any case, we've spoiled enough of one fine day with it." Sabine lighted another cigarette and said with an abrupt change of tone, "About this furniture, Olivia. . . . I don't want it. I've a house full of such things in Paris. I shouldn't know what to do with it and I don't think I have the right to break it up and sell it. I want you to have it here at Pentlands. . . . Horace Pentland would be satisfied if it went to you and Cousin John. And it'll be an excuse to clear out some of the Victorian junk and some of the terrible early American stuff. Plenty of people will buy the early American things. The best of them are only bad imitations of the real things Horace Pentland collected, and you might as well have the real ones."

Olivia protested, but Sabine pushed the point, scarcely giving her time to speak. "I want you to do it. It will be a kindness to me . . . and after all, Horace Pentland's furniture ought to be here . . . in Pentlands. I'll take one or two things for Thérèse, and the rest you must keep, only nothing . . . not so much as a medallion or a snuff-box . . . is to go to Aunt Cassie. She hated him while he was alive. It would be wrong for her to possess anything belonging to him after he is dead. Besides," she added, "a little new furniture would do a great deal toward cheering up the house. It's always been rather spare and cold. It needs a little elegance and sense of luxury. There has never been any splendor in the Pentland family—or in all New England, for that matter."

2

At almost the same moment that Olivia and Sabine entered the old house to lunch, the figures of Sybil and Jean appeared against the horizon on the rim of the great, bald hill crowned by the town burial-ground. Escaped at length from the eye of the curious, persistent Thérèse, they had come to the hill to eat their lunch in the open air. It was a brilliantly clear day and the famous view lay spread out beneath them like some vast map stretching away for a distance of nearly thirty miles. The marshes appeared green and dark, crossed and recrossed by a reticulation of tidal inlets frequented at nightfall by small boats which brought in whisky and rum from the open sea. There were, distantly visible, great piles of reddish rock rising from the endless white ribbon of beach, and far out on the amethyst sea a pair of white-sailed fishing-boats moved away in the direction of Gloucester. The white sails, so near to each other, carried a warm friendliness in a universe magnificent but also bleak and a little barren.

Coming over the rim of the hill the sudden revelation of the view halted them for a moment. The day was hot, but here on the great hill, remote from the damp, low-lying meadows, there was a fresh cool wind, almost a gale, blowing in from the open sea. Sybil, taking off her hat, tossed it to the ground and allowed the wind to blow her hair in a dark, tangled mass about the serious young face; and at the same moment Jean, seized by a sudden quick impulse, took her hand quietly in his. She did not attempt to draw it away; she simply stood there quietly, as if conscious only of the wild beauty of the landscape spread out below them and the sense of the boy's nearness to her. The old fear of depression and loneliness seemed to have melted away from her; here on this high brown hill, with all the world spread out beneath, it seemed to her that they were completely alone . . . the first and the last two people in all the world. She was aware that a perfect thing had happened to her, so perfect and so far beyond the realm of her most romantic imaginings that it seemed scarcely real.

A flock of glistening white gulls, sweeping in from the sea, soared toward them screaming wildly, and she said, "We'd better find a place to eat."

She had taken from the hands of Sabine the task of showing Jean this little corner of his own country, and to-day they had come to see the view from the burial-ground and read the moldering queer old inscriptions on the tombstones. On entering the graveyard they came almost at once to the little corner allotted long ago to immigrants with the name of Pentland—a corner nearly filled now with neat rows of graves. By the side of the latest two, still new and covered with fresh sod, they halted, and she began in silence to separate the flowers she had brought from her mother's garden into two great bunches.

"This," she said, pointing to the grave at her feet, "is his. The other grave is Cousin Horace Pentland's, whom I never saw. He died in Mentone. . . . He was a first cousin of my grandfather."

Jean helped her to fill the two vases with water and place the flowers in them. When she had finished she stood up, with a sigh, very straight and slender, saying, "I wish you had known him, Jean. You would have liked him. He was always good-humored and he liked everything in the world . . . only he was never strong enough to do much but lie in bed or sit on the terrace in the sun."

The tears came quietly into her eyes, not at sorrow over the death of her brother, but at the pathos of his poor, weak existence; and Jean, moved by a quick sense of pity, took her hand again and this time kissed it, in the quaint, dignified foreign way he had of doing such things.

They knew each other better now, far better than on the enchanted morning by the edge of the river; and there were times, like this, when to have spoken would have shattered the whole precious spell. There was less of shyness between them than of awe at the thing which had happened to them. At that moment he wanted to keep her forever thus, alone with him, on this high barren hill, to protect her and feel her always there at his side touching his arm gently. Here, in such a place, they would be safe from all the unhappiness and the trouble which in a vague way he knew was inevitably a part of living.

As they walked along the narrow path between the rows of chipped, worn old stones they halted now and then to read some half-faded, crumbling epitaph set forth in the vigorous, Biblical language of the first hardy settlers —sometimes amused, sometimes saddened, by the quaint sentiments. They passed rows of Sutherlands and Featherstones and Canes and Mannerings, all turned to dust long ago, the good New England names of that little corner of the world; and at length they came to a little colony of graves with the name Milford cut into each stone. Here there were no new monuments, for the family had disappeared long ago from the Durham world.

In the midst of these Jean halted suddenly and, bending over one of the stones, said, "Milford . . . Milford. . . . That's odd. I had a great-grandfather named Milford who came from this part of the country."

"There used to be a great many Milfords here, but there haven't been any since I can remember."

"My great-grandfather was a preacher," said Jean. "A Congregationalist. He led all his congregation into the Middle West. They founded the town my mother came from."

For a moment Sybil was silent. "Was his name Josiah Milford?" she asked.

"Yes. . . . That was his name."

"He came from Durham. And after he left, the church died slowly. It's still standing . . . the big white church with the spire, on High Street. It's only a museum now."

Jean laughed. "Then we're not so far apart, after all. It's almost as if we were related."

"Yes, because a Pentland did marry a Milford once, a long time ago . . . more than a hundred years, I suppose."

The discovery made her happy in a vague way, perhaps because she knew it made him seem less what they called an "outsider" at Pentlands. It wouldn't be so hard to say to her father, "I want to marry Jean de Cyon. You know his ancestors came from Durham." The name of Milford would make an impression upon a man like her father, who made a religion of names; but, then, Jean had not even asked her to marry him yet. For some reason he had kept silent, saying nothing of marriage, and the silence clouded her happiness at being near him.

"It's odd,". said Jean, suddenly absorbed, in the way of men, over this concrete business of ancestry. "Some of these Milfords must be direct ancestors of mine and I've no idea which ones they are."

"When we go down the hill," she said, "I'll take you to the meeting-house and show you the tablet that records the departure of the Reverend Josiah Milford and his congregation."

She answered him almost without thinking what she was saying, disappointed suddenly that the discovery should have broken in upon the perfection of the mood that united them a little while before.

They found a grassy spot sheltered from the August sun by the leaves of a stunted wild-cherry tree, all twisted by the sea winds, and there Sybil seated herself to open their basket and spread the lunch—the chicken, the crisp sandwiches, the fruit. The whole thing seemed an adventure, as if they were alone on a desert island, and the small act gave her a new kind of pleasure, a sort of primitive delight in serving him while he stood looking down at her with a frank grin of admiration.

When she had finished he flung himself down at full length on the grass beside her, to eat with the appetite of a great, healthy man given to violent physical exercise. They ate almost in silence, saying very little, looking out over the marshes and the sea. From time to time she grew aware that he was watching her with a curious light in his blue eyes, and when they had finished, he sat up cross-legged like a tailor, to smoke; and presently, without looking at her he said, "A little while ago, when we first came up the hill, you let me take your hand, and you didn't mind."

"No," said Sybil swiftly. She had begun to tremble a little, frightened but wildly happy.

"Was it because . . . because. . . ." He groped for a moment for words and, finding them, went quickly on, "because you feel as I do?"

She answered him in a whisper. "I don't know," she said, and suddenly she felt an overwhelming desire to weep.

"I mean," he said quietly, "that I feel we were made for each other . . . perfectly."

"Yes . . . Jean."

He did not wait for her to finish. He rushed on, overwhelming her in a quick burst of boyish passion. "I wish it wasn't necessary to talk. Words spoil everything. . . . They aren't good enough. . . . No, you must take me, Sybil. Sometimes I'm disagreeable and impatient and selfish . . . but you must take me. I'll do my best to reform. I'll make you happy. . . . I'll do anything for you. And we can go away together anywhere in the world . . . always together, never alone . . . just as we are here, on the top of this hill."

Without waiting for her to answer, he kissed her quickly, with a warm tenderness that made her weep once more. She said over and over again, "I'm so happy, Jean . . . so happy." And then, shamefacedly, "I must confess something. . . . I was afraid you'd never come back, and I wanted you always . . . from the very beginning. I meant to have you from the beginning . . . from that first day in Paris."

He lay with his head in her lap while she stroked the thick, red hair, in silence. There in the graveyard, high above the sea, they lost themselves in the illusion which overtakes such young lovers . . . that they had come already to the end of life . . . that, instead of beginning, it was already complete and perfect.

"I meant to have you always . . . Jean. And after you came here and didn't come over to see me . . . I decided to go after you . . . for fear that you'd escape again. I was shameless . . . and a fraud, too. . . . That morning by the river . . . I didn't come on you by accident. I knew you were there all the while. I hid in the thicket and waited for you."

"It wouldn't have made the least difference. I meant to have you, too." A sudden impatient frown shadowed the young face. "You won't let anything change you, will you? Nothing that any one might say . . . nothing that might happen . . . not anything?"

"Not anything," she repeated. "Not anything in the world. Nothing could change me."

"And you wouldn't mind going away from here with me?"

"No. . . . I'd like that. It's what I have always wanted. I'd be glad to go away."

"Even to the Argentine?"

"Anywhere . . . anywhere at all."

"We can be married very soon . . . before I leave . . . and then we can go to Paris to see my mother." He sat up abruptly with an odd, troubled look on his face. "She's a wonderful woman, darling . . . beautiful and kind and charming."

"I thought she was lovely . . . that day in Paris . . . the most fascinating woman I'd ever seen, Jean dear."

He seemed not to be listening to her. The wind was beginning to die away with the heat of the afternoon, and far out on the amethyst sea the two sailing ships lay becalmed and motionless. Even the leaves of the twisted wild-cherry tree hung listlessly in the hot air. All the world about them had turned still and breathless.

Turning, he took both her hands and looked at her. "There's something

I must tell you . . . Sybil . . . something you may not like. But you mustn't let it make any difference. . . . In the end things like that don't matter."

She interrupted him. "If it's about women . . . I don't care. I know what you are, Jean. . . . I'll never know any better than I know now. . . . I don't care."

"No . . . what I want to tell you isn't about women. It's about my mother." He looked at her directly, piercingly. "You see . . . my mother and my father were never married. Good old Monsieur de Cyon only adopted me. . . . I've no right to the name . . . really. My name is really John Shane. . . . They were never married, only it's not the way it sounds. She's a great lady, my mother, and she refused to marry my father because . . . she says . . . she says she found out that he wasn't what she thought him. He begged her to. He said it ruined his whole life . . . but she wouldn't marry him . . . not because she was weak, but because she was strong. You'll understand that when you come to know her."

What he said would have shocked her more deeply if she had not been caught in the swift passion of a rebellion against all the world about her, all the prejudices and the misunderstandings that in her young wisdom she knew would be ranged against herself and Jean. In this mood, the mother of Jean became to her a sort of heroic symbol, a woman to be admired.

She leaned toward him. "It doesn't matter . . . not at all, Jean . . . things like that don't matter in the end. . . . All that matters is the future. . . ." She looked away from him and added in a low voice, "Besides, what I have to tell you is much worse." She pressed his hand savagely. "You won't let it change you? You'll not give me up? Maybe you know it already . . . that I have a grandmother who is mad. . . . She's been mad for years . . . almost all her life."

He kissed her quickly. "No, it won't matter. . . . Nothing could make me think of giving you up . . . nothing in the world."

"I'm so happy, Jean . . . and so peaceful . . . as if you had saved me . . . as if you'd changed all my life. I've been frightened sometimes. . . ."

But a sudden cloud had darkened the happiness . . . the cloud that was never absent from the house at Pentlands.

"You won't let your father keep us apart, Sybil. . . . He doesn't like me. . . . It's easy to see that."

"No, I shan't let him." She halted abruptly. "What I am going to say may sound dreadful. . . . I shouldn't take my father's word about anything. I wouldn't let him influence me. He's spoiled his own life and my mother's too. . . . I feel sorry for my father. . . . He's so blind . . . and he fusses so . . . always about things which don't matter."

For a long time they sat in silence, Sybil with her eyes closed leaning against him, when suddenly she heard him saying in a fierce whisper, "That damned Thérèse!" and looking up she saw at the rim of the hill beyond the decaying tombstones, the stocky figure of Thérèse, armed with an insect-net and a knapsack full of lunch. She was standing with her legs rather well apart, staring at them out of her queer gray eyes with a mischievous, humorous expression. Behind her in a semicircle stood a little army of dirty Polish children she had recruited to help her collect bugs. They knew that she had followed them deliberately to spy on them, and they knew that she would pretend blandly that she had come upon them quite by accident.

"Shall we tell her?" asked Jean in a furious whisper.

"No . . . never tell anything in Durham."

The spell was broken now and Jean was angry. Rising, he shouted at Thérèse, "Go and chase your old bugs and leave us in peace!" He knew that, like her mother, Thérèse was watching them scientifically, as if they were a pair of insects.

3

Anson Pentland was not by nature a malicious man or even a very disagreeable one; his fussy activities on behalf of Morality arose from no suppressed, twisted impulse of his own toward vice. Indeed, he was a man of very few impulses—a rather stale, flat man who espoused the cause of Morality because it belonged to his tradition and therefore should be encouraged. He was, according to Sabine, something far worse than an abandoned lecher; he was a bore, and a not very intelligent one, who only saw straight along his own thin nose the tiny sector of the universe in which circumstance had placed him. After forty-nine years of staring, his gaze had turned myopic, and the very physical objects which surrounded him—his house, his office, his table, his desk, his pen—had come to be objects unique and glorified by their very presence as utensils of a society the most elevated and perfect in existence. Possessed of an immense and intricate *savoir-faire* he lacked even a suspicion of *savoir-vivre*, and so tradition, custom, convention, had made of his life a shriveled affair, without initiative or individuality, slipping along the narrow groove of ways set and uninteresting. It was this, perhaps, which lay at the root of Sybil's pity for him.

Worshiping the habit of his stale world, he remained content and even amiable so long as no attack was made upon his dignity—a sacred and complicated affair which embraced his house, his friends, his clubs, his ancestors, even to the small possessions allowed him by his father. Yet this dignity was also a frail affair, easily subject to collapse . . . a sort of thin shell enclosing and protecting him. He guarded it with a maidenly and implacable zeal. When all the threats and pleadings of Aunt Cassie moved him to nothing more definite than an uneasy sort of evasion, a threat at any of the things which came within the realm of his dignity set loose an unsuspected, spiteful hatred.

He resented O'Hara because he knew perhaps that the Irishman regarded him and his world with cynicism; and it was O'Hara and Irishmen like him —Democrats (thought Anson) and therefore the scum of the earth—who had broken down the perfect, chilled, set model of Boston life. Sabine he hated for the same reasons; and from the very beginning he had taken a dislike to "that young de Cyon" because the young man seemed to stand entirely alone, independent of such dignities, without sign even of respect for them. And he was, too, inextricably allied with O'Hara and Sabine and the "outlandish Thérèse."

Olivia suspected that he grew shrill and hysterical only at times when he was tormented by a suspicion of their mockery. It was then that he became unaccountable for what he said and did . . . unaccountable as he had been on that night after the ball. She understood that each day made him more acutely sensitive of his dignity, for he was beginning to interpret the smallest hint as an attack upon it.

Knowing these things, she had come to treat him always as a child, humoring and wheedling him until in the end she achieved what she desired, painlessly and surely. She treated him thus in the matter of refurnishing the house. Knowing that he was absorbed in finishing the final chapters of "The Pentland Family and the Massachusetts Bay Colony," she suggested that he move his table into the distant "writing-room" where he would be less disturbed by family activities; and Anson, believing that at last his wife was impressed by the importance and dignity of his work, considered the suggestion an excellent one. He even smiled and thanked her.

Then, after having consulted old John Pentland and finding that he approved the plan, she began bit by bit to insinuate the furniture of Horace Pentland into the house. Sabine came daily to watch the progress of the change, to comment and admire and suggest changes. They found an odd excitement in the emergence of one beautiful object after another from its chrysalis of *emballage;* out of old rags and shavings there appeared the most exquisite of tables and cabinets, bits of chinoiserie, old books and engravings. One by one the ugly desk used by Mr. Lowell, the monstrous lamp presented by Mr. Longfellow, the anemic water-colors of Miss Maria Pentland . . . all the furnishings of the museum were moved into the vast old attic; until at length a new drawing-room emerged, resplendent and beautiful, civilized and warm and even a little exotic, dressed in all the treasures which Horace Pentland had spent his life in gathering with passionate care. Quietly and almost without its being noticed, the family skeleton took possession of the house, transforming its whole character.

The change produced in Aunt Cassie a variety of confused and conflicting emotions. It seemed sacrilege to her that the worn, familiar, homely souvenirs of her father's "dear friends" should be relegated into the background, especially by the hand of Horace Pentland; yet it was impossible for her to overlook the actual value of the collection. She saw the objects less as things of rare beauty than in terms of dollars and cents. And, as she had said, "Pentland things ought to find a place in a Pentland house." She suspected Sabine of Machiavellian tactics and could not make up her mind whether Sabine and Horace Pentland had not triumphed in the end over herself and "dear Mr. Lowell" and "good, kind Mr. Longfellow."

Anson, strangely enough, liked the change, with reservations. For a long time he had been conscious of the fact that the drawing-room and much of the rest of the house seemed shabby and worn, and so, unworthy of such dignity as attached to the Pentland name.

He stood in the doorway of the drawing-room, surveying the transformation, and remarked, "The effect seems good . . . a little flamboyant, perhaps, and undignified for such a house, but on the whole . . . good . . . quite good. I myself rather prefer the plain early American furniture. . . ."

To which Sabine replied abruptly, "But it makes hard sitting."

Until now there had never been any music at Pentlands, for music was regarded in the family as something you listened to in concert-halls, dressed in your best clothes. Aunt Cassie, with Miss Peavey, had gone regularly for years each Friday afternoon, to sit hatless with a scarf over her head in Symphony Hall listening to "dear Colonel Higginson's orchestra" (which had fallen off so sadly since his death), but she had never learned to distinguish one melody from another. . . . Music at Pentlands had always been a cultural duty, an exercise something akin to attending church. It made no more impression on Aunt Cassie than those occasional trips to Europe when, taking her own world with her, she stayed always at hotels where she would encounter friends from Boston and never be subjected to the strain of barbaric, unsympathetic faces and conversations.

And now, quite suddenly, music at Pentlands became something alive and colorful and human. The tinny old square piano disappeared and in its place there was a great new one bought by Olivia out of her own money. In the evenings the house echoed to the sound of Chopin and Brahms, Beethoven and Bach, and even such barbaric newcomers as Stravinsky and Ravel. Old Mrs. Soames came, when she was well enough, to sit in the most comfortable of the Regence chairs with old John Pentland at her side, listening while the shadow of youth returned to her half-blind old eyes. The sound of Jean's music penetrated sometimes as far as the room of the mad old woman in the north wing and into the writing-room, where it disturbed Anson working on "The Pentland Family and the Massachusetts Bay Colony."

And then one night, O'Hara came in after dinner, dressed in clothes cut rather too obviously along radically fashionable lines. It was the first time he had ever set foot on Pentland soil.

4

There were times now when Aunt Cassie told herself that Olivia's strange moods had vanished at last, leaving in their place the old docile, pleasant Olivia who had always had a way of smoothing out the troubles at Pentlands. The sudden perilous calm no longer settled over their conversations; Aunt Cassie was no longer fearful of "speaking her mind, frankly, for the good of all of them." Olivia listened to her quietly, and it is true that she was happier in one sense because life at Pentlands seemed to be working itself out; but inwardly, she went her own silent way, grieving in solitude because she dared not add the burden of her grief to that of old John Pentland. Even Sabine, more subtle in such things than Aunt Cassie, came to feel herself quietly shut out from Olivia's confidence.

Sybil, slipping from childhood into womanhood, no longer depended upon her; she even grew withdrawn and secret about Jean, putting her mother off with empty phrases where once she had confided everything. Behind the pleasant, quiet exterior, it seemed to Olivia at times that she had never been so completely, so superbly, alone. She began to see that at Pentlands life came to arrange itself into a series of cubicles, each occupied by a soul shut in from all the others. And she came, for the first time in her life, to spend much time thinking of herself.

With the beginning of autumn she would be forty years old . . . on the verge of middle-age, a woman perhaps with a married daughter. Perhaps at forty-two she would be a grandmother (it seemed likely with such a pair as Sybil and young de Cyon) . . . a grandmother at forty-two with her hair still thick and black, her eyes bright, her face unwrinkled . . . a woman who at forty-two might pass for a woman ten years younger. A grandmother was a grandmother, no matter how youthful she appeared. As a grandmother she could not afford to make herself ridiculous.

She could perhaps persuade Sybil to wait a year or two and so put off the evil day, yet such an idea was even more abhorrent to her. The very panic which sometimes seized her at the thought of turning slowly into an old woman lay also at the root of her refusal to delay Sybil's marriage. What was happening to Sybil had never happened to herself and never could happen now; she was too old, too hard, even too cynical. When one was young like Jean and Sybil, one had an endless store of faith and hope. There was still a glow over all life, and one ought to begin that way. Those first years —no matter what came afterward—would be the most precious in all their existence; and looking about her, she thought, "There are so few who ever have that chance, so few who can build upon a foundation so solid."

Sometimes there returned to her a sudden twinge of the ancient, shameful jealousy which she had felt for Sybil's youth that suffocating night on the terrace overlooking the sea. (In an odd way, all the summer unfolding itself slowly seemed to have grown out of that night.)

No, in the end she returned always to the same thought . . . that she would sacrifice everything to the perfection of this thing which existed between Sybil and the impatient, red-haired young man.

When she was honest with herself, she knew that she would have had no panic, no terror, save for O'Hara. Save for him she would have had no fear of growing old, of seeing Sybil married and finding herself a grandmother. She had prayed for all these things, even that Fate should send Sybil just such a lover; and now that her prayer was answered there were times when she wished wickedly that he had not come, or at least not so promptly.

When she was honest, the answer was always the same . . . that O'Hara had come to occupy the larger part of her interest in existence.

In the most secret part of her soul, she no longer pretended that her feeling for him was only one of friendship. She was in love with him. She rose each morning joyfully to ride with him across the meadows, pleased that Sybil came with them less and less frequently; and on the days when he was kept in Boston a cloud seemed to darken all her thoughts and actions. She talked to him of his future, his plans, the progress of his campaign, as if already she were his wife or his mistress. She played traitor to all her world whose fortunes rested on the success and power of his political enemies. She came to depend upon his quick sympathy. He had a Gaelic way of understanding her moods, her sudden melancholy, that had never existed in the phlegmatic, insensitive world of Pentlands.

She was honest with herself after the morning when, riding along the damp, secret paths of the birch thicket, he halted his horse abruptly and with a kind of anguish told her that he could no longer go on in the way they were going.

He said, "What do you want me to do? I am good for nothing. I can think of nothing but you . . . all day and all night. I go to Boston and try to work and all the while I'm thinking of you . . . thinking what is to be done. You must see what hell it is for me . . . to be near you like this and yet to be treated only as a friend."

Abruptly, when she turned and saw the suffering in his eyes, she knew there was no longer any doubt. She asked sadly, "What do you want me to do? What can I do? You make me feel that I am being the cheapest, silliest sort of woman." And in a low voice she added, "I don't mean to be, Michael. . . . I love you, Michael. . . . Now I've told you. You are the only man I've ever loved . . . even the smallest bit."

A kind of ecstatic joy took possession of him. He leaned over and kissed her, his own tanned face dampened by her tears.

"I'm so happy," she said, "and yet so sad. . . ."

"If you love me . . . then we can go our way . . . we need not think of any of the others."

"Oh, it's not so easy as that, my dear." She had never before been so conscious of his presence, of that strange sense of warmth and charm which he seemed to impose on everything about him.

"I do have to think of the others," she said. "Not my husband. . . . I don't think he even cares so long as the world knows nothing. But there's Sybil. . . . I can't make a fool of myself on account of Sybil."

She saw quickly that she had used the wrong phrase, that she had hurt him; striking without intention at the fear which he sometimes had that she thought him a common, vulgar Irish politician.

"Do you think that this thing between us . . . might be called 'making a fool of yourself'?" he asked with a faint shade of bitterness.

"No . . . you know me better than that. . . . You know I was thinking only of myself . . . as a middle-aged woman with a daughter ready to be married."

"But she *will* be married . . . soon . . . surely. Young de Cyon isn't the sort who waits."

"Yes . . . that's true . . . but even then." She turned quickly. "What do you want me to do? . . . Do you want me to be your mistress?"

"I want you for my own. . . . I want you to marry me."

"Do you want me as much as that?"

"I want you as much as that. . . . I can't bear the thought of sharing you . . . of having you belong to any one else."

"Oh . . . I've belonged to no one for a great many years now . . . not since Jack was born."

He went on, hurriedly, ardently. "It would change all my life. It would give me some reason to go on. . . . Save for you. . . . I'd chuck everything and go away. . . . I'm sick of it."

"And you want me for my own sake . . . not just because I'll help your career and give you an interest in life."

"For your own sake . . . nothing else, Olivia."

"You see, I ask because I've thought a great deal about it. I'm older than you, Michael. I seem young now. . . . But at forty. . . . I'll be forty in the autumn . . . at forty being older makes a difference. It cuts short our time. . . . It's not as if we were in our twenties. . . . I ask you, too, because you are a clever man and must see these things, too."

"None of it makes any difference." He looked so tragically in earnest, there was such a light in his blue eyes, that her suspicions died. She believed him.

"But we can't marry . . . ever," she said, "so long as my husband is alive. He'll never divorce me nor let me divorce him. It's one of his passionate beliefs . . . that divorce is a wicked thing. Besides, there has never been a divorce in the Pentland family. There have been worse things," she said bitterly, "but never a divorce and Anson won't be the first to break any tradition."

"Will you talk to him?"

"Just now, Michael, I think I'd do anything . . . even that. But it will do no good." For a time they were both silent, caught in a profound feeling of hopelessness, and presently she said, "Can you go on like this for a little time . . . until Sybil is gone?"

"We're not twenty . . . either of us. We can't wait too long."

"I can't desert her yet. You don't know how it is at Pentlands. I've got to save her, even if I lose myself. I fancy they'll be married before winter . . . even before autumn . . . before he leaves. And then I shall be free. I couldn't . . . I couldn't be your mistress now, Michael . . . with Sybil still in there at Pentlands with me. . . . I may be quibbling. . . . I may sound silly, but it does make a difference . . . because perhaps I've lived among them for too long."

"You promise me that when she's gone you'll be free?"

"I promise you, Michael. . . . I've told you that I love you . . . that you're the only man I've ever loved . . . even the smallest bit."

"Mrs. Callendar will help us. . . . She wants it."

"Oh, Sabine. . . ." She was startled. "You haven't spoken to her? You haven't told her anything?"

"No. . . . But you don't need to tell her such things. She has a way of knowing." After a moment he said, "Why, even Higgins wants it. He keeps saying to me, in an offhand sort of way, as if what he said meant nothing at all, 'Mrs. Pentland is a fine woman, sir. I've known her for years. Why, she's even helped me out of scrapes. But it's a pity she's shut up in that mausoleum with all those dead ones. She ought to have a husband who's a man. She's married to a living corpse.'"

Olivia flushed. "He has no right to talk that way. . . ."

"If you could hear him speak, you'd know that it's not disrespect, but because he worships you. He'd kiss the ground you walk over." And looking down, he added, "He says it's a pity that a thoroughbred like you is shut up at Pentlands. You mustn't mind his way of saying it. He's something of a horse-breeder and so he sees such things in the light of truth."

She knew, then, what O'Hara perhaps had failed to understand—that Higgins was touching the tragedy of her son, a son who should have been strong and full of life, like Jean. And a wild idea occurred to her—that she might still have a strong son, with O'Hara as the father, a son who would be a Pentland heir but without the Pentland taint. She might do what Savina Pentland had done. But she saw at once how absurd such an idea was; Anson would know well enough that it was not *his* son.

They rode on slowly and in silence while Olivia thought wearily round and round the dark, tangled maze in which she found herself. There seemed no way out of it. She was caught, shut in a prison, at the very moment when her chance of happiness had come.

They came suddenly out of the thicket into the lane that led from Aunt Cassie's gazeboed house to Pentlands, and as they passed through the gate they saw Aunt Cassie's antiquated motor drawn up at the side of the road. The old lady was nowhere to be seen, but at the sound of hoofs the rotund form and silly face of Miss Peavey emerged from the bushes at one side, her bulging arms filled with great bunches of some weed.

She greeted Olivia and nodded to O'Hara. "I've been gathering catnip for my cats," she called out. "It grows fine and thick there in the damp ground by the spring."

Olivia smiled . . . a smile that gave her a kind of physical pain . . . and they rode on, conscious all the while that Miss Peavey's china-blue eyes were following them. She knew that Miss Peavey was too silly and innocent to suspect anything, but she would, beyond all doubt, go directly to Aunt Cassie with a detailed description of the encounter. Very little happened in Miss Peavey's life and such an encounter loomed large. Aunt Cassie would draw from her all the tiny details, such as the fact that Olivia looked as if she had been weeping.

Olivia turned to O'Hara. "There's nothing malicious about poor Miss Peavey," she said, "but she's a fool, which is far more dangerous."

Chapter 9

1

As THE MONTH of August moved toward an end there was no longer any doubt as to the "failing" of Aunt Cassie; it was confirmed by the very silence with which she surrounded the state of her health. For forty years one had discussed Aunt Cassie's health as one discussed the weather—a thing ever present in the consciousness of man about which one could do nothing, and now Aunt Cassie ceased suddenly to speak of her health at all. She even abandoned her habit of going about on foot and took to making her round of calls in the rattling motor which she protested to fear and loathe, and she came to lean more and more heavily upon the robust Miss Peavey for companionship and support. Claiming a fear of burglars, she had Miss Peavey's bed moved into the room next to hers and kept the door open between. She developed, Olivia discovered, an almost morbid terror of being left alone.

And so the depression of another illness came to add its weight to the burden of Jack's death and the grief of John Pentland. The task of battling the cloud of melancholy which hung over the old house grew more and more heavy upon Olivia's shoulders. Anson remained as usual indifferent to any changes in the life about him, living really in the past among all the sheaves of musty papers, a man not so much cold-blooded as bloodless, for there was nothing active nor calculating in his nature, but only a great inertia, a lack of all fire. And it was impossible to turn to Sabine, who in an odd way seemed as cold and detached as Anson; she appeared to stand at a little distance, waiting, watching them all, even Olivia herself. And it was of course unthinkable to cloud the happiness of Sybil by going to her for support.

There was at least O'Hara, who came more and more frequently to Pentlands, now that the first visit had been made and the ice was broken. Anson encountered him once in the hallway, coldly; and he had become very friendly with old John Pentland. The two had a common interest in horses and dogs and cattle, and O'Hara, born in the Boston slums and knowing very little on any of these subjects, perhaps found the old gentleman a valuable source of information. He told Olivia, "I wouldn't come to the house except for you. I can't bear to think of you there . . . always alone . . . always troubled."

And in the evenings, while they played bridge or listened to Jean's music, she sometimes caught his eye, watching her with the old admiration, telling her that he was ready to support her no matter what happened.

A week after the encounter with Miss Peavey at the catnip-bed, Peters came to Olivia's room late in the afternoon to say, with a curious blend of respect and confidence, "He's ill again, Mrs. Pentland."

She knew what Peters meant; it was a kind of code between them. . . . The same words used so many times before.

She went quickly to the tall narrow library that smelled of dogs and apples and woodsmoke, knowing well enough what she would find there; and on opening the door she saw him at once, lying asleep in the big leather chair. The faint odor of whisky—a smell which had come long since to fill her always with a kind of horror—hung in the air, and on the mahogany desk stood three bottles, each nearly emptied. He slept quietly, one arm flung across his chest, the other hanging to the floor, where the bony fingers rested limply against the Turkey-red carpet. There was something childlike in the peace which enveloped him. It seemed to Olivia that he was even free now of the troubles which long ago had left their mark in the harsh, bitter lines of the old face. The lines were gone, melted away somehow, drowned in the immense quiet of this artificial death. It was only thus, perhaps, that he slept quietly, untroubled by dreams. It was only thus that he ever escaped.

Standing in the doorway she watched him for a time, quietly, and then, turning, she said to Peters, "Will you tell Higgins?" and entering the door she closed the red-plush curtains, shutting out the late afternoon sunlight.

Higgins came, as he had done so many times before, to lock the door and sit there in the room, even sleeping on the worn leather divan, until John Pentland, wakening slowly and looking about in a dazed way, discovered his groom sitting in the same room, polishing a bridle or a pair of riding-boots. The little man was never idle. Something deep inside him demanded action: he must always be doing something. And so, after these melancholy occasions, a new odor clung to the library for days . . . the fresh, clean, healthy odor of leather and harness-soap.

For two days Higgins stayed in the library, leaving it only for meals, and for two days the old lady in the north wing went unvisited. Save for this single room, there was no evidence of any change in the order of life at Pentlands. Jean, in ignorance of what had happened, came in the evenings to play. But Sabine knew; and Aunt Cassie, who never asked questions concerning the mysterious absence of her brother lest she be told the truth. Anson, as usual, noticed nothing. The only real change lay in a sudden display of sulking and ill-temper on the part of Miss Egan. The invincible nurse even quarreled with the cook, and was uncivil to Olivia, who thought, "What next is to happen? I shall be forced to look for a new nurse."

On the evening of the third day, just after dinner, Higgins opened the door and went in search of Olivia.

"The old gentleman is all right again," he said. "He's gone to bathe and he'd like to see you in the library in half an hour."

She found him there, seated by the big mahogany desk, bathed and spotlessly neat in clean linen; but he looked very old and weary, and beneath the tan of the leathery face there was a pallor which gave him a yellowish look. It was his habit never to refer in any way to these sad occasions, to behave always as if he had only been away for a day or two and wanted to hear what had happened during his absence.

Looking up at her, he said gravely, "I wanted to speak to you, Olivia. You weren't busy, were you? I didn't disturb you?"

"No," she said. "There's nothing. . . . Jean and Thérèse are here with Sybil. . . . That's all."

"Sybil," he repeated. "Sybil. . . . She's very happy these days, isn't she?" Olivia nodded and even smiled a little, in a warm, understanding way, so that he added, "Well, we mustn't spoil her happiness. We mustn't allow anything to happen to it."

A light came into the eyes of Olivia. "No; we mustn't," she repeated, and then, "She's a clever girl. . . . She knows what she wants from life, and that's the whole secret. Most people never know until it's too late."

A silence followed this speech, so eloquent, so full of unsaid things, that Olivia grew uneasy.

"I wanted to talk to you about . . ." he hesitated for a moment, and she saw that beneath the edge of the table his hands were clenched so violently that the bony knuckles showed through the brown skin. "I wanted to talk to you about a great many things." He stirred and added abruptly, "First of all, there's my will."

He opened the desk and took out a packet of papers, separating them carefully into little piles before he spoke again. There was a weariness in all his movements. "I've made some changes," he said, "changes that you ought to know about . . . and there are one or two other things." He looked at her from under the fierce, shaggy eyebrows. "You see, I haven't long to live. I've no reason to expect to live forever and I want to leave things in perfect order, as they have always been."

To Olivia, sitting in silence, the conversation became suddenly painful. With each word she felt a wall rising about her, shutting her in, while the old man went on and on with an agonizing calmness, with an air of being certain that his will would be obeyed in death as it had always been in life.

"To begin with, you will all be left very rich . . . very rich . . . something over six million dollars. And it's solid money, Olivia . . . money not made by gambling, but money that's been saved and multiplied by careful living. For seventy-five years it's been the tradition of the family to live on the income of its income. We've managed to do it somehow, and in the end we're rich . . . very rich."

As he talked he kept fingering the papers nervously, placing them in neat little piles, arranging and rearranging them.

"And, as you know, Olivia, the money has been kept in a way so that the principal could never be spent. Sybil's grandchildren will be able to touch some of it . . . that is, if you are unwise enough to leave it to them that way."

Olivia looked up suddenly. "But why me? What have I to do with it?"

"That's what I'm coming to, Olivia dear. . . . It's because I'm leaving control of the whole fortune to you."

Suddenly, fiercely, she wanted none of it. She had a quick, passionate desire to seize all the neatly piled papers and burn them, to tear them into small bits and fling them out of the window.

"I don't want it!" she said. "Why should you leave it to me? I'm rich myself. I don't want it! I'm not a Pentland. . . . It's not my money. I've nothing to do with it." In spite of herself, there was a note of passionate resentment in her voice.

The shaggy brows raised faintly in a look of surprise.

"To whom, if not to you?" he asked.

After a moment, she said, "Why, Anson . . . to Anson, I suppose."

"You don't really think that?"

"It's his money . . . Pentland money . . . not mine. I've all the money I need and more."

"It's yours, Olivia. . . ." He looked at her sharply. "You're more a Pentland than Anson, in spite of blood . . . in spite of name. You're more a Pentland than any of them. It's your money by every right in spite of anything you can do."

("But Anson isn't a Pentland, nor you either," thought Olivia.)

"It's you who are dependable, who are careful, who are honorable, Olivia. You're the strong one. When I die, you'll be the head of the family. . . . Surely, you know that . . . already."

("I," thought Olivia, "I who have been so giddy, who am planning to betray you all. . . . I am all this!")

"If I left it to Anson, it would be wasted, lost on foolish ideas. He's no idea of business. . . . There's a screw loose in Anson. . . . He's a crank. He'd be giving away this good money to missionaries and queer committees . . . societies for meddling in the affairs of people. That wasn't what this fortune was made for. No, I won't have Pentland money squandered like that. . . ."

"And I," asked Olivia. "How do you know what I will do with it?"

He smiled softly, affectionately. "I know what you'll do with it, because I know you, Olivia, my dear. . . . You'll keep it safe and intact. . . . You're the Pentland of the family. You weren't when you came here, but you are now. I mean that you belong to the grand tradition of Pentlands . . . the old ones who hang out there in the hall. You're the only one left . . . for Sybil is too young. She's only a child . . . yet."

Olivia was silent, but beneath the silence there ran a torrent of cold, rebellious thoughts. Being a Pentland, then, was not a matter of blood: it was an idea, even an ideal. She thought fiercely, "I'm not a Pentland. I'm alive. I am myself. I've not been absorbed into nothing. All these years haven't changed me so much. They haven't made me into a Pentland." But for the sake of her affection, she could say none of these things. She only said, "How do you know what I'll do with it? How do you know that I mightn't squander it extravagantly—or—or even run away, taking all that was free with me. No one could stop me—no one."

He only repeated what he had said before, saying it more slowly this time, as if to impress her. "I know what you'll do with it, Olivia, because I know you, Olivia dear—you'd never do anything foolish or shameful—I know that— that's why I trust you."

And when she did not answer him, he asked, "You will accept it, won't you, Olivia? You'll have the help of a good lawyer . . . one of the best . . . John Mannering. It will please me, Olivia, and it will let the world know what I think of you, what you have been to me all these years . . . all that Anson has never been . . . nor my own sister, Cassie." He leaned across the table, touching her white hand gently. "You will, Olivia?"

It was impossible to refuse, impossible even to protest any further, impossible to say that in this very moment she wanted only to run away, to escape, to leave them all forever, now that Sybil was safe. Looking away, she said in a low voice, "Yes."

It was impossible to desert him now . . . an old, tired man. The bond between them was too strong; it had existed for too long, since that first day she had come to Pentlands as Anson's bride and known that it was the father and not the son whom she respected. In a way, he had imposed upon her something of his own rugged, patriarchal strength. It seemed to her that she had been caught when she meant most to escape; and she was frightened, too, by the echoing thought that perhaps she had become, after all, a Pentland . . . hard, cautious, unadventurous and a little bitter, one for whom there was no fire or glamour in life, one who worshiped a harsh, changeable, invisible goddess called Duty. She kept thinking of Sabine's bitter remark about "the lower middle-class virtues of the Pentlands" . . . the lack of fire, the lack of splendor, of gallantry. And yet this fierce old man *was* gallant, in an odd fashion. . . . Even Sabine knew that.

He was talking again. "It's not only money that's been left to you. . . . There's Sybil, who's still too young to be let free. . . ."

"No," said Olivia with a quiet stubbornness, "she's not too young. She's to do as she pleases. I've tried to make her wiser than I was at her age . . . perhaps wiser than I've ever been . . . even now."

"Perhaps you're right, my dear. You have been so many times . . . and things aren't the same as they were in my day . . . certainly not with young girls."

He took up the papers again, fussing over them in a curious, nervous way, very unlike his usual firm, unrelenting manner. She had a flash of insight which told her that he was behaving thus because he wanted to avoid looking at her. She hated confidences and she was afraid now that he was about to tell her things she preferred never to hear. She hated confidences and yet she seemed to be a person who attracted them always.

"And leaving Sybil out of it," he continued, "there's queer old Miss Haddon in Durham whom, as you know, we've taken care of for years; and there's Cassie, who's growing old and ill, I think. We can't leave her to half-witted Miss Peavey. I know my sister Cassie has been a burden to you. . . . She's been a burden to me, all my life. . . ." He smiled grimly. "I suppose you know that. . . ." Then, after a pause, he said, "But most of all, there's my wife."

His voice assumed a queer, unnatural quality, from which all feeling had been removed. It became like the voices of deaf persons who never hear the sounds they make.

"I can't leave her alone," he said. "Alone . . . with no one to care for her save a paid nurse. I couldn't die and know that there's no one to think of her . . . save that wretched, efficient Miss Egan . . . a stranger. No, Olivia . . . there's no one but you. . . . No one I can trust." He looked at her sharply. "You'll promise me to keep her here always . . . never to let them send her away? You'll promise?"

Again she was caught. "Of course," she said. "Of course I'll promise you that." What else was she to say?

"Because," he added, looking away from her once more, "because I owe her that . . . even after I'm dead. I couldn't rest if she were shut up somewhere . . . among strangers. You see . . . once . . . once. . . ." He broke off sharply, as if what he had been about to say was unbearable.

With Olivia the sense of uneasiness changed into actual terror. She wanted to cry out, "Stop! . . . Don't go on!" But some instinct told her that he meant to go on and on to the very end, painfully, despite anything she could do.

"It's odd," he was saying quite calmly, "but there seem to be only women left . . . no men . . . for Anson is really an old woman."

Quietly, firmly, with the air of a man before a confessor, speaking almost as if she were invisible, impersonal, a creature who was a kind of machine, he went on, "And of course, Horace Pentland is dead, so we needn't think of him any longer. . . . But there's Mrs. Soames. . . ." He coughed and began again to weave the gaunt bony fingers in and out, as if what he had to say were drawn from the depth of his soul with a great agony. "There's Mrs. Soames," he repeated. "I know that you understand about her, Olivia . . . and I'm grateful to you for having been kind and human where none of the others would have been. I fancy we've given Beacon Hill and Commonwealth Avenue subject for conversation for thirty years . . . but I don't care about that. They've watched us . . . they've known every time I went up the steps of her brownstone house . . . the very hour I arrived and the hour I left. They have eyes, in our world, Olivia, even in the backs of their heads. You must remember that, my dear. They watch you . . . they see everything you do. They almost know what you think . . . and when they don't know, they make it up. That's one of the signs of a sick, decaying world . . . that they get their living vicariously . . . by watching some one else live . . . that they live always in the past. That's the only reason I ever felt sorry for Horace Pentland . . . the only reason that I had sympathy for him. It was cruel that he should have been born in such a place."

The bitterness ran like acid through all the speech, through the very timbre of his voice. It burned in the fierce black eyes where the fire was not yet dead. Olivia believed that she was seeing him now for the first time, in his fulness, with nothing concealed. And as she listened, the old cloud of mystery that had always hidden him from her began to clear away like the fog lifting from the marshes in the early morning. She saw him now as he really was . . . a man fiercely masculine, bitter, clear-headed, and more human than the rest of them, who had never before betrayed himself even for an instant.

"But about Mrs. Soames. . . . If anything should happen to me, Olivia . . . if I should die first, I want you to be kind to her . . . for my sake and for hers. She's been patient and good to me for so long." The bitterness seemed to flow away a little now, leaving only a kindling warmth in its place. "She's been good to me. . . . She's always understood, Olivia, even before you came here to help me. You and she, Olivia, have made life worth living for me. She's been patient . . . more patient than you know. Sometimes I must have made life for her a hell on earth . . . but she's always been there, waiting, full of gentleness and sympathy. She's been ill most of the time you've known her . . . old and ill. You can't imagine how beautiful she once was."

"I know," said Olivia softly. "I remember seeing her when I first came to Pentlands . . . and Sabine has told me."

The name of Sabine appeared to rouse him suddenly. He sat up very straight and said, "Don't trust Sabine too far, Olivia. She belongs to us, after all. She's very like my sister Cassie . . . more like her than you can imagine. It's why they hate each other so. She's Cassie turned inside out, as you might say. They'd both sacrifice everything for the sake of stirring up some trouble or calamity that would interest them. They live . . . vicariously."

Olivia would have interrupted him, defending Sabine and telling of the one real thing that had happened to her . . . the tragic love for her husband; she would have told him of all the abrupt, incoherent confidences Sabine had made her; but the old man gave her no chance. It seemed suddenly that he had become possessed, fiercely intent upon pouring out to her all the dark things he had kept hidden for so long.

(She kept thinking, "Why must I know all these things? Why must I take up the burden? Why was it that I should find those letters which had lain safe and hidden for so long?")

He was talking again quietly, the bony fingers weaving in and out their nervous futile pattern. "You see, Olivia. . . . You see, she takes drugs now

. . . and there's no use in trying to cure her. She's old now, and it doesn't really matter. It's not as if she were young with all her life before her."

Almost without thinking, Olivia answered, "I know that."

He looked up quickly. "Know it?" he asked sharply. "How could you know it?"

"Sabine told me."

The head bowed again. "Oh, Sabine! Of course! She's dangerous. She knows far too much of the world. She's known too many strange people." And then he repeated again what he had said months ago after the ball. "She ought never to have come back here."

Into the midst of the strange, disjointed conversation there came presently the sound of music drifting toward them from the distant drawing-room. John Pentland, who was a little deaf, did not hear it at first, but after a little time he sat up, listening, and turning toward her, asked, "Is that Sybil's young man?"

"Yes."

"He's a nice boy, isn't he?"

"A very nice boy."

After a silence he asked, "What's the name of the thing he's playing?"

Olivia could not help smiling. "It's called *I'm in love again and the spring is a-comin'*. Jean brought it back from Paris. A friend of his wrote it . . . but names don't mean anything in music any more. No one listens to the words."

A shadow of amusement crossed his face. "Songs have queer names nowadays."

She would have escaped, then, going quietly away. She stirred and even made a gesture toward leaving, but he raised his hand in the way he had, making her feel that she must obey him as if she were a child.

"There are one or two more things you ought to know, Olivia . . . things that will help you to understand. Some one has to know them. Some one. . . ." He halted abruptly and again made a great effort to go on. The veins stood out sharply on the bony head.

"It's about *her* chiefly," he said, with the inevitable gesture toward the north wing. "She wasn't always that way. That's what I want to explain. You see . . . we were married when we were both very young. It was my father who wanted it. I was twenty and she was eighteen. My father had known her family always. They were cousins of ours, in a way, just as they were cousins of Sabine's. He had gone to school with her father and they belonged to the same club and she was an only child with a prospect of coming into a great fortune. It's an old story, you see, but a rather common one in our world. . . . All these things counted, and as for myself, I'd never had anything to do with women and I'd never been in love with any one. I was very young. I think they saw it as a perfect match . . . made in the hard, prosperous Heaven of their dreams. She was very pretty . . . you can see even now that she must have been very pretty. . . . She was sweet, too, and innocent." He coughed, and continued with a great effort. "She had . . . she had a mind like a little child's. She knew nothing . . . a flower of innocence," he added with a strange savagery.

And then, as if the effort were too much for him, he paused and sat staring out of the window toward the sea. To Olivia it seemed that he had slipped back across the years to the time when the poor old lady had been young and perhaps curiously shy of his ardent wooing. A silence settled again over the room, so profound that this time the faint, distant roaring of the surf on the rocks became audible, and then again the sound of Jean's music breaking in upon them. He was playing another tune . . . not *I'm in love again,* but one called *Ukulele Lady.*

"I wish they'd stop that damned music!" said John Pentland.

"I'll go," began Olivia, rising.

"No . . . don't go. You mustn't go . . . not now." He seemed anxious, almost terrified, perhaps by the fear that if he did not tell now he would never tell her the long story that he must tell to some one. "No, don't go . . . not until I've finished, Olivia. I must finish. . . . I want you to know why such things happened as happened here yesterday and the day before in this room. . . . There's no excuse, but what I have to tell you may explain it . . . a little."

He rose and opening one of the bookcases, took out a bottle of whisky. Looking at her, he said, "Don't worry, Olivia, I shan't repeat it. It's only that I'm feeling weak. It will never happen again . . . what happened yesterday . . . never. I give you my word."

He poured out a full glass and seated himself once more, drinking the stuff slowly while he talked.

"So we were married, I thinking that I was in love with her, because I knew nothing of such things . . . nothing. It wasn't really love, you see. . . . Olivia, I'm going to tell you the truth . . . everything . . . all of the truth. It wasn't really love, you see. It was only that she was the only woman I had ever approached in that way . . . and I was a strong, healthy young man."

He began to speak more and more slowly, as if each word were thrust out by an immense effort of will. "And she knew nothing . . . nothing at all. She was," he said bitterly, "all that a young woman was supposed to be. After the first night of the honeymoon, she was never quite the same again . . . never quite the same, Olivia. Do you know what that means? The honeymoon ended in a kind of madness, a fixed obsession. She'd been brought up to think of such things with a sacred horror and there was a touch of madness in her family. She was never the same again," he repeated in a melancholy voice, "and when Anson was born she went quite out of her head. She would not see me or speak to me. She fancied that I had disgraced her forever . . . and after that she could never be left alone without some one to watch her. She never went out again in the world. . . ."

The voice died away into a hoarse whisper. The glass of whisky had been emptied in a supreme effort to break through the shell which had closed him in from all the world, from Olivia, whom he cherished, perhaps even from Mrs. Soames, whom he had loved. In the distance the music still continued, this time as an accompaniment to the hard, loud voice of Thérèse singing, *I'm in love again and the spring is a-comin'.* . . . Thérèse, the dark, cynical, invincible Thérèse for whom life, from frogs to men, held very few secrets.

"But the story doesn't end there," continued John Pentland weakly. "It goes on . . . because I came to know what being in love might be when I met Mrs. Soames. . . . Only then," he said sadly, as if he saw the tragedy from far off as a thing which had little to do with him. "Only then," he repeated, "it was too late. After what I had done to *her*, it was too late to fall in love. I couldn't abandon her. It was impossible. It ought never to have happened." He straightened his tough old body and added, "I've told you all this, Olivia, because I wanted you to understand why sometimes I am . . ." He paused for a moment and then plunged ahead, "why I am a beast as I was yesterday. There have been times when it was the only way I could go on living. . . . And it harmed no one. There aren't many who ever knew about it. . . . I always hid myself. There was never any spectacle."

Slowly Olivia's white hand stole across the polished surface of the desk and touched the brown, bony one that lay there now, quietly, like a hawk come to rest. She said nothing and yet the simple gesture carried an eloquence of which no words were capable. It brought tears into the burning eyes for the second time in the life of John Pentland. He had wept only once before . . . on the night of his grandson's death. And they were not, Olivia knew, tears of self-pity, for there was no self-pity in the tough, rugged old body; they were tears at the spectacle of a tragedy in which he happened by accident to be concerned.

"I wanted you to know, my dear Olivia . . . that I have never been unfaithful to *her*, not once in all the years since our wedding-night. . . . I know the world will never believe it, but I wanted you to know because, you see, you and Mrs. Soames are the only ones who matter to me . . . and she *knows* that it is true."

And now that she knew the story was finished, she did not go away, because she knew that he wanted her to stay, sitting there beside him in silence, touching his hand. He was the sort of man—a man, she thought, like Michael —who needed women about him.

After a long time, he turned suddenly and asked, "This boy of Sybil's— who is he? What is he like?"

"Sabine knows about him."

"It's that which makes me afraid. . . . He's out of her world and I'm not so sure that I like it. In Sabine's world it doesn't matter who a person is or where he comes from so long as he's clever and amusing."

"I've watched him. . . . I've talked with him. I think him all that a girl could ask . . . a girl like Sybil, I mean. . . . I shouldn't recommend him to a silly girl . . . he'd give such a wife a very bad time. Besides, I don't think we can do much about it. Sybil, I think, has decided."

"Has he asked her to marry him? Has he spoken to you?"

"I don't know whether he's asked her. He hasn't spoken to me. Young men don't bother about such things nowadays."

"But Anson won't like it. There'll be trouble . . . and Cassie, too."

"Yes . . . and still, if Sybil wants him, she'll have him. I've tried to teach her that in a case like this . . . well," she made a little gesture with her white hand, "that she should let nothing make any difference."

He sat thoughtfully for a long time, and at last, without looking up and almost as if speaking to himself, he said, "There was once an elopement in the family. . . . Jared and Savina Pentland were married that way."

"But that wasn't a happy match . . . not too happy," said Olivia; and immediately she knew that she had come near to betraying herself. A word or two more and he might have trapped her. She saw that it was impossible to add the burden of the letters to these other secrets.

As it was, he looked at her sharply, saying, "No one knows that. . . . One only knows that she was drowned."

She saw well enough what he meant to tell her, by that vague hint regarding Savina's elopement; only now he was back once more in the terrible shell; he was the mysterious, the false, John Pentland who could only hint but never speak directly.

The music ceased altogether in the drawing-room, leaving only the vague, distant, eternal pounding of the surf on the red rocks, and once the distant echo of a footstep coming from the north wing. The old man said presently, "So she wasn't falling in love with this man O'Hara, after all? There wasn't any need for worry?"

"No, she never thought of him in that way, even for a moment. . . . To her he seems an old man. . . . We mustn't forget how young she is."

"He's not a bad sort," replied the old man. "I've grown fond of him, and Higgins thinks he's a fine fellow. I'm inclined to trust Higgins. He has an instinct about people . . . the same as he has about the weather." He paused for a moment, and then continued, "Still, I think we'd best be careful about him. He's a clever Irishman on the make . . . and such gentlemen need watching. They're usually thinking only of themselves."

"Perhaps," said Olivia, in a whisper. "Perhaps. . . ."

The silence was broken by the whirring and banging of the clock in the hall making ready to strike eleven. The evening had slipped away quickly, veiled in a mist of unreality. At last the truth had been spoken at Pentlands —the grim, unadorned, terrible truth; and Olivia, who had hungered for it for so long, found herself shaken.

John Pentland rose slowly, painfully, for he had grown stiff and brittle with the passing of the summer. "It's eleven, Olivia. You'd better go to bed and get some rest."

2

She did not go to her own room, because it would have been impossible
to sleep, and she could not go to the drawing-room to face, in the mood
which held her captive, such young faces as those of Jean and Thérèse and
Sybil. At the moment she could not bear the thought of any enclosed place,
of a room or even a place covered by a roof which shut out the open sky.
She had need of the air and that healing sense of freedom and oblivion
which the sight of the marshes and the sea sometimes brought to her. She
wanted to breathe deeply the fresh salty atmosphere, to run, to escape somewhere. Indeed, for a moment she succumbed to a sense of panic, as she had
done on the other hot night when O'Hara followed her into the garden.

She went out across the terrace and, wandering aimlessly, found herself
presently moving beneath the trees in the direction of the marshes and the
sea. This last night of August was hot and clear save for the faint, blue-white
mist that always hung above the lower meadows. There had been times in the
past when the thought of crossing the lonely meadows, of wandering the
shadowed lanes in the darkness, had frightened her, but to-night such an
adventure seemed only restful and quiet, perhaps because she believed that
she could encounter there nothing more terrible than the confidences of
John Pentland. She was acutely aware, as she had been on that other evening, of the breathless beauty of the night, of the velvety shadows along the
hedges and ditches, of the brilliance of the stars, of the distant foaming
white line of the sea and the rich, fertile odor of the pastures and marshes.

And presently, when she had grown a little more calm, she tried to bring
some order out of the chaos that filled her body and spirit. It seemed to her
that all life had become hopelessly muddled and confused. She was aware in
some way, almost without knowing why, that the old man had tricked her,
turning her will easily to his own desires, changing all the prospect of the
future. She had known always that he was strong and in his way invincible,
but until to-night she had never known the full greatness of his strength . . .
how relentless, even how unscrupulous he could be; for he had been unscrupulous, unfair, in the way he had used every weapon at hand . . . every
sentiment, every memory . . . to achieve his will. There had been no fierce
struggle in the open; it was far more subtle than that. He had subdued her
without her knowing it, aided perhaps by all that dark force which had the
power of changing them all . . . even the children of Savina Dalgedo and
Toby Cane into "Pentlands."

Thinking bitterly of what had passed, she came to see that his strength
rested upon the foundation of his virtue, his *rightness*. One could say—
indeed, one could believe it as one believed that the sun had risen yesterday—
that all his life had been tragically foolish and quixotic, fantastically devoted to the hard, uncompromising ideal of what a Pentland ought to be;
and yet . . . yet one knew that he had been right, even perhaps heroic; one

respected his uncompromising strength. He had made a wreck of his own happiness and driven poor old Mrs. Soames to seek peace in the Nirvana of drugs; and yet for her, he was the whole of life: she lived only for him. This code of his was hard, cruel, inhuman, sacrificing everything to its observance. . . . "Even," thought Olivia, "to sacrificing me along with himself. But I will not be sacrificed. I will escape!"

And after a long time she began to see slowly what it was that lay at the bottom of the iron power he had over people, the strength which none of them had been able to resist. It was a simple thing . . . simply that he *believed*, passionately, relentlessly, as those first Puritans had done.

The others all about her did not matter. Not one of them had any power over her . . . not Anson, nor Aunt Cassie, nor Sabine, nor Bishop Smallwood. None of them played any part in the course of her life. They did not matter. She had no fear of them; rather they seemed to her now fussy and pitiful.

But John Pentland *believed*. It was that which made the difference.

Stumbling along half-blindly, she found herself presently at the bridge where the lane from Pentlands crossed the river on its way to Brook Cottage. Since she had been a little girl, the sight of water had exerted a strange spell upon her . . . the sight of a river, a lake, but most of all the open sea; she had always been drawn toward these things like a bit of iron toward a magnet; and now, finding herself at the bridge, she halted, and stood looking over the stone parapet in the shadow of the hawthorn-bushes that grew close to the water's edge, down on the dark, still pool below her. The water was black and in it the bright little stars glittered like diamonds scattered over its surface. The warm, rich odor of cattle filled the air, touched by the faint, ghostly perfume of the last white nympheas that bordered the pool.

And while she stood there, bathed in the stillness of the dark solitude, she began to understand a little what had really passed between them in the room smelling of whisky and saddle-soap. She saw how the whole tragedy of John Pentland and his life had been born of the stupidity, the ignorance, the hypocrisy of others, and she saw, too, that he was beyond all doubt the grandson of the Toby Cane who had written those wild passionate letters glorifying the flesh; only John Pentland had found himself caught in the prison of that other terrible thing—the code in which he had been trained, in which he *believed*. She saw now that it was not strange that he sought escape from reality by shutting himself in and drinking himself into a stupor. He had been caught, tragically, between those two powerful forces. He thought himself a Pentland and all the while there burned in him the fire that lay in Toby Cane's letters and in the wanton look that was fixed forever in the portrait of Savina Pentland. She kept seeing him as he said, "I have never been unfaithful to *her*, not once in all the years since our wedding-night. . . . I wanted you to know because, you see, you and Mrs. Soames are the only ones who matter to me . . . and she *knows* that it is true."

It seemed to her that this fidelity was a terrible, a wicked, thing.

And she came to understand that through all their talk together, the thought, the idea, of Michael had been always present. It was almost as if they had been speaking all the while about Michael and herself. A dozen times the old man had touched upon it, vaguely but surely. She had no doubts that Aunt Cassie had long since learned all there was to learn from Miss Peavey of the encounter by the catnip-bed, and she was certain that she had taken the information to her brother. Still, there was nothing definite in anything Miss Peavey had seen, very little that was even suspicious. And yet, as she looked back upon her talk with the old man, it seemed to her that in a dozen ways, by words, by intonation, by glances, he had implied that he knew the secret. Even in the end when, cruelly, he had with an uncanny sureness touched the one fear, the one suspicion that marred her love for Michael, by saying in the most casual way, "Still, I think we'd better be careful of him. He's a clever Irishman on the make . . . and such gentlemen need watching. They're usually thinking only of themselves."

And then the most fantastic of all thoughts occurred to her . . . that all their talk together, even the painful, tragic confidence made with such an heroic effort, was directed at herself. He had done all this—he had emerged from his shell of reticence, he had humiliated his fierce pride—all to force her to give up Michael, to force her to sacrifice herself on the altar of that fantastic ideal in which he believed.

And she was afraid because he was so strong; because he had asked her to do nothing that he himself had not done.

She would never know for certain. She saw that, after all, the John Pentland she had left a little while before still remained an illusion, veiled in mystery, unfathomable to her, perhaps forever. She had not seen him at all.

Standing there on the bridge in the black shadow of the hawthorns, all sense of time or space, of the world about her, faded out of existence, so that she was aware of herself only as a creature who was suffering. She thought, "Perhaps he is right. Perhaps I have become like them, and that is why this struggle goes on and on. Perhaps if I were an ordinary person . . . sane and simple . . . like Higgins . . . there would be no struggle and no doubts, no terror of simply *acting*, without hesitation."

She remembered what the old man had said of a world in which all action had become paralyzed, where one was content simply to watch others act, to live vicariously. The word "sane" had come to her quite naturally and easily as the exact word to describe a state of mind opposed to that which existed perpetually at Pentlands, and the thought terrified her that perhaps this thing which one called "being a Pentland," this state of enchantment, was, after all, only a disease, a kind of madness that paralyzed all power of action. One came to live in the past, to acknowledge debts of honor and duty to people who had been dead for a century and more.

"Once," she thought, "I must have had the power of doing what I wanted to do, what I thought right."

And she thought again of what Sabine had said of New England as "a place where thoughts became higher and fewer," where every action became a problem of moral conduct, an exercise in transcendentalism. It was passing now, even from New England, though it still clung to the world of Pentlands, along with the souvenirs of celebrated "dear friends." Even stowing the souvenirs away in the attic had changed nothing. It was passing all about Pentlands; there was nothing of this sort in the New England that belonged to O'Hara and Higgins and the Polish mill-workers of Durham. The village itself had become a new and different place.

In the midst of this rebellion, she became aware, with that strange acuteness which seemed to touch all her senses, that she was no longer alone on the bridge in the midst of empty, mist-veiled meadows. She knew suddenly and with a curious certainty that there were others somewhere near her in the darkness, perhaps watching her, and she had for a moment a wave of the quick, chilling fear which sometimes overtook her at Pentlands at the times when she had a sense of figures surrounding her who could neither be seen nor touched. And almost at once she distinguished, emerging from the mist that blanketed the meadows, the figures of two people, a man and a woman, walking very close to each other, their arms entwined. For a moment she thought, "Am I really mad? Am I seeing ghosts in reality?" The fantastic idea occurred to her that the two figures were perhaps Savina Pentland and Toby Cane risen from their lost grave in the sea to wander across the meadows and marshes of Pentland. Moving through the drifting, starlit mist, they seemed vague and indistinct and watery, like creatures come up out of the water. She fancied them, all dripping and wet, emerging from the waves and crossing the white rim of beach on their way toward the big old house. . . .

The sight, strangely enough, filled her with no sense of horror, but only with fascination.

And then, as they drew nearer, she recognized the man—something at first vaguely familiar in the cocky, strutting walk. She knew the bandy legs and was filled suddenly with a desire to laugh wildly and hysterically. It was only the rabbitlike Higgins engaged in some new conquest. Quietly she stepped farther into the shadow of the hawthorns and the pair passed her, so closely that she might have reached out her hand and touched them. It was only then that she recognized the woman. It was no Polish girl from the village, this time. It was Miss Egan—the starched, the efficient Miss Egan, whom Higgins had seduced. She was leaning on him as they walked—a strange, broken, feminine Miss Egan whom Olivia had never seen before.

At once she thought, "Old Mrs. Pentland has been left alone. Anything might happen. I must hurry back to the house." And she had a quick burst of anger at the deceit of the nurse, followed by a flash of intuition which seemed to clarify all that had been happening since the hot night early in the summer when she had seen Higgins leaping the wall like a goat to escape the glare of the motor-lights. The mysterious woman who had disappeared over the wall that night *was* Miss Egan. She had been leaving the old woman alone night after night since then; it explained the sudden impatience and bad temper of these last two days when Higgins had been shut up with the old man.

She saw it all now—all that had happened in the past two months—in an orderly procession of events. The old woman had escaped, leading the way to Savina Pentland's letters, because Miss Egan had deserted her post to wander across the meadows at the call of that mysterious, powerful force which seemed to take possession of the countryside at nightfall. It was in the air again to-night, all about her . . . in the air, in the fields, the sound of the distant sea, the smell of cattle and of ripening seeds . . . as it had been on the night when Michael followed her out into the garden.

In a way, the whole chain of events was the manifestation of the disturbing force which had in the end revealed the secret of Savina's letters. It had mocked them, and now the secret weighed on Olivia as a thing which she must tell some one, which she could no longer keep to herself. It burned her, too, with the sense of possessing a terrible and shameful weapon which she might use if pushed beyond endurance.

Slowly, after the two lovers had disappeared, she made her way back again toward the old house, which loomed square and black against the deep blue of the sky, and as she walked, her anger at Miss Egan's betrayal of trust seemed to melt mysteriously away. She would speak to Miss Egan to-morrow, or the day after; in any case, the affair had been going on all summer and no harm had come of it—no harm save the discovery of Savina Pentland's letters. She felt a sudden sympathy for this starched, efficient woman whom she had always disliked; she saw that Miss Egan's life, after all, was a horrible thing—a procession of days spent in the company of a mad old woman. It was, Olivia thought, something like her own existence. . . .

And it occurred to her at the same time that it would be difficult to explain to so sharp-witted a creature as Miss Egan why she herself should have been on the bridge at such an hour of the night. It was as if everything, each little thought and action, became more and more tangled and hopeless, more and more intricate and complicated with the passing of each day. There was no way out save to cut the web boldly and escape.

"No," she thought, "I will not stay. . . . I will not sacrifice myself. To-morrow I shall tell Michael that when Sybil is gone, I will do whatever he wants me to do. . . ."

When she reached the house she found it dark save for the light which burned perpetually in the big hall illuminating faintly the rows of portraits; and silent save for the creakings which afflicted it in the stillness of the night.

3

She was wakened early, after having slept badly, with the news that Michael had been kept in Boston the night before and would not be able to ride with her as usual. When the maid had gone away she grew depressed, for she had counted upon seeing him and coming to some definite plan. For a moment she even experienced a vague jealousy, which she put away at once as shameful. It was not, she told herself, that he ever neglected her; it was only that he grew more and more occupied as the autumn approached. It was not that there was any other woman involved; she felt certain of him. And yet there remained that strange, gnawing little suspicion, placed in her mind when John Pentland had said, "He's a clever Irishman on the make . . . and such gentlemen need watching."

After all, she knew nothing of him save what he had chosen to tell her. He was a free man, independent, a buccaneer, who could do as he chose in life. Why should he ruin himself for her?

She rose at last, determined to ride alone, in the hope that the fresh morning air and the exercise would put to rout this cloud of morbidity which had kept possession of her from the moment she left John Pentland in the library.

As she dressed, she thought, "Day after to-morrow I shall be forty years old. Perhaps that's the reason why I feel tired and morbid. Perhaps I'm on the borderland of middle-age. But that can't be. I am strong and well and I look young, despite everything. I am tired because of what happened last night." And then it occurred to her that perhaps Mrs. Soames had known these same thoughts again and again during her long devotion to John Pentland. "No," she told herself, "whatever happens I shall never lead the life she has led. Anything is better than that . . . anything."

It seemed strange to her to awaken and find that nothing was changed in all the world about her. After what had happened the night before in the library and on the dark meadows, there should have been some mark left upon the life at Pentlands. The very house, the very landscape, should have kept some record of what had happened; and yet everything was the same. She experienced a faint shock of surprise to find the sun shining brightly, to see Higgins in the stable-yard saddling her horse and whistling all the while in an excess of high spirits, to hear the distant barking of the beagles, and to see Sybil crossing the meadow toward the river to meet Jean. Everything was the same, even Higgins, whom she had mistaken for a ghost as he crossed the mist-hung meadows a few hours earlier. It was as if there were two realities at Pentlands—one, it might have been said, of the daylight and the other of the darkness; as if one life—a secret, hidden one—lay beneath the bright, pleasant surface of a world composed of green fields and trees, the sound of barking dogs, the faint odor of coffee arising from the kitchen, and the sound of a groom whistling while he saddled a thoroughbred. It was a misfortune that chance had given her an insight into both the bright, pleasant world and that other dark, nebulous one. The others, save perhaps old John Pentland, saw only this bright, easy life that had begun to stir all about her.

And she reflected that a stranger coming to Pentlands would find it a pleasant, comfortable house, where the life was easy and even luxurious, where all of them were protected by wealth. He would find them all rather pleasant, normal, friendly people of a family respected and even distinguished. He would say, "Here is a world that is solid and comfortable and sound."

Yes, it would appear thus to a stranger, so it might be that the dark, fearful world existed only in her imagination. Perhaps she herself was ill, a little unbalanced and morbid . . . perhaps a little touched like the old woman in the north wing.

Still, she thought, most houses, most families, must have such double lives—one which the world saw and one which remained hidden.

As she pulled on her boots she heard the voice of Higgins, noisy and cheerful, exchanging amorous jests with the new Irish kitchen-maid, marking her already for his own.

She rode listlessly, allowing the mare to lead through the birch thicket over the cool dark paths which she and Michael always followed. The morning air did not change her spirits. There was something sad in riding alone through the long green tunnel.

When at last she came out on the opposite side by the patch of catnip where they had encountered Miss Peavey, she saw a Ford drawn up by the side of the road and a man standing beside it, smoking a cigar and regarding the engine as if he were in trouble. She saw no more than that and would have passed him without troubling to look a second time, when she heard herself being addressed.

"You're Mrs. Pentland, aren't you?"

She drew in the mare. "Yes, I'm Mrs. Pentland."

He was a little man, dressed rather too neatly in a suit of checkered stuff, with a high, stiff white collar which appeared to be strangling him. He wore nose-glasses and his face had a look of having been highly polished. As she turned, he took off his straw hat and with a great show of manners came forward, bowing and smiling cordially.

"Well," he said, "I'm glad to hear that I'm right. I hoped I might meet you here. It's a great pleasure to know you, Mrs. Pentland. My name is Gavin. . . . I'm by way of being a friend of Michael O'Hara."

"Oh!" said Olivia. "How do you do?"

"You're not in a great hurry, I hope?" he asked. "I'd like to have a word or two with you."

"No, I'm not in a great hurry."

It was impossible to imagine what this fussy little man, standing in the middle of the road, bowing and smiling, could have to say to her.

Still holding his hat in his hand, he tossed away the end of his cigar and said, "It's about a very delicate matter, Mrs. Pentland. It has to do with Mr. O'Hara's campaign. I suppose you know about that. You're a friend of his, I believe?"

"Why, yes," she said coldly. "We ride together."

He coughed and, clearly ill at ease, set off on a tangent from the main subject. "You see, I'm a great friend of his. In fact, we grew up together . . . lived in the same ward and fought together as boys. You mightn't think it to see us together . . . because he's such a clever one. He's made for big things and I'm not. . . . I'm . . . I'm just plain John Gavin. But we're friends, all the same, just the same as ever . . . just as if he wasn't a big man. That's one thing about Michael. He never goes back on his old friends, no matter how great he gets to be."

A light of adoration shone in the blue eyes of the little man. It was, Olivia thought, as if he were speaking of God; only clearly he thought of Michael O'Hara as greater than God. If Michael affected men like this, it was easy to see why he was so successful.

The little man kept interrupting himself with apologies. "I shan't keep you long, Mrs. Pentland . . . only a moment. You see I thought it was better if I saw you here instead of coming to the house." Suddenly screwing up his shiny face, he became intensely serious. "It's like this, Mrs. Pentland. . . . I know you're a good friend of his and you wish him well. You want to see him get elected . . . even though you people out here don't hold much with the Democratic party."

"Yes," said Olivia. "That's true."

"Well," he continued with a visible effort, "Michael's a good friend of mine. I'm sort of a bodyguard to him. Of course, I never come out here. I don't belong in this world. . . . I'd feel sort of funny out here."

(Olivia found herself feeling respect for the little man. He was so simple and so honest and he so obviously worshiped Michael.)

"You see . . . I know all about Michael. I've been through a great deal with him . . . and he's not himself just now. There's something wrong. He ain't interested in his work. He acts as if he'd be willing to chuck his whole career overboard . . . and I can't let him do that. None of his friends . . . can't let him do it. We can't get him to take a proper interest in his affairs. Usually, he manages everything . . . better than any one else could." He became suddenly confidential, closing one eye. "D'you know what I think is the matter? I've been watching him and I've got an idea."

He waited until Olivia said, "No . . . I haven't the least idea."

Cocking his head on one side and speaking with the air of having made a great discovery, he said, "Well, I think there's a woman mixed up in it."

She felt the blood mounting to her head, in spite of anything she could do. When she was able to speak, she asked, "Yes, and what am I to do?"

He moved a little nearer, still with the same air of confiding in her. "Well, this is my idea. Now, you're a friend of his . . . you'll understand. You see, the trouble is that it's some woman here in Durham . . . some swell, you see, like yourself. That's what makes it hard. He's had women before, but they were women out of the ward and it didn't make much difference. But this is different. He's all upset, and . . ." He hesitated for a moment. "Well, I don't like to say a thing like this about Michael, but I think his head is turned a little. That's a mean thing to say, but then we're all human, aren't we?"

"Yes," said Olivia softly. "Yes . . . in the end, we're all human . . . even swells like me." There was a twinkle of humor in her eye which for a moment disconcerted the little man.

"Well," he went on, "he's all upset about her and he's no good for anything. Now, what I thought was this . . . that you could find out who this woman is and go to her and persuade her to lay off him for a time . . . to go away some place . . . at least until the campaign is over. It'd make a difference. D'you see?"

He looked at her boldly, as if what he had been saying was absolutely honest and direct, as if he really had not the faintest idea who this woman was, and beneath a sense of anger, Olivia was amused at the crude tact which had evolved this trick.

"There's not much that I can do," she said. "It's a preposterous idea . . . but I'll do what I can. I'll try. I can't promise anything. It lies with Mr. O'Hara, after all."

"You see, Mrs. Pentland, if it ever got to be a scandal, it'd be the end of him. A woman out of the ward doesn't matter so much, but a woman out here would be different. She'd get a lot of publicity from the sassiety editors and all. . . . That's what's dangerous. He'd have the whole church against him on the grounds of immorality."

While he was speaking, a strange idea occurred to Olivia—that much of what he said sounded like a strange echo of Aunt Cassie's methods of argument.

The horse had grown impatient and was pawing the road and tossing his head; and Olivia was angry now, genuinely angry, so that she waited for a time before speaking, lest she should betray herself and spoil all this little game of pretense which Mr. Gavin had built up to keep himself in countenance. At last she said, "I'll do what I can, but it's a ridiculous thing you're asking of me."

The little man grinned. "I've been a long time in politics, Ma'am, and I've seen funnier things than this. . . ." He put on his hat, as if to signal that he had said all he wanted to say. "But there's one thing I'd like to ask . . . and that's that you never let Michael know that I spoke to you about this."

"Why should I promise . . . anything?"

He moved nearer and said in a low voice, "You know Michael very well, Mrs. Pentland. . . . You know Michael *very* well, and you know that he's got a bad, quick temper. If he found out that we were meddling in his affairs, he might do anything. He might chuck the whole business and clear out altogether. He's never been like this about a woman before. He'd do it just now. . . . That's the way he's feeling. You don't want to see him ruin himself any more than I do . . . a clever man like Michael. Why, he might be president one of these days. He can do anything he sets his will to, Ma'am, but he is, as they say, temperamental just now."

"I'll not tell him," said Olivia quietly. "And I'll do what I can to help you.

And now I must go." She felt suddenly friendly toward Mr. Gavin, perhaps because what he had been telling her was exactly what she wanted most at that moment to hear. She leaned down from her horse and held out her hand, saying, "Good-morning, Mr. Gavin."

Mr. Gavin removed his hat once more, revealing his round, bald, shiny head. "Good-morning, Mrs. Pentland."

As she rode off, the little man remained standing in the middle of the road looking after her until she had disappeared. His eye glowed with the light of admiration, but as Olivia turned from the road into the meadows, he frowned and swore aloud. Until now he hadn't understood how a good politician like Michael could lose his head over any woman. But he had an idea that he could trust this woman to do what she had promised. There was a look about her . . . a look which made her seem different from most women; perhaps it was this look which had made a fool of Michael, who usually kept women in their proper places.

Grinning and shaking his head, he got into the Ford, started it with a great uproar, and set off in the direction of Boston. After he had gone a little way he halted again and got out, for in his agitation he had forgotten to close the hood.

From the moment she turned and rode away from Mr. Gavin, Olivia gave herself over to action. She saw that there was need of more than mere static truth to bring order out of the hazy chaos at Pentlands; there must be action as well. And she was angry now, really angry, even at Mr. Gavin for his impertinence, and at the unknown person who had been his informant. The strange idea that Aunt Cassie or Anson was somehow responsible still remained; tactics such as these were completely sympathetic to them—to go thus in Machiavellian fashion to a man like Gavin instead of coming to her. By using Mr. Gavin there would be no scene, no definite unpleasantness to disturb the enchantment of Pentlands. They could go on pretending that nothing was wrong, that nothing had happened.

But stronger than her anger was the fear that in some way they might use the same tactics to spoil the happiness of Sybil. They would, she was certain, sacrifice everything to their belief in their own rightness.

She found Jean at the house when she returned, and, closing the door of the drawing-room, she said to him, "Jean, I want to talk to you for a moment . . . alone."

He said at once, "I know, Mrs. Pentland. It's about Sybil."

There was a little echo of humor in his voice that touched and disarmed her as it always did. It struck her that he was still young enough to be confident that everything in life would go exactly as he wished it. . . .

"Yes," she said, "that was it." They sat on two of Horace Pentland's chairs and she continued. "I don't believe in meddling, Jean, only now there are circumstances . . . reasons. . . ." She made a little gesture. "I thought that if really . . . really. . . ."

He interrupted her quickly. "I do, Mrs. Pentland. We've talked it all over, Sybil and I . . . and we're agreed. We love each other. We're going to be married."

Watching the young, ardent face, she thought, "It's a nice face in which there is nothing mean or nasty. The lips aren't thin and tight like Anson's, nor the skin sickly and pallid the way Anson's has always been. There's life in it, and force and charm. It's the face of a man who would be good to a woman . . . a man not in the least cold-blooded."

"Do you love her . . . really?" she asked.

"I . . . I. . . . It's a thing I can't answer because there aren't words to describe it."

"Because . . . well . . . Jean, it's no ordinary case of a mother and a daughter. It's much more than that. It means more to me than my own happiness, my own life . . . because, well, because Sybil is like a part of myself. I want her to be happy. It's not just a simple case of two young people marrying. It's much more than that." There was a silence, and she asked, "How do you love her?"

He sat forward on the edge of his chair, all eagerness. "Why . . ." he began, stammering a little, "I couldn't think of living without her. It's different from anything I ever imagined. Why . . . we've planned everything . . . all our lives. If ever I lost her, it wouldn't matter what happened to me afterwards." He grinned and added, "But you see . . . people have said all that before. There aren't any words to explain . . . to make it seem as different from anything else as it seems to me."

"But you're going to take her away?"

"Yes . . . she wants to go where I go."

("They are young," thought Olivia. "They've never once thought of any one else . . . myself or Sybil's grandfather.")

Aloud she said, "That's right, Jean. . . . I want you to take her away . . . no matter what happens, you must take her away. . . ." ("And then I won't even have Sybil.")

"We're going to my ranch in the Argentine."

"That's right. . . . I think Sybil would like that." She sighed, in spite of herself, vaguely envious of these two. "But you're so young. How can you know for certain."

A shadow crossed his face and he said, "I'm twenty-five, Mrs. Pentland . . . but that's not the only thing. . . . I was brought up, you see, among the French . . . like a Frenchman. That makes a difference." He hesitated, frowning for a moment. "Perhaps I oughtn't to tell. . . . You mightn't understand. I know how things are in this part of the world. . . . You see, I was brought up to look upon falling in love as something natural . . . something that was pleasant and natural and amusing. I've been in love before, casually . . . the way young Frenchmen are . . . but in earnest, too, because a Frenchman can't help surrounding a thing like that with sentiment and romance. He can't help it. If it were just . . . just something shameful and nasty, he couldn't endure it. They don't have affairs in cold blood . . . the way I've heard men talk about such things since I've come here. It makes a difference, Mrs. Pentland, if you look at the thing in the light they do. It's different here. . . . I see the difference more every day."

He was talking earnestly, passionately, and when he paused for a moment she remained silent, unwilling to interrupt him until he had finished.

"What I'm trying to say is difficult, Mrs. Pentland. It's simply this . . . that I'm twenty-five, but I've had experience with life. Don't laugh! Don't think I'm just a college boy trying to make you think I'm a roué. Only what I say is true. I know about such things . . . and I'm glad because it makes me all the more certain that Sybil is the only woman in the world for me . . . the one for whom I'd sacrifice everything. And I'll know better how to make her happy, to be gentle with her . . . to understand her. I've learned now, and it's a thing which needs learning . . . the most important thing in all life. The French are right about it. They make a fine, wonderful thing of love." He turned away with a sudden air of sadness. "Perhaps I shouldn't have told you all this. . . . I've told Sybil. She understands."

"No," said Olivia, "I think you're right . . . perhaps." She kept thinking of the long tragic story of John Pentland, and of Anson, who had always been ashamed of love and treated it as something distasteful. To them it had been a dark, strange thing always touched by shame. She kept thinking, despite anything she could do, of Anson's clumsy, artificial attempts at love-making, and she was swept suddenly by shame for him. Anson, so proud and supercilious, was a poor thing, inferior even to his own groom.

"But why," she asked, "didn't you tell me about Sybil sooner? Every one has seen it, but you never spoke to me."

For a moment he did not answer her. An expression of pain clouded the blue eyes, and then, looking at her directly, he said, "It's not easy to explain why. I was afraid to come to you for fear you mightn't understand, and the longer I've been here, the longer I've put it off because . . . well, because here in Durham, ancestors, family, all that, seems to be the beginning and end of everything. It seems always to be a question of who one's family is. There is only the past and no future at all. And, you see, in a way . . . I haven't any family." He shrugged his big shoulders and repeated, "In a way, I haven't any family at all. You see, my mother was never married to my father. . . . I've no blood-right to the name of de Cyon. I'm . . . I'm . . . well, just a bastard, and it seemed hopeless for me even to talk to a Pentland about Sybil."

He saw that she was startled, disturbed, but he could not have known that the look in her eyes had very little to do with shock at what he had told her; rather she was thinking what a weapon the knowledge would be in the hands of Anson and Aunt Cassie and even John Pentland himself.

He was talking again with the same passionate earnestness.

"I shan't let it make any difference, so long as Sybil will have me, but, you see, it's very hard to explain, because it isn't the way it seems. I want you to understand that my mother is a wonderful woman. . . . I wouldn't bother to explain, to say anything . . . except to Sybil and to you."

"Sabine has told me about her."

"Mrs. Callendar has known her for a long time. . . . They're great friends," said Jean. "She understands."

"But she never told me . . . that. You mean that she's known it all along?"

"It's not an easy thing to tell . . . especially here in Durham, and I fancy she thought it might make trouble for me . . . after she saw what had happened to Sybil and me."

He went on quickly, telling her what he had told Sybil of his mother's story, trying to make her understand what he understood, and Sabine and even his stepfather, the distinguished old de Cyon . . . trying to explain a thing which he himself knew was not to be explained. He told her that his mother had refused to marry her lover, "because in his life outside . . . the life which had nothing to do with her . . . she discovered that there were things she couldn't support. She saw that it was better not to marry him . . . better for herself and for him and, most of all, for me. . . . He did things for the sake of success—mean, dishonorable things—which she couldn't forgive . . . and so she wouldn't marry him. And now, looking back, I think she was right. It made no great difference in her life. She lived abroad . . . as a widow, and very few people—not more than two or three—ever knew the truth. *He* never told because, being a politician, he was afraid of such a scandal. She didn't want me to be brought up under such an influence, and I think she was right. He's gone on doing things that were mean and dishonorable. . . . He's still doing them to-day. You see he's a politician . . . a rather cheap one. He's a Senator now and he hasn't changed. I could tell you his name. . . . I suppose some people would think him a distinguished man . . . only I promised her never to tell it. He thinks that I'm dead. . . . He came to her once and asked to see me, to have a hand in my education and my future. There were things, he said, that he could do for me in America . . . and she told him simply that I was dead . . . that I was killed in the war." He finished in a sudden burst of enthusiasm, his face alight with affection. "But you must know her really to understand what I've been saying. Knowing her, you understand everything, because she's one of the great people . . . the strong people of the world. You see, it's one of the things which it is impossible to explain—to you or even to Sybil—impossible to explain to the others. One must know her."

If she had had any doubts or fears, she knew now that it was too late to act; she saw that it was impossible to change the wills of two such lovers as Jean and Sybil. In a way, she came to understand the story of Jean's mother more from watching him than by listening to his long explanation. There must be in her that same determination and ardor that was in her son . . . a thing in its way irresistible. And yet it was difficult; she was afraid, somehow, of this unexpected thing, perhaps because it seemed vaguely like the taint of Savina Pentland.

She said, "If no one knows this, there is no reason to tell it here. It would only make unhappiness for all concerned. It is your business alone . . . and Sybil's. The others have no right to interfere, even to know; but they will try, Jean . . . unless . . . you both do what you want . . . quickly. Sometimes I think they might do anything."

"You mean . . ." he began impatiently.

Olivia fell back upon that vague hint which John Pentland had dropped to her the night before. She said, "There was once an elopement in the Pentland family."

"You wouldn't mind that?" he asked eagerly. "You wouldn't be hurt . . . if we did it that way?"

"I shouldn't know anything about it," said Olivia quietly, "until it was too late to do anything."

"It's funny," he said; "we'd thought of that. We've talked of it, only Sybil was afraid you'd want to have a big wedding and all that. . . ."

"No, I think it would be better not to have any wedding at all . . . especially under the circumstances."

"Mrs. Callendar suggested it as the best way out. . . . She offered to lend us her motor," he said eagerly.

"You discussed it with her and yet you didn't speak to me?"

"Well, you see, she's different . . . she and Thérèse. . . . They don't belong here in Durham. Besides, she spoke of it first. She knew what was going on. She always knows. I almost think that she planned the whole thing long ago."

Olivia, looking out of the window, saw entering the long drive the antiquated motor with Aunt Cassie, Miss Peavey, her flying veils and her Pekinese.

"Mrs. Struthers is coming . . ." she said. "We mustn't make her suspicious. And you'd best tell me nothing of your plans and then . . . I shan't be able to interfere even if I wanted to. I might change my mind . . . one never knows."

He stood up and, coming over to her, took her hand and kissed it. "There's nothing to say, Mrs. Pentland . . . except that you'll be glad for what you've done. You needn't worry about Sybil. . . . I shall make her happy. . . . I think I know how."

He left her, hurrying away past the ancestors in the long hall to find Sybil, thinking all the while how odd it would seem to have a woman so young and beautiful as Mrs. Pentland for a mother-in-law. She was a charming woman (he thought in his enthusiasm), a great woman, but she was so sad, as if she had never been very happy. There was always a cloud about her.

He did not escape quickly enough, for Aunt Cassie's sharp eyes caught a glimpse of him as he left the house in the direction of the stables. She met Olivia in the doorway, kissing her and saying, "Was that Sybil's young man I saw leaving?"

"Yes," said Olivia. "We've been talking about Sybil. I've been telling him that he mustn't think of her as some one to marry."

The yellow face of Aunt Cassie lighted with a smile of approval. "I'm glad, my dear, that you're being sensible about this. I was afraid you wouldn't be, but I didn't like to interfere. I never believe any good comes of it, unless one is forced to. He's not the person for Sybil. . . . Why, no one knows anything about him. You can't let a girl marry like that . . . just any one who comes along. Besides, Mrs. Pulsifer writes me. . . . You remember her, Olivia, the Mannering boy's aunt who used to have a house in Chestnut Street. . . . Well, she lives in Paris now at the Hotel Continental, and she writes me she's discovered there's some mystery about his mother. No one seems to know much about her."

"Why," said Olivia, "should she write you such a thing? What made her think you'd be interested?"

"Well, Kate Pulsifer and I went to school together and we still correspond now and then. I just happened to mention the boy's name when I was writing her about Sabine. She says, by the way, that Sabine has very queer friends in Paris and that Sabine has never so much as called on her or asked her for tea. And there's been some new scandal about Sabine's husband and an Italian woman. It happened in Venice. . . ."

"But he's not her husband any longer."

The old lady seated herself and went on pouring forth the news from Kate Pulsifer's letter; with each word she appeared to grow stronger and stronger, less and less yellow and worn.

("It must be," thought Olivia, "the effect of so many calamities contained in one letter.")

She saw now that she had acted only just in time and she was glad that she had lied, so flatly, so abruptly, without thinking why she had done it. For Mrs. Pulsifer was certain to go to the bottom of the affair, if for no other reason than to do harm to Sabine; she had once lived in a house on Chestnut Street with a bow-window which swept the entrance to every house. She was one of John Pentland's dead, who lived by watching others live.

4

From the moment she encountered Mr. Gavin on the turnpike until the tragedy which occurred two days later, life at Pentlands appeared to lose all reality for Olivia. When she thought of it long afterward, the hours became a sort of nightmare in which the old enchantment snapped and gave way to a strained sense of struggle between forces which, centering about herself, left her in the end bruised and a little broken, but secure.

The breathless heat of the sort which from time to time enveloped that corner of New England, leaving the very leaves of the trees hanging limp and wilted, again settled down over the meadows and marshes, and in the midst of the afternoon appeared the rarest of sights—the indolent Sabine stirring in the burning sun. Olivia watched her coming across the fields, protected from the blazing sun only by the frivolous yellow parasol. She came slowly, indifferently, and until she entered the cool, darkened drawing-room she appeared the familiar bored Sabine; only after she greeted Olivia the difference appeared.

She said abruptly, "I'm leaving day after to-morrow," and instead of seating herself to talk, she kept wandering restlessly about the room, examining Horace Pentland's bibelots and turning the pages of books and magazines without seeing them.

"Why?" asked Olivia. "I thought you were staying until October."

"No, I'm going away at once." She turned and murmured, "I've hated Durham always. It's unbearable to me now. I'm bored to death. I only came, in the first place, because I thought Thérèse ought to know her own people. But it's no good. She'll have none of them. I see now how like her father she is. They're not her own people and never will be. . . . I don't imagine Durham will ever see either of us again."

Olivia smiled. "I know it's dull here."

"Oh, I don't mean you, Olivia dear, or even Sybil or O'Hara, but there's something in the air. . . . I'm going to Newport for two weeks and then to Biarritz for October. Thérèse wants to go to Oxford." She grinned sardonically. "There's a bit of New England in her, after all . . . this education business. I wanted a *femme du monde* for a daughter and God and New England sent me a scientist who would rather wear flat heels and look through a microscope. It's funny how children turn out."

("Even Thérèse and Sabine," thought Olivia. "Even they belong to it.")

She watched Sabine, so worldly, so superbly dressed, so hard—such a restless nomad; and as she watched her it occurred to her again that she was very like Aunt Cassie—an Aunt Cassie in revolt against Aunt Cassie's gods, an Aunt Cassie, as John Pentland had said, "turned inside out."

Without looking up from the pages of the *Nouvelle Revue*, Sabine said, "I'm glad this thing about Sybil is settled."

"Yes."

"He told you about his mother?"

"Yes."

"You didn't let that make any difference? You didn't tell the others?"

"No. . . . Anything I had to say would have made no difference."

"You were wise. . . . I think Thérèse is right, perhaps . . . righter than any of us. She says that nature has a contempt for marriage certificates. Respectability can't turn decay into life . . . and Jean is alive. . . . So is his mother."

"I know what you are driving at."

"Certainly, my dear, you ought to know. You've suffered enough from it. And knowing his mother makes a difference. She's no ordinary light woman, or even one who was weak enough to allow herself to be seduced. Once in fifty years there occurs a woman who can . . . how shall I say it? . . . get away with a thing like that. You have to be a great woman to do it. I don't think it's made much difference in her life, chiefly because she's a woman of discretion and excellent taste. But it might have made a difference in Jean's life if he had encountered a mother less wise than yourself."

"I don't know whether I'm being wise or not. I believe in him and I want Sybil to escape."

Olivia understood that for the first time they were discussing the thing which none of them ever mentioned, the thing which up to now Sabine had only touched upon by insinuation. Sabine had turned away and stood looking out of the window across the meadows where the distant trees danced in waves of heat.

"You spoiled my summer a bit, Olivia dear, by taking away my Irish friend from me."

Suddenly Olivia was angry as she was angry sometimes at the meddling of Aunt Cassie. "I didn't take him away. I did everything possible to avoid him . . . until you came. It was you who threw us together. That's why we're all in a tangle now." And she kept thinking what a strange woman Sabine Callendar really was, how intricate and unfathomable. She knew of no other woman in the world who could talk thus so dispassionately, so without emotion.

"I thought I'd have him to amuse," she was saying, "and instead of that he only uses me as a confidante. He comes to me for advice about another woman. And that, as you know, isn't very interesting. . . ."

Olivia sat suddenly erect. "What does he say? What right has he to do such a thing?"

"Because I've asked him to. When I first came here, I promised to help him. You see, I'm very friendly with you both. I want you both to be happy and . . . besides I can think of nothing happening which could give me greater pleasure."

When Olivia did not answer her, she turned from the window and asked abruptly, "What are you going to do about him?"

Again Olivia thought it best not to answer, but Sabine went on pushing home her point relentlessly, "You must forgive me for speaking plainly, but I have a great affection for you both . . . and I . . . well, I have a sense of conscience in the affair."

"You needn't have. There's nothing to have a conscience about."

"You're not being very honest."

Suddenly Olivia burst out angrily, "And why should it concern you, Sabine . . . in the least? Why should I not do as I please, without interference?"

"Because, here . . . and you know this as well as I do . . . here such a thing is impossible."

In a strange fashion she was suddenly afraid of Sabine, perhaps because she was so bent upon pushing things to a definite solution. It seemed to Olivia that she herself was losing all power of action, all capacity for anything save waiting, pretending, doing nothing.

"And I'm interested," continued Sabine slowly, "because I can't bear the tragic spectacle of another John Pentland and Mrs. Soames."

"There won't be," said Olivia desperately. "My father-in-law is different from Michael."

"That's true. . . ."

"In a way . . . a finer man." She found herself suddenly in the amazing position of actually defending Pentlands.

"But not," said Sabine with a terrifying reasonableness, "so wise a one . . . or one so intelligent."

"No. It's impossible to say. . . ."

"A thing like this is likely to come only once to a woman."

("Why does she keep repeating the very things that I've been fighting all along," thought Olivia.) Aloud she said, "Sabine, you must leave me in peace. It's for me alone to settle."

"I don't want you to do a thing you will regret the rest of your life . . . bitterly."

"You mean. . . ."

"Oh, I mean simply to give him up."

Again Olivia was silent, and Sabine asked suddenly, "Have you had a call from a Mr. Gavin? A gentleman with a bald head and a polished face?"

Olivia looked at her sharply. "How could you know that?"

"Because I sent him, my dear . . . for the same reason that I'm here now . . . because I wanted you to do something . . . to act. And I'm confessing now because I thought you ought to know the truth, since I'm going away. Otherwise you might think Aunt Cassie or Anson had done it . . . and trouble might come of that."

Again Olivia said nothing; she was lost in a sadness over the thought that, after all, Sabine was no better than the others.

"It's not easy to act in this house," Sabine was saying. "It's not easy to do anything but pretend and go on and on until at last you are an old woman and die. I did it to help you . . . for your own good."

"That's what Aunt Cassie always says."

The shaft went home, for it silenced Sabine, and in the moment's pause Sabine seemed less a woman than an amazing, disembodied, almost malevolent force. When she answered, it was with a shrug of the shoulders and a bitter smile which seemed doubly bitter on the frankly painted lips. "I suppose I *am* like Aunt Cassie. I mightn't have been, though. . . . I might have been just a pleasant normal person . . . like Higgins or one of the servants."

The strange speech found an echo in Olivia's heart. Lately the same thought had come to her again and again—if only she could be simple like Higgins or the kitchen-maid. Such a state seemed to her at the moment the most desirable thing in the world. It was perhaps this strange desire which led Sabine to surround herself with what Durham called "queer people," who were, after all, simply people like Higgins and the kitchen-maid who happened to occupy a higher place in society.

"The air here needs clearing," Sabine was saying. "It needs a thunderstorm, and it can be cleared only by acting. . . . This affair of Jean and Sybil will help. We are all caught up in a tangle of thoughts and ideas . . . which don't matter. . . . You can do it, Olivia. You can clear the air once and for all."

Then for the first time Olivia thought she saw what lay behind all this intriguing of Sabine; for a moment she fancied that she saw what it was Sabine wanted more passionately than anything else in the world.

Aloud she said it, "I could clear the air, but it would also be the destruction of everything."

Sabine looked at her directly. "Well? . . . and would you be sorry? Would you count it a loss? Would it make any difference?"

Impulsively she touched Sabine's hand. "Sabine," she said, without looking at her, "I'm fond of you. You know that. Please don't talk any more about this . . . please, because I want to go on being fond of you . . . and I can't otherwise. It's our affair, mine and Michael's . . . and I'm going to settle it, to-night perhaps, as soon as I can have a talk with him. . . . I can't go on any longer."

Taking up the yellow parasol, Sabine asked, "Do you expect me for dinner to-night?"

"Of course, more than ever to-night. . . . I'm sorry you've decided to go so soon. . . . It'll be dreary without you or Sybil."

"You can go, too," said Sabine quickly. "There is a way. He'd give up everything for you . . . everything. I know that." Suddenly she gave Olivia a sharp look. "You're thirty-eight, aren't you?"

"Day after to-morrow I shall be forty!"

Sabine was tracing the design of roses on Horace Pentland's Savonnerie carpet with the tip of her parasol. "Gather them while you may," she said and went out into the blazing heat to cross the meadows to Brook Cottage.

Left alone, Olivia knew she was glad that day after to-morrow Sabine would no longer be here. She saw now what John Pentland meant when he said, "Sabine ought never to have come back here."

5

The heat clung on far into the evening, penetrating with the darkness even the drawing-room where they sat—Sabine and John Pentland and old Mrs. Soames and Olivia—playing bridge for the last time, and as the evening wore on the game went more and more badly, with the old lady forgetting her cards and John Pentland being patient and Sabine sitting in a controlled and sardonic silence, with an expression on her face which said clearly, "I can endure this for to-night because to-morrow I shall escape again into the lively world."

Jean and Sybil sat for a time at the piano, and then fell to watching the bridge. No one spoke save to bid or to remind Mrs. Soames that it was time for her shaking hands to distribute the cards about the table. Even Olivia's low, quiet voice sounded loud in the hot stillness of the old room.

At nine o'clock Higgins appeared with a message for Olivia—that Mr. O'Hara was being detained in town and that if he could get away before ten he would come down and stop at Pentlands if the lights were still burning in the drawing-room. Otherwise he would not be down to ride in the morning.

Once during a pause in the game Sabine stirred herself to say, "I haven't asked about Anson's book. He must be near to the end."

"Very near," said Olivia. "There's very little more to be done. Men are coming to-morrow to photograph the portraits. He's using them to illustrate the book."

At eleven, when they came to the end of a rubber, Sabine said, "I'm sorry, but I must stop. I must get up early to-morrow to see about the packing." And turning to Jean she said, "Will you drive me home? Perhaps Sybil will ride over with us for the air. You can bring her back."

At the sound of her voice, Olivia wanted to cry out, "No, don't go. You mustn't leave me now . . . alone. You mustn't go away like this!" But she managed to say quietly, in a voice which sounded far away, "Don't stay too late, Sybil," and mechanically, without knowing what she was doing, she began to put the cards back again in their boxes.

She saw that Sabine went out first, and then John Pentland and old Mrs. Soames, and that Jean and Sybil remained behind until the others had gone, until John Pentland had helped the old lady gently into his motor and driven off with her. Then, looking up with a smile which somehow seemed to give her pain she said, "Well?"

And Sybil, coming to her side, kissed her and said in a low voice, "Good-by, darling, for a little while. . . . I love you. . . ." And Jean kissed her in a shy fashion on both cheeks.

She could find nothing to say. She knew Sybil would come back, but she would be a different Sybil, a Sybil who was a woman, no longer the child who even at eighteen sometimes had the absurd trick of sitting on her mother's knee. And she was taking away with her something that until now had belonged to Olivia, something which she could never again claim. She could find nothing to say. She could only follow them to the door, from where she saw Sabine already sitting in the motor as if nothing in the least unusual were happening; and all the while she wanted to go with them, to run away anywhere at all.

Through a mist she saw them turning to wave to her as the motor drove off, to wave gaily and happily because they were at the beginning of life. . . . She stood in the doorway to watch the motor-lights slipping away in silence down the lane and over the bridge through the blackness to the door of Brook Cottage. There was something about Brook Cottage . . . something that was lacking from the air of Pentlands: it was where Toby Cane and Savina Pentland had had their wanton meetings.

In the still heat the sound of the distant surf came to her dimly across the marshes, and into her mind came absurdly words she had forgotten for years . . . "The breaking waves dashed high on the stern and rockbound coast." Against the accompaniment of the surf, the crickets and katydids (harbingers of autumn) kept up a fiddling and singing; and far away in the direction of Marblehead she watched the eye of a lighthouse winking and winking. She was aware of every sight and sound and odor of the breathless night. It might storm, she thought, before they got into Connecticut. They would be motoring all the night. . . .

The lights of Sabine's motor were moving again now, away from Brook Cottage, through O'Hara's land, on and on in the direction of the turnpike. In the deep hollow by the river they disappeared for a moment and then were to be seen once more against the black mass of the hill crowned by the town burial-ground. And then abruptly they were gone, leaving only the sound of the surf and the music of the crickets and the distant, ironically winking lighthouse.

She kept seeing them side by side in the motor racing through the darkness, oblivious to all else in the world save their own happiness. Yes, something had gone away from her forever. . . . She felt a terrible, passionate envy that was like a physical pain, and all at once she knew that she was terribly alone standing in the darkness before the door of the old house.

She was roused by the sound of Anson's voice asking, "Is that you, Olivia?"

"Yes."

"What are you doing out there?"

"I came out for some air."

"Where's Sybil?"

For a moment she did not answer, and then quite boldly she said, "She's ridden over with Jean to take Sabine home."

"You know I don't approve of that." He had come through the hall now and was standing near her.

"It can't do any harm."

"That's been said before. . . ."

"Why are you so suspicious, Anson, of your own child?" She had no desire to argue with him. She wanted only to be left in peace, to go away to her room and lie there alone in the darkness, for she knew now that Michael was not coming.

"Olivia," Anson was saying, "come inside for a moment. I want to talk to you."

"Very well . . . but please don't be disagreeable. I'm very tired."

"I shan't be disagreeable. . . . I only want to settle something."

She knew then that he meant to be very disagreeable, and she told herself that she would not listen to him; she would think of something else while he was speaking—a trick she had learned long ago. In the drawing-room she sat quietly and waited for him to begin. Standing by the mantelpiece, he appeared more tired and yellow than usual. She knew that he had worked on his book; she knew that he had poured all his vitality, all his being, into it; but as she watched him her imagination again played her the old trick of showing her Michael standing there in his place . . . defiant, a little sulky, and filled with a slow, steady, inexhaustible force.

"It's chiefly about Sybil," he said. "I want her to give up seeing this boy."

"Don't be a martinet, Anson. Nothing was ever gained by it."

(She thought, "They must be almost to Salem by now.") And aloud she added, "You're her father, Anson; why don't you speak?"

"It's better for you. I've no influence with her."

"I have spoken," she said, thinking bitterly that he could never guess what she meant.

"And what's the result? Look at her, going off at this hour of the night. . . ."

She shrugged her shoulders, filled with a warm sense of having outwitted the enemy, for at the moment Anson seemed to her an enemy not only of herself, but of Jean and Sybil, of all that was young and alive in the world.

"Besides," he was saying, "she hasn't proper respect for me . . . her father. Sometimes I think it's the ideas she got from you and from going abroad to school."

"What a nasty thing to say! But if you want the truth, I think it's because you've never been a very good father. Sometimes I've thought you never wanted children. You've never paid much attention to them . . . not even to Jack . . . while he was alive. It wasn't ever as if they were *our* children. You've always left them to me . . . alone."

The thin neck stiffened a little and he said, "There are reasons for that. I'm a busy man. . . . I've given most of my time, not to making money, but to doing things to better the world in some way. If I've neglected my children it's been for a good reason . . . few men have as much on their minds. And there's been the book to take all my energies. You're being unjust, Olivia. You never could see me as I am."

"Perhaps," said Olivia. (She wanted to say, "What difference does the book make to any one in the world? Who cares whether it is written or not?") She knew that she must keep up her deceit, so she said, "You needn't worry, because Sabine is going away to-morrow and Jean will go with her." She sighed. "After that your life won't be disturbed any longer. Nothing in the least unusual is likely to happen."

"And there's this other thing," he said, "this disloyalty of yours to me and to all the family."

Stiffening slightly, she asked, "What can you mean by that?"

"You know what I mean."

She saw that he was putting himself in the position of a wronged husband, assuming a martyrdom of the sort which Aunt Cassie practised so effectively.

He meant to be a patient, well-meaning husband and to place her in the position of a shameful woman; and slowly, with a slow, heavy anger, she resolved to circumvent his trick.

"I think, Anson, that you're talking nonsense. I haven't been disloyal to any one. Your father will tell you that."

"My father was always weak where women are concerned, and now he's beginning to grow childish. He's so old that he's beginning to forgive and condone anything." And then after a silence he said, "This O'Hara. I'm not such a fool as you think, Olivia."

For a long time neither of them said anything, and in the end it was Olivia who spoke, striking straight into the heart of the question. She said, "Anson, would you consider letting me divorce you?"

The effect upon him was alarming. His face turned gray, and the long, thin, oversensitive hands began to tremble. She saw that she had touched him on the rawest of places, upon his immense sense of pride and dignity. It would be unbearable for him to believe that she would want to be rid of him in order to go to another man, especially to a man whom he professed to hold in contempt, a man who had the qualities which he himself did not possess. He could only see the request as a humiliation of his own precious dignity.

He managed to grin, trying to turn the request to mockery, and said, "Have you lost your mind?"

"No, Anson, not for a moment. What I ask is a simple thing. It has been done before."

He did not answer her at once, and began to move about the room in the deepest agitation, a strange figure curiously out of place in the midst of Horace Pentland's exotic, beautiful pictures and chairs and bibelots—as wrong in such a setting as he had been right a month or two earlier among the museum of Pentland family relics.

"No," he said again and again. "What you ask is preposterous! To-morrow when you are less tired you will see how ridiculous it is. No . . . I couldn't think of such a thing!"

She made an effort to speak quietly. "Is it because you don't want to put yourself in such a position?"

"It has nothing to do with that. Why should you want a divorce? We are well off, content, comfortable, happy. . . ."

She interrupted him, asking, "Are we?"

"What is it you expect, Olivia . . . to live always in a sort of romantic glow? We're happier than most."

"No," she said slowly. "I don't think happiness has ever meant much to you, Anson. Perhaps you're above such things as happiness and unhappiness. Perhaps you're more fortunate than most of us. I doubt if you have ever known happiness or unhappiness, for that matter. You've been uncomfortable when people annoyed you and got in your way, but . . . that's all. Nothing more than that. Happiness . . . I mean it in the sensible way . . . has sometimes to do with delight in living, and I don't think you've ever known that, even for a moment."

He turned toward her saying, "I've been an honest, God-fearing, conscientious man, and I think you're talking nonsense!"

"No, not for a moment. . . . Heaven knows I ought to know the truth of what I've been saying."

Again they reached an impasse in the conversation and again they both remained silent, disturbed perhaps and uneasy in the consciousness that between them they had destroyed something which could never be restored; and yet with Olivia there was a cold, sustained sense of balance which came to her miraculously at such times. She felt, too, that she stood with her back against a wall, fighting. At last she said, "I would even let you divorce me— if that would be easier for you. I don't mind putting myself in the wrong."

Again he began to tremble. "Are you trying to tell me that. . . ."

"I'm not telling you anything. There hasn't been anything at all . . . but . . . but I would give you grounds if you would agree."

He turned away from her in disgust. "That is even more impossible. . . . A gentleman never divorces his wife."

"Let's leave the gentlemen out of it, Anson," she said. "I'm weary of hearing what gentlemen do and do not do. I want you to act as yourself, as Anson Pentland, and not as you think you ought to act. Let's be honest. You know you married me only because you had to marry some one . . . and I . . . I wasn't actually disreputable, even, as you remind me, if my father was shanty Irish. And . . . let's be just too. I married you because I was alone and frightened and wanted to escape a horrible life with Aunt Alice. . . . I wanted a home. That was it, wasn't it? We are both guilty, but that doesn't change the reality in the least. No, I fancy you practised loving me through a sense of duty. You tried it as long as you could and you hated it always. Oh, I've known what was going on. I've been learning ever since I came to Pentlands for the first time."

He was regarding her now with a fixed expression of horrid fascination; he was perhaps even dazed at the sound of her voice, slowly, resolutely, tearing aside all the veils of pretense which had made their life possible for so long. He kept mumbling, "How can you talk this way? How can you say such things?"

Slowly, terribly, she went on and on: "We're both guilty . . . and it's been a failure, from the very start. I've tried to do my best and perhaps sometimes I've failed. I've tried to be a good mother . . . and now that Sybil is grown and Jack . . . is dead, I want a chance at freedom. I'm still young enough to want to live a little before it is too late."

Between his teeth he said, "Don't be a fool, Olivia. . . . You're forty years old. . . ."

"You needn't remind me of that. To-morrow I shall be forty. I know it . . . bitterly. But my being forty makes no difference to you. To you it would be all the same if I were seventy. But to me it makes a difference . . .

a great difference." She waited a moment, and then said, "That's the truth, Anson; and it's the truth that interests me to-night. Let me be free, Anson. . . . Let me go while being free still means something."

Perhaps if she had thrown herself at his feet in the attitude of a wretched, shameful woman, if she had made him feel strong and noble and heroic, she would have won; but it was a thing she could not do. She could only go on being coldly reasonable.

"And you would give up all this?" he was saying. "You'd leave Pentlands and all it stands for to marry this cheap Irishman . . . a nobody, the son perhaps of an immigrant dock-laborer."

"He *is* the son of a dock-laborer," she answered quietly. "And his mother was a housemaid. He's told me so himself. And as to all this. . . . Why, Anson, it doesn't mean anything to me . . . nothing at all that I can't give up, nothing which means very much. I'm fond of your father, Anson, and I'm fond of you when you are yourself and not talking about what a gentleman would do. But I'd give it all up . . . everything . . . for the sake of this other thing."

For a moment his lips moved silently and in agitation, as if it were impossible for him to answer things so preposterous as those his wife had just spoken. At last he was able to say, "I think you must have lost your mind, Olivia . . . to even think of asking such a thing of me. You've lived here long enough to know how impossible it is. Some of us must make a stand in a community. There has never been a scandal, or even a divorce, in the Pentland family . . . never. We've come to stand for something. Three hundred years of clean, moral living can't be dashed aside so easily. . . . We're in a position where others look up to us. Can't you see that? Can't you understand such a responsibility?"

For a moment she had a terrible, dizzy, intoxicating sense of power, of knowing that she held the means of destroying him and all this whited structure of pride and respectability. She had only to begin by saying, "There was Savina Pentland and her lover. . . ." The moment passed quickly and at once she knew that it was a thing she could not do. Instead, she murmured, "Ah, Anson, do you think the world really looks at us at all? Do you think it really cares what we do or don't do? You can't be as blind as that."

"I'm not blind . . . only there's such a thing as honor and tradition. We stand for something. . . ."

She interrupted him. "For what?"

"For decency, for a glorious past, for stability . . . for endless things . . . all the things which count in a civilized community."

He really believed what he was saying; she knew that he must have believed it to have written all those thousands of dull, laborious words in glorification of the past.

He went on. "No, what you ask is impossible. You knew it before you asked. . . . And it would be a kindness to me if you never mentioned it again."

He was still pale, but he had gained control of himself and his hands no longer trembled; as he talked, as his sense of virtue mounted, he even grew eloquent, and his voice took on a shade of that unction which had always colored the voice of the Apostle to the Genteel and made of him a cele-brated and fashionable cleric. Perhaps for the first time since his childhood, since the days when the red-haired little Sabine had mocked his curls and velvet suits, he felt himself a strong and powerful person. There was a kind of fierce intoxication in the knowledge of his power over Olivia. In his vir-tuous ardor he seemed for a moment to become a positive, almost admira-ble person.

At length she said quietly, "And what if I should simply go away . . . without bothering about a divorce?"

The remark shattered all his confidence once more; and she knew that she had struck at the weakest point in all his defense—the fear of a scandal. "You wouldn't do that!" he cried. "You couldn't—you couldn't behave like a common prostitute!"

"Loving one man is not behaving like a common prostitute. . . . I never loved any other."

"You couldn't bring such a disgrace on Sybil, even if you don't care for the rest of us."

("He knew, then, that I couldn't do such a thing, that I haven't the courage. He knows that I've lived too long in this world.") Aloud she said, "You don't know me, Anson. . . . In all these years you've never known me at all."

"Besides," he added quickly, "he wouldn't do such a thing. Such a climber isn't likely to throw over his whole career by running away with a woman. You'd find out if you asked him."

"But he *is* willing. He's already told me so. Perhaps you can't understand such a thing." When he did not answer, she said ironically, "Besides, I don't think a gentleman would talk as you are talking. No, Anson. . . . I don't think you know what the world is. You've lived here always, shut up in your own little corner." Rising, she sighed and murmured, "But there's no use in talk. I am going to bed. . . . I suppose we must struggle on as best we can . . . but there are times . . . times like to-night when you make it hard for me to bear it. Some day . . . who knows . . . there's nothing any longer to keep me. . . ."

She went away without troubling to finish what she had meant to say, lost again in an overwhelming sense of the futility of everything. She felt, she thought, like an idiot standing in the middle of an empty field, making gestures.

Chapter 10

1

Toward morning the still, breathless heat broke without warning into a fantastic storm which filled all the sky with blinding light and enveloped the whole countryside in a wild uproar of wind and thunder, leaving the dawn to reveal fields torn and ravaged and strewn with broken branches, and the bright garden bruised and battered by hail.

At breakfast Anson appeared neat and shaven and smooth, as though there had been no struggle a few hours before in the drawing-room, as if the thing had made no impression upon the smooth surface which he turned toward the world. Olivia poured his coffee quietly and permitted him to kiss her as he had done every day for twenty years—a strange, cold, absent-minded kiss—and stood in the doorway to watch him drive off to the train. Nothing had changed; it seemed to her that life at Pentlands had become incapable of any change.

And as she turned from the door Peters summoned her to the telephone to receive the telegram from Jean and Sybil; they had been married at seven in Hartford.

She set out at once to find John Pentland and after a search she came upon him in the stable-yard talking with Higgins. The strange pair stood by the side of the red mare, who watched them with her small, vicious red eyes; they were talking in that curious intimate way which descended upon them at the mention of horses, and as she approached she was struck, as she always was, by the fiery beauty of the animal, the pride of her lean head, the trembling of the fine nostrils as she breathed, the savagery of her eye. She was a strange, half-evil, beautiful beast. Olivia heard Higgins saying that it was no use trying to breed her . . . an animal like that, who kicked and screamed and bit at the very sight of another horse. . . .

Higgins saw her first and, touching his cap, bade her good-morning, and as the old man turned, she said, "I've news for you, Mr. Pentland."

A shrewd, queer look came into his eyes and he asked, "Is it about Sybil?"

"Yes. . . . It's done."

She saw that Higgins was mystified, and she was moved by a desire to tell him. Higgins ought to know certainly among the first. And she added, "It's about Miss Sybil. She married young Mr. de Cyon this morning in Hartford."

The news had a magical effect on the little groom; his ugly, shriveled face expanded into a broad grin and he slapped his thigh in his enthusiasm. "That's grand, Ma'am. . . . I don't mind telling you I was for it all along. She couldn't have done better . . . nor him either."

Again moved by impulse, she said, "So you think it's a good thing?"

"It's grand, Ma'am. He's one in a million. He's the only one I know who was good enough. I was afraid she was going to throw herself away on Mr. O'Hara. . . . But she ought to have a younger man."

She turned away from him, pleased and relieved from the anxiety which had never really left her since the moment they drove off into the darkness. She kept thinking, "Higgins is always right about people. He has a second sight." Somehow, of them all, she trusted him most as a judge.

John Pentland led her away, out of range of Higgins' curiosity, along the hedge that bordered the gardens. The news seemed to affect him strangely, for he had turned pale, and for a long time he simply stood looking over the hedge in silence. At last he asked, "When did they do it?"

"Last night. . . . She went for a drive with him and they didn't come back."

"I hope we've been right . . ." he said. "I hope we haven't connived at a foolish thing."

"No. . . . I'm sure we haven't."

Something in the brilliance of the sunlight, in the certainty of Sybil's escape and happiness, in the freshness of the air touched after the storm by the first faint feel of autumn, filled her with a sense of giddiness, so that she forgot her own troubles; she forgot, even, that this was her fortieth birthday.

"Did they go in Sabine's motor?" he asked.

"Yes."

Grinning suddenly, he said, "She thought perhaps that she was doing us a bad turn."

"No, she knew that I approved. She did think of it first. She did propose it. . . ."

When he spoke again there was a faint hint of bitterness in his voice. "I'm sure she did. I only hope she'll stop her mischief with this. In any case, she's had a victory over Cassie . . . and that's what she wanted, more than anything. . . ." He turned toward her sharply, with an air of anxiety. "I suppose he'll take her away with him?"

"Yes. They're going to Paris first and then to the Argentine."

Suddenly he touched her shoulder with the odd, shy gesture of affection. "It'll be hard for you, Olivia dear . . . without her."

The sudden action brought a lump into her throat, and yet she did not want to be pitied. She hated pity, because it implied weakness on her part.

"Oh," she said quickly, "they'll come back from time to time. . . . I think that some day they may come back here to live."

"Yes. . . . Pentlands will belong to them one day."

And then for the first time she remembered that there was something which she had to tell him, something which had come to seem almost a confession. She must tell him now, especially since Jean would one day own all of Pentlands and all the fortune.

"There's something I didn't tell you before," she began. "It's something which I kept to myself because I wanted Sybil to have her happiness . . . in spite of everything."

He interrupted her, saying, "I know what it is."

"You couldn't know what I mean."

"Yes; the boy told me himself. I went to him to talk about Sybil because I wanted to make sure of him . . . and after a time he told me. It was an honorable thing for him to have done. He needn't have told. Sabine would never have told us . . . never until it was too late."

The speech left her feeling weak and disconcerted, for she had expected anger from him and disapproval. She had been fearful that he might treat her silence as a disloyalty to him, that it might in the end shatter the long, trusting relationship between them.

"The boy couldn't help it," he was saying. "It's a thing one can't properly explain. But he's a nice boy . . . and Sybil was so set on him. I think she has a good, sensible head on her young shoulders." Sighing and turning toward her again, he added, "I wouldn't speak of it to the others . . . not even to Anson. They may never know, and if they don't what they don't know won't hurt them."

The mystery of him, it seemed, grew deeper and deeper each time they talked thus, intimately, perhaps because there were in the old man depths which she had never believed possible. Perhaps, deep down beneath all the fierce reticence of his nature, there lay a humanity far greater than any she had ever encountered. She thought, "And I have always believed him hard and cold and disapproving." She was beginning to fathom the great strength that lay in his fierce isolation, the strength of a man who had always been alone.

"And you, Olivia?" he asked presently. "Are you happy?"

"Yes. . . . At least, I'm happy this morning . . . on account of Sybil and Jean."

"That's right," he said with a gentle sadness. "That's right. They've done what you and I were never able to do, Olivia. They'll have what we've never had and never can have because it's too late. And we've helped them to gain it. . . . That's something. I merely wanted you to know that I understood." And then, "We'd better go and tell the others. The devil will be to pay when they hear."

She would have gone away then, but an odd thought occurred to her, a hope, feeble enough, but one which might give him a little pleasure. She was struck again by his way of speaking, as if he were very near to death or already dead. He had the air of a very old and weary man.

She said, "There's one thing I've wanted to ask you for a long time." She hesitated and then plunged. "It was about Savina Pentland. Did she ever have more than one child?"

He looked at her sharply out of the bright black eyes and asked, "Why do you want to know that?"

She tried to deceive him by shrugging her shoulders and saying casually, "I don't know. . . . I've become interested lately, perhaps on account of Anson's book."

"You . . . interested in the past, Olivia?"

"Yes."

"Yes, she only had one child . . . and then she was drowned when he was only a year old. He was my grandfather." Again he looked at her sharply. "Olivia, you must tell me the truth. Why did you ask me that question?"

Again she hesitated, saying, "I don't know . . . it seemed to me. . . ."

"Did you find something? Did *she*," he asked, making the gesture toward the north wing, "did *she* tell you anything?"

She understood then that he, marvelous old man, must even know about the letters. "Yes," she said in a low voice, "I found something . . . in the attic."

He sighed and looked away again, across the wet meadows. "So you know, too. . . . *She* found them first, and hid them away again. She wouldn't give them to me because she hated me . . . from our wedding-night. I've told you about that. And then she couldn't remember where she'd hid them . . . poor thing. But she told me about them. At times she used to taunt me by saying that I wasn't a Pentland at all. I think the thing made her mind darker than it was before. She had some terrible idea about the sin in my family for which she must atone. . . ."

"It's true," said Olivia softly. "There's no doubt of it. It was written by Toby Cane himself . . . in his own handwriting. I've compared it with the letters Anson has of his." After a moment she asked, "And you . . . you've known it always?"

"Always," he said sadly. "It explains many things. . . . Sometimes I think that those of us who have lived since have had to atone for their sin. It's all worked out in a harsh way, when you come to think of it. . . ."

She guessed what it was he meant. She saw again that he believed in such a thing as sin, that the belief in it was rooted deeply in his whole being.

"Have you got the letters, Olivia?" he asked.

"No . . . I burned them . . . last night . . . because I was afraid of them. I was afraid that I might do something shameful with them. And if they were burned, no one would believe such a preposterous story and there wouldn't be any proof. I was afraid, too," she added softly, "of what was in them . . . not what was written there, so much as the way it was written."

He took her hand and with the oddest, most awkward gesture, kissed it gently. "You were right, Olivia dear," he said. "It's all they have . . . the others . . . that belief in the past. We daren't take that from them. The strong daren't oppress the weak. It would have been too cruel. It would have destroyed the one thing into which Anson poured his whole life. You see, Olivia, there are people . . . people like you . . . who have to be strong enough to look out for the others. It's a hard task . . . and sometimes a cruel one. If it weren't for such people the world would fall apart and we'd see it for the cruel, unbearable place it is. That's why I've trusted everything to you. That's what I was trying to tell you the other night. You see, Olivia, I know you . . . I know there are things which people like us can't do. . . . Perhaps it's because we're weak or foolish—who knows? But it's true. I knew that you were the sort who would do just such a thing."

Listening to him, she again felt all her determination slipping from her. It was a strange sensation, as if he took possession of her, leaving her powerless to act, prisoning her again in that terrible wall of rightness in which he believed. The familiar sense of his strength frightened her, because it seemed a force so irresistible. It was the strength of one who was more than right; it was the strength of one who *believed*.

She had a fierce impulse to turn from him and to run swiftly, recklessly, across the wet meadows toward Michael, leaving forever behind her the placid, beautiful old house beneath the elms.

"There are some things," he was saying, "which it is impossible to do . . . for people like us, Olivia. They are impossible because the mere act of doing them would ruin us forever. They aren't things which we can do gracefully."

And she knew again what it was that he meant, as she had known vaguely while she stood alone in the darkness before the figures of Higgins and Miss Egan emerged from the mist of the marshes.

"You had better go now and telephone to Anson. I fancy he'll be badly upset, but I shall put an end to that . . . and Cassie, too. She had it all planned for the Mannering boy."

2

Anson was not to be reached all the morning at the office; he had gone, so his secretary said, to a meeting of the Society of Guardians of Young Working Girls without Homes and left express word that he was not to be disturbed. But Aunt Cassie heard the news when she arrived on her morning call at Pentlands. Olivia broke it to her as gently as possible, but as soon as the old lady understood what had happened, she went to pieces badly. Her eyes grew wild; she wept, and her hair became all disheveled. She took the attitude that Sybil had been seduced and was now a woman lost beyond all hope. She kept repeating between punctuations of profound sympathy for Olivia in the hour of her trial, that such a thing had never happened in the Pentland family; until Olivia, enveloped in the old, perilous calm, reminded her of the elopement of Jared Pentland and Savina Dalgedo and bade her abruptly to stop talking nonsense.

And then Aunt Cassie was deeply hurt by her tone, and Peters had to be sent away for smelling-salts at the very moment that Sabine arrived, grinning and triumphant. It was Sabine who helped administer the smelling-salts with the grim air of administering burning coals. When the old lady grew a little more calm she fell again to saying over and over again, "Poor Sybil. . . . My poor, innocent little Sybil . . . that this should have happened to her!"

To which Olivia replied at last, "Jean is a fine young man. I'm sure she couldn't have done better." And then, to soften a little Aunt Cassie's anguish, she said, "And he's very rich, Aunt Cassie . . . a great deal richer than many a husband she might have found here."

The information had an even better effect than the smelling-salts, so that the old lady became calm enough to take an interest in the details and asked where they had found a motor to go away in.

"It was mine," said Sabine dryly. "I loaned it to them."

The result of this statement was all that Sabine could have desired. The old lady sat bolt upright, all bristling, and cried, with an air of suffocation, "Oh, you viper! Why God should have sent me such a trial, I don't know. You've always wished us evil and now I suppose you're content! May God have mercy on your malicious soul!" And breaking into fresh sobs, she began all over again, "My poor, innocent little Sybil. . . . What will people say? What will they think has been going on!"

"Don't be evil-minded, Aunt Cassie," said Sabine sharply; and then in a calmer voice, "It will be hard on me. . . . I won't be able to go to Newport until they come back with the motor."

"You! . . . You! . . ." began Aunt Cassie, and then fell back, a broken woman.

"I suppose," continued Sabine ruthlessly, "that we ought to tell the Mannering boy."

"Yes," cried Aunt Cassie, reviving again. "Yes! There's the boy she ought to have married. . . ."

"And Mrs. Soames," said Sabine. "She'll be pleased at the news."

Olivia spoke for the first time in nearly half an hour. "It's no use. Mr. Pentland has been over to see her, but she didn't understand what it was he wanted to tell her. She was in a daze . . . only half-conscious . . . and they think she may not recover this time."

In a whisper, lost in the greater agitation of Aunt Cassie's sobs, she said to Sabine, "It's like the end of everything for him. I don't know what he'll do."

The confusion of the day seemed to increase rather than to die away. Aunt Cassie was asked to stay to lunch, but she said it was impossible to consider swallowing even a crust of bread. "It would choke me!" she cried melodramatically.

"It is an excellent lunch," urged Olivia.

"No . . . no . . . don't ask me!"

But, unwilling to quit the scene of action, she lay on Horace Pentland's Regence sofa and regained her strength a little by taking a nap while the others ate.

At last Anson called, and when the news was told him, the telephone echoed with his threats. He would, he said, hire a motor (an extravagance by which to gage the profundity of his agitation) and come down at once.

And then, almost immediately, Michael telephoned. "I have just come down," he said, and asked Olivia to come riding with him. "I must talk to you at once."

She refused to ride, but consented to meet him half-way, at the pine thicket where Higgins had discovered the fox-cubs. "I can't leave just now," she told him, "and I don't think it's best for you to come here at the moment."

For some reason, perhaps vaguely because she thought he might use the knowledge as a weapon to break down her will, she said nothing of the elopement. For in the confusion of the day, beneath all the uproar of scenes, emotions and telephone-calls, she had been thinking, thinking, thinking, so that in the end the uproar had made little impression upon her. She had come to understand that John Pentland must have lived thus, year after year, moving always in a secret life of his own, and presently she had come to the conclusion that she must send Michael away once and for all.

As she moved across the meadow she noticed that the birches had begun to turn yellow and that in the low ground along the river the meadows were already painted gold and purple by masses of goldenrod and ironweed. With each step she seemed to grow weaker and weaker, and as she drew near the blue-black wall of pines she was seized by a violent trembling, as if the sense of his presence were able somehow to reach out and engulf her even before she saw him. She kept trying to think of the old man as he stood beside her at the hedge, but something stronger than her will made her see only Michael's curly black head and blue eyes. She began even to pray . . . she (Olivia) who never prayed because the piety of Aunt Cassie and Anson and the Apostle to the Genteel stood always in her way.

And then, looking up, she saw him standing half-hidden among the lower pines, watching her. She began to run toward him, in terror lest her knees should give way and let her fall before she reached the shelter of the trees.

In the darkness of the thicket where the sun seldom penetrated, he put his arms about her and kissed her in a way he had never done before, and the action only increased her terror. She said nothing; she only wept quietly; and at last, when she had gained control of herself, she struggled free and said, "Don't, Michael . . . please don't . . . please."

They sat on a fallen log and, still holding her hand, he asked, "What is it? What has happened?"

"Nothing. . . . I'm just tired."

"Are you willing to come away with me? Now?" And in a low, warm voice, he added, "I'll never let you be tired again . . . never."

She did not answer him, because it seemed to her that what she had to tell him made all her actions in the past seem inexplicable and cheap. She was filled with shame, and tried to put off the moment when she must speak.

"I haven't been down in three days," he was saying, "because there's been trouble in Boston which made it impossible. I've only slept an hour or two a night. They've been trying to do me in . . . some of the men I always trusted. They've been double-crossing me all along and I had to stay to fight them."

He told her a long and complicated story of treachery, of money having been passed among men whom he had known and trusted always. He was sad and yet defiant, too, and filled with a desire to fight the thing to an end. She failed to understand the story; indeed she did not even hear much of it: she only knew that he was telling her everything, pouring out all his sadness and trouble to her as if she were the one person in all the world to whom he could tell such things.

And when he had finished he waited for a moment and then said, "And now I'm willing to chuck the whole dirty business and quit . . . to tell them all to go to hell."

Quickly she answered, "No, you mustn't do that. You can't do that. A man like you, Michael, daren't do such a thing. . . ." For she knew that without a battle life would mean nothing to him.

"No . . . I mean it. I'm ready to quit. I want you to go with me."

She thought, "He says this . . . and yet he stayed three days and nights in Boston to fight!" She saw that he was not looking at her, but sitting with his head in his hands; there was something broken, almost pitiful, in his manner, and it occurred to her that perhaps for the first time he found all his life in a hopeless tangle. She thought, "If I had never known him, this might not have happened. He would have been able to fight without even thinking of me."

Aloud she said, "I can't do it, Michael. . . . It's no use. I can't."

He looked up quickly, but before he could speak she placed her hand over his lips, saying, "Wait, Michael, let me talk first. Let me say what I've wanted to say for so long. . . . I've thought. . . . I've done nothing else but think day and night for the past three days. And it's no good, Michael. . . . It's no good. I'm forty years old to-day, and what can I give you that will make up for all you will lose? Why should you give up everything for me? No, I've nothing to offer. You can go back and fight and win. It's what you like more than anything in the world . . . more than any woman . . . even me."

Again he tried to speak, but she silenced him. "Oh, I know it's true . . . what I say. And if I had you at such a price, you'd only hate me in the end. I couldn't do it, Michael, because . . . because in the end, with men like you it's work, it's a career, which is first. . . . You couldn't bear giving up. You couldn't bear failure. . . . And in the end that's right, as it should be. It's what keeps the world going."

He was watching her with a look of fascination in his eyes, and she knew—she was certain of it—that he had never been so much in love with her before; but she knew, too, from the shadow which crossed his face (it seemed to her that he almost winced) and because she knew him so well, that he recognized the truth of what she had said.

"It's not true, Olivia. . . . You can't go back on me now . . . just when I need you most."

"I'd be betraying you, Michael, if I did the other thing. It's not me you need half so much as the other thing. Oh, I know that I'm right. What you should have in the end is a young woman . . . a woman who will help you. It doesn't matter very much whether you're terribly in love with her or not . . . but a woman who can be your wife and bear your children and give dinner parties and help make of you the famous man you've always meant to be. You need some one who will help you to found a family, to fill your new house with children . . . some one who'll help you and your children to take the place of families like ours who are at the end of things. No, Michael . . . I'm right. . . . Look at me," she commanded suddenly. "Look at me and you'll know that it's not because I don't love you."

He was on his knees now, on the carpet of scented pine-needles, his arms about her while she stroked the thick black hair with a kind of hysterical intensity.

"You don't know what you're saying, Olivia. It's not true! It's not true! I'd give up everything. . . . I don't want the other thing. I'll sell my farm and go away from here forever with you."

"Yes, Michael, you think that to-day, just now . . . and to-morrow everything will be changed. That's one of the mean tricks Nature plays us. It's not so simple as that. We're not like Higgins and . . . the kitchen-maid . . . at least not in some ways."

"Olivia . . . Olivia, do you love me enough to. . . ."

She knew what he meant to ask. She thought, "What does it matter? Why should I not, when I love him so? I should be harming no one . . . no one but myself."

And then, abruptly, through the mist of tears she saw through an opening in the thicket a little procession crossing the meadows toward the big house at Pentlands. She saw it with a terrible, intense clarity . . . a little procession of the gardener and his helper carrying between them on a shutter a figure that lay limp and still, and following them came Higgins on foot, leading his horse and moving with the awkward rolling gait which afflicted him when his feet were on the ground. She knew who the still figure was. It was John Pentland. The red mare had killed him at last. And she heard him saying, "There are some things which people like us, Olivia, can't do."

What happened immediately afterward she was never able to remember very clearly. She found herself joining the little procession; she knew that Michael was with her, and that there could be no doubt of the tragedy. . . . John Pentland was dead, with his neck broken. He lay on the shutter, still and peaceful, the bitter lines all melted from the grim, stern face, as he had been when she came upon him in the library smelling of dogs and wood-smoke and whisky. Only this time he had escaped for good. . . .

And afterward she remembered telling Michael, as they stood alone in the big white hall, that Sybil and Jean were married, and dismissing him by saying, "Now, Michael, it is impossible. While he was living I might have done it. . . . I might have gone away. But now it's impossible. Don't ask me. Please leave me in peace."

Standing there under the wanton gaze of Savina Pentland, she watched him go away, quietly, perhaps because he understood that all she had said was true.

3

In the tragedy the elopement became lost and forgotten. Doctors came and went; even reporters put in an awkward appearance, eager for details of the death and the marriage in the Pentland family, and somehow the confusion brought peace to Olivia. They forgot her, save as one who managed everything quietly; for they had need just then of some one who did not break into wild spasms of grief or wander about helplessly. In the presence of death, Anson forgot even his anger over the elopement, and late in the afternoon Olivia saw him for the first time when he came to her helplessly to ask, "The men have come to photograph the portraits. What shall we do?"

And she answered, "Send them away. We can photograph ancestors any time. They'll always be with us."

Sabine volunteered to send word to Sybil and Jean. At such times all her cold-blooded detachment made of her a person of great value, and Olivia knew that she could be trusted to find them because she wanted her motor again desperately. Remembering her promise to the old man, she went across to see Mrs. Soames, but nothing came of it, for the old lady had fallen into a state of complete unconsciousness. She would, they told Olivia, probably die without ever knowing that John Pentland had gone before her.

Aunt Cassie took up her throne in the darkened drawing-room and there, amid the acrid smell of the first chrysanthemums of the autumn, she held a red-eyed, snuffling court to receive the calls of all the countryside. Again she seemed to rise for a time triumphant and strong, even overcoming her weakness enough to go and come from the gazeboed house on foot, arriving early and returning late. She insisted upon summoning Bishop Smallwood to conduct the services, and discovered after much trouble that he was attending a church conference in the West. In reply to her telegram she received only an answer that it was impossible for him to return, even if they delayed the funeral . . . that in the rôle of prominent defender of the Virgin Birth he could not leave the field at a moment when the power of his party was threatened.

It seemed for a time that, as Sabine had hoped, the whole structure of the family was falling about them in ruins.

As for Olivia, she would have been at peace save that three times within two days notes came to her from Michael—notes which she sent back unopened because she was afraid to read them; until at last she wrote on the back of one, "There is nothing more to say. Leave me in peace." And after that there was only silence, which in a strange way seemed to her more unbearable than the sight of his writing. She discovered that two persons had witnessed the tragedy—Higgins, who had been riding with the old man, and Sabine, who had been walking the river path—walking only because Jean and Sybil had her motor. Higgins knew only that the mare had run off and killed his master; but Sabine had a strangely different version, which she recounted to Olivia as they sat in her room, the day after.

"I saw them," she said, "coming across the meadow. . . . Cousin John, with Higgins following. And then, all at once, the mare seemed to be frightened by something and began to run . . . straight in a line for the gravel-pit. It was a fascinating sight . . . a horrible sight . . . because I knew—I was certain—what was going to happen. For a moment Cousin John seemed to fight with her, and then all at once he leaned forward on her neck and let her go. Higgins went after him; but it was no use trying to catch her. . . . One might as well have tried to overtake a whirlwind. They seemed to fly across the fields straight for the line of elders that hid the pit, and I knew all the while that there was no saving them unless the mare turned. At the bushes the mare jumped . . . the prettiest jump I've ever seen a horse make, straight above the bushes into the open air. . . ."

For a moment Sabine's face was lighted by a macabre enthusiasm. Her voice wavered a little. "It was a horrible, beautiful sight. For a moment they seemed almost to rise in the air as if the mare were flying, and then all at once they fell . . . into the bottom of the pit."

Olivia was silent, and presently, as if she had been waiting for the courage, Sabine continued in a low voice, "But there's one thing I saw beyond any doubt. At the edge of the pit the mare tried to turn. She would have turned away, but Cousin John raised his crop and struck her savagely. There was no doubt of it. He forced her over the elders. . . ." Again after a pause, "Higgins must have seen it, too. He followed them to the very edge of the pit. I shall always see him there, sitting on his horse outlined against the sky. He was looking down into the pit and for a moment the horse and man together looked exactly like a centaur. . . . It was an extraordinary impression."

She remembered him thus, but she remembered him, too, as she had seen him on the night of the ball, slipping away through the lilacs like a shadow. Rising, she said, "Jean and Sybil will be back to-morrow, and then I'll be off for Newport. I thought you might want to know what Higgins and I knew, Olivia." For a moment she hesitated, looking out of the window toward the sea. And at last she said, "He was a queer man. He was the last of the great Puritans. There aren't any more. None of the rest of us believe anything. We only pretend. . . ."

But Olivia scarcely heard her. She understood now why it was that the old man had talked to her as if he were very near to death, and she thought, "He did it in a way that none would ever discover. He trusted Higgins, and Sabine was an accident. Perhaps . . . perhaps . . . he did it to keep me here . . . to save the thing he believed in all his life."

It was a horrible thought which she tried to kill, but it lingered, together with the regret that she had never finished what she had begun to tell him as they stood by the hedge talking of the letters—that one day Jean might take the name of John Pentland. He had, after all, as much right to it as he had to the name of de Cyon; it would be only a little change, but it would allow the name of Pentland to go on and on. All the land, all the money, all the tradition, would go down to Pentland children, and so make a reason for their existence; and in the end the name would be something more then than a thing embalmed in "The Pentland Family and the Massachusetts Bay Colony." The descendants would be, after all, of Pentland blood, or at least of the blood of Savina Dalgedo and Toby Cane, which had come long ago to be Pentland blood.

And she thought grimly, "He was right, after all. I am one of them at last . . . in spite of everything. It's I who am carrying on now."

On the morning of the funeral, as she stood on the terrace expecting Jean and Sybil, Higgins, dressed in his best black suit and looking horribly awkward and ill at ease, came toward her to say, looking away from her, "Mr. O'Hara is going away. They're putting up a 'For Sale' sign on his gate. He isn't coming back." And then looking at her boldly he added, "I thought you might want to know, Mrs. Pentland."

For a moment she had a sudden, fierce desire to cry out, "No, he mustn't go! You must tell him to stay. I can't let him go away like that!" She wanted suddenly to run across the fields to the bright, vulgar, new house, to tell him herself. She thought, "He meant, then, what he said. He's given up everything here."

But she knew, too, that he had gone away to fight, freed now and moved only by his passion for success, for victory.

And before she could answer Higgins, who stood there wanting her to send him to Michael, Miss Egan appeared, starched and rigid and wearing the professional expression of solemnity which she adopted in the presence of bereaved families. She said, "It's about *her*, Mrs. Pentland. She seems very bright this morning and quite in her right mind. She wants to know why he hasn't been to see her for two whole days. I thought. . . ."

Olivia interrupted her quietly. "It's all right," she said. "I'll go and tell her. I'll explain. It's better for me to do it."

She went away into the house, knowing bitterly that she left Miss Egan and Higgins thinking of her with pity.

As she climbed the worn stair carpet to the north wing, she knew suddenly a profound sense of peace such as she had not known for years. It was over and done now, and life would go on the same as it had always done, filled with trickiness and boredom and deceits, but pleasant, too, in spite of everything, perhaps because, as John Pentland had said, "One had sometimes to pretend." And, after all, Sybil had escaped and was happy.

She knew now that she herself would never escape; she had been too long a part of Pentlands, and she knew that what the old man had said was the truth. She had acted thus not because of duty, or promises, or nobility, or pride, or even out of virtue. . . . Perhaps it was even because she was not strong enough to do otherwise. But she knew that she had acted thus because, as he said, "There are things, Olivia, which people like us can't do."

And as she moved along the narrow hall, she saw from one of the deep-set windows the figure of Sabine moving along the lane in a faint cloud of dust, and nearer at hand, at the entrance of the elm-bordered drive, Aunt Cassie in deep black, coming along briskly in a cloud of crape. No, nothing had changed. It would go on and on. . . .

The door opened and the sickly odor of medicines flooded the hallway. Out of the darkness came the sound of a feeble, reed-like voice, terrible in its sanity, saying, "Oh, it's you, Olivia. I knew you'd come. I've been waiting for you. . . ."

THE END

Cold Spring Harbor, Long Island
June 4, 1925
St. Jean-de-Luz, B. P., France
July 21, 1926

A GOOD WOMAN

PART ONE
THE JUNGLE

Chapter 1

SHE FOUND the letter when she returned to the slate-colored house from the regular monthly meeting of the Augusta Simpson Branch of the Woman's Christian Temperance Union. It was eleven o'clock at night and this letter lay, like any quite ordinary and usual letter, on the dining-room table in the dim radiance of gaslight turned economically low in the dome hand-painted in a design of wild-roses. Her first thought as she took off her sealskin tippet was that it must have arrived by the last post, which came at four, and so could have been in her hands seven hours earlier if the slattern Essie had not forgotten to give it to her. But what, she reflected as she removed her hat and jacket, could you expect of a girl of unknown parentage taken from the county poor farm to help around the house in return for her clothing, her board and two dollars a month pocket money? What could you expect from a girl who was boy-crazy? How was such a creature to understand what a letter from Philip meant to her? What could a slut like Essie know of a mother's feelings for her only son?

She knew it was from Philip by the round, boyish handwriting and by the outlandish stamp of Zanzibar. (It would be another for the collection of her brother Elmer.)

Mrs. Downes approached the table with the majestic step of a woman conscious of her dignity and importance in the community; the knowledge of these things lay like a shadow across the sweep of her deep bosom, in the carriage of her head, in the defiant rustle of her poplin bustle and leg-o'-mutton sleeves. It was so easy to see that, in her not too far-distant youth, she had been an opulent beauty in the style of Rubens, less yielding and voluptuous, perhaps, than his Venuses, but of a figure which inclined to overflow. And this beauty in its flowering had not gone unnoticed, for in that far-off day she had been courted by half the eligible, and all the ineligible, men of the town. In the brief moments of depression so rare with a person of such abundant vitality, she comforted herself by thinking, "In any case, I could have been the wife of a county judge, or a bank president, or even of a superintendent of the Mills." But the truth was that she was not the wife of any of them (in fact she had no husband at all) because, by a unique error of judgment forever inexplicable, she had chosen to marry one of the ineligibles, the giddiest but the most fascinating of all her suitors. Now, at forty-eight, she had come to believe that it was better so, that she was more content with the position she had made for herself, single-handed, than as a protected wife who was a mere nobody. The memory of her ancient beauty, hardened long ago into roughly chiseled lines by the struggle to succeed, she had put aside as a negligible affair in comparison to the virtues with which time and trouble had endowed her.

Her sense of satisfaction flowed from many springs, not the least of which was the knowledge that when Mr. Downes saw fit to desert her (she always phrased it thus to herself) he had not left behind a bereft and wilting female. She took satisfaction in the knowledge that she had calmly burnt his note explaining that it was impossible for any man to continue living with so much virtue, and then with equal calm told the world that Mr. Downes had gone away to China on business. Rolling up her sleeves, she had embarked fearlessly upon establishing a bakery to support herself and the two-year-old son who remained, the sole souvenir of her derelict mate.

Indeed, she had not even asked help of her brother, Elmer Niman, the pump manufacturer, who could have helped her easily enough, because she could not bear the thought of giving him an opportunity to say, "I told you so," with regard to Mr. Downes, and because she knew well enough that his penurious nature would never provide her with enough to live upon decently. These were the reasons she set down in her conscious mind; the ones which she did not consider were different—that hers was a spirit not to be chained, and possessed of an energy which could not have been soothed by rocking-chairs and mere housekeeping.

And so, almost at once, the bakery had flourished, and as the Mills brought prosperity and hordes of new citizens to the town, it turned presently into the Peerless Bakery and Lunch Room, and quite recently it had become the Peerless Restaurant, occupying an entire ground-floor at the corner of Maple and Main Streets. She was now known in the town as "an independent woman," which meant that she had no debts, owned her own house, and possessed a flourishing business.

All this she had wrought out of nothing, by her own energy, and far from harboring thoughts of retirement, she still went every day to survey the cooking and to sit near the cash-register during the full stream of noon and evening patronage.

But Mr. Downes, it seemed, fancied himself well out of a bad bargain, for he never returned; and when a year had passed, during which she constantly spoke of his letters and his doings in China, she went to the mausoleum which her brother called his home and told him that she had had no news of Mr. Downes for some months and that she feared something had happened to him in the Orient, which was, as he (Elmer) knew, a sinister place at best. So Elmer Niman, hopeful that some fatal catastrophe had befallen a brother-in-law of whom he disapproved, and to whom he had never spoken, took up the matter with the Government. The ensuing investigation dragged into light two or three stray, light-fingered gentlemen whose last desire was to be unearthed, but found no trace of the missing Mr. Downes—a mystery explained perhaps in Emma's mind by the fact that he had never been in China at all and that she had never received any letters from him.

In due time Mrs. Downes put on mourning and the derelict husband became enveloped in the haze of romance which surrounds one who apparently has met his death among the bandits of the Manchurian mountains. From then on she never spoke of him save as "Poor Mr. Downes!" or "My poor husband!" or to friends as "Poor Jason!" She alluded to a fatally adventurous nature which she had never been able to subdue and which had always filled her with foreboding. And now, twenty-four years later, she had come, herself, to believe that his body had long ago turned to dust in the Gobi Desert. (She had always been rather vague about geography and from time to time distributed his remains over half of Asia.) At the time the affair aggravated her brother's nervous dyspepsia by causing him much fury and agitation, and it cost the Government a large amount of money, but it fixed the legend of Mr. Downes' business trip to China, and so left her with more dignity and prestige than are the lot of a deserted wife.

The sedative effect of more than twenty years had dimmed the fascination of Mr. Downes to a point where it was possible for her to believe that he was, after all, only a scamp who had trifled with her affections and one whom she had never really loved at all—or at least only enough to make the presence of a son respectable in the eyes of the Lord. If he had "lived," she told herself, he would have gone his waggish, improvident way, leaving her and her son somewhat at the mercy of the dyspeptic Elmer; as things stood, she was successful and well off. Her once passionate and rather shameful desire to have him back seemed very remote now; she no longer wanted him to return; her only fear was that he might rise from the grave in which she had placed him with such thoroughness. For years the thought had raised an uneasy feeling in her bosom; but when years passed without a word from him she decided that he must really be dead. There were still moments, however, when she came close to betraying herself by saying, "When Mr. Downes went away"—which could, of course, pass for meaning anything at all.

Each night she thanked God that her son—their son, she was forced to admit—would never know that his father was a scamp. He was a half-orphan to whom she had been both mother and father, and her training (she thanked God again) had left its mark. Her son was a fine young man with no bad habits, smoking, drinking or otherwise, who, married to Naomi Potts (known throughout the churchgoing world as "the youngest missionary of God"), was himself spreading the light among the heathen of that newly discovered land between Victoria-Nyanza and the Indian Ocean. He and Naomi and a third missionary were the first in the field. "In blackest Africa" was the way she expressed it. "My son," she would say proudly, "who is head of a mission in blackest Africa."

No, she reflected frequently, it was impossible to think of Philip, so handsome, so clean, so pure, so virtuous, so molded by her own hand, as the son of Jason Downes. She had succeeded in everything save changing his appearance: he had the same rather feline good looks which had ruined his father by inducing women to fling themselves at his head. (It was a thing she could never understand—how any woman could fling herself at the head of a man, even a man as handsome as Jason had been.)

Chapter 2

THE SIGHT of the letter, so carelessly tossed aside by Essie, filled her with a sense of disappointment: if she had only received it at the proper time, she could have read it to the ladies of the Augusta Simpson Branch. Only an hour before she had "craved the indulgence" of the ladies while she read "one of my son's interesting letters about the work they are doing in blackest Africa." The letter still crackled in her reticule, filling her with an immense pride, for was not the career of Philip, and Philip himself, simply another evidence of her sterling character? If Essie hadn't been a slut she would have had two letters to read.

She drew her solid body up to the table and, clamping on her pince-nez (which for a moment exasperated her by becoming entangled in the white badge of her temperance) she tore open the battered letter and holding it at arm's length because of her far-sightedness, began to read.

At first glance she was disturbed by the brevity of it and by the fact that there was no enclosure from Naomi. Usually Philip wrote pages.

"*Dear Ma:*

"*I write this in great haste to tell you that by the time this reaches you we will be on our way home.*

"*I don't know whether the news has reached you, but there has been an uprising among the tribes to the north of Megambo. They attacked the mission and we narrowly escaped with our lives. I was wounded, but not badly. Naomi is all right. There was a strange Englishwoman who got caught with us. She wasn't a missionary but middle-aged and the sister of a British general. She was seeing the country and doing some shooting.*

"*We sail from Capetown in ten days and ought to be home in time for Christmas. I ought to tell you that I've made a mistake in my calling. I'm not going to be a missionary any longer. That's why I'm coming home. Naomi is against it, but when she saw I was in earnest she came, too.*

"I will try to send you a letter from Capetown, but can't promise. I am very upset and feel sick. Meanwhile love from your devoted son.

"Philip."

For a moment she simply stared at the letter, incapable of any logical thought. Her hand, which never shook, was shaking. She was for a moment, but only a moment, a broken woman. And then, slowly, she read it again to make certain that she had not read it wrongly. On reflection, she saw clearly that he was upset. The letter was hasty and disorderly in composition; the very handwriting had changed, losing its round, precise curves, here and there, in sudden jagged and passionate downstrokes. And at the end he did not write, as he always did, "We pray for you every night."

Beneath the shower of light from the wild-rose dome she tried to fathom the meaning of the letter, struggling meanwhile with a sudden sense of loneliness such as she hadn't experienced since she sat in the same spot years before reading Jason's last letter. Coming home, giving up the work of the Lord in blackest Africa! (Just after she had read aloud before all those women one of his interesting letters.) Philip, who had always placed his hopes unfalteringly in the hope of the Lord. *I've made a mistake in my calling.* What could he mean by that? How could one mistake a call from the Lord?

He was, she saw, in earnest. He had not even waited for a letter from her. If she could only have written she would have changed everything. And there was that hint, so ominous, that he would have left Naomi behind if she chose not to follow him. Something strange, something terrifying, she felt, had happened, for nothing else could explain this sudden deterioration of character. There was no hint of what had caused it, nothing (and her suspicions were bristling) unless it had to do with that Englishwoman. For a moment she felt that she was dealing with some intangible mystery and so was frightened.

After she had grown more calm, it occurred to her that this strange, inexplicable letter might have been caused by the fever that had attacked him twice, that it was a result of the wound he wrote of, or perhaps merely a passing wild idea—only Philip had never had any wild ideas, for you couldn't properly call his ecstatic devotion to God a wild emotion. Once, as a boy, he had had a sudden desire to become an artist, but she had changed him quickly and easily. No, he had always been a good boy who obeyed her. He did not have silly ideas.

During an hour shaken with doubts and fears, one terror raised its head above the others—the terror that after twenty-four years of careful training and control, twenty-four years spent in making him as perfect as his father had been imperfect, the blood of Jason Downes was coming into its own to claim the son which she had come long ago to think of only as her own.

The return of Philip seemed almost as great a calamity as the flight of his father. For the second time in her existence a life carefully and neatly arranged appeared to fall into ruin. How was she to explain this shameful change of Philip's heart to the Reverend Castor, the members of the church, the women who had listened to his letters? It was, she saw, an astonishing, scandalous thing. What missionary had ever turned back from the path shown him by God? What was Philip to do if he was not to be a missionary?

She tried to imagine the confusion and trouble the affair must be causing Naomi, who was the child of missionaries. She had never *really* liked Naomi, but she felt sorry for her now, as sorry as it was possible for a mother to feel for the wife of her son. But Naomi, she thought, almost at once, was quite able to look out for herself, and she must be working on Philip, even now, to turn him back to God. Suddenly she had an unaccustomed feeling of warmth for Naomi. After all, Naomi had had a great success four years ago at the tent meetings. She had converted scores of people then; certainly she could do much to turn Philip from his colossal error and sin.

Her first impulse to take the letter to Elmer died abruptly, as a similar impulse had died twenty-four years earlier. For the present she would say simply that Philip and Naomi were on their way home to rest from their hardships, from the fevers and the wound which Philip had received during a native uprising. She regretted that Philip had not written some details of the affair, because it would have made a most fascinating story. The ladies would have been so interested in it. . . .

Chapter 3

RISING, SHE REMOVED the stamp for Elmer and then thrust the letter itself boldly into the blue flames of the anthracite stove. Then she turned out the gas and with a firm step made her way up the creaking stairs of the house which she owned, free of all mortgage and encumbrance, made so by her own efforts. She had decided upon a course of action. She would say nothing and perhaps by the day Philip arrived he would have been made to see the light by Naomi. Meanwhile his return could be explained by his hardships, his illness and his wound. The poor boy was a hero.

On the way up she remembered that she must reprove Essie about the letter, though, as it turned out, it was perhaps just as well that she hadn't seen it until after the meeting, for she could scarcely have read one of Philip's letters with a whole heart knowing all the while that he was already on his way home, fleeing from the hardships the Lord saw fit to impose. Still Essie must be reproved: she had committed an error.

Again she fell to racking her brain for some explanation of what had happened to Philip. He had never been unruly, undutiful or ungrateful save during that period when he had been friends with Mary Conyngham and it couldn't, of course, be Mary Conyngham's bad influence, since she hadn't

seen him in years and was a woman now with two children and a husband
buried only the day before yesterday.

While she undressed she reflected that she had had a hard day full of
cares, and she thanked God for that immense vitality which never allowed
weariness to take possession of her. She had fought before, and now, with
God's help, she would fight again, this time to save her boy from the heritage
of his father's blood. When she had brushed her short, thin hair and donned
a nightgown of pink outing-flannel with high neck and long sleeves, she
knelt in the darkness by the side of the vast walnut bed and prayed. She
was a devout woman and she prayed every night, never carelessly or through
mere force of habit. Although she did not discount her own efforts, she
looked upon prayer as one of the elements which had made of her life a
success. Religion to Emma Downes was not tainted with ecstasy and mysticism; in her hands it became a practical, businesslike instrument of success. To-night she prayed with greater passion than she had known since
those far-off days (whose memory now filled her with shame) when she had
prayed in the fervor of an unbalanced and frightening passion for Mr.
Downes, that the worthless scamp might be returned to her, for her to
protect and spoil.

She prayed passionately that the Lord might guide the feet of her strayed
boy back in the consecrated paths on which she had placed him; and as she
prayed it occurred to her in another part of her mind that with Philip as the
first in the field she might one day be the mother of the Bishop of East
Africa. And when at last she lay in bed the awful sense of loneliness returned to claim possession of her. For the first time in years she felt an
aching desire for the missing Jason Downes. She wanted him lying there
beside her as he had once done, so that she could share with him this
new burden that the Lord had seen fit to impose upon her.

Chapter 4

THE MISSION, a little cluster of huts, two built of mud and logs and the others
no more than flimsy affairs of thatched reeds, stood at the edge of a tangled
forest, on a low hill above the marshy borders of the tepid lake. All about it
there rose a primeval world, where the vegetation was alternately lush and
riotous or burned to a cinder, and the earth at one season lay soaked with
water and gave off a hot mist and at another turned so dry that the fantastic
birds and animals for hundreds of miles gathered about the life-giving lake
to drink and kill and leave the border strewn with bleaching bones. Once, a
dozen years earlier, the mission had been a post for Portuguese slave-traders,
but with the end of the trade the jungle had once more taken possession,
thrusting whole trees through the decaying thatch and overrunning bar-

ricade and huts with a tangle of writhing vines. It was thus they had come upon it, young Philip Downes and his pale wife, Naomi, and the strange Swede, Swanson, who by some odd circumstance felt that he was called by God from the state of hospital porter to save the heathen from their sin. Of the three, only Naomi, the daughter of missionaries, knew anything of the hostility of such a world. Philip was a boy of twenty-three who had never been outside his own state and Swanson only an enormous, stupid, tow-headed man with the strength of a bull.

It was a world of the most fantastic exaggeration, where the very reeds that bordered the lake were tall as trees and the beasts which trampled them down—the lumbering leviathans of the Old Testament—were, it seemed, de-signed upon a similar scale. In the moonlight the beasts thrust their way by sheer bulk to break great paths to the feeding-grounds along the shore. At times, during the rainy season, whole acres of the shore broke loose and drifted away, each island a floating jungle filled with beasts and birds, to some remote, unseen part of the greenish, yellow sea. One could watch them in the distance, fantastic, unreal ships, alive like the shore with ibis and wild ducks, herons and the rosy paradisical flamingoes whose color sometimes touched the borders of the lake with the glory of the sunrise.

It was here in this world that Philip, with an aching head and a body raw with the bites of insects, found the first glow of that romance with which Naomi, despite her poverty of words, her clumsiness of expression and her unseeing eyes, had managed to invest all Africa. In the beginning, during those first terrible nights, Philip felt the unearthly beauty of the place was dimmed by a kind of horror that seemed to touch all the primeval world about him. It excited him but it also roused an odd, indescribable loathing. It seemed naked, cruel and too opulent. But in the beginning there had been no time to ponder in morbidity over such things; there was only time for work, endless work—the chopping away of the stubborn vines and sap-lings, the strengthening of roofs, the filling-in of gaps in the stockade against thieving natives and prowling animals. For him the work beneath the blazing sun was a ceaseless agony; he had not the slow, oxlike patience nor the clumsy, skillful carpenter's hands of Swanson. There was only work, work, work, with no prospect of conquering the heat, the rains and the horrible vegetation which, possessed of an animal intelligence, sprang up alive where it had been slaughtered only the day before. It seemed to him in moments of blank discouragement that all which remained of their lives must be sacrificed simply in a struggle to exist at all. There would be no time to spread the Word among the black people who watched them, alter-nately shy as gazelles or hilarious as hyenas, from the borders of the forest or the marshes.

He was not a large man—Philip—and his hair was dark, curling close against his small head. His skin, olive-colored like his father's, framed blue eyes that seemed to burn with a consuming, inward fire, the eyes of one who would never be happy. And he was neatly made with light, supple muscles. One would have said that of the three he was the one most fitted to survive in the fantastic, cruel world of Megambo.

And yet (he sometimes pondered it himself) the great blond Swanson, with his pale, northern skin and thin yellow hair, and Naomi with her thin, anemic body and white, freckled skin, seemed not to suffer in the least. They worked after he had fallen with exhaustion, his nerves so raw that he would wander off along the lake lest the seething irritation that consumed him should get the better of his temper. Swanson and Naomi went hopefully on, talking of the day when these rotting huts over which they toiled would give way to houses of brick where sons of negro children would sit learning the words that were to lift them from the sloughs of sin to the blessings of their white brethren. Naomi was even more clever than Swanson. Her courage never flagged and the strange, happy, luminous look in her eyes was never dimmed. She knew, too, the tricks of living in such a world, since, except for two voyages to America to raise money for missions, she had never lived in any other.

They could even sleep, Swanson and Naomi, lost in an abysmal unconsciousness, unmindful of the dreadful sounds that came from the forest, never hearing the ominous rustling of the reeds along the shore, nor the startled, half-human cry of a dying monkey and the steady crunch-crunch of the leviathans pasturing in the brilliant moonlight. They did not hear the roaring of the beasts driven in by the drouth and burning heat from the distant, barren plains. Nothing seemed to touch them, no fear, save that they might fail in their great mission. There were times in those first months when, unable to bear it longer, he burst out to Naomi with the belief that Swanson was only a stupid lout no better than the natives.

And Naomi, taking his hand, would always say, "We must pray, Philip. We must ask God for strength. He will understand and reward our sufferings."

Sometimes he knelt with her while they prayed together for strength. She possessed a sweetness and a calm assurance that at moments made the whole thing all the more unbearable to him.

But no good came of her prayers, not even of the savage remorse which claimed him on such occasions. He was tormented, not alone by a sense of his own weakness, but also by a shameful sense of disloyalty; in that savage world the three of them must cling to each other and to God, even though the place made for them a prison from which there was no escape, wherein their nerves grew frayed from the mere constant association with one another. If they fell asunder, only horror and destruction faced them.

"God," Naomi would say, with the odd, unearthly certainty which colored all her fearless character, "will reward you, Philip. He will reward us all in proportion to our sufferings."

But he found presently, to his horror, that he could not believe what she believed. He felt that he could believe, perhaps, if his sufferings and his reward were both less grandiose. It was harder, too, because there were moments when Naomi and Swanson seemed to him complete strangers who understood nothing of his torments. How could they, whose faith knew no doubts, whose nerves were never worn?

And so, during these first two years, he slipped more and more from a dependence upon God to one upon his mother, who in that smoky mill town on the opposite side of the earth seemed as remote as the Deity Himself. But he could at least write to her, and so ease his soul. He felt that she, who was always right, understood him in a way that was forever closed to Naomi. His mother had suffered and made great sacrifices for his sake. There were no limits to the debt he owed her. In moments when his faith and courage failed, moved more by a desire to please her than to please God, he fancied her, in sudden nostalgic moments, standing near him watching and approving his struggle, always ready to smile and praise. It was that which he needed more than anything—the sympathy which seemed not to exist in Swanson's oxlike body nor in Naomi's consecrated heart. And so he came to pour out his heart to her in long, passionate letters of a dozen pages and she sent him in return the strength he needed.

It was as if the image of Emma Downes hung perpetually above himself and Naomi. From Emma's letters he could see that she never ceased to think of them. She prayed constantly. He could see the pride she had in him to whom she had been both father and mother, teaching him all that he knew of life. He saw that for her sake he must make of this fearsome venture a brilliant, resplendent success, not alone by bringing hundreds of poor, benighted, black souls to Christ, but by rising to the very height of the church. She had allowed him, her only son, to go out of her widowed tragic life whither he had chosen to go, sending him on his way with words only of hope and encouragement. At times it was less his faith in God than his faith in his mother which gave him the courage to go on.

As if the presence of Naomi broke in upon that bond between them, he took the letters off to the borders of the forest to read them again and again in solitude. In waves of homesickness the tears sometimes came into his eyes. He thought of her in a series of odd detached pictures—bending over his crib when he was a little boy, baking him special rolls of pie-crust flavored with cinnamon, working over the ovens until morning in order to have the toys he wanted at Christmas. He owed her everything.

Chapter 5

HE WAS, at twenty-three, a boy singularly innocent of life, and since there were, save for his own sufferings, no realities in his existence, he lost himself with all the passion of adolescence in God and Heaven and Hell. Of love (save for that pure flame which burned for his mother) he knew nothing, nor did he understand, for all the agonies of a sensitive nature, such things as suffering and beauty and splendor. For him, as for Naomi, the flame of faith engulfed all else, but for him the flame sometimes flickered and came near to going out.

He did not know whether he loved Naomi or not, nor what the emotion of love toward her should be. They were brother and sister in Christ and so bound together in Heavenly love. She was his wife by some divine arrangement which slowly began to be clear to him.

It had happened during those months when Naomi, on leave from her father's post, near Lake Tchad, had come to stay as guest in his mother's house, and in that zealous atmosphere, she had seemed a creature bathed in the rosy glow of Heavenly glamour. In the church and at those tent meetings where she spoke from the same platforms as the great evangelist, Homer Quackenbrush, people honored her as something akin to a saint. She was a real missionary, only twenty-three, who had been born in a mission and had never known any other life. He had listened while she spoke in her curious, loud flat voice of her experiences in Africa and slowly she had worked a sort of enchantment upon him. He became fascinated, enthralled, filled by a fire to follow her in her work, to seize the torch (as she described it) and carry it on, unconscious all the while that it was not the faith but something of the mystery and romance of Africa that captured him. He had gone home one night after the singing to tell his mother that instead of seeking a church he meant to become a missionary. Together they had knelt and prayed while Emma Downes, with tears pouring down her face, thanked God for sending the call to her boy.

And then, somehow, he had married Naomi, never understanding that he had consented to the marriage, and even desired it, not because he was in love with Naomi Potts, but with the mystery and color of Africa which clung to her thin, pale figure and her dowdy clothes. The marriage had filled his mother with happiness, and she was always right; she had been right ever since he could remember.

He never knew that he had married without ever having known youth. He had been a boy of an oddly mystical and passionate nature and then, suddenly caught by a wave of wild emotion, he had become overnight a married man. Yet there came to him at odd times the queerest feeling of strangeness and amazement toward Naomi; there were moments when, rousing himself as if from a dream, he found that he was watching her as she went about her work, wondering what she was and how it had come about that at twenty-three he found himself married to her—this stranger who seemed at times so much nearer to Swanson than to himself.

It was difficult to confide in Naomi or even to think of her as an ally. She worked like a man and slept too peacefully; she never had any doubts. Even when she nursed himself and Swanson through the fever (which miraculously passed her by that they might be saved to carry on their work) she went about tirelessly with the expression of a saint on her plain, freckled face. In moments when the chills left his miserable and shaking body for a time, he fancied (watching her) that the Christian martyrs must have had the same serene look in their eyes. You could not look at her without feeling your faith growing stronger. It was better than reading God's Word. . . .

And yet she never seemed quite real, quite human. There was no bond between them save their work.

Chapter 6

IT WAS not prayer that brought them in the end a certain rest and peace, but the coming of the dry season, when for a time Nature changed her plan of torment and gave them a respite. At about the same time there began to steal over Philip the sense of peace that comes of growing used to suffering. They learned how to protect themselves from the insects and how to keep a fire burning all night to frighten away prowling animals, how to outwit the porcupines that attacked their yams and the armies of voracious ants which had twice marched through the compound bent upon devouring the very dwellings over their heads. They succeeded in persuading the natives that they were neither gods nor slave-traders, but only fellowmen come to save them from a vague and awful destiny.

And again it was Naomi who succeeded where Philip failed. It was as if the naked blacks possessed some instinct which told them that he lacked the fire that burned in the heart of Naomi. She had a way of reassuring the black girls who, giggling and slapping one another, hung about the enclosure. With an immeasurable perseverance she drew them into the stockade, where she gave them gaudy trinkets out of her own pitiful stock. And at last one morning Philip returned from shooting ducks to find her telling them stories out of the Bible in a queer jargon made up of signs and Bantu words and the savage, gutteral sounds she had picked up somehow from contact with the natives. Swanson, with all the handicap of a stupid brain, followed in her steps.

It was at the end of the second year when the natives, bored, began to slip away and all their efforts seemed to come to nothing, that Philip became aware of an awful doubt. It seemed to him in the agony of worn nerves that there was a vague and irresistible force which kept drawing Naomi and Swanson nearer and nearer to each other, into an alliance, horribly treasonable in a world of three people, against himself. It was a torturing sensation, not even of honest jealousy which would at least have been clear and definite, but only an inexplicable, perhaps unjustified, feeling of being thrust aside from the currents of understanding which bound them together. Naomi was *his* wife and she obeyed him, as did Swanson, because he was the active defender of their little world; yet even this seemed to draw them together.

Sometimes in a kind of madness he fancied that they plotted against him almost without knowing it, by some secret, unspoken understanding.

It never occurred to him that there was any question of infidelity, for such a thing had no place in their scheme of things. He knew, as he knew that the sun rose each morning, that she was as virginal as the dew which fell on cold nights. Except as they appeared embarrassingly in their contact with the natives such things as lust and love and birth did not exist. Yet there were moments when he seemed to grow dizzy and the whole universe appeared to tremble about him, when he was like a tree shaken in a tempest. He became prey to a vague sense of misery from which he found rest only by tramping for hours along the borders of the lake. At such times it seemed that there lay before him only bafflement and frustration. Once he came to his senses in horror to find himself at the edge of the lake ready to commit the greatest of sins, that of murdering himself, a servant of God.

From then on he suffered a new horror—that he might be going mad.

Sometimes in the night he lay restless and tormented, scarcely knowing what it was that gave him no peace save that it was in some way concerned with Naomi lying in the hut opposite him in the glow of the fire. She slept like a child, her face lighted with the familiar look of bland satisfaction—Naomi whom he had never approached, whom he had never kissed since the day of the wedding years and years ago, it seemed now, in that black and sooty town on the other side of the world. To touch her, to attempt the horrible thing he could not put from his mind, would, he knew, turn their tiny, intense world into a hell and so destroy all they had built up with so much agony and terror.

He was afraid of her for some profound, unnamable reason. In the long, still nights, when every sound took on the violence of an explosion, he had at times a sinister feeling that he stood at the edge of a yawning chasm into which he might precipitate the three of them by so much as crossing the room.

For it had been arranged long ago in the darkened parlor of his mother's house that he and Naomi were never to live together as man and wife, never so long as their minds and bodies were occupied in their consecration to Christ. It was Emma Downes who arranged everything, standing in the parlor on the day of the wedding, talking to a Philip dressed in black and newly ordained both as missionary and bridegroom.

When he thought of his mother it was always as he had seen her on that day—wise, powerful, good and filled with joy and faith, in her purple merino dress with the gold chain attached to Aunt Maria's watch—a woman to whom he owed everything.

He could hear her saying with a strange translucent clarity, "Of course, now that you and Naomi have given yourselves to God, you must sacrifice everything to your work—pleasure, temptations, even" (and here her voice dropped a little) "even the hope of children. Because it is impossible to think of Naomi having a child in the midst of Africa. And any other way would be the blackest of sins. Of course it wouldn't be right for a young girl like Naomi to go to a post with a man she wasn't married to—so you must just act as if you weren't married to her. . . . Some day, perhaps when you have a year's leave from the post, you might have a child. I could take care of it, of course, when you went back."

And then looking aside, she had added, "Naomi asked me to speak to you about it. She's so shy and pure, she couldn't bring herself to do it. I promised her I would."

Sitting on the edge of the narrow sofa, he had promised because life was still very hazy to him and the promise seemed a small and unimportant thing. Indeed he had only a hazy knowledge of what she meant and he blushed at his mother's mention of such "things."

Chapter 7

IT WAS during the third year that the image of his mother began to grow a little blurred. At times the figure on the opposite side of the world seemed less awe-inspiring, less indomitable, less invincible. He wasn't a boy any longer. He had knowledge of life gained from the crude, primitive world about him, and of the intimations born of his own sufferings. It was impossible to exist unchanged amid such hardships, among black people who lived with the simplicity of animals and held obscene festivals dedicated to unmentionable gods of fertility.

He had come to Africa, one might have said, without a face—with only a soft, embryonic boyish countenance upon which life had left no mark; but now, at twenty-six, his features were hardened and sharpened—the straight, rather snub nose, the firm but sensual mouth, the blue eyes in which a flame seemed forever to be burning. The fevers left their mark. There were times when, dead with exhaustion, he had the look of a man of forty. Behind the burning eyes, there was forming slowly a restless, inquiring intelligence, blended oddly of a heritage from the shrewd woman who was always right and of the larky cleverness of a father he could not remember.

Naomi had noticed the change, wondering that he could have grown so old while she and Swanson remained unchanged. There were even little patches of gray at his temples—gray at twenty-six. For days she would not notice him at all, for she was endlessly busy, and then she would come upon him suddenly sitting on a log or emerging from the forest with a queer dazed look in his eyes, and she would say, "Come, Philip, you're tired. We'll pray together."

Prayer, she was certain, would help him.

Once, when she found him lying face down on the earth, she had touched his head with her hand, only to have him spring up crying out, "For God's sake, leave me in peace!" in a voice so terrible that she had gone away again.

The look came more and more often into his eyes. She watched him for days and at last she said, "Philip, you ought to go down to the coast. If you stay on you'll be having the fever."

She was plaiting grass at the moment to make a hat for herself. Standing above her, he looked down, wondering at her contentment.

"But you'll go too?" he asked.

"No . . . I couldn't do that, Philip . . . not just now—in the very midst of our work, at a time like this, Swanson couldn't manage alone and we'd lose all we'd gained. I'm strong enough, but you must go."

"I won't go . . . alone."

She went on plaiting without answering him, and he said at last, "It doesn't make any difference. I'm no good here. I'm only a failure. I'm better off dead."

She still did not cease her plaiting.

"That's cowardly, Philip, and wicked. God hears what you say."

He turned away dully. "I'd go to the coast if you'd go."

"I can't go, Philip. . . . God means us to stay."

The dazed look vanished suddenly in a blaze of fire. "God doesn't care what happens to us!"

Then for the first time she stopped her work. Her hands lay motionless and her face grew white. "You must pray God to forgive you. He hears everything." And then flinging herself down on her knees, she began to pray in her loud, flat voice. She prayed long after he had disappeared into the forest, now running, now walking, scarcely knowing what he did.

He had wanted desperately to go to the coast, partly because he felt tired and ill, but more because it would have been a change from the monotony, a lark, a pitiful groping toward what he had heard people call "a good time." And he couldn't go alone, for staying alone in some filthy town on the Indian Ocean where he knew no one was no better than staying at Megambo. Yet the thought of the coast, however bad it might be, stirred him with a new hunger simply to escape: it was not the coast itself, but the thing for which it stood as a symbol—the great world which lay beyond the barrier that shut in the three of them there on the low hill between the forest and the lake. . . .

In the end he was afraid to go lest he might never come back.

He did not fall ill again with the fever and so give Naomi another proof of her infallibility and her intimacy with God's intentions; and presently he plunged savagely into the ungrateful work among those childish black people whom he loathed, not because God had refilled the springs of his faith, but because it seemed the only way to save himself.

But something queer had happened to him as he watched Naomi fling herself into the dust to pray for him, something which in a way brought him peace, for the night no longer brought with it a cloud of confused and vague desires. It was not actual hatred that took the place of the torments, but only an indifference which closed him in once and forever from Naomi and Swanson. His life became a solitary thing which did not touch the lives of the others.

For as he plunged into the forest a great light burst upon him and he saw that Naomi, rather than leave Megambo, would have let him stay, without a thought, to die in that malarial hole.

Chapter 8

IT WAS the same dry season that marked the beginning of a new life in which he saw things which remained hidden to the others. It had been going on for a long time before he noticed any change beyond the fact that there were occasions when the lake, the distant mountains, and the flamingo-tinted marshes seemed more beautiful than they had been before. He noticed strange colors in the forest and the sound of bees and the curious throb of tom-toms in the village. Things which once he had felt only with the rawness of frayed nerves, he discovered in a new way. It was as if what had been a nightmare was turning into a pleasant, fantastic dream.

And then one day it came upon him suddenly as a sort of second sight, in a flash of revelation which the Prophets would have said descended to him from God; it was a kind of inspired madness which changed the very contours of the world about him, altered its colors and revealed meanings that lay beneath. For a time the lake, the low hills, the forest, all seemed illuminated by a supernatural light.

He had been tramping the borders of the muddy lake since dawn and as the sun, risen now, began to scald away the scant dew, he threw himself down to rest in the precarious shadow of a stunted acacia. Lying on his back he watched the wild bees and the tiny, glittering gnats weaving their crazy patterns through the checkered light and shadow, until presently there swept over him a strange, unearthly sense of peace, in which he seemed to exist no longer as an individual set apart, but only as a part of all the world of bees and gnats and animals and birds all about him. All at once the fears and torments of his mind became no more substantial than the shadows of the parched acacia-leaves. He seemed suddenly to fit into some grand scheme of things in which he occupied but a tiny, insignificant place, yet one in which he knew an odd, luxurious sense of freedom and solitude, cut off from Naomi and Swanson, and from all the things for which they stood as symbols. Dimly he experienced a desire to remain thus forever, half-enchanted, bathed as in a bath of clean cold water, in a feeling of senses satisfied and at peace.

He never knew how long he lay thus, but he was aware, after a long time, of music drifting toward him through the hot, pungent air from somewhere near the borders of the lake. It was a weird, unearthly sound which resolved itself slowly into a pattern of melody sung by high-pitched, whining voices— a melody cast in a minor key, haunting and beautiful in its simplicity, tragic in the insinuation of its haunting echoes. It was brief, too, scarcely a dozen bars in the notation of civilized music, but repeated over and over again until it became a long, monotonous chant. Its few notes belonged to that bare, savage world as the flamingoes and the hippopotami belonged to it.

Sitting up with his brown hands clasped about his knees, he listened, permitting the sound to flow over his tired nerves; and straining his feeble knowledge of the savage tongue, he discovered what it was they were singing. Their reed-like voices repeated over and over again:

> Go down to the water, little monkey,
> To the life of lives, the beginning of all things.
> Go down to the water, little monkey,
> To the life of lives, the beginning of all things.

Slowly he raised himself to his knees and discovered whence the music came. Through a wide gap in the reeds, trampled down by the great beasts of the lake, he caught a distant view of a procession of black women, slim and straight, all of them, as the papyrus that bordered the water. They wore the amulets and the wire ornaments of virgins and carried earthen jars balanced on their heads. At the edge of the water they stooped to fill the jars and raising them to their heads rose and moved up the banks. They were bringing life to the yam plantations, carrying the water from the lake to the parching earth on the high banks.

He knew them; they belonged to a remote village where the activities of Naomi and Swanson had not yet penetrated. Once or twice he had discovered them, perhaps these same black virgins, peering at him from the shelter of the thick forest. But they were different now, touched by a savage dignity that arose from a confidence in their own solitude. One line moved up the bank and the other down, passing and repassing each other in a perfection of repeated contours. They marched to the rhythm of their endless chant, their high-pointed, virginal breasts and slim bodies glistening like black marble in the sun.

> Go down to the water, little monkey,
> To the life of lives, the beginning of all things.

Creeping forward on his hands and knees, he came to an opening which revealed the goal of their march. It was a yam plantation and set in the midst was a grotesque figure, half-man, half-beast, carved of wood and painted in brilliant colors, a monstrous image such as he had seen once at the orgiastic festivals in the village at Megambo. One by one as they passed it, each virgin put down her jar and prostrated herself. Each third one emptied the water over the belly of the obscene god. He knew what it was. By chance, he witnessed a rite not meant for his profane eyes, a religious ceremony which none ever witnessed save the virgins who performed it. There was a black man at Megambo whose eyes had been pierced for having watched the adoration of the god of fertility.

Watching the thing, Philip was seized by a sudden passionate desire to set down in some fashion the beauty of the weird procession, to capture and fix the flow of the repeated contours and the sad splendor of the moaning chant. He wanted passionately to make the world—that great world which lay beyond the ragged coast towns—see the wild beauty which he found in the scene. His brown, thin, young hands felt a fierce hunger for some instrument with which he might draw the scene. The desire struck down, down deep into the past, into the hazy, half-forgotten childhood, when he had made pictures for Mary Conyngham, trying all the while to make her see what he saw in the world about him.

Then, abruptly, while he lay there on his stomach watching, the chanting ceased and the figures of black ivory slipped away like shadows into the dark forest, leaving him alone in a world that had suddenly become translated into something that lay beyond reality, in which every color seemed to have grown brilliant and every leaf and tree-trunk seemed outlined by light. The stagnant lake, lying like brass beneath a flaming sun, took on a beauty he had not seen there before.

It was a strange, new world in which he was still lonely, but in a different way. It no longer held any terror for him. He seemed in a miraculous fashion to understand things which before had been hidden from him.

Chapter 9

IT was noon and the air was filled with a scalding heat when he came at last within sight of the mission. Long before he saw it, there came toward him, on the hot breeze, the familiar sound that was like the droning of a hive of bees, and as he drew nearer he caught sight of Naomi seated beneath the thatched portico of the main hut, on a little platform built for her by Swanson to keep her long skirts out of the dust. Before her on the parched earth sat nine girls shrouded in shapeless sacks of magenta and white calico; they were repeating after her in droning voices the story of the visit of the Queen of Sheba to the court of Solomon. They repeated it in a version translated clumsily by Naomi herself, but out of it they managed somehow to wring an irresistible and monotonous rhythm which caused their supple bodies to sway backward and forward.

She was shrewd, Naomi! She had chosen the story of a black queen.

And then he saw that the performance was being watched by another person, a stranger, white like themselves. It was a woman, dressed like a man save that in place of trousers she wore an extremely short skirt that barely reached the tops of her strong boots. She was tall and thin with a long horse face burned and leathery from exposure to the weather. She stood like a man, with her legs rather well apart, her hands in the pockets of an extremely worn and soiled jacket, watching the spectacle out of a pair of bright blue eyes that were kindled with the light of a great intelligence. She might have been forty-five or sixty: it was impossible to say.

The forest behind her, he suddenly discovered, was alive with negroes who moved about cooking over the coals of a fire, their activities directed by a nervous, yellow man with the hooked nose of an Arab. They were niggers from the North, from somewhere near Lake Tchad.

As he approached, the woman turned sharply and after giving him a searching look, resumed her absorption in the spectacle, saying at the same time in a low voice as if he had entered in the midst of a service that was not to be interrupted, "I am Lady Millicent Wimbrooke. I am on my way south. I asked hospitality for a few hours, as good water is difficult to find."

It was a flat, metallic voice, without color, and after she had spoken, she took no more notice of him. She appeared to be fascinated by the spectacle of Naomi and the black girls repeating their lessons. About the hard mouth there flickered the merest shadow of mockery.

There was something menacing in the presence of the Englishwoman, something which seemed to fill the hot air with an electric tension. It was like having a fragment of some powerful explosive suddenly placed in their midst for a few hours, something which they might regard without touching. Also she was extremely hard and disagreeable.

She ate with them at the crude table fashioned by Swanson, having herself contributed the meat—the tenderest portion of a young antelope shot early that morning on the plains by her own hand. She talked of the country with a sort of harassed intensity as if she hated and despised it and yet was powerless to resist its fascination.

"They're no earthly good, these damned niggers," she said, "they'd all leave me at the clap of a hand to die of starvation and thirst. It's only the Arab's whip that keeps them in order."

Philip felt himself hating her for her arrogance and for the contempt she had for all this world, including themselves, but he sometimes felt as she did about the "damned niggers." He saw Naomi recoil as the words fell from the stranger's thin, hard lips. It was blasphemy to speak thus of their black brothers, of God's children.

But Lady Millicent did give them much valuable information about the Lake tribes and their fierce neighbors in the North. She knew, it appeared, an immense amount about this wild country. She was, she said scornfully, an old maid and she had first come out to this malignant country five years earlier with her brother who had promptly died of fever. She was now making this trip because she had to see the country where only Livingstone and one or two others had been before her.

The Lake tribes, she said, were peaceful black people, who lived by herding a few thin cattle and innumerable scraggy goats brought thither in some time which may well have been as remote as the Deluge. It was fertile land when there was rain and the people were comparatively rich and good-natured. Probably missionaries would find them easy to convert, as they had a childlike curiosity about new stories, and of course the Bible was filled with all sorts of fairy tales. (Again Philip saw Naomi wince and Swanson raise his stupid blue eyes in astonishment and horror.) The Lake people were not warlike; when their fierce neighbors of the North, who lived by robbery and war, came on a raid, the Lake people simply vanished into the bush, taking with them all their possessions, leaving behind only huts which might be burned but could be rebuilt again with little effort. Since the end of the Slave Trade, they had had a long period of peace.

Once Naomi interrupted her by saying, "Our experience with these people has been different. We've used only kindness and it's worked wonders. Of course, they thieve and they lie, but we've only been here three years and in the end we'll make them see that these things are sin."

Lady Millicent laid down her fork. "My dear woman," she said firmly, "niggers haven't any sense of sin. They don't know what you are talking about. My brother used to say the only good nigger is a dead nigger, and the longer I live the more I'm certain of it."

After that a painful silence descended on the table, for it appeared that this stranger seemed intent not only upon disagreeing with them, but even upon insulting them; Naomi and Swanson, his earnest baby's face streaming with perspiration, took it all mildly, even when Lady Millicent observed that "missionaries often made a lot of trouble. In the Northeast where the niggers have given up polygamy, all the extra women have become whores. Instead of sleeping with one man a dozen times a year, they sleep with three hundred and sixty-five different ones. That's what you have done for them up there."

Swanson suddenly burst out in his funny, incoherent fashion, "If I could talk I'd argue . . . but I'm not good at words." Poor Swanson, who could only work for the Lord with his big, sausage-like hands.

But for a moment, when it seemed possible that she was to have a battle, the face of the Englishwoman softened a bit. She looked almost as if she could be fond of Swanson. For Naomi she had only a nostril-quivering contempt.

As for Philip, he sat all the while watching her like a bird fascinated by a snake. Naomi saw that also.

He seemed scarcely able to think in any sensible fashion; he, who had once believed so profoundly, found himself tossed this way and that by conflicting emotions. She made him feel insignificant and sick. It was as if she had the power of destroying all the satisfaction that should have come from their work. He had heard of people like this—unbelieving, wicked scoffers who felt no need for turning to God in search of strength; but he could not quite believe in her, this gaunt, fearless old maid. No one had ever disagreed with them before; no one had ever doubted the holy sanctity of their mission; all the world they had known believed in them and covered them with glory, as Naomi had been covered during the tent meeting in the smoky Town. She had the power of making him ashamed that he was such a fool as to believe he could help the "damned niggers." She made him feel in a disgusting way ashamed of Naomi and poor, stupid Swanson. And then immediately he was ashamed of being ashamed. He had, too, a sudden flash of consciousness that the three of them were helpless, silly babes, facing a terrifying mystery. They were like insects attacking feebly a mountain of granite. To succeed one needed to be as hard as Lady Millicent Wimbrooke.

She disturbed him, too, as an intimation of that world which lay beyond, awaiting him.

After the meal she rose abruptly and summoned two bearers, who set up a collapsible canvas bathtub in one of the huts. When they had filled it with water and she had bathed, she slept for an hour, and then, summoning the Arab, Ali, set the train of bearers in order with the air of a field-marshal, and thanking her hosts, started her caravan on its way through the forest, herself at the head, walking strongly, her short skirt slipping about her bony knees.

When she had gone, the three of them—Swanson, Naomi and Philip—stood at the gate of the enclosure looking after the procession until the last of the bearers was swallowed up in the thick shadows of the forest. Then in silence they returned to their work, disturbed and puzzled by the odd feeling of suspense she left in passing.

Late that afternoon Naomi observed suddenly, "She oughtn't to have stopped here. She is a wicked woman."

Chapter 10

IT WAS long after midnight when Philip was awakened out of a deep sleep by a sound like thunder. Sitting up in his bunk (for he always wakened quickly and sharply) he experienced a feeling of delight that it would rain soon, putting an end to the long, baking drouth. And then slowly he understood that there could be no thunder at this season, and that it was not the sound of thunder; it was too small and sharp and ordered. It was a sound made by man lacking in the grandiosity of the preposterous Nature that dominated Megambo.

Sitting on the edge of the rough bed, he saw the familiar outlines of the mission take form in the darkness—the hut with the eternal insects and animals rustling in the thatch, the bunk opposite where Naomi lay sleeping quietly, all her dislike of Lady Millicent effaced now by the blank look of contentment. He saw the storeroom and Swanson's hut, and last of all the great, lumpy figure of Swanson himself, sitting by a fire that was almost dead. He was asleep with his head sunk between his knees, his great hands hanging like clusters of sausages. (He always fell asleep, careless of danger, certain that God was watching over him.)

It was a clear night, but moonless, when the monstrous trees showed black against the star-powdered sky, and save for the reverberant, thumping sound, silent, as if the unnatural thunder had frightened the very animals to take cover, to listening with hair and ears bristling. Fascinated by the sound, Philip rose and walked out into the enclosure; he wore, in the hut, only a cloth wrapped about his waist, and standing there beside the dying fire he looked and felt a part of all that untamed wild. He was not a big man, but a singularly well-built one, with muscles hard yet supple—a man such as his father must have been when he aroused such turbulent emotions in a breast so chaste as that of Emma Downes.

Listening to the unearthly sound, Philip extended his arms, watching the muscles flex beneath the tanned smooth skin, and suddenly there swept over him a vivid and poignant sense of delight in being alive. He felt the warm life sweeping through him and a sudden fierce pride in a body of which he had never before been conscious. He had a wild desire to leap the flimsy barricade and running, running in the light of the stars, to lose himself in the sable shadows of the forest.

He thought, "I am alive! I am alive!"

He was aware of the things that exist only in the night, of the demons worshipped by the witch-doctor of Megambo, of unearthly creatures that hovered in the shadows of the forest. The scene by the lake returned to him . . . the procession of virgins pouring the fertile waters of the lake over the belly of a repulsive idol.

He thought, "We are bewitched—Swanson and Naomi and I. We will die prisoners without ever having broken the spell."

In the heat of the still night death seemed all about on every side.

"I am awake and yet asleep. I am the only one who sees. . . ."

The strange thunder kept on and on, now near at hand, now far away, rising and falling in volume.

Again the odd, voluptuous feeling of power lying in his own supple body swept over him. Leaning down he touched Swanson's soft, heavy shoulder. "Swanson," he said, and there was no answer. He shook the man savagely, and Swanson, coming out of a deep sleep, stared up at him.

"Yes, I fell asleep again. . . . I can't help it."

"Listen!" Philip commanded.

After a silence, Swanson said, "It's thunder . . . it's going to rain."

"It's not thunder—look at the sky—what is it? You ought to know."

Swanson was humble with that childlike humbleness that always put Philip to shame, as if he said, "I won't be presumptuous. You're much more clever than I am."

"I don't know," he said; "maybe we'd better ask Naomi."

She wakened quickly, catching at once their vague sense of alarm, for Swanson appeared now to be frightened and uneasy for the first time. She, too, listened and said, "I don't know. I never heard it up North in Pa's country. It sounds like drums—like tom-toms. I've heard that sometimes they signal that-a-away."

The three of them—Philip and Swanson still half-naked (for they had forgotten even decency) and Naomi in a long, shapeless calico nightgown—went out again to stand under the open sky by the fire to listen.

After a long time Naomi said, "Yes, it's drums all right. It must mean some kind of trouble."

They slept no more that night and toward morning as the sky beyond the burnished, black surface of the lake began to turn the color of a flamingo's breast, the sound seemed to die away a little, bit by bit, as if it were a long piece of cane being broken off, a morsel at a time. At daylight it died altogether, leaving only a hot, empty stillness, and far away, near the place where Philip had seen the black virgins, the glow which they had mistaken for the rising dawn turned to the gray smoke of a burning village. The gray column spread fan-wise against the horizon until all the bush for miles lay covered by a thick blanket of gray rising above an angry red line. On the surface of the lake the fragile, black silhouette of a canoe jumped for a moment like a water-spider against the horizon, and disappeared.

The sun, dimmed and red, flooded the basin of the lake and the marshes with dull, yellow light, and revealed the village below them—their own village, Megambo—standing silent and deserted. There was no echo of loud, carefree banter, no crowing of cocks, no sound of women screaming at one another over the morning fires. It was silent like a village stricken with a plague wherein all were dead.

As the day advanced it seemed to Philip that they, too, were dead. In that empty world, he could not bring himself to go off alone into a menacing silence where the sound of a rifle-shot might rouse all the forest into life. It was as if thousands of eyes watched them from out of the shadows. He went as far as the village and found there not so much as an earthen pot. A whole people had disappeared, with everything they possessed, as if the earth had swallowed them up.

The hours dragged one into the next while they waited; there was no work, for there were no black people. It was impossible to leave when one did not even know what there was to flee from. Swanson pottered about with his clumsy hands, suffering less than Philip or Naomi. He tried vainly to fill in the silence.

As for Naomi, she seemed to have grown suddenly helpless and dependent, now that the very foundation of her existence, her reason for living was withdrawn. Philip, watching her, found a shameful satisfaction in the sight of Naomi, rudderless and the prey of a nameless terror. Her pale complacence melted into uneasiness. She retired now and then into the hut to pray. She prayed to the Lord to send them some sign by which to interpret the silence and the emptiness. He would, she was certain, perform some miracle as he had done in guiding the Children of Israel out of the Wilderness. He would not abandon them, his chosen servants. She abased herself before God, groveling in the dust as the black women had done before the monstrous idol.

As they watched the distant fire, driven by the changing wind, eating its way toward them, the terror mounted, gnawing at their tired nerves.

The faith of Naomi was rewarded, for at last there came a sign, although it was not in the least religious and came from the most profane and unmystical of all sources. At noon Philip, standing in the gateway, saw emerging from the forest the weather-beaten figure of Lady Millicent Wimbrooke. Across her arm with an air of easy repose lay a rifle. Across her thin back was slung a second gun, and across her flat breast were slung bandolier after bandolier of cartridges. The pockets of her weather-beaten skirt and jacket bulged with more ammunition. She gave the effect of a walking arsenal. Before her, carrying the collapsible bathtub, walked the Arab, Ali, the muzzle of a third rifle pressed into his back.

Watching her, Philip wished that she had not returned, and Naomi, instead of feeling relief at the sight of a white woman, was frightened, more frightened and more resentful than she had been of the silence. It was a nameless fear, but because of that all the more dreadful. Naomi, who believed that all people were the children of God, hated Lady Millicent Wimbrooke.

The invincible spinster appeared to believe that they knew what was taking place in the forest and on the distant plain. She did not speak of the silence. Without greeting them she said, "I must have a bath now, but I can't leave Ali unguarded." She glanced at the three of them and then quickly, with the air of conferring an honor, she handed her rifle to Philip. "Here," she said. "You watch him. If he gets away, he'll make trouble and without him we're lost. He knows the way to the coast. He used to come here in the days of the slave-traders."

She explained briefly that the sound of drums had wakened her in the night and that when she rose to look about, she discovered that not one of her bearers remained. They had vanished into the bush. "They're like that, these damned niggers." She had caught Ali in the act of robbing her and since then she had not left him out of range of her rifle. She finished by saying, "How soon will you be ready to leave?"

It was Naomi who asked, "Leave? Why are we leaving?"

"You can't stay here unless you *want* to die."

The return of the Englishwoman had an amazing effect upon Naomi. The terror seemed to have left her, giving way to a sudden, resentful stubbornness, tinged by hatred.

"God means us to stick to our post," she said. "He will care for us."

Lady Millicent laughed. It was a short, vicious, ugly sound. "You can trust to God if you like. I intend to leave within an hour. I shan't argue it with you, but I mean to take Ali, and without him you'll be lost."

"But why?" Philip asked suddenly. "Is it necessary?"

She gave him a look of utter scorn. "Do you know anything about this country? Do you know what's happened?"

"No," said Philip, meek as a lamb, "I don't."

"Well, they've come down for blood—from the North, and they aren't afraid of any white man and they never heard of God. Besides, before night the fire will be here."

She turned suddenly and poured out a torrent of guttural sounds on the miserable Arab, who turned and entered Swanson's hut.

"If he tries to escape," she told Philip, "just shoot him, and remember I know what I'm talking about . . . I've lived among 'em."

Taking her canvas bathtub, she left them, going down to the Lake.

They knew now what they had to fear, and with the knowledge Naomi seemed once more to gain control of her flagging spirit. There was even color in her cheeks and a new light in her pale eyes. To Philip she seemed almost pretty.

After the Englishwoman had disappeared, she called Philip and Swanson and said, "I am not going to leave. God means us to stay. He has refreshed my spirit."

Philip argued with her. "The Englishwoman knows best; she has lived here."

"She is sent by the Devil to tempt us," said Naomi in a strangely hysterical voice. "She's an evil woman . . . I've prayed and God has answered me." It was difficult to know whether she was stubborn because of faith or because she hated Lady Millicent Wimbrooke.

When Philip didn't answer her, she turned to Swanson. "You'll stay, won't you?"

"If God means us to stay," he answered weakly. "I don't know."

A kind of scorn suddenly colored her voice. "And you, Philip . . . will you stay or will you go off with your friend?"

"What friend?" asked Philip.

"Her," said Naomi, who could not bring herself to say "Lady Millicent."

"Friend?" he echoed. "Why friend?"

"Oh, you know why. You seem to agree with her. You never said a word in our defense."

This was a new Naomi who stood looking at him, a woman excited and hysterical, and desperate, whom he did not recognize. This new Naomi was the martyr prepared to die for a Heavenly crown, moved by some inward fire that was terrifying and quite beyond control and reason. Between them, husband and wife, the chasm had opened again. He saw her suddenly as he had seen her when she was indifferent to the danger of his staying at Megambo—a woman to whom he was less than nothing, who would sacrifice him for the mad faith he no longer shared.

He looked away because he suddenly found her face hard and repulsive, saying, "You're crazy, Naomi. I don't know what you're talking about."

"Oh, yes, I'm crazy, but I know what I mean and you do, too. You've abandoned God and faith. You're like her now."

She was growing more and more excited. It struck him suddenly that she was jealous of Lady Millicent—that strange, battered, weather-beaten old maid; but the idea was too fantastic. He put it away. She might, perhaps, be jealous because the Englishwoman had picked him as the one who was most sane, but it couldn't be more than that. Before he was able to answer, he saw Lady Millicent herself entering the gate and barring it behind her. She looked in at the door of Swanson's hut. "He's pretending to be asleep," she said. "I know the Arab tricks."

Then wiping the sweat from her face, she said, "We may have to fight for it. There's a band of them painted like heathen images coming along the lake." Again she addressed Philip. "Do you know how to use a gun?"

"Yes."

"The others," she asked, indicating Naomi and Swanson, "are they any good?"

"No."

Naomi came forward. "Philip, I forbid you to kill." She placed herself suddenly between him and Lady Millicent, but the Englishwoman pushed her aside.

"This is no time for rot!" She gave such a snort that it seemed to him sparks must fly from her nostrils. "I can't defend all of you . . . with two able-bodied, strong men."

"We're missionaries," said Philip. "We didn't come to kill the poor heathen but to save."

"Well, I mean to kill as many as possible."

Suddenly there was the cannon-like report of an old-fashioned musket, and a bullet sang past them, embedding itself in the thatch of Swanson's hut. Philip saw Lady Millicent thrusting a rifle on Swanson to guard the wily Arab—Swanson who couldn't bear to kill a rat. There was another report and the slow whistle of a bullet. Then he found himself suddenly on the forest side of the stockade, beside the Englishwoman. There was a rifle in his hands and he heard her saying, "Don't fire till they get clear of the forest—then they'll have no shelter."

She was crouching behind the barricade like an elderly leopard, peering toward the forest. The bathtub lay where she had tossed it aside. Through a gap in the wall he saw seven black men, hideously painted and decorated with feathers, running toward them. He raised the rifle and some one seized his arm. It was Naomi, screaming, "Don't! Don't! Thou shalt not kill!"

He heard the hoarse voice of Lady Millicent calling out, "If you want to live, fire! Fire *now!*"

He struck Naomi savagely, pushing her into the dust. She lay there praying hysterically. He fired. He heard Lady Millicent firing. He saw one black man after another pitch forward and fall. She was (he thought) an excellent shot. The voice of Naomi praying wildly rose above the noise, the shots and the wild cries of the attacking niggers. Then all at once, those who remained alive turned and ran for the forest. He took careful aim, and one of them fell, kicking grotesquely. There was another report beside him, and the second fell on the edge of the forest. He saw the last of them turn and fire his musket. Then something struck him on the head like the blow of a club.

He heard a great voice calling, "I want to *live!* I want to *live!*" and all the world about him exploded with a great flash of light.

Chapter 11

HE WAKENED with the acrid tang of smoke in his nostrils, conscious of a slow, gliding motion, to find himself being carried on the back of Swanson. They were moving along a narrow path bordered by tall dry grass. At the head marched Ali followed by Lady Millicent, her rifle pressed against his trembling spine, her salvaged bathtub slung across her flat shoulders; and close behind came Naomi, still in her wide hat of thatched grass, her long, grotesque calico skirts muddy and wet to the waist from wading some stream. They had escaped with Lady Millicent's arsenal of ammunition and the clothes on their backs. The sun had slipped below the distant mountains and they walked through a twilight dimmed by the clouds of smoke borne toward them by a rising wind.

He got down at once and set out to follow them, feeling weak and shaky, until Lady Millicent (whom Naomi watched with the expression of one observing the source of all evil) provided a drink from the flask which she carried on her hip.

They marched in silence, racing against the fire and the rising wind, in the knowledge that if they reached the river before dark they were safe; and Philip, his bandaged head filled with a sickening ache, managed slowly to reconstruct what had happened since he was wakened by the thunderous echo of tom-toms. It all returned to him slowly, bit by bit, with an increasing vividness which reached its climax in the image of a hideously painted black man kicking grotesquely as he lay on his face by the edge of the forest.

The image somehow cleared his head and he was conscious slowly of a new and thrilling sensation of freedom. Presently he understood what it was: he had killed the men he had come to turn to God and he was never going back to that inferno beside the brassy lake. It was all over now. He hadn't even any faith. He was free and fearless. He had killed a man—perhaps three or four men. (He would never know whether he or Lady Millicent was the better shot.) But it did not matter. He was free and he was alive. Even the ache in his sick body seemed to fade into silence.

The little column before him had halted suddenly and as he moved up he found them standing about the body of a black girl that lay on its face full in the middle of the path. Swanson, bending down, turned the naked body over and they saw that she was young, straight, and beautiful in her savage way. By the wire ornaments Philip recognized her as one of the virgins from the village near the lake—perhaps one of those he had watched pouring water over the belly of the idol. There was no mark on her; they could not tell how she died. And they left her lying there because there was no time. The leopards would come to bury what was left of her after the cruel fire had passed. There would be a fête for the leopards with all those black men who lay outside the barricade.

As they turned to hurry on, the Englishwoman pointed behind them to a great column of flame and smoke. "Look," she said. "There's the mission."

With a little sigh, Naomi sank down in the middle of the path and began to weep hysterically. It was Philip who knelt beside her and lifted her up, trying to comfort her. They hurried on, his arm about her waist. She only addressed him once and then it was to say, "I can't help it, because it's the end of me—the end of everything." He had never seen her like this—broken, trembling and frightened.

At that moment he felt toward her for the first time as he supposed husbands must feel toward their wives. He pitied her, but his pity could not stifle the fierce wave of delight that welled up deep inside him. He turned to look for the last time at the columns of flame and smoke and was seized by a savage joy in the spectacle. He found it wildly beautiful, for he saw it with that new vision which had come to him by the lake; but that was not the reason why he felt this intoxicating happiness.

He was free. He meant to live, to have his youth. He meant never to go back.

PART TWO
THE SLATE-COLORED HOUSE

Chapter 1

LONG AGO Mrs. Downes had followed the example of other thrifty house-holders and painted her dwelling that peculiar slate-gray which gave the whole town so depressing an aspect. It was a color which did not show the marks of the soot that rose from the blast-furnaces and chimneys to fall and fall again over the community. The color, however, in the case of Emma's house, seemed to extend to the inside, to lie in some peculiar fashion in the very warp and woof of the place. Being a woman of affairs she was seldom at home save when she returned to sleep and so the breath of conviviality scarcely touched its walls. The nearest approach occurred on the occasion, once each year, when she opened the place to entertain the Minerva Circle. Then she flung open the massive oak doors which separated the dining-room from the parlor and had in bleak rows of collapsible chairs, hired from McTavish, the undertaker, to support the varying weights of her fellow club members.

The refreshments were provided from the kitchens of her own restaurant —an assortment of salads, sandwiches and ice creams familiar enough to the regular patrons, but exciting and worldly novelties to ladies who did their own cooking or at best had only rather incompetent hired girls. But even this occasion was not one which left behind those ghosts of gayety which haunt the pleasant houses of the blessed; it was at best a gathering of tired, middle-aged women seated on hard chairs who wrestled with worries over children and husbands, while one or another of their fellow-members read from a rustling paper the painfully prepared account of her trip to the Yellowstone, or if the occasion was an intensely exciting one, of her voyage to Europe. Sometimes, it is true, Emma Downes rose to announce that she would read one of the interesting letters from her son, for these letters came vaguely under the head of geography and foreign travel, just as at the meetings of the Woman's Christian Temperance Union, they came hazily under the classi-fication of temperance. And as many of the members belonged to both or-ganizations and were also friends of Emma, they sometimes heard the same letter several times.

No one ever dined or lunched with Emma. She had no meals at home, as she took no holidays save Sunday, when it was the tradition to lunch with Elmer, who, she sometimes reflected, was certainly rich enough from the profits of his pump works to set a better table. In Emma there was a streak of sensuality which set her apart from her brother—she liked a comfortable house and good food (it was really this in the end which made the Peerless Restaurant a triumphant success). But there was evidence of even deeper fleshliness, for the brief interlude of Mr. Downes—that butterfly of passion—had shaken her life for a time and filled it with a horrid and awful uneasiness.

In the parlor, above the tiled mantelpiece, there hung an enlarged photograph of the derelict husband from which he looked out as wooden and impassive as it was possible for a photographer to make him. Yet life had not been altogether extinguished, for there was in the cocky tilt of the head and the set of a twinkling eye which could not be extinguished, in the curve of the lip beneath the voluminous dragoon mustaches, something which gave a hint of his character. He was, one could see, a swaggering little man, cock-of-the-walk, who had a way with women, even with such game as the invincible Emma—a man who was, perhaps, an odd combination of helplessness and bravado, a liar doubtless and a braggart. On the occasions of Minerva Circle meetings a vase of flowers always stood beneath the picture, a gesture touching and appropriate, since all that remained of Mr. Downes lay, as every one knew, somewhere in China and not in a well-ordered grave among the dead of his wife's family.

Chapter 2

IT WAS to this bleak and cheerless house that Philip and Naomi returned one winter night in the midst of a blizzard which buried all the town in snow and hid even the flames of the blast-furnaces which were always creeping distressingly nearer to Emma Downes' property.

All the way from Baltimore during two days and a night of traveling in one dreary day-coach after another they had sat sullenly side by side, rarely speaking to each other, for Philip, driven beyond endurance, had suddenly lost his temper and forbidden her to speak again of going back to Megambo. For a time she had wept while he sat stubbornly staring out of the window, conscious of the stares of the two old women opposite, and troubled by suspicions that Naomi was using her tears to shame him before their fellow-passengers. When there were no more tears left she did not speak to him again, but she began to pray in a voice just loud enough for him to hear. This he could not forbid her to do, lest she should begin to weep once more, more violently than ever, but he preferred her prayers for his salvation to her weeping, for tears made him feel that he had abused her and sometimes brought him perilously near to surrender. He tried to harden his heart by telling himself that her tears and prayers were really bogus and produced only to affect him, but the plan did not succeed because it was impossible to know

when she was really suffering and when she was not. Since that moment
when he pushed her aside into the dust and fired at the painted niggers, a
new Naomi seemed to have been born whom he had never known before. It
was a Naomi who wept like Niobe and, turning viciously feminine, used
weakness as a horrible weapon. There were moments when he felt that she
would have suffered less if he had beaten her daily.

She had been, as Emma hoped, "working over him" without interruption
since the moment at Zanzibar when Lady Millicent bade them a curt good-by
and Philip told her that he meant never to return to Megambo nor even be a
missionary again. She was still praying in a voice just loud enough for him
to hear when she was interrupted by his saying, "There's Ma, now—standing
under the light by the baggage-truck."

Emma stood in the flying snow, wrapped warmly in a worn sealskin coat
with leg-o'-mutton sleeves, peering up at the frosted windows of the train.
At first sight of her a wave of the old pleasure swept Philip, and then gradually it died away, giving place to a disturbing uneasiness. It was as if the sight
of her paralyzed his very will, reducing the stubbornness which had resisted
Naomi so valiantly, to a mere shadow. He felt his new-born independence
slipping from him. He was a little boy again, obeying a mother who always
knew best.

It was not that he was afraid of her; it lay deeper than fear, a part of his
very marrow. He was troubled, too, because he knew that he was about to
hurt her, whom he wanted to hurt less than any person in the world. Naomi
did not matter by the side of his mother; what happened to Naomi was of no
importance.

She saw them at once, almost as if some instinct had led her to the exact
spot where they got down. Naomi she ignored, but Philip she seized in her
arms (she was much bigger than he, as she had been bigger than his father).
The tears poured down her face.

"Philip," she cried. "My boy! Philip!"

From the shadow of a great pile of trunks a drunken baggage hustler
watched the scene with a wicked light of amusement in his eye.

Then she noticed Naomi, who stood by, shivering in her thin clothes. For a
moment there was a flash of hostility in her eye, but it passed quickly, perhaps because it was impossible to feel enmity for any one who looked so pale
and pitiful and frightened. Philip, noticing her, too, suspected that it was not
the cold alone that made her tremble. He knew suddenly that she was terrified by something, by his mother, by the sound of the pounding mills, of the
red glow in the sky—more terrified than she had been in all the adventure by
the burning lake. And all at once he felt inexplicably sorry for her. She had a
way of affecting him thus when he least expected it.

"Come," said Emma, composed and efficient once more. "You're both
shivering."

The transfer to a smelly, broken-down cab was accomplished quickly, since missionaries have little need for worldly goods and Philip and Naomi had only what they had bought in Capetown.

On the way up the hill, the snow blew in at the cracks of the cab windows, and from time to time Emma, talking all the while, leaned forward and patted Philip's knees, her large face beaming. Philip sat back in his corner, speaking only to answer "Yes" or "No." No one paid any heed to Naomi.

Elmer Niman was waiting for them at the slate-colored house, seated gloomily in the parlor before the gas-logs by the side of his wife, a fat, rather silly woman, who was expecting hourly her second child, conceived, it seemed, almost miraculously after an hiatus of ten years and conscientious effort in that direction. Emma held her in contempt, not only because she was the wife of her brother, but because she was a bad housekeeper and lazy, who sat all day in a rocking-chair looking out from behind the Boston fern in her bow-window, or reading sentimental stories in the women's magazines. Moreover, Emma felt that she should have accomplished much sooner the only purpose for which her brother had married—an heir to inherit his pump works. And when she gave the matter thought, she decided, too, that Mabelle had deliberately trapped her brother into matrimony.

But there was no feeling of hostility between them, at least not on Mabelle's side, for it might have been said that Mabelle was not quite bright and so never felt the weight of her sister-in-law's contempt. At the moment she simply sat rocking mildly and remarking, "I won't get up—it's such an effort in my condition"—a remark which brought a faint blush into Naomi's freckled cheeks.

As soon as Philip saw his uncle—thin, bilious and forbidding—standing before the gas-logs—he knew that they all meant to have it out if possible at once, without delay. Uncle Elmer looked so severe, so near to malice, as he stood beneath the enlarged photograph of Philip's jaunty father. There was no doubt about his purpose. He greeted his nephew by saying, "Well, Philip, I hadn't expected to see you home so soon."

For a second the boy wondered whether his mother had told Uncle Elmer that he had come back for good, never to return to Africa, but he knew almost at once that she had. There was a look in his cold eyes which, as Philip knew well, came into them when he fancied he had caught some one escaping from duty.

He and Naomi were thrust forward to the fire and he heard his mother saying, "I'll have Essie bring in some hot coffee and sandwiches," dimly, as in a nightmare, for he was seized again with a wild surge of the fantastic unreality which had possessed him since the moment when he fell unconscious beside the barricade. The very snow outside seemed unreal after the hot, brassy lake at Megambo.

He thought, "Why am I here? What have I done? Am I dreaming, and really lie asleep in the hut at Megambo?" He even thought, "Perhaps I am two persons, two bodies—in two places at the same time. Perhaps I have gone insane." Of only one thing was he certain and that was of a strange, intangible hostility that surrounded him in the persons of all of them, save perhaps of Aunt Mabelle, who sat rocking stupidly, unconscious of what they were set upon doing to him. He knew the hostility that was there in the cold eyes of Uncle Elmer, and he knew the hostility that was in Naomi, and it occurred to him suddenly that there was hostility even in the way his mother had patted his knees as they rode through the blizzard.

They talked of this and that, of the voyage, the weather, the prodigious growth of the town and the danger of strikes in the Mills (for every one in the town lived under the shadow of the pounding mills), and presently Emma said, "But you haven't told us about the uprising. That must be a good story."

Philip said, "Let Naomi tell it. She can do it better than I."

So Naomi told the story haltingly in the strong voice which always seemed strange in so fragile a body. She told it flatly, so that it sounded like a rather bad newspaper account made up from fragments of mangled cables. Once or twice Philip felt a sudden passionate desire to interrupt her, but he held his peace. It was the first time that he had heard her talking of it, and she didn't see it at all. He wanted to cry out, "But you've forgotten the sound of the drums in the night! And the sight of the fire on the plains!" He thought his mother might understand what he saw in it, but Uncle Elmer wouldn't. He decided to save it to tell his mother when they were alone. It was *his* story, *his* experience; Naomi had never shared it at all.

He heard Naomi saying, "And then we came to the coast—and—and that's all there is to it."

"But what about the Englishwoman?" his mother was asking.

"Oh, she went away north again—right away—I must say we were glad to be rid of her. I didn't care for her at all—or Swanson either. She was hard and cruel—she didn't like us and treated us like fools, like the dirt under her feet, all except Philip. I think she—well, she liked him very much."

At the end her voice dropped a little and took on a faint edge of malice. It was a trick Philip had only noticed lately, for the first time during the long voyage from Capetown. It hung, quivering with implications, until Philip burst out:

"Well, if it hadn't been for her we'd all be dead now. I don't know about you, but I'm glad I'm alive. Maybe you'd rather be dead."

Naomi made no answer. She only bowed her head a little as if he had struck her, and Uncle Elmer said, "What about Swanson? What's happened to him?"

Naomi's head, heavy with its mass of sandy hair, raised again. "Oh," she said, "*he* went back to Megambo. *He* didn't want to desert the post. He thought all the natives were depending on him."

"Alone?"

"Yes, all alone."

For a moment the silence hung heavy and unpleasant; Philip, miserable and tortured, sat with his head bowed, staring at the Brussels carpet. It was his mother who spoke.

"I must say it was courageous of him. When I saw him before you all left I didn't think much of him. He seemed stupid. . . ."

"But he has faith," said Naomi, "and courage. He was for not raising a hand during the attack. He didn't want to kill, you see."

Sitting there, Philip felt them beating in upon him, mercilessly, relentlessly, and he was afraid, not of any one of them but because all of them together with the familiar sight of the room, the veneered mahogany furniture, the red wallpaper, even his father's photograph with the flowers beneath it, made him feel small and weak, and horribly lonely as he had sometimes felt as a little boy. He kept saying to himself, "I'm a man now. I won't give in—I won't. They can't make me."

And then Uncle Elmer launched the attack. His method aimed, as if by some uncanny knowledge, at Philip's weakest part. He began by treating him as a little boy, humoring him. He even smiled, an act so rare with Uncle Elmer that it always seemed laden with foreboding.

"And what's this I hear about your not going back, Philip—about your changing your mind?"

Philip only nodded his head without speaking.

"You mustn't think of it too much just now. Just forget about it and when you're rested and better everything will come out all right."

Then Philip spoke. "I'm not going back."

But Uncle Elmer pondered this, still humoring him as if he were delirious or mad.

"Of course, it's a matter of time and rest. I've always felt toward you as I would toward my own son—if I had one." (Here Aunt Mabelle bridled and preened herself as if flattered by being noticed at last, even by implication.) "I'm thinking only of your own good."

"I'm not going back," repeated Philip dully.

The singsong voice of Uncle Elmer went on: "Of course, once you've had the call—there's no mistake. You can't turn back from the Lord once you've heard the call."

"I never had the call."

"What do you mean? You can't imagine a thing like that. Nobody ever imagined he heard the Lord calling him."

"It's true, though—I must have imagined it."

He couldn't say, somehow, what he wanted to say, because it wasn't clear in his own mind. He *had* thought he had heard the call, but now he saw it wasn't really so at all. He felt vaguely that his mother was somehow responsible for the feeling.

Uncle Elmer waited for a time, as if to lend weight to his words.

"Do you understand that it is a great sin—to abandon the Lord's work—the greatest sin of which a human creature can be guilty?"

Philip was trembling now like a man under torture. He couldn't fight back, somehow, because he was all confused, inside, deep down in his soul. It was as if his brain were all in knots.

"I don't know what is sin and what isn't. I've been thinking about it—I used to think of it for hours at a time at Megambo, I couldn't do my work for thinking of it—I don't know what is sin and what isn't, and you don't either. None of us know."

"We all know, Philip. The Bible tells us."

(Yes, that was true. The Bible had it all written down. You couldn't answer a thing like that.)

"He's lost his faith," said Naomi.

"You must pray, Philip. I pray when I'm in doubt—when I'm in trouble. I've prayed when I've been worried over the factory, and help always came."

"I can't explain it, Uncle Elmer. It's a spiritual thing that's happened to me . . . I couldn't go back—not now!"

Uncle Elmer's eyebrows raised a little, superciliously, shocked.

"A spiritual thing? To turn your back on God!"

"I haven't said that—" How could he explain when "spiritual" meant to them only Uncle Elmer's idea of "Biblical"? "I mean it is something that's happened to my spirit—deep inside me."

How could he explain what had happened to him as he lay in the rushes watching the procession of black girls? Or what had happened as he stood half-naked by the dying fire listening to the drums beating against the dome of the night? How could he explain when he did not know himself? Yet it was an experience of the spirit. It had happened to his soul.

He kept repeating to himself, "I won't—I won't. They can't make me." He saw his mother watching him with sad eyes, and he had to look away in order not to weaken and surrender.

Then Naomi's flat voice, "I've prayed—I've pled with him. I never cease to pray." She had begun to weep.

Philip's jaw, lean from illness and dark from want of shaving, set with a sudden click. His mother saw it, with a sudden sickening feeling that the enlarged photograph above his head had come to life. She knew that jaw. She knew what it meant when it clicked in that sudden fashion.

"It's no use talking about it—I won't go back—not if I burn in Hell."

Uncle Elmer interrupted him, all the smoothness gone suddenly from his voice. "Which you will as sure as there's a God above!"

The thin, yellow, middle-aged man was transformed suddenly into the likeness of one of the more disagreeable Prophets of the Old Testament. He was cruel, savage, intolerant. Emma Downes knew the signs; she saw that Elmer was losing his temper and beginning to roll about in the righteousness that made him hard and cruel. If he went on against that set, swarthy jaw of Philip, only disaster could come of it. They would lose everything.

"We'd all better go to bed; it's late and we're all worn out—Philip and Naomi most of all. There's no hurry about deciding. When Philip's well again—"

They meant to postpone the struggle, but not to abandon it. They bade each other good-night and Aunt Mabelle, rising from her rocking-chair with difficulty, smiled and insisted on kissing Philip, who submitted sullenly. Secretly she was pleased with him as she was always pleased when she saw some one get the better of Elmer.

As the door closed beneath the horrid glare of the green-glass gas-jet, Uncle Elmer turned.

"And what will you do, Philip, if you don't go back? You'll have to start life all over again."

"I don't know," Philip answered dully. But he did know, almost, without knowing it. He knew deep down within the very marrow of his bones. There was only one thing he wanted to do. It was a fierce desire that had been born as he lay beneath the acacia-tree watching the procession of singing women.

Chapter 3

WHEN UNCLE ELMER and Aunt Mabelle, walking very carefully on account of Aunt Mabelle's "condition," had gone down the path into the flying snow, Emma said, "We'll all go to bed now. You're to have the spare-room, Philip, Naomi will sleep with me."

"No, I can't sleep yet. I'm going to sit up a while."

"Then put out the gas when you come to bed. It gets low toward morning and sometimes goes out by itself."

Naomi went off without a word, still enveloped in the aura of silent and insinuating injury, and Philip flung himself down on the floor before the gas-log, as he had always done as a boy, lying on his stomach, with the friendly smell of dust and carpet in his nostrils, while he pored over a book. Only to-night he didn't read: he simply lay on his back staring at the ceiling or at the enlarged photograph of his father, wondering what sort of man he had been and whether, if he were alive now, he would have helped his son or ranged himself with the others. There was a look in the eye which must have baffled a man like Uncle Elmer.

Upstairs, directly overhead, Naomi and Emma prepared for bed in silence. Only once did either of them speak. It happened when Emma burst out with admiration as Naomi let down the heavy mass of dull reddish hair. They both undressed prudishly, slipping on their outing-flannel nightgowns before removing their underwear, and hastily, because the room was filled with damp chill air. Emma lent her daughter-in-law one of her nightgowns, for Naomi had no use for outing-flannel in East Africa, and possessed only a sort of shapeless trousseau of patterned calico. The borrowed garment gave her the air of a woman drowning in an ocean of cotton-flannel.

After the gas was extinguished, they both knelt down and prayed earnestly,

and toward the same end—that the Lord might open Philip's eyes once more
and lead him back to his duty.

The moment the blankets were drawn about their chins, they began to
talk of it, at first warily, feeling their way toward each other until it became
certain that they both wanted the same thing, passionately and without division of purpose. Naomi told her mother-in-law the whole story—how she
had worked over him, how she had even made the inarticulate Swanson summon courage to speak, how she had prayed both privately and in public, as
it were, before Philip's eyes. And nothing had been of any use. She thought
perhaps the wound had injured his brain in some way, for certainly he was
not the same Philip she had married; but once when she had suggested such
a thing to him, he had only attacked her savagely, saying, "I'm just as sane
as you are—wanting to go back to those dirty niggers."

"Dirty niggers," Naomi said, was an expression that he had undoubtedly
picked up from the Englishwoman. She always spoke of the natives thus, or
even in terms of profanity. She smoked cigars. She used a whip on her bearers. In fact, Naomi believed that perhaps she was the Devil himself come
to ruin Philip and in the end to drag him off to Hell.

"I would have gone back without Philip," she said, "but I couldn't go alone
with Swanson, and I felt that the Lord meant me to cleave to Philip and
reclaim him. That would be a greater victory than the other."

Emma patted her daughter-in-law's thin hand. "That's right, my dear. He'll
go back in the end, and a wife ought to cleave to her husband." But there
was in the gesture something of hostility, as there had been in her touching
Philip a little while before. It was as if she said, "All the same, while he's
here, he belongs to me."

And then Emma, listening, said, "Sh! There he comes now up the stairs."

They both fell silent, as if conscious that he must not know they lay
there in the darkness plotting (not plotting, that was a word which held
evil implications) but planning his future, arranging what would be best
for him body and soul—a thing, they knew, which he could not decide in
his present distracted state of mind. They both fell silent, listening, listening, listening to the approaching tread of his feet as they climbed the creaking stairs, now at the turn, now in the upper hall, now passing their door.
He had passed it now and they heard him turning the white china knob
of the door into the dismal spare-room.

He would think they were both asleep long ago.

They talked for a while longer, until Naomi, worn by the wretched journey in a day-coach and lulled by the warmth with which the great vigorous
body of Emma invested the walnut bed, fell asleep, her mouth a little open,
for there had never been a surgeon anywhere near her father's mission to
remove her adenoids. But she did not sleep until Emma had learned beyond
all doubt that in this matter Naomi was completely on her side; and that
there was no possibility of children to complicate matters. Naomi was still
a virgin, and somehow, in some way, that was a condition which might be

made use of in the battle. She was not certain of the manner, but she felt the value of Naomi's virginity as a pawn.

Nor did she fall asleep at once. She suffered from a vague, undefined sense of alarm, which she had not known in more than twenty years of life wherein men played no rôle. She had not suffered thus since the disappearance of her husband. He seemed to have returned to her now with the return of her son. Philip, she saw, was a child no longer, but a man, with a little gray already in his black hair, terrifyingly like his father in appearance.

It was more, too, than appearance, for he had upon her the same effect that his father had had before him—of making her feel a strange desire to humor, to coddle him, to go down on her knees and do his bidding. He was that sort of man. Even Naomi seemed at moments to succumb to the queer, unconscious power. Lying there in the darkness Emma determined resolutely to resist this disarming glamour, for she had lost his father by not resisting it. She must make the resistance for her own and for Philip's good, though it would have been a warmer and more pleasant, even a voluptuous feeling to have yielded to him at once.

One thing, she saw, was clear—that Philip did not mean to run away as his father had done. He had returned to fight it out, with his dark jaw set stubbornly, because there was in him something of herself, which his father had lacked, something which, though she could not define it, filled her with uneasiness. She, the invincible Emma, was a little frightened by her own son.

And it touched her that he seemed so old, more, at times, like a man of forty than a boy of twenty-six: his face was lined, and his mouth touched by bitterness. He was no longer her little boy, so soft and good-looking, with that odd, blurred haze of faith in his blue eyes. He had a face now and the fact disturbed her, she could not tell why. He had been a little boy, and then, all at once, a man, with nothing in between.

At last—even after Philip, lying tormented in the spare bedroom, had fallen asleep, she dropped into an uneasy slumber, filled with vague alarms and excursions in which she seemed to have, from time to time, odd disturbing glimpses of a Philip she had never known, who seemed to be neither boy nor man, but something in between, remarkably like his worthless scamp of a father, who lived always to the full.

Chapter 4

THE TOWN stood built like Rome upon Seven Hills, which were great monuments of earth and stone left by the last great glacier, and on these seven hills and in the valleys which surrounded them a whole city, created within the space of less than a century, had raised houses and shops, monstrous furnaces spouting flame and smoke and cavernous sheds black and vast as the haunts of legendary monsters, where all day and night iron and steel drawn from the hot bellies of the furnaces was beaten into rails and girders, so that other towns like it might spring into existence almost overnight. The Mills and furnaces could not, it seemed, work fast enough, so there were always new ones building, spreading out and out, along the borders of the railroad which touched the Atlantic Ocean on one side and the Pacific on the other.

It was not a pretty town. The sun rarely rose unobscured by clouds of hanging black smoke: the air was never still day or night from the vibrations of that gigantic beating and pounding. There was no house nor building unstained by long streaks made by the soot which fell like black manna from the skies. But it was a rich town, fabulously rich and busy as an ant-hill overturned carelessly by the foot of man. People were always crawling in and out of the Mills, up the long hill to the Main Street that was bordered by hundreds of little shops which sold cheap clothing and furniture, swarming over the bright steel threads of the railroads and through the streets in the dark region known as the Flats, which was given over to the slave ants brought in from foreign countries to work day and night without light or air. On the hills, at a little distance, dwelt those who in a way subsisted upon the work of the slave ants—all the little merchants, the lawyers, the bankers who were rich because the world about them was rich, because the little world was a hive of activity where men and women were born, and toiled, and lived and died endlessly. For them it was not a struggle to exist. It was scarcely possible not to succeed.

It had made even Emma Downes rich in a small way. The money seemed forever pouring out, rolling off: one had only to find a clear spot and stand there waiting to catch what rolled towards it.

On the seven hills the ants had their social life, divided into caste upon caste. In the Flats the slave ants had no existence at all. They seldom climbed the hills. One never saw them. But on the hills there were ants of all sorts, and odd reasons determined why they were what they were: sometimes it was money, sometimes ambition, sometimes clothes, sometimes the part of the ant-hill which they occupied, sometimes the temple in which they worshipped. They fussed over these things and scurried about a great deal in their agitation.

At the bottom of the heap were the slave ants who had no existence and at the top was an old woman who occupied a whole hill to herself and was content to live there surrounded on all sides by the black, dark mills and the workers. She was a sort of queen ant, for she was a disagreeable, scornful old woman, and she made no effort. She was immensely rich and lived somberly in a grand manner unknown elsewhere in the Town; but it was, too, more than this. She was scornful and she inspired awe. Her name was Julia Shane. She had been born a queen ant.

Emma Downes did not know her. It is true that she had seen the old woman often enough in a mulberry victoria drawn by high-stepping black horses, as she passed the Peerless Restaurant; she had seen her sitting very straight and grim, dressed in mauve and black, or wrapped comfortably in sables. Sometimes her daughters rode with her—the one who was religious and worked among the people of the Flats, and the one who lived in Paris and was said to be fast.

There were reasons, of course, why they did not know each other—antlike reasons. Emma lived in the wrong part of the Town. She was the sister of Elmer Niman, who was a pious man with a reputation for being a sharp dealer. Emma and Elmer cared nothing for the things on which the old woman spent insanely great sums of money, such things as pictures and carpets and chairs. To Emma, a chair was a chair; the fancier it was, the prettier and more tasteful it must be. And Emma went to a church that was attended by none of the fashionable ants, and the old woman went to no church at all. Emma was President of the Woman's Christian Temperance Union, which the old lady considered not only as great nonsense, but as an impertinent effort to fly in the face of Nature. Emma had a missionary son, and to Julia Shane missionaries were usually self-righteous meddlers. (The old lady had never even heard of Naomi Potts, "the youngest missionary of the Lord in darkest Africa.") There was reason upon reason why they never met. Emma thought her a wicked old thing, who ought to be reformed, and Julia Shane didn't know that Emma existed.

It was immensely complicated—that antlike world.

For Philip it was no more complicated now than it had been in his childhood, when he had gone his own shy, solitary way. He had been lonely as a child, with the loneliness which all children know at moments when they are bruised and hurt: only with him it seemed always to have been so. It may have been the domination, even the very presence, of a woman so insensitive and crushing as Emma Downes that bruised and hurt him ceaselessly and without consciousness of relief. It was worse, too, when she was your mother and you adored her.

He had been happiest in moments when, escaping from his mother and the slate-colored house, he had gone off to wander through the fields beyond the Town or along the railway tracks among the locomotives. It was the great engines which he liked best, monsters that breathed fire and smoke, or sat still and silent in the cavernous roundhouse, waiting patiently to have bolts tightened, or leaks soldered, so that they might go on with their work. They did not frighten him as they might have frightened some children: they seemed ferocious but friendly, like great ungainly dogs. They terrified him less than Uncle Elmer or the preacher, Mr. Temple. (Mr. Temple was gone now and another younger, more flowery man named Castor had taken his place.)

By some miracle he had been able to keep his secret from his mother and continued, even when he was grown, to wander about for hours among the clanging wheels and screaming whistles during his holidays from the theological seminary. Some childish cunning had made him understand that she must never know of these strange expeditions, lest she forbid them. She was always so terrified lest something happen to him.

In all his childhood he could remember having had only two friends—one of them, McTavish, the undertaker, was kept as much a secret as the friendly locomotives had been; for Philip, even as a child, understood that there was something about the fat, jovial man which Emma detested with a wild, unreasonable fury.

The other was the black-haired, blue-eyed, tomboyish Mary Watts, who lived a dozen blocks away in a more fashionable part of Town where each house had its big stables and its negro coachmen and stable boys. She was older than he by nearly two years, and much stronger: she detested girls as poor weak things who liked starched skirts and dickies of white duck that were instruments of torture to any one who liked climbing and snowball fights. So she had recruited Philip to play on the tin roof of the carriage shed and build the house high up in the branches of the crabapple tree. He always felt sorry for her because she had no mother, but he saw, too, with a childish clarity, that it was an advantage to be able to do exactly as you pleased, and build the tree-house as high in the air as you liked, far up among the shiny little red apples where it made you thrillingly sick to look over the edge.

But this friendship was throttled suddenly on the day (it was Philip's twelfth birthday) they went to play in the hay-loft. They had been digging in the fragrant hay and building tunnels, and feeling suddenly tired and hot, they lay down side by side, near the open door. In the heat, Philip, feeling drowsy, closed his eyes and listened to the whirring of the pigeons that haunted the old stable, happy, contented and pleased in a warm, vague way to be lying there beside his friend Mary, when suddenly he heard his mother's hearty voice, and, opening his eyes, saw her standing at the top of the stairs. He could see that she was angry. She said, "Philip, come home at once—and you, Mary, go right in to your aunt. You ought to be ashamed of yourself!"

She swept him off without another word and at home she shut him in the storeroom, where she talked to him for an hour. She told him he had done a shameful thing, that boys who behaved like that got a disease and turned black. She said that he was never to go again to Mary Watts' house or even to speak to her. She told him that because he had no father she must be both father and mother to him, and that she must be able to trust him in the hours when she was forced to be at the bakery earning money to feed and clothe them both.

When she had finished, Philip was trembling, though he did not cry, because men didn't behave like babies. He told her he was sorry and promised never to speak to Mary Watts again.

And then she locked him in for an hour to ponder what she had said. He didn't know what it was he had done: he only felt shameful and dirty in a way he had never felt before, and terrified by a fear of turning black like those nigger boys who lived in the filthy houses along the creek by the Mills.

When Emma came back to release him from the storeroom prison, she forgave him and, taking him in her arms, kissed and fondled him for a long time, saying, "And when you're a big boy and grown up, your mother will always be your girl, won't she?"

She seemed so pleasant and so happy, it was almost worth the blind pain to be able to repent and make promises. But he never had the fun of playing again with Mary Watts. He went back to his beloved engines. Sometimes he played ball, and he played well when he chose, for he was a smallish, muscular boy, all nerves, who was good at games; but they never interested him. It was as if he wanted always to be alone. He had had friends, but the friendships had ended quickly, as if he had come to the bottom of them too soon. As a little boy there was always an odd, quizzical, affectionate look in his eye, and there were times when, dreaming, he would wander away into mazes of thought with a perpetual air of searching for something. He, himself, never knew what it was.

And then at seventeen, taciturn, lonely and confused, he had stumbled upon God. The rest was easy for Emma, especially when Naomi came unexpectedly into their lives. Sometimes, in bitter moments, she had thought of Philip as a symbol of vengeance upon his errant father: she had kept him pure and uncontaminated by the world. She had made of him a model for all the world to observe.

Chapter 5

WHEN, on the morning after his return, Philip went out of the door of the slate-colored house, and down the walk through the drifted snow, he knew suddenly that he was more lonely, more aimless than he had ever been. The blizzard was over, and the sky lay cold and gray above the curtain of everlasting smoke. At the gate he hesitated for a moment, wondering which way he would turn; and then abruptly he knew that it made no difference; there was no one that he wanted to see, no one with whom he could talk. He knew that in the house behind him there were two women who thought it shameful for him to be seen at all in the streets. They had even hoped, no doubt, that he would not show himself so soon. Even people who knew the story Emma had told of illness and wounds and a holiday, would think that he ought to have stuck at his post and fought it out there.

People, he knew—at least the people of their sort who were church-goers —were like that: they were willing to pile glory upon visiting missionaries, but they gave money grudgingly and expected missionaries to stick to their tasks. The money they gave warmed their hearts with a wicked Roman Catholic sense of comforts bought in Heaven. They would think he ought not to have returned until he had earned a proper holiday. For himself he did not care, especially since he knew he was far more wicked than they imagined, but with his mother and Naomi it was different. At the sight of Naomi, sitting pale and miserable across the table from him at breakfast, he had been stricken suddenly with one of those odd twinges of pity which sometimes delivered him into her hands, bound and helpless. When he thought of it now—how near he had been to yielding—he was frightened. Such odd, small things could turn a whole life upon a new path.

He closed the gate and turned towards the left, without thinking why he had chosen that direction until he found himself turning down the long hill to the Flats. He was going towards his beloved locomotives exactly as he had done a dozen years earlier when he could think of no one he wanted to see in all the Town; and suddenly he was almost happy, as if he were a boy of twelve once more, and not a man of twenty-six who had lost more than ten precious years of life.

It struck him, as he waded through heaps of snow already blackened by soot, that the Town had changed: it was not, in some subtle way, the same place. Where once it had seemed a dull, ugly Town, friendly because it was so familiar, it now seemed rather exciting and lively, and even thrilling. It was so alive, so busy, so filled with energy. As he descended the hill the impression grew in intensity. The pounding of the Mills, the leaping red flames above the furnace chimneys, the rumbling, half-muffled clamor of the great locomotives—all these things gave him a sudden, tremendous feeling of life. He saw for the first time, though he had passed them a thousand times in his life, those long rows of black houses where the mill-workers lived huddled together in squalor. He saw one or two sickly geraniums behind the glass, a crimson featherbed hung from a window, a line of bright clothes all dancing frozen and stiff as dead men in the cold wind.

For a moment he halted on the bridge that crossed Toby's Run and, standing there, he watched the great cranes at work lifting, with a weird animal intelligence, their tons of metal, picking up a burden in one place and setting it down in another. The air smelled of hot metal and the pungent tang of coal-smoke. Beneath him the stream, no longer water, but a flowing mass of oil and acids and corrosion, moved smoothly along: in a stream so polluted even ice could not freeze along the banks. Beyond the mills and piled low on the top of its patrician hill the mass of Shane's Castle showed itself against the leaden sky. It had been red brick once, but long ago it had turned black. There were only dead trees in the park surrounding it.

It all stood out sharp and clear—the houses, the river, the furnaces, the great engines, the lonely, quiet homes on the hills; and suddenly he knew what it was that made the difference. The Town seemed a new, strange place because of that queer thing which had happened to him at Megambo. The scales had fallen from his eyes. He remembered how suddenly he had seen the lake, the forest, the birds, in a new way, as if outlined by light; and that odd, sensual feeling of strength, of vigor, of life, overwhelmed him again, as it had done while he stood naked in the moonlight listening to the ominous drums. For a moment he fancied that he heard them once more, but it was only the pounding of the Mills. It was new to him after having been away for so long; the sound hadn't yet come to be a part of the silence which one did not hear because it was always there.

As he turned away he caught a glimpse of a pale, tall figure all in gray turning a corner down one of the sodden streets of the mill-workers. After a moment he recognized it slowly: it was Irene Shane, the daughter of Old Julia—the daughter who had given all her life and her money to work among the poor of the Flats. He remembered her then—she was the one who had started a club-house and a school where the foreigners, the Hunkies and Dagoes, might learn to speak English and their wives might learn to save the babies who died like flies. She carried it on herself, with only the aid of a Russian mill-hand, because people in the Town wouldn't give money. He remembered his mother's having mentioned it in a letter. "The Church was against it," she wrote, "because it took time and money away from foreign missions."

He looked after the thin figure until it disappeared into one of the houses, and then turned away. As he walked he found himself thinking of Mary Watts. His mother had written that Mary Watts had something to do with the club-house, until she married the new superintendent of the mills. He must ask his mother what had become of Mary Watts. Of course, she was Mary Conyngham now. . . . It was odd, but she was the only person in the Town that he wanted to see. At last he had thought of some one.

On his way up the hill once more, he passed, near the establishment of McTavish, the undertaker, the tall, powerful, middle-aged figure of the Reverend Castor bound upon some errand. He was a rather handsome man, a little pompous but with a kind face, who was quite bald and wore the hair which the Lord had spared him very long and wound about his head, in a way calculated to conceal his baldness. People said he was a good man, and a fiery preacher with a wife who had been a complaining invalid for fifteen years and rarely left her bed. Philip scarcely knew him, though it was he who had married himself and Naomi and blessed them when they left for Africa. The clergyman did not see him now and Philip slipped by unnoticed.

From behind the glass of the Funeral Parlor, he knew that McTavish and his cronies had seen him. They sat in there hugging the stove, a group of middle-aged and elderly men who played checkers or rummy and gossiped all day. It was a great place for news, since most deaths were reported at once to the fat, good-natured McTavish. Every one was buried by McTavish; he was the one who laid the hill-ants to rest deep in the gravel of the seventh of these glacial hills. McTavish never went to church and the big iron stove was known, even on Sunday, as the nucleus of a band of shocking atheists and mockers. McTavish seemed to understand at once whether the one he had come to bury was loved or whether it was simply a relative from whom you were likely to inherit. He was a bachelor who had no life save that which centered about the iron stove; yet he knew the Town in a way that no one else knew it because he was always near to the root of all things.

Philip knew that the group about the stove were saying, "There goes Emma Downes' boy who went to Africa for a missionary. He was always a queer one—not a bit like Emma."

And then they would launch into talk about the old story of Jason Downes and his fantastic disappearance into the depths of China, where he had escaped in the end the last ministrations of McTavish. They knew everything, those old men. Each one was a walking history of the Town.

Philip, half a block off now, began to feel that sense of life which somehow sustained them. He began to feel people, ambitions, jealousies, loves and hatreds, stirring all about him in a strange, complicated maze.

Naomi was waiting for him, dressed to go out. She had put on a thick blue veil because, Philip suspected, she did not want to be recognized.

"Your Ma wants us to eat at the restaurant," she said, and together they set out in silence.

Miraculously they met no one on the way, and once inside the big, white, clean restaurant, Emma led them to the table where, shielded by a screen from draughts, she always ate. The restaurant began to fill with customers —clerks, lawyers, mill-employees, shopkeepers, farmers and their wives in from the country for the day—all lured by the excellent food supplied by Emma. After a time the tables were all filled and people stood waiting their turn. It was marvelous, the success of Emma. Dishes clattered, orders were shouted, the cash-register clanked and banged unceasingly. She was proud of the place and happy there: it was clear that she could not imagine living away from such a hubbub and din.

While they were eating the stewed dried corn which she gave her customers in place of the usual insipid canned variety, she asked, "What did you do this morning, Philip?"

"I went for a walk."

"Where?"

"In the Flats."

"You might have chosen a handsomer part of the Town. You might have gone out to see the new Park."

He didn't tell her about the locomotives. Once he had kept it a secret because she would have forbidden him to return to them. Now, he kept his secret for some other reason: he did not know quite what it was. He only knew that Emma and Naomi must not know of it. It would only make them believe that he was completely crazy.

Presently, when they had reached the squash pie, he asked, "What's become of Mary Watts?" And at the same moment he felt himself blushing horribly, for in some way the memory of the imprisonment in the storeroom returned to claim him unawares, and make him feel a shameful little boy unable to look his mother in the eye. Only he understood now: he knew what lay beneath the ancient, veiled accusations. . . .

"Oh, she's had a sad time," said Emma. "You know she married the superintendent of the Mills—John Conyngham—a man fifteen years older than she was, and every one thought it was a good match. But he died—three weeks ago—while you were on the ocean, leaving her with two small children. They've some money, but not very much. The Watts house was sold when old Watts died—to pay his debts. She's living with Conyngham's sister, who's quite well off. They're in the old Stuart house in Park Avenue. Old Stuart lost all his money hanging on to too much land, so they bought the house off him. I guess Conyngham wasn't a very good husband—I used to see his bicycle sitting in front of Mamie Rhodes' house. There couldn't have been much good in that—men like Mamie Rhodes too well."

She knew it all, the story in all its details, even to Mamie Rhodes, at whose name women in the Town were wont to bristle. No one *knew* anything about Mamie: it was just that she was much too young for her years, and did something to men—nobody knew just what it was—that made her very popular.

"And what was he like?" asked Philip.

"Conyngham," said Emma, "John Conyngham? He was handsome, but I never liked his looks. I'd never trust a man that looked like that."

What she meant was that there was something about John Conyngham that reminded her of the derelict Mr. Downes, and that the sight of him had always disturbed her in a terrifying way. She couldn't bear to look at him.

"He died of pneumonia," she said above the clatter of the dishes and the prosperous banging of the cash-register. "They say he caught it coming home in the rain from Mamie Rhodes' on Thanksgiving night."

Philip listened and the dull red still burned under the dark skin. He was aware that the two women were watching him, secretly, as they might watch a man who was a little unbalanced: they had been doing so without cessation since his return. They were a little like two purring cats watching prey all innocent of their intentions.

Chapter 6

IT WAS impossible, of course, for the three of them to continue playing the game of hide-and-seek, pretending that Philip and Naomi had not returned or that Philip was too ill to go out; it was impossible for Naomi to go about forever disguised by a thick veil. Even Emma's eternal policy of allowing things to work themselves out appeared after a month to be productive of no result, for Philip's "mental condition" showed no signs of improvement.

He remained, rocklike, in his determination, while the two women watched, stricken with uneasy fears because the Philip whom they had once known so well that they could anticipate and control his every impulse, now seemed a creature filled with vague and mysterious moods and ideas that lay quite beyond the borders of their understanding.

Their watching became at times unbearable to him, for it gave him the suffocating sense of being a maniac who was not to be trusted alone. He took to spending more and more time away from the house, either walking the country roads or wandering through the black Flats where he was safe from encountering any one or anything, save the gray figure of Irene Shane, going her tireless rounds. Once he had a glimpse of the old lady herself— Irene's mother—riding by wrapped in sables on the last ride she was ever to take.

A sense of waiting, more definite, more intense, than the tension of the long day at Megambo, settled over the slate-colored house. It was broken on the fourth Sunday after Philip's return when the three of them lunched, as usual on boiled mutton, at Uncle Elmer's. It was a gloomy lunch, tainted by the sense of Philip's sin. The gloom enveloped all of them, save Aunt Mabelle and her ten-year-old daughter, Ethel, who showed already signs of resembling her mother in feebleness of character and inertia of mind. The room was, through a lack of windows, dark, and under the fog of smoke that enveloped the Town it became even more cavernous and dreary; but Elmer Niman never permitted his wife to waste gas in illumination. One groped for food in the dark, while Elmer talked of the low pressure occasioned by the sad waste of gas in the Town.

The break came only after considerable preparation on the part of Emma. She said, quite casually, "I saw Reverend Castor yesterday. He came into the restaurant to see me."

"He's not looking as well," put in Aunt Mabelle. "It must be a strain to have an invalid wife. It's not natural for a man to live like that."

Elmer interrupted her, feeling perhaps that she was bound toward one of those physiological observations which she sometimes uttered blandly and to the consternation of all her world.

"He is a good man. We are fortunate in having him."

"God will reward him for his patience," observed Emma.

"I talked to him day before yesterday," said Naomi. "I think I may go to sing in the choir while we are on our holiday."

Vaguely Philip began to sense the existence of a plot, conceived and carried out with the express purpose of forcing him to do something he had no desire to do. It seemed to him that they had rehearsed the affair.

"There is an empty place on the alto side," observed Emma. "They could use a good strong voice like yours."

"Of course," said Naomi, "it's so long since I've sung—not since I used to lead the singing at the revival meetings."

"And Philip—he used to sing."

"He never does now. He wouldn't help me teach the natives at Megambo."

Philip, listening, fancied that he caught a sympathetic glance from Aunt Mabelle. She was silly and stupid, but sometimes it seemed to him that she had flashes of uncanny intuition: she had, after all, had great experience with the tactics of Elmer and his sister. She sat opposite Philip, eating far too much, lost in cowlike tranquillity. She was still bearing patiently the burden which by some error in calculation had been expected hourly for more than a month. Only yesterday she had said, "I expect little Jimmy will have all his teeth and be two years old when he is born!"—a remark that was followed by an awkward silence. Married to another man she would undoubtedly have had ten or fifteen children, for she was born to such a rôle.

"That's how I met Elmer," she said brightly, "singing in the choir. I used to sing alto, and he sang bass. He sat right behind me and his foot. . . ."

"Mabelle!" said Elmer.

She veered aside from the history of a courtship which always engaged her with a passionate interest. "Well, I've always noticed that lots of things begin in church choirs. There was that Bunsen woman who ran off with. . . ."

Emma trod upon her, once more throttling her flow of reminiscences. "That's right, Naomi," she said, "it'll help pass the time while you're waiting." And then, polishing her spoon with her napkin (an action which she always performed ostentatiously as an implication upon the character of Mabelle's housekeeping) she said, "By the way, he's planned a Sunday night service which is to be given over entirely to you and Naomi—Philip. Think of that. It's quite an honor." (She would sit well down in front that night where she could breathe in all the glory.) "I told him, of course, that you'd be delighted to do it."

"Yes," said Naomi, "he spoke to me about it. We'll tell our experiences." The prospect of so much glory kindled a light in the pale eyes—the light of memories of revival meetings when she had been the great moving force.

Then Philip spoke for the first time. "I won't do it—I'm through with all that."

There was a horrible silence, broken only by the clatter of a fork dropped by little Ethel on her plate.

"What do you mean?"

"I told you all that before. I thought you must have understood by now. I can't go on saying it forever."

"But, Philip . . . you can't refuse a good man like the Reverend Castor. You can't when he's been so kind. He always prayed for you and Naomi every Sunday, publicly, as if you were our special missionaries."

There was only silence from Philip. The dark jaw had hardened suddenly.

"When we were all looking forward to it so much," added Emma.

Then suddenly there came to him a faint suspicion—shadowy and somewhat shameful—of what it was all about. They were looking forward to an orgy of public notice and glory, to sitting bathed in the reflected light while he talked about Africa to a congregation of faithful admirers. He even suspected that this was the reason they were so determined to ship him back to Africa. They would find glory in his sufferings. He was angry suddenly, even hostile.

"You can tell him I won't do it."

"But, Philip, you must tell him yourself."

"I don't want to see him."

Here Uncle Elmer took a hand, using the familiar tactics. "Of course, I can understand that—Philip's not wanting to see him." He grimaced suddenly at Emma to let him manage it. "I'll speak to Reverend Castor myself. I'll explain about Philip's condition."

For a second Philip grew hot with anger; he even pushed back his chair from the table as if to rise and leave. It was, oddly enough, Aunt Mabelle who restrained him. He fancied he caught a sudden twinkle in her round eyes, and the anger subsided.

Another painful silence followed, in which Rose, the negro maid-of-all-work, placed the Floating Island violently before Aunt Mabelle to be served. The room grew darker and darker, and presently Uncle Elmer said, "I suppose, Philip, if you intend to stay here you'll be looking for some sort of work. It will mean, of course, starting life all over again."

"Yes."

"Of course you could teach—a young man with a good education like yours. It cost your mother a lot of work and trouble to educate you."

"Yes."

"But if you can't get such work right away, I could make a place in the factory for you. Of course," and here Uncle Elmer smiled his most condescending smile, "of course, with your kind of training you wouldn't be much good at first. You'd have to learn the business from the ground up. You could begin in the shipping department."

It was the first time any of them had admitted even a chance of his not returning to Africa; but they did not mean to yield, for Emma said, "That perhaps would help him over this nervous trouble."

And then Philip shattered everything with an unexpected announcement. It was as if a bomb had exploded in the dust and shadows beneath the table.

"I've already got a job," said Philip. "I'm going to work to-night at midnight."

"To-night—at midnight?" asked Emma. "What on earth do you mean?"

"I'm going to work in the Mills. I've got a job."

"The Mills! You're crazy. What do you mean—the Mills?"

"I mean the Mills," said Philip, looking at his plate. "It's all been settled."

Suddenly Naomi began to cry, at first silently, and then more and more noisily, as if all the dammed emotions of months had given way. Emma rose to comfort her, and Aunt Mabelle, murmuring, "Oh, dear! Oh, dear!" helplessly pushed the water-pitcher across the table. Little Ethel, conscious of the strain of the whole meal, and frightened by the outburst of hysterics, began to cry too, so that Aunt Mabelle became occupied in comforting her.

Philip, able to stand it no longer, rose and, flinging back his chair, said, "Damn!" in a loud voice, and walked out of the house. His swearing moved Naomi to new outbursts. She began to cry about the Englishwoman—the source of all her troubles.

It was all horrible, and it was the last time that Philip ever entered his uncle's house.

When he returned late that night he found them all waiting for him in the parlor, ready to attack once more, but they accomplished nothing. He went upstairs and changed his clothes. When he came down, he was dressed for the Mills in an old pair of trousers, an old coat and a flannel shirt. Aunt Mabelle, round and sloppy, was standing in the ghoulish light of the green lamp. The others were all seated in the parlor gloomily, as if brooding over the problem of a daughter gone astray.

From the shadows, Aunt Mabelle seized his arm, "Is it true? Is Naomi going to have a little baby?"

Philip looked at her with a sudden astonishment. "No," he said savagely. "Who gave you such an idea?"

Aunt Mabelle seemed to shrink into herself, all softness and apology. "I didn't know . . . I just couldn't understand a woman carrying on like that if she wasn't."

Chapter 7

IT WAS more than an hour before the midnight shift began at the Mills, and during that hour Philip walked, sometimes running, along the empty streets, through the falling snow, all unconscious of the cold. He was for a time like a madman living in an unreal world, where all values were confused, all emotions fantastic and without base: in his tired brain everything was confused—his love for his mother, his hatred for his uncle, his pity for Naomi, and his resentment at all three of them for the thing they were trying to do. He wanted to run away where he might never see any of them again, yet to run away seemed to him a cowardly thing which solved nothing. Besides, if he ran away, he would never see Mary Conyngham, and Mary had in some odd fashion become fixed in his mind, an unescapable part of the whole confusion. He *must* see Mary Conyngham, sometime, in some way.

He was afraid to stay, depressed by the feeling that whenever he returned to the house, he was certain to find them there—waiting, watching him. Why, a man could be driven to insanity by people like that who treated him always as if he were mad.

But worst of all, he had no longer any faith in God: there was nothing of that miraculous essence which seemed to take from one's shoulders all the burden of doubt and responsibility. He couldn't say any longer, "I will leave it to God. He will devise a way. Whatever happens, He will be right. I must accept His way." He knew, sharply, completely, for the first time, that a faith must be born in himself, that he had taken up his own life to mold in his own fashion: there was no longer that easy refuge in a God, Who would arrange everything. If he had trusted to God now he would have been on his way to Africa, disposed of, not by God, but by the hands of his mother and Naomi and Uncle Elmer.

He could be a coward and weak no longer.

After he had gone a long way he found himself on a height that seemed strange to him, in that part of the Town which lay just above the Flats. It was not strange, of course, for he had stood on the same spot a hundred times before. It was strange only because he was in an odd fashion a new person, born again, a different Philip from the one who had stood there as a boy.

The sight that lay spread out below him suddenly brought a kind of peace: he stopped running, and grew calm and, watching it, he succumbed slowly to its spell. By night, the hard, angular lines of that smoky world melted into a blue mystery, pierced and spotted here and there by lights—the great blue-white lights of the arc-lights in the Mill yards, the leaping scarlet flames that crowned the black furnaces, the yellow lights plumed with steam of the great locomotives moving backward and forward like shuttles weaving a vast carpet with the little signal-lights, red and yellow and mauve and green, set like jewels in a complicated design. In the darkness the grim blacks and grays took on color. Color and light lay reflected from the canopy of smoke and steam that hung above the whole spectacle. Piercing the glow of light, rose the black columns of the chimneys and furnaces.

Above it all rose the endless sound of pounding, like the distant booming of a gigantic surf, pierced now and again by the raucous, barbaric squeals of a locomotive.

Halted and given poise by the sight, he stood for a long time looking down into the very center of the roaring hive, forgetting himself suddenly and all his fantastic troubles; and slowly an odd thing happened to him. He felt strong: he wasn't any longer puzzled and afraid. It was as if there lay in the turbulent scene some intoxicating sense of power which took the place of his missing faith. The spectacle beneath him became alive with a tremendous sense of vitality and force that he had not found in all his mystical groping toward God. This thing that lay below him was real, he knew, real in a solid, earthly fashion, created by men in the face of hostile Nature, free of any weak dependence upon a Power which at best had only a doubtful existence. Yet the awful power of this world created by the feeble hand of man was in an odd fashion like the power of the lake, the forest, the sounds of life on the hill at Megambo.

Hazily there came to him the feeling that here lay his salvation, and presently he was overcome by an intense desire to plunge deep into the very midst of the whirling maelstrom of noise and heat and light and power.

Hurrying, he descended the hill, crossing the little river of oil and corruption, passing a great open space covered with cinders, beneath the white glare of lights hanging high above him, until he came at last to a high fence and a gate where he explained who he was and showed his card. He had an odd feeling that he should have said simply, "I have come here to save myself," as if the Italian gatekeeper would have known what he meant.

Inside this barrier the sound of pounding grew more and more violent. He went past one cavernous shed and another and another until he came to the one marked with a gigantic number in white paint—17. The yard, the shed, all the world about him was swarming with men—big, raw-boned men with high cheekbones, little, swarthy men, black men, men with flat, Kalmuck noses, some going towards the sheds, some moving away from them. Those who moved homeward were so black with sweat and soot that one could not tell which were negroes and which were white.

Stepping through a doorway, he found himself in a vast cavern echoing with sound, that reached up and up until its height became lost in smoke and shadows. High up, near the top, great cranes with white lights like piercing eyes, and tiny, black figures like ants climbing over them, moved ceaselessly back and forth, picking up tons of metal and putting it down again with a tremendous clatter. Here and there along the sides stood furnaces out of which men were drawing from time to time great piles of metal all rosy-white with heat. Flames leaped out of the ovens, licking the sides and casting fantastic shadows over the powerful, half-naked figures of the workers. The gigantic sound of hammering reverberated through the black cavern.

After a moment Philip addressed a thin, swarthy man with burning eyes. "Where is Krylenko?" he asked. But the man understood no English. "Krylenko," he repeated, shouting, above the din, "Krylenko."

The thin man grinned. "Oh, Krylenko," and, pointing, indicated the figure of a powerful, blond man, who stood leaning on a crowbar before an oven a little way off. He was, like the others, naked to the waist, and his white skin was already streaked with soot and sweat. When he turned, Philip saw that he was young, younger even than himself, and that his eyes were blue beneath a great mop of hair so yellow that it had the appearance of having been bleached. The eyes were intelligent.

In English with only a shadow of an accent he told Philip to strip off his coat and shirt and take up a crowbar. In a moment he was standing there with the others, indistinguishable among so many workers. He was half-naked, as he had been beside the fire at Megambo, and the same voluptuous sense of power swept through him. It was oddly terrifying, this cavern filled with flame and smoke and sweating men. It was oddly like the jungle.

Chapter 8

BEHIND HIM in the slate-colored house Aunt Mabelle waited, yawning and wishing for bed, while Elmer and Emma and Naomi sat in silence, pondering whether their battle had been completely lost. They sat in silence, and Naomi sometimes dried her red-rimmed eyes and sobbed, because there was nothing to say, nothing to do. It was all so much worse than they had expected. With Philip living, as one might have said, in hiding, life could still be endured, and one could go on pretending, pretending, pretending, that he was merely ill, and one day would go back to Megambo to the glory and justification of them all. No one of them really believed any longer in the pretense of Philip's illness. Tacitly they would pretend to believe it because it was a good weapon: they would not even admit their doubts to each other. But from the moment he sprang up from Uncle Elmer's table they knew that he was quite in his right mind, and knew exactly what he meant to do. He was in his right mind, but he was a strange, unmanageable Philip.

And now he had disgraced them in a new and shameful way by going to work, not in an office over columns of figures, or even into a polite business such as Uncle Elmer's pump works, but by plunging straight into the Flats, into the Mills to work with the Hunkies and Dagoes. It was a thing no American had ever done. It was almost as if he had committed theft or murder.

After they had sat thus for more than an hour, always beneath the larky gaze of the "late" Mr. Downes, Uncle Elmer rose at last and making himself very thin and stiff as a poker, he said, "Well, Em, I've decided one thing. If Philip doesn't come to his senses within two weeks, I'm through with him forever. You can tell him that—tell him I give him just two weeks, not an hour more—and then I'm through with him. After that I never want to see him again, or hear his name spoken. And when he gets into trouble from his wicked ways, tell him not to come to me for help."

He expected a response of some sort from his sister, but there was only silence, while she sat grimly regarding the carpet. It seemed that he felt a sudden need for an answer, even though he must strike at her unchivalrously upon a wound which he must have believed cured long ago.

"You see," he said, "all this comes of making a marriage long ago that I was against. I knew what I was talking about when I warned you against Jason Downes."

For a moment she did not answer him, but when she spoke it was to upset him, horribly, by one of those caprices to which women are prey. It may have been because of the strain of the day, but it was more probable that there still was left the embers of her old, inexplicable passion for the worthless Mr. Downes, embers fanned into flame by the return of Philip.

She said, "Very well, Elmer. I'll tell him, but you can consider everything over between you and me, too. I don't want to see you again. If you can't speak to Philip, you needn't speak to me either. I should never have told you. You haven't done anything at all but make things worse."

For a time he only stared at her out of round eyes that were like blue marbles. "Well!" he said, coughing. "Well! I've done my duty. Don't say that I haven't."

"A lot of good it's done," said Emma with bitterness, "a lot of good. . . ."

She seemed, the indomitable Emma, very near to tears. In her corner Naomi snuffled so that they would take some notice of her.

He had meant to make his exit with a cold dignity, and a sense of injury, but Aunt Mabelle stood across his path. Unable any longer to keep up the battle against sleep, she was dozing peacefully in her rocking-chair, unconscious even of the scene that had taken place. She had to be prodded and spoken to sharply, and at last she wakened slowly to profuse apologies, and a walk home with a husband who never addressed her.

Her child was born the following day. Early in the evening before Elmer came home from the factory, she came to see Naomi, to discover what had happened on the night before, during her nap. (She had a way of "running in" on Naomi. They liked each other.) While she was talking the pain began, and Naomi went at once to fetch a cab. It arrived quickly, and Mabelle bustled into it, was driven home at top speed. But haste was of no use; she was carried upstairs by the cab driver and the butcher's boy, and before the doctor arrived the child was born. Naomi had never seen anything like it: the whole business took less time than with the native women at Megambo.

"I'm like that," Mabelle told her; "it only takes a minute."

The child was small and rather puny, to have been born of such an amiable mountain as Mabelle. It was a boy, and they called him James after his grandfather.

Emma called on her sister-in-law and sent broths and jellies from the restaurant, but she did not speak to her brother.

She told the news to Philip when he wakened to go to work, and he looked at the floor for a long time before he said, in a low voice, "Yes—that's fine. He wanted a boy, didn't he?"

Something in his eye as he turned away made Emma lay a hand on his arm.

"Philip," she said in a low voice, "if you're *really* never going back to Africa, I mean *really* not going back—you might have a child of your own."

"Yes," he answered, "I might."

That was all he said, but Emma in all her bluntness had divined the thought that came to him so quickly. He wanted a child with all the hunger of a deeply emotional nature; what she did not divine was that he did not want a child with Naomi for the mother. He couldn't bear to think of it, and he went to work that night sick at heart, plunging into the work like a man leaping from an unbearable heat into a deep pool of cool water. In that fiercely masculine world, he found pleasure in the soreness of his muscles, in the very knowledge that he would, when the day was finished, fall into a deep slumber, wearied to death, to find a world in which would be no troubles.

Chapter 9

NAOMI, too, had suffered in her own complaining fashion. After a life passed in a fierce activity, the empty days began to hang upon her spirits like leaden weights. As far back as she could remember her life had been a part, as the daughter and then the wife of a missionary, of a struggle against heat and disease and ignorance, her soul always warmed by the knowledge that she was doing God's work, that the pain and discomforts of the body were as nothing in comparison to the ecstasies of the soul. Save for a few weeks, she had never known life in the civilized world, and now in the midst of it there seemed to be no place for her. She tried dusting and cleaning the slate-colored house (there was no cooking to do, for they ate always at the restaurant), but there was no satisfaction in it. She came in a few days to hate it. She tried making garments to be shipped to the missions, long nightgowns with which to clothe the nakedness of savages, but her fingers were clumsy, and she found herself as indifferent a seamstress as she was a housekeeper. The tomblike silence of the house depressed her, and in these first weeks she dreaded going out, lest she should meet women who would ask after her plans. After a time she found herself seated like Aunt Mabelle for hours at a time, staring out of the windows at the passers-by.

After the scene at Uncle Elmer's there seemed for a time no solution of their troubles. She plunged into choir singing, where her loud, flat voice filled a much-needed place; and she went without Philip to talk at the Sunday Evening Service of her experiences in Africa. Emma was there and Uncle Elmer, treating the congregation to the spectacle of a brother and sister who occupied the same pew without speaking to each other. But somehow everything was changed, and different from those glorious days so short a time before when the sound of her voice had moved whole congregations to a frantic fervor. The assembly-room now showed great gaps of empty seats, like missing teeth, along the sides and at the back. Naomi wasn't any longer a great attraction as "the youngest missionary of the Lord in darkest Africa": she was a woman now, a missionary like any other missionary. And there were, too, strange rumors circulating through the flock of the quarrel between Emma and her brother and other rumors that Naomi and Philip weren't really missionaries at all any longer, but had both deserted the cause forever. There were a hundred petty bits of gossip, all magnified and sped on their way by friends of Emma who resented the reflected glory in which she bathed herself.

No, something had gone wrong, and the whole affair seemed stale and flat, even the little reception afterward. Emma, of course, stood with the Reverend Castor and Naomi, while members of the congregation filed past. Some congratulated Naomi on her work and wished her fresh successes; one or two asked questions which interested them specially—"was it true that a nigger king had as many as eighty wives?" and, "did they actually eat each other, and if so how was the cooking done?" Emma was always there, beaming with pride, and answering questions before Naomi had time to speak. The Reverend Castor from time to time took Naomi's hand in his and patted it quite publicly, as if she were a child who had recited her first piece without forgetting a line. He kept saying, between fatherly pats, "Yes, the Lord has brought our little girl safely home once more. He has spared her for more work."

But it was a failure: it had none of the zest of those earlier meetings, none of the hysterics and the wild singing of *Throw Out the Life Line* and *The Ninety and Nine*, and other hymns that acted as powerful purges to the emotions. The occasion was dampened, too, by the curiosity of various old ladies regarding the absence of Philip; they kept asking question upon question, which Emma, with much practice, learned to parry skilfully. "He didn't feel well enough to make the effort. You see, the fever clings on—that's the worst part of it."

For she was squeezing the last drop of triumph before the débâcle; and of course she always believed in the depths of her soul that Philip *would* go back to Africa some day. She meant, in the end, to accomplish it as she had already accomplished the things she desired—all save the recovery of Mr. Downes.

But it was Naomi who suffered most, for behind the mild and timid exterior there lurked an ironclad egotism which demanded much of the world. It demanded more attention and enthusiasm than had been her share at the Sunday Evening Service; it demanded respect and, curiously enough, evidence of affection (it was this last rather pitiful hunger that drew her close to Aunt Mabelle). She understood well enough that Emma had no affection: what capacity for love Emma possessed was all directed toward Philip. And before many weeks had passed Naomi knew bitterly that although she lived in the same house with her husband and his mother she really occupied no more of a place in it than Essie, the poor-house slavey. But Aunt Mabelle was kind to her, and would come and sit for hours rocking and gossiping, occasions when the only interruption was the periodic cry of the pallid baby, which Mabelle stifled at once by opening the straining bombazine of her bosom and releasing the fountain of life.

This last was a spectacle which Naomi came to regard with a faint and squeamish distaste. She grew to have a passionate dislike for the pallid infant that lay gorged with milk in Mabelle's ample lap. Even the frank and open manner of the black women had never accustomed her to the exposé in which Mabelle indulged with such an air of satisfied pride.

"I've always had plenty of milk," Mabelle would say, as she settled back comfortably. "The doctors say I've enough for any three normal children."

Naomi, indeed, had spent half her life in an effort to conceal black nudity in yards of cheap calico.

But deeper than any of these flurried emotions lay the shadowy knowledge that the pallid child was in a way a reproach to herself, and a vague symbol of all the distasteful things that lay before her, for she felt that sooner or later the tangle would end in bringing her to the state of a wife in reality, of facing even perhaps the business which Mabelle managed with such proud composure. In the midst of the wilderness at Megambo she was still safe, protected by the fantastic sense of honor that lay in Philip; but here in this complicated world of which she knew nothing, when each day she felt her security, her fame, her glory, slipping from under her feet, the thing drew constantly nearer and nearer. If she could not force Philip to return, the day would come when with all her glory and prestige faded and bedraggled, she would no longer be a missionary, but only Philip's wife.

There were moments when, on the verge of hysteria, she thought of leaving them all and going back alone to Africa; but when the moments passed, she found herself strangely weak and incapable of action. For a strange and frightening thing had begun to happen. At Megambo when Philip had always been gentle and submissive, it was herself who dominated and planned. They were comrades in the work of the Lord, and Philip rarely reached the point of being irritable. In those days he had meant no more to her than the clumsy Swanson. Save that he was tied to her by law, he might have been only another worker in the mission. And now it was changed somehow; and Philip ignored her. There were whole days when he never spoke to her at all—days and nights spent in working in the black Mills and sleeping like a dead man to recover from the profound weariness that attacked him.

This new Philip frightened her in a way she had never been frightened before. She found herself, without thinking, doing little things to please him, even to attract his notice. There were still moments when, wrapping herself in the shroud of martyrdom, she flung herself, the apotheosis of injured womanhood, before him to be trampled upon; but they were not profitable moments, for they no longer had any effect upon him; and so, slowly they came to be abandoned, since it seemed silly thus to abase herself only to find that she had no audience. It frightened her, for it seemed that she was losing slowly all control of a life which had once been so neatly and thoroughly organized. She wanted desperately to regain her ancient hold over him, and in the lonely moments when Mabelle was not there she sometimes awakened in horror to find herself sitting before the gigantic walnut mirror letting down the masses of her long, straight, reddish hair, trying it in new ways, attempting to discover in what position her face seemed prettiest. And then, filled with disgust at her own wickedness, she would fling herself on the walnut bed and burst into a passion of tears and prayer, to arise at last strangely calm and comforted. Surely God would not abandon her—Naomi Potts, who had given all her life to God. Sometimes she fancied that she, instead of Philip, was the one whose brain was weak; for no sane woman could do the things she had done.

Slowly, imperceptibly, the curious power of the Mills had begun to make itself felt. It was as if Philip, returning from the Flats at noon each day, brought with him, clinging to his very clothes, traces of the fascination which they held for him. It was not that she herself felt any of the fascination, for she regarded the Mills with a growing hatred: it was only that they fixed upon Philip himself some new and tantalizing quality. She liked to see him come home at noon, hard and unshaven, blackened by soot and sweat. Sitting in her rocking-chair by the window, the sight of him as he swung along, his head bowed a little, filled her with odd flutterings of pleasant emotion. She felt at times that strange weakness which so often attacked Emma una-wares—of wanting to yield and spoil him by caresses and attention. She had strange desires to fling herself down and let him trample upon her, not in the old, dramatic sense, but in a new way, which seemed to warm her whole body.

This new Philip, hard and thin, returning from the Mills with his flannel shirt open upon his bare chest, disgusted and fascinated her. And then when the knob turned and the door opened, all the little speeches she had planned, all the little friendly gestures, seemed to wither and die before his polite coldness.

He would say, "I'll wash up and we can go right away to eat," or "Tell Essie to bring some hot water."

There was nothing more than that. Sometimes it seemed to her that he treated her as a servant whom he scarcely knew.

It came, at length, to the point when she spoke of it, timidly and with hot blushes, to Aunt Mabelle. She said she wanted to be kind to Philip, she wanted to be friendly with him, but somehow she couldn't. He was so changed and cold and hard. If she could only get him back to Africa everything would be all right: they had been happy there, at least she had been, and as for Philip, he didn't seem any happier now that he was doing what he wanted to do. He never seemed happy anywhere, not since the day they had arrived at Megambo.

Mabelle, rocking little Jimmy, listened with the passionate interest of a woman who found such a conversation fascinating. She led Naomi deeper and deeper into the mire and at last, when she had considered all the facts, she said, "Well, Naomi, it's my opinion that you ought to have a child. Philip would like a baby. He's that kind. I know them when I see them. Now, my Elmer hates children. They get in his way and I think they make him feel foolish and awkward, God alone knows why. But Philip's different. He ought to have a lot of children. He'd love 'em, and it would be a tie be-tween you."

Naomi raised the old difficulty. "But if we go back to Africa—we can't take a little baby there."

"Well, you'd have to work that out, of course. Em would take care of it. She'd find time somehow. She can do anything she sets her mind to." Naomi, it seemed, wouldn't meet her eye and Aunt Mabelle pushed on, with the tact and grace of a walrus. "Did you ever see a doctor to find out why you hadn't had one? A doctor can help sometimes."

Naomi was suddenly pale and shaking. Without looking at Mabelle she said in a low voice, "I don't have to see the doctor to find out why."

Mabelle's rocking-chair paused in its monotonous bobbing. "You don't mean to say you've been doing sinful things to prevent it—you, Naomi Downes, a missionary!"

Naomi, wringing her hands, said, "No, I don't know what you mean. I haven't been doing sinful things. . . . I . . . we couldn't have had a baby . . . we've—we've never lived together."

The rocking-chair still remained quiescent, a posed symbol of Mabelle's shocked astonishment. "Well, I don't know what you mean. But it seems sinful to me if a man and wife don't live together. What does the Bible say? Take unto yourself a wife and multiply. Look at all the begats."

Naomi burst out, "We meant to . . . some day. Only we couldn't out there in Africa."

"Well, you ought to have taken a chance." Mabelle seemed outraged and angry for the first time in all Naomi's friendship with her, and it was only after a long time that the rocking-chair began once more its unending motion. The baby, startled by a sudden cessation of the soothing motion, set up a cry and Mabelle, loosening ten of the twenty-one buttons that held together her straining basque, quieted it at once.

"What do you expect?" asked Mabelle rhetorically. "What do you expect? A man isn't going on courting forever for nothing—especially after he's married to a woman. He'll get tired after a while. Philip's a man like any other man. He's not going on forever like this. He isn't that kind. Any woman can tell in a glance—and he's the kind that can wrap a woman around his thumb." Then, being a woman whose whole philosophy was based upon her own experience, she said, "Why, even my Elmer wouldn't stand it, like as not. He's not much at things like that and he's always ashamed of himself afterwards. I guess it was a kind of duty with him—still he's a man." And turning back again to the subject at hand, she asked, "Did you ever know about Philip's father? Why, that man was like a rabbit. You'd better look out or you'll lose him altogether."

It was the longest single speech Mabelle had made in years, and after it she sat rocking herself for a long time in profound meditation. Naomi cried a little and dried her eyes, and the baby fell back into a state of coma. The chair creaked and creaked. At last Mabelle got up heavily, deposited the sleeping child on the sofa, and put on her jacket and hat.

"Take my advice, Naomi," she said. "It can't go on like this. If you don't want to lose him, you'll do what I say. I'm a good judge of men and Philip is worth keeping. He's better than his Ma, Pa, Uncle Elmer, or any of 'em. I wish I was married to such a man."

Chapter 10

EMMA in these days found relief in a vast activity. The restaurant business kept growing and growing until at last she secured a long lease on the shoe store next door and undertook the necessary alterations. She was in and out of the place a score of times a day, watching the carpenters, the plumbers and the painters, quarreling with the contractor and insisting that pipes should be placed where it was impossible to place them and pillars spaced so that there would be a permanent danger of the roof falling in upon her customers.

She was active, too, in her church work and contributed half a wagon load of cakes and pies to the annual June church fair. The Minerva Circle met at her house and Naomi was introduced to those members whom she did not know already, and so launched in a series of sewing parties which she attended in a kind of misery because on account of Philip she could not answer honestly the persistent questions of her new women "friends." And Emma kept up as well her fervent activities as President of the Woman's Christian Temperance Union, carrying war into the enemy's country, trying to drive whisky from a country of mills and furnaces where every other corner was occupied by a saloon. She even called upon Moses Slade, Congressman of the district, and lately become a widower, in his great box-like house set back among the trees on Park Avenue. It was an odd call which began with open hostility when she urged him to wear a white ribbon and declare himself at once on the side of God and Purity.

But Slade, being a politician, felt that Fortune had not yet sided with God and Purity, and declined the honor with a great flow of eloquence for which he was famed. There was much talk of his being chosen to represent the majority of the people, and as yet the majority seemed unfortunately ("the human race is naturally wicked and must be educated to goodness—we must not forget that, Mrs. Downes") still on the side of gin.

He was a man of fifty, with a great stomach and massive feet and hands, who had a round, flat face and a broad, flat nose, with odd little shifty eyes. He was bald in front, but what remained of the once luxuriant black locks was now worn, loose and free, bobbed in a style which women came, shockingly, to adopt years afterward.

He received Emma in his study, a room with red walls, set round with mastodon furniture in mahogany and red leather. In the beginning he was taken aback by the vigor and power of Emma's handsome figure.

She said to him, "The day will come, Mr. Slade, when you will have to vote on the side of purity if you wish to survive—you and all your fellow-members."

And he replied, "That, Mrs. Downes, is what I am waiting for—a sign from the people. You may tell your members that my heart is with them but that I must not lose my head. A sign is all I'm waiting for, Mrs. Downes —only a sign."

Emma, feeling that she had gained at least half a victory, turned the conversation to other things. They discussed the Republican chances at the coming election, and the lateness of the summer, the question, as it was called, of "smoke abatement" and, of course, the amazing growth and prosperity of the Town. They found presently that they saw eye to eye on every subject, for Emma was in her own way a born politician. Congressman Slade observed that since the death of his wife (here a deep sigh interrupted his observation) life had not been the same. To lose a woman after thirty years! Well, it made a gap that could never be filled, or at least, it was extremely unlikely that it would be filled. And now his housekeeper had left, leaving him helpless.

Emma, in her turn, sighed and murmured a few words of condolence. She knew what it was to be alone in the world. Hadn't she been alone for more than twenty years? Ever since Mr. Downes, going to China to make a fortune for himself and his son, had been killed there. They hadn't even found his body, so that she hadn't even the consolation of visiting his grave. That, of course, was a great deal. Congressman Slade ought to be thankful that he had his wife's grave. It helped. In a way, it made the thing definite. It was not like the torturing hope in which she had lived for twenty years. . . . Yes, more than twenty years, hoping all the while that he might not be really dead. Oh, she understood. She sympathized.

"But as to the housekeeper, Mr. Slade, don't let that trouble you. Come and take your meals at the restaurant. I'd be delighted to have you. It would be an honor to have you eat there."

"I'll take up your offer," he said, slapping his knee almost jovially. "I've heard how excellent it is. But, of course, I'll pay for it. I couldn't think of it otherwise."

For a moment, there appeared in the manner of Emma the faintest hint of an ancient coquetry, long forgotten and grown a little stale. It was a mere shadow, something that lurked in the suspicious bobbing of the black ostrich plumes in her hat.

"Oh, don't think of that," she said. "It would be a pleasure—an honor."

She rose and shook his hand. "Good-by, Mr. Slade, and thank you for letting me waste so much of your time."

"It was a pleasure, madam, a pleasure," and going to the door, he bowed her out of his widowed house.

When she had gone, Moses Slade returned to his study and before going back to his work he sat for a long time lost in thought. The shadow of a smile encircled the rather hard, virtuous lips. He smiled because he was thinking of Emma, of her fine figure and healthy, rosy face, of the curve of the full bosom, and the hips from which her dress flowed away like the waters of a fountain.

From the very moment of Minnie's death—indeed, even long before, during the dragging, heavy-footed years of her invalidism—he had been thinking, with a deep sense of guilt, of a second marriage. The guilt had faded away by now, for Minnie had been in her grave for two summers and he could turn his thoughts in such a direction, freely and with a clear conscience. After all, he was a fine, vigorous man, in his prime. People talked about fifty-five as old age—a time when a man should begin to think of other things; but people didn't know until they *were* fifty-five. He had talked like that himself once a long while ago. And now, look at him, as good a man as ever he was, and better, when it came to brains and head. Why, with all the experience he had had. . . .

As he sat there, talking to himself, his earnestness became so great that his lips began to move, forming the words as if he were holding a conversation, even arguing, with another Moses Slade, who sat just across from him in the monstrous chair on the opposite side of the desk. He must, he felt, convince that other Moses Slade.

He went on talking. Look at Mrs. Downes! What a fine woman! With such noble—(yes, noble was the only word)—such noble curves and such a fine, high color. She, too, was in her prime, a fine figure of a woman, handsomer now than she had been as a skinny young thing of eighteen. There was a woman who would make a wife for a man like himself. And she had sense, too, running a business with such success. She'd be a great help to a man in politics.

He began prodding his memory about her. He remembered the story of her long widowhood, of Mr. Downes' mysterious death. Yes, and he even remembered Downes himself, a whipper-snapper, who was no good, and had a devastating way with women. (Memories of a hot-blooded youth began to rise and torment him.) Well, she was better off without him, a no-good fellow like that. And what a brave fight she'd made! She was a fine woman. She had a son, too, a son who was a missionary, and—and— Why, come to think of it, hadn't the son given it up and come home? That didn't sound so good, but you could keep the son out of the way.

The truth was that Moses Slade really wanted a skinny young thing of twenty, but a Congressman who wrote "Honorable" before his name couldn't afford to make a fool of himself. He couldn't afford to marry a silly young thing, or ever get "mixed up" with a woman. A man of fifty-five who kept wanting to pinch arms and hips had to be careful. If he could only pinch, just one pinch, some one like—well, some one as plump as Mrs. Downes, he'd feel like a boy again. He felt that youth would flow back again into him through the very tips of the pinching fingers. It wasn't much—just wanting to pinch a girl. Why did people make such a fuss about it?

He almost convinced himself that a full-blown rose like Emma Downes was far better than a skinny young thing. There was, too, of course, the Widow Barnes, who lived next door, still in her prime, and with a large fortune as well.

He took up the Congressional Record, and tried to lose himself in its mountains and valleys of bombast and boredom, but in a little while the book lay unnoticed on his heavy thighs and he was arguing with the other Moses Slade across the desk.

Suddenly, as if he had been roused from a deep sleep, he again found himself talking aloud. "Well," he thought, "something has got to be done about this."

Chapter 11

MEANWHILE EMMA, walking briskly along beneath the maples of Park Avenue, found her mind all aglitter with interesting projects. She often said that she always felt on the crest of the wave, but to-day it was even better than that; she felt almost girlish. Something had happened to her, while she sat with Moses Slade, consoling him and accepting his consolations. He had noticed her. She marked the look in his eye and noticed the fingers that drummed impatiently the fine edge of his black serge mourning trousers. A man behaved like that only when a woman made him nervous and uneasy. And as she walked, there kept coming back to her in a series of pictures all the adventures of a far distant youth, memories of sleighrides and church suppers, of games of Truth and Forfeits. There was a whole gallery of young men concerned in the flow of memories—young men, tragically enough, whom she might have married. They were middle-aged or oldish now, most of them as rich and distinguished as Moses Slade himself. Somehow she had picked the poorest of the lot, and so missed all the security that came of a sound husband like Slade.

Well (she thought), she wasn't sorry in a way, for she had been happy, and it wasn't too late even now to have the other thing—wealth, security. She'd made a success of her business, and could quit it now with the honest satisfaction of knowing it hadn't defeated her—quit it, or, better still, pass it on to Philip and Naomi, if he were still sure that he wouldn't go back to Megambo. Perhaps that was the way out—to let him take it off her shoulders, and so bring him out of those filthy mills where he was disgracing them all. But then (she thought), what would she do with no work, nothing on which to center her life? It wasn't as if she were tired: she'd never felt as well in her life as in this moment moving along under the slightly sooty maples. No, she couldn't settle down to doing nothing, sitting at home rocking like Naomi and Mabelle. (She fairly snorted at the thought of Mabelle.) Of course, if she married again, married some one like Moses Slade—not Moses Slade, of course (she scarcely knew him), but some one like him. Such a thing wasn't impossible, and with a husband of his age marriage couldn't be very unpleasant. She could go to Washington and do much good for such causes as temperance and woman suffrage.

And then, abruptly, her thoughts were interrupted by the voice of some one speaking to her.

"How do you do, Mrs. Downes?" Looking up, she saw it was Mary Watts . . . now Mary Conyngham . . . looking pale and rather handsome in her widow's clothes.

"Why, Mary Watts, I haven't seen you in ever so long."

There was a certain gush in Emma's manner that was too violent. The cordiality of Mary Watts had, too, the note of one who disliked the object of her politeness. (Emma thought, "She usually pretends not to see me. She's only stopped me because she wants to ask about Philip.")

"I've been away," said Mary; "I had the children in the South. That's why you haven't seen me."

"Yes, now that you speak of it, I do remember reading it in the paper."

And Mary, who never possessed any subtlety, went straight to the point. "I hear," she said, "that Philip has come home."

"Yes, he's been home for some time."

"It is true that he's working in the Mills . . . as a day laborer?"

("What business is it of yours?" thought Emma.)

"Yes, it's a notion he had. I think he wants to find out what it's like. He thinks a missionary ought to know about such things."

"I suppose he'll be going back to Africa soon?"

"Oh, yes. I think he's impatient to be back."

"His wife's here, too?"

"Yes, she's here."

"I've never met her. Perhaps I'd better call."

"Yes, she's always there. She doesn't go out much."

There was an awkward pause and Mary, looking away suddenly, said, "Well, good-by, Mrs. Downes. Remember me to Philip."

"Of course," said Emma. "Good-by."

Once after they had parted, Emma looked back to watch Mary. She looked handsome (Emma thought), but sad and tired. Perhaps it was the trouble she had had with Conyngham and Mamie Rhodes . . . carrying on so. Still, she didn't feel sorry for Mary: you couldn't feel sorry for a girl who had such superior airs. She was always stuck-up—Mary Watts; and she'd better not try any of her tricks on Philip.

Her thoughts flew back to Philip. Something had to be done about him. He'd been home for nine months now, and people were beginning to talk; they were even beginning to find out about the Mills. (Why, Mary Watts knew it already.) Being so busy with the new addition to the restaurant and the church and the Union affairs, she hadn't done her best by him these last few weeks; she'd been neglecting her duty in a way. It wasn't too late for him to go back to Megambo—why, he might still become Bishop of East Africa. If he didn't, it would go to that numbskull, Swanson, as first in the field.

And instead of that, he was working like a common Dago in the Mills.

And Naomi, she wasn't any help at all. Funny, too, when she'd always thought Naomi could look out for herself and manage Philip. Instead, she seemed to grow more spineless every day—almost as if she were siding with Philip. She was getting just like Mabelle, sitting around all day in a trance, rocking. Something had to be done.

Then, for no reason at all, unless it happened through that train of memories fired by the behavior of Moses Slade, which led back to her youth, she thought of Naomi's preciously guarded virginity.

Perhaps (she thought) if they had a child, if Philip and Naomi lived together as man and wife, they would all have a greater hold upon him. A man with a *real* wife and children wasn't as free as a man like Philip, who had no responsibilities (now that he'd become so strange), save those imposed by the law. Perhaps he would come to love Naomi and do things to please her. He'd come in time to want things from her. A thing like that did give you a hold over a man: it was a precarious hold, and you had to be very clever about it, but it was something, after all. If there was a child, she (Emma) could take charge of it when Philip and Naomi went back to the place God had ordained for them.

As she walked, the idea grew and grew. Why (she wondered) hadn't it occurred to her before, as the one chance left? Naomi would hate it, and probably refuse at first, but she must be made to understand that it was her duty, not only as a wife (there were plenty of passages in the Bible to prove it), but as an agent of God. Why, it was almost another case of Esther and Ahasuerus, or even Judith and Holofernes. Look what they had done for God!

Yes, there was a chance of managing Philip, after all. If they fixed on him such new responsibilities, it might bring him to his senses.

Suddenly, in the midst of these torrential thoughts, she found herself at the very door of her own house, and, entering, she called out, "Naomi! Naomi!" in her loud, booming voice.

From her rocking-chair by the window, Naomi rose and answered her. She had been crying, perhaps all the afternoon, and her pale eyes were swollen and rimmed with red.

"Naomi," she said, flinging aside her hat and jacket, "I've had a new idea about Philip. I think we've been wrong in our way of managing him."

Chapter 12

AT THE SAME MOMENT, Philip was walking along the road that led out into the open country, talking, talking, talking to Mary Conyngham.

He had met her in a fashion the most natural, for he had gone to walk in the part of the town where Mary lived. There were odd, unsuspected ties between the people who lived on the Hill and those who lived in the Flats, and he had come to know of her return from Krylenko, his own foreman; for Krylenko had heard it from Irene Shane, who had seen Mary herself at the school that Irene kept alive in the midst of the Flats. Krylenko told him the news while they sat eating their breakfast out of tin pails and talking of Irene Shane. Once he heard it, there was no more peace for Philip: he thought about her while he worked, pulling and pushing great sheets of red-hot metal, while the thick smoke blew in at the windows of the cavernous shed. All through the morning he kept wondering what she was like, whether she had changed. He kept recalling her face, oval and dark, with good-humored blue eyes and dark hair pulled back in a knob at the back of her small head. That was the way he remembered her, and he tormented himself with doubts as to whether she had changed. She wasn't a girl any longer; she was the mother of two children, and a widow. She had been through troubles with her husband.

At lunch he scarcely spoke to Naomi and his mother, and he never uttered the name of Mary Conyngham, for something made him cautious: he could not say what it was, save that he felt he oughtn't to speak of her before the other two. He had to see Mary Conyngham; he had to talk with her, to talk about himself. He couldn't go on any longer, always shut in, always imprisoned in the impenetrable cell of his own loneliness. It was Mary Conyngham who could help him; he was certain of it.

He left Naomi at the door of the restaurant, telling her that he meant to go for a walk. He would return later to sleep. No, he didn't feel tired. He thought a walk would do him good.

And then, when he had left her, he walked toward the part of the town where Mary lived, and when he reached her street, he found that he hadn't the courage even to pass her house, for fear she might see him and wonder why he was walking about out there on the borders of the town. For an hour he walked, round and round the block encircling her house, but never passing it. It wasn't only that she might think him a fool, but she might be changed and hard. If she had changed as much as he himself had changed, it would only be silly and futile, the whole affair. But he couldn't go on forever thus walking round and round, because people would think him mad, as mad as his mother and Naomi believed him.

Crossing the street, he looked up, waiting for a wagon to pass, and there on the opposite side stood Mary Conyngham. She did not see him at once, perhaps (he thought) because she had not expected to see him, and so had not recognized him. She was wearing a short skirt, known as a "rainy daisy," though it was a bright, clear day. She looked pale, he thought, and much older—handsomer, too, than she had once been. All the tomboyish awkwardness had vanished. She was a woman now. For a moment he had a terrible desire to turn and run, to hide himself. It was a ridiculous thought, and it came to nothing, for as the wagon passed she saw him, and, smiling, she crossed the street to meet him. His heart was beating wildly, and the rare color came into his dark cheeks.

"Philip," she said, "I've been wondering where you were."

It gave him the oddest sensation of intimacy, as if the meeting had been planned, and he had been waiting all this time impatiently.

They shook hands, and Mary said, "I've just left your mother." And Philip blushed again, feeling awkward, and silly, like a boy in his best clothes, who didn't know what to do with his hands. He was dressed like a workman in an old suit and blue cotton shirt.

Suddenly he plunged. "I came out here on purpose. I wanted to see you."

"Have you been to the house?"

"No," he hesitated. "No . . . I've just been walking round, hoping to run into you."

It was five years since they had last seen each other, and longer than that since they had really been friends. Talk didn't come easily at first. Standing there on the corner, they made conversation for a time—silly, banal conversation—when each of them wanted to talk in earnest to the other.

At last Philip said, "Are you in a hurry? Could I come home with you?"

"No, I'm not in a hurry. I've left the children with Rachel . . . Rachel is my sister-in-law. We share expenses on the house. But I don't think we better go home. Are you tired?" she asked abruptly.

"No."

"Because if you aren't, we might go for a walk. I was afraid you might be, after working all night at the Mills."

For a moment Philip looked at her sharply. "How did you know I was in the Mills?"

She laughed. "Krylenko told me. I saw him yesterday. He was helping Irene teach English to a lot of dirty and very stupid Poles."

"He's a nice fellow—Krylenko. I didn't know there were such men down there."

"Nobody knows it without going down there. Shall we walk a bit?"

They set out along Milburn Street, past the row of houses surrounded by green leaves and bright trees. It was the hill farthest from the Mills and the soot seldom drifted so far. As they drew nearer and nearer to the open fields, the queer sense of restraint began a little to melt away. They even laughed naturally as they had done years before when they had played together.

"It was a funny thing," said Philip. "I've been wanting to see you ever since I came back. That's why I came out here this afternoon—on a chance of meeting you. I came as soon as I heard you were home."

He was walking with his hands clasped behind him, his dark brows puckered into a fine line with the effort he was making. He didn't know how to talk to women, at least women like Mary, and, in spite of their old, old friendship, he felt shy with her. With her dead husband and her two children, she seemed so much older and wiser. Some odd, new complication had entered their relationship which made it all difficult and confused. Yet she seemed to take it calmly, almost sadly.

"Tell me," she said presently. "Philip, tell me about yourself. You don't mean to go back?" She halted and looked at him squarely.

"No, I don't mean to go back." And all at once he found himself pouring out to her the whole story. He told her how he hated it all from the beginning, how he had begun to doubt, how the doubts had tortured him; how he had prayed and prayed, only to find himself slipping deeper and deeper. He told her of the morning by the lake, of the terrible night of the drums, of the coming of the queer Englishwoman, and the fight that followed, in which his last grain of faith had gone. Suddenly, he realized that he was telling the whole story for the first time. He had never spoken of it before to any one. It was as if all the while, without knowing it, he had been saving it for Mary Conyngham.

"And so," she said, "you've come back to stay. Do you think you'll stay?"

He shrugged his shoulders. "I don't know. There's nothing else to do."

"And why did you go to work in the Mills?"

"I don't know. At least, I didn't know at the beginning."

"Was it because you wanted to work among the people in the Flats?"

"No . . . no . . . I'm through with meddling in other people's lives."

There was a bitterness in his tone which Mary must have guessed had some relation to the woman she had left a little while before; only Philip had always adored his mother. Emma Downes boasted of it.

"I think I went into the Mills," he was saying, "because I had to find something solid to get hold of . . . and that was the solidest thing I could find. It's awfully solid, Mary. And it's beginning to do the trick. At first I hadn't faith in anything, least of all myself, and now I've got something new to take its place. It's a kind of faith in man—a faith in yourself. I couldn't go on always putting everything into the hands of God. It's like cheating—and people don't do it really. They only pretend they do. If they left it all to God, I suppose things would work out somehow; but they don't. They insist on meddling, too, and when a thing succeeds then God is good and he's answered their prayers, and if it fails, then it is God's Will. But all the while they're meddling themselves and making a mess of things."

"And you don't mean ever to go back to the church?"

For a moment he didn't answer. Then he said in a low voice, "No . . . I don't believe any longer—at least, not in the way of the church. And the church—well, the church is dead so far as the world is concerned. It's full of meddling old women. It might disappear to-morrow and the world would go on just the same. That's one thing about the Flats. . . . Down there you get down to brass tacks. You know how little all the hubbub really means."

"Do people know how you feel?"

"No, they just think I'm a little mad. I've never told any one any of this, Mary, until now."

She looked at him shyly. "Your blue shirt suits you better than your black clothes, Philip. I always thought you weren't made for a preacher."

He blushed. "Perhaps . . . anyway, I feel natural in the blue shirt." He halted again. "You know, Mary, it's been the queerest thing—the whole business. It's as if I never really existed before. It's like being born again—it's painful and awful."

They were quite clear of the Town now. It had sunk down behind the rolling hills. They sat down side by side presently on the stone wall of the bridge that crossed the brook. The water here was clear and clean. It turned to oil further on, after it had passed through the Flats. For a time they sat in silence, watching the sun slipping down behind the distant woods that crowned Trimble's Hill. In the far distance the valley had turned misty and blue.

Presently Mary sighed suddenly, and asked, "And your wife? What's to be done about her? She's a missionary, too, and she still believes, doesn't she?"

A shadow crossed Philip's face. "Yes, that's the trouble. It's made such an awful mess. She's always lived out there. She's never known any other life, and she doesn't know how to get on here. That's the trouble. Sometimes I think she ought to go back . . . alone, without me. She'd be happier there."

For a moment there was a silence, and Philip fancied that she began to say something, and then halted abruptly; but he couldn't be certain. It may have only been the noise of the brook. He looked at her sharply, but she rose and turned her back.

"We'd better start back," she said. "It will be getting dark."

For a long time they walked side by side in silence—an odd silence in which they seemed to be talking to each other all the while. It was Mary who actually spoke.

"But you don't mean to go on forever in the Mills? Have you thought what you want to do?"

Again he waited for a long time before answering her. It must have seemed to Mary that he was being shy and cautious with her, that despite the pouring out of his story, there was still a great deal that he had kept hidden away. He had the air of a man who was afraid of confidences.

At last he said, "I don't know whether I ought to speak of it, but I do know what I want to do. It sounds ridiculous, but what I want to do is . . . is . . . paint." He blurted it out as if it required an immense effort, as if he were confessing a sin.

"Pictures?" asked Mary. "Do you know anything about it?"

"No . . . not very much. I've always wanted to, in a way. A long time ago, when I was a boy, I used to spend all my time drawing things." His voice fell a little. "But as I grew older, it seemed foolish . . . and the other thing came up . . . and I did that instead. You see, I've been drawing a bit lately. I've been drawing in the Flats—the engines and cranes and chimneys. They always . . . well, they fascinated me as far back as I can remember." When she did not answer, he said, "You remember . . . I used to draw when I was a kid . . ."

For a time she considered this sudden, fantastic outburst, and presently she said, "Yes, I remember. I still have the picture you made of Willie, the pony . . . and the tree-house. . . ." And then after another pause. "Have you thought about a teacher?"

"No . . . but . . . don't think I'm conceited, Mary . . . I don't want a teacher. I want to work it out for myself. I've got an idea."

She asked him if she might see some of the drawings.

"I haven't shown them to any one," he said. "I don't want to yet . . . because they aren't good enough. When I do a good one . . . the kind I know is right and what I meant it to be, I'll give it to you."

His secret, he realized suddenly, was out—the secret he had meant to tell no one, because he was in a strange way ashamed of it. It seemed so silly for any one in the Town to think of painting.

The odd, practical streak in Mary asserted itself. "Have you got paints? You can't get them here in the Town."

"No . . . I haven't needed them. But I'll want them soon. I want to begin soon."

"I'm going to Cleveland on Monday," she said. "I'll get them there . . . everything you need. You'd never find them here."

And then, since he had let escape his secret, he told her again of the morning by the lake at Megambo, and the sudden, fierce desire to put down what he saw in the procession of black women carrying water to the young plantations. He tried to tell her how in a way it had given him a queer sense of religious ecstasy.

It was almost dark now, and the fragrance of the garden on the outskirts of the Town filled the air.

Mary smiled suddenly. "You know," she said, "I don't think you really hated Africa at all. It wasn't Africa you hated. You loved it. And I don't think you mean to stay here all your life. Some day you'll be going back."

He left her in the shadows as the older of her children, a towheaded girl of three, came down the path to meet her, calling out her name.

On returning to the slate-colored house, he opened the door to find Naomi awaiting him.

"Supper is ready," she said. "I sent Essie to the restaurant for it, so you wouldn't have to walk up there."

He thanked her, and she answered, "I thought you'd be tired after walking so long."

"Thank you. I did take a long walk. I wanted to get into the open country."

While they ate, sitting opposite each other, beneath the glow of the dome painted with wild-roses, he noticed that she was changed. She seemed nervous and uneasy: she kept pressing him to eat more. She was flushed and even smiled at him once or twice. He tried to answer the smile, but his face seemed made of lead. The effort gave him pain.

Suddenly he thought, "My God! She is trying to be nice to me!" And he was frightened without knowing why. It was almost as if, for a moment, the earth had opened and he saw beneath his feet a chasm, vague and horrible, and sinister.

He thought, "What can have changed her?" For lately there had grown up between them a slow and insinuating enmity that was altogether new. There were moments when he had wanted to turn away and not see her at all.

She poured more coffee for him, and he became aware suddenly that his nerves were on edge, that he was seeing everything with a terrible clarity—the little freckles on the back of her hand, the place where the cup was chipped, the very figures and tiny discolorations of the ornate wallpaper.

"Your mother won't be home till late," she said. "She's gone to report her talk with Mr. Slade to the ladies of the Union."

He wondered why she had told him something which he already knew. But he was kind to her, and tried not to seem different, in any way, from what he had always been. He was sorry for Naomi more than ever since her life had become such an empty, colorless thing.

At last he was finished, and thanking her again, he left her helping Essie to clear away the table, and went upstairs with a strange feeling that she had stayed behind to help only because she didn't want to be alone with him.

Undressing, he lay for a long time in the darkness, unable to sleep because of the acuteness which seemed to attack all his senses. He heard every small noise in the street—the cries of the children playing in the glare of the arc-lights, the barking of dogs, the distant tinkle of a piano. Slowly, because he was very tired, the sounds grew more and more distant, and he fell asleep.

He slept profoundly, as a man drowned in the long exhaustion of the Mills. He was awakened by something touching him gently at first, as if it were part of a dream. It touched him again and then again, and slowly he drifted back to consciousness. Being a man of nerves, he awakened quickly, all at once. There was no slow drowsiness and clinging mists of slumber.

He opened his eyes, but the room was in complete blackness, and he saw nothing. It must have been late, for even the sounds of the street had died away, to leave only the long pounding of the Mills that was like the silence. Somewhere, close at hand, there was a sound of breathing. For a second he thought, "I have died in my sleep."

Then the thing touched him again. It was a bit of metal, cold and rigid, not longer than a finger. And in a sudden flash he knew what it was—a metal hair-curler. The thing brushed his forehead. He knew then, quickly. It was Naomi come to him to be his wife. She was bending over him. The darkness hid her face. She made no sound. It was unreal, like something out of a dream.

Chapter 13

IN THE MILLS Philip had come to know the men who worked at his oven, one by one, slowly, for they were at first suspicious of him as a native from the Hills who came to work among them. It was Krylenko more than any of them who broke down the barrier which shut him away from all those others. Krylenko, he came presently to understand, was a remarkable fellow. He was young, not perhaps more than twenty-five or six, a giant even among the big Poles, who worked with the strength of three ordinary men. There was a magnificence about his great body, with its supple muscles flowing beneath the blond, white skin. Naked to the waist, and leaning on his great bar of iron, there were times when he seemed a statue cut in the finest Parian marble. It was this odd, physical splendor that gave him a prestige and the power of leadership, which would have come to nothing in a stupid man; but Krylenko was intelligent, and hidden within the intelligence there lay a hard kernel of peasant shrewdness. He knew what it was he wanted and he was not to be turned aside; he was, Philip had come to understand, partly the creation of Irene Shane, that pale, transparent wraith, who spent all her days between the Flats and the great, gloomy house known as Shane's Castle. She had found him in her night class, a big Russian boy with a passion for learning things, and she had taken him to help her. She had perhaps discerned the odd thing about Krylenko, which set him apart from the others, that he had a vision. He had no ambition for himself, but his queer, mystical mind was constantly illuminated by wonderful plans of what he might do for his people. By this, he did not mean his own country people, but all the hordes of workers who dwelt in the rows of black houses and spent half their lives in the Mills. To him they were, quite simply, brothers—all the Poles, the Lithuanians, the Italians, the Croats, even the negroes who came up from the South to die slowly working over the acid vats. In his own Slavic way he had caught a sense of that splendor of the Mills which sometimes overwhelmed Philip. Only Krylenko saw, what was quite true, that the people in the Flats belonged to another world from those on the Hill. They made up a nation within a nation, a hostile army surrounded and besieged.

He meant to help his people to freedom, even by doing battle, if circumstance demanded it. At times there was about him the splendor of the ancient prophets.

It was for this reason that he stayed in the pounding-sheds, as a simple foreman, refusing to go elsewhere, though he could have had after a time one of the easy places in the shipping-rooms. He might have been one of those men who, "working their way from the bottom of the ladder," turned to oppress his own people. There were plenty of shrewd, hard-headed, pitiless men like that—men such as Frick and Carnegie, who had interests in these very Mills. Only he wasn't concerned for himself. He had a queer, stupid, pig-headed idea of helping the men about him; and he was one of those fantastic men to whom Justice was also God.

He had his own way of going about it; and he was not a sentimentalist. He knew that to get things in this world, one had to fight; and so he had gone quietly about organizing men, one here, one there, into the dreaded unions. It had to be done secretly, because he would have been sent away, blacklisted and put outside the pale if the faintest suspicion of his activity reached the ears even of the terrified little clerks who talked so big. There were meetings sometimes in the room over Hennessey's saloon, with men who wandered into town on one train and out on the next. It was a slow business, for one had to go carefully. But even with all the care there were whispers of strange things going on beneath the rumbling surface of the Flats. There were rumors which disturbed the peace of the stockbrokers, and stirred with uneasiness the people on the Hill—the bankers, the lawyers, the little shopkeepers—all the parasite ants whose prosperity rested upon the sweat of the Flats. There were, too, spies among the workers.

They even said on the Hill that old Julia Shane and that queer daughter of hers had a finger in the pie, which was more than true, for they did know what was happening. In their mad, fantastic way they had even given money.

There was always a strange current of fear and suspicion running beneath the surface, undermining here and there in places that lay below ground. In the first weeks Philip had become aware slowly of the sinister movement. He came to understand the suspicions against him. And then abruptly, bit by bit, perhaps because of his own taste for solitude and his way of going off to sit alone in a corner eating his own lunch, Krylenko had showed signs of friendliness, stifled and hindered in the beginning by the strangeness which set apart a dweller in the Flats from one on the Hill. One by one, the other men came to drop their suspicions and presently Philip found himself joining in their coarse jokes, even picking up snatches of their outlandish tongues. He came, in a way, to be one of them, and the effect of the communion filled him with a sense of expansion, almost as if he could feel himself growing. In a life dedicated to loneliness, he felt for the first time that warm, almost sensual feeling of satisfaction in companionship. He came to understand the men who worked at his own oven—Sokoleff, who drank whisky as if it were water, and sweated it all out as fast as he drank it, Krylenko himself, who was in love with an Italian girl who couldn't marry him until her orphaned brothers and sisters were grown, and Finke, the black little Croat who sometimes lost his head and talked wildly about revolution. And a dozen others—simple, coarse men, whose lives seemed plain and direct, filled too with suffering, though it was of a physical sort concerned with painful work, and childbirth, and empty stomachs, and so unlike that finer torture which Philip himself suffered.

And presently he found that the Mills were saving him—even his brain: the grimness, the bitter tang of the black life in the Flats, presented a savage reality which was to him like a spar in the open sea. There was no reality, he thought sometimes, even in his marriage to Naomi. It was all shadowy and unreal, filled with sound and fury which seemed baseless and even silly, when one thought of this other life of fire and steel. His own existence had been a futile, meaningless affair of vapors, swooning and ecstasies.

And then on the morning after Naomi had come to him, Krylenko fixed it for him to join the Union. To Philip it was a move that took on a significance out of proportion with the reality: it had an importance which for the others was lacking. He had entered the sinister conspiracy against his own people on the Hill; it marked the closing of a door behind him. He was certain now never to turn back.

All night and all morning he scarcely spoke to Krylenko and Finke and Sokoleff. He worked beside them, silent and sweating, his mind and soul in a confused state of alternate satisfaction and torment. Once or twice, he caught himself smiling into the depths of the burning ovens, like an idiot. He was smiling because of what had happened there in the dark in his room, with the pleasure of a boy come at last of age. It filled him with an odd, warm feeling of satisfaction and power. He was at last a man, like those others, Finke and Sokoleff and even Krylenko, who took such things as part of the day's routine, as they took eating and drinking. For them, a thing so commonplace couldn't mean what it meant to him. It couldn't give them that strange feeling of being suddenly set free after a long imprisonment. It couldn't mean a fever bred of long restraint that was vanished. And slowly through the long hours by the hot ovens his nerves grew relaxed and his mind cleared. The memory of the hot, tormenting nights at Megambo seemed distant and vague now. He was, as he had said to Mary Conyngham, being slowly born again. Something tremendous had happened to him. He was aware of a new strength and of a power over women, even women like his mother, and Naomi, terrified and hysterical in the darkness. He was free. A great light like a rocket had burst in the darkness.

At noon when the whistles blew, Krylenko, tucking in his shirt, said, "Come on and have a drink. . . . We gotta celebrate, all of us."

For a moment Philip hesitated. He had never drunk anything, even beer, but now there seemed a difference. What the hell difference did it make if you drank or not? These men about him all drank. It was the only pleasure they had, most of them, except what they found in the dismal, shuttered houses of Franklin Street. There was a reason now to drink. They would think he was celebrating his entrance into the Union, and all the time he'd be celebrating the other thing which they knew nothing about, which they wouldn't even understand.

"Yes," he said, "I'll go."

Hennessey's saloon stood at the corner of Halstead Street and the Erie tracks, just at the foot of the hill crowned by Shane's Castle. It was open night and day, and always filled with smoke and noise and drunken singing. Noise was its great characteristic—the grinding, squeaking sound of brakes on the endless freight-trains that passed the door, the violent, obscene voices of protesting drunks, the pounding of the Mills, and the ceaseless hammering of the tinny mechanical piano that swallowed nickels faster and faster as the patrons grew drunker and drunker. The only silence seemed to hang in a cloud about Mike Hennessey, the owner, a gigantic Irishman, with a beefy red face and carroty hair. He wasn't the original Hennessey. The founder, his father, was long since dead. In his day the famous Hennessey's had been only a crossroads saloon. There were no mills and furnaces. His customers were farmers. This silent Mike Hennessey knew his business: he watched men get drunker and drunker while the cash-register banged and jangled. He never spoke. He was afraid of no man, and he had a very special scorn for the Dagoes and their way of using knives to fight. He paid five hundred dollars a month to the mayor, which made the police both blind and deaf to the noise and lights of the saloon which had no closing hours, and a thousand more to veil in purity his row of shuttered houses in Franklin Street. There was a hard, flinty look in his cold blue eyes, that said: "I know the price of everything in this bedlam of a Town. Every man and woman has a price."

But the hard blue eyes which never changed, widened ever so slightly for a brief second as the swinging doors opened and Philip came in with Finke and Krylenko and Sokoleff.

They sat at a table in the corner, where the mechanical piano growled and jangled. It was the full tide of drinking in the saloon, the hour when one shift of workers had left and another, dog-tired and black with soot, had only arrived. Most of them came unwashed from the Mills and their black faces together with the drifting smoke and clatter of sound gave the place the aspect of some chamber in Hell. The four companions began by drinking whisky, all of them but Philip perfectly straight. They would, Krylenko said, drink beer afterward to finish up.

The whisky, even diluted, burned and then warmed him. Finke and Sokoleff drank steadily, one glass after another, until the alcohol presently killed their weariness and Sokoleff began to grow hilarious and Finke to talk of revolution. For them the bad liquor took the place of rest, of sleep, of food, of cleanliness, even of decency. In the Flats it was useless to search for any decent thing, because comfort, food and warmth were not to be found there. Finke and Sokoleff had learned long ago that they lay only at the bottom of a glass filled many times with the rot-gut whisky that Hennessey sold.

Krylenko only drank a little and then said he must go, as he had to see Giulia before he went to bed. The great Ukrainian had washed himself carefully all over with cold water at the Mills, while the other three waited, Finke and Sokoleff standing by and making Rabelaisian jokes about his preparations for the courtship. Krylenko took it with good-natured tolerance, but there was an odd, shining look in his small, clear blue eyes.

Philip, sitting in a faint, warm haze, remembered the scene with pleasure, conscious that he belonged to them now. He was a member of the Union, one of them at last, but more than that he had become like them a man. He was drinking with them to celebrate.

Krylenko, taking leave of them, touched Philip on the shoulder. "You better go home now and get some sleep."

"No," said Philip; "I'm going to stay a while."

The big Russian's great hand closed on his shoulder with a powerful but gentle pressure. "Look here, Philip," he said, "you ain't like these two. You can't stand it. You better go home now. They're just a pair of hogs. Nothing hurts 'em."

But Philip felt hazy enough to be stubborn and a little shrewd. He sided with Finke and Sokoleff, who kept protesting noisily. He meant to have one more drink—beer this time—and then he'd go.

Krylenko, shaking his big yellow head, went off to see Giulia, and, as Philip watched his great shoulders plowing their way through the mob, something odd happened to him. It was as if a light had gone out; instead of feeling jolly and a bit wild, he was seized in the grip of melancholy. He wanted suddenly to weep. He remembered what Krylenko had said about hogs, and, staring in a queer daze at Finke and Sokoleff, he saw them by some fantastic trick of the mind as two pigs with smutty faces thrusting their noses into the big drinking-glasses. He wanted suddenly to rise and wash himself all over with cold water as Krylenko had done—to wash away the smoke, the smell of sweat and the noise that filled the room. He didn't want to talk any more or listen to the lewd jokes which Finke and Sokoleff kept on making about Krylenko's courtship. He sat silently and stared into space.

And as the fumes of the alcohol filled his brain, the impulse to wash himself grew stronger and stronger. He came to feel vaguely that there were other things beside the soot and sweat that he wanted to wash away, and slowly he knew what it was. He wanted to wash away with cold water the memory of the night before, the fantastic memory of what had happened with Naomi.

Finke and Sokoleff had forgotten him. The one had gone off to stand by the bar talking red revolution, and the other was shouting wildly to stop "that Gott-damned piano." The room seemed to expand and then contract, growing vast and cavernous like the Mill shed and then pressing in upon him, squeezing the horrible noise tight against his ear-drums. He felt sick and filled with disgust. Suddenly he knew that he was drunk and he knew that he hadn't meant to be. It had happened without his knowing it. He was drunk, and last night he had slept with a harlot. Oh, he knew now. It sickened him. It might just as well have been a harlot, one of those women out of Hennessey's shuttered houses. It would have been better, because he wouldn't have to go back to a woman like that: he'd never see her again. And he wouldn't have that queer little knot, like a cramp in a weary muscle, that was almost hatred for Naomi.

The drunker he got, the clearer it all seemed. And then suddenly his tired brain gave way. He fell forward and buried his face in his hands. He knew now and he began to weep drunkenly. He knew now, because he had learned in a strange way during the darkness of the slate-colored house. He knew why it was that he had had to see Mary Conyngham; he knew why he had walked with her into the open country. He was in love with Mary Conyngham; he had been in love with her ever since he could remember. And it was Naomi who shared his bed.

Disgust enveloped him in physical sickness, and the old desire to wash himself in cold water returned passionately. What Krylenko had said was true. "You ain't like these two—just a couple of hogs." Krylenko knew with that shining look in his blue eyes. Krylenko had his Giulia, and he, Philip, had nothing . . . less than nothing, for he had bound himself in a terrible, sickening fashion to Naomi. It was all horrible. He was drunk and he wanted suddenly to die.

Some one touched his shoulder, and he raised his head. It was Hennessey, looking down at him out of the cold blue eyes.

"Look here," he said. "You're drunk enough. Get out of here and go home. Your Ma is Emma Downes, and I don't want to get mixed up with a hell-cat like her."

For a second Philip was blinded by rage. He wanted to kill Hennessey for the insult to his mother. He tried to get up, but he only knocked his glass on the floor, and then fell down beside it. He tried again to rise, and then Hennessey, cursing, bent over and picked him up as if he'd been a child, and carried him, plowing through the heat and confusion, out the swinging doors. In the open air, he placed him on his feet, holding him upright for a moment till he got a sense of his balance. Then, giving him a little push, he said, "There now. Run along home to your Ma like a good little boy. Tell her not to let her little tin Jesus come back again to Hennessey's place if she don't want him messed up too much to be a good missionary."

Chapter 14

IN THE SLATE-COLORED HOUSE, the Minerva Circle was seated on the collapsible chairs from McTavish's listening to a paper by Mrs. Wilbert Phipps on her visit to the Mammoth Caves of Kentucky. To overcome the boredom, some thought about their children and their husbands, or even the hired girl, filling in the time until the dreary reading was over, and they might fall back again into gossip and recipes and children's ailments. It was the price they paid for the honor which came to each of them every eighteen months of standing before the Minerva Circle and reading a paper to which no one listened.

The folding-doors between the parlor and the sitting-room had been opened and those leading from the parlor to the hall were closed. Upstairs Naomi lay in bed with her hair still in steel curlers: she was too ill to come down. She had wept hysterically all the night and most of the morning. When Emma had tried to comfort her with vague, soothing words about matrimony, nothing had made any difference. It was only Aunt Mabelle's visit, colored by great chunks of wisdom and frankness drawn from her own experience and conferences with many other married ladies upon a subject which she always found absorbing, that reduced Naomi at length to a calmer state of mind. And Mabelle was sitting by her now, nursing the baby, and pouring forth details of her own history, in an effort to forestall fresh outbursts.

Downstairs, in the dining-room and kitchen, Emma bustled about, scolding the slattern Essie, and thinking that it was just like Naomi to have chosen such a busy and awkward occasion for following her advice. So Emma had to look after all the refreshments herself. She was putting out the plates of fruit salad on the dining-room table, when she heard the knob of the front door turn. Pausing in her work, she saw the door open, gently and carefully, as Philip entered. His foot caught on the carpet, he tripped and fell.

In the next moment she knew. He was drunk. He couldn't get to his feet.

Behind the closed doors of the parlor the thin, refined voice of Mrs. Wilbert Phipps was saying, "And then the guide caught some fish in a net and showed them to us. They proved most interesting, as they were quite without eyes, and therefore blind. It seems that living so long in the darkness the eyes shriveled up in succeeding generations until they disappeared. I remember saying to Wilbert: 'Think of it! These fish are quite blind!'"

Philip, struggling to his feet, heard the word "blind." "Yes, I was blind too. But I'm not any longer. Naomi made a man of me. She made a man of me."

He laughed wildly, and Emma, clapping a hand over his mouth, put her arm about his shoulders and guided him up the stairs. She helped to undress him and put him to bed. She knew all the little knacks of doing it: she had learned long ago by caring for his father.

He didn't speak to her again, and buried his face in the pillow, biting into it with his strong, even teeth.

Belowstairs, Mrs. Wilbert Phipps was finishing her paper. "And so," she was saying in the flat voice she adopted for such occasions, "that was the visit that Mr. Phipps and I made to the Mammoth Cave. It was most interesting and not expensive. I advise you ladies all to make it at the earliest opportunity. We can never know enough of the geographical marvels of this, the greatest, freest and most noble nation under the protection of God."

Emma got down just in time. She congratulated Mrs. Phipps on the fascination of her paper, and regretted being able to hear only a little of it, but what she heard made her want to hear more: it was so fascinating. She did not say that the only part she heard was a sentence or two dealing with blind fishes.

It was Aunt Mabelle who "brought Naomi round." She had that quality of soft, insensitive people which, if allowed to expose itself long enough, becomes in the end irresistible. Aunt Mabelle was in her way a philosopher, possessing indeed even the physical laziness which gives birth to reflection. She was neither happy nor unhappy, but lived in a state of strange, cowlike contentment, which knew neither heights nor depressions. She was surprised at nothing, and through her long rocking-chair contemplation upon life and love, birth and death, she had shared the confidences of so many women that such behavior as Naomi's did not strike her as remarkable, but only to be listed in the vast category of human folly.

"Don't think you're remarkable or different," she told Naomi. "You're just like any other woman."

It was Aunt Mabelle who led Naomi into the routine of matrimony as a tried and experienced working elephant leads another, freshly captured, into the routine of piling teak logs and pushing carts. She made it all seem the most natural thing in the world.

But it was only after a week of hiding and of sudden outbursts of tears that Naomi returned to Philip—a new and uncomplaining Naomi curiously broken and acquiescent. Aunt Mabelle noticed the difference with the little round blue eyes that seemed too stupid and sleepy to notice anything; she saw that something very odd had happened to Naomi: nothing that was very odd in her (Mabelle's) experience in such cases, but odd only because it had happened to Naomi. It was as if she had found suddenly some reason for existence in a world where before she had no place, as if she enjoyed this newly discovered marital relationship.

Emma, too, noticed the difference—that Naomi began to take an interest in her appearance, and even went so far as to buy some ribbons and bits of lace which she sewed awkwardly on her somber woolen dresses. Her anemic cheeks at moments even showed the shadow of color. She went almost briskly to her choir rehearsals and made a feeble attempt at resuming her manufacture of calico mother-hubbards.

It was, thought Emma, working itself out. She was not one to discuss such things, and yet she knew that Naomi had followed her advice. Why, Naomi was almost like a bride. She was certain in the end to gain a hold over Philip, for he was not the sort whose eye wandered: he never looked at another woman. He wasn't like his father. Emma told herself these things twenty times a day. (And she knew things which she would never admit knowing.) If things went well, he was certain to come round in the end, for there was nothing like a wife and family to bring a man to his senses. When he was older and perhaps Bishop of East Africa, and the youngest bishop of the church, he would thank his mother for all her strength of will. He would look back and understand then how right she had been at the time when, for a moment, his foot had strayed from the path. Then God would bring her her just reward.

There was one thing she did not understand—the intoxication of Philip. At first she succumbed to righteous fury, filled with a wild desire to punish him by shutting him in the storeroom as she had done when he was a little boy. All the night after she had helped him up the stairs, she lay awake, pondering what she should do. The thing had frightened her in a fashion she did not understand: it was an event which seemed to thrust upward out of the shadowy depths of heritage, imperiling all her carefully made plans. It gave her for the first time a sense of awe for her son, because it opened vistas of behavior of which she did not believe him, a boy so carefully brought up, capable. It was this fear which led her into paths of caution, and prevented her from pouring out a torrent of reproach. When a week passed and then another without any repetition of the disgraceful episode, she settled back into her old sense of confident security. Philip was her boy, after all. She could trust him. And fortunately no one had seen him drunk; no one knew.

But it troubled her that he never spoke of it. His silence hurt her. Always he had told her everything, shared all his secrets and plans with her, and now he shut her out of everything. He was polite and kind to herself and to Naomi, but he never told them anything.

Still, he seemed to be less restless now, even if he was more silent. He was beginning, she thought, to soften a little. In the end, when it was all settled and he had returned to the arms of the Lord, she could perhaps sell her restaurant business and give herself over completely to missionary work and her clubs.

It wasn't that she had given up the idea of matrimony; it was only that she had laid it aside for the moment, since Moses Slade had said nothing in the least definite. He had been encouraging, and very friendly; he had taken her at her word and come to have his meals at the restaurant. On the occasion of his third visit, she said, "Perhaps you'd rather eat in my corner? A man like you, who is so prominent, is always stared at so."

So he had come to take his meals in the corner behind the screen, arriving after one, so that he never interfered with the family lunch of Philip, Naomi and herself. Sometimes she sat with him while he ate great plates of meat and potatoes and huge slices of pies. He was a vigorous man and an enormous eater. They talked usually of politics, and she thought more than once, "Of course, some people might think such a marriage undignified, but it wouldn't matter, because of all the influence I'd have. As the wife of a Congressman in Washington, I'd be a power for good."

They returned sometimes to the subject of their widowhood and loneliness, and once he seemed almost on the verge of speaking, when she was called to the telephone to speak to Mrs. Wilbert Phipps about her paper.

After a time she again urged him not to pay for his meals. It would be a pleasure, she said, to have such a distinguished man as her guest. One meal more or less meant nothing in the ocean of her prosperity. But he was wily and insisted that he could not impose upon her generosity. And then one morning she received from him a letter, saying that he had been called back to Washington suddenly, and would not be able to see her before leaving. He said nothing of marriage; it was a very polite, but a very cautious letter. And Emma resolved to put him out of her mind, and never again to ask him to have his meals at the Peerless Restaurant.

Chapter 15

WHEN PHILIP AWOKE to the sound of the alarm-clock on the night that followed the scene in the hall, he was quite sober again, though his head ached horribly. He was alone in the darkness and suffered from a wretched feeling of shame. It was as if he had plunged into some pit of filth which still clung to him, despite all the washing in the world. It was a conviction of shame, almost of sin, stronger than he had known since, as a little boy, he had listened to one of Emma's terrifying lectures upon purity and the future life. It concerned what had happened on the night before in this very room, it concerned Hennessey's saloon, and the memory of Hennessey's hard voice, "Go on home to your Ma!" and the vague memory of something which had happened in the hall while a voice said something about blindness. He wakened in the exact position in which he had fallen asleep, with his face half buried in the pillows. He was dirty and unshaven. Slowly he remembered the events of the day before, one by one, but, fitting them together, he could not see how they had brought him here, soiled and filled with a sense of horror.

While he dressed, he tried to fathom what it was that had caused a collapse so sudden and complete, and it seemed to him that it all had very little to do with the chain of things that had happened yesterday; it lay deeper than that. It went back and back into the past. There were moments when it seemed to him that he had been moving towards this night ever since he had been born. It was as if he had no power because he did not even know what it was.

At the Mills, Sokoleff and Finke and Krylenko were already by the oven. They greeted him, as they always did, without comment. Of his drunkenness they said nothing, Sokoleff and Finke perhaps because they were themselves too drunk to have noticed it. He had arrived, sober and ashamed, with the fear that they would use it as an excuse of coarse jokes. And now they did not even remember. For them a thing like that was part of the day's business, just as rabbit-like love and its various counterfeits were things which one took for granted.

He didn't talk to them, even while they all sat eating their lunches. It was as if something had robbed him of the very power of speech. And he felt that they were more remote now and strange than they had ever been, even on the first night he had come there to work by the glowing ovens.

Only Krylenko seemed to understand anything at all. He laughed, and said, "You feel pretty bad after yesterday. Well . . . you'll sweat it out. You get over it quick like that. You can drink like a hog but you sweat it all out right away."

He grinned feebly and said nothing, but he remembered what Krylenko had said, "You ain't like those other fellows." It was true: he wasn't like them, and at the moment he wanted to be like them more than all else on earth. It seemed to him that salvation lay in drinking like a hog and living like a rabbit. He couldn't do it, because something walled him in and shut him away from that fierce turbulent current of life which he felt all about him and could never enter. It was the old hunger, more clear now and understandable, which had driven him to the Mills, seizing him on the night he stood on the Hill looking down upon the miraculous beauty of the Flats at night.

He knew now that he wasn't even free. Naomi hadn't freed him after all, and his celebration had been all for nothing, a bitter joke. He was still the same, only with a strange sense of having been soiled. Weary and sick and disgusted, he felt suddenly like a little child who wanted comforting, only it never occurred to him now to turn to his mother as he had once done. Something had happened, some mysterious snapping of the bonds which bound them together. He found himself wishing with a passionate feeling of self-reproach that he might not see her again. It was partly shame and partly because his love for her had vanished in some inexplicable fashion. It struck him with horror that he had no love any longer either for her or for Naomi. The one he respected because he owed her so much: she was so much stronger and more valiant than himself. The other he pitied because he understood through pitying himself that she, too, must be miserable.

He worked on in silence passionately, straining in every muscle, shoving and pushing the hot steel, until the patches of soot in the sides of the shed began to turn gray with the light of dawn. The sweat that streamed down his body seemed in some way to purify his soul, and at last he grew so weary that all his troubles seemed to lose themselves in the terrible heat and clamor of the pounding hammers.

Only one thing remained in his weary mind, and that was a fierce desire to see Mary Conyngham. If he saw her, he would have peace, because she would understand. She seemed to him like a cool lake into which he could plunge, bathing his whole soul, and his body too, for he understood now what love could be if the woman was Mary Conyngham. *Naomi had made a man of him.* . . .

But it was impossible ever to see her again, because he had nothing to offer her. He belonged now to Naomi, beyond all doubt. Naomi was his wife, she might even be the mother of his child. What could he offer to Mary Conyngham?

For Emma had done her work well. Her son *was* a decent sort, and not at all like his father.

In the weeks that followed he did not see Mary Conyngham. As if she had understood what happened during that walk into the open country, she sent him the paints she had bought, with a little note asking him to take them as a present from her on his return from Africa. She sent them to him at the Mills by the hand of Krylenko, and so put an end to the shameful hope that he would see her when she returned. It was marvelous how well she understood, and yet the very knowledge of her understanding made it all the more unbearable, for it was as if she said, "I know what has happened," and tragically, in the voice that seemed so much sadder than it had once been, "There's nothing to be done."

He kept the box of paints and brushes at Krylenko's boarding-house where he came to be regarded with a kind of awe by the Ukrainians as an odd mixture of artist and lunatic. Without thinking why, he kept the whole affair a secret from Naomi and his mother. He told them that the afternoons when he worked, painting and rubbing out, painting and rubbing out, among the rows of dirty houses, were spent in walking or doing extra work at the Mills. It became slowly a sort of passion into which he poured his whole existence. It was only in those hours when he worked horribly to put on bits of canvas and wood that strange, smoky glamour which he found in the Flats, that he was able to forget Mary Conyngham and the dull sordid sense of uneasiness which enveloped all his existence in the slate-colored house. No one save Krylenko saw anything he painted, and Krylenko liked it all, good, bad and indifferent, with all the overwhelming vitality of his friendly nature. (He had come in a way to treat Philip as a child under his special protection.) Sometimes he puzzled his head over the great messes of black and gray and blue, but he saw, oddly enough, what Philip was driving at.

"Yes," he'd say, rubbing his nose with his huge hands. "It's like that . . . that's the way it *feels*. That's what you're after, ain't it?"

He never went again to Hennessey's saloon, although the memory of Hennessey's epithet clung and rankled in his brain. "I don't want to get mixed up with that hell-cat." He could, he thought, go and shoot Hennessey, but no good would come of it; nothing would be accomplished, and life would only become more horrible and complicated. He couldn't fight Hennessey, for the Irishman could break him across his knee. Once, a long while ago, when he was a boy, he would have flung himself at Hennessey, kicking and biting and punching, to avenge the insult to his mother, but all that seemed to belong vaguely to another life which no longer had anything to do with him. The epithet festered in his brain because there were times when it led to horrible doubts about his mother—that perhaps she wasn't, after all, so good and noble and self-sacrificing. It gave him a sudden, terrifying glimpse of what she must seem to others outside that circle in which she moved and had her whole existence. But that was only because they didn't know her as he knew her . . . for the good woman she was. At moments he even felt a fierce resentment toward her because she stood somehow between him and that rich savor of life which he felt all about him. If she had not existed he could have gone to Hennessey's place as much as he liked, drinking as much as he pleased. He could have come nearer to Sokoleff and Finke and even Krylenko.

She must be a powerful woman when a man like Hennessey feared her. . . . Hennessey, he thought sometimes, who was like some beast out of that other cruel jungle at Megambo.

As he lost himself more and more deeply in the effort to catch in color the weird fascination of the world about him, the anguish of the life at Megambo began to fade into the shadows of the existence which had belonged to that other Philip, who began to seem so strange and distant. Sometimes, the sight of his mother returning from church, or the sound of Naomi pounding the tinny piano and singing revival hymns in her loud voice (as if she were trying to recapture some of her past glory), brought to his mind a sharp picture of the other Philip, pale and shy and silent, dressed always in dark clothes—a Philip who worshipped a mother who was never wrong and respected a wife who had no fear of the jungle; and the picture gave him an odd flash of pity, as if the image had been that of some stranger. His life now wasn't exactly happy, but it was better than the life of that other Philip, for now he stood with his feet fairly planted on the ground; it was an existence that was real, in which he was aware of a sinfulness that was really a temptation toward sin. He wasn't tortured any longer by battling with shadows. There were times when he was forced to laugh (a trifle bitterly) at the memory of a Philip who had suffered at his own doubts and agonies over the awful prospect of turning his back upon the church. It was finished, but no one would believe him, no one, except Mary Conyngham.

He came to accept the attentions of Naomi, for he could not see what else there was to do, and after a time it became a relationship which he managed to fit into the scheme of things as he went to work seven days a week and ate three meals a day; but there was no joy in it, save that obscure satisfaction which came of knowing that like other men he had a woman who belonged to him.

They never spoke of it to each other: it was a thing which happened silently in the night, as if they both were ashamed, and afterward Philip still had the strange feeling that in some way he had been soiled. It was, after all, exactly such a relationship as he might have had with any of the women in Franklin Street. If it was different, it was only because Naomi was in love with him, and this love of hers sometimes frightened him, because it made him more than ever her prisoner. There sometimes came into her eyes that same look of shining rapture that he had seen there in the days when she was giving her life to God at Megambo. You could see it in the way she watched him. Yet the word love had never been spoken between them, and the possibility of children had never been uttered.

It was as if all her adoration of God had been turned upon Philip.

Presently he began to drink, taking a glass on his way to work, and another on his way home, but he did not go to drink with any of the men from his own furnace. He did not go to Hennessey's; he went to a saloon where the back room was filled with Polish girls and no one had ever heard of Emma. The whisky made him feel jolly and forget the slate-colored house. He got there the feeling that he was himself, Philip Downes, for the first time in his life, as if at last he had been completely born. No one in the place had ever heard of the other Philip. It was only an illusion which came to him while the alcohol had possession of his brain, and so he came to drink more and more regularly because it made him happy. With a glass or two he was able to forget the life he shared with Naomi.

Chapter 16

HE WAS SITTING one afternoon in Krylenko's room working on a view of the Flats which included the oily creek, a row of battered houses, and a glimpse of furnaces. For two days he had worked on it, and out of the lines and color there began to emerge something which he recognized with a faint sense of excitement as the thing he had been searching for. It grew slowly with each stroke of the brush, a quality which he could not have described, but something which he felt passionately. He was beginning a little to succeed, to do something which he would want to show, not to the world, but to . . . to . . . Mary Conyngham. He would send it to her as a gift, without a word. Certainly she wouldn't mind that. She would understand it as she understood all else. As he worked, his passion for painting and his love for Mary Conyngham became in a strange fashion blended and inextricable. It was as if he were talking to her with the line and color, telling her all the choked, overpowering, hot emotions that were kindled when he thought of her.

Presently, as the light began to fail, he put down his brushes, and, taking up his worn coat and hat, he closed the door to return to the slate-colored house. In that sudden exultation, even the prospect of encountering Naomi did not depress him. Feeling his way along the greasy hallway smelling of boiled cabbage and onions, he descended the stairs and stepped into the street. It was that hour between daylight and darkness, when sharp contours lose their hard angles, and ugliness fades mysteriously into beauty—the hour in the Flats when all the world changed magically from the squalor of daylight into the glowing splendor of the night.

Outside, the street was alive with dirty, underfed children. There seemed to be myriads of them, all drawn like moths out of the darkness towards the spots of light beneath each street-lamp. A great, ugly Ukrainian sat on the steps rocking gently and playing a Little Russian song on a wheezy concertina.

For a moment, while Philip stood in the shadow of the doorway, looking down the long vista of the hot, overcrowded street, he felt again the old, poignant sense of the richness, the color that was born simply out of being allowed to live. And then suddenly he became aware of a familiar presence close at hand, of a voice heard in the twilight above the clamor of children, which made him feel suddenly ill.

Before the doorway of the next house he could see the dim figure of Irene Shane, a pale gray figure which seemed at times almost a ghost. The other woman he could not see in the hard reality, but he saw with all the painful clearness of an image called up by the sound of her soft voice. It was Mary Conyngham calling on some sick baby. He listened, hiding in the shadow, while a Polish woman talked to her in broken English. Then suddenly she turned away and with Irene Shane passed so near to the doorway that he could have touched her.

She was gone, quickly, lost in the crowd. He hadn't run after her and cried out what was in his heart, because he was afraid. His whole body was shaking; and he burned with a fire that was at once agony and delight, for the thing that had happened with Naomi made this other pain the more real and terrible.

For ten minutes he sat on the step of Krylenko's boarding-house, his head in his hands. When at last he rose to climb the hill, all the sense of exhilaration had flowed away, leaving him limp and exhausted. For weeks he had worked twelve hours a day in the Mills, painted while there was still daylight, and slept the little time that remained; and now he knew suddenly that he was horribly tired. His body that was so hard and supple seemed to have grown soft and heavy, his legs were like sacks of potatoes. Near the top of the hill, before the undertaking parlor of McTavish, he felt so ill that he had suddenly to sit down. And while he sat there he understood, with a cold horror, what had happened to him. It was the Megambo fever coming back. The street began to lose its colors, and fade into shadows of yellow before his eyes.

Behind him the door opened, and he heard a booming voice asking, "Anything the matter, Philip? You look sick."

Philip told McTavish what it was, and felt a feeble desire to laugh at the thought of being succored by the undertaker.

"I know," said McTavish. "It used to come back on me in the same way. I got a touch of it in Nicaragua, when I was a boy." Here he halted long enough to grunt, for he had bent down and was lifting Philip in his corpulent embrace bodily from the steps. He chuckled, "I was a wild 'un then. It's only since I got so damned fat that the fever left me."

He put Philip in one of the chairs before the stove. There was no fire in it now, but the door was left open for the old rips to spit into the ashes.

"You look sick—yellow as paint."

Philip tried to grin and began to shiver.

"It's nothing. I've often felt like this." The memory of the old fever took possession of him, setting his teeth on edge at the thought of the chill-hot horrors and all the phantasmagoria of jungle life which it invoked. Out of the terror of sickness, one thought remained clear—that perhaps this was the best way out of everything, to die here in the chair and let McTavish prepare what remained of him for the grave. He wouldn't then be a nuisance to any one, and Naomi, free, could go back to Megambo.

McTavish was pouring whisky down his throat, saying, "That'll make you stop shaking." And slowly warmth began to steal back. He felt dizzy, but a little stronger.

"I'll take you home," said McTavish, standing off and looking at him. "You know a fellow like you oughtn't to be working in the Mills. Why, man, you're thin as a fence-rail. I've been watching you when you went past—getting thinner and thinner every day. And you're beginning to look like an old man. A fellow of your age ought to be getting drunk and giving the girls a time. I wish to God I was twenty-six again."

He finished with a great booming laugh, which was meant to be reassuring, but which Philip, even through the haze of illness, knew was meant to hide his alarm. He gave Philip another drink, and asked suddenly, "What's the matter with you, anyway? There's something wrong. Why, any fool can see that." Philip didn't answer him, and he added, "You don't mean to go back to Africa. That's it, ain't it? I guessed that long ago, in spite of everything your Ma had to say. Well, if you was to go back like this, it'd be the end of you, and I propose telling your Ma so. I knew her well enough when she was a girl, though we don't hold much with one another now."

Philip suddenly felt too ill to speak to any one, to explain anything. McTavish had lifted him up and was carrying him toward the door, "Why you don't weigh no more than a woman—and a little woman at that."

He felt himself being lifted into McTavish's buggy. The fat man kept one arm about him, and with the other drove the horses, which on occasions pulled his hearse. At length, after what seemed to Philip hours, they drew up before the slate-colored house.

It was Emma herself who opened the door. McTavish, the debaucher of young men, she saw, had got Philip drunk, and was delivering him to her like a corpse.

"What does this mean?" she asked.

Philip managed to say feebly, "I haven't been drinking."

McTavish, still carrying him, forced his way past her into the hall. "Where do you want to put him? You've got a pretty sick boy here, and the sooner you know it the better."

They carried him upstairs and laid him on his and Naomi's bed. Naomi was in the room, and Mabelle was with her, and as they entered, she got up with a wild flutter of alarm, while McTavish explained. Philip asked for water, which Naomi went to fetch, and McTavish led Emma with him into the hall.

Downstairs, they faced each other—two middle-aged people, born to be enemies by every facet of their characters; yet, oddly enough, McTavish had once been a suitor for Emma's hand in those far-off days when Emma had chosen such a hopeless mate as Jason Downes. Sometimes, drawing deep out of his own experience, the philosophic McTavish had wondered how on earth he had ever fallen in love with Emma, or how she had come to be in turn the abject slave of such an amiable scamp as Downes. It made no sense, that thing which got hold of you, brain and body, in such a tyrannical fashion. (He was thinking all this again, as he stood facing the ruffled Emma beneath the cold glow of the green Moorish light.)

"Look here, Em," he was saying, "that boy has got to have a little peace. You let him alone for a time."

"What do you mean? What does a man like you, John McTavish, know about such things?"

The fat undertaker saw in a swift flash that the invincible Emma was not only ruffled, but frightened.

"Well, you know what I mean. The boy ain't like you. That's where you've always made a mistake, Em . . . in thinking everybody is like yourself. He's a bundle of nerves—that boy—and sensitive. Anybody with half an eye can see it."

"I ought to know my boy." She began to grow dramatic. "My own flesh . . . that I gave birth to . . . I ought to know what's good for him, without having to be told."

McTavish remained calm, save for an odd wave of hatred for this woman he had desired thirty years ago. "That's all right. You ought to know, Em, but you don't. You'd better let him alone . . . or you'll be losing him . . . too."

The last word he uttered after a little pause, as if intentionally he meant to imply things about the disappearance and death of Mr. Downes. She started to speak, and then, thinking better of it, checked herself, buttoned her lips tightly, and opened the front door with an ominous air.

"No, I ain't going till I've finished," he was saying. "I know you, Em. I've known you a long time, and I'm telling you that if you love that boy you'll stop tormenting him . . . you'll do it for your own good. If he gets well, I think I'll take a hand myself."

He went through the door, but Emma remained there, looking after the fat, solid form until it climbed into the buggy, and drove off, the vehicle swaying and rocking beneath the weight of his three hundred odd pounds.

She was frightened, for she felt the earth slipping away from under her feet as it had done once before, a long time ago. The whole affair was slipping away, out of her control. It was like finding herself suddenly in quicksand.

Upstairs in the darkened room, Aunt Mabelle, left alone with Philip, pulled her rocking-chair to the side of the bed. She had news, she thought, which would cheer him, perhaps even make him feel better.

"Philip," she said softly. "Philip." He turned his head, and she continued, "Philip, I've got good news for you. Are you listening?"

Philip nodded weakly.

"Naomi is going to have a little baby . . . a little baby. Think of that!" She waited, and Philip said nothing. He did not even move.

"Aren't you glad, Philip? Think of it . . . a little baby."

He whispered, "Yes . . . of course . . . I'm glad," and turned his face into the pillow once more.

Aunt Mabelle, excited by her news, went on, "You won't have to wait long, because she's already about four months along. She didn't want to talk about it. She wasn't even sure what was the matter, but I dragged it out of her. I thought she was looking kind of peaked."

Then the door opened, and Emma and Naomi came in together. Naomi crossed to the bed, and, bending over Philip, said, "Here's the water, Philip." He stirred and she put her arm under his head while he drank. It seemed to him that all his body was alive with fire.

When he had finished, Naomi did an extraordinary thing. She flung herself down and burying her head against his thin chest, she began to sob wildly, crying out, shamelessly before Emma and Mabelle, "You mustn't be sick, Philip. You mustn't die . . . I couldn't live without you now. You're all I've got. . . . No . . . no . . . you mustn't die." She clung to him with terrifying and shameless passion. "I couldn't live without you . . . I couldn't . . . I couldn't . . . I'll never . . . leave you." Her long, pale hair came unfastened and fell about her shoulders, covering them both. "I'll never leave you. I'll do whatever you want."

It was Emma who seized her by force and dragged her off him; Emma who, shaking her, said in a voice that was horrible in its hatred, "You fool! Do you want to make him worse? Do you want to kill him?"

And Naomi cried out, "He's mine now. He's mine! You tried to poison him against me. You can't take him away from me any more. He belongs to me!"

It was horrible, but to Philip the scene had no reality; it came to him through the haze of his fever, as if it had been only an interlude of delirium.

When Naomi grew a little more calm, Aunt Mabelle said to her in a whisper, "I told him."

Naomi, still sobbing, asked, "Was he glad?"

"As pleased as Punch," said Aunt Mabelle. "It always pleases a man. It makes him feel big."

On the bed Philip lay shivering and burning. The room appeared to swell to an enormous size and then slowly to contract again till it was no bigger than a coffin. After a time, it seemed to him that he was already dead and that the three women who moved about the room, undressing him, fussing with the window-curtain, talking and sobbing, were simply three black figures preparing him for the grave. A faint haze of peace settled slowly over him. He would be able to rest now. He would never see them again. He was free.

Chapter 17

IT WAS NOT, after all, the old Megambo fever, but typhoid which had been lurking for months in the filth of the Flats. Irene Shane knew of it and Mary Conyngham and one or two doctors who were decent enough to take cases for which there was little chance either of pay or glory. It was typhoid that had brought Mary and Irene to talk to the Polish woman in the doorway next to Krylenko's boarding-house. Typhoid was a word that existed in an aura of terror; a disease which might strike any of the Hill people. So long as it happened in the Flats (and the fever lurked there winter and summer) it did not matter. But with Philip it struck at the people on the hills. The news spread quickly. There was another case and then another and another. The newspapers began to talk of it and suddenly the Town learned that there were sixty cases in the Flats and that eleven Hunkies and Dagoes were already dead.

When Emma first heard that the illness was typhoid, she snorted and said, "Of course! What could you expect? He got it working in the Flats among those Hunkies and Dagoes. They throw all their slops right into the streets. They ought to be shut off and a wall placed around them. They always have typhoid down there. Some day they'll have a real epidemic and then people will wake up to what it means—bringing such animals into a good clean country!"

The doctors, summoned by Emma in her terror, told her that Philip's case was doubly serious because he had already had fever twice in Megambo and because his whole body was thin and sick. He fell into a state of stupor and remained thus. He seemed to have no resistance.

For days terror racked Emma and Naomi. Each of them prayed, secretly and passionately, begging God to spare the life of the man who became suddenly the only possession in the world which they cherished. And out of their fight there was born a kind of hostility which made their earlier distrust of each other fade into oblivion. There were hours and days when they scarcely addressed each other, when it seemed that the slightest disagreement might hurl them into open warfare. Mabelle was always in the house, moving about, comforting Naomi and exasperating Emma by her sloppy ways.

Indeed, the perpetual sight of Mabelle and her squalid overfed brat in her neat house filled Emma with a distaste to be equaled only by such a calamity as the discovery of vermin in one of her beds. But she found herself suddenly delivered into Mabelle's hands; for Mabelle was the only person who could "do anything with" Naomi. If Emma approached her, she grew tense and hysterical. And it was, of course, impossible to think of ridding herself of both: you couldn't turn from your home the woman who was to be the mother of your grandchild.

Mabelle she hated, too, for her passionate and morbid absorption in the subjects of love and childbirth; she seemed to Emma to stand as a symbol of obscenity, who must as such have tortured her brother Elmer. She was a symbol of all that side of life which Emma had succeeded in putting out of her mind for so many years.

But there was one other person who had the power of calming Naomi. This was the Reverend Castor, who, since Naomi's condition prevented her from appearing in the choir, came himself two or three times a week to comfort her and inquire after her husband. Except for Mabelle, he seemed to be Naomi's only friend.

"He is," she told Emma, "a very sympathetic man, and he reminds me of my father. He is just the same build and bald in the same way."

The Reverend Castor had a beautiful voice, low and mellow and filled with rich inflections which Mrs. Wilbert Phipps had once spoken of as an "Æolian harp." He could have had, people said, a great success as an Evangelist, but he was so devoted to his bedridden wife that he would not leave her, even for such a career. The church, they said, was indeed fortunate to keep him, even though it was at the price of his own misfortune. Words of condolence and courage spoken in the rich voice had a strange power of rousing the emotions. Once or twice Emma had come upon him sitting in the twilight of the parlor talking to Naomi of illness and faith, of death and fortitude, in so moving a fashion that the tears came into her eyes and a lump into her throat. And he was a good man—a saint. One felt it while talking to him. He was a man who believed, and had devoted his whole life to the care of a sick wife.

Sometimes Mabelle lingered long after the hour when she should have been in her kitchen preparing supper for Elmer. There were in the Reverend Castor's voice intimations of things which she had never found in her own chilly husband.

As Naomi's time drew nearer, the conversation of Mabelle grew proportionately more and more obstetrical.

They compared symptoms and Mabelle's talk was constantly sprinkled with such remarks as, "When I was carrying Jimmy," or, "When Ethel was under way." She even gave it as her opinion that Naomi, from the symptoms, might be having twins.

She appeared to have a strange, demoralizing effect upon Naomi, for the girl came presently to spend all the day in a wrapper, never bothering to dress when she rose. And Emma discovered that for days at a time she did not even trouble to take off the metal bands which she used for curling her long, straight hair. The two of them sat all day long in rocking-chairs while little Jimmy, who was beginning to walk a little, crept from one piece of furniture to another. He had already ruined one corner of the Brussels carpet in the parlor.

Meanwhile, in the great walnut bed Philip lay more dead than alive. There were long periods when he recognized no one and simply lay as if made of stone, white, transparent, with a thin, pinched look about the temples. The lines seemed to have faded from his face, giving him a pathetic, boyish look. The only life lingered in the great dark eyes which in his fever were larger and more burning than ever. The doctors who came and went sometimes shook their heads and expressed belief that if the patient could be got to show any interest in the life about him there was hope. But he appeared to have no desire to recover. Even in those moments when his wife gave way and, weeping, had to be taken from the room, he only stared at her without speaking.

Failing to take into account the terrible vitality which came to him from Emma and the toughness of that father whom none of them had ever seen, they marveled that he could go on living at all. Yet week after week passed when he grew no better or worse. None of them knew, of course, about Mary Conyngham and how the thought of her sometimes came to him and filled him with a fierce desire to live. When his sick brain cleared for a little while, he knew with a strange certainty that he could not die leaving her behind, because in some way life would be left incomplete. It was a thought which troubled him, as he was troubled when he could not get a picture to come right because he was not yet a good painter.

And then one day Emma's own doctor took her aside in the hall and said, "There's one thing you must understand, Mrs. Downes. No matter how much your son wants to return to Africa, you mustn't let him go. If he gets well and tries to go back, it will be the end of him. I know he'll want to go back, but it'll be suicide to send him where there's fever."

When the doctor had gone, Emma put on her hat and jacket and went for a walk. It was a thing she never did, for there were no moments in her busy life to be wasted simply in walking; but there seemed no other way to find solitude in a world filled with Naomi and Mabelle, little Jimmy and the trained nurse. She had to be alone, to think things out.

She saw clearly enough that, whatever happened, there was now no chance of Philip's going back to Africa and the knowledge filled her with a blank, inexplicable feeling of frustration. But after she had grown more calm, she began to feel more like herself and thus more able to cope with her troubles.

Philip could not go back, and he was to have a child. But if he could not go back to duty, neither, she saw, must he be allowed to return to the Flats. The one, surely, was just as dangerous as the other, and the Mills carried with them a sense of failure and disgrace. No, up to now she had been patient in the belief that he would return to his senses; but the time for patience had passed.

The old feeling of her own strength and righteousness began to return to her in great surging waves of confidence.

John McTavish! What did he know of her husband's weakness? Or Philip's weakness? How could he know that both of them were the sort who had to be guided? John McTavish! (She snorted at the thought.) A waster, a vulgar man, about whom gathered the riffraff of the Town. What had he ever done for the good of any one?

She had a sudden desire to see Moses Slade. Somehow she felt he'd understand her problem and approve her strong attitude. There was a man who did things. A distinguished man! A man who'd made his mark! Not a good-for-nothing like John McTavish.

The old possibility of marrying Moses Slade kept stealing back over her. Through pride and a faint sense of being a woman rejected, she tried not to think of it, but it was no good trying to put it out of her mind because it was always stealing back upon her unawares. Perhaps if she sent him a postcard, a pretty view of the new park, it would serve to remind him of her without being, properly speaking, a piece of forwardness. The temptation kept pricking her. It would be splendid to be the wife of a Congressman, and it would solve the difficulty of Philip. She could turn over the restaurant to him and Naomi.

Nearly two hours passed before she returned to the house, but in that time all life seemed to have become subdued and conquered once more. It had all been worked out. She sat down at once and wrote a perfectly impersonal message to Congressman Slade on the back of a picture postcard of the new monument to General Tecumseh Sherman that adorned dubiously the new park. On the way to the restaurant she posted it. As she left the house she heard Naomi sobbing alone in the corner of the darkened parlor, and a great wave of contempt swept over her for people who were not strong enough to manage their own lives.

On the same night the Reverend Castor led his congregation, or a fraction of it, in addressing to the Lord words of supplication and entreaty on behalf of "their brother Philip Downes, who lay at the point of death." He begged that Philip, who had sacrificed his health, might be spared "to carry on the noble work among the black and sinful children of the great African continent."

As he prayed, with arms extended and face upturned to heaven, the fine nose, the shapely dome of his head and imposing expanse of his chest, took on a classic, moving dignity. As the sonorous voice, trembling with emotion, rolled over the heads of his flock more than one woman felt herself slipping dimly into the grip of strange disturbing emotions.

He prayed longer than usual, painting for the Lord a moving and luxurious picture of the trials suffered by His servant; in Old Testament phrases he finished by calling the attention of God to the suffering of Naomi, who sat at home, ill herself, praying for the life of the husband she loved with such noble and selfless devotion.

When he had finished, there were tears in all eyes, and Emma, seated near the back, was sobbing in a warm mist of suffering and glory. In some way his eloquence had purified them all. It was as if each one of them had passed with Philip through the flame of suffering. They felt purged and clean and full of noble thoughts, almost ready at last to enter the Kingdom of Heaven.

The sound of "Amens!" trembled in the air and before it had died away completely, Miss Swarmish, an old maid with a mustache, struck out several loud chords on the tinny piano and in her booming voice led them in singing, *Throw Out the Life Line!* They sang with militant enthusiasm, their voices echoing in the vast, damp basement of the church. It was an oblique glorification of Philip, the renegade, who lay unconscious in the slate-colored house. It was as if they, too, were forcing him back.

When they had finished the orgy of music and the Benediction was spoken, the usual stir was silenced suddenly by Emma's rich voice. She had risen to her feet at the back of the room and was standing with her hands clasped on the back of the chair before her.

"Brothers and sisters," she was saying, in a voice rich with emotion, "I know that all of you feel for me in the illness of my son. I have felt for some time that I should speak to you about him" (here, overcome by feeling, she coughed and hesitated) "to make an answer to the talk that has come to my ear from time to time. I feel that to-night—to-night is the time—the occasion ordained by God. I have very little to say. You know that his health has been wrecked forever by his work among our ignorant, sinful brothers in Africa. He is lying at the point of death. Your prayers have touched me to the depths of my heart, and if it is God's will, surely they will help towards his recovery." (Here she hesitated once more.) "People wondered why he came back. It was because his health was ruined. People wondered why he went into the Flats to work. It was because he wanted to know the life there. He has been through a great spiritual struggle. He fell ill because he was tormented by the wish to go back to his post, to those ignorant black men who live in darkness. If he recovers . . ." (her voice broke suddenly) "if he recovers . . . he can never go back. The doctors have told me that it would be nothing short of suicide. He has given his health, perhaps his life, in carrying forward our great purpose of sending the light to heathen."

She hesitated for a moment as if she meant to say more, and then sat down abruptly, too overcome for speech. For a moment there was silence, and then one by one women began to gather about her, sobbing, to offer comfort. It was a touching scene, in which Emma managed to control herself after a time. Surrounding her, they moved out of the church in a sort of phalanx. Two or three of them even followed her a little way down the street. But it was her brother, Elmer, who accompanied her home. In his stiff, cold way he proposed to let bygones be bygones.

"At a time like this," he said, "it's not right for a brother and sister to quarrel." And then, after an awkward silence, "I've no doubt that when Philip is well again, he'll come to his senses and behave himself."

He stopped at the slate-colored house for Aunt Mabelle, who had come over to sit with Naomi, and before they left, all of them, even Naomi, seemed to have changed in some way, to have grown more cheerful, as if the Heavenly joy of the prayer-meeting still clung like perfume to their very garments. Things, they all felt, were beginning to work themselves out.

Chapter 18

WHEN HE HAD CLOSED the roll-top desk in his study and locked the door after him, the Reverend Castor turned his steps toward the parsonage, still lost in the exalted mood which, descending miraculously upon the congregation, had risen to a climax in the noble words of Mrs. Downes. There was a lump in his throat when he thought of the goodness of women like her. She'd had a hard life, bringing up her boy, feeding and clothing him, and finding time, nevertheless, to care for his soul and give herself to church work. It was women like her who helped you to keep your faith, no matter what discouragements arose.

For a moment, a suspicion of disloyalty colored his meditations and he thought, "If I had only been blessed with a wife like Emma Downes!"

But quickly he stifled the thought, for such wickedness came to him far too often, especially in the moments when he relaxed and allowed his mind to go its own way. The thing seemed always to be lying in wait, like a crouching animal stealing upon him unawares. "If only I'd had some other woman for a wife!" The thing had grown bolder and more frequent as the years piled up. He would be fifty years old in another month. It kept pressing in upon him like the pain of an aching tooth. Soon he'd be too old to care. And he would die, having missed something which other men knew. He was growing older every day, every minute, every second . . . older, older, older.

In a sudden terror, he began to repeat one of the Psalms in order to clear his mind and put to rout the grinning, malicious thought. He said the Psalm over three times, and then found that God had sent him strength. Walking the dark, silent street, he told himself that there were others far worse off than he. There was poor Naomi Downes with the husband she worshipped dying hourly, day and night, in the very house with her. She, too, had courage, though she wasn't as strong as her mother-in-law. She wasn't perhaps as fine a character as Emma, but there was something more appealing about her, a weakness and a youth that touched your pity. It was terrible to see a young girl like that with her husband dying and a baby coming on. He remembered that he must go again to-morrow and pray with her. It was odd (he thought) how little prayer seemed to comfort her—a girl like that who was a missionary and the daughter of missionaries. He must have a talk with her and try to help her. . . . She seemed to be losing her great faith. . . .

He was on the front porch of the parsonage now, turning his key in the lock, and something of the wild emotion of the prayer-meeting still clung to him. It had been a glorious success. He was still thinking of Naomi as he closed the door, and heard a whining voice from the top of the stairs.

"Is that you, Samuel?"

He waited for a moment and then answered, "Yes, my dear."

"What kept you so late? I've been frightened to death. The house was full of noises and I heard some one walking about in the parlor."

"We prayed for Philip Downes," he said, turning out the light.

The whining voice from above-stairs took on an acid edge. "And you never thought about your poor suffering wife at home all alone. I suppose it never occurs to you to pray for *me!*"

He stood in the darkness, waiting, unwilling to climb the stairs until her complaints had worn themselves out. The voice again: "Samuel, are you there?"

"Yes, Annie."

"Why don't you answer me? Isn't it enough to have to lie here helpless and miserable?"

"I was turning out the light."

"Well, I want the hot-water bottle. You'll have to heat water. And make it hot, not just lukewarm. It's worse again. It's never been so bad."

As he went off to the kitchen, fragments of her plaints followed him: "I should think you'd have remembered about the hot-water bottle!" And, "If you'd had such pain as mine for fifteen years. . . ."

Yes, fifteen years!

For fifteen years it had been like this. The old wicked thought came stealing back into his mind. If only he had a wife like Emma Downes or her daughter-in-law, Naomi . . . some one young like Naomi. He was growing older, older, older. . . .

He began again to repeat the Psalm, saying it aloud while he waited by the stove for the kettle to boil.

Chapter 19

IN THE FLATS the number of deaths began to mount one by one with the passing of each day. When disease appeared in any of the black, decaying houses, it had its way, taking now a child, now a wife, now a husband, for bodies that were overworked and undernourished had small chance of life in a region where the very air stank and the only stream was simply an open sewer. Doctors came and went, sometimes too carelessly, for there was small chance of pay, and to the people on the Hill the life of a worker was worth little. The creatures of the Flats were somehow only a sort of mechanical animal which produced and produced and went on producing.

The churches went on sending missionaries and money to the most remote corners of the earth; the clergymen prayed for the safety of their own flocks, while their congregations sat frightened and resentful, believing that somehow the people in the Flats had caused the catastrophe. It could not be (they reasoned) that God would send such a calamity upon a Town so God-fearing.

Irene Shane and Mary Conyngham closed their school because there was no longer any time to teach when people were ill and dying to right and left. Mary sat night after night at the beds of the dying. She saw one of Finke's thirteen children die and then another and another. She listened to his cursing and drunken talk of revolution, and all the while she knew bitterly enough that those of the family who remained would be happier because they would have more to eat.

The Mills went on pounding and pounding; they were building new furnaces and new sheds. There seemed no end to it. It did not matter if people in the Flats died like flies, because there were always more where they came from—hordes of men and women and children who came filled with glorified hopes to this new country.

One day Mary read in the papers that the man who owned the Mills, himself a German immigrant, had built himself a marble palace on Fifth Avenue and would now divide his time between Pittsburgh and New York. He was becoming a gentleman: he had engaged an expert, a cultivated man of taste, to fill his New York house with pictures brought from Europe. The Town *Gazette* printed an editorial drawing a moral from the career of the great magnate. See what could be done in this great land of God-given opportunity! A man who had begun as an immigrant. But it said nothing of the foundations on which the marble palace rested. It appeared to have arisen miraculously with the aid and sanction of God, innocent of all connection with the stinking Flats.

Mary, watching the spectacle about her, felt her heart turning to stone. If she was to be saved from bitterness, it would only be, she believed, through the touching faith of the ignorant wretches about her. She came to feel a sympathy for the cursing of a man like Finke: she herself even wanted at times to curse. She understood the sullen drunkenness of men like Sokoleff. What else was there for them to do? Something—perhaps a sense of dull misery, perhaps a terror of death—had slowly softened their resentment toward herself and Irene Shane. Once they had been looked upon as intruders come down from the Hills to poke about in filthy hallways and backyards filled with piles of rubbish and rows of privies. But it was no longer possible to doubt them. The two women, gently bred and fastidious, slept night after night at the school in the midst of the Flats. They sat up night after night by the beds of the dying.

There were times when Mary wondered why Irene Shane poured out all her strength in succoring these wretched people. She sensed deep in Irene a strange kind of unearthly mysticism which made her seem at times stubborn and irritable. It was a mysticism strangely akin to that groping hunger which had always tormented Philip. The likeness came to her suddenly one night as she sat by the bed of one of Finke's dying children. It seemed to her a strange and inexplicable likeness in people so different. Yet it was true—they were both concerned with shadowy problems of faith and service to God which never troubled the more practical Mary. And Irene, she fancied, was prey to a sense of atonement, as if she must in some way answer to God for the wickedness of a father long dead and a sister who was, as the Town phrased it, "not all she should have been." There was, too, that hard, bitter old woman who lay dying and never left Shane's Castle—old Julia Shane, the queen ant of all the swarming hive.

As for herself, Mary knew well enough why she had come to work in the Flats: she had come in order to bury herself in some task so mountainous and hopeless that it would help her to forget the aching hurt made by John Conyngham's behavior with Mamie Rhodes. It required a cure far more vigorous even than a house and two children to make her forget a thing like that.

She had been, people said, a fool to put up with such behavior. But what was she to do? There were the children and there was her own devotion to John Conyngham, a thing which he had thrown carelessly aside. It wasn't even as if you suffered in secret: in the Town a thing like that couldn't be kept a secret. The very newsboys knew of it. She had found a sort of salvation in working with Irene Shane. People said she was crazy, a woman with two small children, to go about working among Hunkies and Dagoes; but she took good care of her children, too, and she supplied the people in the Flats with what no amount of such mystical devotion as Irene Shane could supply: she had a sound practical head.

She was an odd girl (she thought) when you came to consider it, with a kind of curse on her. She had to have some one to whom she could give herself up completely, pouring out all the soul in a fantastic devotion. John Conyngham had tired of it, perhaps (she sometimes thought) because he was a cold, hard, sensual man who had no need for such a thing. A woman like Mamie Rhodes (she thought bitterly) suited him better. If she had been married to Philip, who needed it so pathetically. . . .

In the long nights of vigil, she thought round and round in circles, over the same paths again and again. . . . And before many nights had passed she found herself coming back always to the thing she knew and tried constantly to forget . . . that it had been Philip whom she loved always, since those very first days in the tree-house. It seemed to her that at twenty-eight her life, save for her children, was already at an end. She was a widow with only memories of an unhappy married life behind her and nothing to hope for in the future. Philip was married and, so Krylenko told her, about to have a child of his own. She didn't even know whether he even thought of her. And yet, she told herself, fiercely, *she did know*. He had belonged to her always, and she knew it more than ever while they had sat on the bridge, during that solitary walk into the open country.

Philip was *hers*, and he was such a fool that he would never know it. He was always lost in mooning about things that didn't matter. *She* could save him: she could set straight his muddles and moonings. He needed some one who thought less of God and more of making a good pie and keeping his socks darned.

She herself had never thought much about God save when her children were born and her husband died, and even then she had been only brushed by a consciousness of some vast and overwhelming personal force. Life, even with its pain, seemed a satisfactory affair: there was always so much to be done, and it wasn't God that Philip needed but pies and socks and a woman who believed in him.

She knew every day whether he was better or worse and she found herself, for the first time in all her life, praying to God to spare his life. She didn't know whether there was a God or whether He would listen to one who only petitioned when she was in need, but she prayed none the less, believing that if there *was* any God, He would understand why it was she turned to Him. If He did not understand, she told herself rebelliously, then He was not worthy of existing as God.

She did not go to the slate-colored house, though she did ask for news on one occasion when she met Emma in the street. She understood that Emma had resented her friendship for Philip, even when they were children, and so avoided seeming to show any great interest. But she heard, nevertheless, sometimes from Krylenko who had even gone to the door to inquire, and sometimes from the doctor, but most of the time it was McTavish who kept her informed.

McTavish was the only person whom she suspected of guessing her secret. After she had stopped day after day at his undertaking-parlors, he looked at her sharply one day out of his humorous little blue eyes, and said, "If Philip gets better, we've got to help him." Then he hesitated for a moment and added, "Those two women are very bad for him."

He was, she understood, feeling his way. When she agreed, by not protesting, he went on, "You ought to have married him, Mary, when you had a chance."

"I never had a chance."

"I thought perhaps you had. . . . I understand. She began her dirty work too soon."

Mary knew well enough whom he meant by "she." It struck her that he seemed to hate Emma Downes with an extraordinary intensity.

"Still it may work out yet," he said. "Sometimes things like that are a little better for waiting."

She did not answer him, but spoke about the weather, and thanked him and said good-by, but she felt a sudden warmth take possession of all her body. "*Still it may work out yet.*" He never spoke of it again, but when she came in on her way up the hill, he always looked at her in the same eloquent fashion. It was odd, too, that the look seemed to comfort her: it made her feel less alone.

It was from Krylenko that she first heard news of the catastrophe that was coming: he told her and Irene Shane, perhaps because he had confidence in them, but more, perhaps, because he knew that in the end they were the only ones beyond the borders of the Flats to whom he might look for sympathy. The news frightened her at first because there had never been any strike in the Town and because she knew that there was certain to be violence and suffering and perhaps even death. She understood that the spirit which moved the big Ukrainian was an eternal force of the temper which had made bloodshed and revolution since the beginning of time. It shone in his blue eyes—the light of fanaticism for a cause. The thing, he said, had been brewing for a long time: any one with half an intelligence could have seen it coming. And Mary knew more than most, for she knew of the hasty, secret meetings in the room over Hennessey's saloon with men who came into the Town and out again like shadows. She watched the curious light in Krylenko's eyes in turn kindle a light in the pale eyes of an unecstatic old maid like Irene Shane. She felt the thing spreading all about her like a fire in the thick underbrush of a forest. It seemed to increase as the plague of typhoid began to abate. In some mysterious way it even penetrated the secure world settled upon the Seven Hills.

She had, too, a trembling sense of treason toward those whom the Town would have called her own people—but her heart leaped on the day when Krylenko told her that Philip, too, was on their side. He was, the Ukrainian said, a member of the new Union: they had celebrated his joining months ago at Hennessey's saloon. It made Philip seem nearer to her, as if he belonged not at all to the two women who guarded him. Krylenko told her on the day when every one was certain that Philip was dying, and it served to soften the numb pain which seemed to blind her to all else in the world.

In the afternoon of the same day, Irene Shane said to her, "My mother is dying, and I've cabled to my sister, Lily, to come home."

Chapter 20

WHEN MOSES SLADE was not in Washington, he always went on Sundays to the Baptist Church which stood just across the street from Emma's house of worship. It was not that he was a religious man, for he had enough to do without thinking about God. The service bored him and during the sermon he passed the time by turning his active mind toward subjects more earthly and practical, such as the speech he was to make next week at Caledonia, or what answer he would have for the Democratic attack upon his vote against the Farmers' Relief Bill. (How could they understand that what was good for farmers was bad for industry?) In the beginning, he had fallen into the habit of going to church because most of his votes came from churchgoing people: he went in the same spirit which led him to join sixteen fraternal organizations. But he had gone for so long now that he no longer had any doubts that he was a religious, God-fearing man. (In Washington it did not matter: he could sit at home on Sunday mornings in old clothes drinking his whisky with his feet up on a chair while he read farm papers and racing news.)

Of all the citizens of the Seven Hills, he alone appeared in the streets on Sunday mornings clad in a Prince Albert and a top-hat. Any other citizen in such a fancy-dress costume would have been an object of ridicule, but it was quite proper that he—the Honorable Moses Slade, Congressman—should be thus garbed. He carried it off beautifully; indeed, there was something grand and awe-inspiring in the spectacle of the big man with thick, flowing hair and an enormous front, standing on the steps of the First Baptist Church, speaking to fathers and mothers and patting miserable children imprisoned in stiff Sunday clothes.

On one hot September Sunday he was standing thus (having just patted the last wretched child) when the doors of the church opposite began to yield up its dead. Among the first to descend the Indiana limestone steps appeared the large, handsome figure of Emma, dressed entirely in dark clothing. Moses Slade noticed her at once, for it was impossible not to notice such a magnetic personage, and he fancied that she might go away without even knowing he was there. (He would never learn, of course, that she had hurried out almost before the last echo of Reverend Castor's Benediction had died away, because she knew that the Baptist Church was always over a little before her own.)

In that first glance, something happened to him which afterward made him feel silly, but at the moment had no such effect. A voice appeared to say, "I can't wait any longer," and excusing himself, he hurried, but with an air of dignity, down the steps of his church, and, crossing the street in full view of the now mingling congregations, raised his glistening top-hat, and said, "Good-morning, Mrs. Downes."

Emma turned with a faint air of surprise, but with only the weakest of smiles (for was she not in sorrow?) "Why, Mr. Slade, I didn't know you were back."

"May I walk a way with you?"

"Of course, it would be a pleasure."

Together they went off beneath the yellowing maples, the eyes of two congregations (to Emma's delight) fastened on them. One voice at least, that of the soured Miss Abercrombie, was raised in criticism. "There's no fool," she observed acidly, "like an old one."

When they had gone a little way beyond the reach of prying eyes and ears, Moses Slade became faintly personal in his conversation.

"I appreciated your sending me that postcard," he said.

"Well, I thought you'd like to see the new monument to General Sherman. I knew it was unveiled while you were away, and seeing that you took so much interest in it. . . ." Her voice died away with a note of sadness. The personal touch had filled them both with a sense of constraint, and in silence he helped her across the street, seizing her elbow as if it were a pump-handle.

Safely on the opposite side, he said, "I was sorry to hear of the illness of your son. I hope he's better by now."

Emma sighed. "No . . . he's not much better. You see, he gave up his health in Africa working among the natives." She sighed again. "I doubt if he'll ever be well again. He's such a good boy, too."

"Yes, I always heard that."

"Of course, he may not live. We have to face things, Mr. Slade. If God sees fit to take him, who am I to be bitter and complain? But it isn't easy . . . to have your only son. . . ." She began to cry, and it occurred to Moses Slade that she seemed to crumple and grow softly feminine in a way he had not thought possible in a woman of such character. He had never had any children of his own. He felt that she needed comforting, but for once words seemed of no use to him—the words which always flowed from him in an easy torrent.

"You'll forgive me, Mr. Slade, if I give way . . . but it's gone on for weeks now. Sometimes I wonder that the poor boy has any strength left."

"I understand, Mrs. Downes," he said, in a strange, soft voice.

"I always believe in facing things," she repeated. "There's no good in pretending." She was a little better now and dabbing her eyes with her handkerchief. Fortunately, no one had passed them: no one had witnessed the spectacle of Emma Downes in tears, walking with Congressman Slade.

Before the slate-colored house, they halted, and Mr. Slade asked, "Would you mind if I came in? I'd like to hear how the boy is."

She left him in the parlor, sitting beneath the enlarged portrait of the late Mr. Downes, while she went off up the stairs to ask after Philip. Naomi and Mabelle were there talking, because Naomi no longer went out on account of her appearance, and Mabelle, who always went to sleep in church, avoided it whenever possible. Emma did not speak to them, but hurried past their door to the room where Philip lay white and still, looking thin and transparent, like a sick little boy.

Downstairs, in the darkened parlor, Moses Slade disposed his weight on the green plush, and, leaning on his stick, waited. His mind seemed to be in utter confusion, his brain all befogged. Nothing was very clear to him. He regarded the portrait of Emma's husband, remembering slowly that he had seen Downes years ago, and held a very poor opinion of him. He had been a clever enough fellow, but he never seemed to know where he was going. Emma (he had begun already with a satisfactory feeling of warmth to think of her thus) was probably well rid of him. She had made a brave struggle of it. A fine woman! Look how she behaved about this boy! She believed in facing things. Well, that was a fine, brave quality. He, too, believed in facing things. He couldn't let her go on alone like this. And he began to think of reason after reason why he should marry Emma Downes.

She was gone a long while, and presently he found his gaze wandering back to the portrait. The dead husband seemed to gaze at him with an air of mockery, as if he thought the whole affair was funny. Moses Slade turned in his chair a little, so that he did not look directly at the wooden portrait.

And then he fell to thinking of Philip. What was the boy like? Did he resemble his father or his mother? Had he any character? Certainly his behavior, as far as you could learn, had been queer and mysterious. He might be a liability, yes, a distinct liability, one which was always making trouble. Perhaps he (Moses Slade) ought to go a little more slowly. Of course the boy might die, and that would leave everything clear, with Emma to console. (He yearned impatiently to console her.) It was a wicked thought; but, of course, he wasn't actually *hoping* that the boy would die. He was only facing things squarely, considering the problem from every point of view as a statesman should.

Again he caught the portrait smirking at him, and then the door opened, and Emma came in. She had been crying again. He stood up quickly and the old voice said, "I can't wait any longer." He took her hand gently with a touch which he meant to be interpreted as a sympathetic prelude to something more profound. She didn't resist.

"Well?" he asked.

Emma sank down on the sofa. "I don't know. They thought he'd be better to-day, and . . . and, he isn't."

"You mustn't cry—you mustn't," he said in a husky voice.

"I don't know," she kept repeating. "I don't know what I'm to do. I'm so tired."

He sat down beside her, thankful suddenly that the room was dark, for in the darkness courtship was always easier, especially after middle-age. He now took her hand in both his. There was a long silence in which she gained control of herself, and she did not withdraw her hand nor resist in any way.

"Mrs. Downes," he said presently in a husky voice. "Emma. . . . Mrs. Downes. . . . I have something to ask you. I'm a sober, middle-aged man, and I've thought it over for a long time." He cleared his throat and gave her hand a gentle pressure. "I want you to marry me."

She had known all along that it was coming. Indeed, it was almost like being a girl once more to see Moses Slade, man-like, working his way with the grace of an elephant toward the point; but now it came with the shock of surprise. She couldn't answer him at once for the choke in her throat. For weeks she had borne so much, known such waves of sorrow, that something of her unflagging spirit was broken. She thought, "At last, I am to have my reward for years of hard work. God is rewarding me for all my suffering."

She began to cry again, and Moses Slade asked quickly, "You aren't going to refuse—with all I can give you. . . ."

"No," she sobbed, and, leaning forward a little, as if for support, placed her free hand upon his fat knee. "No . . . I'm not going to refuse . . . only I can't quite believe it. . . . I've had such a hard time. I'd begun to think that I should never have a reward."

Suddenly he leaned over and took her awkwardly in his arms. She felt the heavy metal of his gold watch-chain pressing into her bare arm, and then she heard footsteps descending the stairs in the hallway. It was Mabelle going home at last. She was certain to open the door, because Mabelle couldn't pass a closed door without finding out what was going on behind it.

"Wait!" said Emma, sitting up very straight. "You'd better sit on the other chair."

Understanding what it was she meant, he rose and went back to the green plush. The steps continued, and then, miraculously, instead of halting, they went past the door and out into the street.

The spell was broken, and Moses Slade suddenly felt that he had made a fool of himself, as if he had been duped by an adventuress.

"It's Mabelle," said Emma, who had ceased weeping. "My brother Elmer's wife. She has such a snoopy disposition, I thought we'd better not be found . . . found . . . well, you understand." She blew her nose. "You've made me happy . . . you don't know what it's like to think that I won't have to go on any more . . . alone . . . old age is all right, if you're not alone. . . ."

"Yes, I understand that!" He was a little upset that she treated the affair as if they were an elderly pair marrying for the sake of company in adjoining rocking-chairs. That wasn't at all the way he had looked upon it. In fact, he had been rather proud at the thought of the youthful fervor which had driven him to cross the street a little while before. By some malicious ill-fortune, Mabelle's footsteps had cut short the declaration at the very moment when he had been ready to act in such a way as to establish the whole tone of their future relationship.

"Yes, I understand that," he repeated, "but there's no use talking about old age. Why, we're young—Emma—I suppose I can call you Emma?"

She blushed. "Why, yes, of course."

"You wouldn't mind if I called you just Em? That was my mother's name, and I always liked it."

"No, don't call me Em. It's a name I hate—not on account of your mother, of course . . . Moses."

She couldn't think why she objected to the name: she had been called Em all her life, but somehow it was connected with the vague far-off memory of the romantic Jason Downes. He had called her Em, and it seemed wrong to let this elderly, fleshy man use the same name. It seemed vaguely sacrilegious to put this second marriage on the same basis as the first. She had *loved* Jason Downes. She knew it just now more passionately than she had ever known it.

"You understand," she said, laying one hand gently on his.

"Yes, of course, Emma."

They were standing now, awkwardly waiting for something, and Moses Slade again suddenly took her in his arms. He pinched her arm, ever so gently—just a little pinch; and then he began at once to make a fool of himself again.

"When shall it be?" he asked. "We must fix a date."

She hesitated for a moment. "Don't ask me now. I'm all confused and I've had so much to worry me. We mustn't be hasty and undignified—a man in your position can't afford to be."

"We can be married quietly . . . any time. No one would know how long I'd been courting you." Then he suddenly became romantic. "The truth is that I've wanted to marry you ever since that day you came to see me. So it's been a long time, you see."

For a moment she was silent and thoughtful. At last she said, "There's one thing we ought to consider, Moses. I don't know about such things, but you'll know, being a lawyer. It's about my first husband. You see they never found his body out there in China. They only know he disappeared and must have been killed by bandits. Now what I mean is this . . . he mightn't be dead at all. He might have lost his mind or his memory. And if he turned up . . ."

Moses Slade looked at her sharply. "You *do* want to marry me, don't you, Em . . . I mean Emma. . . . You're not trying to get out of it?"

"Of course I want to marry you. I only mentioned this because I believe in facing things."

"How long has he been gone?"

"It's twenty-four years this January. I remember it well. It was snowing that night, just after the January thaw. . . ."

He checked what would have been a long story by saying, "Twenty-four years . . . all alone without a husband. You're a brave little woman, Emma." He made a clicking sound with his tongue, and looked at her fondly. "Well, that's a long time . . . long enough for him to be considered dead under law. But we'll have him declared dead by law and then we won't have to worry."

Emma was staring at the floor with a curious fixed look in her eyes. At last she said, "Do you think that would be right? He might still be alive. He might come back."

Moses Slade grew blustering, as if he were actually jealous of that shadow of the man who kept looking down at him with an air of sardonic amusement.

"It won't make any difference if we declare him dead. Besides, he hasn't got any right to you if he *is* alive."

It wasn't that she was simply afraid he might return; the source of her alarm went much deeper than that. She felt that she couldn't trust herself if he did return; but of course she couldn't explain that to Moses.

"It wasn't quite that," she murmured, and, conscious that the remark didn't make sense, she asked quickly, "How long ought it to take?"

"A couple of months."

"We could be married after that?"

"Yes, as soon as possible."

Moses Slade took her hand again. "You've made me a happy man, Emma. You won't regret it." He picked up his hat. "I'd like to call to-night. Maybe you'd go to evening service with me?"

"No, I think we'd better not let any one know about it till it's settled."

"Maybe you're right. Well, I'll come to the restaurant to-morrow for lunch."

He kissed her again, a bit too ardently, she felt, to be quite pleasant, and they went into the hall. At the same moment the figure of Naomi appeared, descending the stairs heavily. She was clad only in a nightgown and a loose kimono of flowered stuff. Her hair, still in curl-papers, lay concealed beneath a kind of mob-cap of bright green satin, trimmed with soiled lace. It was impossible to avoid her.

"Naomi," said Emma, in a voice of acid, "this is Mr. Slade—Moses, my daughter-in-law, Naomi."

Naomi said, "Pleased to meet you." Moses Slade bowed, went through the door, and the meeting was over.

When the door closed, Emma stood for a moment with the knob in her hand. Naomi was watching her with a look of immense interest and curiosity strangely like the look that came so often into the eyes of Mabelle when curiosity about the subjects of love and childbirth became too strong for her feeble control.

"Is that Mr. Slade . . . the Congressman?" asked Naomi.

"Yes, it is." There was something in Naomi's look that maddened her, something that was questioning, shameless, offensive, and even accusing.

"What made him come to see us?"

Emma controlled herself. She felt lately that it was all she could bear always to have Naomi in the house.

"He came to ask about Philip."

"I didn't know that he knew Philip."

"He didn't, but he's an old friend of mine." The lie slipped easily from her tongue.

"Philip's better," Naomi answered. "He opened his eyes and looked at me. I think he knew me."

"Did he speak?"

"No, he just closed them again without saying anything."

Emma moved away from the door as Naomi turned into the dining-room. "Naomi," she called suddenly, "is the Reverend Castor coming this afternoon?"

"Yes . . . he said he was."

"Surely you're going to put on some clothes before he comes?"

"I was going to fix my hair."

"You must put on some clothes. I won't have you going about the house all day looking like this—half dressed and untidy. You're a sight! What will a man like Mr. Slade think—a man who is used to Washington where there's good society."

Naomi stared at her for a moment with an unaccustomed look of defiance in her pale eyes. (Emma thought, "Mabelle has been making her into a slattern like herself.")

"Well, in my condition, clothes aren't very comfortable. I think in my condition I might have some consideration."

Emma began to breathe heavily. "That has nothing to do with it. When I was in your condition I dressed and went about my work every day. I wore corsets right up to the end."

"Well, I'm not strong like you. . . . The doctor told me . . ."

Emma broke in upon her. "The doctor didn't tell you to go about looking like a slattern all day! I wish you'd tell Mabelle for me that I'd like to come home just once without finding her here."

The fierce tension could not endure. When it broke sharply, Naomi sat down and began to cry. "Now you want to take her away from me," she sobbed. "I've given up everything to please you and Philip . . . everything. I even gave up going back to Megambo, where the Lord meant me to be. And now I haven't got anything left . . . and you all hate me. Yes, you do. And Philip does too sometimes. . . . He hates me. . . . You wanted me to marry him, and now see what's come of it. I'm even in this condition because you wanted me to be." She began to cry more and more wildly. "I'll run out into the street. I'll kill myself. I'll run away, and then maybe you'll be happy. I won't burden you any longer."

Emma was shaking her now, violently, with all the shame and fury she felt at Moses' encounter with this slatternly daughter-in-law, and all the contempt she felt for a creature so poor spirited.

"You'll do no such thing, you little fool! You'll brace up and behave like a woman with some sense!"

But it was no good. Naomi was simply having one of her seizures. She grew more hysterical, crying out, "You'd like to be rid of me . . . both of you. You both hate me. . . . Oh, I know . . . I know . . . I'm nothing now . . . nothing to anybody in the world! I'm just in your way."

Emma, biting her lip, left her abruptly, closing the door behind with ferocious violence. If she had not gone at once, she felt that she would have laid hands on Naomi.

Moses Slade, bound toward his own house, walked slowly, lost once more in a disturbing cloud of doubts. With Emma out of sight, the ardent lover yielded place to the calculating politician. He suffered, he did not know why, from a feeling of having been duped. The sight of Naomi so untidy and ill-kempt troubled him. He hadn't known about the child. The girl must be at least seven months gone, and he hadn't known it. Of course (he thought) you couldn't have expected Emma voluntarily to mention a subject so indelicate. Nevertheless, he felt that she should have conveyed the knowledge to him in some discreet fashion. Even if the boy did die, the

situation would be just as bad, or worse. If he left a widow and a child. . . .
He felt suddenly as if in some way Emma herself had tricked him, as if she
herself were having a child, and had tricked him into marrying her to protect
herself. . . .

In a kind of anguish he regretted again that he had been so impetuous
in his proposal to the widow Barnes that he had shocked her into refusal.
She wasn't so fine-looking a woman as Emma, but she was free, without
encumbrances or responsibilities, without a child. Of course, Emma would
never know that in the midst of his courtship he had been diverted by the
prospect of Mrs. Barnes. She would never know what had been the reason for
the months of silence. . . .

Chapter 21

SINCE THE RECONCILIATION, the Sunday dinner at Elmer Niman's had again
been resumed, and Emma, on her way there, suffered as keenly from doubts
as her suitor had done on his homeward journey. Now that the thing was
accomplished, or practically so, she was uneasy. It was not, she reflected, a
simple thing to alter the whole course of one's life at her age. There would
be troubles, difficulties, for Moses Slade was not, she could see, an easy man
to manage. To be sure, he was less slippery than Jason had been: a Congressman could never run off and disappear. But, on the other hand, he was as
rocklike and solid as his own portly figure.

She faced the thing all the way to Elmer's house, examining it from every
possible angle, except the most important of all—the angle of ambition. In
the bottom of her heart, hidden and veiled by all the doubts and probings,
there lay a solid determination to marry Moses Slade. The restaurant was a
complete success, enlarged to a size commensurate with the possibilities of
the Town. Nothing more remained to be done, and she was still a healthy,
vigorous woman in the prime of life. As the wife of Moses Slade, new vistas
opened before her. . . . There had never been any doubt about her course
of action, but she succeeded in convincing herself that she was going slowly
and examining every possibility of disaster.

What she found most difficult to bear was the lack of a confidante. Even
though, as she admitted to herself, it was silly to think of such a thing as
love between herself and Moses, she had nevertheless an overwhelming desire to share the news with some one. It was almost as strong as the feeling
she had experienced twenty-seven years earlier after accepting Jason's declaration. She could not, she felt, go in safety beyond the borders of a discreet
hinting to any of her woman friends: a mere rumor soon spread among them
with the ferocity of a fire in a parched forest. Naomi was the last person
to tell, especially since that queer Mabelle look had come into her eyes. And

her brother? No, she couldn't tell him, though she supposed he would be pleased at her marrying so solid a man. It wasn't clear to her why she couldn't bring herself to tell him, save that it was connected vaguely with the memory of his behavior on the occasion of announcing her engagement to Jason. He might behave in the same fashion again; and on the first occasion he had only forgiven her when Jason had vindicated his opinion by disappearing. Elmer, she knew, loved to say, "I told you it would end like this."

There remained only Philip, and he was too ill to be told; but when she thought of it, she began to doubt whether she would have told him if he had been well.

It was the first time since his return that she had had need to confide in him, and now she found herself troubled by the feeling that it wouldn't be easy. Until now she had gone bravely on, ignoring the changes in their relations as mother and son, but now that a test had arisen, she saw that there had been a change. She saw, despite herself, that he had become in a way a stranger—her boy, who had always loved her, whom she worshipped with a maternal passion too intense to be put into words. Her boy, whose very character she had created as she had created his flesh, had become a stranger with whom she couldn't even discuss her own plans. Once he would have believed that whatever she did was right.

As she thought of it, she walked more rapidly. Why, she asked herself, had this happened to her? Hadn't she given all her life to him? Hadn't she worked her fingers to the bone? Hadn't she watched and guarded him from evil and sin, kept him pure? Had she ever thought of anything but his welfare and saving him from the pitfall of his father's weaknesses? A lump came into her throat, and a moisture into her eyes. What had she done to deserve this?

She felt no resentment against him. It was impossible to blame him in any way. He was a good boy, who had never caused her any trouble—not trouble in the real sense, for his doubts about his calling were temporary, and perhaps natural. Since he could never go back to Africa, he would in the end settle down with some church of his own. He might even perhaps become a bishop, for certainly he was more clever than most preachers, a thousand times more clever than the Reverend Castor, and more of a gentleman, more of what a bishop ought to be. And after this illness perhaps he would see the light once more. Perhaps the Lord had sent this illness for just that reason.

No, Philip was a perfect son. She was sure that he still loved her.

She tried to hate the Mills, but that was impossible, and in the end the suspicion came to her that the change was due in some way to Naomi. It must be Naomi. She had always thought that Naomi disliked her. Why, she didn't know. Hadn't she done everything for Naomi? Hadn't she treated her as if she were her own daughter?

And her only reward was spite and jealousy.

While she thought of it, it occurred to her that the change in Philip—

the *real* change—his slipping away from her—had begun at the time that Naomi became his wife in more than name: until that time he had always been her boy who adored her. Suddenly, she saw it all clearly; it was Naomi for whom she had done everything, who had stolen Philip from her.

Her tears were dried by the time she reached her brother's front step, but the lump in her throat was still there, and it remained all through the lunch, so that at times she felt that she might suddenly weep, despite herself. In her sorrow, she paid little heed to her brother's usual long speeches, or to Mabelle's idiotic interruptions. But she was able to despise Mabelle with a contempt which made any previous emotion pale by comparison. Because Mabelle was Naomi's friend, she, too, seemed responsible for what had happened.

After lunch, when Mabelle had gone out to the kitchen for a time, Emma took her brother aside in the grim parlor, and said, "Elmer, I have something to ask of you."

He looked at her sharply, in a way in which he had looked at her for years on occasions when he thought she might be asking for money. It had never yet happened, but the unguarded look of alarm had never wholly died since the moment that Jason Downes left his wife penniless.

"It's not what you think," said Emma coldly. "It's only about Mabelle. I want you to keep her from coming to the house so often."

"But why, Emma?"

"You don't know that she spends all her days there. I never go home without finding her . . . and I think she's bad for Naomi . . . just now."

"How bad for her?"

He was standing with his hands clasped behind him, watching her. For a moment she looked squarely into his eyes, hesitating, wondering whether she dared speak the truth. Then she took the plunge, for she felt suddenly that Elmer would understand. There was a bond between them not of fraternal affection (for there were times when they actually disliked each other), but a tie far stronger. He would understand what she meant to say, because he was, in spite of everything, very like her. They were two people who had to rule those about them, two people who were always right. She knew that he understood her contempt for Mabelle as a woman and as a housekeeper; the fact that Mabelle was his wife made little difference.

"You'll understand what I mean, Elmer. You know that Mabelle doesn't keep house well. You know she's . . . well, lazy and untidy. And that is why she's bad for Naomi. Naomi wasn't meant for a wife and mother, I'm afraid. She's a miserable failure at it. I'm trying to put character into her, to make something of her . . . but I can't, if Mabelle's always there. She undoes all I can do."

He unclasped his hands, and, after a moment, said, "Yes, I think I know what you mean. Besides, Mabelle ought to be at home looking after her own house a little. You'd think that she couldn't bear the sight of it. She's always gadding." He turned away. "She's coming now. I'll speak to her, and if she still bothers you let me know."

Mabelle came through the swinging beaded portières. "It's too bad Naomi couldn't come, too, for lunch. It's a pity she feels like she does about being seen in the street. I have tried to make her sensible about it. Why, when I was carrying Ethel . . ."

Both of them gave her black looks, but Mabelle, seating herself at once in the rocking-chair, rattled on without noticing.

Chapter 22

THE INSPIRATION came to Emma at the evening service, when she was struck again by the quality of sympathy in the voice and countenance of the Reverend Castor. He, of course, was the one with whom to discuss the problem of her marriage. He would understand, and he would be able, as well, to give her advice. Nor did he ever betray all the ladies of his congregation who came to him with their troubles. And he had been so sympathetic over Philip's long illness, showing so deep a solicitude, calling at the house three or four times a week.

Almost at once she felt happier.

At the end of the service, she waited until he had shaken hands with all the congregation, smiling and making little jests with them, as if he had not done so twice a day for fifty-two Sundays a year, ever since he had felt the call. When they had all gone, she said, "Could I take a moment of your time, Reverend Castor? I want advice over something that worries me."

It was a request he heard often enough, from one woman after another—women who asked advice upon every subject from thieving hired girls to erring husbands. There were times when he felt he could not endure listening to one more woman talk endlessly about herself. It wearied him so that he wanted to flee suddenly, leaving them all, together with the handshaking and the very church itself, behind him forever. Sometimes he had strange dreams, while he was awake, and with his eyes wide open, of fleeing to some outlandish place like those marvelous islands in the South Seas where there were none of these things. And then to calm his soul, he would tell himself cynically that even in those islands there were women.

He led her to his study, which he had been driven to establish at the back of the church, since there was no peace in the parsonage from the complaining voice above-stairs. There the two of them sat down. It occurred to Emma that he looked very white and tired, that there were new lines on his face. He couldn't be an old man. He wasn't much older than herself, yet he was beginning to look old. It was, she supposed, the life he led at home. A clergyman, of all people, needed an understanding, unselfish wife.

"And now," he was saying, "I'm always pleased to help, however I can in my humble way."

He was a good man, who never sought to evade his duty, however tired he was. He wanted, honestly, to help her.

She began to tell him, constructing an approach to the fact itself by explaining what a lonely, hard life she had had since the death of her husband in China. She touched upon the Christian way in which she had brought up her boy, and now (she said) that he was a grown man and married and would soon have a parish of his own (since he could not return to Africa) she would be left quite alone. She wanted the rest which she had earned, and the companionship for which she would no doubt hunger in her old age. These were the reasons why she had accepted the offer of Moses Slade. Yet she was troubled.

She leaned back in her chair and sighed. What did he think? Could he help her to decide?

The study was a gloomy room, lighted in the daytime by a single sooty Gothic window and at night by a single jet of gas. There was a roll-top desk, a long heavy table, a cabinet where the choir music was kept, and two or three sagging, weary leather chairs. Before he answered her, the tired eyes of the Reverend Castor rested for a time on the meager furniture as if he had lost himself in deep thought. She waited. This attitude was, however, merely professional, and wholly misleading. He was not in deep thought. He was merely thinking, "She doesn't want advice. She only wants to talk about herself. Whatever I say will make no difference. She means to marry him, no matter what happens."

But because this was his work he spoke at last, setting forth one by one all the arguments she had repeated to herself earlier in the day, concluding with the remark, "The reasons on the other side you have put very well yourself."

Emma stirred in the springless leather chair. "Then what do you advise?"

"Mrs. Downes, it is a matter that no one can decide but yourself. Pray God to help you, and do what you think is right."

He was troubled, and, in a vague way, disturbed and unhappy, because in the back of his mind the worm of envy was at work, gnawing, gnawing, gnawing—a sinful worm that gave him no peace. Moses Slade was free to marry again, and he had chosen Emma Downes. He had thought of Emma Downes for himself, in case . . . (the wicked thought returned to him again like a shadow crossing his path) . . . in case Annie's illness carried her off at last. It seemed to him that all the world was going past him, while he remained behind, chained to a complaining invalid.

Emma rose, and, after he had turned the gas out and locked the door, they went out together. It was a clear, quiet night, when for once there seemed to be no soot in the air, and the stars seemed very close. For a moment they both stood listening, and at last Emma said, "Am I right, or am I growing deaf? Do the Mills sound very far away to-night . . . sort of weak?"

He listened, and then said, "Yes, it's queer. They sound almost faint."

There was another silence. And Emma gave a low, groaning sound. "Maybe that's it . . . maybe they've gone out on strike."

"There'll be trouble," said the Reverend Castor. "It makes me kind of sick to think of it."

They bade each other good-night, and went their ways, the Reverend Castor hurrying along, because he was more than an hour late. He knew that when he arrived she would be out of her bed, standing at the upper window looking for him, her mind charged with the bitter reproaches she had thought out to fling at him, torturing sarcasms dealing with what had kept him so long in the study. She had an obsession that he meant to be unfaithful to her; she never ceased to hint and imply the most odious things. She was always accusing him of disgraceful things about women. . . .

As he came nearer and nearer to the parsonage, he was seized by a terrible temptation to turn away, to disappear, never to enter the doors of his home again. But a man of God, he knew, couldn't do a thing like that. And now God—even God—seemed to be deserting him. He couldn't drive these awful thoughts from his mind. He began desperately to repeat his Psalm.

Turning past the hedge, he saw that there was a light in the upper window, and against the lace curtains the silhouette of a waiting figure, peering out eagerly.

When Emma entered the house, she discovered that all the lights were on, that Philip had been forgotten, and that his nurse and Mabelle were with Naomi, who was being forced to walk up and down. Mabelle sat giving advice and saying repeatedly that she never had such trouble even with her first baby. In a little while, the doctor came, and seven hours later Mabelle's predictions were vindicated, for Naomi gave birth at last to twins, a boy and a girl. At about the same hour the last echo of the pounding at the Mills died away into silence, and the last fire in the blast-furnace died into ashes. In the room next to Naomi's, Philip opened his eyes, called for a drink of water, and for the first time in four months knew that his head was clear and that his body was not burning or shaking. It was an extraordinary thing, the nurse observed, as if his children coming into the world had called him back to life.

He came back to consciousness out of a strange country peopled with creatures that might have haunted a Gothic nightmare, creatures who seemed as confused and unreal as the fantastic world on which they moved. Sometimes his mother was present, moving about, oddly enough, against the background of the jungle at Megambo, moving about among the niggers, converting them in wholesale lots. At times she would disappear suddenly, to return almost at once, driving before her with Lady Millicent Wimbrooke's rawhide whip whole troops of natives, dressed completely, even to bonnets and shoes, like the people one saw in Main Street. And then she would feed them at the Peerless Restaurant, which seemed to have been set up intact on the borders of the gloomy forest. Once Lady Wimbrooke appeared herself with her portable-bath and rifle, and shooting about her carelessly, she drove all of them, including Emma, out of the restaurant into Main Street, which appeared miraculously to have sprung up just outside the door. Once outside, he discovered that all of them—Emma herself and the niggers, were walking stark naked in the car-tracks in the middle of the street. He, himself, seemed to be carrying a banner at the head of the parade on which was written in fiery letters, "Let God look out for himself. We will do the same." And at the corner he found Mary Conyngham waiting to keep a tryst, and neither he nor she seemed to take any notice of the fact that he was as naked as the day he was born.

And Naomi was there, too, always in the background, only she was not the Naomi he knew, but a large woman with a soft, powerful body, like Swanson's, above which her pale face peered out comically from beneath a sunbonnet woven of reeds. Once or twice he had mistaken her for Swanson playing a joke on him.

At other times he seemed to be back in the Mills, or in Hennessey's saloon, where Emma entered presently and broke all the mirrors; and then all of them were suddenly squeezed out of the doors to find themselves in the jungle, which appeared to have sprung up all about them, impenetrable save for a single path in which was stuck a cast-iron guide-post, reading, "To the Mills." The air was filled with the sound of distant thunder, but he could not make out whether it was the distant sound of tom-toms, or the pounding of monstrous steel hammers. Oddly enough, it seemed quite natural, as if the trees, the jungle and the Mills belonged thus together.

And Mary Conyngham was always there. It seemed that she was married to him, and that they had somewhere a family of children which he had never seen and could not find.

Once he witnessed a horrible sight. He saw Emma pursuing the black virgin who had long ago been eaten by the leopards. The virgin, naked, save for her ornaments of copper wire, ran to the lake, and across the water, skimming the surface like a kingfisher of ebony, and, as Emma gave chase, she sank like a stone, disappearing beneath the brassy surface without a sound.

For a long time after he returned to life, memories of the dead, nightmarish world clung to him like wisps of the haze that sometimes veiled the lake at Megambo in the wet season. He did not know how long he had been ill, and at times it seemed to him that he had died and was not living at all. His body felt light as air, but when he tried to raise it, it failed him, slipping back in a miserable weakness. And then, bit by bit, as the memories of the delirium faded into space, the hard, barren world about him began to take shape . . . the starched lace curtains at the windows, which Emma kept clean despite all the soot, the worn rocking-chair, the table at the side of the bed crowded with medicines, and, finally, the strange figure of the nurse. And then he understood that Naomi must be somewhere near at hand, and his mother. He had a vague feeling that they must have become old now, and gray, after all the years he had been ill.

It was Emma whom he saw first, and recognized. She came into the darkened room, and stood silently by the side of the bed until he, conscious that there was some one near him, opened his eyes, and said in a weak voice, "Is that you, Ma?"

Without answering him, she fell on her knees beside the bed and took his head in her hands, kissing him passionately again and again on his forehead. She wept and said over and over again, "Philip, my boy! The Lord has given me back my boy!"

There was something frightening in the wildness of her emotion. The nurse, hearing her weeping, came in to warn her that she must be calm, and Philip said weakly, "It's all right. I understand. She's always been like that."

Once it would never have occurred to him to speak thus, as if he were detached from her and stood quite apart, protecting her. Protecting Emma! Something had happened to him during that long night of four months' delirium.

When his mother had gained control of herself once more, she sat down by the side of the bed, and, taking his hand, she held it clasped passionately in hers, while she sat looking at him, without once speaking. For some reason, he could not look at her, perhaps because in the intensity of her emotion she was asking from him a response which he could not give. He was ashamed, but it was impossible to pretend. Instead of any longer seeming almost a part of her, he was detached now in a strange, definite fashion. In his weakness, it seemed to him that he was seeing her for the first time and he was ashamed and sorry for her. He knew that before long she, too, would understand that there was a difference, that in some way their relationship had been broken forever. The old Philip was dead, and the new one suddenly pitied her from a great distance, as he pitied Naomi. It was as if the weakness gave him a clairvoyance, a second sight, which illuminated all the confusion of mind that had preceded the long night.

Lying there, with his eyes closed, her passionate cry, "Philip, my boy!" burned itself into his brain. He was, he knew, unworthy of that consuming love she had for him.

After a long time he heard her asking, "Philip, are you awake?"

"Yes, Ma." But he did not open his eyes.

"I have some good news that will delight you."

What could it be? Perhaps she had arranged his return to Megambo. She would think that was good news.

"It's about Naomi. You're a father now, Philip . . . twice a father, Philip. You've two children. They were twins."

The knot of perplexity which had been tormenting his brain suddenly cleared away. Of course! That was what he couldn't remember about Naomi. She had been going to have a baby, and now she had had two. Still he did not open his eyes. It was more impossible now than ever. He did not answer her, and presently Emma asked, "You heard what I said, Philip?"

"Yes, Ma."

"You're glad, aren't you?"

He answered her weakly, "Of course . . . why, of course, I'm glad."

Again there was a long silence. He was ashamed again, because he had been forced to lie, ashamed because he wasn't proud, and happy. His mother sat there trying to raise his spirits, and each thing she said only drove them lower. In that curious clarity of mind which seemed to possess his soul, he knew with a kind of horror that he had wanted to waken alone, free, in a new country, where he would never again see Naomi, or his mother, or the lace curtains, or the familiar, worn rocking-chair. That, he saw now, was why he had wanted to die. And now he was back again, tied to them more closely than ever.

At last he said in a low voice, "It was like Naomi, wasn't it . . . to have twins?"

"What do you mean?"

He hesitated a moment, and then said, "I don't know . . . I'm tired . . . I don't know."

Again a silence. Deep inside him something kept urging him to break through all this web which seemed to be closing tighter and tighter around him. The last thought he could remember before slipping into the nightmare returned to him now, and, without knowing why, he uttered it, "There won't be any more children."

"Why?" asked Emma. "What are you trying to say?"

"Because I don't mean to live with Naomi ever again. It's a wicked thing that I've done."

She began to stroke his forehead, continuing for a long time before she spoke. She was having suddenly to face things—things which she had always known, and pretended not to know. At last she said, "Why is it a wicked thing to live with your lawful wife?"

The world began to whiz dizzily about his head. Odd flashes of light passed before his closed eyes. It seemed to him that he must speak the truth, if he were ever to open them again without shame.

"Because she's not really my wife . . . she's just like any woman, any stranger . . . I never loved her at all. I can't go on . . . living like that. Can't you see how wicked it is?"

Emma was caught in her own web, by the very holy principles she upheld—that it was wrong to marry some one you did not love. It was this same thing which disturbed her peace of mind about Moses Slade.

"You loved her once, Philip, or you wouldn't have married her."

"No, I didn't know anything then, Ma." The color of pain entered his voice. "Can't you see, Ma? I wasn't alive then. I never loved her, and now it's worse than that."

The stroking of his forehead suddenly ceased. "I don't know what you're talking about, Philip. . . . We'd better not go on now. You're tired and ill. Everything will be different when you are well again."

For a second time there came to him a blinding flash of revelation. He saw that she had always been like that: she had always pushed things aside to let them work themselves out. An awful doubt dawned upon him that she was not always right, that sometimes she had made a muddle of everything. A feeling of dizziness swept over him.

"But it will break her heart, Philip," she was saying. "She worships you. . . . It will break her heart."

Through a giddy haze he managed to say, "No . . . I'm so tired. . . . Let's not talk any more." He felt the nightmare stealing back again, and presently he was for some strange reason back at Megambo, sitting under the acacia-tree, and through the hot air came the sound of voices singing, in a minor key:

> "Go down to the water, little monkey,
>   To the life of lives, the beginning of all things."

He thought wildly, "I've got to get free. I must run . . . I must run."

Emma, holding his hand, felt the fever slipping back. She heard him saying, "Go down to the water, little monkey," which clearly made no sense, and suddenly she sprang up and called Miss Bull, the nurse.

"It's odd," said Miss Bull, white and frightened, "when he was so much better. Did anything happen to upset him?"

"No," said Emma. "Nothing. We barely talked at all."

The nurse sent Essie for the doctor, reproaching herself all the while for having allowed Emma to stay so long a time by the bed. But it was almost impossible to refuse when a woman like Mrs. Downes said, "Surely seeing his mother won't upset him. Why, Miss Bull, we've always been wonderful companions—my boy and I. He never had a father, you see. I was both mother and father to him." Miss Bull knew what a gallant fight she'd made, for every one in the Town knew it. A widow, left alone, to bring up her boy. You couldn't be cruel enough to stop her from seeing her own son.

When the doctor came and left again, shaking his head, Emma was frightened, but her fright disappeared once more as the fever receded again toward morning, and when at last she fell asleep, she was thinking, "He doesn't belong to her, after all. He's never belonged to her. He's still my Philip." There was in the knowledge a sense of passionate triumph and joy, which wiped out all else—her doubts about Moses Slade, her worry over Philip's future, even the sudden, cold terror that gripped her as she felt the fever stealing back into his thin, transparent hand. He didn't belong to Naomi. Why, he almost hated her. He was still her boy. . . . And she had defeated Naomi.

In the darkness the tears dampened the pillow. God had not, after all, forsaken her.

PART THREE
THE STABLE

Chapter 1

AT THE BACK of the great Shane house there clustered a little group of build-ings arranged in plantation style. There were a laundry, a kennel, an office and a stable with a double row of box-stalls. The whole was overgrown with dying vines and was connected with the big white-trimmed brick house by a sort of gallery, roofed but open on the sides. The buildings were empty now, since the old woman had taken to her canopied bed, save for the pair of fat old horses who never went out any more and now stood fat and sleek, groomed carefully each day by the old negro who acted as groom and general factotum. One daughter had given up her life to the poor and the other to the great world and no one cared any longer if the hinges rusted on the stable doors and the great wrought-iron gates sagged at the entrance to the park. Ghosts haunted the place—the ghost of the wicked old John Shane who had built the Castle, the ghosts of all the great who had stayed at the Castle in the glamorous days before the coming of the black Mills. Old Julia Shane lay dying, aloof, proud, rich and scornful. Nobody cared. . . .

When the strike came the whole park fell into a state of siege, walled in on the one side by the Mills and on the other by the filthy houses of the steelworkers. The warfare raged just outside its borders. Sometimes in the night a shot sounded in the darkness. But neither side invaded the ter-ritory: it remained in some mysterious way neutral and sacred, as if the lin-gering spirit of the old woman who lay dying in the smoke-blackened house held the world at bay. The doctor came twice daily, making his way bravely through the black district of the strike; once each day, the old nigger Hen-nery went timorously across the Halstead Street bridge to fetch food. Irene Shane and sometimes Hattie Tolliver, a cousin who came to "take hold," went in and out. Otherwise the place lay deserted and in solitude, waiting.

Early in December, when the first blackened snow lay among the dead trees of the park, Irene Shane and Mary Conyngham visited the stables. It was the first time Irene had gone there since she was a young girl and kept a pony called Istar. To Mary Conyngham it was a strange place never before visited. They were accompanied by the old nigger Hennery.

Above the stalls of the fat horses there was a room once occupied by a coachman, which now lay empty save for a table, two or three chairs, an iron stove and a bed. At each end of the room there was a big window partly covered by the vines that overran the whole building. It was here that the two women and the old negro came.

Irene, dressed in her shabby gray clothes, opened the door of the harness-closet, looked inside, and then regarded the room with a sweeping glance. "This ought to serve, very well," she said.

Mary was pleased. "It's perfect, I should think."

"Put those newspapers in the stove, Hennery, and light them," said Irene. "He can't work here unless there's some means of heat."

The papers went up in a burst of flame. The stove worked perfectly.

The two women looked at each other. "Will you tell him, then?" asked Mary.

"Yes . . . Krylenko will tell him. I don't know him at all."

Suddenly Mary kissed the older woman on the cheek. It was an odd, grotesque gesture, which failed of all response. It was like kissing a piece of marble to kiss a woman like Irene Shane.

"Thank you, Irene," she said.

Irene ignored the speech, and turned to the old negro. "Clean the room out, Hennery. There's a Mr. Downes coming here to paint now and then."

"What? Pitchers?" asked Hennery.

"Yes, pictures. He's to come and go as he likes. You needn't worry about him."

They left him raising clouds of dust with a worn stable-broom. It did not strike him that there was anything extraordinary in the arrangement. He had come to Shane's Castle a buck nigger of eighteen, when John Shane was a bachelor. He was sixty-five now. Anything, he knew, might happen at Shane's Castle. Life there possessed a sort of subterranean excitement.

As he swept he kept thinking that Miss Lily was already on her way home from Paris, coming to see her Mammy die. She hadn't been home in seven years. When Miss Lily came home, everything was changed. All the excitement seemed to rise above the surface, and all life changed and became a tingling, splendiferous affair. Even the presence of death in the Castle couldn't dampen the effect of Miss Lily.

Chapter 2

WITH THAT first fall of snow the fever began to lose a little its hold upon the twice-stricken community. As it waned the new terror came to take its place—a terror that, like the fever, rose out of the black of the Flats.

Bristling barriers of ugly barbed-wire sprang up overnight and for days each train brought in criminals shipped from the slums of a dozen cities to protect the sheds and furnaces. In the beginning it was neither the strikers, nor the men who owned the Mills, but the Town itself which suffered. Business in the shops bordering the diseased area fell off; but, far worse than that, there began to occur one after another, with terrifying regularity, a whole series of crimes. Houses were broken into, a woman was attacked at twilight in the raw, new park, two fat business men were held up and beaten, and the Farmers' and Industrial Bank, the institution of the corrupt Judge Weissman, was robbed and then quickly failed under mysterious circumstance. It was the gunmen brought in to make war on the strikers who committed the crimes, but it was the strikers who were accused. Save for Philip and Mary Conyngham, and perhaps McTavish, they had no friends on the Hills. The Shanes could not be counted, since they stood apart in an isolation of their own. A panic-stricken community began to imagine innumerable horrors. The newspapers wrote editorials predicting anarchy and dissolution. They talked of the "sacred rights of property" and used clouds of similar high-sounding phrases. Moses Slade, seeing perhaps a chance to harvest new crops of votes by "standing by his community in such a crisis," returned to head a sort of vigilance committee whose purpose was to fasten all crime upon the strikers.

By this heroic act he soon rose high in the esteem of Emma, so high indeed that it seemed to wipe out all her doubts concerning her marriage. It was an action of which she approved with all her spirit. She herself went about talking of "dirty foreigners" and the need of making laws to exclude them from a nation favored by God, until Moses took her aside and advised her not to talk in such a vein, because the very strength of the Mills depended on new hordes of cheap labor. If they throttled immigration, labor would rule. Didn't she understand a simple thing like that?

She understood. Moses Slade seemed to her a paragon. "Why," she told Philip, "he understands all the laws of economics."

Philip, restless and convalescent, listened to her in silence. He even met the Honorable Moses Slade, who eyed him suspiciously as a cat and asked about his future plans.

"I haven't any," said Philip. "I don't know what I mean to do," and so put Moses Slade once more upon a bed of pins and needles concerning Emma's qualifications as a bride.

The omnipresence of the Congressman's name in Emma's conversation had begun to alarm Philip. He saw presently that she meant to tell him something, and after a time he came to guess what it was. He saw that she was breaking a way through his prejudices and her own; and in that odd sense of detachment born of the fever he faced the idea with disgust. It was not only that he disliked Mr. Slade; it seemed to him that there was something disgraceful in the idea of his mother marrying again after so many years. It was in a strange way a disloyalty to himself. Moses Slade was a new ally in the forces against him. The idea came to torment him for hours at a time, when he was not pondering what was to be done about Naomi, how he could escape from her without hurting her too deeply.

The two women, Naomi and his mother, hovered over him with the solicitude of two women for a man whom they had snatched from death. In
these first days when he came downstairs to sit in the parlor there was always
one of them with him. Naomi left him only long enough to nurse the twins.
She was, as Mabelle observed, very fortunate, as she was able to feed them
both, and there were not many women, Mabelle remarked with a personal
pride, who could say the same. And under Mabelle's guidance Naomi adopted
the same methods: the moment the twins set up a wail they were fed into
a state of coma. Mabelle had great pride in them, as if she had played in
some way a part in their very creation. She was always in the house now,
for Emma's request and Elmer's commands were of no avail against her instinct for human companionship. With the twins crying and little Jimmy
running about, the house seemed overrun with children. And little Jimmy
had turned into what Mabelle described as "a whiner."

"I don't know what to do about him," she said. Her method was to cuff
him over the head, thus changing the whine instantly into a deafening squall.

Naomi used her own convalescence as an excuse for clinging to the soiled
flowered kimono and the green mob-cap.

It was a state of affairs which could not long endure and the climax arose
on the afternoon when Emma, returning unexpectedly, found a scene which
filled her with horror. In his chair by the window sat Philip, looking white
and sick. Behind him on the sofa Naomi in wrapper and mob-cap fed the
twins. Little Jimmy sat on the floor pulling photographs out of the album at
the back of the family Bible. Draping the backs of the mahogany chairs hung
white objects that were unmistakably diapers. Two of the objects were even
hung to dry upon the very frame of Jason Downes' enlarged photograph!

For a moment Emma simply stood in the doorway in a state of paralysis.
At the sight of her Naomi sat up defiantly and Mabelle smiled blandly.
Philip, wearily, did not even turn to witness the picture. And then, quickly,
like a bird of prey, Emma swooped upon the diapers, gathering them up in a
neat roll. Then she turned on Naomi.

"It's the last time I want this to happen in my house." She seized the
family Bible from Jimmy, who began to squall, setting off the twins like
matches brought too close to a fire. "I won't have it looking like a bawdy-
house," she cried. "With you sitting here all day in a wrapper, like a chippy
waiting for trade." Words that she would have denied knowing came to her
lips in a stream.

This time Naomi did not weep. She sprang up from the sofa as if to
attack Emma. "Take care what you say! Take care what you say! You old
hypocrite!"

Emma turned suddenly to Philip. "You hear what she called me!"

And Naomi, like an echo, cried, "You heard what filthy names she called
me."

Mabelle, terrified, rolled her cowlike eyes, and tried to stifle Jimmy's
screams. Philip did not even turn. He felt suddenly sick.

Naomi was saying, "If I hadn't all the work to do. . . . If I had the right kind of husband—"

Emma interrupted. "I took care of my child and did all the work as well. I never complained or made excuses."

"You didn't have twins. . . . Sometimes my back fairly breaks. Oh, if I had the right kind of husband, I wouldn't be in your dreary old house!"

Emma turned again, "Philip . . . Philip. . . ."

But Philip was gone. She saw him, hatless and without an overcoat, running through the snow that had begun to come down slowly and softly as a white eiderdown.

Chapter 3

HE ONLY STOPPED running when he grew so weak that he could no longer make an effort. He had gone, without knowing why, in the direction of the Mills, and presently he found himself, with a savage pain just beneath his heart, sitting on the steps of McTavish's undertaking parlors. It was almost dark, and the air was cold and still; he felt it creeping about him as the heat went out of his body. He knew that if he caught cold he would die and suddenly he wanted to live, horribly. It was as if that sickening scene had in some way released him from the bondage of the two women. They seemed all at once to belong to another world in which he played no rôle, a world strange and horrible and fantastic. Even the twins did not seem to be his children, but creatures born somehow of the two women and all they stood for in his tired mind. They were two squalling tomato-colored infants in whom he could take no interest—a judgment sent by fate as a punishment for his own weakness and indecision. He grew bitter for the first time and out of the bitterness there was born a new strength.

Sitting there in the softly falling snow, he resolved to go his own way. He couldn't desert Naomi and his children, but he could tell her that he was through with her once and for all. And he saw suddenly the whole sickening depth of the tangle—that it was her fault no more than his, that she had suffered as much as himself, that perhaps in the end she would suffer more, because (he knew it with a kind of disgust) she *loved* him with all her soul and body.

Beating his arms against his body, he rose and turned the handle of the door. McTavish was inside, alone, sitting by the stove. At the sound of the handle turning, he looked up and grinned.

"Hello, Philip," he said, and then quickly, "What the hell are you doing out without a coat or hat?"

Philip grinned, and the very grin hurt his face, as if it had been frozen by the cold. "I came out in a hurry . . . I wanted to borrow a coat and hat off you."

McTavish rose and stretched his great arms, yawning, watching Philip all the while. "Driven out?" he asked at last, with a sharp look.

"Yes," said Philip quietly. "Driven out." He knew suddenly that McTavish understood. He remembered all at once what he had said, "I knew your Ma before you were born. You can't tell me anything about her."

"Here," suddenly the undertaker was pouring whisky. "Here, drink this. I'll get you a coat."

He disappeared into that portion of the establishment where the dead were kept, and returned in a moment bearing a coat and hat. The curious, pungent odor of the place clung to him.

"Here," he said. "It's all I've got. You couldn't wear my clothes. You'd be drowned in them." He laid the coat and hat on a chair by the stove. "These ought to about fit you. They belonged to Jim Baxter, who got bumped off at the grade-crossing while comin' home drunk last week. His wife has never come for 'em. I guess he won't need a coat where he is now." He sat down and took Philip's wrist, feeling the flow of blood. "Feel better now? Your heart seems all right."

"I've always been strong as an ox."

"It ain't the same after you've had a fever."

They sat in silence for a moment and then McTavish asked, "You don't mind wearin' a dead man's clothes?"

"No," said Philip. "No." Anything was better than going back to the slate-colored house.

"When you're in my business, you get over squeamish feelings like that. Dead men and live ones are all the same, except you know the dead ones are mebbe missing a lot of fun."

"No . . . I don't mind, Mr. McTavish." Philip looked up suddenly. "There's one thing you could do for me. You could send word around to the house that I'm not coming home to-night."

A grin lighted up the big face. "Sure I will. . . . I'll take the word myself." After a pause, "Where will you go?"

"I don't know . . . somewhere." He rose and put on Jim Baxter's coat and hat. "I'm going down to the Flats now."

"Your friends have been raising hell down there."

"Yes . . . that's why I want to go down there now. . . . They'll think I'm dead."

"No . . . they won't think that. That Dago friend . . . Krylenko . . . is that his name? He's been asking for you, and Mary Watts . . . Mary Conyngham she is now, she's been asking, too . . . almost every day."

He must have seen the sudden light come into Philip's eye, for he said suddenly, turning to the window, "There's a good girl . . . a brave one, too."

"Yes," said Philip.

"She's the kind of a wife a man ought to have. There aren't many like her."

"No."

There was a long silence and McTavish said, "They can't win down there . . . everything's against 'em. It'll be over in two months and a lot of 'em never be able to get work within ten miles of a mill ever again."

Philip said nothing. He thrust his hands deep into the pockets of Jim Baxter's coat.

"They tried it too soon. They weren't strong enough. They'll win some day, but the time isn't yet."

Philip looked at him sharply. "I'm on their side. I know what it's like down there. Nobody else knows, except Irene Shane and Mary Conyngham."

"Does your Ma know it?" asked McTavish, with a grin.

"She must know it. She pretends not to."

"And the Reverend Castor?"

"No . . . I suppose he doesn't."

Philip thanked him abruptly, and went out of the door. When he had gone, McTavish poked up the fire, and sat staring into it. "I'm a regular old woman in some ways," he thought, "trying to meddle in people's affairs. But it needs a whole army to cope with Em."

Chapter 4

OUTSIDE, the world of the Flats lay spread out before him no longer alive with flame and clamor, but still now and cold and dead beneath the softly falling snow. There was no glow of fire; no wheel turned. Only the locomotives shrieked and puffed backward and forward over the shining rails. The streets were alive with people: they stood in little groups in the snow. On the bridge a little knot of them surrounded a speaker unknown to him, who harangued them in three tongues, urging them not to lose faith. At Hennessey's corner the lights cast a glow over the fallen snow—it was really white now that there was no longer any soot—and the tinny piano sent forth its showers of brassy notes into air that was no longer filled with the pounding of gigantic hammers. And the saloon was filled to the doors. Now and then a drunken Pole or Croat fell through the doors into the street. He saw what McTavish meant. They weren't strong enough yet. They were so weak that Hennessey alone could defeat them: his banging cash-register could swallow up their strength. He was a better friend of the Mill owners than all the men brought in to break the strike.

As he followed the path that lay among the garbage heaps by the side of the oily brook, it occurred to him that it was odd how strong he felt on this first sally from the house. He was strong, and suddenly so content that he forgot even the scene from which he had fled, running like a madman. It was as if he gained strength from treading the very soil of the Flats, as if it came to him from the contact of all these human creatures battling for existence. And among them he was lost, alone as he had been on those rare happy hours at Megambo when he had gone off into the jungle at the peril of his life. The snow fell all about him, silently, into the oil-muffled brook.

Crossing a vacant lot where the rubbish lay hidden beneath a carpet of snow, he came at last to the familiar doorway which he had not seen since the night six months before when he stood hidden in its shadow listening to the voice of Mary Conyngham. Feeling his way along the dark passageway, smelling of coal-gas and cabbage, he came at last to Krylenko's door. He knocked and the familiar voice called out something in Russian.

Pushing open the door, he saw Krylenko sitting on the edge of his iron bed with his head in his hands. There was no light in the room, but only the reflection of a rubbish fire some one had built in the yard outside the house. For a moment Philip stood leaning against the door, and when Krylenko did not raise his head, he said, "It's me . . . Philip Downes."

When he saw Krylenko's face, he knew that the strike was lost. Even in the reflected firelight, he seemed years older. He was thin, with deep lines on either side of his mouth.

"Oh, it's you, Feeleep. . . . I thought it was the old woman."

He rose and put a match to the gas and then peered closely into Philip's face, with the look of a man waking from a deep sleep.

"It's you. . . . Sit down."

Philip knew the room well. It was small and square, with no furniture save a bed, two pine chairs and a washstand. Above the bed there was a shelf made by Krylenko himself to hold the dangerous books that Irene Shane and her mother had given him . . . John Stuart Mill and Karl Marx and a single volume of Nietzsche.

"And how do you feel . . . huh?" asked Krylenko, seating himself once more on the bed.

"All right. Look at me."

"Kind-a skinny."

"You, too."

"Yeah! Look at me!" Krylenko said bitterly. "Look at me. . . . A bum! A failure! No job! Nothing."

"It's not as bad as that."

"It will be." He looked up. "Did yuh pass Hennessey's place?"

"Yes."

"Well, you see what it is . . . trying to make a lot of pigs fight. All they want is to quit work and get drunk. That's all it means to them."

"It's not over yet."

"It will be . . . I'm gonna fight it to the end. They're startin' to operate the B chain to-night . . . a lot of niggers from the South that ain't organized." He got up and went over to the window, standing with his back to Philip.

"We can make trouble for another month or two and then I'm finished, and me . . . I'm out of a job for good . . . down . . . on the blacklist. You know what that means."

It was an eloquent back, big, brawny and squared with defiance, despite all the tone of despair in his voice. The rumpled, yellow hair fairly bristled with vitality and battle. Philip thought, "He's not done yet. He's going on. He's got something to believe in . . . to fight for. For him it's only begun. He's got a giant to fight . . . and I'm fighting only two women."

Suddenly Krylenko turned. "Look," he said. "Look," pointing out of the window. "That's what they're up to now. They've bought up all the loose houses and they're turning the strikers out in the snow . . . on a night like this, God damn 'em. Look!"

Philip looked. Across the street in the falling snow lay a pitiful heap of odds and ends of some Slovak household . . . pots, kettles, battered chairs, blankets, a mattress or two. A woman and four small children, none of them more than six, stood drearily watching.

"And it's a hell of a thing to do. . . . A free country, hell! It belongs to a lot of crooked rich men." Suddenly, he thrust his big fist through the pane of glass and the tinkling fragments fell into the snow in the yard. "We're finished this time . . . but we've only begun!" He laughed. "The windows don't matter. They bought this house, too. A lot of niggers are movin' in to-morrow."

The blood was running from his cut knuckles and he bound them round silently with a red cotton handkerchief. Presently, he said, "You're looking for your paints and pictures. . . . They ain't here. . . . Mrs. Conyngham took 'em away."

"Mrs. Conyngham!"

"Yeah. . . . She came and got 'em herself. She's fixed up a place for you up at Shane's Castle . . . in the stable. I was to tell you and I forgot. She did it when she heard about the Mills buyin' up this row of houses. It's in the stable and you're to go up there whenever you want. There's a stove and everything."

He spoke in agitation, as though the paints, the pictures, were nothing compared to his own troubles. A little thing, of no use! Suddenly he turned, "And you, what are you goin' to do?"

"When?"

"Now you're finished, too. They've done with you, too. You're one of 'em. Don't forget that."

Yes, that was a thing he hadn't thought of. There must be people in the Town who hated him the way they hated the Shanes, and perhaps Mary Conyngham . . . as renegades, traitors. And while he waited there in the squalid room, watching Krylenko sitting with his head buried in his hands, there came to him for the first time a curious, intoxicating sense of satisfaction in being one of that odd little band—Krylenko, the saintly Irene, the dying old woman in Shane's Castle, and Mary Conyngham. The wind had begun to rise, and with it little gusts of snow swirled in through the broken window. He thought suddenly, "We are the leaven in the lump." He was not quite certain what he meant by that; he only knew that the lump was concerned vaguely with that mass of materialism and religion which made the character of the Town . . . a religion tamed and shopworn and subdued to commercial needs, a faith worn down to the level of convenience. Groping, it seemed to him that he was beginning to emerge at last, to be born as a soul, an individual.

"I mean to paint," he said suddenly.

"That won't feed you . . . and your children."

"No . . . I'll manage somehow." Nothing seemed impossible . . . nothing in the world . . . if he could only shake himself free. He thought, without any reason, "Krylenko is no more one of the mill workers than I am. If he were really one of them, he would be drunk now in Hennessey's place. There is something which sets him apart. . . . He isn't one of them either. He's as unhappy as I am."

Looking up, he asked suddenly, "And what about Giulia? Are you going to marry her?"

Without raising his hand, Krylenko answered, "No . . . that's finished now. If we'd won, it would have been all right. But now . . . it's no good . . . I'll be nothing but a tramp and bum."

He spoke in a strange, dead voice, as if he were saying, "It's a snowy night," as if something had died in him.

"No . . ." he repeated. "That's all finished. But you . . . you've got everything before you . . . and that girl . . . Mrs. Conyngham. . . ." He looked up suddenly, "She has faith in you . . . that's something." He looked at the great, nickeled watch he carried. "I've gotta go now. I've got to see about putting up tents for all of 'em who've been thrown out of their houses. It's a hell of a night to live in a tent." Rising, he took up his black felt hat. "What are you going to do?"

Philip wakened suddenly out of a haze of thought. "Me! I want to stay here to-night."

"Here in this room?"

"Yes."

"All right. . . Turn in there." He pointed to the rickety iron bed. "I'll be out most of the night, gettin' coal and blankets. See you later."

When he had gone, Philip felt suddenly ill again, and hopelessly weary. He lay down on the bed wrapped in Jim Baxter's overcoat, and in a moment fell asleep.

At two, when Krylenko finally returned, there was a little drift of snow by the broken window. Going over to the bed, he stood for a time looking down at Philip, and then, with a great gentleness, he lifted him, and, drawing out the blanket, laid it over him, carefully tucking in the edge to keep out the cold. When he had finished, he lay down, keeping well over to the edge in order not to disturb Philip. It was all done with the tenderness of a strong man fostering the weak, of a great, clumsy father protecting a little boy.

Chapter 5

IN THE MORNING Philip awakened to find Krylenko already gone. It was still snowing as he went out into the empty street and made his way toward the shed where there was always hot coffee for the strikers and their families. He stood there among them, drinking his coffee and feeling the old sense of satisfaction of being in a world stripped bare to those things which lay at the foundations of life. This was solid, with a rawness that bit into the soul. He took out a pencil and on a bit of newspaper began to sketch fragments of the scene about him—a Croat woman who was feeding coffee to her three small children out of a clumsy teacup, a gigantic, bearded Slovak and his wizened, tubercular wife, a baby wrapped in the ragged remains of a pair of overalls, a thin, white, shivering girl, with the face of a Madonna. They were simply sketches, reduced to the very skeletons of drawing, yet they were in a way eloquent and moving. He felt intoxicatingly sure of his hand, and he saw all at once that they were the best things he had ever done. Set down on the face of columns of printing, they caught the cold misery and the dumb bravery of these puzzled, wretched people, suffering silently in the midst of a hostile, foreign country. Looking at the sketches, he saw that by some ironic chance he had chosen to draw directly upon an editorial condemning them. He began to read. The fragment was torn, and so had no beginning. ". . . sacred rights of property must be protected against the attacks of men little better than brutes who have come, infected with poison of socialism and anarchy, to undermine the institutions of a great, free and glorious nation favored by God. These wretches must be treated as they deserve, without consideration, as beasts bent upon tearing down our most sacred institutions and destroying our God-given prosperity."

It was signed in bold black type with the name MOSES SLADE. He was quite safe in his attack, thought Philip: foreign-born mill workers had no votes.

A hand touched Philip's shoulder and a voice said, "Give me that." It was Krylenko. "I can use it," he said. "I know just where it belongs."

He gave it to Krylenko without a word.

From the steaming coffee-shed he made his way through a street filled with people and bordered with pitiful little heaps of shabby household goods like that which he had seen from Krylenko's window the night before. He passed Hennessey's place and, crossing the railroad tracks, came within the area of the Mills. It was silent here. Even the trolleys had ceased to run since one car had had its windows shattered. Beyond this he came to the

great iron fence that shut in the park of Shane's Castle. At the gates he
turned in, following the drive that ran between rows of dead and dying
Norway spruce up to the house that crowned the hill. It was silent in the
park and the falling snow half veiled the distant gables and odd Gothic
windows of the big house. Among the dead trees it occurred to him that there
was a peace here which did not exist elsewhere in the whole Town. It was
an enchanted place where a battered old woman, whom he had seen but
once or twice, lay dying.

Following the drive, he passed the wrought-iron portico and the little
cast-iron Eros who held a ring in his outstretched hand and served as a
hitching-post. The towering cedars that gave the place a name—Cypress
Hill—which all the world had long ago forgotten, loomed black and melancholy against the sky. And, turning the corner, he came suddenly within
sight of the stables.

Before the door an old negro swept away the falling snow with a worn
and stubby broom. He did not hear the approach of Philip, for he was
deaf and the snow muffled the sound of footsteps. It was only when Philip
said "Good-morning" that he turned his head and, grinning, said, "You must
be Mr. Downes."

"Yes."

"The room's all ready for you."

The old man, muttering to himself, led the way. At the top of the stairs, he
said, "If I'd knowed you was a-comin' I'd a-had a fire."

The place was all swept and in order and in one corner stood all the
things which Mary Conyngham had carried there from Krylenko's room.
The sight of them touched him with emotion, as if something of Mary herself clung to them. He wanted to see her more than he wanted anything in
the world. He stood looking out of the window while the old nigger waited,
watching him. He was sure that in some way she could wipe out the sickening memory of that awful scene. The window gave out over the Mills, which
lay spread out, cold and desolate and silent, save for the distant K section,
where smoke had begun to drift from the chimneys. He would paint the
scene from this window, in all its dreary bleakness—in grays and whites and
cold blues, with the faintest tinge of pink. It was like a hell in which the
fires had suddenly burned to cold ashes. No, he must see Mary. He had to see
her. He couldn't go on like this. It wasn't possible for any human creature
to be thirsty for so long—thirsty for peace and honesty and understanding.

He began to see himself in the mawkish light of one who suffered and
was put upon, and what had been impossible before began in the light of
self-pity to seem possible.

He had (he knew) to go back to the slate-colored house. Turning, he said
to the old nigger, "I'm coming back," and then halting, he asked, "How's
Mrs. Shane?"

"She ain't no better, sir. She's dying, and nothin' kin save her." Suddenly the black face lighted up. "But Miss Lily's come back. She came back last night."

"Yes?"

"You don't know Miss Lily, mebbe."

"No. . . . I've seen her years ago riding through the Town."

"Then you don't know what she's like. . . . The old Missie can die now that Miss Lily's come home. She jus' couldn't die without seein' Miss Lily."

Philip scarcely heard him. He was thinking about his own troubles, and Lily Shane was a creature who belonged to another world whose borders would never touch his own. Even as a boy, looking after her as she rode in the mulberry victoria up Park Avenue, it never occurred to him that he would ever come nearer to her. There was something magnificent about her that set her apart from all the others in the Town. And there was always the wicked glamour that enveloped one who, it was whispered, had had a child out of wedlock and then declined to marry its father.

How could Lily Shane ever touch the world of Uncle Elmer and Naomi and Emma and Mabelle? No, she did not exist for him. She was like one of the actresses he had followed furtively along Main Street as a boy, because a mysterious, worldly glamour clung to those ladies who appeared in town one night and disappeared the next into the great world. No creature could have been more remote than these coryphées from the slate-colored house and the prayer-meetings of the Reverend Castor.

Chapter 6

IT WAS the Reverend Castor himself who greeted Philip on the doorstep when he reached home at last. Philip would have avoided him, but the clergyman was coming down the path as he turned into it and so there was no escape.

He greeted Philip with a smile, saying, "Well, it's good to see you about again, my boy. We had a bad time over you . . . thought you weren't going to make the grade."

Philip grinned. "I'm not so easy to be rid of." He felt a sudden refreshing sense of superiority over the preacher, strange in all his experience. It was simply that he had no longer any awe of him as a man of God.

The Reverend Castor coughed and answered, "Oh! My dear boy. We didn't want to be rid of you. That's the last thing. . . ." He protested nervously and added, "I just dropped in for a moment to see how your wife was doing . . . and the twins. You ought to be proud, my boy, of two such fine babies . . . two. Most people are thankful for one."

"I would have been, too."

"You don't mean you aren't delighted with what God has sent you?"

"No . . . of course not . . . I was only making a joke." It hardly seemed honest, Philip thought, to give God the credit for the twins.

"I suppose we'll be having Mrs. Downes back with us in the choir soon. . . . Since Mrs. Timpkins has moved to Indianapolis I've asked your wife to be the leader and the librarian of the music."

"Yes . . . she ought to be back soon. She seems strong again."

There was an awkward silence, and the Reverend Castor's kindly blue eyes turned suddenly aside. He started to speak and then halted abruptly and seized Philip's hand a second time. "Well, good-by. I must be off."

He was gone quickly, and for a moment Philip stood looking after him, puzzled by his strange, nervous manner. He was sorry for this poor man, whom he had always disliked. It was a sorrow he could not explain, save that his life must be a hell with a wife like his, and all the women of the parish on his neck. He did his duty, the Reverend Castor. He never shirked. It was good of him to call on Naomi. She would like such attention from the head of her church. It would bring back to her, Philip thought, some of the old glory and importance that had waned steadily since the night they had got down from the train, shivering, and fearful of what lay before them.

And she would be pleased at being asked to lead the choir and take care of the music. It was odd what little things brought happiness to her. She had need of the little things, for he meant to hurt her. He was certain now that it was the only way out. It would be easier for her to face the truth.

He found her sitting in the parlor where the Reverend Castor had left her. She was dressed for the first time since the twins were born, and she had been crying. As he entered, she came over to him and, putting her arms about his neck, pressed her head against Jim Baxter's overcoat, and said, "I'm ashamed, Philip . . . I want to die. I couldn't help it yesterday. It's the way I feel! I feel so tired."

The whole action disturbed him horribly. She had never done such a thing before; she had never done more than kiss him chastely. He freed himself and, still holding her hands, said, "I understand. It's all over now and I understand."

She began to cry again helplessly, pitifully. "You'll forgive me? You'll forgive me?"

"There's nothing to forgive. I understand it." He pushed her gently into a chair, and sat down beside her, silently, wondering how he could bring himself to say what he *had* to say.

"It's because I'm so unhappy, Philip. . . . I've been unhappy ever since we left Megambo . . . ever since that Englishwoman stopped there. I wish to God we'd never seen her."

"Let's not think about her. She had nothing to do with it."

"And it's so awful in this dreary house. I'm nothing here, Philip. . . . I'm less than a hired girl. Your Ma hates me. . . ." He tried to speak, but she cried out passionately, "I can't go on living here . . . I can't . . . I can't."

As he sat there, all his horror of scenes, of that wretched scene in the same room the evening before, swept over him. It was like a physical sickness rising into his throat and choking him. He was confused, too, with a sense of impotent rage.

"And after you ran away she told Mabelle she was never to enter the house again. . . . Now I haven't any one."

No, she hadn't any one, but she didn't know yet how alone she really was. "Naomi," he said quietly. "Naomi . . . listen to me . . . try to control yourself."

"Yes. . . . Yes. . . . I'm trying to." Her pale, homely face was even paler with weeping. Her eyes were swollen beneath the transparent lashes and her nose was red.

"Naomi . . . would you like to have a house of your own?"

"Oh, Philip . . . yes."

"I don't mean a whole house, but a place to live . . . two or three rooms where you'd be away from my mother."

"Yes . . . yes. I'd do better. I'd take care of things . . . if I had a chance in my own place. Oh, Philip—if you'd only be kind to me."

He stroked her hand suddenly, but it was only because he pitied her. "I try to be kind, Naomi."

"You've been so hard to me . . . just like a stone—ever since we left Megambo. Oh, I knew it . . . I knew even when. . . ." She broke off suddenly, without finishing. Philip looked away, sick with misery. He pitied her, but he could not love her. She went on and on. "Out there I had something to live for . . . I had my work. I loved it. It was the only life I'd ever known. It was everything. And here . . . there's nothing. I don't know how to live here."

"There are the children," he said in a quiet voice.

"Yes . . . but that's not what I mean. It's my soul I'm thinking of. It's rotting away here. . . ."

"Mine was rotting at Megambo." She did not answer him, and he said, "There's church work to do, and now Reverend Castor wants you to lead the choir."

"But it's not the same, and they're all jealous of me . . . all those women . . . jealous because I'm more important because I've been a missionary, and jealous because Reverend Castor shows me favors. Oh, I know. I don't belong here, and they don't want me here. Oh, I don't know what's to become of me!"

There was a long silence, in which they sat there, dumbly trying to find some way out of the hopeless muddle, trying to patch together something which was now in tatters, if it had ever existed at all. Philip's thin jaw was set in that hard, stubborn line that made even his mother afraid.

"Naomi," he said presently, "I'll get you a place to live. It won't be much, for I haven't much money, but you'll be free . . . to do what you please. Only . . . only, Naomi . . . I . . . I . . ." Suddenly, his head fell forward, and he buried his face in his hands. In a voice that was hardly audible he said, "I don't want to live with you any longer. It's . . . it's all over."

For a long time there was no sound in the room, save the ticking of the great onyx clock beneath the picture of Jason Downes. Naomi didn't even sob; but presently she said, in a voice like the voice of a deaf person, "Philip, you mean you're going to leave me?"

"No," he said slowly. "No . . . it's not that exactly. I shan't leave you. I'll come and see you every day and the children—only I won't sleep in the house. I'm going to sleep where I work."

In the same dead voice she asked, "You're not going back to the Mills?"

"No, I'm not going back to the Mills . . . they wouldn't have me now. I'm going to paint. . . ."

"Pictures?"

"Yes . . . pictures. That's what I've always wanted to do and now . . . now, nothing can stop me." There was in his voice a sudden cold rasp, as of steel, which must have terrified her. He thought, "I've got to do it, if I'm to live. I've got to do it."

She said, "But you could have a good congregation. You could preach."

"No, that's the last thing I could do. I'm through with all that."

"Oh, my God! Oh, my God!"

He raised his head, and saw that she was biting her handkerchief. "Naomi," he said. "Naomi," and the sound of her name seemed to precipitate a sudden climax. She fell on her knees and beat them with her fists.

"You won't do that, Philip. You can't . . . you can't leave me for everybody to mock at. Say that you won't . . . I was wrong in the beginning, but now I'll do anything. I'll lie down and let you walk over my body!"

"Naomi," he said. "Please! For God's sake!"

"Oh, don't you see! It's different now . . . I love you. Don't you see that makes it different?"

"It can't make it different, Naomi. I can't pretend what isn't true . . . it's a thing a man can't do."

Suddenly she stopped sobbing and looked up at him, her face all white and contorted. "You can't say that! You can't mean it! It isn't true!"

"It's true, Naomi. I can't help myself. I wish to God I could!"

"And you didn't love me . . . even . . . even then?"

He made a heroic effort. "No . . . not even then."

She flung herself on the floor, pressing her face against the carpet, moaning and moaning. Kneeling down, he picked her up bodily and laid her on the sofa. Bending over her—

"Naomi . . . listen to me. It's not my fault. It's not yours. It's all a muddle. Nobody's to blame."

Then she sat up suddenly. "Yes, there is. It's your mother who's to blame. She made me marry you. It all began with that. I didn't want to . . . I didn't want to marry any one, but I wanted to have a mission of my own. She did it. She's to blame, and now she hates me. She thinks I've stolen you from her."

She buried her face in the cushions and lay sobbing. After a time, Philip said, "Naomi . . . listen to me. You didn't steal me from her."

"Who did then?" said Naomi's muffled voice.

"I don't know. It just happened. I suppose it's one of the things that happen in life. I've grown up now. I've grown up since we went to Megambo. That's all. I know my own mind now."

"Oh, you're hard, Philip . . . harder than flint." She sat up slowly. "I'll do anything for you. You can wipe your feet on me. I can't let you go now . . . I can't . . . I can't!" She began suddenly to laugh. "I'll do anything! I'll prove to you I can keep house as well as your mother. I'll show you how I can care for the children. They're your children, too. I'll learn to cook . . . I'll do anything!"

He did not answer her. He simply sat staring out of the window like an image carven of stone. And he was saying to himself all the while, "I can't yield. I daren't do it. I can't—not now." And all the while he felt a kind of disgust for the nakedness of this love of Naomi's. It was a shameful thing. And during all their life together he had thought her incapable of such love.

She kept moaning and saying, over and over again, "I've got nothing now. I'm all alone . . . I've got nothing now."

He rose, and laid a hand on her shoulder. "I'm going now, Naomi. I'm not going to the restaurant. I'll come back this afternoon. It'll be all right. We'll work it out somehow."

She looked up at him. "You've changed your mind?"

"No, I don't mean that. No, it's better this way."

"I'll show you, Philip, what a good wife I can be."

He picked up his hat, Jim Baxter's hat, and suddenly he thought, "The old Philip is dead—as dead as Jim Baxter. I've dared to do it."

Aloud he said, "Let's not talk any more now. I'll be back in an hour or two when you feel better."

Then he went away, and outside the house, among the lilacs, he was suddenly sick.

Chapter 7

HE FOUND a tiny flat of three rooms over a drugstore halfway up the hill from the railway station. It had been occupied by the family of a salesman who traveled for a house which manufactured false teeth. He had been promoted to a western territory where, with the great boom in the silver mines, the market for gold teeth had risen enormously.

He was a little fat man, with enormous black mustaches, all aglow with his promotion. "It's the best gold tooth territory in America," he told Philip.

The apartment rented for thirty dollars a month. The bubbling salesman would leave the furniture behind for two hundred and fifty dollars. Philip could move in the day after to-morrow.

He left the place, his whole body warmed by the satisfaction of having acted, of having done something definite. But the thing was not settled yet, because his mother still remained to be told.

He found her in the kitchen of the restaurant, superintending the preparation of mince-meat according to a recipe of her own which eliminated all intoxicating liquors. Standing over the negress who did the work, she was the essence of vigor and authority, her face crimsoned by the heat of the place, her hair all in disorder.

"Ma," he said to her. "I have something I want to discuss with you."

After bidding the negress wait until she returned, she followed him quickly, surprised and troubled by the look in his eye and the set of his jaw. The talk took place at the table behind the screen where Moses Slade came every day to eat.

"It's about Naomi, Ma . . . I've taken some rooms for her to live in. She won't trouble you any longer. We'll move out on Tuesday."

She looked at him for a moment in astonishment. "But, Philip," she said, "you ought to have consulted me. You mustn't do that. We can't even think of it."

"The rent is paid. I've bought furniture."

"Where did you get the money?"

"I used what Grandpa left me."

"I thought you'd pledged the interest on that to the mission."

"I've taken it back. I took it back before I was sick."

She didn't say anything for a long while. She saw suddenly that he was changed, more hardened even than she had feared. He didn't even come to her any longer for advice. He had shut her out altogether. At last she said, "But, Philip, what will people think—when I've a house big enough for you all?"

"I don't care any longer what people think. I can't go through any more scenes like yesterday. Besides, a man has a right to his own house."

"But, Philip . . . my house is your house. I've worked all these years and sacrificed. . . . Oh, you don't know what it's meant sometimes. I wouldn't even let Uncle Elmer help me—so that you'd have the house for your own. It wasn't for myself. . . . I could have got along somehow."

He looked away from her at the mustard-pot in the center of the table. "You know that you can't get on with Naomi—and she hates living in your house."

"I can try . . . we can both try. If only she'd take a little interest and not make the place into a pigstye."

"You know she won't change."

"Philip, I'll do anything . . . I'll put up with Naomi . . . I won't say a word, only don't leave me now after all the years when I'm an old woman."

She saw the stubborn jaw set in a hard line. The sight of it stirred a sudden, turbulent emotion: it was his father's jaw over again, terrifying in its identity. What had she done to deserve such treatment from these two men to whom she had given up all her life without once a thought of herself? She had worked for them, sacrificed. . . .

Philip was saying, "It won't make any difference. Even if you and Naomi never spoke to each other. You'd be hating each other all the time. Don't you see? That's what I can't stand."

She reached over and touched his hand. "Philip . . . once you used to come to me with everything, and now . . . now you treat me like a stranger . . . me, your own mother. Why don't you come to me? I want to share your life, to be a part of it. It's all I live for. You're all I've got."

He felt her trying to capture him once more. What she said was true . . . you couldn't deny it. She had given her whole life to him. Every word she spoke hurt him.

"I don't know, Ma. Nothing has happened except maybe that I'm grown up now. I'm a man. I've got to decide things for myself."

It was that hard, brutal jaw which she couldn't overcome. It had thwarted her always. With Jason, when his jaw was set thus, it was as if his heart had turned to stone.

"Where did you go last night?"

He told her, and the answer frightened her. In the Flats, in a Dago's boarding-house, her son had passed a night.

"Where did that coat come from?"

"It belonged to Jim Baxter, who was killed at the grade-crossing last week. I borrowed it from McTavish."

"So you've been seeing him."

"Yes, he told you I wouldn't come home, didn't he?"

"Yes," she said, with a sudden flash of anger. "Yes . . . he told me. I wish you wouldn't see so much of him, Philip. He's a wicked man."

He made no response to this sudden, feeble sally of the old authority. He had, she discovered with awe, that old trick of his father's—of not answering in an argument unless he had something to say. It was an unfair method, because it always kept the argument upon the level of reason, excluding all the force of the emotions.

"And I'm not coming home any more to sleep, Ma. That's all finished."

He must have seen the look of fear in her eyes. It was that look he had seen there whenever, for a moment, she seemed to lose control of that solid world she had built up.

"But, Philip . . . it's your house . . . your own home. You've never had any other." He said nothing, and she asked, "Where are you going to sleep?"

Slowly, and then carefully, so that it would hurt her as little as possible, he told her about the stable at Shane's Castle, and his plan of painting. She listened, half believing that she could not be in her right mind, that what she heard was only part of a nightmare. She kept interrupting him, saying, "But, Philip, you never told me . . . I didn't know," and when he had finished, she said abruptly, "That wasn't the plan I had for you, Philip; I've been talking with Reverend Castor and he thinks we could arrange to get you a good congregation."

"No . . . that's all finished. It's no use even talking of it."

She went on, ignoring him. "And if that didn't please you, I thought . . . well, you could take the restaurant because, well . . ." she looked away from him, "you see, I'm thinking of getting married."

She saw his face grow red with anger. "Not to that humbug, Moses Slade!"

"Yes, Philip. But it's wrong of you to call him a humbug. He's a distinguished man, a good man, who stands for the best in the community."

"He's a hypocrite and a humbug!"

An uncontrollable rage took possession of him. It was impossible that he was to have Moses Slade, the humbug who had written that editorial about the strike, for a stepfather. No, it was outlandish, too impossible, that a good woman like his mother should be taken in by that lecherous old rip.

"Philip," she was saying. "You don't understand. I've been alone always . . . except for you—ever since your father died. It would be a good marriage, a distinguished marriage, and I wouldn't be alone in my old age."

"You couldn't marry him. You couldn't marry a fat old man like that."

He fancied that he saw her wince. "It isn't a question of love, Philip, at our age. It's companionship. I'm very fond of him, and he's been thoughtful—so thoughtful all the time you were sick."

"It's disgusting!"

It was odd, what had happened—that he found himself for the first time in his life taking a high hand with his mother. It was an intoxicating sensation.

"If I give him up, I'll be giving up a great opportunity for good. As a Congressman's wife, there's no end to the things I could accomplish. . . ." She began to cry. "But I'll give him up . . . I'll give him up if you won't turn your back on your poor mother. I'd do anything for you, Philip. You're all I've got, and I hoped for so much—to see you one of the great men of the church, a Christian leader, fighting on the side of God."

"It's no good, Ma. I won't go back to that."

One of the waitresses appeared suddenly from behind the screen. "Mrs. Downes . . ." she began.

"Go away! Go away! I'll talk to you later."

The girl disappeared.

"And that isn't all, Ma. I'm not going to live with Naomi any more. I'm through with that. I meant what I said when I was sick."

"Philip—listen to me, Philip!"

"No . . . I'll come to see her and the children. But I'm through."

"What will people think? What will they say?"

"You can tell them I've got a night job. . . . Nobody'll know, except Aunt

Mabelle, where Naomi is going to live. Nobody will see me come or go. It's in Front Street."

"Front Street! Why, that's on the edge of the Flats! You can't do that!"

He looked at her for a long time in despairing silence. "My God, Ma! Can't you see? Can't you understand?.From now on, I'm going to stand on my own. I'm going to work things out. I've got to get out of this mess. . . . I've *got* to."

He rose abruptly, and put on his coat.

"Philip," she asked, drying her eyes, "where are you going now?"

"I'm going to buy blankets for myself."

"Philip, listen to me. For God's sake, listen! Don't ruin everything. I've a right to something. I'm your mother. Doesn't that mean anything?"

He turned for a moment hesitating, and then quickly said, "Ma, don't talk like that, it isn't fair."

Without another word, he put on his hat and hurried out of the restaurant.

Once outside, the cold air cleared his head, and he was thankful that he had been hard as a stone. Again he was sorry for Emma in a vague, inexplicable fashion; she could never understand what it was that made him hard. She couldn't see why he had to behave thus.

"I wish to God," he thought bitterly, "that I'd had a mother who wasn't a fine woman. Life would have been so much easier. And I can't hurt her . . . I can't. I love her."

And suddenly he saw that in all their talk together nothing had really been settled. Nothing had been changed or decided.

Chapter 8

HE WENT that night to sleep in the room above the stable, and on the following Tuesday Naomi and the twins moved into the three rooms above the drugstore in Front Street. Emma stayed home from the restaurant all day, going and coming to and from the newly established household. She did and thought of everything, so that Naomi in the end gave up, and, sitting on the imitation-tapestry davenport, simply watched her mother-in-law arrange the new household. Mabelle was there, too, with little Jimmy, in the way most of the time, or making suggestions which Emma ignored. She was a creature whose feelings were not easily hurt and all Emma's bitter remarks seemed to have left no trace. When they had left Naomi with the three rooms in order, she even walked home with Emma, dragging the tired and whining Jimmy behind her.

As she hurried through the darkness after Emma's tall, robust form, she panted, "Well, things might go better now. I always think young people ought to start out in a house of their own."

"Yes," said Emma, certain from the remark that Naomi hadn't told Mabelle the whole truth.

"It's funny what a change has come over Philip. He's much nicer than he used to be."

"What on earth do you mean by that, Mabelle?"

Here Jimmy set up a yell—"I don't wanna walk! I wanna be carried!"

"All right, dear, only you mustn't cry. Little men don't cry."

"Well, I do. I'm tired. I don't wanna walk!"

"All right, dear." She bent down and picked up the child. He continued to whine, but at least their progress was not retarded.

"If he were my child, Mabelle," said Emma, "I'd just leave him sitting on the curb till he got good and ready to walk. I never had any trouble with Philip. He's always been *obedient* and respectful."

"But Jimmy's delicate, and I'd rather carry him than have him whine."

"He's whining in any case," said Emma, acidly.

Mabelle was puffing now beneath her burden and the long steps of Emma. But she managed to say, "What I mean about Philip is . . . that he's more masterful now. He's a man. He's the kind of a man that women have a right to be afraid of."

Emma snorted. "Don't talk such rot, Mabelle. If you'd read less trash."

"It's funny about him taking up with the Shanes."

Naomi *had* told her, then, about the stable. And Mabelle was a sieve: whatever you told her poured right on through. "He hasn't taken up with the Shanes. He's simply using their stable to work in. That's not the same thing. Why, he barely knows them—except that half-crazy old maid, Irene. And he doesn't know the others at all."

"Then it must be that Mary Conyngham. She's friends with them."

"Mary Conyngham!" repeated Emma. "Mary Conyngham! Why, he hasn't seen her in years!" But the shock of the name turned her suddenly thoughtful, so that she walked at a slower pace, mercifully for Mabelle.

"Well, he *might* have seen her," persisted Mabelle. "She's mixed up with Irene Shane's school for the Dagoes and Hunkies. They all belong to the same crowd . . . all thinking they can make something out of a lot of bums." For a moment she was so completely winded that she could not speak. When she recovered her breath, she said, "I remembered the other night that they'd been sweet on each other once."

Still Emma walked furiously in silence, and presently Mabelle said, "Of course, I didn't say anything about her to Naomi. She might be upset just now."

"No," said Emma, "and don't say anything to her about it or to any one else. It's nonsense."

"Well, I didn't know. I was just interested in Philip, and Naomi, and in his queer behavior, and I always find that when a man goes off his head like that, there's a woman about somewhere."

"I forbid you, Mabelle, to speak of it to any one." She halted and took

Mabelle by the shoulder. "You understand? That's the way silly talk gets started."

Mabelle was silent as they resumed their way, but presently she said, "That Lily Shane . . . she's come home to see the old woman die."

"They're a bad lot, all of 'em," said Emma, "and I guess she's the Jezebel of the lot."

"I hate to see a good boy like Philip getting mixed up with people like that."

"He's not getting mixed up, I tell you."

"What am I to tell people about him, Em, if they ask me?"

"Tell them that he's going to be an artist. You might say, too, that he has a fine talent, and later he's going to New York to study."

She had thought it all out. There was only one method—"to take the bull by the horns." If Philip wasn't one day to be a bishop, he might be a great artist and paint great religious pictures like the man who did the Sistine Madonna or the Flight into Egypt.

The voice of Jimmy interrupted her thoughts. "Aren't we nearly home? I'm hungry!"

"Yes, dearie. That's your house right there. . . . See the one with the red light in the window?"

"I don't like Aunt Em. I wish she'd go away."

"Shh! Jimmy! Shh! He's tired, Em, that's all—the poor little thing."

They reached the house with the red light in the window, and bade each other good-night.

"Remember what I said," was Emma's final word.

After she left the gate, only one thought occupied the mind of Emma, the thought that it was Mary Conyngham who had stolen Philip from them both —from herself and Naomi. "Mary Conyngham, of course," she told herself. "What a fool I've been not to think of her before! It *would* be like her and her superior ways. The Watts always thought nobody good enough for 'em but the Shanes—that bawdy old woman and her two daughters—one a lunatic and the other a harlot. Yes, Mary Conyngham could carry on to her heart's content there in the Flats, and no one would know of it. The Shanes would only help her. Shane's Castle had been like a bawdy-house in the days when old John Shane was still living."

She was in a savage humor, born partly of her irritation at Naomi's helplessness, and partly of disgust at Mabelle's feeble-minded chatter; and now she had found an object on which to pin it. It was Mary Conyngham who lay at the root of everything: it explained why Mary had stopped her that day to ask about Philip.

"Mabelle," she thought, "is a dangerous woman, going about and saying things like that when she *knows* nothing."

Mabelle was a constructive gossip. Having nothing to keep her occupied, she sat about all day thinking up things, putting two and two together, pinning odd pieces of stories together to construct a whole, but she *did* have (thought Emma) an uncanny way of scenting out scandal; her only fault was that she sometimes told the story before in fact it had happened. She came upon a scrap, the merest suspicion of some dubious story, and presently after days of morbid brooding it reappeared, trimmed and garnished to perfection, with such an air of reality about it that if it wasn't true, it might easily have been.

It was the uncanny faculty of Mabelle's that really troubled Emma. Her suspicion of Mary Conyngham frightened her even while it gave her satisfaction. It occurred to her that Philip was now quite beyond control, as his father had sometimes been. Anything might happen. She dared not think of it. For a moment she felt the quick shadow of foreboding, of some tragedy that lay ahead, beyond the power of anything to prevent.

She shook it off quickly, thinking, "That is nonsense. I can still bring Philip to his senses."

Inside the house, she prepared her own supper, and spent an hour in clearing up her own house, putting from sight every trace of Naomi.

At nine o'clock Moses Slade came to call. He was in a furious temper. He brought with him a labor periodical, called *The Beacon*.

"It was marked," he said, "and sent to me through the mail."

Opening it, he showed her the desecration of his most admired editorial. It was a fragment of the local newspaper, stained and torn, which read, ". . . sacred rights of property must be protected against the attacks of men little better than brutes, etc., etc.," and signed in large black letters MOSES SLADE. On the face of the printing some irreverent hand had made a series of drawings in pencil—a Croat woman feeding her three small children with coffee out of a clumsy tin cup, a gigantic, bearded Slovak and his wizened, tubercular wife, a baby wrapped in the remains of a ragged pair of overalls, a thin, shivering girl with the face of a Madonna. The whole had been photographed and reproduced.

Underneath them was a line which read, "These are the brutes of the Honorable Moses Slade who have endangered our most sacred institutions and destroyed our God-given prosperity." And beside it was a caricature of Slade himself, gross, overdressed, with flowing locks and a leering expression, beneath which was written: "Puzzle—find the beast on these two pages."

He banged the table with his hamlike fist. "By God, I'll find out who did it, and make him pay for his impudence! I'm not a force in this Town for nothing!"

Emma turned faintly pale, but she only said, "It's shameful, I think, Moses, but what can you expect from such people? They have no respect for our institutions . . . our excellent Congressmen."

But she knew well enough who had made the drawing.

Chapter 9

IN THE FLAT in Front Street, Philip put the last chair in place, washed his face and hands at the sink in the kitchen, and went in to look at the sleeping twins. They lay side by side, fat, rosy, healthy children, such as women like Naomi or Mabelle were certain to bear. He was alone in the room, and, after a time, he bent down and touched the fine, soft dark hair that covered their small, round heads. They were like him, and so, he supposed, like his father, with eyes that one day would be the same clear blue. It struck him suddenly that there was something ruthless in the operation of Nature which took no account of all the structure of habits and laws of man. It took no account of the fact that he had never loved Naomi, or that neither of them had really wanted these children. Nature had wanted children, and it did not matter how they were created, so long as the act of creation occurred. All man's ideas of love, of lawful wedlock, of sentimentality, had nothing to do with it. And it was impossible to imagine stronger, healthier children.

He fell to stroking the soft head of the little girl, and, slowly, in her sleep, she stirred and, groping with a fat, pink hand, found one of his fingers, and clutched it tightly. Something in the touch of the soft, plump hand melted him suddenly. She was so soft, so helpless, reaching out trustfully. And for the first time he felt a sudden quick pride and delight. These were *his* children; he knew that he loved them, despite everything, Naomi and his mother and all the trouble he had been through. They were *his* to care for and protect and set on their way in life. That was a wonderful thing. When he thought of it, he was frightened; and yet (he reflected) he would perhaps understand far better than most fathers how to help them. He had learned, he thought, bitterly, by his own blundering.

The little girl still clung tightly to his finger, and presently he found himself smiling, without knowing it. He was, oddly enough, suddenly happy, and conscious that no matter what fate befell him, it was good to be alive. He wasn't sorry any longer that he had helped to bring into existence these two fat, funny little morsels of life. He almost laughed, and then, bending down, he kissed first one and then the other on the tops of their round, dark little heads. They were his: he was a father. And it had happened without his wanting it, almost without his understanding how it had happened.

He was still bending over them when the door opened and, with a sense of falling spirits, he heard Naomi come in. Ever since that horrible day in his mother's parlor, she had made an effort to dress completely and neatly, but somehow it was impossible for her to accomplish it entirely. Little wisps of sandy hair fell down over the back of her high tight collar. Her white petticoat, showing itself an inch or two below her skirts, dragged on the floor. There was a smudge of the dust left behind by the dental salesman's wife on one side of her face. She might set herself in order a dozen times a day, but always, in some mysterious way, she was in disarray. At Megambo, it hadn't made any difference: in a place like that such things were lost in the whole cataclysm of disorder. But here in a civilized place, it was different. It was as if Naomi could not cope with the problems of decent living.

At the sound of the opening door, Philip straightened up quickly, as if ashamed to be found thus, caressing his children. But Naomi had seen him, and smiled—an odd, twisted, pitiful smile, which was like a knife turned in his flesh, for behind it lay a whole regiment of ghosts, of implications. It was as if he saw suddenly what happiness there might be in life, if he himself had been different, if Naomi had been a different woman, if he had only been able to love her. He couldn't change: he saw again how ruthless a thing Nature could be. Some one had meddled with her plans, and so the misery resulted. It was not that he thought these things: the whole impression happened far more quickly than any process of thought. It was a sudden, pitiful flash of illumination. What hurt him most was the faint hint of bitterness in her smile, a hint almost of mockery, a shadow which had crossed her pale, freckled face without her knowing it. But until now, he hadn't thought her capable of suffering in that way.

It frightened him by making him feel weak and yielding.

Perhaps if she had been a more clever woman, she could in that moment have changed the whole course of his life. Long afterward when he thought of the scene (and it always remained one of his clearest memories of her) he saw that it *could* have been done. But then he saw that if she had been a more clever woman he might have loved her in the beginning.

She came over and stood by his side. "What are we to call them, Philip? We've never even spoken of it." She said it in a flat voice, as if they had been puppies or kittens, and not children—*his* children—at all.

"I don't know."

"I've been thinking about the girl. Your mother would like to call her Emma, but I'd like it if you'd call her Naomi."

He knew before she had finished what she had meant to say, and he knew, too, that he hated both names. To go on for the rest of his life, even as an old man, calling his child "Emma" or "Naomi". . . .

"She's your child, too, Naomi. You have a choice in the matter."

"I wanted you to be pleased." There was a humbleness in her voice which made him feel ill.

"And the boy—have you thought of him?"

"I want to call him Philip, of course."

(No, he couldn't do that: it was like wishing them bad luck.)

"No, I hate the name of Philip. You can call the girl Naomi. You bore her, and you've more of a right to name her than Ma has. But—no, we won't call the boy Philip. We'll think of something else."

"I'd like to have her called Naomi . . . and then you'd think of me sometimes, Philip."

He looked at her sharply. "But I do think of you. Why should you say that?"

"Oh, I don't know . . . just in case anything happened to me. That's why I'd like to call him Philip."

"No . . . no . . . any other name."

He took up his hat. "What are you going to do with the twins on Sundays and choir practice nights?"

"I don't know. I'd thought of asking Mabelle to stay with them . . . but she lives such a long way off. Maybe I'd just better give it up."

"No, you mustn't do that. I'll come and stay with them. I'd like to."

"You don't mind my leading the choir, Philip?"

"No, of course not."

"Because I want you to be pleased. I want it to be a new start now, here in this new house."

He didn't answer, and after an awkward pause, she said, "I wouldn't go at all, but I think Reverend Castor needs me. He's got so many worries. Yesterday when I was talking to him, he began all at once to cry . . . not out loud, but the tears just came into his eyes. His wife's an awful woman. He's been telling me about her. And now that Mrs. Timpkins has moved away, there's no one to take the choir who knows anything about music."

"Of course, go by all means."

He was glad for two reasons, because he knew she liked the importance of leading the choir, and because he would have these evenings alone with the children—*his* children—who had been born in reality as he stood looking down at them a moment before.

"Good-night, Naomi," he said abruptly.

"Philip. . . ."

"Yes."

"Philip, you won't stay?"

"No, Naomi. . . . It wouldn't look right."

There was a pause.

"Sometimes you're like your mother, Philip."

He went out and in his agitation found himself half-way down the flimsy pine stairway before he remembered his overcoat. When he returned and opened the door of the little flat, he heard the sound of sobbing, a horrible choked sound, coming from the bedroom. She had not made a scene. She had not wept until he was gone, for she was trying to please him.

Chapter 10

It was a clear night, and very cold, when the moonlight painted the snow and the black houses of the Flats with a luminous blue light. As he walked, the hard-packed snow creaked and whined beneath his heels. The stars, for all their brilliance, seemed infinitely remote. As he walked, a little cloud of frozen breath trailed behind him.

By the railroad-tracks and in the narrow streets that bordered them, the Flats were empty. The houses stood silent and black. The fires, the little piles of household goods, were gone now, and with them the miserable, shivering women and children. At Hennessey's corner there was the usual blaze of light, the jagged clamor of the mechanical piano, and the sound of drunken voices behind the swinging-doors. The lights, the sounds, hurt him in an inexplicable fashion, filling him with an acute and painful sense of loneliness.

It was an emotion which changed, as he entered the park, to one of vague fear. Inside the rusted gates the park lay frozen and solitary in the brilliant moonlight. The deep shadows were blue along the drive, black where the outline of a dead tree fell across the snow. The bits of statuary—the Venus of Cydnos, the Apollo Belvedere, the cast-iron Cupid—all had little caps and collars of frozen snow. The windows of the big house lay shuttered and dark, save for a room in the corner where little bars of yellow light filtered out. It was perhaps the room where Lily Shane sat waiting for her mother to die.

As he turned the corner on the stable side, there came to him all at once a feeling that he was not alone in the park. There were other creatures there, too, not human perhaps, but the ghosts of all the men and women who had been there in the gaudy days of the Castle when the trees were still alive, and the garden neatly kept, and the stable filled with horses. There had always been a mystery about the place, and for him, who had never seen the place while it was alive, it was a mystery enveloped in a romantic glamour. He understood suddenly how people are able to invest a place with the character of their own existence. It was the wicked old John Shane, dead so long that he had become a legend, and his dying widow, who owned this silent frozen park filled with dead trees. . . . It would still be theirs and theirs alone long after they had turned to dust, until at last the house was pulled down and the park buried beneath clamorous steel sheds and roaring furnaces. And even then . . . as long as there remained alive one person who remembered them, the place would be known as Shane's Hill, where once the Castle stood. It was an odd sort of immortality. . . .

He saw, too, that the slate-colored house was like his mother: she had stamped it forever as her own, and that the huts at Megambo were oddly like Naomi, who had been so happy in them. And he saw suddenly why he had hated both places and how in a way they explained both his mother and Naomi, and the power they both possessed of making him wretched. This cold park and the silent house, peopled by creatures that were dead, seemed a dark and sinister place, yet it had, too, a sense of splendor, of barren grandeur, that for more than half a century had dominated the Town. It existed still in the very midst of the clamorous Mills.

The stable was silent, save for the sound of the fat horses tramping in their stalls, and in his room overhead the stove still burned, filling the room with warmth. It was a plain enough room, empty save for the iron cot where he slept, a table, two chairs and his painting materials. Yet for him a pleasant place. He had for the first time in all his life a sense of coming home. It was his; and it suited him with its barren emptiness. It was like the cell of a monk, bare and cold, and free of everything which might distract from a contemplation of the great mystery.

He did not trouble to light the kerosene lamp. The cold moonlight flooded in through the window, casting in black filigrees on the bare floor the shadow of the drooping vines that fell across the panes. Against the walls and ceiling the flames in the belly of the stove cast another pattern, different, outlined of warm and glowing light.

For a long time he stood there, his hands clasped behind him, looking out of the window, seized once more by the enchantment of the beauty with which the night invested all the expanse of the Flats. Far off, under the shadow of one of the seven hills, the flames of the furnaces in the Jupiter plant raised an arc of glowing light. He saw in his imagination all the spectacle that existed there—the bodies of the black men, the dancing shadows cast by the glaring lights, the angry hiss and bubble of boiling white-hot metal. He could smell the curious, pungent odor of burning coke. He saw the movement, the unearthly splendor, the immense energy that filled the whole scene.

Just beneath the hill, the sheds and furnaces lay in black shadows. There were fires there, built by the Mill guards, that burned like the red eyes of giants asleep in the velvety darkness. There was the sudden wild screech of an express locomotive, and a long serpent-like monster, lighted from within like a firefly, rushed through the darkness.

He was glad suddenly to be alone, for the solitude brought him a strange peace like the peace that had come to him at times when he went alone at dawn along the borders of the lake at Megambo. It was the peace of complete aloofness, of detachment from all that troubled him—a mysterious exaltation like death perhaps, in which no one could share. No, not even Mary Conyngham. . . . Mary Conyngham. . . . He found himself repeating the name idly in his brain. Now, in this moment of solitude, even Mary Conyngham did not trouble him. It was as if he were free suddenly of his body and existed only as a spirit.

Presently, he put his hand across his eyes, pressing them with a kind of anguish. He knew that he believed again; he knew that he had always believed. He had never lost his faith. It was only that until now he had followed a bogus God. It was only that he didn't believe in that harsh, commonplace, ugly God of Naomi and Emma and the Reverend Castor. It was a different sort of God—One who was concerned with a kind of beauty and splendor which they did not know . . . the beauty of all that scene outspread below him, of that savage energy which cast a distant glow against the sky; it was the beauty of those two children, his children, called into existence because

He willed it, the sinister beauty of the park and of people like old John
Shane and his widow who lived on even after they were dead and dying, the
beauty even of that coffee-shed filled with shivering women and children, and
the fires in the street. He was the God, too, of those black women pouring
the water of the burning lake over the belly of an obscene idol—a God concerned with the whole glowing tragic spectacle of living.

Presently his hands dropped to his side once more, and, looking out of
the window, he saw that the park was no longer empty. There was some one
there—a woman—walking up and down in the moonlight. She was wrapped
in furs and she was no ghost, for in the cold air, the moonlight and the frost
of her breath made a little halo about her uncovered head. She was walking
round and round the ruined dead English garden, which must have had its
own ghosts of larkspurs and foxgloves and lavender and mint and primulas—
all the ghosts of flowers long dead, killed by the soot of the Mills.

And then all at once, he divined who the woman must be. She was Lily
Shane, walking in the moonlight.

She turned at last, and, going carelessly through the deep snow, returned
to the big, darkened house.

Philip lay down on the iron cot, and toward morning he fell asleep. But
in the long hours while he lay there, watching the pattern of warm light on
the ceiling, he became aware slowly of a whole new world born of a strange,
mystical understanding, that had come to him as he stood by the window in
the brilliant moonlight . . . a world which belonged to him alone, which
none could intrude upon or destroy. He fell asleep in peace, aware vaguely
that for a time he had escaped from Naomi and Uncle Elmer, from Mabelle—even from his own mother.

It was at noon on the following day that old Julia Shane fell into a sleep
from which she did not awaken. The old nigger, standing in the snow by
the stable door, told him the news. The old man wept like a little child. "It's
the end of something, Mr. Downes," he said. "It's all over now, and I expect
I ain't got much longer on this earth, myself. It ain't the same no longer."

All that day Philip stayed in the room above the stable, struggling passionately, with his stubborn jaw set like a steel trap, over paints and canvas,
trying to capture, while the mood was still on him, the strange things he
had seen in the dead park and the desert of silent Mills beyond. But in the
end, when it grew too dark to work any longer, there was only a mass of
blacks and grays, blues and whites, upon the canvas.

At eight o'clock, he went to the Flats to sit with the twins while Naomi
went to choir practice.

Chapter 11

THE CHOIR MET in the room of the church which was given over on the Sabbath to "the infant class" of the Sunday School for children under six. It was a large, barren room, with large chromos of Biblical scenes decorating the walls—the soldiers of Moses returning from the Promised Land, Moses smiting the Rock, the same as an Infant being discovered in the Bulrushes by a Princess dressed in garments as gaudy and inaccurate as those of a music-hall Cleopatra, Noah and his family receiving the Dove and Olive Branch. In the center of the room two dozen lilliputian chairs sat ranged in a circle, save on the occasions of choir practice, when a dozen adult chairs were brought in from the main Sunday School room to accommodate members of the choir.

Naomi arrived early, and, admitting herself with the private key that was her badge of office, turned on the gas and seated herself at the upright piano. There was no piano in the flat by the railroads, and she fell at once to playing, in order to recover her old careless facility. She had no sense of music; yet music was to her only what wine is to some temperaments: it served to unlock the doors of the restraining prison which forever shut her in. She played relentlessly in showers of loud, banging notes, heedless of discord and strange harmonies; and the longer she played, the more shameless and abandoned became the character of her playing. To-night she played from a none too sure memory *The Ninety and Nine* and *Throw Out the Life Line* (her favorites) and then *I'm a Pilgrim, I'm a Stranger*, which always made her want to cry, and then with a strong arm and a loud pedal she swept into *Ancient of Days*, which filled her with the strangest, emotional grandeur. There was a splendor in it which made her feel noble and heroic: it filled her with a sense of beauty and power. She saw herself vaguely as a barbarian queen, like Sheba, riding on an elephant, surrounded by guards and servitors. The image in her mind bore a strange resemblance to her memory of a highly painted artificial blonde, clad principally in sequins and crimson satin, whom she had once seen riding an elephant in the circus parade—a lady advertised as "the ten-thousand-dollar beauty." But always when she had finished *Ancient of Days*, and the last note had died away, she was left with a melancholy feeling of depression and a sense of wickedness. The world about her became after one of these musical debauches a sad and unbearable place.

To-night, alone in the bare, unattractive room, she poured into the music all the pent-up emotions of days . . . all her hatred of Emma, her fear of the new life on which she had embarked, but, most of all, that curious passionate half-wicked feeling she had for Philip. Beneath the spell of *Ancient of Days* this emotion for him seemed to become purified and free of all restraint. She poured into the banging, careless chords all the things which she could never bring herself to tell him—how the sight of him standing by the crib had made her feel suddenly ill with warm voluptuous feeling, how there were times when she wanted to lie down before him and beat her head on the floor to show him how she felt, how she wakened out of a sound sleep in the midst of the night with her hands aching to touch his face and his dark hair. In the splendor of the hymn it was as if all those things were realized. For a time she *was* that fantastic, barbaric queen of her imagination and Philip was her lover, dressed like one of the soldiers in the chromo of the return from the Promised Land, and sometimes in an overwhelming wave of wickedness she saw him as she had seen him on the night of the drums, standing half naked by the light of the dying fire.

It was thus that she saw him to-night, and, as if she meant to preserve the wild romantic feeling, she played and sang the whole hymn over again in her loud, flat voice. She was wildly happy, for in the end it seemed that Philip really belonged to her, and that they were alone once more by the lake at Megambo. They weren't even missionaries and Swanson wasn't there. And he loved her.

When she had finished, the spell clung to her until the last chord, held deliberately by the use of the loud pedal, died away, leaving her weak and exhausted, and prey suddenly to the horrible, sickening depression. She let her head fall forward on the piano. She wanted to cry, but she couldn't cry, because people would be coming in at any moment. And suddenly she felt the touch of a hand on her shoulder and a voice saying, "That was splendid, Mrs. Downes! That's the sort of music that will bring them to the Lord!"

It was the Reverend Castor. He had come in quietly, without a sound, and had been sitting there all the while listening to her while she desecrated the sanctity of a hymn with all her fleshly emotions. She tried to gain control of herself, and, without looking up, mopped her eyes and nose with her handkerchief. But it was no good: when she looked up he saw that she had been crying. She was blushing with shame, and the color made her seem almost pretty.

"Why, you've been crying!" he said.

She choked, recovered herself, and answered, "Yes . . . I . . . I can't help it. . . . It always makes me cry—that hymn."

He laid a big, bony, masculine hand on her shoulder. "But you mustn't cry . . . Mrs. Downes. You mustn't cry. . . . It's something to be joyful over."

She looked (he thought) so young and pitiful and unhappy. If it were only possible to comfort her, to take her on his knee as if she were a little child. It was no more than that, this feeling toward her. He wanted to comfort her. But you couldn't do that, of course, especially if you were a preacher.

"I watched your face while you were singing," he said. "It was a beautiful sight . . . so filled with joy and hope and exaltation . . . like the face of one who has seen a vision. It was an inspiration—even to me, a man of God."

She thought, "Oh, I *am* wicked. I *am* wicked!" And aloud, suddenly, without knowing why, she said, "Oh, I'm so unhappy!"

"But why, Naomi?"

He had called her by her name, without thinking, and suddenly he was frightened. He always thought of her thus, as if she had been his own child, and now the thought had slipped into words. He saw that she had noticed it, for she was blushing and avoided his eyes. She did not answer his question, and suddenly he said, "You mustn't mind that . . . that . . . Mrs. Downes. . . . It only means . . . that . . . well, I always think of you as Naomi because I think of your mother-in-law as *the* Mrs. Downes."

Still looking away, she answered, "I know . . . I know. . . . It's all right. You may call me that if you want, only . . . only not in front of the others. I didn't. . . . I think it would make me feel less alone."

And then the door creaked, and Mrs. Wilbert Phipps came in. The Reverend Castor began fingering the piles of music, and Naomi began again to pound the piano with an hysterical violence.

"Good-evening, Mrs. Phipps."

"Good-evening, Reverend Castor."

"I've been looking over the anthems for next Sunday."

"We haven't sung O *the Golden, Glowing Morning* for a long while."

"No . . . but that's an Easter hymn!"

"But we *have* sung it before on other occasions . . . it's so moving."

"What do you think, Mrs. Downes?"

Naomi stopped in the midst of her playing. "I think it would be fine. It's so full of joy."

One by one the others arrived. Each had his favorite, some song which he or she found moving. Naomi, troubled and unhappy, yielded to their choice. She was not, it was plain to be seen, to be a leader save in name alone. The eleven singers took their seats. There was a rustling of music and Naomi plunged noisily into:

> "O *the Golden, Glowing Morning!*
> *Stars above and Stars adorning!*"

The voices rang out loud and clear, filling the infants' classroom with a wild joy that seemed almost improper in so bare and chaste a place. They went on through a whole program of anthems and hymns, singing more and more loudly. At last, as the clock banged out eleven, the orgy of music came to an end, leaving them tired but happy, and filled with a strange excitement. At the piano, Naomi turned away to collect the sheets of music. There was a bustle of farewells and small talk and, one by one, or in pairs, the singers drifted out. It had been a happy evening: the happiness of these evenings in the infants' classroom held the choir together. In all the dreary Town of slate-colored houses, the weekly orgy of singing provided a half-mystical joy that elsewhere did not exist. It was, for all the pious words that were chanted, a sort of pagan festival in which men and women found a wild, emotional abandon. It was from choir practice that Mrs. Swithers had run off with the county auditor, leaving behind a husband, an aged mother and three small children.

The music was kept in a cabinet in the Reverend Castor's study, and before the others had all gone, Naomi hurried off to place it there. The depression had begun to settle over her once more, leaving her a prey to uneasiness. The drawer of the cabinet was jammed, and while she pulled and tugged at it, she heard the singers in little groups passing the door. She heard the dry Mrs. Wilbert Phipps say in a curious, excited voice, "No, Hanna, you mustn't say that here. Wait until we get out," and then the banging of the door. She pulled and tugged desperately at the drawer. The door banged again, and again. Without thinking, she counted the number of times it had closed . . . ten times! They must all have gone, and she was left alone. She knew suddenly that she must escape before the Reverend Castor appeared. She could not stay alone with him there in the study. She could not. She could not. . . . Suddenly, in a wave of terror, she let the music slip to the floor, and turned to escape, but at the same moment the Reverend Castor came in. He stood for a second, looking at her with a queer, fixed expression in his kindly gray eyes, and then he said, gently, "What is it, Naomi? Did I frighten you?"

In her struggle with the drawer, her hat had slipped to the back of her head and her hair had fallen into disarray. Her pale face was flushed once more.

"No," she said. "I just couldn't get that awful drawer open."

"I'll do it for you."

She couldn't escape now. She couldn't run past him out of the door. It would be too ridiculous. Besides, she had a strange, wicked desire not to escape. She sat down on one of the shabby leather chairs and put her hat straight. The Reverend Castor stooped without a word and gathered up the music, and then, with one hand, he opened the drawer easily. She saw it happen with a chill of horror. It was as if the drawer had betrayed her.

She rose quickly and said, "It *really* wouldn't open for me. It *really* wouldn't. . . . I tried and tried." (He would think she had planned it all.)

But when he turned toward her, he said gently, "Yes, I know. It's a funny drawer. It sticks sometimes like that." He was so calm and so . . . usual, she had suddenly, without knowing why, a queer certainty that he understood what was happening there deep inside her, and was trying to still her uneasiness. The knowledge made her want to cry. If only for a second Philip would treat her thus. . . .

He was rubbing his hands together. "Well, that *was* what I call a real choir practice. We've always needed some one like you, Naomi, to put spirit into them. It's the way you make the piano talk. Why, it was like a new choir to-night."

She looked away from him. "I tried my best. I hope they liked it."

"It was wonderful, my child."

There was a sudden, awkward silence, and Naomi said nervously, "Well, I ought to be going."

She moved toward the door, and the Reverend Castor took up his hat and coat. "I'll walk with you, Naomi. I want some air."

Despite herself, she cried out in a sudden hysteria, "No, no. You mustn't do that."

"But it isn't safe down there by the railroads."

"Oh, I'm not afraid." She kept moving slowly toward the door.

"But I don't mind the walk, Naomi. It's no walk for a strong man like me."

"Oh, it isn't that. . . ." She hesitated for a moment. "I don't mean that. . . . I don't know how to explain, only . . . only you never walked home with Mrs. Timpkins when she was leading the choir . . . and . . . you see, if any one saw us. . . ."

He looked suddenly at the floor, and a great sigh escaped him—a heart-breaking sigh, filled with the ghosts of disillusionment, of misery and disappointment.

"Yes . . . I know," he said gently. "I understand."

The door closed behind her, and she was outside in the snow. She kept hearing the sigh. It haunted her as she hurried, confused and out of breath, down the long hill. She felt so sorry for him . . . a kind, good man like that. And all at once she began to cry silently. There was no sound, but only tears and a lump in her throat.

Chapter 12

THE SUSPICION of Mary Conyngham, planted by Mabelle in the mind of Emma, lay there for days, flourishing upon fertile soil until at last it took on the sturdy form of reality and truth. In her pain at Philip's coldness toward her and in her anger at the spectacle of an existence which had become as disorderly and unmanageable as her own house during Naomi's presence in it, the thought of Mary Conyngham seldom left her. It burned her mind as she sat behind the cash-register, while she lay in bed at night alone in the house she had meant always to be Philip's house. It gave her no peace. What right, she asked herself, had Mary Conyngham to steal her boy? Bit by bit, she built up the story from that one shred of gossip dropped by Mabelle.

She saw now that the name of Mary Conyngham explained everything. Mary had never gone to church, and perhaps hadn't any faith in God, and so she had aggravated Philip's strange behavior. It was probably Mary or the thought of her, that put into Philip's head that fantastic idea of going to work in the Mills, in a place which had nearly cost him his life. She must have seen him almost every day. Why, she was even friendly with the Polacks and Dagoes. Who could say what things she hadn't been guilty of down there in the Flats, where no decent person ever went? There was probably truth in the story that Irene Shane slept with that big Russian—what was his name—who had had the boldness to come to the very door when Philip was ill. No, all sorts of orgies might go on in the Flats and no one would ever know. It was awful, degrading of Philip, to have mixed himself up with such people.

And presently she began to suspect that Mary lay at the source of Philip's behavior toward Naomi. A man didn't give up living with his wife so easily unless there was another woman. A man didn't do such things. Men were different from women. "Why," she thought, "I've lived all these years without a man, and never once dreamed of re-marrying. I gave up my life to my son."

It was Jason's fault too (she thought). It was Jason's bad blood in Philip. The boy wouldn't have behaved like that if it hadn't been for his father before him. That was where the weakness lay.

And now Mary probably came to see him at that room over the stables at night, and even in the daytime, because there was nothing to stop her coming and going. No one in the Flats would care, especially now, in the midst of the strike, and the Shanes wouldn't even take notice of such a thing. Shane's Castle had always been a sort of bawdy-house, and with the old woman dead the last trace of respectability had vanished. . . .

She remembered, too, that Mary hadn't been happy with her husband. Being married to a man like that who ran after women like Mamie Rhodes did something to a woman. Why, she herself could remember times when Jason's behavior made her, out of revenge, want to be unfaithful to him; and if it could happen to her (Emma) why, what would be the effect on a godless woman like Mary Conyngham?

For a time she considered boldly the plan of going to Philip himself and forcing him to give up Mary Conyngham. Surely she could discuss a thing like that with her own son, to whom she had been both father and mother. There must be, no matter how deeply it lay buried, still a foundation of that sound and moral character which she had labored so long to create. "If only," she thought, "I could make him feel again as he once felt. If only I could get through to the *real* Philip, my Philip, my little boy." But he was hard, as hard as flint.

Twice she planned to go alone to the stable of Shane's Castle, and once she got as far as the bridge before she lost courage and turned back. Always a shadow rose up between her and her resolution—the shadow of that day when, hidden by a screen in the corner of the restaurant, she had pled with him passionately, only to find herself beating her head against a wall of flint, to hear him saying, "You mustn't talk like that. It's not fair"; to see the thin jaw set in a hard line. No, she saw that it was impossible to talk to him. He was so strange and unruly that he might turn his back on her forever. The thought of it filled her with terror, and for two nights she lay awake, weeping in a debauch of self-pity.

But one thing was changed. In all the trouble with Philip, her doubts over marrying Moses Slade seemed to have faded away. At times when she felt tired and worn she knelt in her cold bedroom and thanked God for sending him to her. They could be married in two more months, and then . . . then she would have some one to comfort her. She couldn't go to him with her troubles now, lest the weight of them should frighten him. No, she saw that she must bear all her suffering alone until God saw fit to lift the cross from her shoulders.

One afternoon when Moses Slade had left, still breathing fire and thunder against Krylenko, she sat for a long time alone behind the screen, in the restaurant, looking out of the window. Her eyes saw nothing that passed, for she was seeing far beyond such things as shop-fronts and trolley-cars. She was thinking, "What has come over me lately? I haven't any character any more. I'm not like Moses, who goes on fighting like an old war horse. I've let things slide. I haven't faced things as I should. I've humored Philip, and see what's come of it. When I kept hold on the reins everything went well, and now Philip's ruining himself and going straight to the Devil. I should never have allowed Naomi to leave the house. She's wax in his hands, with all her softness—she can never manage him and he needs to be managed just as his father did. If I'd treated his father the way Naomi treats Philip . . . God knows what would have happened."

She began automatically to stack the dishes on the table before her, as if she had gone back to the days when the restaurant had been only a lunch-room and she had herself waited on her customers.

"I must take hold," she told herself. "There's only one thing to do . . . only one thing. . . . I must go and see Mary Conyngham. I must talk to her face to face and have it out. He's my son. I bore him. I gave him life, and I have a right to save him."

A kind of feverish energy took possession of her. It seemed that she could no longer sit there seeing the whole structure of her life going to ruin. She would save Philip. She would die knowing that he was a bishop. She would marry Moses Slade and go to Washington and work there to save the country from chaos, from drink, from strikes. She would rise in the end, triumphant as she had always been. She had been weak: she had rested at the time when she should have worked. She needed to act. She *would* act, no matter what it cost her. She *would* save Philip and herself.

In a kind of frenzy she seized her hat and coat and left the restaurant.

It was a warm day when the snow had begun to melt and the pavement was deep with slush. She hurried, wet to the knees, fairly running all the way, so that by the time she reached Mary Conyngham's house her face was scarlet and wet with sweat.

Mary was in, but she was upstairs with the children, and the hired girl bade her wait in the parlor. There she seated herself on a rosewood chair, upholstered in horsehair, to mop her face and set her hat straight. And slowly the room began to have a strange effect upon her. Though the room itself was warm, it was as if she had come into a cool place. The rosewood furniture was dark and cool, and the great marble slab of the heavy mahogany commode. The wax flowers and the glass dome that protected them were cool, and the crystal chandelier and the great silver-bordered mirror. The whole room (queer and old-fashioned, Emma thought indignantly) was a pool of quiet . . . a genteel room, a little thread-bare, but nevertheless possessed of an elegance all its own.

It exerted the queerest effect on Emma, dampening her spirits and extinguishing the indignation that a little while before had roared in her bosom like the flames in the belly of one of the furnaces. She began suddenly to feel tired again and filled with despair.

"It's like her to keep an older woman waiting," she thought. "Probably she knows well enough why I've come."

She began to tap the carpet with the toe of her shoe and at last she rose and began to walk about, as if she felt that only by activity could she throw off from her the softening effect of that quiet room. She halted presently before the oval portrait, framed in gilt, of Mary's mother, a very pretty woman, with dark hair and a spirited eye . . . a woman such as Mary might have been if she hadn't married that John Conyngham and had her spirit subdued. Well (thought Emma) she seemed nevertheless to have too much spirit for her own good or the good of any one else.

She was standing thus when Mary came in, dressed in a mauve frock, and looking pale and a little nervous. Emma thought, "She knows why I've come. It's on her conscience. She's afraid of me already."

"I'm sorry, Mrs. Downes," said Mary, "but my sister-in-law has gone out, and I couldn't come down until both children were asleep."

It was odd, but her voice had upon Emma the same effect as the room. It seemed to sap the foundations of her assurance and strength by its very gentleness. It was strange how subdued and quiet Mary seemed, almost as if (Emma thought suspiciously) she had forgotten her early troubles and was now shamelessly and completely happy. Feeling that if she did not begin at once, she would not accomplish her plan, Emma plunged.

"It's about Philip I've come to see you," she said. "I knew that you were interested in him."

Mary admitted the interest shamelessly.

"I don't know what's happened to him. He's so changed . . . not at all the boy he used to be."

"Yes, he's very different. . . . I think maybe he's happier now."

"Oh, he's not happy. No one could be happy in his state of mind. Why, he's even abandoned God. . . . Something, some one has gotten hold of him."

The shadow of a frown crossed Mary's smooth brow. She had the air of waiting . . . waiting. . . . She said, "Perhaps I've chosen the wrong word. I mean that he seems on a more solid foundation."

"Do you call what he's doing solid?"

"If it's what he wants to do."

"He doesn't know his own mind."

"I mean he's more like the real Philip. I think he *is* the real Philip now."

Emma's fingers began to strum the arm of her chair nervously. "I don't know what you're talking about, but if you mean that the old Philip wasn't real, why, I think you're saying a crazy thing. It's this new one who's queer. Do you mean to insinuate that I, his own mother . . . the one who bore him . . . who gave him life, doesn't know who the real Philip is?"

It was clear that she was "working herself up." Mary did not answer her at once, but when she raised her head, it was to say, with a curious, tense quietness, "No . . . if you want the truth, Mrs. Downes, I don't think you know Philip at all. I think that's really what's the matter. You've never known him."

Emma found herself suddenly choked and speechless. "Do you know what you're saying? I've never had any one say such a thing to me before . . . *me*, his own mother! Why, do you know what we've been to each other . . . Philip and me?" She plunged into a long recital of their intimacy, of the beautiful relationship that had always existed between them, of the sacrifices she had made. It went on and on, and Mary, listening, thought, "That's how she talks to him. That's why he can't get free of her." Suddenly she hated Emma. And then she heard Emma saying, in a cold voice, "Of course, I suppose in one way you do know him better than I do—in one way."

"What are you trying to say?"

"You know what I mean. You ought to know . . . you . . . you . . . who have stolen him away from me and from his own wife."

Mary's fingers dug suddenly into the horsehair of her chair. She felt a sudden primitive desire to fling herself upon Emma, to pull her hair, to choke her. The old tomboyish spirit, dead for so long, seemed suddenly to breathe and stir with life. She thought quickly, "I mustn't. I mustn't. It's what she'd like me to do—to put myself on a level with herself. And I mustn't, for Philip's sake. It's all bad enough as it is." She grew suddenly rigid with the effort of controlling herself. She managed to say in a quiet voice, "I think you're talking nonsense. I think you're a little crazy."

"Crazy, am I? That's a nice thing to say!"

"I have talked to Philip just once since he came home, and that was on the day I met you in the street. I didn't try to find him. He came to me."

"Do you expect me to believe that?"

"It's the truth. Beyond that I don't care what you believe."

"I want you to leave him alone."

Suddenly Mary stood up. "I *was* leaving him alone. I meant never to see him, but I won't leave him alone any longer. He would have been mine except for you. He's belonged to me always and he needs me to protect him. No, I won't leave him alone any longer."

All at once she began to cry, and turning, she ran from the room and up the stairs. Emma, left behind on the horsehair sofa, felt suddenly foolish and outwitted. She was certain that Mary meant not to come back, but she remained in the cool, quiet room for a long time, as if her dignity demanded such an action. And at last, baffled and filled with a sense of flatness, she rose and walked out of the house.

The whole visit had been a failure, for it hadn't come properly to a climax. It was ended before it began. But she had (she felt) done her best, all that a mother could do to save her only son. She had laid herself open to insult. . . . A block from Mary's house she discovered that in her agitation she had forgotten her gloves. She halted abruptly, and then resumed her way. They didn't matter. They were old gloves, anyway.

She couldn't bring herself to go back and enter that depressing house again.

Upstairs in the room where the two children were asleep in their cribs, Mary lay on the bed and wept. Until this moment her love had seemed a far-off, distant thing, to be cherished sadly and romantically as hopeless, but now, all at once, it had become unbearably real. She saw Philip in a new way, as some one whom she might touch and care for with all the tenderness that had been wasted upon John Conyngham. She saw him as a lonely man who wanted one thing above all else from a woman, and that was understanding; and it was tenderness that she wanted to give him more than all else on earth. In the midst of her grief and fury, she meant to have him for her own. It seemed to her suddenly that it was only possible to free him from that terrible woman by sacrificing herself. If she gave herself—soul and body and heart—to Philip, she could save him. "He is mine," she kept sobbing, half-aloud. "He is mine . . . my own dear Philip." Why (she asked herself) should she care at all for gossip, for the sacrifice of her own pride, for all the tangle that was certain to follow? He needed her, though she doubted whether the fact had ever occurred to him, and she needed him, and it had been so ever since they were children, and would be so when they were old. All at once she felt a sudden terror of growing old. She seemed to feel the years rushing by her. She knew that she could not go on thus until she died.

And after a little while, when her sobbing had quieted a little, she began to see the thing more coldly. She saw even that Philip was fantastic and hopeless, trying to escape as much from himself as from his mother and from Naomi. She saw even that he was impossible. She doubted whether there was in him the chance of happiness. Yet none of it made any difference, for those were the very reasons perhaps why she loved him. They were the reasons too, perhaps, why at least three women—his mother, his wife and herself—had found themselves in a hopeless tangle over him. It was simply that without knowing it he made demands upon them from which they could not escape. He had even touched Irene Shane in whose cold life men played no part. Mary loved him, she saw now, without reason, without restraint, and she knew that because she loved him she must save him from his own weakness and lead him out of his hopeless muddle into the light.

Because she was a sensible woman, the sudden resolution brought her a certain peace. She coldly took account of all the things that might follow her decision, and knew that she was decided to face them. She *had* to help him. It was the only thing that mattered.

As she stirred and sat up on the edge of the bed, the youngest child moved and opened its eyes, and Mary, in a sudden burst of joy, went over and kissed it. Bending down, she said, "Your mother, Connie, is a wicked woman." The child laughed, and she laughed too, for there was a sudden peace and delight in her heart.

Chapter 13

PHILIP HAD SPENT the morning of that same day among the tents where the strikers lived in the melting snow. He had made sketches, a fragment here, a fragment there—tiny glimpses that were in their own way more eloquent than the lifting of the whole curtain. They were a weekly affair now, done regularly on a fragment of some denunciating speech or editorial. They appeared weekly in the *Labor Journal*. Now he chose an editorial in which the Chairman of the Board of Mill Directors made a speech filled with references to Christ and appeals to end the strike and return to an era of Peace on Earth; now it was an address from the Governor of the State—a timid man, a bit of a fool, and destined one day to be President of the Nation. Moses Slade suffered twice more, for his pompous bombastic speeches made irresistible subjects for burlesque. But, as the weeks passed, Philip found himself less and less interested in making propaganda for the workers, and more and more concerned with the purity of his line. The room above the stable came to be papered in sketches made on bits of newsprint or fragments of butchers' brown paper. A frenzy of work took possession of him, and for whole days at a time he never left the place, even to see his children. There were even times when he forgot the very existence of Mary Conyngham. But he did go faithfully twice a week to stay with the twins so that Naomi might go to choir practice. It was, he knew, the only pleasure which lay in his power to give her.

The importance of the thing appeared to make her happy, and to diminish the aching sense of strain that was never absent when they were together. She began, little by little, to grow used to a husband whose only activities were those of a nursemaid, but she still tried pathetically to please him. She made a heroic effort to dress neatly and keep the house in order (although there were times when he spent his whole visit to the twins in putting closets in order and gathering the soiled clothing into piles), and she never spoke any more of his coming back to her. The only fault seemed to be a jealousy which she could not conquer.

She kept asking him questions, disguised in a pitiful air of casualness, about what the Shanes' house was like, and whether he thought Lily Shane as beautiful a woman as she was supposed to be. Once she even asked about Mary Conyngham. He always answered her in the same fashion—that he had never been inside the Shanes' house, and did not know Lily Shane, and had spoken to Mary Conyngham but once since he had come home. Sometimes he fancied that it was more than mere jealousy that prompted her questions: he thought, too, there was something in them of wistful curiosity about a world filled with people she would never know. She still had the power of rousing a pity which weakened him like an illness.

He did tell her at last that he *had* seen Lily Shane three or four times walking in the park, once in the moonlight, and that he thought she was a beautiful woman; but he never told her how the figure of Lily Shane was inextricably a part of that strange illuminating vision that came to him as he stood by the vine-clad window. It was, he believed, the sort of thing no one would understand, not even Mary. Naomi would only think him crazy and go at once to tell his mother. They would begin all over again humoring him as a madman or a child. No, he did not know Lily Shane, and yet he did know her, in a strange, unearthly, mystical fashion, as if she stood as a symbol of all that strange, sensuous world of which he had had a single illuminating intuition as he stood by the window. It was a world in which all life was lived on a different plane, in which tragedies occurred and people were happy and unhappy, but it was a world in which success and happiness and tragedy and sorrow were touched by grandeur. There was in it nothing sordid or petty, for there were in it no people like Uncle Elmer and Naomi and Mabelle. One could enter it if one knew how to live. That, he saw, was a thing he must learn—how to live, to free himself of all that nastiness and intolerance and pettiness of which he had suddenly become aware. He had to escape from all those things which the old Philip, the one who was dead, had accepted, in the blindness of a faith in a nasty God, as the ultimate in living.

This new Philip, prey to a sickening awareness, had been working all the morning in the Flats and ate with Krylenko at the tent where the homeless strikers were fed soup and coffee and bread, and, on returning to the stable, he lay down on the iron bed and fell asleep. He did not know how long he lay there, but he was awakened presently by a curious feeling, half a dream, that some one had come into the room with him. Lying quietly, still half-lost in a mist of sleep, he became slowly aware that some one was walking softly about beyond the screen. Rising, he pushed it aside and, stepping out, saw who it was. Standing in the shadow near the window, peering at the drawings, was Lily Shane, hatless, with her honey-colored hair done in a knot at the back of her neck, her furs thrown back over her shoulders. At the sound of his step, she turned slowly and said, "Oh! I thought there was no one here. I thought I was alone."

It was a soft voice, gentle and musical, exactly the right voice for such a figure and face. At the sound of it, he was aware suddenly that he must appear ridiculous—coatless, with his hair all rumpled. It was the first time he had ever spoken to such a woman, and something in her manner—the complete calm and assurance, the quiet, almost insolent lack of any apology, made him feel a gawky little boy.

"I . . . I was asleep," he said, desperately patting down his hair.

She smiled. "I didn't look behind the screen. Hennery told me you hadn't come in." But there was a contradiction behind the smile, a ghost of a voice which said, "I *did* look behind the screen. I knew you were there."

And suddenly, for the first time, Philip was stricken by an awful speculation as to how he looked when asleep. He knew that he was blushing. He said, "It doesn't matter. It's your stable, after all."

"I didn't mean to disturb you. I've stayed longer than I meant to . . . but—you see . . ."—she made a gesture toward the drawings—"I found all these more fascinating than I expected. I knew about you. My sister told me . . . but I didn't find what I expected. They're so much better. . . . You see, it's always the same. I couldn't believe it of the Town. Can any good thing come out of Nazareth?"

He began to tremble a little. He'd never shown them to any one save Krylenko, who only wanted pictures for propaganda and liked everything, good and bad. And now some one who lived in a great world such as he could scarcely imagine, thought they were good. Suddenly all the worries, the troubles, slipping from him, left him shy and childlike.

"I don't know whether they're good or bad," he said, "only . . . only I've *got* to do them."

She was standing before the painting of the Flats seen from the window, over which he had struggled for days. She smiled again, looking at him. "It's a bit messy . . . but it's got something in it of truth. I've seen it like that. It was like that one moonlight night not so long ago. I was walking in the garden . . . late . . . after midnight. I noticed it."

She sat down in one of the chairs by the stove. "May I stay and talk a moment?"

"Of course."

"Sit down too," she said.

Then he remembered that he was still without a coat, and, seizing it quickly, he put it on and sat down. His mind was all on fire, like a pile of tinder caught by a spark. He had never seen anything like this woman before. She wasn't what a woman who had led such a life should have been. She wasn't hard, or vulgar, or coarse, as he had been taught to believe. She must have been nearly forty years old, and yet she was fresh as the morning. And in her beauty, her voice, her manner, there was an odd quality of excitement which changed the very surface of everything about her. Her very presence seemed to make possible anything in the world.

She was saying, "What do you mean to do about it?"

"About what?"

She made a gesture to include the drawings. "All this."

It seemed to him for the first time that he had never thought of what he meant to do about it. He had just worked, passionately, because he had to work. He hadn't thought of the future at all.

"I don't know . . . I want to work until I can find what I know is here . . . I mean in the Mills and in the Flats. And then . . . some day . . . I . . . I want to go back to Africa. . . . I've been to Africa, you know. I was a missionary once." He thought that from the summit of her worldliness she might laugh at him for being a missionary; but she didn't laugh. She clasped her hands about her knee, and he saw suddenly that they were very beautiful hands, white and ringless, against the soft, golden sables. He wanted to seize a pencil and draw them.

She didn't laugh at him. She only said, "Tell me about that . . . about Africa . . . I mean."

And slowly he found himself telling the whole story, passionately, as he had never told it before, even to Mary Conyngham. He seemed to find in it things which he hadn't seen before, strange lights and shadows. He told it from beginning to end, and when he had finished, she said, looking into the fire, without smiling, "Yes, I understand all that. I've never been religious or mystical, but I've always had my sister Irene. I've seen it with her. You see I'm what they call a bad lot. You've probably heard of me. I'm only thankful I'm alive and I try to enjoy myself in the only world I'm sure of."

He went on, "You see, when I've learned more, I want to go back and paint that country. It had a fascination for me. I guess I'm like that Englishwoman . . . Lady Millicent . . . the one I told you about. She said there were some people who couldn't resist it."

When he finished, he saw that all his awe of her had vanished. He knew her better than any one in the world, for she had a miraculous way of understanding him, even those things which he did not say. The desire for the jungle and the hot lake swept over him in a turbulent wave. He wanted to go at once, without waiting. He was thirsty for a sight of the reedy marshes. The procession of black women moved somehow across the back of the room beyond Lily Shane. He was hot all at once, and thirsty for the water they carried up the slope to the parched ground.

She understood what he was trying to tell her . . . she had caught a magnificence, a splendor, that was not to be put into words. He wasn't afraid any more, or shy. It was as if she existed in an aura of contagious lawlessness.

She took out a cigarette from a lacquered box. "Do you mind if I smoke?"

"No."

"I didn't know. . . ."

He watched her curiously. There lay in the soft curve of her body, in the long slim leg crossed over the other, in the curve of the fur thrown back across her shoulders, in the poise of her arm, all the perfection of some composition designed and executed by a great artist. It was a kind of perfection he had never dreamed of, something which had arisen mysteriously during years out of the curious charm of her own personality. It was, too, a completeness born of the fearlessness which he had sensed for a moment by the window. Suddenly he thought, "Some day I shall be of that world. I shall succeed and become great. And Mary, too, will share it."

He had almost forgotten Mary, but it was only, he told himself shamefully, because she had been there with him all the while. It was almost as if she were a part of himself: whatever happened to him must happen also to her. It was not that he had fallen in love with this stranger, or even that he desired her: the emotion was something far beyond all that, a sort of dazzled bewilderment shot through with streaks of hope and glamour which brought near to him that world in which people were really alive.

Suddenly he summoned all his courage. He said, blushing under his dark skin, "I want to draw you. I want to make a picture of you."

She moved a little and smiled.

"No," he said, quickly. "Like that. Don't move."

He wanted to capture the grace and elegance of the pose, so that he might have it always, as a little fragment, caught and held, of this thing which he knew to exist, beyond his reach. She sat quietly. "Yes, of course . . . only it's almost dark now . . ."

He seized a pencil and a bit of paper, working swiftly, as he had done at the soup-kitchen. He must hurry (he thought) or she would be gone again back to Paris. She appeared presently to have forgotten him, and sat, with the remnant of the cigarette hanging from her long white fingers, while she stared into the fire. There was a curious sense of repose in the whole body, and a queer sadness too. She might have been quite alone. He had the feeling that she had forgotten his existence.

He worked nervously, with long, sure strokes, and with each one he knew that he was succeeding. In the end he would fix her thus forever on a fragment of paper. And then suddenly he heard some one enter the stable below, and, fumbling with the door, open it and hurry up the steps. He went on, pressed by the fear that if he were disturbed now the thing would never be finished. He *had* to have it. It would be a kind of fetish to keep off despair.

It was Lily Shane who moved first, stirred perhaps by a sense of being watched. As she moved, Philip turned too, and there, half-way up the stairs where she had halted at sight of them, stood Naomi, staring.

She was breathless, and beneath a carelessly pinned hat, from which wisps of hair escaped, her face showed red and shining as a midsummer day. For one dreadful moment the three remained silent, staring at each other. Lily Shane stared with a kind of bored indifference, but there was in Naomi's eyes a hurt look of bewilderment. Suddenly she turned back, as if she meant to go away again without speaking to either of them. Philip knew the expression at once. She had looked thus on the day that Lady Millicent appeared out of the forest with the Arab marching before her. It was the look of one who was shut out from something she could not understand, which frightened her by its strangeness.

It was Lily Shane who moved first. The burnt cigarette dropped from her fingers and she stamped on it. The action appeared to stir Naomi into life. "Philip," she said. "I came to tell you that your Pa has come home."

Chapter 14

IT WAS Emma herself who saw him first. Returning flustered and upset from the call upon Mary Conyngham, she entered the slate-colored house closing the door stormily behind her. She would have passed the darkened parlor (where since Naomi's departure the shades were always kept drawn to protect the carpet), but, as she explained it afterward, she "felt" that there was some one in the room. Peering into the darkness, she heard a faint sound of snoring, and, as her eyes grew accustomed to the darkness, she discerned the figure of a man lying on her best sofa, with his feet resting on the arm. He was sleeping with his mouth open a little way beneath a black mustache, waxed and curled with the care of a dandy.

As she stood there in the midst of the room, the figure in the shadows took form slowly, and suddenly she knew it . . . the dapper, small body, dressed so dudishly, the yellow waistcoat with its enormous gold watch-chain, and cluster of seals. She knew, with a sudden pang, even the small, well-shaped hand, uncalloused by any toil, that lay peacefully at rest on the Brussels carpet. For a second she thought, "I've gone suddenly crazy from all the trouble I've had. What I'm seeing can't be true."

It took a great deal of courage for her to move toward the sofa, for it meant moving in an instant, not simply across the Brussels carpet, but across the desert of twenty-six years. It meant giving up Moses Slade and all that resplendent future which had been taking form in her mind only a moment before. It was like waking the dead from the shadows of the tomblike parlor.

She did not lack courage, Emma; or perhaps it was not courage, but the headlong thrust of an immense vitality which now possessed her. She went over to the sofa and said, "Jason! Jason Downes!" He did not stir, and suddenly the strange thought came to her that he might be dead. The wicked idea threw her into an immense confusion, for she did not know whether she preferred the unstable companionship of the fascinating Jason to the bright future that would be hers as the wife of Moses. Then, all at once, she saw that the gaudy watch-chain was moving up and down slowly as he breathed, and she was smitten abruptly by memories twenty-six years old of morning after morning when she had wakened, full of energy, to find Jason lying beside her sleeping in the same profound, conscienceless slumber.

"Jason!" she said again. "Jason Downes!" And this time there was a curious tenderness in her voice that was almost a sob.

He did not stir, and she touched his shoulder. He moved slowly, and then, opening his eyes, sat up and put his feet on the floor. He awakened lazily, and for a moment he simply sat staring at her, looking as neat and dapper as if he had just finished an elaborate toilet. Again memory smote Emma. He had always been like this: he had always wakened in the mornings, looking fresh and neat, with every hair in place. It was that hair-oil he persisted in using. Now that he'd come home, she would have to get antimacassars to protect the furniture against Jason's oily head.

Suddenly he grinned and said, "Why! Hello! It's you, Em." It wasn't a sheepish grin, but a smile of cocky assurance, such as was frozen forever upon the face of the enlarged portrait.

"Jason . . . Jason! Oh, my God! Jason!" She collapsed suddenly and fell into the mahogany-veneer rocker. It was a strange Emma, less strange perhaps to Jason Downes than she would have been to the world outside, for suddenly she had become all soft and collapsed and feminine. All those twenty-six years had rolled away, leaving her helpless.

As if he had left the house only that morning, he sat on the arm of the chair and kissed her. He patted her hands and said, "You mustn't cry like that, Em. I can't bear to hear you. It breaks me all up."

"If you knew how long I'd waited!" she sobbed. "Why didn't you even write? Why didn't you tell me you were coming?"

He seemed a little proud of himself. "I wanted it to be a surprise."

He led her to the sofa and sat there, patting her hand and smiling, and comforting her while she wept and wept. "A surprise," she echoed. "A surprise . . . after twenty-six years. . . ." After a time she grew more calm, and suddenly she began to laugh. She kept saying at little intervals, "If you knew how I've waited!"

"I'm rich now, Emma," he said with the shadow of a swagger. "I've done well out there."

"Out where . . . Jason?"

"Out in Australia . . . where I went."

"You were in Australia?" He wasn't in China at all, then. The story was so old that she had come to believe it, and with a sudden shock of horror she saw that they would now have to face the ancient lie. He hadn't been in China, and he hadn't been killed by bandits. Here he was back again, and you couldn't keep a man like Jason shut up forever in the house. The Town would see him. She began once more to cry.

"There, there, Em!" he said, patting her hand again, almost amorously. "Don't take it so hard. You're glad I did come back, ain't you?"

"I don't know . . . I don't know. You don't deserve anything . . . even tears . . . after treating a wife the way you've treated me. Don't think I'm crying because I'm glad you're back. It's not that. I ought to turn you out. I'd do it, too, if I was an ordinary woman."

She saw then that she still had to manage everything, including Jason. She saw that he was as useless as he had always been. She would have to "take hold." The feminine softness melted away, and, sitting up, she blew her nose and said, "It's like this, Jason. When you went away, I said you'd gone to China on business. And when you didn't come back, I said I hadn't had any letters from you and something must be wrong. You see I pretended I heard from you regularly because . . . I wanted to protect you and because I was ashamed. I didn't want people to think you'd deserted me after everybody had warned me against you. And so Elmer. . . ."

"And how's he?" said Jason. "Cold boiled mutton, I call 'im."

"Wait till I finish my story, Jason. Try to keep your mind on what I'm saying. And so Elmer set the Government to investigating. . . ."

"They were looking for me? The *United States Government* itself?" There was in his voice and manner a sudden note of gratification at his importance.

"Yes . . . they hunted all over China."

Jason was grinning now. "It's lucky they was looking in China, because I was in Australia all the time."

"And they said you must have been killed by bandits . . . so I put on black and set out to support myself and Philip."

"Why didn't old pious Elmer help you out? I wouldn't have gone away, except that I knew 'e was rich enough to look out for you."

"Elmer's tight, and besides I didn't want him to be pitying me and saying, 'I told you so' every time I asked him for a cent."

"And Philip? You haven't told me about him yet."

"We'll come to him. We've got to settle this other thing first. You see, Jason, we've got to do something about that lie I told . . . it wasn't really a lie because I told it for your sake and Philip's—to protect you both."

"Yes, it is kind-a awkward." He sat for a moment, trying to bring his volatile mind into profitable operation. At last he said, "You oughtn't to have told that lie, Em."

"I told you why I told it. God will understand me if no one else will."

"Now, Em, don't begin on that line. . . . It was always the line I couldn't stand. . . . You ain't no bleedin' martyr."

She looked at him with a sudden suspicion. "Jason, where did you pick up this queer talk . . . all the queer words you've been using?"

"Australia, I guess . . . living out among the cockneys out there." He rose suddenly. "Em, I can't sit any more in this dark. I can't think in a tomb." He went over and drew up the window-shades. As the fading winter light filled the room, he looked around him. "Why, it ain't changed at all! Just the same . . . wedding parlor suite and everything." His glance fell on the wall above the fireplace. "And you still got my picture, Em. That was good of you."

She showed signs of sobbing again. "It's all I had. . . ."

He was looking at the picture with a hypnotic fascination. "It's funny, I ain't changed much. You'd never think that picture was taken twenty-six years ago." He took out a pocket mirror and began comparing his features with those in the enlarged photograph. What he said was true enough. Time had left no marks on the smooth, good-looking face, nor even on a mind that was like a shining, darting minnow. He was as slim and dapper as ever. The hair was much thinner, but it was still dark, and with the aid of grease and shrewd manipulation you couldn't tell that he was really bald. Emma, watching him, had an awful suspicion that it was dyed as well; and the elegant mustaches too. She would be certain to discover, now that he had come back to share the same room and bed. She had a sudden, awful fear that she must look much older than he.

"I'm a little bald," he said ruefully, "but nothing very much."

"Jason," she said sternly. "Jason . . . we've got to settle this thing . . . now . . . before we do anything else. Did any one see you?"

"No, I don't think so." He replaced the pocket mirror with a mild, comic air of alarm at the old note of authority in her voice.

"You must think of something . . . you're better at such things than I am." He had, she remembered, the proper kind of an imagination. She knew from experience how it had worked long ago when he had given her excuses for his behavior.

He looked at her with an absurd air of helplessness. "What can we say? I suppose you could say I lost my memory . . . that I got hit on the head." Suddenly a great light burst upon the empty face. "I *did* get a fall on the steamer going out. I fell down a stairway and for three days I didn't know a thing. A fall like that might easily make you lose your memory. . . . A thing like that *might* happen." As if the possibilities of such a tale had suddenly dawned upon him, his face became illumined with that look which must come at times into the faces of great creative artists. He said, "Yes, I *might* have lost my memory, not knowing who I was, or where I came from, and then, after twenty-six years, I got another fall . . . how? . . . well out of the mow on my ranch in Australia, and when I came to, I remembered everything—that I had a wife in America. It's true—it might happen. I've read of such things."

Listening to him, Emma felt the story seemed too preposterous, and yet she knew that only heroic measures could save the situation. The bolder the tale, the better. It was, as he said, a story that *might* be true. Such things *had* happened. She could trust him, too, to make the tale a convincing one: the only danger lay in the possibility of his doing it *too* well. It occurred to her in the midst of her desperate planning that it was strange what wild, incredible things had happened in her life . . . a life devoted always to hard work and Christian living.

Jason's glittering mind had been working rapidly. He was saying, "You see, there's the scar and everything." He bent down, exposing the bald spot that was the only sign of his decay. "You see, there it is—the scar."

She looked at him scornfully, for the crisis of her emotion had passed now, and she was beginning to feel herself once more. "Now, Jason," she said, "I haven't forgotten where that scar came from. You've always had it. You got it in Hennessey's saloon."

For a second the dash went out of him. "Now, Em, you're not going to begin on that, the minute I get home." And then quickly his imagination set to work again, and with an air of brightness, as if the solution he had thought of vindicated him completely, he said, "Besides I wasn't bald in those days and nobody ever saw the scar. And the funny thing is that it was on that exact spot that I fell on the boat. It enlarged the scar." He looked at her in the way he had always done when he meant to turn her mind into more amiable channels. "Now, isn't that queer? It enlarged the scar."

It was clear that she meant not to be diverted from the business at hand. "I suppose that's as good a story as any. We've got to have a story of some kind. But you must stick to it, Jason, and don't make it too good. That's what you always do . . . make it too good." (Hadn't she, years ago, trapped him time after time in a lie, because he could not resist a too elaborate pattern of embroidery?)

She said, "But there's one thing I've got to do right away, and that is send word to Naomi to tell Philip."

"Who's Naomi?"

"She's Philip's wife."

"He's married?"

"He's been married for five years."

He made a clucking sound. "We're getting on, Em."

"And there's more than that. You're a grandfather."

The smooth face wrinkled into a rueful expression. "It's hard to think of myself as a grandfather. How old is the child, or the children?"

"They're twins."

He chuckled. "He did a good job, Philip."

"Now, Jason. . . ."

"All right, but how old are they?"

"Four months . . . nearly five."

"I must say that Philip took 'is time about it. Married five years. . . . Well, we didn't waste any time, did we, Em."

"Jason!"

She hated him when he was vulgar. She decided not to go into the reasons why Philip and Naomi had been married four years without children, because it was a thing which Jason wouldn't understand—sacrificing the chance of children to devote yourself to God. There was nothing spiritual about Jason. It was one of his countless faults.

"But who did 'e marry, Em? You haven't told me."

"Her name was Naomi Potts. You wouldn't know who she was. Her people were missionaries, and she was a missionary too."

"Oh, my God!"

"I won't have you blaspheming."

"And what's Philip like?"

"He was a missionary too. . . . He was three years in Africa . . . until his health broke."

"Oh, my God!" He grew suddenly thoughtful, moved perhaps by the suspicion that she had succeeded in doing to his son what she had failed to do to him.

She was at the door now. "I won't listen to you talking like that any longer." She turned in the doorway. "Don't go out till I come back. You mustn't be seen till we've worked this thing out. I've got to send word to them all."

When she had gone, he picked up his hat, took a cigar from his vest pocket and lighted it. In the hallway, he shouted at her, "Are we still using the same room, Em? I'll just move in my things and wash up a bit."

In the sitting-room Emma sat down and wrote three notes—one to Naomi, one to Mabelle, and the third to Moses Slade. With a trembling hand she wrote to him, "God has sent Jason, my husband, back to me. He came to-day. It is His will that we are not to marry. Your heartbroken Emma."

She summoned the slattern Essie, and, giving her instructions of a violence calculated to impress Essie's feeble mind, she bade her deliver the three notes, Mr. Slade's first of all. But once outside the sight of Emma, the hired girl had her own ideas of the order in which she meant to deliver them, and so the note to Moses Slade arrived last. But it made no difference, as the Honorable Mr. Slade, bearing a copy of the *Labor Journal*, was at the same moment on his way to Emma's to break off the engagement, for he had discovered the author of the libelous drawings. The latest one was signed boldly with the name, "Philip Downes." He never arrived at Emma's house, for on his way he heard in Smollett's Cigar Store that Jason Downes had returned, and so he saved himself the trouble of an unpleasant interview. For Essie, in the moment after the returned prodigal had made known to her his identity, had put on a cast-off hat of Emma's and set out at once to spread the exciting news through the Town.

When she returned at last from delivering the three notes, Emma was "getting Jason settled" in the bedroom he had left twenty-six years before. Essie, tempted, fell, and, listening outside the door, heard him recounting to his wife a wonderful story of having lost his memory for a quarter of a century. But one thing tormented the brain of the slattern Essie. She could not understand how Emma seemed to know the whole story and to put in a word now and then correcting him.

At the sound of Emma's footsteps approaching the door, Essie turned and, fleeing, hid in the hall closet, from which she risked her whole future by opening the door a little way to have a look at the fascinating Mr. Downes. Her heart thumped wildly under her cotton blouse at the proximity of so romantic a figure.

Chapter 15

IT SEEMED that something in the spirit of the irrepressible Jason Downes took possession of the house, for Emma turned almost gay, and at times betrayed signs of an ancient coquetry (almost buried beneath so many hardening years) in an actual tendency to bridle. For the first time since Jason had slipped quietly out of the back door, the sallow dining-room was enlivened by the odors, the sounds, the air of banqueting: a dinner was held that very night to celebrate the prodigal's return. Elmer came, goaded by an overpowering curiosity, and Mabelle, separated for once from Jimmy, her round, blue eyes dilated with excitement and colored by that faintly bawdy look which so disturbed Emma. And Philip was there, of course, and Naomi, paler than usual, dressed in a badly fitting new foulard dress, which she and Mabelle had "run up at home" in the hope of pleasing Philip. The dress had been saved for an "occasion." They had worked over it for ten days in profound secrecy, keeping it to dazzle Philip. It was thick about the waist, and did not hang properly in the back, and it made her look all lumpy in the wrong places. In case Philip did not notice it, Mabelle was to say to him, "You haven't spoken about Naomi's pretty new dress. She made it all herself—with her own hands." They had carefully rehearsed the little plot born of Mabelle's romantic brain.

But when Naomi arrived at the slate-colored house, she took Mabelle quickly into a corner and said, "Don't speak of the dress to him." And when Mabelle asked, "Why not?" she only answered, "You can do it later, but not to-night. I can't explain why just now."

She couldn't explain to Mabelle that she was ashamed of the dress, nor why she was ashamed of it. She couldn't say that as she stood on the stairs of the stable and saw a handsome woman, in a plain black dress, with her knees crossed, and furs thrown back over her fine shoulders, that the pride of the poor little foulard dress had turned to ashes. She couldn't explain how she had become suddenly sick at the understanding that she must seem dowdy and ridiculous, standing there, all red and hot and disheveled, staring at them, and wanting all the time to turn and run, anywhere, on and on, without stopping. She couldn't explain how the sight of the other woman had made the foulard dress seem poor and frowzy, even when she put on the coral beads left her by her mother, and pinned on the little gold fleur-de-lys watch her father had given her.

When she first arrived, she kept on her coat, pretending that the house was cold, but Emma said, "It's nonsense, Naomi. The house is warm enough," and the irrepressible Mabelle echoed, "That's what I say, Emma. She ought to take it off and show her pretty new dress."

Naomi had looked quickly about her, but Philip hadn't been listening.

He was standing with Uncle Elmer beside his father, who was in high spirits, talking and talking. He wouldn't notice the dress if only she could keep people from speaking of it.

She hadn't spoken of Lily Shane to Philip. All the way back to the flat by the railroad they had talked of nothing but his father and the poor bits of information she had been able to wring from the excited Essie; and when they arrived it was to find Mabelle waiting breathlessly to discuss it with them. She had been already to the slate-colored house and seen him with her own eyes. She didn't stay long (she said) because she felt as if she were intruding on honeymooners. Did they know that he had lost his memory by a fall on the boat going out to China, and that it had only come back to him when he had a fall six months ago out of the mow on his ranch in Australia? Yes, it was Australia he had been to all this time. . . .

She went on and on. "Think of it," she said. "The excitement of welcoming home a husband you hadn't seen in twenty-six years . . . like a return from the dead. I don't wonder your Ma is beside herself."

Naomi heard it all, dimly, as if all Mabelle's chatter came to her from a great distance. She should have been excited, but she couldn't be, with something that was like a dull pain in her body. She could only keep seeing Lily Shane, who made her feel tiny and miserable and ridiculous—Lily Shane, whom Philip said he didn't even know, and had never spoken to. Yet he knew her well enough to be making a picture of her. He never thought of making a picture of his own wife.

She felt sick, for it was the first time she had ever seen herself. She seemed to see at a great distance a pale, thin, freckled woman, with sandy hair, dressed in funny clothes.

And then she would hear Mabelle saying through a fog, "Your Ma wants you to come right up to supper. You can get Mrs. Stimson—the druggist's wife—to sit with the twins."

Mabelle hurried off presently, and Mrs. Stimson came in duly to sit with the twins. She gave up the evening at her euchre club because the excitement of sitting up with the grandchildren of a man who had returned after being thought dead for twenty-six years was not to be overlooked. She would hear all the story at first hand when Philip and Naomi returned, before any one else in the Town had heard it. She could say, "I sat with the twins so that Philip and Naomi could go to supper with Mr. Downes himself. I heard the whole thing from them."

As they went up the hill to the slate-colored house, Naomi said nothing, and so they walked in silence. She had begun to understand a little Philip's queer moods, and she knew now that he was nervous and irritable. She had watched him so closely of late that she had become aware of a queer sense of strain which once she had passed over unnoticed. She had learned not to speak when Philip was like that. And as they climbed the hill, the silence, the strain, seemed to become unbearable. It was Philip who broke it by crying out suddenly, "I know what you're thinking. You're thinking I lied to you about Lily Shane. Well, I didn't. Before God, I never spoke to her until to-day, and I wouldn't have, even then, but she came to my room without my asking her."

For a moment, she wanted to lie down in the snow and, burying her face in it, cry and cry. She managed to say, "I wasn't even thinking of her. Honestly I wasn't, Philip. And I believe you."

"If that's so, why do you sulk and not say anything?"

"I wasn't sulking. I only thought you didn't want to talk just now."

"I hate it when you act like a martyr." This time she was silent, and he added, "I suppose all women do it . . . or most women . . . it's what Ma does when she wants to get her way. I hate it."

She thought, "He said 'most women' because he meant all women but Lily Shane." But she was silent. They did not speak again until they reached the slate-colored house.

It wasn't really Naomi who lay at the bottom of his irritation, but the thought of his father. The return troubled him. Why should he have come now after twenty-six years? It was, he thought, almost indecent and unfair, in a way, to his mother. He tried, when he was not talking to Naomi, to imagine what he must be like—a man who Emma said had gone out to China to make money for his wife and child, a man who adored her and worshipped his son. He was troubled, because the moral image created by his mother seemed not to fit the enlarged, physical portrait in the parlor. In these last years he had come to learn a lot about the world and about people, and one of the things he had learned was that people *are* like their faces. His mother was like her large, rather coarse and energetic face; Naomi was like her pale, weak one; and Lily Shane and Mary and Uncle Elmer and even Krylenko and McTavish were like theirs. It was impossible to escape your own face. His father, he thought, couldn't escape that face that hung in the parlor.

When the door opened and he stepped into the parlor, he saw that his father hadn't escaped his face. He felt, with a sudden sensation of sickness, that his father was even worse than his face. It was the same, only a little older, and the outlines had grown somehow dim and vague from weakness and self-indulgence. Why, he thought again, did he ever come back?

But his mother was happy again. Any one could see that.

And then his father turned and looked at him. For a moment he stared, astonished by something in the face of his son, something which he himself could not perhaps define, but something which, with all the sharp instincts of a sensual nature he recognized as strange, which had little to do with either himself or Emma. And then, perhaps because the astonishment had upset him, the meeting fell flat. The exuberance flowed out of Jason Downes. It was almost as if he were afraid of his son—this son who, unlike either himself or Emma, was capable of tragedy and suffering. His eyes turned aside from the burning eyes of his son.

"Well, Philip," he said, with a wild effort at hilarity, "here's your Pa . . . back again."

Philip shook hands with him, and then a silence fell between them.

But it was Jason Downes who dominated the family gathering. Philip, silent, watched his father's spirits mounting. It seemed to him that Jason had set himself deliberately to triumph over his dour, forbidding brother-in-law, and to impress his own son. It was as if he felt that his son had a poor opinion of him, and meant to prove that he was wrong in his judgment.

He told the whole story of the voyage out, of his fall down a companion-way, and the strange darkness that followed. Once more he bowed his head and exhibited the scar.

"But," said the skeptical Elmer sourly, "you always had that scar, Jason. You got it falling on the ice at the front gate."

"Oh, no. The one before was only a small one. The funny thing was that I struck my head in exactly the same place. Wasn't that queer? And then when I fell out of the mow I hit it a third time. That's what the doctors in Sydney said made it so serious." For a moment, conscious that the embroidering had begun, Emma looked troubled and uneasy.

And Mabelle, with a look of profound speculation, asked, "And what if you hit it a fourth time? Would that make you lose your memory about Australia?"

Jason coughed and looked at her sharply, and then said, "Well, no one could say about that. If it happened again, it would probably kill me."

"Well," said Mabelle, "I must say I never heard a more interesting story . . . I never read as interesting a one in any of the magazines . . . not even in the *Ladies' Home Journal*."

For a moment Philip wanted to laugh at Mabelle's question, but it wasn't a natural desire to laugh: it sprang from a blend of anger and hysterics. He loathed the whole party, with Mabelle and her half-witted questions, his mother with all her character gone in the silly blind admiration for her husband, Uncle Elmer and his nasty, mean questions, and Naomi, silent, and looking as if she were going to cry. (If only she wouldn't sulk and play the martyr!) And Mabelle's half-witted questions were worse than Uncle Elmer's cynical remarks, for they made him see suddenly that his father *was* lying. He was creating a whole story that wasn't true, and he was enjoying himself immensely. If it *was* a lie, if he had deliberately deserted his wife and child, why had he come back now?

Jason went on and on, talking, talking, talking. He told of his ranch of eighteen hundred acres and of the thousands of sheep he owned and of the sixty herders employed to take care of them. He described the long drouths that sometimes afflicted them, and told a great deal about Melbourne and Sydney.

"Your Pa," he said, addressing Philip, "is an important man out there." And the implication was, "You don't think much of him, but you ought to see him in Australia."

But Philip was silent, and thought, "He's probably lying about that, too," and, as the conversation went on, he thought, "He's never said anything about women out there. He's never spoken about that side of his life, and he's not the kind to leave women alone."

"And I suppose you'll be wanting to take Emma back to Australia," said Uncle Elmer, regarding Jason over his steel-rimmed spectacles.

"No . . . I won't be doing that. After all, her life is here, ain't it? I shall have to go back from time to time to look after my affairs, but . . ."

"Don't speak of that now," Emma interrupted, "when you've only just arrived."

"But we have to face these things," said Jason.

Suddenly Emma turned away from the table to the doorway where Essie, in terror of interrupting the party, yet fascinated still by the spell of Jason's narrative, stood waiting. She was standing, as she always stood, on the sides of her shoes.

"What is it, Essie? What are you standing there for?"

"There's a man come to see Mr. Downes."

"What does he want?"

"He's from the newspaper."

"Tell him to come back to-morrow."

But Jason had overheard. He rose with the napkin still tucked into the fawn-colored vest. "No, Essie. . . . Tell him I'll speak to him now."

"But, Jason. . . ."

"Yes, Em. . . . I might as well get it over."

There was no holding him now; but Emma succeeded in thrusting forward a word of advice.

"Remember, Jason, what the newspapers are like. Don't tell them too much."

A shadow crossed her face, and Philip thought suddenly, "Ma knows he's lying too, and she's afraid he'll overdo it." And then a more fantastic thought occurred to him—that she knew for a good reason that he was lying, that perhaps she had planned the lie to cover up an earlier one.

"I must say it's all very remarkable . . . how Jason's affairs have turned out," said Elmer. "I never would have thought it."

"You never believed in him," said Emma, with an air of triumph, "and now you see."

To Philip the whole room, the table, the people about it, the figure of the slattern Essie standing in the doorway, all their petty boasting and piety and lying, became suddenly vulgar and loathsome. And then, almost at once, he became ashamed of himself for being ashamed, for they were *his* people. He had no others. It was a subtle, sickening sort of torture.

Chapter 16

EMMA WAS herself forced to go in at last and send away the newspaper man, for Jason would have kept him there the rest of the night, telling a story which became more and more embroidered with each rash recounting. And when, at last, the reporter had gone, the others came in and sat about while Jason continued his talk. But the evening died slowly, perhaps because of Elmer's suspicions, or Naomi's curious depression, or Philip's own disgust and low spirits. Jason found himself talking presently against a curious, foreboding silence, of which he took no notice. Only Emma and Mabelle were still listening.

It was Elmer who at last broke up the party, pushing the rotund and breathless Mabelle before him. In the door Mabelle turned, and, shaking her head a little coquettishly, said, "Well, good-night, Jason. Good-night, Emma. I feel like I was saying 'good-night' to a honeymoon couple." And the bawdy look came into her eyes. "There'll never be any second honeymoon for Elmer and me. We've got our family now and that's all done."

Still tittering, she was dragged off by her husband. When she had gone, Jason said, "Mabelle is a cute one, ain't she, and a funny one too, to be married to a mausoleum like Elmer."

"Now, Jason, it's all patched up between you and Elmer. There's no use beginning all over again."

Naomi and Philip had put on their wraps, and were standing by the door, when Jason suddenly slapped his son on the back. "We've got to get better acquainted, son. You'll like your Pa when you know him better. Nobody can resist him." He winked at Emma, who turned crimson. "Ain't it so, Em. Least of all, the ladies." And then to Philip again, "I'll come and see you in the morning."

Philip turned quickly. "No, I'll come and fetch you myself. You wouldn't find the way."

"I want to see the twins the first thing."

"I'll come for you."

He had resolved that his father was not to come to the stable. He saw that Emma hadn't even told his father that he wasn't living with his wife. The stable had suddenly become to him a kind of temple, a place dedicated to that part of him which had escaped. There were things there which his father wouldn't understand, and could only defile. The stable belonged to him alone. It was apart from all the others—his father, his mother, Naomi, Uncle Elmer and Aunt Mabelle.

Emma was standing before Naomi, holding her coat open, so that she might examine the dress underneath. She was saying, "You must come up some afternoon, Naomi, and I'll help you make the dress right. It hangs all

wrong at the back, and it's all bunchy around the armholes. You could make
it all right, but, as it is, it's . . . it's sort of funny-looking."

All the way back to the Flats neither of them spoke at all: Philip, because
there was a black anger and rebellion burning in him, and Naomi, because
if she had tried to speak, she would have wept. She felt as though she were
dead, as if in a world made up of Philip and his father and Emma she no
longer had any existence. She was only a burden who annoyed them all. And
the dress . . . it was only sort of "funny-looking."

He left Naomi at the door of the flat with an abrupt "good-night." It was
after midnight, and the moon was rising behind the hill crowned by Shane's
Castle, throwing a blue light on the mist that hung above the Flats. In the
far distance the mist was all rosy with the light from four new furnaces that
had begun once more to work. The strike was slipping slowly into defeat, and
he understood that it meant nothing to him any longer. He had almost
forgotten Krylenko.

As he passed through the rusted gates of the park, there drifted toward
him from among the trunks of the dead trees, a faint, pungent odor that
was hauntingly familiar and, as he climbed the drive between the dead trees,
it grew stronger and stronger, until at last he recognized, in a sudden flash
of memory which brought back all the hot panorama of the lake and the
forest at Megambo, that it was the smell of gunpowder, the smell that clung
to his rifle when he had stood there by the barricade beside Lady Millicent
killing those poor niggers. It was a faint, ghostly smell that sometimes died
away altogether and sometimes came in strong waves on a warm breeze filled
with the dampness of the melting snow.

At the top of the hill, the big house lay dead and blind, without a sign
of life, and, as he turned the corner, he saw that near the stable lay the
remnants of a fire which had burnt to a heap of embers. His foot touched
something that was wet and slippery. He looked down to discover a great
stain of black on the snow. For a moment he stared at the stain, fascinated,
and suddenly he knew what it was. It was a great stain of blood.

In the distance, among the trees, he discerned a light, and after a moment
he discovered a little group of men . . . three or four . . . carrying a lantern,
which they held high from time to time, as if searching for something. And
then, all at once, as he moved forward again, he almost stepped upon a
woman who lay in the snow at the entrance to the rotting arbor covered
with the vines of the dying wistaria. She lay face down with one arm above
her head in a posture that filled him for a moment with a sense of having
lived through this same experience before, of having seen this same woman
lying face down . . . dead . . . for she was unmistakably dead. He knelt
beside her, and, turning the body on its side, he remembered suddenly. She
lay like the black virgin they had found dead across the path in the tall
grass at Megambo . . . the one they had left to the leopards.

Trembling, he peered at the white face in the moonlight. The woman
was young, and across one side of the face there was a little trickle of blood

that came from a hole in the temple. She was dressed in rags, and her feet were wrapped in rolls of sacking. She was the wife or daughter of some striker. It occurred to him suddenly that there was something pitifully lonely in the sight of the body left there, forgotten, by the embers in the dead park; it had the strangest effect upon him. He rose and tried to call to the little group of searchers, but no sound came from his throat, and he began suddenly to cry. Leaning against one of the pillars of the arbor, he waited until his body had ceased to tremble. It was a strange, confused feeling, as if the whole spectacle of humanity were suddenly revealed in all its pathos, its meanness, its grandeur, and its cruelty. It was a brilliant flash of understanding, but it passed almost at once, leaving him weak and sick. And then, after a moment, he found his voice again, and shouted. The little party halted, and looked about, and he shouted a second time. Then they came toward him, and he saw that two of them carried shotguns and that one of them was McTavish.

The woman was dead. They picked her up and laid her carefully on one of the blackened marble benches of the garden, and McTavish told him what had happened. In the Town they had forbidden the strikers to hold meetings, hoping thus to break the strike, but the Shanes, Irene and Lily (for the old woman was dead), had sent word to Krylenko that they might meet in the dead park. And so the remnant of those who had held out in the face of cold and starvation had come here to listen to Krylenko harangue them from a barrel by the light of a great fire before the stables. There had been shouting and disorder, and then some one inside the Mill barrier —one of the hooligans (they hadn't yet discovered who did it) turned a machine-gun on the mob around the fire. It had only lasted an instant—the sharp, vicious, staccato sound, but it had taken its toll.

"It's a dirty business," concluded McTavish in disgust. He wasn't jolly tonight. All the old, cynical good-humor had gone out of him, as if he, too, had seen what Philip saw in that sudden flash as he leaned against the decaying arbor.

They took a shutter from the windows of the stable and, placing the body of the girl upon it, set off down the hill between the dead walls of the pine-trees. For a long time Philip stood in the soiled, trampled snow, looking after them, until a turn in the drive hid the lantern from view behind the pine-trees.

Chapter 17

THE ROOM above the stable was in darkness, but as he came up out of the staircase he saw that there was a woman sitting by the window, silhouetted against the moonlight beyond. He thought, "It must be Lily Shane, but why is she here at this hour of the night?" And then a low, familiar voice came out of the darkness, "It's only me, Philip . . . Mary." She spoke as if he must have known she was there, waiting for him.

He struck a match quickly and lighted the kerosene lamp, at which she rose and came over to him. By the flickering, yellow light he saw that she had been crying.

"It's been horrible, Philip. I saw it all from the window while I was waiting for you."

"I know . . . we just found a dead woman in the snow."

He was possessed by a curious feeling of numbness, in which Mary seemed to share, as if the horror of what had taken place outside wiped out all the strangeness of their meeting thus. Death, it seemed, had brushed by them so closely that it had swept away all but those things which lay at the foundation of existence—the fact that they loved each other, that they were together now, and that nothing else was of any importance. They were, too, like people stunned by horror. They sat by the stove, Philip in silence, while Mary told him what she had seen. For a long time it did not even appear strange to him that she should be there in his room at two o'clock in the morning.

He heard her saying, "Who was the woman they killed?"

"I don't know. She looked Italian."

There was a long silence and at last it was Mary, the practical Mary, who spoke. "You must wonder why I came here, Philip . . . after . . . after not seeing you at all for all this time."

He looked at her slowly, as if half-asleep. "I don't know. I hadn't even thought of it, Mary . . . anything seems possible to-night, anything seems possible in this queer park." And then, stirring himself, he reached across the table and touched her hand. She did not draw it away, and the touch gave him the strangest sense of a fathomless intimacy which went back and back into their childhood, into the days when they had played together in the tree-house. She had belonged to him always, only he had been stupid never to have understood it. He could have spoken out once long ago. If only he, the *real* Philip, had been born a little sooner, they would both have been saved.

And then, suddenly, he knew why she had come, and he was frightened. He said, "You heard about my father?"

She started a little, and said, "No."

"He came back to-night. It was awful, Mary. If he'd only stayed away! If he'd never have come back. . . ."

So he told her the whole story, even to his suspicion that his father was a liar, and had deserted him and his mother twenty-six years before. He told her of the long agony of the reunion, describing his father in detail. And at the end, he said, "You see why I wish he'd never come back. You *do* see, don't you, Mary . . . if he'd stayed away, I'd never have thought of him at all, or at least only as my mother thought of him. But he isn't like that at all. I don't see how she can take him back . . . how she can bear to have him about."

She wanted to cry out, "Don't you see, Philip? Don't you see the kind of woman she is? If you don't see, nothing can save you. She's worse than he is, because he's harmless." But she only said quietly, "Perhaps she's in love with him. If that's true, it explains anything."

"Maybe it's that. She must be in love with him."

Mary thought, "Oh, Philip! If you'd only forget all the things that don't matter and just live, you'd be so much happier!" She wanted him to be happy more than anything in the world. She would, she knew, do anything at all to make him happy.

Presently she said, "She came to see me this afternoon, Philip . . . your mother. That's why I'm here now. She said horrible things . . . that weren't true at all. She said . . . she said . . . that I'd been living with you all along, and she'd just found out about it. She said that I came here to meet you in the stable. She's hated me always . . . just because I've always been fond of you. She said I'd tried to steal you from her."

For a moment he simply sat very still, staring at her. She felt his hand grow cold and relax its grasp. At last he whispered, "She said that? She said such things to you?"

"Yes . . . I ran away from her in the end. It was the only thing I could do."

Then all at once he fell on his knees and laid his head in her lap. She heard him saying, "There's nothing I can say, Mary. I didn't think she'd do a thing like that . . . and now I know, I know what kind of a woman she is. Oh, I'm so tired, Mary . . . you don't know how tired I am!"

She began to stroke his dark hair, and the sudden thought came to her with horror that in her desire for vengeance upon Emma Downes, it was not Emma she had hurt, but Philip.

He said, "You don't know what it is, Mary—for months now . . . for years even, I've been finding out bit by bit . . . to have something gone that you've always believed in, to have some one you loved destroyed bit by bit, in spite of anything you can do. I tried and tried, but it was no good. And now . . . I can't hold out any more. I can't do it . . . I hate her . . . but I can never let her know it. I can never hurt her . . . because she really loves me, and it's true what she says . . . that she did everything for me. She fed and clothed me herself with her own hands."

Again Mary wanted to cry out, "She doesn't love you. She doesn't love any one but herself!" and again she kept silent.

"And now it's true . . . what she said . . . you've stolen me away from her, Mary. She's made it so. I'm through now . . . I can't go on trying any more."

Still stroking his head, she thought, "He's like a little boy. He's never grown up at all." And she said, "I was so angry, Philip, that I came here. I didn't care what happened; I only thought, 'If she thinks that's the truth, it might as well be, because she'll tell about it as the truth.' I didn't care any longer for anything but myself and you."

His head stirred, and he looked up at her, seizing her hands. "Is that true, Mary?" He kissed her hand suddenly.

"It's true . . . or why else should I be here, at this hour?" He was hopeless, she thought: he didn't live for a moment in reality.

He hadn't even thought it queer of her to be sitting there in his room long after midnight with his head on her knees. And suddenly she thought again, "If I'm his mistress, I can save him from her altogether. Nothing else can break it off forever."

He was kissing her hands, and the kisses seemed to burn her. He was saying, "Mary, I've loved you always, always . . . since the first time I saw you, but I only knew it when it was too late."

"It isn't too late, Philip. It isn't too late."

He was silent for a time, but she knew what he was thinking. He wasn't strong enough to take life into his own hands and bend it to his own will, or perhaps it wasn't a lack of strength, but only a colossal confusion that kept him caught and lost in an immense and hopeless tangle. Until to-night she hadn't herself been strong enough to act, but now a kind of intoxicating recklessness had seized her—the sober, sensible Mary Conyngham. She meant to-night to take him and comfort him, to make them both, for a little time, happy. To-morrow didn't matter. It would have been better if there were no to-morrow, if they could never wake at all.

It was Philip who spoke first. After a long silence, he said in a whisper, "I can't do it, Mary . . . I can't. It isn't only myself that matters. It's you and Naomi too. It isn't her fault any more than mine."

For a moment she wished wickedly that he had been a little more like John Conyngham, and then almost at once she saw that it was his decency, the very agony of his struggle, that made her love him so profoundly. And she was afraid that he would think her wicked and brazen and fleshly. It was a thing she couldn't explain to him.

There were no words rich enough, strong enough, to make him understand what it was that had brought her here. She had thought it all out, sitting for hours there by the window, in the light of the rising moon. She had felt life rushing past her. She was growing old with the passing of each second. She had seen a man killed, and afterwards Philip had himself come upon the body of a dead woman lying in the snow. Nothing mattered, save that they come together. What happened to her was of no consequence. Some terrible force, stronger than either of them, had meant them for each other since the beginning, and to resist it, to fight against it unnaturally as Philip was doing, seemed to her all at once a black and wicked sin.

He freed himself suddenly and stood up. "I can't do it, Mary. I'll go away. . . . You can spend the night here and leave in the morning. No one in the Town will know you haven't spent the night at Shane's Castle."

"Where will you go?"

"I'll go to the tents. I'll be all right."

She suddenly put her hand over her eyes, and, in a low voice, asked, "And . . . what's to come after, Philip?"

"I don't know . . . I don't know. I don't know what I'm doing."

"We can't go on . . . I can't . . ."

"No . . . I'd rather be dead."

Suddenly, with a sob, she fell forward on the table, burying her face in her hands. "You belong to your mother still, Philip . . . you can't shake off the hard, wicked things she's taught you. Oh, God! If she'd only died . . . we'd have been married to each other!"

She began to cry softly, and, at the sound, he stopped the mechanical business of buttoning his coat, and then, almost as if he were speaking to himself, he said, "Damn them all! We've a right to our happiness. They can't take it from us. They can't . . ."

He raised her face from the table and kissed it again and again with a kind of wild, rude passion that astonished her, until she lost herself completely in its power. Suddenly he ceased, and, looking at her, said, "It doesn't matter if to-morrow never comes. I love you, Mary . . . I love you. That's all that matters."

They were happy then, for in love and in death all things are wiped out. There, in the midst of the dead and frozen park, she set him free for a little time.

Chapter 18

THE MORNING CAME quickly in a cold gray haze, for the furnaces, starting to work one by one as the strike collapsed, had begun again to cover the Flats with a canopy of smoke. It was Mary who went first, going by the back drive, which led past the railway-station. And with her departure the whole world turned dark. While she had been there with him, he was happy with the sense of security that is born of companionship in adventure, but as her figure faded presently into the smoke and mist that veiled the deserted houses of the Flats, the enchantment of the night gave way to a cold, painful sense of actuality. The whole night had been, as some nights are in the course of lives that move passionately, unreal and charged with strange, intangible currents of fire and ice. During that brief hour or two when he had slept, years seemed to have passed. The figure of his father had become so remote that he no longer seemed cheap and revolting, but only shallow and pitiful. Even the memory of McTavish and the two men with the lantern standing over the dead woman in the snow was dim now and unreal.

It was only the sight of the trampled, dirty snow, the black spot where the fire had been and the pool of blood at the turn of the drive that made him know how near had been all these things which had happened during the night. And the park was no longer beautiful and haunted in the moonlight, but only a dreary expanse of land filled with dead trees and decaying arbors. The old doubts began slowly to torment him once more—the feeling of terror lest Naomi should ever discover what had happened, and the knowledge that he had betrayed her. There was, too, an odd new fear that he might become such a man as his father. It was born in that cold, gray light, of a sudden knowledge that deep inside him lay sleeping all the weaknesses, all the sensuality, of such a man. After what had happened in the night, he saw suddenly that he might come like his father to live in a shallow world that shut out all else. He was afraid suddenly, and ashamed, for he had been guilty of a sin which his father must have committed a hundred times.

Yet he had, too, an odd new sense of peace, a soothing, physical, animal sort of peace, that seemed to have had its beginnings months ago, in the moments of delirium when he had wanted to live only because he could not die without knowing such an experience as had come to him in the night. It was, he supposed, Nature herself who had demanded this of him. And now she had rewarded him with this sense of completeness. Nature, he thought, had meant his children to be Mary's children, too; and now that couldn't be . . . unless . . . unless Naomi died.

It was a wicked thought that kept stealing back upon him. It lay in hiding at the back of his mind, even in the last precious moments before Mary had left, when she stood beside the stove making the coffee. He had thought again and again, "If only Naomi died . . . we could be like this forever." Watching her, he had thought, despite all his will to the contrary, of what love had been with Naomi and what with Mary. And he had told himself that it wasn't fair to think such things, because he had never loved Naomi: at such moments he had almost hated her. Yet she had loved him, and was ashamed of her love, so that she made all their life together a sordid misery. And Mary, who had been without shame, had surrounded her love with a proud and reckless glory. Yet, in the end, it was Mary who hid, who stole away through the black houses of the Flats as if she had done a shameful thing, and it was Naomi who bore his children. For a moment he almost hated the two helpless little creatures he had come so lately to love, because a part of them was also a part of Naomi.

As he stood by the window, all wretched and tormented, he saw coming across the trampled snow the battered figure of Hennery. He was coming from the house, and his bent old figure seemed more feeble and ancient than it had ever been before. He entered the stable, and Philip heard him coming painfully up the stairs. At the sight of Philip, he started suddenly, and said, "You scared me, Mr. Downes . . . my nerves is all gone. I ain't the same since last night." He took off his hat and began fumbling in his pockets. "I got a letter for you . . . that strike feller left it for you . . . that . . . I doan' know his name, but the feller that made all the trouble."

He brought forth a piece of pale mauve paper that must have belonged to Lily Shane, but was soiled now from contact with Hennery's pocket.

"He was in the house all night," said Hennery, "a-hiding there, I guess, from the police, and he's gone now."

Then he was silent while Philip opened the note and read in the powerful, sprawling hand of Krylenko:

"I've had to clear out. If they caught me now, they'd frame something and send me up. And I'm not through fighting yet. The strike's bust, and there's no good in staying. But I'm coming back. I'll write you from where I go.

"Krylenko."

He read it again and then he heard Hennery saying, "It was a turrible night, Mr. Downes . . . I guess it was one of those nights when all kinds of slimy things are out walkin'. They're up and gone too . . . both of them . . . the girls, Miss Lily and Miss Irene. And they ain't comin' back, so Miss Lily says. She went away, before it was light, on the New York flier. Oh, it was a turrible night, Mr. Downes . . . I've seen things happenin' here for forty years, but nothin' like last night . . . nothin' ever."

He began to moan and call on the Lord, and Philip remembered suddenly that the half-finished drawing of Lily Shane had disappeared. She had carried it off then, without a word. And slowly she again began to take possession of his imagination. For a moment he tried to picture her house in Paris where his drawing of her would be hung. She had gone away without giving him another thought.

Hennery was saying over and over again, "It was a turrible night . . . something must-a happened in the house too. The Devil sure was on the rampage."

He stood there, staring out of the window, suffering from a curious, sick feeling of having been deserted. "By what? By whom?" he asked himself. "Not by Lily Shane, surely, on whom I had no claims . . . whom I barely knew." Yet it was Lily Shane who had deserted him. It was as if she had closed a door behind her, shutting him back into the world of Elmer and his mother and Jason Downes. The thing he had glimpsed for a moment was only an illusion. . . .

Chapter 19

WHEN HENNERY had gone off muttering to himself, Philip put on his coat and went out, for the room had become suddenly unendurable to him. He did not know why, but all at once he hated it, this room where he had been happy for the first time since he was a child. It turned suddenly cold and desolate and hauntingly empty. Running down the stairs, he hurried across the soiled snow, avoiding the dark stain by the decaying arbor. He went by that same instinct which always drove him when he was unhappy towards the furnaces and the engines, and at Hennessey's corner he turned toward the district where the tents stood. They presented an odd, bedraggled appearance now, still housing the remnant of workers who had fought to the end, all that little army which had met the night before in the park of Shane's Castle. Here and there a deserted tent had collapsed in the dirty snow. Piles of rubbish and filth cluttered the muddy field on every side. Men, women and children stood in little groups, frightened and helpless and bedraggled, all the spirit gone out of them. There was no more work for them now. Wherever they went, no mill would take them in. They had no homes, no money, no food. . . .

Lost among them, he came presently to feel less lonely, for it was here that he belonged—in this army of outcasts—a sort of pariah in the world that should have been his own.

At the door of one of the tents, he recognized Sokoleff. The Ukrainian had let his beard grow and he held a child of two in his arms—a child with great hollow eyes and blue lips. Sokoleff, who was always drunk and laughing, was sober now, with a look of misery in his eyes. Philip shook his free hand in silence, and then said, "You heard about Krylenko?"

"No, I ain't heard nothin'. I've been waitin' for him. I gotta tell him a piece of bad news."

"He's gone away."

"Where's he gone?"

Philip told him, and, after a silence, Sokoleff said, "I suppose he had to beat it. I suppose he had to . . . but what are we gonna do . . . the ones that's left. He's the only one with a brain. The rest of us ain't good for nothin'. We ain't even got money to get drunk on."

"He won't forget you."

"Oh, it's all right for him. He ain't got nobody . . . no children or a wife. He ain't even got a girl . . . now."

For a moment the single word "now," added carelessly after a pause, meant nothing to Philip, and then suddenly a terrible suspicion took possession of him. He looked at Sokoleff. "What d'you mean . . . now?"

"Ain't you heard it?"

"What?"

"It was his girl, Giulia . . . that was killed last night."

Philip felt sick. In a low voice he asked, "And he didn't know it?"

"I was to tell him, but nobody's seen him. I'm damned glad he's went away now. I won't have the goddamned dirty job. He'll be crazy . . . crazy as hell."

And then Philip saw her again as he had seen her the night before, lying face down in the snow . . . Krylenko's Giulia.

"She oughtn't to have went up there," Sokoleff was saying. "But she was nuts on him . . . she thought that he was the best guy on earth, and she wanted to hear his speech. . . ." The bearded Slovak spat into the snow. "I guess that was the last thing she ever heard. She musta died happy. . . . That's better than livin' like this."

And Krylenko had been hiding in Shane's Castle all night while Giulia lay dead in the snow outside.

The sick baby began to cry, and Sokoleff stroked its bare head with a calloused paw covered by black hair.

All at once Philip was happy again; even in the midst of all the misery about him, he was gloriously, selfishly happy, because he knew that, whatever happened, he had known what Krylenko had lost now forever. He thought suddenly, "The jungle at Megambo was less cruel and savage than this world about me."

Chapter 20

To JASON DOWNES the tragedy in the park of Shane's Castle had only one significance—that it tarnished all the glory of his astonishing return. When the papers appeared in the morning, the first pages were filled with the news of "the riot precipitated by strikers last night." It recounted the death of a Pole and of Giulia Rizzo, and announced triumphantly that the strike was broken at last. And far back, among the advertisements of Peruna and Lydia Pinkham's Compound, there appeared a brief paragraph or two announcing the return of Jason Downes, and touching upon the remarkable story of his accident and consequent loss of memory. There were, doubtless, people who never saw it at all.

But he made the most of his return, walking the round of all the cigar-stores and poker-rooms which he had haunted in his youth. He even went to Hennessey's saloon, beginning to thrive again on the money of the strike-breakers. But he found no great triumph, for he discovered only one or two men who had ever known him and to the others he was only Emma Downes' husband, whom they barely noticed in the excitement of discussing the riots of the night before. Even his dudishness had dated during those long twenty-six years: he must have heard the titters that went up from poolroom loafers at the sight of the faun-colored vest, the waxed mustaches and the tan derby. He was pushed aside at bars and thrust into the corner in the poolrooms.

Half in desperation, he went at last to find an audience in the group of old men who sat all day about the stove of McTavish's undertaking-parlors. They were old: they would remember who he was. But even there the clamor of the tragedy drowned his tale. He found the place filled with Italians—the father and the seven orphaned brothers and sisters of Giulia Rizzo. The father wept and wrung his hands. The older children joined him, and the four youngest huddled dumbly in a corner. It was Jason's own son, Philip, who was trying to quiet them. He nodded to his father, gave him a sudden glance of contempt, and then disappeared with McTavish into the back room where the undertaker had prepared Giulia for her last rest. For a moment Jason hung about hopefully, and then, confused and depressed by the ungoverned emotions of the Italians, he slipped out of the door, and up the street toward the Peerless Restaurant. He was like a bedraggled bantam rooster which had lost its proud tail-feathers, but as he approached the restaurant he grew a bit more jaunty: there was always Em who thought him wonderful. . . .

Behind the partition of the undertaking-rooms, Philip and McTavish stood looking down at Giulia. The blood had been washed away and her face was white like marble against the dark coil of her hair. She was clothed in a dress of black silk.

"It was her best dress," said McTavish. "The old man brought it up here this morning."

Philip asked, "Are they going to bury her in the Potters Field? Old Rizzo hasn't got a cent, with all these children to feed."

"No, I've arranged that. I fixed it up with the priest. She had to be buried in consecrated ground . . . and . . . and I bought enough for her. I ain't got any family, so I might as well spend my money on something."

Chapter 21

PHILIP SAW his father at the restaurant, but there was little conversation between them, and Emma kept talking about the riot of the night before, observing that, "now that the police had tried something besides coddling a lot of dirty foreigners, the strike was over in a hurry."

At this remark, Philip rose quietly and went out without another word to either of them. At home he found the druggist's wife sitting with the twins. Naomi, she said, was out. She had gone to see Mabelle. Mrs. Stimson wanted more details of his father's return, and also news of what had happened at Shane's Castle. After answering a dozen questions, he went away quickly.

At four o'clock his father came and saw the twins, diddling them both on his feet until they cried and Mrs. Stimson said, with the air of a snapping-turtle, "I'm going to leave them with you. Naomi ought to have been home two hours ago, and I've got a household of my own to look after." (Even for her poor Jason appeared to have lost his fascination.)

At seven when Philip came in to sit with the twins while Naomi went to choir practice, he found little Naomi crying and his father asleep in the Morris-chair by the gas stove. Jason had removed his collar and wrapped himself in a blanket. With him, sleeping was simply a way of filling in time between the high spots in existence: he slept when he was bored, and he slept when he was forced to wait.

Holding the baby against him, and patting its back softly, Philip approached his father and touched him with the toe of his shoe. "Pa!" he said. "Pa! Wake up!"

Jason awakened with all the catlike reluctance of a sensual nature, stretching himself and yawning and closing his eyes. He would have fallen asleep a second time but for the insistence of Philip's toe, the desperate crying of the child, and Philip's voice saying, "Wake up! Wake up!" There was something in the very prodding of the toe which indicated a contempt or at least a lack of respect. Jason noticed it and scowled.

"I just fell asleep for a minute," he said. "It couldn't have been long." But all the cocksureness had turned into an air of groveling apology.

"Where's Naomi?"

"She went off to Mabelle's." He took a pair of cigars from the yellow waistcoat and asked, "Have a cigar?"

"No. Not now." Philip continued to pat the baby's fat back. Suddenly he felt desperate, suffocated and helpless. The cry of the child hurt him.

He said, "She's been at Mabelle's all day."

"I do believe she said she'd be back after choir practice." He lighted the cigar and regarded the end of it thoughtfully. Philip began to walk up and down, and presently his father said, without looking at him, "You ain't living with Naomi, are you? I mean here in this house? You ain't sleeping with her?"

"No . . . I'm not."

"I thought so. Your Ma was trying to make me believe you was." He cocked his head on one side. "But I smelled a rat . . . I smelled a rat. I knew something was wrong."

Philip continued his promenade in silence.

"How'd you ever come to hook up with Naomi?"

"Because I wanted to . . . I suppose."

Jason considered the answer thoughtfully. "No, I don't believe you did. I ain't very bright, but I know some things. No man in his right mind would hook up to anything as pious as Naomi. . . ." He saw that Philip's head tossed back and his jaw hardened, as if he were going to speak. "Now, don't get mad at your Pa . . . your poor old Pa . . . I know you don't think much of 'im, but he's kind-a proud of you, just the same. And he don't blame you for not living with Naomi. Why, the thought of it makes me kind-a seasick."

Again a silence filled by little Naomi's heartbroken crying.

"Why, she ought to be home now looking after her children instead of gadding about with preachers and such. Your Ma was always pious, too, but she was a good housekeeper. She never allowed religion to interfere with her bein' practical."

Philip, distracted, unhappy, conscience-stricken, and a little frightened at Naomi's queer avoidance of him, was aware, too, that his father was saying one by one things he'd thought himself a hundred times. It occurred to him that Jason wasn't perhaps as empty and cheap as he seemed. It was almost as if an affection were being born out of Jason's hopeless efforts toward an understanding. If only little Naomi would stop squalling. . . .

His father was saying, "No, I'm proud of you, my boy. D'you know why?"

"No."

"Because of the way you stand up to your Ma. It takes a strong man to do that, unless you learn the trick. I've learned the trick. I just let her slide off now like water off a duck's back. I just say, 'Yes, yes,' to her and then do as I damned please. Oh, I learned a lot since I last saw her . . . a hell of a lot. There's a lotta women like her . . . especially American women—that don't know their place."

The baby stopped screaming, sobbed for a moment, and then began again.

"It wasn't her piousness that drove me away. I could have managed that. It was her way of meddlin'."

Philip stopped short and turned, looking at his father. "Then you *were* running away from us when you fell and hit your head?"

"I wasn't runnin' away from *you*."

Philip stood in front of the chair. "And you didn't lose your memory at all, did you?"

Jason looked up at him with an expression of astonishment. "No . . . of course not. D'you mean to say she never told you the truth . . . even you . . . my own son?"

"No . . . I guess she was trying to protect you . . . and made me believe my father wasn't the kind to run away." (The cries of the baby had begun to beat upon his brain like the steel hammers of the Mill.)

"Protect me, hell! It was to protect herself. She didn't want the Town to think that any man would desert her. Oh, I know your Ma, my boy. And it would have took a hero or a nincompoop to have stuck with her in those days." He knocked the ash from his cigar, and shook his head sadly. "But I oughtn't to have run away on your account. If I'd 'a' stuck it out, you wouldn't have got mixed up in the missionary business or with Naomi either. You wouldn't be walkin' up and down with that squallin' brat—at any rate, it wouldn't be Naomi's brat. I guess the missionary business was her way of gettin' even with me through you." He shook his head again. "Your Ma's a queer woman. She's got as much energy as a steam engine, but she never knows where she's goin', and she always thinks she's the only one with any sense. And my, ain't she hard . . . and unforgivin' . . . hard as a cocoanut!"

"She forgave you and took you back."

"But she's been aching to do that for years. That's the kind of thing she likes." His chest swelled under the yellow vest. "Besides, I always had a kind of an idea that she preferred me to any other man she's ever seen. Your Ma's a passionate woman, Philip. She's kind of ashamed of it, but deep down she's a passionate woman. If she'd had me about all these years she wouldn't have been so obnoxious, I guess."

The baby had ceased crying now, and, thrusting its soft head against the curve of Philip's throat, was lying very still. The touch of the downy little ball against his skin filled him with pity and a sudden, warm happiness. The poor little thing was trusting him, reaching out in its helpless way. He didn't even mind the things that his father was saying of his mother. He scarcely heard them. . . .

"I thought," said Jason, "that we'd cooked up that story about my memory for the Town and for old pie-faced Elmer. I thought she'd tell you the truth, but I guess she don't care much for the truth if it ain't pleasant."

Philip continued to pat little Naomi, more and more gently, as she began to fall asleep. In a low voice he asked, "You're going to stay now that you've come back, aren't you?"

"No, I gotta go back to Australia."

Philip looked at his father sharply. "You aren't going back to stay, are you?"

"I gotta look after my property, haven't I?"

"Why did you ever come back at all?"

Jason considered the question. "I suppose it was curiosity . . . I wanted to see my own son, and well . . . I wanted to see what had happened to your Ma after all these years, and then it is sort of fun to be a returned prodigal. Nothing has happened to your Ma. She's just the same. She accused me of bein' drunk this morning when I'd only had a glass. She carried on something awful."

"Have you told her you're going back to stay?"

"No . . . I've just told her I'm going back." He looked at Philip suddenly. "I suppose you think I'm lyin' about all that property in Australia. Well, I ain't. I'll send you pictures of it when I get back . . . I ought to have brought them. I can't guess why I didn't."

He rose and put on his coat. "I'd better be movin' on now, or she'll be sayin' I've been hangin' around bars. Have you eaten yet?"

"Yes . . . at the railroad lunch counter."

"That's a hell of a life for a married man."

He stood for a moment looking at little Naomi, who lay asleep on Philip's shoulder. Then, shyly, he put out his finger and touched the downy head gently. "They're fine babies," he said. "I wouldn't have thought a poor creature like Naomi could have had 'em."

Philip laid the child gently beside her brother and stood looking down at them.

"Philip," his father began. Philip turned, and, as if the burning gaze of his son's eyes extinguished his desire to speak, Jason looked away quickly, and said, "Well, good-night." He turned shyly, and Philip, aware that he was trying to pierce through the wall that separated them, felt suddenly sorry for him, and said, "Yes, Pa. What was it you meant to say?"

Jason coughed and then with an effort said, "Don't be too unhappy . . . and if there's somebody else . . . . I mean another girl . . . why, don't torture yourself too much about it. Your Ma has made you like that. . . . But she's got queer ideas. We ain't alive very long, you know, and there ain't any reason why we should make our brief spell miserable."

Philip didn't answer him. He was looking down again at the children, silent, with the old, queer, pinched look about the eyes, as if he were ill again. He saw suddenly that his father wasn't such a fool, after all, and he *was* human. He was standing there with his hat in his two hands, looking childish and subdued and very shy.

Philip heard him saying, with another nervous cough, "Well, good-night, Philip."

"Good-night."

The door closed and Philip sank down wearily into a chair, resting his head on the edge of the crib. Presently he fell asleep thus.

Chapter 22

ON THAT NIGHT the singing at choir practice reached a peak of frenzy. While Philip sat sleeping beside the crib, Naomi was pounding her heart out on the stained celluloid keys of the tinny piano in the Infants' Classroom. She played wildly, with a kind of shameless abandon, as if she wanted to pour out her whole story of justification; and the others, taking fire from her spirit, sang as they had never sung before.

During the afternoon, the old Naomi—the stubborn, sure Naomi of Megambo—had come to life again in some mysterious fashion. She even put on the new foulard dress in a gesture of defiance to show them—Philip and his mother—that, however "funny-looking" it might be, she was proud of it. And then neither of them had seen her wearing it, Philip because she was avoiding him, and Emma because chance had not brought them together. She had gone up to Mabelle's bent upon telling her that she had come to the end of her endurance. She had meant to ask Mabelle's advice, because Mabelle was very shrewd about such matters.

And then when she found herself seated opposite Mabelle she discovered that she couldn't bring herself to say what she meant to say. She couldn't humble her pride sufficiently to tell even Mabelle how Philip treated her. She had finally gone home and then returned a second time, but it was no use. She couldn't speak of it: she was too proud. And she knew, too, that whatever happened she must protect Philip. It wasn't, she told herself, as if he were himself, as he had been at Megambo. He was sick. He really wasn't responsible. She cried when she thought how she loved him now; if he would only notice her, she would let him trample her body in the dust. Mabelle's near-sighted blue eyes noted nothing. She went on rocking and rocking, talking incessantly of clothes and food and a soothing syrup that would make little Naomi sleep better at night.

During the day she had formed a dozen wild projects. She would go back to Megambo. She would return to her father, who was seventy now, and would welcome her help. She would run off to a cousin who lived in Tennessee. She would join another cousin who was an Evangelist in Texas: she could play the piano and lead the singing for him. In any of these places she would find again the glory she had known as Naomi Potts, "youngest missionary of God"; she wouldn't any longer be a nobody, unwanted, always pushed aside and treated as of no consequence.

But always there were the twins to be considered. How could she run off and forget them? And if she did run away, Emma and perhaps even Philip would use it as a chance to rid themselves of her forever. She fancied that she saw now how Emma had used her, willing all the while to cast her off when she was no longer of any service. She told herself again and again, as if she could not bring herself to believe it, that she loved the twins—that she loved them despite her aching back and the hours she was kept awake by their crying. But she remembered that she had never been tired at Megambo: no amount of work had tired her. She hadn't wanted the twins: she'd only gone to Philip because Mabelle and Emma told her that she must and because Mabelle said that men liked children, and that going to Philip would give her a hold over him. And now . . . see what had come of it! Philip scarcely noticed her. Before she lived with him, it hadn't mattered to her, but now—now she always carried a weight about inside her. Her heart leaped if he took the least notice of her.

No, she saw it all clearly. She must run away. She couldn't go on, chained down like a slave. But if she ran away, she'd lose Philip forever, and if she stayed, he might come back to her. The children belonged to both of them. They were a bond you could never break, the proof that once, for a little time, he belonged to her. She saw that he, too, was chained after a fashion. He belonged to her in a way he belonged to no other woman. In the sight of the Lord any other woman would always be a strumpet and a whore.

At last, as it was growing dark, she found herself sitting on a bench in the park before the new monument to General Sherman. It was raining and her coat was soaked and her shoes wet through. The rain ran in little trickles from her worn black hat. It was as if she had wakened suddenly from a dream. She wasn't certain how she came to be sitting on the wet bench with the heavy rain melting the snow all about her. She thought, "I must have been crazy for a time. I can't go on like this. I've got to talk to some one. I've got to . . . I've got to!" She began to cry, and then she thought, "I'll speak to the Reverend Castor to-night after choir practice. He'll help me and he's a good man. He'll never tell any one. He's always been so kind. It was silly of me to think things about him. I was silly to be afraid of him. I'll talk to him. I've got to talk to some one. He'll understand."

When the practice was finished, the Reverend Castor came out of the study to bid the members good-night. In the dim light of the hallway, as Naomi passed him, he looked at her and smiled. She saw that his hands were trembling in a way that had come over him lately, and the smile warmed her, but at the same time weakened her. There was a comfort and a kindliness in it that made her want to cry.

Once inside the study, she found that the drawer of the cabinet was jammed again, as it had been on that first night. While she tugged at it, she heard him outside the door saying good-night one by one to the choir. Putting down the music, she began again to struggle with the drawer, and then suddenly, as if the effort was the last she could make, she collapsed on the floor and began to weep.

She heard the door open and she heard the Reverend Castor's deep, warm voice saying, "Why, Naomi, what's the matter?"

She answered him, without looking up. "It's the drawer," she said. "It's stuck again . . . and I'm . . . I'm so tired."

He went over to the cabinet and this time he was forced to struggle with it. "It's really too heavy for you, my dear girl . . . I'll fix it myself in the morning." He replaced the music and when he attempted to close the drawer again it stuck fast. "Now it won't close at all. But I can fix it. I'm handy about such things."

His hands were trembling, and he looked white and tired. He talked with the air of a man desperately hiding pits of silence. When he turned, Naomi still sat on the floor, her body bent forward. Her worn, rain-soaked hat had fallen forward a little, and she was sobbing. He sat down in the great stuffed leather chair. It was very low, so that he was almost on a level with her.

"My poor child," he asked, "what is it? Is it something I can help?"

"I don't know. I wanted to talk to some one. I can't go on. I can't . . . I can't."

He laid his big hand on her shoulder with a gentleness that seemed scarcely real, and, at the touch, she looked up at him, dabbing her eyes with a handkerchief that had been soaked with tears hours earlier. As she looked at him, some old instinct, born of long experience with unhappy women, took possession of him. He said, "Why, you've got a new dress on, Naomi. It's very pretty. Did you make it yourself?"

For a second a look almost of happiness came into her face. "Why, yes," she said. "Mabelle helped me . . . but I made most of it myself."

His other hand touched her shoulder. "Here," he said, "lean back against my knee and tell me everything that's making you unhappy. . . ." When she hesitated, he said, "Try to think of me as your father, my child. I'm old enough to be your father . . . and I don't want to see you unhappy."

She leaned against his knee with a sudden feeling of weak collapse. It was the first time any one had been kind to her for so long, and, strangely enough, she wasn't afraid of him any longer. The old uneasiness seemed to have died away.

"Tell me, my child."

The damp handkerchief lay crushed into a tiny ball in her red, chapped hand. For a long time she didn't speak, and he waited patiently until she found words. At last she said, "I don't know how to begin. I don't know myself what's happened to me . . . I don't know. Sometimes I think I must be black with sin or going crazy . . . sometimes I can't think any more, and I don't know what I'm doing. . . . It was like that to-day . . . all day. . . . I've been going about like a crazy woman."

And then, slowly, she began, in a confused, incoherent fashion, to tell him the whole story of her misery from the very beginning at Megambo when the Englishwoman had suddenly appeared out of the forest. It all seemed to begin then, she said, and it had gone on and on ever since, growing worse and worse. She hadn't any friends—at least none save Mabelle; and the others didn't want her to see Mabelle. Besides, Mabelle didn't seem to help: whatever she advised only made matters worse.

The Reverend Castor interrupted her. "But I'm your friend, Naomi . . . I've always been your friend. You could have come to me long ago."

"But you're a preacher," she said. "And that's not the same thing."

"But I'm a man, too, Naomi . . . a human being."

And then she even told him about Emma while he interrupted her from time to time by saying, "Can it be?" and, "It hardly seems possible—a woman like Emma Downes, who has always been one of the pillars, the foundation-stones, of our church! How much goes on of which we poor blind creatures know nothing."

And Naomi said, "I know. No one will ever believe me. They'll all believe that I'm nothing and that she's a good, brave woman. I can't fight her, Reverend Castor. I can't . . . and sometimes I think she tries to poison him against me."

The trembling hand came to rest once more on her shoulder. There was a long silence, and presently he said, in a low voice, "I know, my child . . . I know. I've suffered, too . . . for fifteen years."

She had begun to sob again. "And now there are other women . . . more than one, I'm sure. I pray to God for his soul. I pray and pray to God to return him to me . . . my Philip, who was a good man and believed in God. He's changed now. I don't know him any more. To-night I don't think I love him. I've come to the end of everything."

He began to pat her shoulder, gently, as if he were comforting a child, and for a long time, they stayed thus in silence. At last he said, "I've suffered, too, Naomi . . . for years and years. . . . It began almost as soon as I was married, and it's never stopped for an hour, for a moment since. It gets worse and worse with each year." Suddenly he covered his face with his hands and groaned. "I pray to God for strength to go on living. I have need of God's help to go on at all. I, too, need some one to talk to." His hands dropped from his face, and he placed one arm about her thin, narrow shoulders. She did not draw away. Still sobbing, she let her whole weight rest against him.

She was so tired, and she felt so ill. A strange, gusty and terrifying happiness took possession of the tired, nerve-racked man. Just to touch a woman thus, to have a woman kind to him, to have a woman who would trust him, was a pleasure almost too keen to be borne. For fifteen acid years he had hungered for a moment, a single moment, like this. He did not speak, conscious, it seemed, that to breathe might suddenly shatter this fragile, pathetic sense of peace.

Naomi had closed her eyes, as if she had fallen asleep from her long exhaustion; but she wasn't sleeping, for presently her pale lips moved a little, and she said in a whisper, "There's nothing for me to do but run away or kill myself . . . and then I'll be out of the way."

He did not tell her at once, without hesitation, that she was contemplating a great sin. He merely kept silent, and, after a time, he murmured, "My poor, poor child . . . my tired child," and then fell once more into silence. They must have remained thus for nearly an hour. Naomi even appeared to fall asleep, and then, starting suddenly, she cried out. His arm ached, but he did not move. He was, it seemed, past such a small discomfort as an aching arm. And he was struggling, struggling passionately, with a terrible temptation, conscious all the while that each minute added to the bitterness of the reproaches that awaited him on opening the parsonage door. It was long after eleven o'clock, and he should have returned ages ago. He thought, "I can't go home now. I can never go home again. I can never open that door again. I would rather die here now. One more time might drive me mad . . . I mightn't know what I was doing . . . I might. . . ."

The free hand again closed over his eyes, as if to shut out the horrible thing that had occurred to him. Naomi had opened her eyes and was looking up at him. For a second he thought, "Has she seen what was in them?"

Her lips moved again. "I don't care what happens to me any longer."

Suddenly, without knowing what he was doing, he bent down and took her in his arms, "Naomi . . . Naomi . . . do you mean that? Answer me, do you mean that?"

She closed her eyes wearily. "I don't care what happens to me."

He held her more tightly, the odd, gusty pleasure sweeping over him in terrifying waves. "Naomi . . . will you . . . will you go away . . . now . . . at once, and with me?"

"You can do with me what you want, if you'll only be kind to me."

"We've a right to be happy. We've suffered enough." She did not answer him, and he said, "God will understand. He's merciful. We've had our hell here on earth, Naomi . . . Naomi . . . listen to me! Will you go now . . . at once?" A curious, half-mad excitement colored his voice. "I've got money. I've been putting it aside for a long time, because I've thought for a long time I might want to go away . . . I've been saving it, a dime and a quarter here and there where I could squeeze it. I've got more than two hundred dollars. I thought that sometime I'd have to run away. But I meant to go away alone . . . I never knew . . . I never knew." He began abruptly to cry, the tears pouring down the lined, tired face. "We'll go somewhere far away . . . to South America, or the South Sea Islands, where nobody will know us. And we'll be free there, and happy. We've a right to a little happiness. Oh, Naomi, we'll be happy."

She appeared not to have heard him. She lay in a kind of stupor, until, raising her body gently, he stood up and lifted her easily into the big leather chair, where she lay watching him, her eyes half-closed, her mouth set in a straight, hard line, touched with bitterness.

The Reverend Castor moved quickly, with a strange vigor and decision. The trembling had gone suddenly from his hands. His whole body grew taut and less weary, as if he had become suddenly young. He had the air of a man possessed, as if every fiber, every muscle, every cell, were crying out, "It's not too late! It's not too late! There is still time to live!" He approached the desk, and, unlocking the drawer, began taking out money—a thin roll of bills, and then an endless number of coins that tinkled and clattered as they slid into his pockets. There must have been pounds of metal in dimes and nickels and quarters. He filled his vest pocket with cheap cigars from a box on the desk, and then, turning, went over to Naomi, and, raising her from the chair, smoothed her hair and put her hat straight, with his own hands. Then he kissed her chastely on the brow, and she, leaning against him, murmured, "Take me wherever you like. I'm so tired."

For a moment they stood thus, and presently he began to repeat in his low, rich, moving voice, *The Song of Songs*.

"*For, lo, the winter is past, the rain is over and gone. The flowers appear on the earth; the time of the singing of birds is come, and the voice of the turtle is heard in our land. . . .*"

The words had upon her a strange effect of exaltation, the same that had come over her when she sat by the piano, carried away by her emotions. She wasn't Naomi any longer. Naomi seemed to have died. She was a gaudy Queen, and Solomon in all his glory was her lover. She seemed enveloped by light out of which the rich, vibrant voice was saying, "*Until the day break, and the shadows flee away, turn, my beloved, and be thou like a roe or a young hart upon the mountains of Bether.*"

A little while after, as the clock on the firehouse struck midnight, the door of the study closed, and two figures hurried away into the pouring rain. They were a tired, middle-aged preacher and a bedraggled woman, in a queer, homemade dress of figured foulard, and a soaked coat and hat; but there was a light in their eyes which seemed to illumine the darkness and turn aside the rain.

Chapter 23

PHILIP WAKENED slowly, conscious of being stiff and sore from having slept in a cramped position, and thinking, "It must be late. Naomi will be home soon." And then, looking up at the clock, he saw that it was after one. He rose and went over to it, listening for the tick to make certain that it was working properly. He looked at his own watch. It, too, showed five minutes past one. He listened for a moment to the sound of the rain beating upon the tin roof and then he went into the other two rooms. They were empty, and, suddenly, he was frightened.

Giving a final look at the twins, he seized his hat, and, hurrying down the steps, roused the long-suffering Mrs. Stimson and told her that Naomi hadn't yet come home. He begged her to leave her door open, so that she might hear the twins if they began to scream, and without waiting to hear her complaints he rushed out into the rain.

It fell in ropes, melting the snow and running off down the hill in torrents. To-morrow, he knew dimly, there would be a flood in the Flats. The water would rise and fill the stinking cellars of the houses. Those few families who lived in tents must already be soaked with the cold downpour. The streets were deserted, and the shops and houses black and dark. Once he caught the distant glint of light on the wet black slicker of a policeman. Save for this, he seemed to be alone in a town of the dead.

From a long way off he saw the light in the church study, and the sight of it warmed him with quick certainty that Naomi must still be there. Some urgent thing, he told himself, had arisen at choir practice. He ran down the street and through the churchyard, and at the door of the study he knocked violently. No one answered. The place was empty. He opened the door. A drawer of the cabinet stood half-open with a pile of music thrust into it carelessly. A drawer of the desk was open and empty. The gas still flickered in the corner. Passing through the study, he went into the church itself. It was dark, save for a dim flare that made the outlines of the windows silhouettes of gray set in black. The empty church frightened him. He shouted, "Naomi! Naomi!" and, waiting, heard only an echo that grew fainter and fainter . . . "Naomi! . . . Naomi! . . . Naomi! . . ." until it died away into cold stillness. Again he shouted, and again the mocking, receding echo answered him. . . . "Naomi! . . . Naomi! . . . Naomi! . . ." His own voice, trembling with terror, came back to him out of the darkness: "Naomi! . . . Naomi! . . . Naomi!"

He thought, "She's not here, but she might be at the parsonage. In any case, Reverend Castor will know something." And then, "But why did he go away leaving the gas lighted and the study unlocked?" He turned back and, running, went through the dark church and the lighted study out into the rain.

There was a light still burning in the parsonage, and as he turned into the path he saw that a figure, framed against the light, stood in the upper window. At first he thought, "It's Reverend Castor," and then almost at once, "No . . . it's his wife. She's waiting for him to come home."

He knocked loudly at the door with a kind of desperate haste, for a terrible suspicion had begun to take form. Whatever had happened to Naomi, every moment was precious: it might save her from some terrible act that would wreck all her life and the Reverend Castor's as well. He knocked again, and then tried the door. It was locked, and he heard an acid voice calling out, "I'm coming. I'm coming. For Heaven's sake, don't break down the door!"

The key turned, and he found himself facing a figure in a gray flannel dressing-gown, dimly outlined by the slight flicker of gas. He could barely distinguish the features—thin, white and pinched . . . the features of a woman, the Reverend Castor's wife.

"Who are you . . . coming at this hour of the night to bang on people's doors?" It was a thin, grating voice. As his eyes grew accustomed to the light, he saw a face of incredible repulsion. It was a mean face, like that of a malicious witch.

"I'm Philip Downes. I'm trying to find my wife. She didn't come home from choir practice."

A look of evil satisfaction suddenly shadowed the woman's face. "She wasn't the only one that didn't come back. Like as not they're still there, carrying on in the church. I guess it wouldn't be the first time."

He didn't care what she was saying, though the sound of her voice and the look in her cold blue eyes made him want to strangle her.

"They aren't there. I've just come from the church."

He fancied that he heard her chuckle wickedly, but he couldn't be certain. He heard her saying, "Then he's done it. I always knew it would happen."

He seized her by the shoulders. "Done what? What do you mean?"

"Let go of me, young man! Why, he's run off with your wife, you fool! I always knew he'd do it some day. Oh, I knew him . . . Samuel Castor . . . I haven't been married to him for fifteen years for nothing!"

He wanted to shake her again, to make her talk. "If you knew, why didn't you tell me?"

"Because it might have been any woman. It wasn't just your wife. I wasn't sure who it would be." She began to laugh again, a high, cackling laugh. "I told him he'd do it. I told him so every night. I knew it was going to happen." She seemed to find delight in her horrible triumph.

"Where have they gone?"

"How do I know where they've gone? He's gone to hell for sure now, where he can't torment me any more. He's left me—a poor invalid . . . without a cent or any one to look after me. God knows what'll become of me now. But he's done it. I always told him he would. He's a fine man of God! He's left a poor invalid wife . . . penniless and sick."

There was a kind of wild delight in her voice and manner, as if she had been trying all these years to destroy him and had at last succeeded. She seemed to receive this last calamity as the final crown of her martyrdom. She was happy. To Philip it seemed suddenly that by wishing it, by thinking of nothing else for fifteen years, she had made the thing happen—just as it was Emma who had made happen the thing she wanted to believe— that Mary had stolen him from her.

He waited no longer. He ran past the malicious figure in the greasy dressing-gown, out again into the rain. He heard her saying, "He didn't even think of my hot-water bottle . . . the scoundrel . . ." and then the horrible voice was drowned by the sound of the downpour.

Without quite knowing how he got there, he found himself, soaked and shivering, inside the baggage-room at the railway station. Everything else was closed, but in the shadows among the gaudy, battered trunks of some theatrical company, the baggageman dozed quietly. He was shaken into consciousness to find a madman standing before him, white and trembling, and dripping with water.

"Tell me," Philip asked, "did any one leave the Town on the one o'clock?"

The man looked at him sleepily, and growled something about being wakened so roughly.

"Tell me. I've got to know!"

He scratched his head. "Why, yes. I do mind somebody gettin' on the one o'clock. Come to think of it, it was what's-his-name, the preacher."

"Reverend Castor?"

"Yes . . . that's the one . . . the big fellow."

"Was he alone?"

"I dunno. . . . He was alone for all I know. I didn't see no one else."

Philip left him, and, outside, stood for a moment in the shelter of the platform shed, peering into the distance where the gleaming wet rails disappeared into the dimness of fog and jewel-like signal lights. And all at once he hated the Flats, the Mills, the whole Town, and then he laughed savagely: even his beloved locomotives had betrayed him by carrying Naomi off into the darkness.

There was nothing to do now. What was done was done. He was glad he hadn't gone to the police to find her. If they didn't know, it would keep the thing out of the papers for a little time, and the two of them might come back. There was only that crazy old woman in the parsonage who need be feared; it was impossible to imagine what she might do. He hadn't really thought of her until now, and, as he walked through the rain, up the hill again, to his mother's house, her horrid image kept returning to him as she stood in her greasy dressing-gown screaming at him in triumph, "I knew it would happen some day. I always told him he'd do it!"

He thought, "I never knew it was as bad as that. No one knew." It seemed to him that God would forgive a man any sin who must have suffered as the Reverend Castor.

He was no longer conscious of the downpour, for he was already as wet as if he had jumped into the brook, and as he walked, all the deadly sickness of reaction began to sweep over him. He was tired suddenly, so tired that he could have lain down in the streaming gutter in peace; the whole thing seemed suddenly to lose all its quality of the extraordinary. In his weariness it seemed quite a usual experience that a man should be searching the Town for a wife who had run away with the preacher. It was as if the thing hadn't happened to himself, but as if he saw it from a great distance, or had heard it told him as a story. To-morrow (he thought), or the next day, they would be telling it everywhere in the Town, in every cigar-store and poolroom, about the stove at McTavish's undertaking-parlors. They would hear of it even in Hennessey's saloon. All at once a sudden flash of memory returned to him —of Hennessey standing above him, saying, "Run along home to your Ma like a good little boy. Tell her not to let her little tin Jesus come back to Hennessey's place, if she don't want him messed up too much to be a good missionary . . . I don't want to be mixed up with that hell-cat."

In that queer mood of slackness, he was certain now of only one thing —that he could stay no longer in the same Town where Naomi and the Reverend Castor had lived, where Giulia Rizzo had been killed, where that pathetic uprising of workmen asking justice had been beaten down. He couldn't stay any longer in the same place with his own father. He wanted to go away, to the other side of the earth. Any place, even the savage, naked jungle at Megambo was less cruel than this black and monstrous Town.

At the slate-colored house he hammered on the door for twenty minutes without getting any answer, and at last he went to the side of the house and tossed stones against the window behind which his mother and father were passing what Mabelle called "a second honeymoon." After a moment a head appeared at the window, and his mother's voice asked, "Who's there? For God's sake, what's the matter?"

"It's Philip . . . let me in!"

She opened the door to him in her outing-flannel gown and a flowered wrapper which he had never seen her wear before. It was, he supposed, a best wrapper which she had kept against the homecoming she had awaited for years. Her head was covered coquettishly by a pink boudoir cap trimmed with lace. As he closed the door behind him, she said, "For God's sake, Philip. What's the matter? Have you gone crazy?"

He smiled at her, but it was a horrible smile, twisted and bitter, and born of old memories come alive, and of a disgust at the sight of the flowered wrapper and the coquettish lace cap. "No, I'm not crazy this time—though I've a right to be. It's about Naomi . . . she's run away. . . ."

"What do you mean?"

"And she hasn't gone alone. She's run away with the Reverend Castor."

"Philip! You *are* crazy. It's not true!"

"I'm telling you the truth. *I know*."

She sat down suddenly on the stairs, holding to the rail for support. "Oh, my God! Oh, my God! What have I done to deserve such a thing? When will God bring me to the end of my trials?"

He made no move to comfort her. He simply stood watching, until presently she asked, "How do you know? There must be a mistake . . . it's not true."

Then he told her bit by bit the whole story, coldly and with an odd, cruel satisfaction, so that no doubt remained; and for the first time in his memory he saw her wilt and collapse.

"You see, Ma, there can't be any doubt. They've gone off together."

Suddenly she seemed to make a great effort. She sat up again and said bitterly, "I always thought something like this would happen. She was always flighty . . . I discovered that when she lived here. She wasn't any good as a wife or as a mother. She wouldn't nurse her own children. No . . . I think, maybe, you're well rid of her . . . the brazen little slut."

"Don't say that, Ma. Whatever has happened is our fault. We drove her to it." His words were gentle enough; it was his voice that was hard as flint.

"What do you mean? How can you accuse me?"

"We treated her like dirt . . . and it wasn't her fault. In some ways she's better than either of us."

She looked at him suddenly. "You're not planning to take her back if she comes running home with her tail between her legs?"

"I don't know . . . I have a feeling that she'll never come back."

"Leaving her children without a thought!"

"I don't suppose she left them without a thought . . . but sometimes a person can be so unhappy that he only wants to die. I know . . . I've been like that. Besides, she never wanted the children any more than I wanted them."

"How can you say such a wicked thing!"

His face looked thin and pinched and white. The water, all unnoticed, had formed a pool about his feet on the immaculate carpet of Emma's hall. He was shaking with chill. He was like a dead man come up out of the sea. And deep inside him a small voice was born, which kept saying to him, "It's that ridiculous woman in a flowered wrapper and pink cap who lies at the bottom of all this misery." It was a tiny voice, but, like the voice that the Reverend Castor had tried to still by repeating Psalms, it would not die. It kept returning.

"It's not wicked. It's only the truth . . . and it's only the truth I care about to-night. I don't give a damn for anything else in the world . . . not for what people think, or about what they say. They can all go to hell for all I care." His face was white and expressionless, like the face of a man already dead. It was the voice that was terrible.

"You needn't swear, Philip." She showed signs of weeping. "And I never thought my boy would turn against his own mother—not for any woman in the world."

"Now don't begin that. I'm not your boy any longer. I've got to grow up sometime. I'm not turning against you. I'm just sick to death of the whole mess. I'm through with the whole thing."

She wiped her eyes with a corner of the ridiculous flowered wrapper, and the sight made him want to laugh. The tiny voice grew more clamorous.

She was saying, "I won't wake your Pa and tell him. He's no good at a time like this." (Philip thought, "I don't know. He might do better than any of us.") "And I'll dress and come down to the twins. And you ought to get on some dry clothes." She rose, turned all at once into a woman of action. "I'll take care of the twins."

"No," he said abruptly. "I can do that."

"You don't know about their bottles."

"I *do* know . . . I've done them on the nights Naomi went to choir practice. I don't want you to come . . . I want to be alone with them."

"Philip . . . I'm your mother. . . . It's my place. . . ."

"I want to be alone with them. . . ."

He looked so wild that she seized his shoulders and said, "You're not thinking anything foolish, are you?"

"I don't know what I'm thinking. I can't bear to think of her running off like that. I can't bear to think of how we treated her. . . . If you mean that I'm thinking of killing myself, I'm not . . . I can't do that. I've got to think of little Philip and Naomi. If it wasn't for them . . . I might do anything."

Suddenly in wild hysteria, she put her arms about him, crying out, "Philip! Philip! My boy! Don't say such things—it's not you who's talking. It's some one else . . . it's a stranger . . . somebody I never knew . . . somebody I didn't bear out of my own body." She shook him passionately. "Philip! Philip! Wake up! Be your old self . . . my son. Do you hear me, darling? You *do* love me still. Tell me what's in your heart . . . what the voice of your real self is saying."

In the violence of her action, the pink lace cap slipped back on her head, exposing a neat row of curl-papers, festoons and garlands (thought Philip in disgust) of their second honeymoon. He didn't resist her. He simply remained cold and frozen, one cold, thin hand thrust into his pocket for warmth. Then suddenly the hand touched something which roused a sudden train of memory, and when at last she freed him, he drew out a pair of worn gloves.

"I think I'll go home now," he said in the same frozen voice. "Before I go, I must give you these. Mary Conyngham sent them to you. I think you left them at her house when you went to call." It was as if he said to her, "It's true . . . what you thought about Mary and me. It's true . . . now."

She took the gloves with a queer, mechanical gesture, and without another word he turned and went out, closing the door. When he had gone, she sat down on the steps again and began to weep, crying out, "Oh, God! Oh, God! What have I done to deserve such trouble! Oh, God! Have pity on me! Bring my son back to me!"

Suddenly, in a kind of frenzy, she began to tear the gloves to bits, as if they were the very body of Mary Conyngham. In the midst of her wild sobbing, a voice came out of the dark at the top of the stairs, "For Heaven's sake, Em, what are you carrying on about now?"

It was Jason standing in his nightshirt, his bare legs exposed to the knees. "Come on back to bed. It's cold as Jehu up here."

By the time Philip reached the Flats, the rain had begun to abate a little, and the sky beyond the Mills and Shane's Castle to turn a pale, cold gray with the beginning of dawn. The twins were awake and crying loudly. Poking up the fire in the kitchen range, he prepared the bottles and so quieted them before taking off his soaked clothing. The old feeling of being soiled had come over him again, more strongly even than on the day in Hennessey's saloon, and when he had undressed and rubbed warmth back into his body, he drew hot water from the kitchen range, and, standing in a washtub by the side of the cribs where he could restore the bottles when they fell from the feeble grasp of the twins, he scrubbed himself vigorously from head to foot, as if thus he might drive away that sordid feeling of uncleanness.

At last he got into the bed beside the cribs—the bed which he had never shared with Naomi, and to which it was not likely that she would ever return. He had barely slept at all in more than two days, but it was impossible to sleep now. His mind was alive, seething, burning with activity like those cauldrons of white-hot metal in the Mills; yet he experienced a kind of troubled peace, for he had come to the end of one trouble. He knew that with his mother it was all finished. In the moment he had given her the gloves, he knew that he didn't love her any more, that he no longer felt grateful to her for all that she had done for him. There was only a deadness where these emotions should have been. It was all over and finished: it would be better now if he never saw her again.

And the twins . . . they must never go to her; whatever happened, she must never do to them what she had done to him. He would protect them from her, somehow, even if he died.

The day that followed was one of waiting for some sign, some hint, some bit of knowledge as to the whereabouts of Naomi and the Reverend Castor. Like the day after a sudden death in a household, it had no relation to ordinary days. It was rather like a day suspended without reality in time and space. Philip went about like a dead man. His father came and sat with him for a time, silent and subdued, and strangely unlike his old exuberant self.

It was Emma alone who seemed to rise above the calamity. "It is," she said, "a time for activity. We must face things. We mustn't give in."

She went herself to call upon the editors of the two newspapers and by some force of threats and tears she induced them to keep silence regarding the affair until some fact was definitely known. It was a triumph for her, since neither editor had any affection for her, and one at least hated her. From the newspaper offices she went at once to call upon the invalid in the parsonage. She found the miserable woman "prostrated," and in the care of Miss Simpkins, head of the Missionary Society. Before five minutes had passed, she understood that she had arrived too late. Miss Simpkins had been told the whole story, and in turn had communicated it, beyond all doubt, to a whole circle of hungry women. The invalid was still in the same state of triumph. It seemed to Emma that she saw no disgrace in the affair, but only a sort of glory and justification. It was as if she said, "People will notice my misery at last. They'll pay some attention to me. They'll give up pitying him and pity me for a time." It was impossible to argue with her. When Emma left, she said to herself savagely, "The old devil has got what was coming to her. She deserved it."

Once a trickle of the scandal had leaked out, there was no stopping it: the news swept the Town as the swollen waters of the brook flooded the pestilential Flats. It reached Mary Conyngham late in the afternoon. For a time she was both stunned and frightened, as if the thing were a retribution visited with horrible speed upon herself and Philip. And then, quickly, she thought, "I must not lose my head. I've got to think of Philip. I've got to help him." She fancied him haunted by remorse and self-reproaches, creating in his fantastic way all manner of self-tortures. One of them at least must keep his head, and she was certain that the one wouldn't be Philip. And she was seized with a sudden terror that the calamity might shut him off from her forever: it was not impossible with a man like Philip who was always tormenting himself about troubles which did not exist. She found to her astonishment that she herself felt neither any pangs of conscience nor any remorse. What she had done, she had done willingly, and with a clear head: if there had ever been any doubts they were over and done with before she had gone to the stable.

She dared not, she knew, go and see him, and thus deliver herself into the hands of his mother; for she knew well enough that Emma would be waiting, watching for just such a chance. She would want to say to Philip, "You see, it's the judgment of God upon you for your behavior with Mary Conyngham." For a second there came to Mary a faint wish that she had never turned Emma's accusation into truth, but it died quickly. She knew that nothing could ever destroy the memory of what had happened on the night of the slaughter in the dead park.

She decided at last to write to him, and late that night, after she had torn up a dozen attempts (because writing to a man like Philip under such circumstances was a dangerous business) she finished a note and sent it off to him. She wrote: "My Darling . . . I can't come to you now. You know why it is impossible. And I want to be with you. It is killing me to sit here alone. If you want to meet me anywhere, send word. I'd go to hell itself to help you. You mustn't torment yourself. You mustn't imagine things. At a time like this, you must keep your head. For God's sake, remember what we are to each other, and that nothing else in the world makes any difference. I love you, my boy. I love you . . . Mary."

Then she addressed the note, and, as a safeguard against Emma, printed "*Personal*" in large letters on the outside of the envelope. It was too late to find any one to deliver the note and the post-office was closed. At last she put on a hat and coat and went herself to leave it under the door of the drugstore, where the druggist would be certain to deliver it in the morning. When she came home again, she lay down in the solitude of the old Victorian parlor, and before long fell asleep. It was two o'clock when she wakened, frightened, and shivering with cold.

Mr. Stimson, the druggist, found the letter in the morning, and laid it aside until he had swept out the store. Then he had breakfast and when a Pole with a cut on the side of his head came in to have it bandaged, he quite forgot the letter. It was only after ten o'clock when a boy came bringing a telegram for Philip that he remembered it suddenly. The note and the telegram were delivered together.

The telegram was brief. A man and woman believed to be Samuel Castor and Mrs. Philip Downes were found dead by suicide in a Pittsburgh boarding-house. Would Mr. Downes wire instructions, or come himself. It was signed, "H. G. Miller, Coroner."

Chapter 24

THE ROOMING-HOUSE stood in one of the side streets in the dubious quarter that lay between the river wharfs and the business district—a region of Pittsburgh once inhabited by middle-class families, and now fallen a little over the edge of respectability. It was one of a row of houses all exactly alike, built of brick, with limestone stoops, and all blackened long ago by the soot of mills and furnaces. Number Twenty-nine was distinguished from the others only by the fact that the stoop seemed to have been scrubbed not too long ago, and that beside the sign "Rooms to Let to Respectable Parties," there was another card emblazoned with a gilt cross and bearing an inscription that was not legible from the sidewalk. Philip and McTavish, peering at the house, noticed it, and, turning in at the little path, were able to make out the words. The card was stained and yellow with age, and beneath the cross they read, "JESUS SAID, 'COME UNTO ME.'"

For a moment, McTavish gave Philip an oblique, searching look, and then pressed the bell. There was a long wait, followed by the sound of closing doors, and then a tired little woman, with her hair in a screw at the back of her head, stood before them, drying her hands on a soiled apron.

Philip only stared at her, lost in the odd, dazed silence that had settled over him from the moment the telegram had come. He seemed incapable of speech, like a little child in the care of McTavish. It was the fat undertaker who lifted his hat and said, "This is Mr. Downes, and I'm the undertaker." He coughed suddenly, "The Coroner told us that . . . they had left some things in the room."

The little woman asked them in, and then began suddenly to cry. "I've never had such a thing happen to me before . . . and now I'm ruined!"

McTavish bade her be quiet, but she went on and on hysterically. In all the tragedy, she could, it seemed, see only her own misfortune.

"You can tell me about it when we're upstairs," said McTavish, patting her arm with the air of a bachelor unused to the sight of a woman's tears, and upset by them. "Mr. Downes will wait down here."

Then Philip spoke suddenly for the first time. "No . . . I'm going with you. I want to hear the whole thing. I've . . . I've *got* to know."

There was a smell of cabbage and onions in the hallway. As McTavish closed the door, the whole place was lost in gloomy shadows. The tired woman, still sobbing, and blowing her nose on the soiled apron, said, "It's upstairs."

They followed her up two flights of stairs to a room at the back. It was in complete darkness, as if the two bodies were still there, and as she raised the window-shade there came into view a whole vista of dreary backyards littered with rubbish and filled with lines of newly washed clothing. The gray light revealed a small room, scarcely a dozen feet square, with a cheap pine table, a wash-bowl, pitcher and slop-jar, two chairs and a narrow iron bed. On the walls hung a bad print of the Sermon on the Mount and a cheaply illuminated text, "Come unto Me, all ye that labor and are heavy laden." The bed was untouched, save for two small depressions at the side away from the wall.

Near the door there were little rolls of torn newspaper—the paper (Philip thought, with a sudden feeling of sickness) with which they had stuffed the cracks of the door to imprison the smell of gas. A newspaper and a Bible lay on the table beside the wash-bowl.

"I left everything just as it was," said the woman; "just as the Coroner ordered."

Those two depressions on the side of the bed suddenly took on a terrible fascination for Philip. It was as if they were filled by the forms of two kneeling figures who were praying.

"Here's the bag they brought," said the woman. She bent down and opened it. "You see it was empty. If I'd known that . . . but how was I to know?" It was a cheap bag made of paper and painted to imitate leather. It stood in a corner, mute, reproachful, empty.

Philip was staring at it in silence, and McTavish said again, "Maybe you'd better go downstairs and wait."

For a moment there was no answer, and then Philip replied, "No, I mean to stay. I've got to hear it."

The woman began to tell her story. They had come to the rooming-house about nine o'clock in the evening. "I remember the hour because Hazel— that's the girl that helps me with the house—had finished the dishes and was going to meet a friend." She had one room empty, and she was only too glad to rent it, especially to a clergyman. Oh, he had told her who he was. He told her he was the Reverend Castor and that the woman with him was his wife. They were, he said, on their way east, and came to the rooming-house because he had heard Mr. Elmer Niman speak of it once as a cheap, clean, respectable place to stay at when you came to Pittsburgh. "You see," she explained, "I'm very careful who I take in. Usually Methodists and Baptists. They recommend each other, and that way I do a pretty good business, and it's always sure to be respectable." She sighed and said, "It wasn't my fault this time. I never thought a preacher would do such a thing, and being recommended, too, by Mr. Elmer Niman."

They went, she said, right up to their room, and, about half-past ten, when Hazel came back, she heard voices singing hymns. "They weren't sing-ing very loud . . . sort of low and soft, so as not to disturb the other roomers. So I thought it was a kind of evening worship they went through every night, and I didn't say anything. But one of my other roomers came to me and complained. I was pretty near undressed, but I put on a wrapper and went up to tell them they'd have to be quiet, as other people wanted to sleep. They were singing, *Ancient of Days*, and they stopped right away. They didn't even say anything."

The woman blew her nose again on her apron, sighed, and went on. "So I went to sleep, and about one o'clock my husband came in. He's so crippled with rheumatism he can't work much and he'd been to a meeting of the Odd Fellows. It must have been about one o'clock when he waked me up, and after he'd gotten into bed and turned out the light, I told him that I'd rented the empty room. And he said, 'Who to?' and I told him a Reverend Castor and his wife. He sat up in bed, and said, 'His wife!' as if he didn't be-lieve me, and I said, 'Yes, his wife!' And then Henry got out of bed and lit the gas, and went over to his coat and took out a newspaper. I thought it was kind-a funny. He opened it, and looked at it, and said, 'That ain't his wife at all. It's a woman who sings in his choir. The scoundrel, to come to a respectable house like this!' And then he showed me the newspaper, and there it all was about a preacher in Milford who'd run away with a choir singer. And there was his name and everything. You'd have thought he'd have had the sense to take some other name if he was going to do a thing like that."

McTavish looked at her quietly. "I don't think he'd ever think of a thing like that. He was a good man. He was innocent."

The woman sniffed. "I don't know about that. But it seems to me a good man wouldn't be trapsin' around with another man's wife."

The look in McTavish's eyes turned a little harder. When he spoke, his voice was stern. "I know what I mean. *He was a good man.* He had a hellion for a wife. She deserved what she got and worse."

Something in the quality of his voice seemed to irritate the woman, for she began to whine. "Well, you needn't insult me. I was brought up a good Christian Methodist, and I'm a regular churchgoer, and I know good from bad."

McTavish turned away in disgust. "All right! All right! Go on with your story."

"Well," said the woman, "Henry—that's my husband—said, 'You must turn them out right away. We can't have the house defiled by adulterers!'" Her small green eyes turned a glare of defiance at McTavish. "That's what they were—adulterers."

"Yes," said McTavish wearily. "There's no denying that. But go on."

"So I got up, and went to their room and knocked. I smelled gas in the hall and thought it was funny. And then I knocked again and nobody answered. And then I got scared and called Henry. He was for sending for somebody to help break down the door, and then I turned the knob and it was open. They hadn't even locked it. It just pushed open, easy-like. The room was full of gas, and you couldn't go in or strike a match and you couldn't see anything. But we left the door open, and Henry went to get the police. And after a time I went to open the window, and when I pulled up the window-shade and the light from the furnaces came in, I saw 'em both a-lyin' there. He was sort of slumped down beside the bed and she was half on the bed a-lyin' on her face. They'd both died a-prayin'."

The thin, dreary voice died away into silence. McTavish looked at Philip. He was sitting on one of the stiff pine chairs, his head sunk on his chest, his fingers unrolling mechanically bit by bit the pieces of newspaper with which the door had been stuffed. Automatically he unrolled them, examined them and smoothed them out, putting them in neat piles at his feet. They were stained with tears that had fallen silently while he listened. And then, suddenly, he found what he had been looking for. He handed it to McTavish without a word, without even raising his head.

It was a scrap torn hastily to stuff the door, but in the midst of it appeared in glaring headlines:

"PREACHER ELOPES
WITH MISSIONARY

*Romance begins at choir
practice. Woman a
former Evangelist*"

The editors had kept their word to Emma, but the story had leaked out into the cities nearby.

McTavish read it in silence, and turned to the woman. Philip did not even hear what they were saying. He was thinking of poor Naomi lying dead, fallen forward on the bed where she had been praying. It was poor Naomi who had made that ghastly depression in the gray-white counterpane. He saw what had happened. He saw them coming in, tired and frightened, to this sordid room, terrified by what they had done in a moment of insanity. He saw them sitting there in silence, Naomi crying because she always cried when she was frightened. And perhaps he had taken the newspaper out of his pocket and laid it on the table and as it fell open, there was a headline staring at them. They must have seen, then, that they were trapped, that they could neither go on nor turn back. In their world of preachers and Evangelists and prayer there was no place for them. And presently they must have noticed the print of the Sermon on the Mount, and at last the framed text—"Come unto Me, all ye that labor and are heavy laden. . . ." They must have seen the text written in letters of fire, inviting them, commanding them—"Come unto Me, all ye that labor and are heavy laden. . . ." It must have seemed the only way out. And then they had sung hymns until the harpy had knocked at the door and bade them be silent.

The depression in the bed kept tormenting him. The two figures kneeling there, praying, praying for forgiveness, until one of them slumped down, unconscious, and the other was left alone, still praying. . . . Which one of them had gone first? He hoped it was Naomi, for she would be so frightened at being left alone. For the one who was left alone, those last moments must have seemed hours. And Naomi must have been frightened. She was destroying herself—a sin which once she had told him was the unforgivable.

He saw then that the faith which had given her strength in that far-off unreal world at Megambo must have been failing her for a long time. It must have died before ever she set out on the mad journey that ended in this wretched room. Or she must have been mad. And then, all at once, the memory of her figure kneeling in the dust of the Mission enclosure rose up and smote him. He saw her again, her face all illumined with a queer, unearthly light. She had been ready then to die by the bullets of the painted niggers. She should have died then, happy in the knowledge of her sacrifice. He had saved her life—he and that queer Englishwoman—only that she might die thus, praying alone, lost, forgotten. . . .

She should have died at Megambo—a martyr.

Suddenly he heard the voice of the tired little woman, "And here is her hand-bag." She held it out to McTavish, a poor morsel of leather, all hardened and discolored by the rain. "That's how we found her address. It was written on a card."

McTavish opened it mechanically, and turned it upside-down. A few coins rattled out. He counted them . . . eighty-five cents. The woman opened a drawer of the table. "And here is his." The worn wallet contained a great amount of silver and ninety odd dollars in bills. They had meant to start life again with ninety odd dollars.

"They must have been mad," said McTavish. He touched Philip's shoulder. "Come . . . we'd better go."

Philip rose in silence, and McTavish turned toward the Bible that lay open on the table. "Was that theirs?" he asked.

"No, that's mine. I keep Bibles in all my rooms."

McTavish turned toward the door, and she said, "The bag . . . ain't you going to take the bag?"

McTavish turned toward Philip.

"No," said Philip. "You may keep it."

The woman frowned. "I don't want it. I don't want any of their things left in my house. I've suffered enough. They ruined me. I don't want my house polluted."

McTavish started to speak, and then thought better of it. He simply took up the bag and followed Philip. They went down the two flights of odorous stairs and out of the door. The policeman who had accompanied them was waiting on the sidewalk. As the door closed, they heard the woman sobbing and calling after them that she, an honest, God-fearing woman, had been ruined.

In silence they turned their backs on the dingy house, with the sign, "Rooms to Let to Respectable Parties," and the emblazoned text, "JESUS SAID, 'COME UNTO ME. . . .'"

Half-way down the block, McTavish said, "You mustn't think about it, Philip. You mustn't brood. You had nothing to do with it."

"How can I help thinking about it?" He could only see them kneeling there by the bed praying until the end, innocent save that they had tried to escape from a life which circumstance or fate had made too cruel for them to bear. They had died without ever knowing the happiness which had come to him and Mary. He saw bitterly that there was not even any great dignity in their death, but only a pathos. They had not even known a poor tattered remnant of human happiness. They had simply run away, fleeing from something they could not understand toward something that was unknown.

"How can I ever think of anything else?"

Chapter 25

THE REVEREND CASTOR was buried from his own house, and Naomi from the flat over the drugstore. Emma had proposed that the services should be held in the slate-colored house, but Philip refused. It seemed wrong that Naomi should enter it again, even in death. He would not even allow any mourners save the family. His mother and father were there, Jason in a curious state of depression, more than ever like a bedraggled bantam rooster, and Mabelle bringing both Ethel and little Jimmy, who kept asking in loud whispers where Cousin Naomi had gone, and why he wasn't supposed to speak of her. Mabelle herself repeated over and over again, "I can't believe it. She was so cheerful, though she did seem a bit nervous and fidgety that last day. She came twice to see me. I suppose she wanted to tell me something," and, "What strikes me as funny is that nobody ever suspected it. There wasn't any talk about them at all. It was like a flash out of the blue." It was impossible to silence her tongue. Even during the service she whispered to Jason, "Don't she look pure and sweet? You just can't believe that things like this happen. Life is a funny thing, I always say. It was just like a flash out of the blue."

And "pie-faced" Elmer was there too, all in dingy black. He read the service, looking like the Jewish god of vengeance. He only spoke once or twice in a ghoulish whisper, but his eyes were eloquent. They said, "You see the wages of sin . . ." and, "This is what comes of Philip abandoning God."

Once the service was interrupted when little Philip, wakened by the singing of *Crossing the Bar* by the hired quartet, stirred in his crib and began to cry.

Naomi was buried in the dress of figured foulard. Mabelle observed that in the coffin it looked all right. Naomi, she said, looked so young and so natural.

Chapter 26

THE MILLS BEGAN once more to pound and roar. The flames of the furnaces again filled all the night sky with a rosy glow. The last miserable remnants of the strikers drifted away and the tent village disappeared, leaving only a vacant lot, grassless and muddy with the turn of winter. The strike and the slaughter in the park of Shane's Castle, even the tragedy of Naomi and the Reverend Castor, were at last worn to shreds as subjects of conversation. Life moved on, as if all these things counted for nothing, as if the Shanes, and Krylenko, poor Giulia Rizzo, Naomi and the Reverend Castor, had never existed. In the church, Elmer Niman read the services until a suitable preacher was found. The bereft and invalid Mrs. Castor disappeared in the obscurity of some Indiana village, where she went to live with a poverty-stricken cousin.

As for Philip, he stayed on in the flat, hiring an old negress, whom McTavish knew, to care for the twins. A sort of enchantment seemed to have taken possession of him, which robbed him even of his desire to go away. Emma came nearly every day to question old Molly about the children, to make suggestions and to run her finger across tables in search of dust. She did not propose that he return to the slate-colored house, for she seemed now to be afraid of him, with the fear one has of drunkards or maniacs—a fear which had its origin in the moment he had taken the worn gloves from his pocket and given them to her. There was, too, a wisdom in the fear, a wisdom which had come to her from Jason on that same night, after she had returned to the marital bed.

For Jason had said to her, when she had grown calm, "Em, you never learn anything. If you lived to be a hundred, you'd still be making a mess of things."

And she had cried out, "How can you say such a thing to me . . . after all I've suffered . . . after all I've done? It's you who've made a mess of your life."

"My life ain't such a mess as you might think," he had replied darkly. "But let me tell you, if you don't want to lose that boy altogether, you'll let him alone. He ain't no ordinary Town boy, Em. He's different. I've found that out. I don't know how we produced 'im. But if you don't want to lose him, you'll let him alone."

She didn't want to lose him. There were times when she hardened her heart toward him, thinking he was ungrateful and hard to allow a hussy like Mary Conyngham to stand between him and his mother; and again she would think of him as her little boy, her Philip, for whom she would work her fingers to the bone. But she was hurt by the way he looked at her, coldly, out of hard blue eyes, as if she were only a stranger to him. She felt him slipping, slipping from her, and at times she grew cold with fear. She "let him alone," but she could not overlook her duty toward him and his children. They were, after all, her grandchildren, and a man like Philip wasn't capable of bringing them up properly, especially since he had lost his faith. And with a mother like theirs, who had such bad blood, they would need special care and training . . . she resolved not to speak of it for the moment, but, later on, when they were a little older. . . .

But it was Mabelle who was the most regular visitor at the flat. She came with a passion for always being in the center of things; she clung to the tragedy, and came every day to break in upon Philip's brooding solitude, to chatter on and on, whether he listened or not. She brought little Jimmy's old toys for the twins, and she dandled them on her knee as if they were her own. There were times when Philip suspected her of being driven by a relentless curiosity to discover more of what had happened on the terrible day, but he endured her; he even began to have an affection for her, because she was so stupid and good-natured.

She was sitting there one morning, playing with little Philip and little Naomi, when she said suddenly, "You know I often think that all that trouble in the park at Shane's Castle . . . killing all those people . . . had something to do with Naomi's being so upset. You see, when she heard that morning about the people being killed there, she got worried about you. She was nearly crazy for fear that something had happened to you, and she went herself to the stable to find you, and when she didn't find you there she was sort of crazy afterward. She came up and talked to me in a crazy way until she heard from your Pa that he'd seen you at Mc-Tavish's. When I think of it now, I see that she was sort of unbalanced and queer, though I didn't notice it at the time."

Philip, barely listening to her, took little notice of what she was saying, for he had come long ago to allow her to rattle on and on without heeding her; it was only a little while afterward that it had any significance for him. It was as if what she had said touched some hidden part of his brain. When she had gone, and he began indifferently to think of it, it seemed to him that he remembered every word exactly as she had spoken it. The words were burned into his mind. *"She was nearly crazy for fear something had happened to you, and she went herself to the stable to find you."*

When Mabelle had gone, he could think of nothing else.

Since the morning after the slaughter in the park, he had never returned to the stable. The place which he had once thought of as belonging to himself alone was spoiled now: it had been invaded by Lily Shane and poor Naomi, and even by Mary . . . even by Mary. There were times when he resented her having come there, and times, too, when his remorse over Naomi made him feel that Mary had come deliberately, to tempt him, that what they had done was not a beautiful, but a wicked thing, which would torment him until he died. The place was spoiled for him, since it had come in a ghastly way to stand as a symbol of all those things which he believed had driven Naomi into madness.

But he knew, too, that he must return one day to the stable. It was filled with his belongings, the sketches pinned to the walls, the unfinished canvas of the Flats at night on which the paint must long since have caked and turned hard. (He knew now that it would never be finished, for he could never bring himself to sit there again by the window, alone, watching the mists stealing over the Mills.) After Mabelle had gone, he kept thinking that Naomi was the last one to enter the place. It was as if her spirit would be there awaiting him.

And then all at once there came to him a sudden terrifying memory: he had gone away that morning leaving behind unwashed the dishes he and Mary had used at breakfast. He had sent Mary away, promising to wash them himself, and then, troubled by the remorse of the gray dawn, had gone off, meaning to do it when he returned. They were still lying there—the two plates, the two coffee-cups, the very loaf of bread, turned hard and dry, and nibbled by the mice. And Naomi had gone there, "crazy for fear something had happened" to him. She had seen the remnants of that breakfast. In all the uproar and confusion he had forgotten. . . . She had known then; she must have known before she ran away. . . .

For a moment he thought, "I must be careful, or I shall go crazy. It must feel like this to lose one's mind." He thought, "It was I who did it. I drove her away. I killed her myself. She thought that I was lying to her all along. I wasn't lying. I wasn't lying. I was telling her the truth. . . . It would have been the truth, even now, to the end, if Mary hadn't come then. She must have been crazy. Both of us must have been crazy."

And then, after a time, he thought, "I've got to be calm. I've got to think this thing out." There wasn't, after all, any reason why there shouldn't have been two plates and two cups. Any one might have been having breakfast with him . . . any man, Krylenko, or even McTavish. Oh, it was all right. There couldn't have been anything wrong in that.

And then he thought bitterly, "But if it had been Krylenko, Naomi wouldn't have believed it. She'd be sure it was a woman. She'd think it was Lily Shane . . . Lily Shane, who wouldn't have looked at me. She was jealous of Lily Shane."

None of it was any good—none of this self-deception. It wasn't a man who had had breakfast with him. It was a woman—Mary Conyngham, only Naomi had believed it was Lily Shane. Thank God! It wasn't the same as if he and Mary together had driven her away to death in that horrible rooming-house. He'd never have to think of that after he and Mary were married. Naomi had believed the woman was Lily Shane.

Suddenly he pressed his hands to his eyes, so savagely that for a moment he was blinded. "I'm a fool. It's just the same, even if she did think that it was some other woman."

The stable began to acquire for him a horrid fascination, so powerful that he could no longer stay away from it. He *had* to return, to see the place with his eyes, to see the tell-tale cups and plates. Perhaps (he thought) some miracle had happened. Old Hennery might have removed them after he left, or perhaps he had himself washed them and put them away in the harness-closet without remembering it. Such a thing could happen. . . . In all the tragedy, all the confusion, the ecstasy of those few hours, he might have done it, without knowing what he did. Or afterwards, in all the stress of what had happened, he might have forgotten. Such things had been known to occur, he told himself, such lapses in the working of a brain. There were, after all, moments of late when he was not certain of what was happening—whether he was alive or dead, or whether Naomi had really killed herself, praying by the side of that wretched bed. . . .

But immediately he said, "I'm a fool. I'm like my father. I'm not thinking of what *did* happen, but what I wish had happened. It's like his story of losing his memory."

When the old negress Molly returned from marketing, he gave her the twins and went off like a madman to the stable. He traversed the area of the Mills, passed Hennessey's place, and entered the dead park, but when he came to the stable, it took all his courage to enter.

He climbed the creaking stairs with his eyes closed, groping his way until he stood at the top. Then he opened them and looked about.

The place had a wrecked and desolate look. The dust and the soot of the Mills, filtering in through the decaying windows, covered everything.

At some time during the storm the roof had begun to leak, and the water, running down the walls, had ruined a dozen sketches and soaked the blankets on the bed, and in the middle of the room on the table stood the coffee-pot, the dried loaf of bread gnawed by the mice, the soiled cups and plates, and a saucer with rancid butter on it.

There wasn't any doubt of it—the things were there, just as they had been left by him and Mary.

He sat down weakly in one of the chairs by the table, and lighted a cigarette. Suddenly he leaned back with his eyes closed. He didn't care any longer. He was tired. He had come (he thought) to the end of things, and nothing any longer made any difference—neither his mother, nor his father, nor Naomi, nor even Mary. He wanted only to be alone forever, to go off into some wilderness where there was no human creature to cause him pain. He wanted to be a coward and run away. In solitude he might regain once more that stupid faith which had once given him security. It wasn't that he'd ever again be glad to be alive: it was only when you believed you could make God responsible in a way for everything. Whatever happened, it was the Will of God. He hadn't been alive: it was only when he had turned his back on God that he had begun to understand what it meant to be alive. And now that, too, was past: he saw now that he wasn't strong enough to live by himself. He was, after all, a coward, without the courage of a person like Mary. She had, he saw, no need of a God to lean upon. No, he wasn't even like his father, whom no tragedy had the power to touch. He was like her—like his mother. He needed God as an excuse. She was safe: nothing could touch her, nothing could ever change her. She always had God to hold responsible. . . .

The forgotten cigarette, burning low, scorched his fingers, and, dropping it, he stepped on it mechanically, and, rising from the chair, saw suddenly a woman's handkerchief lying on the table among the dishes. It lay there, folded neatly, beneath a covering of dust and soot. He thought, "It must have been Naomi's. She must have dropped it here." The thing exerted an evil fascination over him. He wanted to go away, but he couldn't go, until he knew whose handkerchief it was. It couldn't have been Lily Shane's, for he or Mary would have noticed it. It couldn't have been Mary's: for she wouldn't have gone away from the table with it lying there, neat and unused, in full sight on the table. It must have belonged to Naomi. He wanted to go away without even looking, but he had not the strength. It lay there tormenting him. He would never have any peace if he went away in ignorance.

At last his hand, as if it moved of its own will, reached out and picked it up. It left behind a small square free of dust on the surface of the table. It was a tiny handkerchief, frail and feminine, and in the corner it was marked with initials. They were . . . M.C. There wasn't the slightest doubt. . . . M.C. . . . M.C. . . . Mary Conyngham.

He saw then what must have happened—that Mary had dropped it somewhere in the room, and Naomi, searching for some clue, had found it and left it lying behind on the table. It was Naomi's hand that had placed it there on the table, Naomi's hand that had last touched it.

Naomi had known who the woman was. In the next moment he had, in some unaccountable way, a curiously clear vision of an iron bed with a small depression where some one had knelt to pray.

After a long time, he rose, and, leaving the handkerchief on the table, went down the stairs once more. He never returned again to the room above the stable.

Chapter 27

WHILE PHILIP SAT in the dust and soot of the dead stable, his father waited for him at the flat. He danced the twins for a time on his knee, and set them crowing by giving a variety of imitations of birds and animals which he had learned in Australia, but, after a time, the old spirit flagged. He wasn't the same gay, blithe creature that Emma found awaiting her in the darkened drawing-room. Even the waxed mustaches seemed to droop a little with weariness. For Jason was growing old in body, and he knew it. "My sciatica," he said, "will not let me alone."

"For an active, nervous man like me," he had told Emma only that morning, "there ain't much left when his body begins to get old."

Even his return home had been in a way a failure. He began now to think he ought never to have come back. Emma was the only one pleased by his return. "You'd have thought," he told himself, "that she'd have forgotten me long ago and taken to thinking about other things." It was pretty fine to have a big, handsome woman like Emma give you all her devotion. Yes, she was glad enough to see him, but there was his boy, Philip, whom he hardly knew. He'd never get to know Philip: he couldn't understand a boy like that. And this Naomi business. It was too bad, and of course it was a scandal, but still that didn't make any difference in the way you enjoyed living. The truth was that Philip ought to be kind-a glad to be rid of her. It wasn't a thing he could help, and he'd behaved all right. If there *was* another woman, Philip had kept it all quiet. There wasn't any scandal. And now, if he wanted to marry her, he could—if she wasn't married too. No, he couldn't understand Philip. Emma had done something to him.

The return was a failure. He hadn't even had any glory out of it, except on that first night when he'd had his triumph over pie-faced Elmer; but who wanted a triumph over a thing like Elmer? No, he'd been forgotten, first in the excitement of the riot when they'd killed a couple of dirty foreigners, and then by Naomi running off and killing herself with a preacher. Em wouldn't let him say that preachers were a bad lot but he had his ideas, all the same. The Town had forgotten all about him—him, a man who lost his memory, and who had been thought dead for twenty-six years. Of course he hadn't *quite* lost his memory, but he might have lost it. . . .

And then he was homesick. The Town wasn't home to him any more. It was no more his *real* home than Philip was his *real* son, or Emma his *real* wife.

He was thinking all these things, mechanically rolling a ball back and forth to the twins, when Philip came in. At first Jason didn't notice him, and when he did look up, the drawn, white look on the face of his strange son frightened him. He tried to jest, in a wild effort to drive away that sense of depression.

"Well, here I am," he said brightly. "Back again like a bad penny." Philip didn't answer him, and he said, "I just ran in to say I'm going home day after to-morrow."

"Home?" asked Philip, with a look of bewilderment.

"Yes . . . home to Australy."

"Oh." Then the boy pulled himself together with an effort. "But I thought this was your home."

"No . . . not really. You see, I've lived out there most of my life. And this darned Town has changed so, it don't seem the same any longer. It's all full of new people . . . and foreigners. Most of 'em have never heard of me."

"What'll Ma think?"

"I don't know. I haven't told her, but she knows I had to go back some day. She'll think I'm comin' back. She'll have that to look forward to."

"You're not coming back . . . ever?"

"It ain't likely. They say an animal wants to go home when he's dying. Well, that's me. I want to go home."

"But you're not dying."

"No, but I ain't as young as I once was. I don't want there to be no mistake." He appeared to grow even more dejected. "If I'm out there, I'll know where I am. It's no place for a man like me here in this Town. Why, there ain't room to breathe any more." He took a cigar out of his yellow waistcoat pocket and offered it to Philip, who refused it instinctively, and then accepted it, moved by the pathetic effort at friendliness. The little man wanted to tell him something; he wanted to treat him as a son, to create suddenly a bond that had never existed. He held a match for the cigar and then lighted his own. "It's like this, Philip," he said. "I've been thinking it over. You don't want to stay in this Town any more?"

"No."

"It's no place for a fella like you any more than it is for one like me. We've got to have room to breathe and think. I often think that. It's a nasty place, this Town—no room for a fella to do as he wants . . . always somebody a-watchin' of 'im."

Philip scarcely heard what he was saying, but he did notice the return of the haunting, half-comic accent. It was the first time that he had ever seen his father grave, the first time a serious thought had ever pierced the gay, shiny surface. And suddenly he felt a queer affection for the little man. Jason was making so great an effort that his face had turned red as a turkey-cock's.

"It's like this, Philip. . . . Why don't you come away with me to Australia? It's a fine life, and I'm rich out there." He waited for a moment, and when Philip didn't answer, he said, "You could begin all over again—like a new person. I know you could, because I did it myself . . . I started all over." Again he waited. "There's nothing to keep you, is there? No woman?"

He always thought of women first—his father. Philip turned slowly. "Yes . . . there is."

"Does she count as much as that?"

"Yes."

"You could marry her and take her along, couldn't you? She ain't a married woman, is she?"

"No."

"She'd be likely to go with you?"

"Yes, she'd go anywhere I chose, I guess."

"She must be the right sort."

There was a pause, and Jason struck suddenly at the thing that had been hanging over both of them like a shadow. "Out there, you'd be where your Ma couldn't put her nose in."

"Oh, I'm going away. . . . I'm not going to stay here."

Jason suddenly brightened. "Then come along with me. I'd even wait till you could get away. We ought to get better acquainted, Philip, and you'd like it out there." He laid a hand suddenly on Philip's arm. "I'll tell you something, if you promise not to tell your Ma . . . at least not till I'm gone."

He looked searchingly at Philip, who asked, "What is it?"

"You mustn't tell. You've got to promise."

"No, I won't tell."

"You've got brothers and sisters out in Australia!"

Jason looked at him with an air of expectancy, but Philip only looked puzzled.

"What on earth do you mean by that, Pa?"

"You wouldn't be alone out there. You see I've got a family there too. . . . You'd have brothers and sisters there."

"But you're married to Ma."

"That's all right. I ain't a bigamist. I've just never been married to Dora—that's my other wife. She knows about Em. I told her everything.

I guess she always liked me so much that not being married didn't matter."

The little man put his head on one side. At the thought of Dora his depression seemed to vanish. As for Philip, he simply stared, failing to live up to such an announcement. It neither surprised nor shocked him, for the whole thing seemed completely unreal, as if he were holding the fantastic conversation in a dream. It was the other thing that was real—the sight of the room in disarray with Mary's handkerchief laid on the table by the hand of Naomi . . . the memory of the sordid bed with the depression in the gray coverlet.

"You don't seem surprised," said his father.

"No. . . . No. . . . Nothing surprises me any more. I suppose if you wanted to have a family out there, it was all right. You can't expect a man to stop living." (He was right then: his father had had a woman out there.)

"But you see, Philip, they're your brothers and sisters . . . your father's children."

Philip made an effort. "How many of them are there?"

Jason's yellow waistcoat swelled with pride. "Three boys and two girls," he said. "Nobody can say I haven't done my part in helping the world along. All strapping big ones too. The youngest . . . Emma . . . is thirteen."

"Emma!"

"Yes. I called her after your Ma. I always liked the name, and I always liked your Ma too, when she's not having tantrums."

Suddenly Philip wanted to laugh. The desire arose from a strange mixture of pain and mirth. It was ridiculous.

"The others are Jason, Henry, Hector and Bernice. It was Dora who named the others. Dora's a wonderful woman . . . like your Ma in a way, only Dora understands me."

There was a long, sudden silence, in which Philip thought, "If I'd only done as he did, everything would have been all right. He's happy and he's been free . . . always. I was weak and cowardly. I didn't do one thing or the other, and now there's no way out."

"You see what I mean," said Jason. "You'd have a home out there, and a family too. You wouldn't be going alone into a new country." He looked at his son wistfully. "You'd better come with me . . . woman or no woman."

"No, Pa . . . I can't. I've got to marry the woman, and I want to go to a new country . . . alone." His face was gray and drawn suddenly. "I've got to do it . . . it's the only thing."

"You'd better think it over, Philip."

"I've thought it over . . . I've been doing nothing else."

His father took up the tan derby. "And you won't tell your Ma, will you?"

"I won't tell her . . . ever. You needn't worry."

"You can tell her when I'm gone . . . I don't want to face her, that's all."

Jason went out, all depressed once more. Philip wasn't his boy at all. Emma had done something to him.

When he had gone, Philip sat down and began to laugh. He felt sick inside, and bruised. "Oh, my God! And I've got three brothers and two sisters in Australia! And that's where he got the accent. He got it from Dora!"

Chapter 28

THAT NIGHT he sat with Mary in the Victorian drawing-room, planning their future. It was the first time he had ever entered the house, and he found the quiet, feminine sense of order in the big room soothing and pleasant, just as Emma had found it melancholy and depressing. But he hadn't come to her to be comforted and petted, as he had always done before: he was a different Philip, pathetic, and yet hard, kindly, yet cold in a way, and aloof. He did not speak of the stable, nor even of Naomi, and Mary, watching him, thought, "Perhaps I'm wrong. Perhaps after all he's been sensible and put all that behind him," and then, in the next moment, she saw him close his eyes suddenly. She knew what he was seeing . . . that room in the boarding-house where Naomi had died. "They ought never to have let him go there," she thought. "If any of them had any common sense, they wouldn't have let him do it." But she knew, too, that no one could have stopped him. He had gone because he saw it as his duty, a kind of penance: he was the sort who would never spare himself anything. . . .

And, reaching over, she touched his hand, but there was no response. After a time, he said, "It's all right, Mary. It's just a headache. I've been having them lately."

They couldn't marry and stay there in the Town with every eye watching them, waiting for some bit of scandal: but Philip seemed obsessed with the idea that they must be married at once. At first she thought it might be because he wanted her so much, and then she saw that it was for some other reason, which she could not discover.

She asked him why they must hurry, and he said, "Don't you want to be married? Don't you care any longer?"

"Of course I do, Philip. You ought to know that."

"Besides, I can't bear staying here any longer."

But even that, she felt, wasn't the real reason. She did not press him, and together they planned what they were to do. The lease on Mary's house was finished in a month, and she could go away with her sister-in-law, Rachel, and the two children, to Kentucky, where a sister of her mother's lived. And then, quietly, Philip could send the twins there, and come himself. He would bring old Molly to help care for them.

"Rachel loves children," said Mary, "and she'll never be separated from mine. She'd like two more in the household." (Only she wished they weren't Naomi's children . . . they would always be reminding him of Naomi. It seemed impossible to be rid of Naomi. The shadow of her was always there, coming between them.)

After a long silence, she said suddenly, "You *do* want to marry me, don't you, Philip?"

As he answered, it seemed to him that he came back from a great distance. "Marry you? Marry you? Why, of course I do. What have you been thinking of? What have I just been saying?"

"I don't want it to be because you think you have to . . . because of that night at the stable."

"No . . . no . . . of course not. I want to marry you. I couldn't think of *not* doing it. Where did you get such an idea?"

"I don't know . . . only you're so queer. It's as if I didn't make any difference any more . . . as if you could do without me."

For a moment he turned cross. "That's nonsense! And you know it. I can't help being like this . . . I'll be better later on."

"I don't know."

But he did not try to convince her. He simply sat staring into the shadows of the old room and at last he said, "And then when everything is settled, I want to go back to Africa . . . to Megambo."

"You can't do that, Philip . . . you mustn't. It would be like killing yourself. You can't go back where there's fever." She wanted to cry out wildly, desperately, against the vague, dark force, which she felt closing in about her.

"That's all nonsense," he said. "Doctors don't know everything. I shan't get the fever. I've got to go back. I want to go back there to paint . . . I've *got* to go back."

"You hated the place. You told me so."

"And you said once that I really liked it. You told me that some day I'd go back. Do you remember the day we were walking . . . a few days after I came home? You were right. I've got to go back. I'm like that queer Englishwoman."

"You won't go . . . leaving me alone."

"It wouldn't be for long . . . a year, maybe."

She did not answer him at once. "A year," she thought. "A year! But that's long enough. Too long. Anything could happen in a year. He might. . . ." Looking at him as he lay back in the old horsehair sofa, he became unbearably precious to her. She seemed to see him for the first time—the thin, drawn, tormented face, the dark skin, the high cheekbones, the thin lips, even the tired eyelids. He didn't know she was watching him. He wasn't perhaps even thinking of her. He looked young, like a boy . . . the way he had been long ago at twenty, when he was still hypnotized by Emma. She thought, "I can't lose him now just when we've a chance of being happy. I can't. I can't. He's mine . . . my Philip." He was free now of his mother, but he was still a captive.

She took his hand and pressed it against her cheek. "Philip, my Philip," she said. Opening his eyes, he looked at her for a moment lazily, and then smiled. It was the old shy smile she had seen on that solitary walk into the country. And then he said slowly what Naomi had once said— "I'm tired, Mary dear, that's all. . . ." She drew his head to her shoulder and began stroking it slowly. She thought, "It's odd. My grandmother would turn in her grave if she knew. Or maybe she'd understand. He's been mine always, since the beginning. I mean to keep him."

And yet she knew that he was in that very moment escaping her. She knew again the terrifying sensation of fighting some dark and shadowy thing which she could neither see nor feel nor touch.

"Philip," she said softly. "Philip."

"Yes."

"I'm going with you to Africa."

A little pause, and then— "You'd hate it there. You'd be miserable."

She saw suddenly that he had wanted to go alone, to hide himself away. She was hurt and she thought, "I can't let him do it. I've got to fight to save us both."

Aloud she said, "I wouldn't mind anything, Philip, but I've got to go with you. That's all I care about."

"There's the children."

"I've thought of that. I've thought of everything. We can leave them with Rachel and old Molly." She would make the trip a lark, a holiday. She would care for him every moment, and even see that he took the proper drugs. She would fight the fever herself. Nothing could touch him if she were there to protect him. She could put her own body and soul between him and death.

"You're sure you want to go, Mary?"

"Of course I'm sure. It's the only thing I want . . . never to be separated from you again. Nothing else makes any difference."

But this time she did not ask him whether he really wanted her. He smiled at her again. "A poor, weak fool like me doesn't deserve such a woman."

She kissed him, thinking, "Yes, my dear, you're poor and weak, and a bit of a fool, but it doesn't make any difference. Maybe that's only why I love you so much that it breaks my heart."

For a moment, it seemed to her that he again belonged to her, body and soul, as he had belonged to her on that terrible, beautiful night in the stable. She knew now. She understood that strange, sad happiness that always seemed to envelop the wicked Lily Shane.

Chapter 29

WHEN HE TOLD Emma the next day that he meant to marry Mary Conyngham, she turned suddenly white about the lips, and for once she was silent for a time before speaking. She must have seen that she had lost him forever, that she had lost even her grandchildren; but she had never yet surrendered weakly and she did not surrender now. She held her tongue, moved perhaps by the memory of Jason's, "You never learn anything, Em. You'd better leave the boy alone, if you ever expect to see him again."

She only said, "You might have waited a respectable time, so people wouldn't talk. Why, Naomi's hardly cold in her grave. You certainly don't owe her much, but. . . ."

"No one need know. We're going away. We'll keep it a secret if you like."

She softened a little. "Why couldn't you wait a little time?" (Mary might die or he might grow tired of her, if he would only wait.)

He looked at her steadily. "I've waited too long already, years too long."

"And now that your Pa's going back to Australia for a time, I'll be alone . . . I won't have anybody. It's hard when you're beginning to be old to find your life hasn't come to anything . . . all the struggle gone for nothing."

He saw that she was beginning to "work herself up" in the old fashion that she always used as a last resort. He knew the signs, and he didn't care any longer. She couldn't touch him that way. The trick had worn itself out, and he saw her with a strange, cruel clarity. One thing, however, did soften him . . . "now that your Pa is going back to Australia for a time. . . ." She didn't know that she would never see Jason again.

"I'll come sometimes to visit you," he said. "You won't lose me."

"But it's not the same, Philip. When a girl marries, she still belongs to her mother, but when a boy marries, he is lost forever."

"But, Ma, I was married before."

"But that didn't count. Naomi didn't make any difference. She was always a sort of poor thing."

PART FOUR
THE JUNGLE

Chapter 1

THEY MADE a part of the journey from the coast by the feeble half-finished railway that had only lately thrust its head like a serpent through the wilderness that had been untouched when Philip with Naomi and Swanson and Lady Millicent had made their way on foot to the coast. It was the end of the rainy season, before the coming of the burning heat, and Mary saw the country at its best, when it was still green and the earth still damp and pungent. The railroad came to an end abruptly, for no reason at all, in a clump of scrubby trees, and here they passed the second night in a shack shared by the East Indian guards. Long after nightfall, Mary heard the first roar of a lion—a strange, spasmodic, coughing sound, that came nearer and nearer until the frail wall of the shack trembled with the reverberation. Sitting up in bed, she fancied that she heard the beast circling the little shed. It came so near that she listened to the sound of its wheezing breath . . . a queer, brutal sound, that created a sudden vision of slobbering, ruthless jaws.

In the morning, she found the footprints of the beast in the damp earth, great toed prints pressed deep by the weight of the tawny body. And again the terror seized her, this time a terror less of the beast than of the dark thing for which he seemed to stand as a symbol. She knew as she stood looking down at the tracks in the earth that what had happened just before dawn was not a nightmare, but reality. It was part of this life which she was entering. Every day would be like this. She said nothing to Philip. She succeeded in behaving as if the night had been the most usual thing in the world. For she was aware that she must not disturb the peace that seemed to settle over him, slowly, with each mile that brought them nearer to Megambo and the brassy lake. He appeared no longer to be tired and troubled; yet he was not the old, gentle, dependent Philip she had always known. It was still a new one she had never seen before—a Philip who seemed still and quiet, who seemed at times to be looking far beyond the world that lay all about them. Twice she had discovered him thus staring across the scrub-covered plains, as if he were enchanted by the sense of vast emptiness.

She never shattered his moods by so much as a word, yet she was frightened, for at such times he seemed to withdraw far beyond her into a strange mystical world of his own where she had no part. Once she awakened in the night to find him sitting by the side of the fire, awake, looking up at the dome of cobalt sky powdered with stars. She lay there for a long time watching him. He turned toward her, and she closed her eyes quickly, pretending to be asleep. The old terror seized her that he was escaping her in an unearthly fashion that left her powerless.

On the fourth day, at the crest of a low hill covered with thorn-trees, Philip halted the little train of bearers, and said to her, "That ought to be the lake and Megambo." He pointed into the distance where the plain seemed to break up into a group of low hills covered with trees, and then far beyond to turn into the dark line of a real forest. At an immense distance, out of the heat, the mountains appeared like a mirage. She stared for a long time, and presently she saw that what at first she had believed to be only sky was in reality a vast lake. As she looked, it seemed in a way to come alive, to be striking the reflection of the sky from a surface made of metal. It was a dark, empty country, wild and faintly sinister in its stillness.

Chapter 2

IT WAS Swanson who saw them coming and went out to meet them on the edge of the forest. He had heard the news from a black runner on his way up the lake to join a party of German engineers who were bound inland. He was so changed that Philip looked at him for a moment with the air of a stranger. He was much thinner and had lost most of his hair. As if to compensate the loss, he had grown an immense sandy beard, which gave him the air of a comic monk. But the slow, china-blue eyes were the same, and the way of talking slowly, as if he were always afraid that his tongue would run faster than his dull brain.

Philip said, "This is my wife," and the shadow of Naomi suddenly fell on the three of them. "You got my letter?"

Poor Swanson had turned crimson, and stood awkwardly, holding his battered straw hat in his sausage-like hands. "No," he stammered. "No—what letter?"

For a moment there was a terrible silence. They both saw that he had expected Naomi. He had thought all the while that the woman he saw from afar off with the train of bearers that wound along the river was Naomi . . . coming back. And it was true. She *had* come back. She had returned in the strangest way to take possession of them all. She was there in the stupid, puzzled eyes of Swanson, in the confusion of Mary, in the tragic silence of Philip.

It was Philip who spoke suddenly. "Naomi is dead!" And Mary thought bitterly, "She isn't dead! She isn't dead! This place belongs to her. This strange man wishes that I were Naomi."

"We've missed you," said Swanson dully.

"I'll tell you about it . . . later, when we're settled. Let's be moving on now."

"I'm glad you've come back. I got no letter from you; I only knew from the Germans who came through a week ago." Swanson had suddenly the air of a child who has forgotten the poem that he was to recite before a whole audience of people. He was aware, in his dull way, that he had blundered.

Philip said quickly, "I'm not coming back to work . . . at least not as a missionary. That's all finished."

"We never get any news out here," said Swanson humbly. "I didn't know."

"Are you alone?"

"No . . . there's a new man. Murchison . . . he's a preacher. He's doing Naomi's work."

(Naomi! Naomi! Naomi!)

"Let's go on now," said Philip. He shouted at the bearers an order to march, and as they walked, Philip said, "We passed a train of bearers in the distance yesterday . . . over beyond the Rocks of Kami. Who was it?"

For a moment Swanson was silent. He scratched his head. "Oh, that . . . that . . . it must have been that queer Englishwoman's train . . . going back alone."

They were entering the borders of the real forest, where the moist earth was covered by a tangle of vines and a pattern of light and dark. Philip asked, "Why . . . alone?"

"She died three days ago . . . of the fever. Murchison would have sent her away if she hadn't been sick. She abused missionaries. She said we were spoiling her country."

"Yes . . . she thought it belonged to her."

The shadows grew thicker and thicker all about them. They walked in silence, save for the occasional chatter of a monkey.

"It was the third time she'd been back," said Swanson.

"She must have been quite old."

"About sixty, maybe. She told Murchison to stop praying over her. 'Stop slobbering over me,' is what she said."

"Yes . . . she would say that. Where did you bury her?"

"Down the lake . . . by the lagoon."

By the lagoon . . . the spot where Philip had come upon the black women carrying water from the lake. It was a beautiful spot, a quiet place to rest.

"She asked to be buried there. She liked the place."

They walked in silence until suddenly through the trees and the tangle of vines the glittering lake became visible, and a moment later the clearing on the low hill where Philip had once fought back the ravenous jungle. There was no trace of the old mission that had been burned; there were two new huts, larger than the old, built by the patient Swanson of mud and of stones dragged up from the river-bed in dry season.

Mary, watching Philip, knew what he was seeing. Naomi . . . Naomi. The place belonged to her in a strange, inexplicable fashion. She saw suddenly that Naomi perhaps belonged in a place like this with a stupid man like Swanson . . . a man who was all faith, too stupid even to have doubts.

On a platform before one of the huts a strange figure sat before a table reading aloud in the native tongue some long harangue which was repeated after him by ten or a dozen black girls who sat swaying monotonously to the rhythm of their own voices. The sound was droning and monotonous, like the sound of a hive of bees.

"That's Murchison," said Swanson. The figure was dressed in a black suit like an undertaker, with a high white celluloid collar gaping about a reed-like neck, which it no longer fitted. On his head was a stiff straw hat, yellowed with age. He wore steel-rimmed spectacles that in the heat had slipped well down upon a long nose.

"He's dressed up to greet you," said Swanson.

The black girls, all save one or two, had ceased their buzzing and were staring now with pokes and giggles at the newly arrived procession. The Reverend Mr. Murchison halted the two dutiful girls who were going mechanically on with their lesson, and stepped down from his throne. He was an ugly little man with a sour expression.

He shook hands and to Mary he said, "I suppose you'll want to take back your girls. I've been teaching them while you were away. We've made a good deal of progress, I guess. . . ."

There was a silence and Mary said:

"But I'm not Naomi . . . Naomi is dead."

The Reverend Mr. Murchison passed lightly over his error. "Like true children of God," he said, "let us kneel here in the dust and humbly thank Him for having brought you safely through a perilous journey."

The little man flopped duly to his knees, followed by Swanson. Mary waited, watching Philip, and then she saw him kneel along with the others. He didn't protest. He knelt and bowed his head. She knew suddenly why he was doing this—because it would have pleased Naomi. Then she knelt, too, with the old fear in her heart. She was afraid, because he was praying. . . . He kept slipping further and further. . . .

"O Just and Almighty God," said the dry, flat voice of the withered Mr. Murchison, "we thank Thee for having brought these poor humble travelers safely through their perilous journey. . . ." Swanson knelt dumbly, his head bowed. It was the gnatlike Mr. Murchison who ruled the mission. But it was the meek Swanson who was the servant of God. Mary saw all at once the vast and immeasurable difference.

Chapter 3

PHILIP MADE no effort to paint. The box containing his things lay forgotten in a dark corner of the hut, and for three days he went out to spend hours wandering alone along the shores of the tepid lake. Mary only waited, fighting a queer unnatural jealousy of the ghost that walked with him. And on the fourth night she was awakened by his voice saying, "Mary, I feel ill. I'm afraid I've caught the fever again." It was a voice peaceful and full of apology.

By noon the fever had taken possession of his thin body, and by evening he lay still and unconscious. For three days and three nights Mary sat beside him, while Swanson fumbled with his medicines, and kept saying in his kind, clumsy way, "He'll be all right now. You mustn't fret. Why, he's strong as an ox. I've seen him like this before." She sat by the bed, bathing Philip's thin face, touching his head gently with her hand. In her weariness she deceived herself, thinking at times, "He's cooler now. It will pass," but in the end she always knew the bitter truth—that the fever hadn't passed. It was always there, burning, burning, burning the little life that remained.

Sometimes in his delirium he talked of Lady Millicent and Swanson, but nearly always of Naomi. She was always there, as if she, too, stayed by the side of the crude bed . . . watching.

In the middle of the fourth night, when Swanson had come in to look at him, Philip stirred slowly, and opened his eyes. For a moment he looked about him with a bewildered look in the burning blue eyes, and then he reached out weakly, and took her hand. "Mary," he said, "my Mary . . . always mine since the beginning."

He asked her to get a pencil and a block of paper out of his box, and then he said, "I want you to write something for me. I'll tell you what it is. . . ." When she returned, he lay silent for a time, and then he said, "It's this, Mary. Listen. . . . Write. . . . I think it ought to go like this. . . . 'Whatever happens, after my death, I mean that my children, Philip and Naomi . . . whom I had by my first wife, Naomi Potts, are never to be left in the care of my mother, Emma Downes.'" He hesitated for a moment, and then weakly murmured, "'The same is my wish with regard to any child who may be born after my death . . . of my second wife, Mary Conyngham.'" Again he paused. "'This is my express wish.'" He beckoned with his eyes to Swanson. "Raise me up," he said. "Here, Mary, give me the pencil and the paper." She held the drawing-block for him while the thin, brown hand wrote painfully the words "Philip Downes."

The pencil dropped to the floor. "Now, Swanson . . . you must sign it as witness. . . ." Swanson laid him back gently and then wrote his own name and went quietly out.

As his grotesque figure shut out from the doorway the blue of the African night, she knelt beside him, and, pressing the dry, hot hands against her cheek, she cried out, "But you're not going to die, Philip. . . . You're not going to die! I won't let you!" She would hold him by her own will. Anything was possible in this strange, terrifying world by the lake.

"No . . . Mary . . . I'm not going to die. I only wanted to make certain."

The room grew still, and all at once she found herself praying. Her lips did not move, but she was praying. She was ashamed to have Philip hear her, and she was ashamed, too, before God that she should turn to Him only when she had desperate need. But none of these things made any difference. In her terror and anguish she prayed. God would hear her. He would know and understand if he were a good God.

Then suddenly she felt his hand relax ever so little, gently, and she said softly, "Philip! Philip!"

After a long silence, he said, "Yes . . . Mary," and pressed her hand feebly. "I'm here."

"Philip . . . I think there is to be a child. . . . You must live on his account."

"I'm glad, Mary . . . I mean to live. I mean to live."

She fell to praying again, and again she felt the thin hand relax. This time it slipped slowly from her cheek.

"Philip! Philip!"

He did not answer, and again she called, "Philip! Philip!"

His eyes were closed, but he still breathed. She began to pray once more, pressing her body close to his. She never knew how long she knelt there, but presently she knew that the thin, brown hands were no longer hot. The fever had gone out of them, and she thought suddenly, "The thing has passed, and he is safe." But the coolness turned slowly to a strange dead chill. She raised her head and looked at him. He seemed asleep, but he was so still. She touched his face, and the head fell a little to one side. The mouth opened. And then she knew. . . .

Without a sound, she slipped to the dusty earth beside the cot. She tasted the earth with her lips, but she did not even raise her head.

When she came out of the hut to find Swanson, it was still dark, although a faint rim of light had begun to show above the surface of the lake. Near the opening in the barricade, the night fire had burned to a glowing pile of embers. For a long time she stood there beneath the stars, listening to the mysterious sounds of the African night, on the very spot where Philip had once stood, half-naked, listening to the sound of the drums, lost in a strange, savage delight at the discovery of being alive and young and a man. And at last there came to her the feeling that she was not alone, but surrounded by the creatures who filled all the night with their sense of life. She was not alone, for Naomi was there, too. This strange world belonged to Naomi. She herself was only an intruder.

A sound of birds churring in the darkness roused her, and she went off to find Swanson. He was asleep in his hut and he wakened slowly, clumsily. For once, understanding without being told, he rose and followed her.

As the gray turned to rose above the lake, and the sounds of the waking forest grew more distinct, she knelt by the side of the cot while Swanson prayed, and slowly she came to understand that in his simplicity he was a good man, akin in his selfless simplicity, to the wild things in the gloomy forest that surrounded them. She understood, too, that Philip had meant to die thus, that he had come here to the spot where death was certain. But she saw, too, that he had really died long ago, on the night that had followed their happiness in the room above the stable. She didn't hate Naomi: she had never hated her.

The morning light began to filter in through the doorway, and the spaces below the thatching. She stirred and took up the drawing-block on which Philip had written his name. No, it was not Naomi that she hated. . . .

Two days later they buried him beneath the acacia not far from the fresh grave of the battered old Lady Millicent, on the spot where once, for the first time, he had known a blinding intimation of what life might be. He had known it again afterward—once as he stood in the moonlight listening to the drums, and again, on the day the wicked Lily Shane came to the stable; and then at last on the night he returned to find Mary waiting in the darkness.

It was the simple Swanson who read the service, because Mary wished it; for the Reverend Mr. Murchison made her think of Christians like Emma Downes and her brother, Elmer Niman. . . . It was the Reverend Mr. Murchison who would be the first Bishop of East Africa.

Chapter 4

WHEN EMMA returned home one night from the restaurant to find a letter from Madagascar addressed in a strange handwriting, she knew what had happened. For a long time, she sat at the dining-room table, staring at the letter, for the sight of it threw her into one of those rare moods when for a moment she gave herself over to reflection and so came unbearably near to seeing herself. She had known all along that it was certain to happen, yet the knowledge had not prepared her in any way. It seemed as hard to bear as if he had been killed suddenly by some terrible accident in the Mills.

He had not told her he was returning to Megambo until he had gone, when it was too late for her to act; and now she knew that he had died without ever seeing the letter she had sent, as it were, into space, to follow him in time to turn him back. He had died, she saw, without even knowing at all she had written, begging him not to be so hard, to think of her as his mother who was willing to sacrifice everything for his happiness. She would (she had written) forgive Mary, and try her best to behave toward her as if Mary were her own daughter. What more could she have done? To forgive Mary who had stolen him from her?

As she sat there the dull pain of a hopeless loneliness took possession of her. Here she was, at fifty, beginning for the first time to feel tired and in need of companionship, and she had no one—not even her own grandchildren. It was cruel, she told herself, to have suffered as she had suffered, with no reward but this—to end life alone after struggling for so long, always bent upon doing the right thing. Surely she had lived as God meant her to live, a Christian life filled with sacrifice to individuals and duty. Surely no one since Job had been so bitterly tried . . . no husband . . . no son . . . alone.

And presently her blunt, strong fingers tore open the envelope, and she read the letter. It was brief, almost like a cablegram . . . a few lines which told her what she already knew, that Philip, her little boy, was dead. The sight of the word "dead" and the name "Mary Downes" signed at the end, filled her with a sudden wave of bitterness that swept away all her sorrow. It was Mary who had stolen him from her like a thief. What could be more sinful than to steal from a mother a son for whom she had sacrificed her whole life? It was Mary who had destroyed him in the end, by filling his head with strange ideas, and leading him back to Africa. She was finished now with Mary. She would like to see Mary dead. And some day (perhaps it had happened already) Mary would receive the wandering letter and read, "I will even forgive Mary and try to treat her as if she were my own daughter." Then perhaps for a moment she would feel remorse over what she had done.

The letter lay crumpled in her work-stained hand. She began suddenly to weep, falling forward and burying her head in her arms beneath the glow of the gas-dome, painted with wild-roses. She had suffered too long. . . . She kept seeing Philip as a little boy. . . .

After midnight, when she had ceased to weep, she rose, and, turning out the light, went up the creaking stairs of the home she had made her own by the labor of her own hands . . . the house (she thought bitterly) she had meant for Philip. She had done everything for his sake.

Alone in her own room, she thought, "I must not give in. I must go on. God will in the end reward me." The old spirit began to claim her.

She put on mourning (a thing her conscience had not permitted her to do when Naomi died), and in the Town people said, "Poor Emma Downes! She has had almost too much to bear. It is a life like hers that makes you sometimes doubt God . . . a good woman like that deserves a better reward." She even had a letter from Moses Slade.

Only McTavish did not join in the pity. To him it seemed that the chain of her calamities was as inevitable as a Greek tragedy. It was not God, but

Emma herself, who had created them. And he saw what the others did not, that Emma was by no means a broken woman.

And, after a time, she came even to create a certain glory out of Philip's death, for she found that people believed he had gone back to Megambo to take up his old work, and so had gone back to certain death and martyrdom. She did not disillusion them: it could not, surely, be wrong to let them believe that her Philip was a martyr. Philip, who must now be with God, would understand. And, sitting in church, she knew that people about her thought of him as her martyred son. He had not lived to be Bishop of East Africa, but he had died a martyr. . . .

There remained, however, one more blow. Two months after Philip's death, she received a second letter, in a strange handwriting, this time from Australia. As she opened it, there fell out a photograph on a picture postcard. It was the photograph of seven people, all of them strangers save Jason, who sat in the middle of the front row beside a large, rather coarse and plain woman, whose hand rested on his shoulder. At the bottom was written: "*Upper row: Jason, Henry, Hector. Lower row: Bernice, old Jason, self and Emma.*"

It was "self and Emma" which startled her. Who was "self," and who was "Emma"?

She read:

"*Dear Madam:*

"*I am writing because I knew you would be interested in the details of Jason's death. . . .*"

(Jason's death! Jason dead!)

"*He died a month ago on board ship coming home. . . .*"

(Coming home! What did it mean—coming home? This house was Jason's home!)

"*He died from a fall down some steps. I guess he had been taking a drop too much. You know how Jason was. And he hit his head where he had fallen once before. You remember the scar he had. Well, that's where he hit himself. He didn't ever become conscious again, and died two days later.*

"*I know you will be wondering about the postcard. Well, it is me and Jason and our five children. No, Jason was no bigamist. We was never married. He came to my father's ranch looking for work twenty-four years ago. The eldest, Jason, is twenty-two come Michaelmas. He wasn't much good as a worker, but he was good company and the ranch was a lonely place, so Pa kept him on. He told such good stories. And the following spring—I was eighteen then, but developed like a woman of twenty-five, he seduced me. I guess I wanted to be seduced. You know what a way Jason had with women. My only complaint against him as a husband was that it was hard to keep him in order. Well, when Pa found out that I was in the family way, he was hoppin' mad, and I didn't care, because I was off my nut about Jason. Pa said he had to marry me, and Jason said he couldn't, because he already had a wife. So then when Pa had cooled down a bit, he said we was all to go to Sydney, and pretend we was married there, and if Jason ever deserted me he'd go after him with a gun and shoot him. The way it was about here then, it didn't make much difference if you was married or not. It was kind of wild. So we pretended we was married because Pa was a believer and a Primitive Methodist.*

"Well, at the time Pa died, we had four children, and he left everything to me, I being his only child, and heir. Emma was born after he died. Maybe you'll think it was funny about her name. It was Jason who wanted to call her Emma. He said he'd like to because it made him think of old times. I said it was all the same to me, though I wanted to call her Opal.

"Jason must have told you that he was rich and owned a lot of land. He was always a liar. Well, it ain't true. He didn't own a square foot of land, and he never made a ha'penny in all the time he was my husband. I even gave him the money to go back to America to see you. He wanted to go so bad I couldn't say no to him. I guess he was curious about that son of his in America, and maybe he wanted to see you, too. I just wanted you to know this, so you wouldn't think there was any money coming to you or your son.

"I always speak of him as my husband. He may have been married to you, but he was really mine. He was happy out here and I need never to reproach myself for anything I did while he was alive. He always belonged to me and as I've often told him, before he passed away, that counts for more than all the banns and marriage certificates in the world. That's why I didn't mind his paying you a brief visit. I KNEW he'd come back to me.

"Well, I can't think of any more that ought to be said. He often spoke of you kindly. The worst he ever said was, 'Em had an unfortunate temperament.' I think that was how he put it. He was embalmed on ship, and at his funeral looked very natural. He was a remarkable young-looking man for his age. Well, I will stop now.

> *"Yours respectively,*
> *"Dora Downes.*
> *"(Mrs. Jason Downes.)*

"Postscriptum. The picture is good of all except me and Emma. I never did photograph well. It was a thing Jason always said—that photographs never did me justice."

When she had finished reading, Emma took up the postcard and looked again at the three strapping sons and the two robust daughters, but her chief interest lay in the figure of Dora Downes (Mrs. Jason Downes!). She was a healthy, rather plain woman, with an enormous shelflike bosom on which her fat double chin appeared to rest. Beside her, Jason appeared, small and dapper and insignificant, like a male spider beside the female who devours her mate after he has filled Nature's demands.

"She must have been plain always," thought Emma. "She's really a repulsive woman."

Then she rose and, going into the kitchen, lifted an iron plate from the stove, and thrust into the coals the letter and the picture postcard, sending them the way of that other letter left by Jason twenty-seven years earlier.

One thing in the letter she could not forget—"*I knew he'd come back to me.*"

It was a little more than a year later that Moses Slade and Emma Downes were married quietly in Washington, but not so quietly that Sunday newspapers did not have pictures of the bride and bridegroom taken outside the church. They had come together again, through the strangest circumstances, for Moses, still unmarried, had found himself suddenly involved with Mamie Rhodes, who Emma had once said "did something to men." He was, in fact, so involved that blackmail or the ruin of a career seemed the only way out . . . the only way save marriage with some woman so prominent and so respectable as to suffocate any doubts regarding his breach of morality. "And what woman," he had asked himself, "fitted such a rôle as well as Emma Downes, who was now a widow . . . a *real* widow whose troublesome son was dead." He saw with his politician's eye all the protection she could give him as a prominent figure, known for her moral strictness and respectability, pitied for the trials she had borne with such Christian fortitude. Such a woman, people (voters) would say, could not marry him if the stories about Mamie Rhodes were true.

So he had gone to Emma and, confessing everything, thrown himself upon her mercy. For five days she kept him in doubt, and terror, lest she refuse, and in the end she accepted, but only at a price . . . that it should remain, as she expressed it, "a marriage in name only."

In the end, she subdued even Moses Slade. It was in reality Emma who sat in his seat in the House of Representatives. It was Emma who cast his votes. She became, in a small way, a national figure, concerned always with moralities and reforms. She came into a full flowering as chairman or member of a dozen committees and movements against whisky and cigarettes, and for Sunday closing. She made speaking tours, when she was received by palpitating ladies who labored in vain to sap the robust vitality of their country. There were times when her progress became a marvel of triumph. She was known as a splendid speaker.

But the apotheosis of her glory was reached in the war, when she offered her services as a speaker to right and to left—to aid recruiting, or Y.M.C.A. funds, to attack Bolshevism and denounce the barbarous Huns. She had a marvelous speech which began on a quavering note: "I had a son of my own once, but he gave his life as a martyr in Africa, fighting the good fight for God and home and Christian faith, even as all our boys are fighting to-day against a whole race, a whole nation bent upon spreading murder and destruction across the face of God's bright earth. (Cheers.) If my son were alive to-day, he would be over there, on the rim of the world (cheers), etc., etc."

It was in making this speech that she wore herself out. The end came on a wet, chill night in Kansas City, when, speaking on behalf of the Y.M.C.A., she was taken with a chill. Moses Slade came from Washington to be at her bedside, and so was there at the end to tell her that "she'd given her life as much as any soldier who fell in Flanders Field."

She was buried in the Town, alone, for the grave of her husband was in Australia, and that of her son beside a tepid lake in East Africa. The funeral service, in the enthusiasm of the war, became a sort of public festival, done to the titanic accompaniment of the Mills, which pounded now as they had never done before, to heap up piles of shells in the dead, abandoned park of Shane's Castle. It was an end which she would have liked. The new preacher, more sanctimonious but less moving than the Reverend Castor, made a high-flown and flowery funeral oration. He did it skilfully, though it was a difficult thing to speak of her trials and still not raise the ghosts of Naomi and the Reverend Castor. But the ghosts were there: they troubled the minds of every member of the congregation.

In conclusion, he said in a voice rich with enthusiasm, "She never lost her faith through trials more numerous than are the lot of most. She gave her son to God and her own life to this great cause which is so near to the heart of us all. She was brave and courageous, and generous and tolerant, but she fought always for the right like a good soldier. She never had any doubts. She was, in brief, all that is meant when our hearts lead us to say of some one, 'She was a good woman. . . .'"

It was in the following year that the Town bought the Castle from Lily Shane who had never returned to it since the night of the riot. The Town demolished the place and even dug away the hill itself to make a site for the new railway station. When the wreckers attacked the stable they found a room whose walls were covered with pencil sketches. By the window stood a half-finished painting black with soot and dust. On the table there was a coffee-pot, several soiled plates, and a fragment of something which turned out to be bread. Nearby beneath a layer of soot lay a woman's handkerchief of fine linen marked with the initials M.C.; one of the workmen took it home to his wife. The other things—the sketches and the painting—were thrown into a heap and burned on the very spot where eight years before there had been another fire in the snow.

THE END